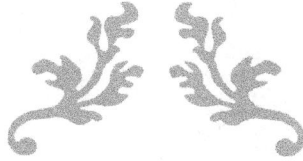

THE HUNCHBACK'S GIFT

Book IV of The Stillness Series

Stirring the Stillness
Stilling the Stillness
Stillness
The Hunchback's Gift
Flames of Extinction

Richard Lee Ferguson

Tenebris Lux Publishers
(Silentium Press)

First Edition
Published in July 2024
Copyright © Richard Lee Ferguson, 2024

10 9 8 7 6 5 4 3 2 1

ISBN 979-8-9881446-0-1

Printed in the United States of America

Cover Design: Bookfly Design, James Egan

Frontspiece Illustration: Brian Bowes Illustration, Brian Bowes

Table of Contents

BOOK I: MING-HUÀ

ACKNOWLEDGEMENTS

May humankind always be remembered for the irrefutably wondrous gifts it possessed, and may it be forgiven for the irreparable devastation it wrought.

PRINCIPAL CHARACTERS

Progenitors

John Powers
Bai Meiying (Powers)
Michael Powers
Child of Buddha

Homo dimensiones

Tamara Powers
Ming-huà Powers
Pythia Powers
Tara Powers
Abassi Powers
Zhang Yan
Mr. Tang
Eleos Powers
Harihara

Guides

Lady Oracle
Siren Rung (Scarecrow)
Buandelgereen
Altan
Queequeg (Mongol)
Temulun (boxer dog)
Bataar

Metaphors

God
Goddess

Intermediates

Matthew Weston (Zookeeper)
Siyabonga
Kholwa
Walter Monroe
Anne Monroe

Homo sapiens

Doctor Jared Paine
Luciana
Elena
Mateo
Rogelio
Busisine Okoro
Thato
Lance Romellion
John Rochelle
Judith Simmons
Mr. Lootens
Margaret Feldman
Mr. Chu
Koamalu
Doctor Feng
Ruth
Doctor Richard Carlson
Harold Burton
Ben Solokov
Roger Arlington
Amygdala
Angel Cake
Pepper Spray
Mpho
Kungawo
Edward Golden
White thunder
Jasmine (Crazy) Walker
Agent Saunders
Agent Dunlap

FOREWORD

Query: If you believe humans pose an existential threat to other species, as well as to the planet itself, then what might be the next evolutionary step, orchestrated or not, that would give rise to a successor species? How to unravel the ubiquitous human presence without simultaneously destroying the rest of the planetary ecosystem? Such a successor species, by random chance or intentional design, must possess much greater cognitive and emotional capacities in order to thwart the human proclivity for global destruction. What would it be like for those first few confused generations of advanced individuals who would be surrounded by a sea of slow-witted but resourceful *Homo sapiens*? How would they survive the human penchant for fearing otherness and the relentless instinct to exterminate it?

Whether the guiding force that would effectuate this evolutionary change is Nature, Superior Alien, God or Gods, Goddess or Goddesses, here is an Interesting Conundrum:

How to replace *Homo sapiens* with a more advanced species peacefully and with a minimum of suffering? In other words, not *drive* humans to extinction, but *dilute* their genes to insignificance. There is precedent for such top-down genetic engineering. Human biologists eliminate dangerous pests by introducing mutant strains that breed with the targeted species to produce offspring harboring the desired genetic makeup. Generations later, the original species is superseded. This is analogous to the way *Homo sapiens* interbred with and eventually replaced *Homo neanderthals* (whose genes currently reside in the human genome only as faintly echoing ghosts.)

A new form of consciousness must necessarily arise—one in which strange Voices with immense power reverberate in superior minds the way strange Voices once arose in the minds of early *Homo sapiens*. Voices that are mistakenly diagnosed as schizophrenia, but are, in fact, the stirrings of a superior species. How disorienting those first expressive Voices in the mind! How astonishing those first feats of awesome predictive power! So it must be for our successors. The Stillness Series is the story of one possible path to such a cataclysm.

Thus goes humanity gentle into that still night. . . .

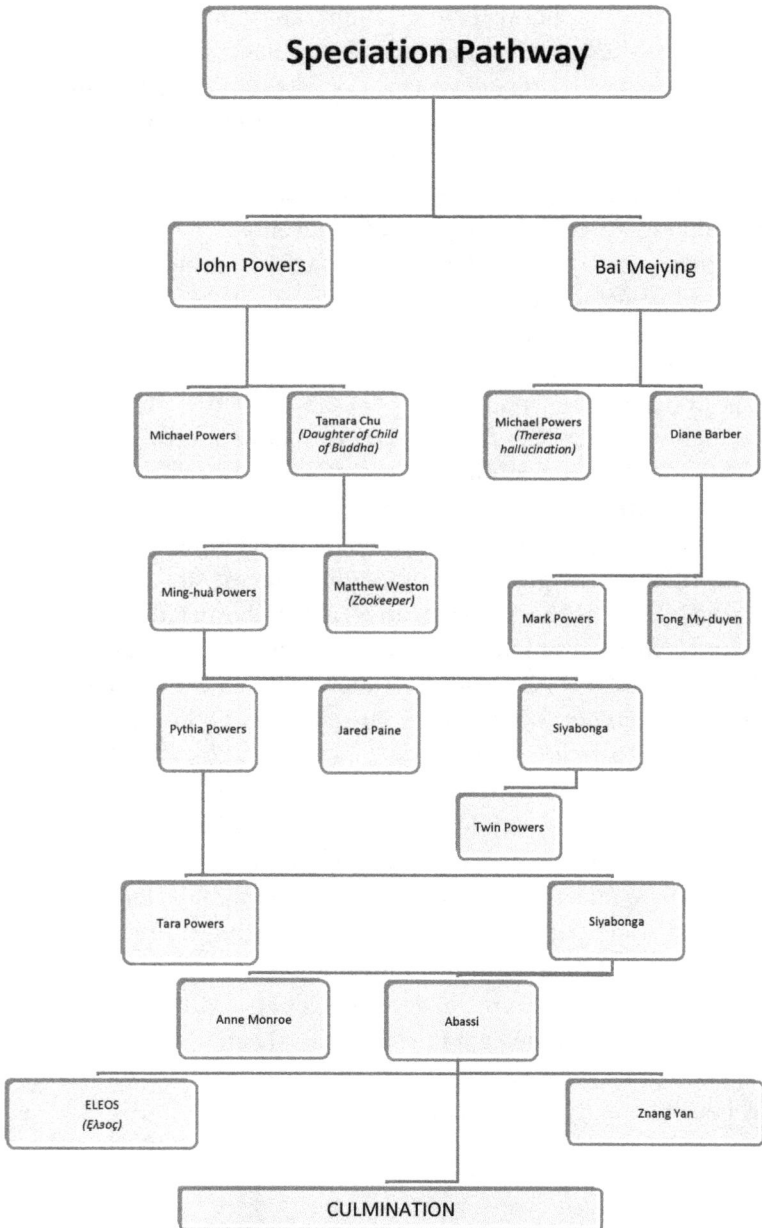

Speciation Pathway

John Powers

Bai Meiying

Michael Powers

Tamara Chu
(Daughter of Child of Buddha)

Michael Powers
(Theresa hallucination)

Diane Barber

Ming-huà Powers

Matthew Weston
(Zookeeper)

Mark Powers

Tong My-duyen

Pythia Powers

Jared Paine

Siyabonga

Twin Powers

Tara Powers

Siyabonga

Anne Monroe

Abassi

ELEOS
(Ἔλεος)

Znang Yan

CULMINATION

PROLOGUE

On a dreary afternoon, in one of the dingy back streets of San Francisco's Tenderloin district, three young men, known in the neighborhood as vicious drug dealers, are seen at various locations running and screaming as if chased by demons. This in and of itself would be odd, since these men are no strangers to violence and scrupulously adhere to the male ethos of taciturn stoicism. No. The odd thing is that not a one of them possesses arms. Witnesses will testify that they all had arms the previous day, but now have only stumps. Odder still, the stumps are not bloody. No. They appear as if the men had been born without arms, or at least had them amputated years ago. All they can babble when questioned is the extraordinary claim that a hunchbacked girl is responsible. Along with their arms, their minds appear gone as well.

All except for one . . . .

Book I – Ming-huà

Chapter 1: The Island

~ A Secret ~

Far out into the depths of the forest, on an isolated island off the coast of Washington State, a young hunchbacked girl lives alone in a primitive two-bedroom cabin. Though appearing roughhewn and ramshackle from without, the inside is kept clean and orderly. Few furnishings exist other than a well-stocked kitchen, crude wooden table, four-poster bed in the main bedroom and a smaller one in the guest room, colorfully painted nightstand, free standing closet, and assorted chairs. One chair, an apparent favorite, squats solidly on four short, gracefully curved legs. Its faded upholstery covers an overstuffed backrest that bears a deep, bowl-like impression perfectly formed to accommodate the girl's hump. An unfinished coverlet with protruding knitting needles enfolds the little end table near the chair. Oil lamps hang from various hooks, ready to be lit when darkness makes reading or delicate handwork difficult. It is late afternoon and the young hunchback is currently on her knees, bent over an elaborately carved wooden trunk she keeps at the foot of her bed. She mutters to herself as she rummages through the contents. Occasional sighs of frustration escape her lips as she digs deeper.

"Where are you?" she asks. Often, very often, she talks to herself. Being alone for many years has honed her skills at passing the time without feeling bored or adrift. Her conversations with herself are often rather long and convoluted, but today she is more succinct in her utterings.

"There you are, silly thing. What were you doing way down there?"

She pulls out a packet of letters bound together with twine, and returns to her favorite chair. Setting the packet on her lap, she gently unties the knot and leafs through the tumbled, unbound envelopes. She scans the postage dates stamped in the corners. Some of the envelopes are addressed to her in finely scripted English, others in gracefully coiled Chinese calligraphy. All are from her mother. She closes her eyes and picks a random envelope, carefully setting the rest atop the coverlet where she has smoothed the folds to make a flat space. Afternoon shadows from the towering Douglas fir trees have enveloped the cabin in gloomy dark, so she rises and lights an oil lamp hanging above the chair, then sits again and peruses the familiar handwriting with a sigh of pleasant anticipation. This one is dated over two years ago and the address is written in spidery English letters. Still, she waits to pull out the letter, enjoying the anticipation. Ever since that terrible incident when she was a little girl, she has learned to repress her eagerness and tamp down her impatience. These skills are not mere matters of expediency. No. To her, they are matters of life and death.

"Well, open it, open it Ming-huà," she says to herself.

"All in good time."

Ming-huà's father died when she was a young child. She keeps a black and white photograph of her parents in the trunk, but her mother (also a hunchback) never discussed the subject of her father. Even after innumerable attempts to raise the topic, her mother flatly refused. Any mention of him met with strict silence. Finally, out of the blue on Ming-huà's thirteenth birthday, her mother casually revealed the shattering news that he had been a wandering businessman who suffered dreadfully from mental illness, eventually dying in an institution. Stunned, Ming-huà asked a string of questions, but her mother again refused to answer or elaborate in any way, vowing that further questioning would be useless. Ming-huà continued to try, but her mother remained faithful to her vow. Further mention of him was strictly *verboten*. However, Ming-huà remained stubbornly persistent. After months of pestering, she finally learned her father suffered from schizophrenia. Beyond that, her mother would not elaborate. Researching the illness on her own, she woke up every day dreading to discover voices chattering unspeakable things in her head. Fortunately, this never happened. But, to her horror, she had already discovered an affliction that terrified her far more than schizophrenia. It was due to this affliction that her mother exiled them to such a far-away spot.

"Well, are you ever going to read it?"

"Quiet Ming-huà! Look at that silly squirrel outside running up and down the trunk of that tree. In the dusk, you can just make him out. Such a big tail! Ow!" Ming-huà instinctively puts her hand over her stomach. "That hurts. It hurts. What a hungry little fellow."

Usually, Ming-huà feels only a steady vibration from her hump, but there have been many times when a surge of electric shocks jarred her into awareness of something amiss in the surrounding world. Right now, she feels that type of jolt, one she is quite familiar with. It is the stab of hunger, transmitted through the receptors in her back by the frantic little squirrel. She immediately becomes uneasy and wants to disengage from the unpleasant sensation, but she has never been able to turn off these bursts of suffering. Only intense concentration on some other object has succeeded in alleviating the disturbing signals that so often afflict her mind. As a little girl, she puzzled over the vibrations and the surges, knowing them to be significant but always beyond her ability to fathom. Eventually, she came to accept them. Her mother, however, noticed her unique sensitivity growing in its power; and with this increased power, it correspondingly strengthened in its ability to cause Ming-huà empathetic pains. It soon became obvious these pains originated from the suffering of any creature in close proximity. Her mother made the determination that being around people in a big city was the problem. They had to get away from the distressing exigencies and violent emotional swings of a dense human population. Such proximity, her mother reasoned, had overloaded the sensitive receptors in her daughter's hump and had begun exerting a morbid sway over her extraordinary mind. She watched Ming-huà sink into a mire of ever-increasing bouts with torment and sorrow, all transmitted by those unhappy souls around her. Ming-huà's mother hesitated to pack up and leave, mainly for lack of opportunity and means. Only following a first horrifying incident that left no choice did she take her daughter to this isolated place. After living together in the cabin for a couple of years, on her sixteenth birthday, her mother suddenly informed Ming-huà she must leave her daughter and travel to a magic cave where she would vanish from this existence and never return. Ming-huà would, by some unspoken, terrible necessity, be left on her own. Her mother's last act consisted of turning over a bank account that would automatically provide Ming-huà sufficient funds every month to cover expenses, and perhaps a little more if her daughter lived frugally.

[4]

Now, three years later, Ming-huà has adapted to an utterly isolated life beyond all expectations of change.

"Come on, can't see the silly fellow any longer. He's run up the tree with his treasure. Open it."

"Yes, it's time."

She slowly removes the letter, carefully unfolds it, and briefly scans the words without reading, as might a thirsty woman pause in appreciation before taking deep swallows from a cool glass of water.

~ The First Horrifying Incident ~

Years earlier, who would have thought her troubles began with a favorite doll? When still a very young child, Ming-huà became attached to a ragdoll sewn together by her mother. It had been stuffed with poly fiber and clothed in a dress of extravagant colors. The chubby calico face had a permanent smile painted on. Its eyes were distinctly Asian, and its black locks of coiled fabric cascaded around its head. The moment the completed doll was presented, Ming-huà held it close to her chest, slept with it, and carried it everywhere. She wanted to give it a name, but of all those that came to mind none satisfied. One bright day the solution emerged like a thunderbolt from some unknown patch of Ming-huà's imagination. After this epiphany, the name "Miss Gladflower" could be heard repeated by the little hunchback girl with regularity.

"Miss Gladflower, time for tea."

"Miss Gladflower, let's go for a walk."

"Miss Gladflower, you seem sad today."

"Miss Gladflower, tell me about your boyfriend."

And so on. . . .

~

But one dreary afternoon, when left momentarily unattended on the lawn, Miss Gladflower fell prey to a neighborhood dog who, before being chased away, left the doll with a serious wound on her back. The pretty fabric had pulled loose and stuffing bulged out. After the dog had been safely shooed off, Ming-huà grabbed the unfortunate Miss Gladflower and retreated to her room where she performed emergency surgery. She tried pushing the stuffing back into the body, but it would not stay and kept bulging out in a most horrible manner. Ming-huà recognized the resemblance immediately.

"Ugly hunchback!" she cried. "Ugly hump!"

Some signal from her own hump jolted her mind, and she stared at the doll in anger.

"I want you to be gone, ugly hunchback!"

It dissolved into thin air.

Completely disappeared.

Not a trace remained.

Her heart stopped and she could only stare at an empty lap where Miss Gladflower used to be.

Ming-huà heard her mother gasp from behind. "It is come!"

She watched in stupefied horror as her mother clapped her hands over her face and moaned loudly, "Now we must leave! We must leave and never come back!"

These impassioned words terrified her, but she was in a state of shock. With her mother's threat to leave and never come back, she stared at the empty place where the doll had been and wished it back.

Nothing.

She concentrated hard.

Nothing.

Her power worked in only one direction. This discovery tore something from her soul that itself, like Miss Gladflower, could never be returned. Ming-huà howled in abject terror. No matter how many times she asked what her mother meant by "it is come", no answer ever came. After the incident, life for her became a whirl of confusion; packing, moving, stopping, unpacking, starting, resting, running, always with no particular destination except for some unspecified, isolated location. Only the desert (Ming-huà later realized it represented the most obvious choice) seemed eliminated from her mother's list of possibilities. Ming-huà never learned why, but whenever her mother mused aloud about the desert as a solution, the dismissive words, "No, no. Too many ghosts!" quickly followed. To Ming-huà, this utterance gave an inexplicable expression of finality to the problem.

Often, when frustrated over some difficulty, her mother would say, "I wish your father were with us now."

Ming-huà briefly passed through her mind the notion of what it must be like to have a husband, then merely smiled serenely back at her mother. How could she miss a schizophrenic father? The very word conjured visions of spooky madness. Still, he must have been an outcast, like her. This fact, at least, provided some connection to him.

Since her earliest years, in spite of possessing a quite strikingly beautiful face, Ming-huà had come to accept her self-perceived ugliness. For as long as she can remember she had given up on ever attracting a boyfriend, or being involved in any romantic affair, even a momentary one. Although many had been wonderstruck by her gorgeous features, she rejected their advances as evidence of pity. Instead, she chose to view the world like an old woman long since divested of her sexual charms, whose life is very much lived with both feet planted firmly on undeceived ground. Without unnecessary relational complications, she fully recognized the absurdity and evanescence of life's struggles. Grandmothers can afford to be wise. Ming-hua's charm lay in her utter absence of idyllic dreams and grandiose plans. Only the massive anomaly of her hump interfered with living the entirety of her young life as a self-possessed seventy-year-old.

Through a veritable maze of endless roads, cheap motels, and the byzantine movements of her mother, they found themselves in the State of Washington. While contemplating the desirability of settling in Canada, or going farther north to Alaska, a string of obscure islands off the coast drew her attention. After researching all of them, and visits to a handful, she settled on the most isolated and pristine. Persevering over the objections of a hesitant real estate agent, she insisted the choice of that distant island was irrevocable, and demanded he find a suitable plot of land with a minimally habitable structure. It took a long time to locate. Finally, on a lonely parcel in the middle of the forest, the real estate agent reluctantly showed her a rather broken-down cabin, far from any other human habitation. He tried to talk her out of it, emphasizing the dangers of a single woman raising a child alone, with no electricity and no neighbors to give comfort. Worse, there were no schools to educate her daughter.

After listening politely, her mother said, "No, it is perfect, thank you. We will do just fine."

The agent knew of a handyman that would make the cabin more habitable.

"Yes, yes, that would be good."

Had Ming-huà's mother and herself not been hunchbacks, the agent would have more strongly objected, perhaps even refused to be involved. However, he concluded hunchbacks were a species unto themselves, and like some sort of Neanderthals, could survive more readily in harsh conditions than normal people. With the deal quickly struck and arrangements made, the cabin was soon transformed into a cozy retreat by the talented handyman (who became quite close with the two odd females).

Mother and daughter prepared to move in.

~

Meanwhile, for the past year, Ming-huà had been experimenting with her power. Alternately terrified of it, yet fascinated by it, she tested herself by focusing her attention on a variety of small inanimate objects.

"Be gone," she would whisper.

Nothing.

"Be gone!" she commanded.

Nothing.

After spending so much time trying and failing to duplicate her obliteration of Miss Gladflower on more innocuous objects, Ming-huà gave up and tried, in her clumsy way, to move on to other childish things. Nevertheless, such innocent bliss could not be recaptured. A pall hung over her, a kind of dread that colored her once open and happy view of life. Assailed by her mother's frantic quest and flailing actions, her emotions slowly migrated inward where she assiduously nurtured a self-sufficient tranquility (to such an extent she could pass muster at a medieval nunnery). Sweet and pliable, silent and contemplative, she followed her mother uncomplainingly, and spent most of her time in a state of silent contentment.

However, a second incident occurred that drastically reinforced her sense of otherness. Just before they moved to the island cabin, she sat in her motel room sewing a torn blouse the way her mother taught her. Ming-huà pricked her finger, drawing blood, so she sucked on it to stop the bleeding. Satisfied it had been staunched, she began anew but once again pricked her finger in the same spot, hurting much worse and drawing even more blood.

"Ow! Stupid needle!" she cried. "Stupid stupid needle!"

It disappeared.

Gone.

Nowhere to be found.

Stunned, Ming-huà again sucked her finger in wonder and thought to herself, *So, that's it! I must be angry to make things disappear. Anger is what does it!*

At first, this idea pleased her, as she had solved the mystery.

Now when I get angry, I can make things go away.

But after further reflection, she again felt a childish terror. *What if I get angry at mother? No, no, no, no. I must never get angry. Never!*

The thought that she might make her mother, or some other innocent being cease to exist curdled her blood and made her even more inwardly drawn. She now approached life as carefully as a person with hemophilia approaches a bramble bush. This self-imposed monastic existence only intensified when they moved to the cabin. Yet, far from feeling confined, Ming-huà was instantly entranced by the surrounding forest, and fell easily into a quiet, ascetic life. The endless green whispering of the trees soothed her. As wonderful as the trees, the forest animals, abundant in their diversity and effortless in their movements, delighted her beyond words. Her mother, watching her progression like a hawk, took great comfort in Ming-huà's silent joy, and planned the date when she would leave her daughter forever. Thus, shortly after turning sixteen, Ming-huà found herself completely alone. Once, on a stormy night when her loneliness and anger at being deserted got the better of her, she made her mother's picture vanish. Again, the evidence of her power horrified her and made her withdraw even farther into her own world. This was no devil-child, whipped to cruel frenzy by the unleashing of her destructive power. No. This very power terrified her and drove her generous spirit into deeper solitude lest she inflict intentional or unintentional harm on others.

She mustn't slip again. Ming-huà felt quite content to spend the remainder of her years living anonymously in a small cabin surrounded by forest. Only the letters from her mother remained as fragile, loving ties binding her to another human being.

~ Post Office ~

Nevertheless, unpleasant memories of her power rarely return as time passes in repetitious predictability. Now, habituated to her island solitude, Ming-huà slowly finishes reading her mother's letter, then reads it again and with a satisfied sigh, carefully refolds it and slips it inside the envelope. Retying the bundle of letters, she steps lightly back to the trunk and places them deep in a corner. She closes the lid and for a moment runs her fingers over carved scenes decorating the top.

"Tomorrow is post office day," she reminds herself, then returns to her favorite chair to spend some hours knitting before going to bed.

Once a month Ming-huà walks to the post office pulling a red wagon to collect groceries and what little mail is in her box. Her mother's letters have long ago stopped coming. The only mail of any consequence are bills and her monthly statement showing the deposit of funds from some mysterious source. After picking up the mail, she goes to the small grocery store and stocks up on food. These excursions are almost always uneventful, and the little talking she engages in with other humans is brief and awkward for all parties. Nevertheless, even such minimal human contact is welcome, and Ming-huà deliberately limits her time around people so that their internal angers, frustrations, sufferings and pains merely give the white noise in her hump a somewhat grating, raspy tone.

Ming-huà awakes early, and because the walk into town is long and tiring, she makes a hearty breakfast to last until dinner. In the absence of human companionship, her thoughts are necessarily focused only on the immediate needs and observations of the moment. Preparing food, working in her garden, and alternately sewing, knitting, and quilting occupy the bulk of the day. A trip to the post office always disrupts this monotonous schedule, and so have taken on the characteristics of an adventure far exceeding its actual significance. To an outside observer, the only noticeable sign that this is a special day would be an increase in the chattiness of Ming-huà's self-directed soliloquies.

"So sorry, little eggs, that I have to put you in this hot skillet, but a body has to eat. Just know it is all for the good. I will use your nutrients for good purposes, and you will sacrifice your snug little home in the shell for the betterment of the world . . . I hope. I must remember not to get angry, especially today. I will be around people. Only people are in danger. Not my animal friends, no matter how cruel they can sometimes be. But, not to worry, I have never yet gotten angry in town. People are usually either nice or ignore me altogether . . . particularly after they see my hump. I recognize many of them now, and we always exchange pleasantries. Not to worry, Ming-huà. All will be well."

In this manner she carries on a discussion with herself throughout breakfast. However, once she steps out of the cabin, grabs the handle of her little wagon, and starts down the path, she stops chattering and attends to the sounds of the forest. Always, she first listens for the wind whispering through the needles of the fir trees. Once perceiving that familiar sound, she picks up on a variety of birds making their usual ruckus. Her hump seems alive to the various life forms, and its usual low-key hum comes alive and commences a pleasant sing-song rhythm. Only the eternal lower chords of universal hunger and the jolts of sudden, violent death contribute a slightly ominous, bass gravitas to the chorus. Ming-huà embraces her sense of belonging in this natural world, one that is devoid of human pettiness, greed, ignorance, and casual cruelty. It is that other world, that human world, where her type will never belong. Still, in spite of the satisfaction found in solitude, she does look forward to seeing her own kind again. Even the awkward curiosity her misshapen body attracts is not enough to keep her entirely a hermit. It rarely occurs to Ming-huà that she feels sorry for herself. The few pangs of self-pity she does feel invariably arise when around loving couples or happy families. In those instances, her hump sheds its darker tones and soars in soprano majesty. However, instead of making her happy, this exquisite music elicits only sadness and depression, which Ming-huà ascribes to the deceptive feedback of her brain, not to the eternally truthful emanations from her hump.

Now, as she walks, Ming-huà feels unwelcome excitement, an emotion she is unaccustomed to, for it is always followed by disappointment and a feeling of being let down by the universe. Unfortunately, this feeling of disillusionment is an affliction she always carries back to her cabin after trips to the post office. Unwilling to dwell on such self-fulfilling prophecies, she initiates a discussion with the passing woods.

"Such a pleasant walk. All of you giants are so kind to line my stroll with your majestic presence." She bows politely and looks up at the boughs of a nearby fir where a noisy squirrel is scolding her for violating its space.

"Oh, don't be silly! I'm leaving soon enough. Be nice."

On she walks, excitement tinged with nervousness growing more palpable in spite of her self-admonishments to remain calm. As she reaches the outskirts of town, houses reveal themselves and the dirt path abruptly becomes a paved road. When the houses become more numerous, she sees a few people working outside and waves. They wave back, staring a bit longer than they normally would at a person strolling by. Ming-huà's hump remains a stable hum, and she takes no offense at the curious spectacle she must appear to those who rarely see her. Often, when subjected to surreptitious scrutiny by others, her hump will send inharmonious chords, but she has learned to pay no attention and go on with her business as if all were normal and unremarkable.

"Hello!" she calls to a person who pauses while raking a garden.

"Hello!" comes the reply.

Unknown to Ming-huà, every townsperson knows who she is and how much they talk amongst themselves about the "odd young hunchback girl" who lives alone far out in the forest. Children and teenagers, of course, have convinced themselves she is a witch with supernatural powers. There is, however, a split of opinion about whether she is a good witch or an evil one. It used to be that some brave young souls would steal at night to her cabin and watch for supernatural, "witch-things" like dancing with a broomstick and chanting covens of grotesque witches sacrificing an animal, or a human. But nothing ever happened, except she would come onto her porch and ask them if they wanted to come inside and listen to her read aloud. At first, it was assumed this constituted a ploy to lure them in and be sacrificed. However, a few heroes agreed, and she really did just read to them. As a result, the practice of spying on her cabin fell into disuse due to the dry content of her books and the boredom they induced.

When Ming-huà nears the one-street business district, friendly but reserved verbal niceties increase, as do the stares. Still, she is pleased. Her hump only occasionally registers the jarring emotions of a passing individual whose unhappiness or anger disrupts the placid hum, but her visit proceeds with a minimum of fuss. Ming-huà enjoys the civilities exchanged between her and the townspeople, as they are appropriately brief and non-threatening. Inside the post office, she sees familiar faces retrieving their mail, but there is one individual she does not recognize, and whose entire demeanor is out of place in this rural outpost. He reminds her of the scarecrow in a movie her mother shared many years earlier, except he is dressed nicely and wears no floppy hat. Nevertheless, his attention is entirely focused on her and does not quickly look away like most people when she makes eye contact. She nods, and he nods in return, smiling all the while just like that movie scarecrow. Ming-huà is used to stares, but his gaze is different. Very different. Her hump is awash with confusing waves of indecipherable impressions emanating from this strange man.

Pretending to look through her mail, she waits for him to leave. But he doesn't. He just stands and stares while others walk around his deceivingly immoveable figure. She notices he does not merely stand, with arms in a normal position. Instead, he seems to be in constant movement while remaining in the same spot, as if his joints were all made of rubber. *Like the scarecrow*, she thinks. Preferring to wait until he is gone, she pretends to be absorbed in her mail but he continues to stare, his odd body atwitch with restless movement. Finally, Ming-huà forces herself to pass by him as she leaves. Instead of stepping aside, he dances a little jig and slides in front of her, nodding. The smile never leaves his face, *like the scarecrow. Like Miss Gladflower.*

"Hello, Ming-huà," he says calmly.

Her hump's receptors shift into overdrive, but the information received by her brain is garbled and incomprehensible. Neither good nor bad. Neither happy nor sad. Neither this nor that. A contradictory enigma.

"Hello," she mumbles under her breath while continuing to move awkwardly toward the door. Her thoughts are a jumble of confusion, and to escape becomes her only imperative. She manages to slip by him and make it out of the building. He follows, and yet he does not simply follow. No. Rather, he dances after her, spinning his arms and waving his hands at odd angles. Now, for once she is not the center of attention, as a handful of people in front of the post office pause to admire his performance. Ming-huà wants to take the opportunity to hurry away unnoticed with her wagon in tow and finish shopping so she can avoid this extraordinary character. Some perverse feeling wants her to stay and demand how he knows her name, but she is far too intimidated and shy for such a bold move. As she separates from the little crowd and retrieves her wagon, she hurries to the grocery store, nervously glancing behind to make sure he does not follow.

Ming-huà is anxious to return to the safety of her little cabin, so she rushes to complete her shopping and quickly leave town with groceries in tow. Unfortunately, this is hunting season, and there are more customers than usual who have arrived on the island to shoot deer. She waits in a long line at the cash register, all the while being ogled by strangers. At last, she pays, loads her wagon, and quickly heads down the street. To her relief, the scarecrow is nowhere to be found. When the end of the paved road is reached, she relaxes and slackens her pace. Still, she occasionally looks back to make sure no one is following. Now, with the security of knowing her forest friends are all around, she falls into a comfortable stride and turns her attention to the mystery of the scarecrow and how he knows her name.

~ A Second Terrible Incident ~

Thus lost in thought, a sudden rush of excited yells and coarse laughter erupts some distance away, shattering her reverie. Ming-huà is aware a creek runs parallel to the path and this is where the ruckus seems to originate, but dense foliage blocks her view. Unsettled by the crude noises, she quickens her pace, intent on ignoring the commotion and assuming they come from a group of rowdy tourists having an outdoor gathering. Somehow, an ominous rumbling from her hump indicates otherwise. Her nerves are on full alert, and she longs to put the noise far behind. But without warning, her hump sends a series of viciously painful jolts into her brain, and she doubles over in agony. As the shouting and roaring continue, she forces herself to gain control over her body and rushes off the path toward the spot where, she now assumes, a person is in distress. When she reaches the edge of the creek, a bewildering scene unfolds before her eyes.

Two young males, dressed in camouflaged khakis, are knee deep in the creek, leaning over something churning desperately beneath them in the water. Ming-huà cannot make out what is happening, so she takes a few steps closer. To her horror, she realizes the men are drowning a struggling fawn. They are laughing, probably drunk, encouraging each other to keep the poor fawn's head beneath the water and roaring playful obscenities when the tiny nose slips their hold and tries to breath in some air.

Without thinking any further, Ming-huà 's confusion turns to rage as she watches the obscene pleasure these evil men are deriving from such pointless and heartless murder. If she hesitates even a few seconds longer, the little fawn will be dead, so her entire wrath is loosed upon its tormentors.

In an instant the two men are gone.

Disappeared.

Just like Miss Gladflower.

Their bodies dissociated and the rich molecules and atoms that comprised them dispersed into the environment where they might serve better purposes.

Not a trace left. No clothes. Nothing. Only two hunting rifles lying on the bank remain as evidence the men once existed at this spot in space and time.

Ming-huà carefully lifts the exhausted fawn out of the water and steadies her on the bank, where her mother awaits at a discreet distance in alert anticipation. It is only then that the full horror of what she had just done dawns upon the shaken young hunchback.

~

As if escaping a murder scene, Ming-huà runs back to the path and stands looking down its dirt length toward the cabin. Her legs will no longer obey her commands, and she feels faint. Knowing she must get as far away from this spot as possible, she nonetheless plops stupefied on a fallen log and buries her face in her hands, heaving dry sobs (tears will not come to help wash away the guilt). She does not know how much time passes, but she must have sunk into some sort of stupor, for she awakes to the lengthening shadows of dusk and sees a man standing over her, smiling.

It is the scarecrow.

He dances a little jig and proclaims, "I know what just happened."

Ming-huà stares at him in shock.

"Believe me, I know. It was a good thing to do. That is why I followed you today. Don't worry, it is good! They did not suffer, and the suffering they inflicted on the world is over! Kaput!"

Much to Ming-huà's consternation, he again dances a jig. The smile never leaves his face. He looks up the path toward the town. "It is time we go."

"Where?" asks Ming-huà dumbly.

"To your quaint little wooden castle, of course. Those two who are no longer two will soon be missed. Sooner or later there will be people coming. When that happens, you want to be away from this spot."

"But—" Ming-huà starts to object.

"Innocence itself. You are innocence itself. Even Miss Gladflower knew that when you made her disappear."

Ming-huà trembles in the face of this absurdity. This dream. This nightmare. She can only mutter, "Who are you?"

He holds out his hand to help her up. "Come! It is late. We must be on our way. I will tell you as we walk."

She takes his hand and they start off together in silence, Scarecrow pulling her wagon. "You can't stay at my place," she finally says.

"Of course. Never intended to stay at your place. But, nonetheless, we need to talk. Oh yes, we need to talk. But certainly not here. Not at the scene of the . . . well, of your reconfiguration."

"Reconfiguration?"

"Yes, reconfiguration. You just rearranged a few atoms here, a few molecules there, and *voilà!*"

Ming-huà feels sick. "I killed them."

"You reconfigured them." He glances at her in alarm as she slows her pace. "Are you sick? Do you need to vomit?"

"No," she replies miserably. "I wish I did."

He contorts his body into a dramatic pose.

"Who are you?" she asks again.

"My name is Siren Rung."

In her misery, she dryly chuckles. "What?"

"Siren Rung."

"A funny name . . . sounds oddly familiar."

"It should." He laughs as at an inside joke.

"Why should it?"

"No reason. Let's keep walking, it's getting dark."

Ming-huà's legs move, but she feels queasy and weak. She shudders, wraps her arms around her body, and tries to erase all thoughts from her mind, but her hump reverberates with an unfamiliar, grating buzz. Her trembling continues all the way to the cabin.

~

[16]

Once inside, Ming-huà collapses on a straight back chair. She tries to keep her body rigid while her mind struggles to cope, but the shaking becomes uncontrollable. If she keeps asking questions, perhaps her nerves will calm.

"I know your name now, but who are you?" In spite of her struggles to maintain some semblance of calm, the words come out a stuttering mess.

Siren Rung looks at her with a degree of pity. "As your father would say, it is the Time of Shaking."

"My father! You knew him?" Again, the words are staccato, as if it takes some effort to spit them out with clear enough pronunciation to make them understood.

Revelations have come too fast and furious for poor Ming-huà to absorb. Her trembling increases to an alarming degree, and she succumbs to more violent shaking, even causing her normally equable visitor to quickly grab a blanket off the bed and wrap it around her as one might do for a freezing person. Between clattering teeth, Ming-huà attempts to repeat her questions, viewing them as crucial lifelines to reality. It takes her multiple times to finally force out the words, albeit stretched loosely apart by abrupt pauses and deep intakes of breath.

"Who are you? How do you know my father?"

Apparently encouraged by her perseverance, he dances another little jig, this one far less exuberant, edged in its movements with a hint of sorrow. With one leg lifted in the air and hands raised heavenward, he freezes the pose and glares at her dramatically.

"As I told you, I am Siren Rung, and I knew your father very well. We all did. By the way, call me Sy."

Ming-huà is not listening, her attention drawn to her own suffering and the two men whose faces, cruel as they were, expressed a humanity that, to her, must have possessed some deeper quality of redemption. Surely they must have had some quality of goodness! They may have had wives and children. And to have caused them to simply vanish! The agony of having committed such an atrocity is unbearable to her.

Ming-huà tries to return her attention to the visitor's words, but she feels dizzy, and her bones and muscles melt away, no longer able to prop up her body. She feels herself slipping downward. . . .

~ Aftermath ~

Ming-huà is awakened by a persistent knocking at the door. She is surprised to find herself in bed, nightgown on, covers drawn around her neck, sunlight flooding the room. Her mind is sluggish and she slowly remembers certain terrible events, but is unclear how long ago they happened, or whether they happened at all. *A dream. It was a dream. Thank God!* But the knocking continues in intensity, and she knows it does not arise from any dream. She quickly rises and throws on a robe.

Cracking open the door, she sees the town sheriff and a handful of men standing behind.

"Hello Mr. Turner," she says in a growly voice.

He tips his hat. "Hello Miss Powers. Sorry to bother you. May I come in?"

Ming-huà pulls her robe tighter around her neck and keeps the door cracked open just enough to see his face. "Oh, I'm so sorry, I just got up. What is it?"

"Well, we have reports of missing persons. Two men. White males. They were hunting near your cabin. We found their guns, but they are still missing. Can I come in, please?"

No dream no dream no dream oh God no dream.

She keeps the door only cracked open. "I don't know anything about it, sheriff."

"Did you see any men around yesterday?"

"No. I went to town, to the post office and shopping, and came straight back here. I didn't see anything."

"Their guns were near the creek that runs close to your place. Did you hear anything?"

"Like what?"

"Voices, gunfire, you know, anything?"

"Sorry Mr. Turner. No."

"Are you sure?"

"I'm sure."

He hesitates, then says haltingly, "Well . . . if you saw or heard nothing, I guess there is not much to say, is there?"

"No."

"Well, if you remember something, anything, please call me. Here's my card. Call me if you think of anything, no matter how insignificant you think it might be. Will you do that, Miss Powers?"

She takes the card. "Yes. Yes, I will," adding vaguely, "I have no phone."

He turns to leave and says, "Come on, boys, let's keep searching." Over his shoulder he acerbically utters, "Thanks for your time."

Ming-huà does not respond. She closes the door and moves as in a daze to the comfort of her overstuffed chair. Settling in, she replays the events of the previous day with a clear reenactment of details that are mesmerizing in their horror. She feels oppressed by the stale air and opens a window. As she does so, a squirrel begins chattering in a nearby tree.

"Silly squirrel, so early to be so talkative." These words are muttered instinctively, automatically, her thoughts now focused on something else. Something important.

"Where is the scarecrow?"

She looks down at her robe, then scans the room and sees her clothes from the previous day neatly folded on the night table.

"Who is scarecrow?"

The trembling starts again, and Ming-huà quickly goes to the kitchen and busies herself preparing breakfast. "Keep busy, Ming-huà," she says out loud. "Keep busy and focus on what you are doing. Nothing can be done now. Nothing."

She hears the squirrel again, and says, "Oh, if only I were you. If I had only hunger to think about. Only hunger! Not. . . . "

~

It is afternoon, and in her misery, Ming-huà takes to the garden and pulls weeds with single-minded purpose. The physical work feels good, and she lapses into a rhythm, unmindful of anything around her. When the faces of the two men materialize in her imagination, she doubles her efforts at pulling and tossing, pulling and tossing.

Often, when the wind rustles a branch or an inquisitive deer steps on a twig, Ming-huà stops her labor and looks around . . . for what? The sheriff? The two men who have reassembled? No. She looks for the scarecrow. *How fitting!* she thinks bitterly. *A scarecrow in my garden, scaring away . . . who knows?*

[19]

Days pass in this fashion. With an innocent conscience torn away so brutally, her quiet contentment and symbiotic relationship with the natural world seems a distant memory. *Murder is not natural*, she reminds herself daily. *My animal friends do not murder. I am the canker that now afflicts this forest.* No more does she carry on long conversations with herself, as if she shunned her own existence. An echoing remorse at her loss, and the ever-present fear of exposure, are her constant companions. Although sinking deeper in her own pain, and with a single-minded intent to exile herself even farther from the human race, there exists only one person she longs to see.

Still no scarecrow. . . .

Once, Sheriff Turner stopped by her garden and asked if she remembered anything, but she replied with a simple, "No," and he never returned. She dared not inquire about the search, or the missing men's background. Just a simple "No" and she was cleared of any wrongdoing by everyone but herself. Guilt has worked its magic and eroded even the small amount of confidence left to defend against despair. Her hump continues preternaturally silent. A barely perceptible hum the only reminder it exists at all. Proof, to her, that estrangement from the world must be permanent and inexorable. She cannot sleep nor can she eat, and gradually her strength dwindles to the point she gives up working in the garden. Her greatest fear looms just over the horizon, when she must return to town and expose herself to the living. Or, alternatively, she can simply wait and let herself die. Appropriate punishment for murder. Better yet, she tries to dissociate herself, as she did to those poor men. But, as always, her power does not work on her own body. So, she takes to her bed and wastes away as, she feels, fitting and proper for a murderess.

~

"It's time to leave."

The voice comes from some distant place, barely discernable to her ears.

"Come, come, Ming-huà! It's time to go!"

Nearer. Familiar.

She feels her head lifted and a spoon with warm soup put to her lips. "Drink. It's time to go. Drink!"

Pillows are fluffed and she is helped to sit up in bed. More spoonsful of soup. She sips. It tastes good.

[20]

"Goodness gracious, girl! You're skin and bones! That's no way to travel. Drink more!"

More is given. More is consumed. The room is warm and her caretaker remains a fuzzy smudge. She sleeps. Two days pass between sleep and soup. Her strength returns. Her hump buzzes with unusual energy. One afternoon, she focuses.

"Scarecrow," she murmurs. "I thought it was you."

"Scarecrow! No, no, no, my dear. It is Sy."

He dances a lively jig. "I'm no scarecrow. See me whirl! I keep the crows away better than any scarecrow!"

He affects an exaggeratedly deep bow. "It is Sy . . . Siren Rung, at your service. And we must leave!"

"Leave? Why?"

"*Goddess* says so."

"What?" The word makes Ming-huà freeze up inside. Her muscles tighten and her mind struggles to make sense of her reaction.

"*Goddess*?" she blurts.

"Never mind. It is enough that we must leave."

A sudden terrible thought prods her to sit up. "Are they coming for me?"

"They?" He laughs knowingly. "No, no. It is not, 'they who are coming for you'! Instead, you, my dear, are going to them!"

"I don't understand."

"Nor do I, but I never understand *Her*. Nevertheless—"

"*Her*?"

He shakes his head irritably. "Never mind! You are The Daughter. Get a bit stronger. Eat. Eat! Tomorrow, we go, come hell or high water!"

"But this is my house!"

"Correction, it is no longer your house. It is your prison."

Ming-huà sinks back and assumes a sour face. "As it should be. This is where my crime was committed. The corpses of those two men were little more than a stone's throw away."

"No, little hunchback. There were no corpses, remember? You simply reconfigured the innumerable constituents of their bodies and freed them for other, better purposes. In the meantime, you stopped the terrible suffering of a poor little fawn and obliterated the animate machinery of evil that disguised itself as these men."

[21]

"I will not play *God*."

At this, Sy roars with laughter and slaps his knees in delight. "*God*? Oh, that is rich! That is hilarious! Hilarious! If only you knew what a good joke that is." He dances another jig, throwing his arms outward and craning his head heavenward. "You hear that, Great Lady? She doesn't want to play *God* while *God* plays with her! Marvelous! Delicious!"

"Stop!" cries a startled Ming-huà.

He abruptly stops and turns his fierce eyes upon her. "Do you believe in *God*?"

She hesitates. "No," she whispers.

"And *Goddess*?"

For some reason, the memory of her mother pops into her head, and the mention of *Goddess* reverberates in her hump as a profound clarion call, deafening as one of Quasimodo's bells. She is thrown into utter bewilderment and cannot say a word.

"Well?" he prompts.

Still, she remains speechless.

"Never mind! Tomorrow we leave!"

Ming-huà is shaken back to reality by his raucous behavior and loud voice.

"Look. . . Mr. Rung—"

"Call me Sy."

"Look, Sy, I don't know anything about you. I have no intention of leaving my home. In fact, I want you to leave. Please!"

Sy falls quiet and stares at her with an unreadable glint in his eyes. "What does your hump say?"

"What?"

"Your hump. What does it say?"

"What do you know about my hump?" she stammers.

"Everything. And you're supposed to be The Daughter? Ha! You are just as silly as that squirrel you always talk with. Your hump nurtures a seed that has been planted since your grandparents were around. It is now sprouting. Thus, it is time for a gardener. Me!"

Dancing another loose-jointed jig, he cackles, "Scarecrow with a green thumb! I'm beginning to like that moniker after all! From now on you can call me Scarecrow!"

[22]

Ming-huà falls silent as her last remaining willpower caves in upon itself, leaving her too weak to make further demands he leave. Observing her weakness, Sy's face suddenly darkens and all pretense at lightheartedness falls away to reveal a somber, intimidating presence. He leans over her and speaks in the harsh growl of a disturbed lion, his eyes frozen daggers unveiled now for the first time.

"Ming-huà, you have a power that is unique in the world. It is your fate to possess this power. However, no longer can you hide it away in this place; its once safe and pleasant environs are now disturbed by . . . unexplained disappearances. Humans abhor unexplained things, and they will move heaven and earth to explain them, even if incorrectly. It is time you test the limits of your power's potential. Now, misshapen child, you must venture out into the larger world of people; a world full of deadly traps and elaborate snares. You must! Unbeknownst to you, that cursed hump is a blessing, and it can make things vanish, but it can also make things be reborn, and all the while it sings the Music of the Spheres— music which it is your task in life to decipher properly. Your grandmother could decipher the taps from a Precious Object. Your mother could decipher the echoes of space and time in magic caves. Your father, in the depths of his so-called schizophrenia, never gave up his quest to decipher the wishes of *Goddess*. It is your fate to do the same. It is your destiny."

He straightens up, a mischievous smile softening the harshness of his glare. "And that destiny will be paid for. You will find your anonymous financial guardian will double and triple the amount of money deposited in your account. A dream! Enough to finance a dozen quests! By the way, your little cabin will continue to be paid for . . . just in case. And what about this clever sorcerer, yours truly Siren Rung? Ah! He is descended from other sorcerers whose life threads are entwined with those of your parents and grandparents. Siren Rung will gleefully dance ahead of you on your journeys, grabbing every opportunity to take what evil the world has to offer and in return, poke both its eyes in jest! Oh, yes, he will step back and laugh at this old world's teary blinks and sputtering outrage." He pauses for effect. "After all, you are The Daughter."

Ming-huà listens submissively. "I have many questions," she says softly. "But, not now."

"No, not now," he agrees. "I will give you another day or two to rest, eat, and reflect. But then, we are off."

[23]

"All right, I will go." She can barely believe her own words.

"Good! I'll return in two days. Be packed. One suitcase only, or a backpack. Nothing else. Ah! I forget! You have a built-in backpack. No matter! We leave early. Be ready."

She watches him walk jauntily down the path, his nimble form hazy in the twilight. As he fades away, riddles, like swarms of butterflies, flutter in an undulating cloud around his lanky, scarecrow body. Oddly enough, she is not startled by this vision. Instead, the riddles act as lures drawing her into his orbit. She is her mother's daughter.

~ Leaving the Island ~

Later that night, lying in bed, Ming-huà struggles to understand the meaning behind Siren Rung's rather disjointed rambling. A few words had penetrated: "mother", "father", "grandmother", "grandfather", "quest", "*Goddess*", but she now has no energy to try and flesh out the portentous significance binding them into a coherent whole. She simply decides to give herself over to this decidedly outlandish man, come what may. He will relieve the burden of coping with the desiccating grind of an everyday life weighed down by guilt and murder. As she reflects on these notions, she is surprised how quickly and completely, heart and soul, she has succumbed to his siren call. She remembers saying, "All right, I will go," as if someone else spoke the words. Perhaps the response came from her hump's command, or maybe from the ghostly voice of her mother, but once spoken, the words consummated the total surrender she had been unconsciously seeking. Yet surprisingly, in the totality of her defeat, she sees an unexpected glimmer of hope. In a fleeting moment of surrender, everything in her world precipitously turned on a dime, but rather than feeling dazed, she now views the future with a degree of reawakened confidence, albeit as yet with no clear purpose. Her beloved forest would continue, but she would be gone, the awful spirits of her two victims left behind to haunt those who cannot be haunted. As of now, her old life is ended. It matters little that she does not comprehend the meaning behind the beaded necklace of shimmery words strung together by Siren Rung. What matters now is how to deal with an uncertain future. From the darkness outside, Ming-huà hears a squirrel . . . the same squirrel? . . . chattering away. *He's scolding me again, telling me to leave. I've outlived*

*my usefulness here. No, that's not quite right. I've lost the right to live
here.*

~

When Sy comes for her, Ming-huà had been sitting in her favorite,
overstuffed chair for hours, a small suitcase primly beside it on the floor,
both waiting patiently. Before his arrival, she had been luxuriating in all
the rich objects that inhabited what was once her comfortable universe.
That universe, although now ostensibly spread before her eyes in the
present, had already become a memory. It encompassed the outside, the
forest, all her animal friends and confidantes—indeed her entire life—yet
she remains tearless. No sentimentality must be indulged in by a
murderess! *Does it become easier?* she wonders about murder. Through
the window, she catches sight of Sy approaching in a lightheaded, dancing
gait. "I suppose we will find out," she muses aloud, a sorrowful, brief
throwback to her happier days of long soliloquies. Ming-huà has begun to
view the world in the sulky manner of a young girl who has lost her
virginity to a boy whose heartless lies have only just been discovered.
Now, she stands to greet Sy with a determination borne of resignation, and
calls out an invitation to enter. As he opens the front door, she is startled
to see her two murdered victims peering in through a side window.
Momentarily frightened, Ming-huà twists away from the sight, and notices
Miss Gladflower sitting on the same overstuffed chair she had just vacated.
It seems the ghosts have taken over, and lost no time in doing so, she
thinks. Abruptly her body stiffens in protest over these uninvited specters,
and swivels back toward the window. She shouts angrily, "You evil men
should not have tried to kill that helpless fawn!" She is astonished at her
own violent outburst, and turns her head sharply to look back at the chair.
In a much softer tone, she admonishes the doll, "And Miss Gladflower, I
am sorry, but you should not have lost your stuffing in such an insulting
manner! I will leave you all to your own devices. Haunt an empty cabin,
if you wish. I will go with this absurd man to face whatever fate has in
store!" Before Sy's admiring eyes, she picks up her suitcase and storms
past him out the door, leaving the little cabin in her wake.

~

It is a while before Ming-huà works up the courage to ask, "Where
to?"

Without breaking stride, Sy answers, "To the mainland."

"After that?"

"After that? To a magnificent city, of course!"

Ming-huà 's spirits fall. "A city?" she asks pathetically.

"Yes, with lots and lots of people. We really must have you dive into the deepest part of the icy river. Sink or swim!"

"It is not whether I sink or swim that worries me," says Ming-huà. "What if I get angry? What if I let slip something I cannot take back? I can't face another. . . incident."

Sy assumes a tragic face. "I know what worries you, little hunchback. That's as it should be. But you are destined for greater things than the *wee sleekit, cow'ring timorous beastie* your fears make of you."

Ming-huà shakes her head ruefully. "This cursed power has plowed my own field and uprooted my own comfy house. Your foolish behavior will not make me laugh off the awful deed I have done. Shame on you! Two men are dead."

They walk in silence for a while. Ming-huà suddenly pauses and asks, "Did they have families? I have been too scared to read, or inquire in any way."

Sy closes his eyes and shakes his head disapprovingly. "Here is the paved road. We're almost to town. I suggest we stop at the post office to make sure they have a forwarding address."

"You already know the address we're going to?"

"Of course. *She* thinks of everything." He rummages through his pocket. "Here it is."

Taking Sy's proffered note, Ming-huà asks, "*She*?"

"Not now. We'd best hurry or we'll miss the next boat to the mainland!"

In spite of his entreaty, Ming-huà stops and looks back down the tree-lined path. Sy rests a hand on her shoulder and gives a gentle squeeze. "Regrets?"

She allows herself to be pulled back from her reverie. "All I have are regrets."

~

As usual, when they enter the town, Ming-huà's hump begins to vigorously hum, its intensity rising and falling as she passes people on the street. She zips into the post office and retrieves a couple of envelopes and uses Sy's note to fill out a forwarding address form, and rejoins the scarecrow figure fidgeting outside. Once safely on board the boat that will take them to the mainland, Sy visibly relaxes while Ming-huà sits on a bench enjoying the view, her mind grasping at whatever pleasing scene might offer a peaceful, soothing balm to her restless hump. She focuses only on the surface of the water, for she knows to plumb the depths, where dwell the creatures of the sea, there is hunger, violent death, and painful disease. Avoiding unpleasantness is now the singular imperative driving her actions. Sy watches her and feels pangs of regret that she will soon be forcefully dragged away from her comforts and driven into a world where her survival will be severely tested. He knows the incident with the two hunters is only the beginning of the process.

Chapter 2: Introduction to the City

~ First Impressions ~

It has been years since Ming-huà set foot on the mainland, and immediately her senses are overwhelmed by a frantic activity that does not exist on the island. Her hump is ablaze with the fleeting emotions of passers-by, while her mind reels at the chaotic movements of people and their machines, racing this way and that, all with cryptic purposes and single-minded obsessions. Ming-huà feels like a child on her first day of school, panic stricken and driven by instinct to return to the safety of home. Nevertheless, in spite of her trepidation, she grits her teeth and soldiers on. But before taking many steps, she plops her suitcase on the ground and sits dizzily on a curb. Sy dances back and forth impatiently, exhorting her to breathe deeply.

"Hurry up, little one! We have places to go, people to see, a bus to catch!"

Ming-huà waves her arm weakly. "Let me rest for a minute."

"You're too young to be tired."

"I'm not tired, I'm frightened. I can't breathe. I need time."

Those passing by crane their necks and gawk at Ming-huà's hump. Sy meets these rude rubberneckers with an accusatory glare, but the hunchback is painfully aware of her otherness. Now, she rises and mutters, "Let's go," determined to escape the feeling of being a spectacle, or worse, a carnival exhibit. Sy hails a cab and she climbs into the safety of its cocoon, avoiding the eyes of the driver ogling her in the rear-view mirror.

"They are not staring at your hump," says Sy. "You will never believe it, but they are marveling at your glorious beauty; your gorgeous face, luxurious hair, luminous eyes, queenly bearing. All of you! Magnificent!"

Ming-huà can only scoot farther down in the seat, unwilling to look out the window at the restless hive buzzing past. Before she knows it, they arrive at the bus terminal, jostling in a disorganized line where Sy finally makes it to the counter and purchases two tickets to San Francisco.

An old, diesel-spewing bus awaits, and as they board, Ming-huà notices her fellow passengers are a rather motley looking group, none of whom take any notice of her deformity. Most of them are exiles themselves, drab and inward turning, left behind by the flashier members of a wealthy society. Sitting among them, she is saddened by their disappointments and failures singing an off-key, melancholic dirge through her hump. For the first time since leaving the island, she feels at home among these fellow cast-offs. Miles roll by, towns come and go, and Ming-huà falls in and out of sleep. Sy never sleeps, chattering the entire way with other passengers, speaking to each in turn by gliding effortlessly into their individual language idiosyncrasies as easily as slipping on and off a cloak. As for Ming-huà, low-key pain and isolation are the sad chords that reverberate in her hump; chords she has long recognized and made peace with. Perhaps, she thinks, it is the reason she feels comfortable with the people in this mournful bus.

Once, in the midst of a long, desolate stretch of scrubland, she awakes just in time to see a coyote loping in the distance. Sharp pangs of hunger and a fierce determination to find prey doubles her over in pain. How different the desperate, never-to-be-satiated craving for food by non-human animals, compared to the slow burn of human suffering! Agony quick and agony gradual everywhere!

"No, Ming-huà, not so," says Sy.

"What?"

"There is a notion among many that one cannot experience joy without first experiencing suffering. Many of your grandmother's comrades often discussed this conundrum. Do you believe it?"

Ming-huà shakes her head, still feeling the coyote's bitter knot of starvation. "I don't know."

Sy shrugs, but she feels a tremor deep within her hump. "How do you know about my grandmother?"

He breaks into a raucous laugh. "If you only knew!" he cries. He jumps into the aisle and assumes a ridiculous, twisted, operatic pose. "If you only knew!"

His antics elicit a smattering of applause from the passengers.

As Ming-huà watches, she briefly questions Scarecrow's sanity, but remembers her own father had suffered from schizophrenia, and must have also acted crazy. She also recalls Sy mentioning something about her

[29]

grandfather being part of a quest. *Like my grandfather,* she wonders, *is Sy embarked on some mysterious quest? But what kind of quest? And what kind of quest was my grandfather on? Mother knows. Why won't she tell me? What spectacle did papa make of himself? Was he viewed as a freak, like me? Like mother? Sy is also a bit of a freak. Am I truly a freak? I hear no voices, see no hallucinations, suffer from no delusions. Or do I? No, I am worse! My condition is worse! My hump and its ability to detect things, things that are suffering, is worse. My destructive power is worse. My deformity is worse! Oh, yes yes yes. My condition is much worse!*

In her distress, Ming-huà remembers her mother once described her as a "one-trick pony", born with a saddle on her back, but no rider. Yes, she circles the carnival ring riderless. Around and around. But now, Sy has grabbed the reins and has ridden her out of the comfy cozy cabin that now seems so distant. For better or worse, she is inexorably moving toward some unknown fate. Visions of disaster flood her mind, and she feels helpless to turn back. Yes, she decides, her condition is much worse than her father's or grandfather's must have been, and trembles at her powers. Certainly those powers will unleash something terrible on the world. They will lead to her life and those of unknown others come crashing down in a death-spiral.

When the bus enters the outer suburbs of San Francisco, her hump comes alive with a surge of confusing signals—a mishmash of conflicting human sensations, all overloading her ability to process. At the central bus terminal, she staggers to a waiting taxi with the help of Sy, who supports and guides her protectively. He barks the address to the driver, clearly anxious to reach their destination for the sake of his protégé's increasingly debilitating condition. The taxi pulls in front of their destination at the top of one of San Francisco's most prestigious hills. Sy pays the driver and helps Ming-huà step out. She looks up to behold a magnificent Victorian house rising in stately grandeur. Multiple turrets loom majestically against the sky, while a gorgeous wrap-around porch accentuates the inviting nature of the building's charms: swirling curves, fish-scale shingles, and lovely bays, all providing an intimate allure that to Ming-huà seem irresistible. The house proudly stands atop a steep hill overlooking San Francisco Bay. To her further delight, the grounds are a luscious mix of shrubs, flowers, and ornamental trees that seamlessly merge to form an organic extension of the architecture itself. A wave of familiarity passes over Ming-huà, though she had never seen this place before. Her anxiety falls away.

Sy produces a key from nowhere and unlocks the front door. Passing through the ornate foyer, Ming-huà is overcome by the regal grandeur of the house. She turns to Sy in wonder.

"Is this where we will stay?" she asks in a hopeful voice.

His concern for her state of mind melts away in a paroxysm of relieved laughter and spontaneous dance.

"Yes! Yes, little hunchback! You are home! All the ghosts that inhabit this place are rooting for you. In fact, here you are loved by spirits and spooks alike!"

She blinks in disbelief. Even her hump vibrates soothingly, as if corroborating Sy's words. After a brief tour, Sy escorts her to a magnificent bedroom on the second floor.

"Don't worry, my room is at the other end of the hall. For purposes of propriety, in case anyone asks, I am your uncle. Now, unpack, wash up, and come down to the little anteroom I showed you. We will have tea and discuss plans. In future, that is where we will meet to discuss the day's events. It is the favorite of all our ghost friends."

"Who are these ghosts?"

Scarecrow contorts his body in the most absurd of poses. "You'll see. Yes, you'll see! Now, unpack, unwind, wash up, and join me downstairs to detoxify, demystify, reoxify, and—dare I say it—deify."

In spite of herself, Ming-huà has to laugh. "I have no idea what you are talking about."

"Of course not! Nor could certain dead psychiatrists and aged detectives. But that is neither here nor there. Do you drink?"

"What?"

"Drink! Drink! You know, alcohol, booze, spirits, nectar-of-the-gods, liquor, demon drink, grog, hooch, firewater?"

Ming-huà remains dumbstruck.

"Well, girl?"

Nothing.

Sy assumes a tragic face. "Whiskey, whiskey!"

"No," she finally blurts.

Scarecrow crumples to the ground in a heap and moans. "Not your father's daughter! Woe is me. Not your father's daughter! Ah well, tea it is." He half rises and slinks crestfallen out of the room, calling over his shoulder, "Half an hour, downstairs, we talk!"

Not even Sy's bizarre antics and strange words hinder the feeling of comfort and safety this house conveys. She shudders at the sea of suffering and anger in the surrounding multitudes that must even now be crashing against the outer walls of this sanctuary, trying to reach her hump. But all is quiet. *It seems the house projects some sort of membrane or force-field that protects my hump from being assailed,* she thinks. *No need to overthink it. Just enjoy while I can!* Still, beneath the calm, she has never been more cognizant of the latent power that she fears will, at some point, demand release. Never has she felt more frightened, yet strangely exhilarated at the knowledge. With these turbulent thoughts, she showers and goes downstairs to talk with Scarecrow.

~ The Plan ~

Sy stands with a drink in his hand and invites Ming-huà to sit.

"Not as comfy as your favorite chair back on the island, but hopefully will do."

As she sits, he gulps the last of his drink and pours a cup of tea.

"Here you are," he says, looking slightly disgusted at its contents. "For what it's worth."

"Thank you."

"Now, Ming-huà, we must talk."

"Okay."

"Are you listening very carefully?"

"Yes."

"And your hump?"

She smiles. "It is content."

"Good, because it will soon be tested."

Ming-huà visibly tenses. "How?"

"Starting tomorrow, we will go for long walks together. We will go to different parts of the city. We will pass many people. There will be many many emotions flooding your hump. Some happy and joyous, to be sure, but most full of stress, anxiety, fear, hatred, anger, suffering, suffering, suffering."

Ming-huà recoils. "Why must I do this?"

"Conditioning, my dear. You are in training."

"For what?"

He waves his hand dismissively. "Later. Now, as part of your training, I want you to do something else."

She waits.

"This is the most important point: every day you must spend a great deal of time . . . well, how do I put it? . . . you must spend hours each day practicing, like a concert pianist . . . like your grandmother."

"My grandmother?"

"Yes, on your father's side."

"She was a pianist?"

"The best."

"Did she have . . . I mean, was she. . . . ?"

"No, but her beauty was unsurpassed even without a hump."

Ming-huà chews on this revelation for a while. "What must I practice? I can't play the piano."

"No, but you can perform a different kind of music. You carry a piano within. Your hump, a part of you, is like a grand piano. It interprets the music of the masses. That makes you the instrument itself."

"What must I practice?" Ming-huà asks again, this time with suspicion hardening her tone.

Scarecrow pours a drink for himself and dances a lively jig without spilling a drop. "Did you notice what I just did?"

"You danced about quite foolishly, like you always do."

"No, no! What else?"

"I don't know."

"The Daughter," he says dismissively under his breath. "Look, I controlled this glass while cavorting about. Not a drop spilled. Control! That is the key!"

Ming-huà waits patiently for clarification.

"You see," he continues. "Your power is like my dance. All movement. But if not controlled, it disturbs everything around . . . like a tornado; undirected and destructive chaos. Your job, little one, is to learn how to control your power."

"Fine. How?"

"We know it is triggered by anger. Now we must teach your power to temper the anger with justice. As the Bard said, 'The quality of mercy is not strained.'"

"I don't understand."

"In short, Ming-huà, you must develop your current ability to . . . reconfigure . . . with the ability to tailor the severity of the sentence to the severity of the crime."

Ming-huà shakes her head in confusion.

Sy gives a snort of impatience. "I'll be blunt. You must learn to remove a hand, a foot, an arm, a finger, rather than all-or-nothing obliteration."

Ming-huà's eyes grow large. "But I don't want to reconfigure anyone, as you put it. Not anyone at all! I never want to use my power again."

"This is why you are The Daughter. Look, the fact is you will use it. Inevitable. Anger is fundamental. Even you can't escape it. Ask those two hunters. Anger has driven revolutions, rebellions, murders, divorces, and any number of untold suicides. No, you are not immune. Even with your kind and gentle nature, anger is a major pathway in your brain, inexorably connected to your hump."

"What if I never get angry?"

"Ah, that is why we will go for walks. It marks the beginning of your training."

"Leading to?"

Scarecrow pirouettes, but this time angrily, emptying his glass in a prodigious guzzle. "Leading to very dark places, places where *She* has made a vow to . . . never mind! Leading to you being as much a virtuoso as your grandmother."

"Sy, I cannot control my anger, let alone my power. I've tried."

"I know, but that was then and this is now. Our task is to merge anger with justice. You see, a judge should not let personal anger interfere with a just verdict. So, you must elevate injustice to anger, and then direct the anger back to the injustice by imposing justice."

"I think you have had too much to drink."

"Not enough. Anyway, that is our mission. Our mission starts now!"

Before Ming-huà can react, he grabs her hand and forces it onto the table. As she struggles to free his grip, a hammer appears, raised in his other hand, poised to come down with a terrible blow.

"First!" he shouts. "First I must break the bones in your hand!"

[34]

"Don't!" she cries, but to her horror, he viciously brings the hammer down on her outstretched hand. Her eyes instinctively close at the coming blow.

~

When Ming-huà opens her eyes, Sy is smiling. He releases her unharmed and waves his empty hands in her face.

"See? The hammer is gone. You made it go away. It is reconfigured. Kaput!"

"But . . . but I was not only afraid of the hammer," she stammers. "I was more afraid of you."

"Ha! You see, little hunchback, fear and anger are Siamese twins."

"But why didn't you . . . disappear. I wanted you to!"

His expression darkens. "I am here for a reason. You can no more reconfigure me than you can reconfigure yourself. But the hammer . . . well, that is a different story."

Ming-huà, heart still pounding, shakes her head wonderingly.

"Now, imagine I was a murderer," says Sy. "Imagine the hammer was a knife, or a gun. We will train you not to remove the entire person, but his hand only, as well as the knife or gun. Doing that, you now have achieved justice with mercy."

"But—"

Sy holds up a cautionary hand. "And just as importantly, there is no pain associated with the removal. Just *a priori*—gone! Now the perpetrator is not a murderer, but is nonetheless *ex post facto* punished for his intent."

Ming-huà can only continue to shake her head. Numbed by the entire scheme. Yet, her hump remains quiescent, a vessel filling with his words, containing them as they deepen. She resists.

"Mr. Rung, I am not fit for this. I'm just a deformed girl who wants to go home in peace."

His face transforms into a fierceness reminiscent of when he raised the hammer. "Peace! No, hunchback! You will never have peace! Not even on your precious island. You left behind the obliterated remains of two men. Fool!"

Ming-huà cringed back in her chair.

Sy continues in a calmer voice. "Imagine if you had the power to only remove their hands. They would still be alive, the fawn would be alive, and their families still whole. Justice served. Worse suffering averted."

This constitutes the first indication Ming-huà has that the men had families. She closes her eyes, horrified at the consequences of her unthinking deed.

Oh, if I could be rid of this curse! she thinks.

"You will never be rid of it, little one," says Sy in a soft, sympathetic tone.

"You can read minds?"

"You can read Charles Dickens?"

"Who are you, really?"

He slips back into his operatic clown routine and leaps gracefully. "A scarecrow! Nothing much more to me than to Miss Gladflower!"

"But I could make Miss Gladflower disappear."

"Ah, I am made of stronger stuff! . . . or should I say stuffing?"

"Mr. Rung—"

"Ah ah," he wags a finger. "Sy, if you please. Or Scarecrow. Whichever."

"Sy, unfortunately I am not. I would like to go back to the island."

"To the island?"

"Yes."

"It is gone."

Ming-huà blinks uncomprehendingly.

"It is gone," he repeats.

"How? Oh my *God*! Did I. . . . "

Sy laughs. "No, no. I mean, it no longer exists for you."

"Sy, I'm over eighteen. I can decide. You cannot stop me."

Scarecrow is silent for a long moment, then says, "Come with me."

"Where?"

"Just come."

She follows him to the front door. He opens it and steps out, inviting her to join him. She hesitates.

"Come on, I'll be right here. I won't push you down the steps or close the door on you. Come on."

She steps out. . . .

~ Into the Depths ~

Ming-huà finds herself back in the anteroom, sitting in the same chair. Sy stands over her with another drink in his hand.

"What happened?" she asks.

"I see you're still a bit dazed."

She rubs her forehead. "Yes. What happened?"

"You fainted."

Her hump is faintly vibrating in clashing, discordant, ugly notes.

"Here," says Sy, handing her a fresh cup of tea.

Slowly, the unpleasant, scratchy noise from her hump subsides.

"It will be that way from now on, and even worse on your island," says Sy nonchalantly.

"Why worse on the island?" she asks.

"You are exiled. A stranger in a strange land. Adrift. The island is now beyond the horizon, and the currents carry you farther and farther away even as we speak. Your only hope to see it again is to sail all the way around the Great Sphere, only then, when your journey ends, will you return to its beginnings."

"When I die," she says in disgust.

"No, when you are reborn."

He prances around in circles. "Enough of this philosophical rubbish! Enjoy the night, because tomorrow we start!"

Sy peers at her expectantly. "Now do you want a drink?"

"Sy, it is still morning."

He shakes his head. "Look out the window."

She does.

It is dark.

Scarecrow laughs. "You were out longer than you think."

Next morning, Sy calls her to breakfast.

"Ready?" he asks after she takes her last bite.

"Yes." Her voice is strong, determined.

Sy jumps up and pirouettes. "I see sleep has fortified you! Let's go then!"

When they step outside, her hump remains quiet, and she suspects Sy had something to do with yesterday's overwhelming cacophony. Without time to think further, they start walking.

~

At first, Ming-huà feels no discomfort. Although the San Francisco wind is chilly, the sky is an iridescent blue, and the reassuring warmth of the sun penetrates her hump. Birds are happily chirping and she assumes there must be ample food available to satiate their hot-blooded appetites. But as they descend the hill toward the bowels of the city, familiar echoes of dense human crowds prick her consciousness. Her hump stirs to the innumerable discords of big-brained passions. A kaleidoscope of conflicting sensations builds steadily when they commingle with the mass of humanity packed together in the busiest streets; tourists, workers, shoppers, cops, transients, homeless, couples, families, and the full panoply of every other category of person. Her hump goes almost silent, as if a giant breaker switch had been tripped. Now she feels almost fully anesthetized to her surroundings, dazed and numb to the throngs who appear propelled in all directions by giant, intricately elaborate conveyers designed by a mad architect. Sy keeps glancing at her blank stare, but his pace never falters. Periodically, intense emotions such as sharp pain, violent anger, bleak sadness, hopeless depression, unbounded joy, euphoric love, even ecstasy, penetrate like jolts from a pinched nerve. When this happens, she lets out a cry, but Sy keeps steadily on.

Eventually, as they enter the Tenderloin district, one of the most dreadfully run-down parts of San Francisco, he instinctively slips his arm through her elbow. His caution is not unwarranted. They pass by many alleyways, all dark and strewn with trash and feces, sheltering every manner of tattered person, male and female, young and old, all aware they constitute the disposable detritus of a rich society reeking of perfume and deodorant in disposable excess. Here, the mix of despair, hopelessness, anger, and hostility, break through the discomforting but endurable white noise from her hump and brutally assail what little is left of her resistance. It is too much to bear. She stumbles around a corner and leans over to vomit. Still registering no emotion, Sy tells her to let it come. After spitting the last tendrils of mucous, she issues a long, piteous moan.

With this sad sound, his cold distance breaks down and he rubs her hump sympathetically.

"All right, little hunchback, let's go home now," he says. "Besides, it will be dark soon. We have walked enough. We're done for the day."

[38]

"Sorry," she whispers. "I am not strong enough."

"No worries. You just vomited up the undigested remains of the world's psychic gristle. We'll be home soon. Eh? Okay?"

"Yes, please. Let's go."

Sy continues to rub her hump with his healing hand and she feels a soothing release; a grounding that mercifully dissipates the stomach-churning toxicity that has collected. On the way, they pass a few street performers. Ming-huà signals Sy to stop, and she watches them with childlike pleasure.

"Yes, that's right," he says. "Not all is bleak and desolate. There is joy in the world. There is hope. It is the needless suffering that must be confronted. That is why you are here. You are truly The Daughter."

"Shhh," Ming-huà scolds him. "Just listen to the music. I already feel better. No more of that nonsense about The Daughter. I don't even know what that means."

"Yes, well—"

"Shhhhhh!"

"Okay, okay."

~

Upon entering the comforting shelter of the house, Ming-huà rushes upstairs, seemingly rejuvenated.

"I must bathe," she calls from the top of the stairs. "But afterward, we should sit and . . . how do you say? . . . debrief."

Sy stares in astonishment as she disappears into the bathroom. "How is it possible she is so resilient?" he says aloud. "She recovers so quickly! Maybe she is The Daughter after all." He dances a jig and looks upward. "Eh, *Goddess*? Maybe You're right! Another few days and she will be ready to meet Lady Oracle, right?"

After speaking these words, Sy cranes his head as if to hear a voice from far away. "Yes, I see," he says. "No rest for her, eh?" He shakes his head doubtfully. "Okay, I'll make her tea and set her to work. But be careful Great Lady. If my intuition is correct, *You* need to lighten up a bit. Give her time. She is, after all, *Your* vessel, but she may crack, as did *Your* previous . . . designee."

~

At the same time Sy is having his conversation seemingly with the air, Ming-huà stands under the shower and wonders at her state of mind.

[39]

While vomiting in that alley, she vowed never again to follow Sy. Never! Her sole desire centered on immediately returning to the comfort of her island, regardless of the consequences, and live out her life in some semblance of peace. But on the way back, something happened to make her change. Perhaps it was Sy's magical hand soothing the restless beasts in her hump, perhaps it was the hump itself, perhaps it was the street musicians, perhaps something else. Whatever it was, she now felt resolved to see Scarecrow's . . . what to call it? . . . experiment, to its conclusion. Ming-huà reacted to this new found resolve in amazement, and no small amount of suspicion. It ran counter to her most cherished disposition— that of spiritual and physical solitude.

Still engaged in pondering these mysteries, Ming-huà suddenly realizes she has been standing like a statue under the shower holding a bar of soap. Focusing all her attention, she orders it to disappear.

Nothing.

Try again.

Nothing.

She smiles sheepishly. "Guess I'm not mad at you enough. Or afraid of you enough."

She lifts the soap close to her face. "Go ahead, threaten me."

Then she has an alarming thought. "What if I eat you, and you taste so disgusting, I make you disappear?"

The thought briefly intrigues her, but she places it back in the dish. "No. Can't do it. Foolish foolish girl!"

With this last bit of silliness, she steps out of the shower, gets dressed, and goes downstairs to join Scarecrow.

When she joins him in the anteroom, he looks up with bleary eyes, already having quaffed any number of bourbons.

"No need for a long discussion," he says. "We will continue our walks tomorrow. Meanwhile, continue your exercises."

"Okay. For how long do we go on these walks."

"Until you're ready."

"For what?"

"Until you're ready." He coughs and mumbles, "That's all I have to say. Tomorrow we leave at the same time. Good night."

~

And so, for over a week, Sy and Ming-huà walk through all parts of San Francisco, her reactions remaining a mix of nauseousness to horror to pleasure. But as each day passes, Sy seems to grow more distant. There are times he reverts to his old, clowning self, but she grows suspicious that something dreadful hangs over him. Each night, he insists she "do her exercises" and try and make objects disappear, which she is never able to accomplish. When she informs him of her failures, he shrugs and says, "Just takes time." But one day, after a particularly strenuous walk, he tells her to meet him in the anteroom as usual.

~

When she enters, Sy is sitting with a drink in his hand, looking quite glum.

"There's tea in the pot there," he says. "Help yourself. I'm too comfortable."

"Thank you."

"Ming-huà, you still have work to do."

"I know, but I'm tired and want to sit for a minute."

"Well, you need to do your exercises."

"Not now."

"Have your tea first. Rest a moment, then I want to show you something."

Ming-huà notices he is nervous, something she has never seen in him before. She tenses. "What?"

"Well, remember our little discussion about the purpose of your exercises, of controlling your powers?"

"Of course, you want me to take off an arm rather than the entire person, or something like that."

"And remember I said you must practice, you must train like a pianist to be able to . . . well, control what you reconfigure?"

"Yes."

"Wait here."

Sy slowly leaves the room, shaking his head as he goes. When he returns, he is cradling a rabbit.

Ming-huà jumps up in alarm. "I'm not going to make a rabbit disappear! Never!"

"Of course not. That is not what I'm asking."

"Then what?"

[41]

Before she has time to think, he brutally pins the rabbit on a table, holds its head down, and brandishes a knife.

"No!" she shrieks.

As the rabbit struggles and squeals, he raises the knife.

"*God*, no!" she cries again, knocking over an end table as she rushes to save it.

Sy plunges the knife down.

She hears the rabbit emit a high-pitched scream.

Chapter 3: Awakening

~ Novice ~

Ming-huà stands trembling, arms wrapped around her body, watching Sy carry the healthy rabbit out of the room. Tears of relief roll down her cheeks. When he returns, a wide grin lights up his face, and he prances joyfully around her, crying out, "New life, no knife! New life, no knife!"

"I don't know how I did it."

Sy chuckles. "Of course not, but you did it! You did great! Now, you're Peter Rabbit's best friend!"

"Would you have done it?"

"Done what?"

She shoots him a look of impatience. "Would you?"

He turns solemn. "What do you think?"

She shakes her head, unwilling to play. "Would you?"

"If I say 'yes', you'll hate me for being so cruel. If I say 'no', you won't believe I'll do it next time."

"Next time?"

"Ming-huà, when the knife disappeared, my entire body tingled. If I had been a normal person, I would have been . . . you know, reconfigured. We must work harder to control your savior impulses. Next time I want only my hand to feel pinpricks."

"How can I? There is no time to think."

"Wrong. Train yourself. Remember your grandmother's gift. She could play the most difficult compositions by musicians like Liszt and Beethoven because her fingers had been trained not to hesitate."

"But I am not her."

"Her blood and the blood of your father are in your veins. You are The Daughter. The ability is there. Hidden. You must learn."

"The blood of a concert pianist and a schizophrenic flow through my veins? It can never be. I am simply a deformed woman with a deformed power. Best left to die out."

"Tell that to Peter Rabbit! Tell it to that fawn you saved."

Ming-huà shakes her head doubtfully.

"I may have a solution that will speed up the process, if you're willing to take the place of our furry friend."

Her eyes widen. "You mean threaten me with a knife?"

"No, of course not, just threaten you with pain. We know pain can trigger the power."

"Pain leads to fear, or anger."

"Exactly. We know your power is triggered by both. Believe me, Ming-huà, I don't want to spend the next few weeks or months threatening cute animals. Besides, we have bigger fish to fry, and you need to be ready. Do you trust me?"

"No."

Sy jumps skyward and clicks his heels, then pulls his best operatic pose and roars with laughter. "Smart girl! Smart girl!"

She remains unamused.

"Seriously, Ming-huà, my plan will not entail much pain. Just a little, but hopefully enough. Enough. Let's see if it works. Even if it doesn't, it won't leave you permanently damaged, just a little pain is all."

"I'll think about it."

~

That night, Ming-huà evaluates the complex mix of emotions roiling her mind. On the one hand, she feels a new and unfamiliar tinge of pride in her power. What if she really could control it and use it for good? On the other hand, she remains horrified at the possibility she might inadvertently snuff out an innocent life. Unable to sleep, she creeps downstairs to the room where Sy keeps the rabbit. She pulls a chair close to the cage and stares into the dark interior. Its huge, luminous eyes reflect the dim light and stare back at her fearfully.

"I won't hurt you friend," she whispers. "In fact, I saved your little bunny life. Tell me, what does it feel like not to have so many complicated worries? You're just like my friends in the forest. Food, shelter, a mate— you require so little, but you fear so much. We humans require so much more, and fear so much more. Our fears are endless, stretched out over time and space in a thousand different ways. Your fears are so limited, but oh so deep! Your lives are richer for it, little friend. Every second you feel deeply; every second you survive the impossible; every second you live on the knife edge, all the time dreadfully suffering from gnawing hunger or fear of a predator. Believe me, I know. My hump tells me all. It's telling me that now. You are so afraid."

Ming-huà shivers. *So afraid!*

Maybe that's why you want to live so badly, fewer the worries, the worse they are? No, no. Non-human animals don't commit suicide. Do you little fellow? Suffering is suffering. All around.

"Yes, that's right," comes Scarecrow's voice whispering close to her ear. "Suffering everywhere. That is why you're here. You are The Daughter."

Ming-huà jumps at his words and looks at him with her hand over her heart. "Sy, you have to stop scaring me like that. If you can read my mind, keep it to yourself, or better yet, explain to me what this Daughter business is. No more deflections."

"You're not ready. Have you thought about it?"

"It?"

"My experiment? Remember, pain?"

"I need to think about it."

"I thought that's what you were doing."

"In a way, I suppose."

"And?"

"I don't know, Sy. I haven't decided."

"You know, in the basement, I have a boa constrictor."

Ming-huà's heart flutters.

"I had planned to use it for the next step."

"Boa constrictors eat rabbits," Ming-huà murmurs.

"Yes."

"You wanted me to make the boa constrictor disappear?"

"I was a thought."

"No! Are you crazy! I will not kill living things. Period. I want to go back to the island. Now! This is too much."

"Which is why I suggest we try my pain idea. The object that would give you pain is not alive."

"How does it work?" As soon as she asks the question, Ming-huà is furious with herself for letting curiosity weaken her resolve.

"Well, the trick is to make the object that would cause you pain only half of the total object. Remember, the point is for you to develop the ability to reconfigure only part of something. So, I have rigged up a very primitive object. If it works, no experimenting on living creatures."

"What is it?"

"I have to finish it first. Tomorrow I will show you. Time for us both to sleep."

"How can I sleep after this?"

"Try. At any rate, I am going to bed. You can stay and continue your conversation with Peter if you want."

"I will." She looks at him significantly. "He's better company than some I know. But, Sy, I warn you now. If you refuse to clue me in on this 'Daughter' business, I will leave."

"If we succeed, think of the good you can accomplish—the suffering you can relieve."

Ming-huà shakes her head. "No, Scarecrow, there is an old saying that perfectly applies here: the road to hell is paved with good intentions."

Sy laughs humorlessly. "You have it backwards, hunchback. The road to good intentions is paved with hell. Good night."

Ming-huà watches Sy leave, then turns to the rabbit. "I will take the pain, little Peter. I'll never let him sacrifice you to a snake. But I will sacrifice myself." She looks deeply into the rabbit's bright eyes. "Question is, why am I willing to do this? Why? I fear it is pride, little one. Pure pride. Still, what if I actually can use my power to make a difference? To reduce suffering? Is that not reason enough? Achilles' *hubris* or Buddha's compassion? Perhaps they are just two sides of the same coin."

~

Next morning at breakfast, Sy announces they will remain at home and perform the experiment.

Ming-huà has spent the night steeling herself, and she is prepared. "Okay, how does it work?"

He rises quickly, afraid of giving the hunchback time to change her mind. On the way out of the room he calls, "Let me show you."

Sy returns carrying something hidden in his palm. Holding a fist out to her, his fingers unfold to reveal a strange object. She peers more closely. One half is an oblong shaped, rather sharp stone, and the other half is a broken egg shell. One rounded end of the rock is seated inside the shell, and the other sharper end sticks out, as if it was in the process of being born.

Ming-huà looks at him questioningly.

"You will be laying down and I will hold this high above your forehead. Once I let it go, it will fall far enough for the stone to cause quite a bit of pain. If the stone disappears, the empty egg shell will do no damage whatsoever. Primitive, but effective, I think."

Ming-huà objects. "Sy, I will never be able to make either the stone or the shell disappear."

"Why do you say that?"

She shrugs. "I don't know. It just seems too silly."

"But painful if you fail."

"Yes, but I don't think my power works like this."

"Won't know until we try. We already know your power works when you suffer pain, but here is the key: you must keep your eyes open until the moment I drop it. Then you will know it is on its way. I count on you to react. You must direct your power only against the stone, not the shell, otherwise we will be back to square one. Understand?"

"Okay, but let's get it over with so we can move on."

Sy has her lay on the couch and holds the object high above her head.

Ming-huà begins to realize how much the stone will hurt falling from such a distance.

"That's too high," she objects.

But the words have hardly left her mouth when he suddenly lets it go.

She instinctively closes her eyes.

Nothing.

The entire object has disappeared mid-flight.

Ming-huà stares up at Sy speechless, while he claps his hands. "Okay!" he cries. "Partial success! We know you can reconfigure the entire object. Now you must learn to reconfigure only the stone."

She sits up woozily, feeling drained, as she always does after using her power, so does not respond.

"You're tired," Sy observes. "Rest a little, then we try again. The world contains an endless supply of stones and eggs. We repeat for however long it takes!"

Ming-huà wants to object. She wants to call off this entire absurd nonsense. She wants to tell him she is unwilling to continue. Instead, she hears herself saying, "Yes, let's keep trying."

"That's the spirit! You are The Daughter! Truly! I have already prepared more of these strange little objects."

"You knew I would fail?"

"Quite the contrary! You succeeded. Now you simply have to learn not to succeed so much!"

"I can try."

Sy runs out of the room and returns with another object, this one almost identical to the last. "I'm calling these little gems stoshells. Now, lay back down. Lay back down. Let's try again."

Again, he holds it above her head, only this time, he asks, "Are you ready?"

"Yes."

It drops.

It disappears.

Nothing is left.

"It's okay!" cries Sy. "I have plenty more where those came from. Again!"

"No," she says. "Each time, I get more tired. No more today."

"Okay, you're right," he replies.

"Give me your hand." He helps her rise and directs her to a chair. "I'll pour myself a drink and yourself some nice, hot tea."

As he walks across the room to the decanter table and reaches for an empty glass, he suddenly whips around and savagely throws another stoshell directly at her head, shouting, "Only the rock!"

She screams.

It disappears.

All of it.

"Damn!" he exclaims. "I thought maybe. . . . "

Ming-huà collapses in the chair. "No more, Sy, no more."

"Yes, yes, no more today. Tomorrow we start again. We'll go for a walk and when we return, we'll try again."

[48]

"For how long?"

"As long as it takes."

A week passes during which Sy repeats the experiment multiple times a day. Every time, the entire stoshell vanishes. Ming-huà is exhausted and discouraged, but Sy seems more and more enthused.

"Closer! We're getting closer!" he exclaims after each failure.

And after each exclamation, Ming-huà objects with a weary reply. "No, we're not. I cannot control it."

Then, one day, a breakthrough.

~ Graduation ~

Sy is holding another stoshell over her head as usual, rambling on about her mental state and whether she is more effective when surprised or when given a little more time to prepare. In the middle of a sentence, he unexpectedly drops it.

When Ming-huà opens her eyes, a half eggshell wobbles on her forehead.

Sy dances around like a madman, clapping his hands and shouting, "You did it! You did it!"

Ming-huà is stunned. She sits up, letting the shell fall into her hand, and rotates it curiously. Even the part of the stone that had been seated inside the shell is gone! How is that possible? Her power seems attuned to something more refined than the gross outcome of simply wishing half an object gone. *How can it be so discriminating? Impossible!*

Evan as she ponders these conundrums, Sy whirls and throws another stoshell at her head.

She lets out a shrill cry and reacts.

No stone.

Shell remains, having fallen harmlessly to the floor in mid-flight.

Once more Sy prances about. "Success again! Again! Pianist reborn! Virtuoso! Magnificent! You are ready! Ready!"

Ming-huà slumps back on the couch, watching Sy with a mix of pride and fear. What have they unleashed? Can she turn it off? A vision of Pandora's box flashes through her mind. No going back. No toothpaste back in the tube. On a whim, Ming-huà looks at Sy's collection of stoshells and wishes them gone.

Nothing.

She is not surprised.

Ming-huà closes her eyes and thinks, while Scarecrow's celebrations fade in the background.

She realizes her power is limited, or perhaps has a universal safety catch. Unbridled reconfiguration of atoms and molecules directed mainly by the amygdala is too dangerous. However, curbing this power would be like a bus fitted with a governor; the driver is prevented from going faster than a predetermined speed, no matter how hard the accelerator is pushed. Yes, that must be it. Fear and anger, those are the ingredients of suffering. Fear of failure, fear of poverty, fear of hunger, fear of pain, fear of ridicule, fear of powerlessness, fear of losing power, fear of predators, fear of love, fear of losing love, fear of being fearful . . . the list is endless. When fear is triggered, so also is anger. Anger at failure, anger at those who succeed, anger at poverty, anger at pain, anger at ridicule, anger at powerlessness, anger at those who exercise power, anger at predators, anger at rejection, anger at withdrawn love, anger at being angry . . . the list is parallel to fear, and equally endless. No wonder her non-human friends live their lives far beyond human capacity to understand. The equations that govern their lives are far simpler, and far deeper than the Rube Goldberg equations that mimic complexity but elude efficacy. Yes, humans are lesser beings with greater capacity for fear and still greater capacity for anger. As Nietzsche pointed out, humans are the only species to make promises, and the only species to break them.

All of these thoughts, and many more, pass through Ming-huà's brain, and eventually her thoughts turn to the linage that flows backward to her father and grandmother. *Father was a schizophrenic, so was he more than human, or less? If I am The Daughter, as Sy insists, my father must hold the key. Or mother? Or both? Or is it grandmother?*

Ming-hua's perplexing questions become too much. She opens her eyes and looks at Scarecrow, who in turn is openly staring at her.

"What are you thinking?" he asks.

"Tell me about my father. Tell me about my grandmother. Tell me about this title you have given me—The Daughter. I deserve to know."

"Ask your mother."

"She always refused to tell me anything. Now she is gone. There is only you."

"No."

[50]

Ming-huà is startled by his bluntness, and manages to croak out the question, "Why?"

"We have passed a milestone. We must move on. No looking back. It is about time for you to meet someone."

"Who?" Ming-huà is irritated with herself for asking. Scarecrow is diverting her once again. Why does she continue to put up with it? She fears it is nothing more complicated than pride. When she realizes he has not answered, she asks again. "Who?"

"Lady Oracle."

Ming-huà laughs in spite of herself. "Silly name. Is she some sort of old hippie? I mean, we are in San Francisco, right?"

"No, she is not exactly 'an old hippie' as you say. But she is someone quite special, in spite of the silly name."

"Will she throw more things at my head?"

Sy laughs. "Actually, yes, just not stoshells."

"What then?"

"Once you meet Lady Oracle, you will visit the saddest, the poorest, the dregs of humanity."

Ming-huà lets out a groan. "I am not interested in visiting this type of humanity. I have already experienced extreme poverty and isolation. I do not need to see more."

"It is important to continue your exercises."

"I am too frightened at how my hump will react."

"Exactly!"

"No, I do not want to visit the saddest people."

"Then we will visit the cruelest."

"No. That is much worse!"

"Well then, we will visit those most passionately interested in the salvation of humanity."

"Salvation?"

"Do you not want to save yourself?"

"I have no idea what you're talking about. I want you to answer my questions."

"Or you'll leave?" Sy says these words in the form of a challenge, or a dare.

Ming-huà takes no more than a second to respond. "No."

"Good. You were right when talking to Peter Rabbit. Pandora's box is open. You will visit the saddest and the cruelest of humans. Lady Oracle will show you the way. Now that you are released from the box, you must go where the winds blow."

"I don't understand any of this."

"You must go where *She* directs."

"*She?*"

Sy throws up his arms. "No more questions!" His words are harsh. "You are no longer a novice! It is time to leave the cloister."

"Lady Oracle?"

He nods affirmatively.

"I don't want to see her," says Ming-huà with firmness.

"*Goddess*, you are stubborn!"

They argue. Back and forth they go. Ming-huà eventually admits she is terrified of being subjected to such sensory abuse.

Sy cuts her off with a scornful laugh. "Don't you see, foolish hunchback! Humans are infested with vermin. Their so-called higher emotions—love, intellect, altruism—are neural parasites. Diseased. Once the disease spreads and infects others, love turns to hate, intellect becomes the curse of all life on earth, and altruism is extended beyond its intended purpose in order to justify holocausts! Thus suffering. Suffering of an immense scale. That is where you come in. *His* addiction must be broken once and for all!"

"Whose addiction?"

"Never mind. Forget I said that. All you need to know is that you have a chance to relieve some of the suffering. Can't you get that through your thick hunchbacked skull? Damn it!"

Ming-huà listens with head lowered as if savaged by violent winds. Her mind focuses on the two men drowning the fawn. *Sy is doing the same thing to me*, she thinks. *Except I'm powerless to make him disappear.*

"What are you doing to me?" she asks weakly.

"Ming-huà, what would you have me do? Should I take you to evangelical Christians to expunge your demons, or to Catholic priests to exorcise them? Perhaps neurosurgeons to remove them, or psychiatrists to make contact with them? They all share the same misconception: condemn that which they do not understand! Same nonsense they did to your father! Same to your mother! Why? Fear, of course."

"But my animal friends are also fearful, and they are not bad for being afraid."

"And your human friends?"

"I have none."

"That is not true."

"If you were my friend, you would support my returning to the island and forgetting all this."

"But I am not your friend."

Ming-huà is taken aback by this naked admission. "You see?" she mutters.

"Reducing universal suffering is more important than relieving the individual sufferer."

"How can you achieve one without the other?"

"Such is life's paradox. Such is science's power. Such is *God*'s lie. And such is *Goddess's raison d'etre*."

"What does all this have to do with me?"

"You are no longer a novitiate. Time to go out into the world and confront the paradox. Increase the power of science. Expose *God*'s lies. Obey *Her* wishes."

From his pocket, Sy suddenly pulls out a stoshell and flings it viciously at her head. An empty half-eggshell falls harmlessly to the floor.

"You have the means. Now use it to save all the fawns of the world."

~

Lying awake in bed that night, Ming-huà feels herself slipping into an abyss so wide and deep that she loses sight of the rim on which she stood just hours ago. Hurdling through space, her psyche, her sense of self, stretches like a bungee cord to the breaking point, and she breathlessly waits to hear the final snap.

~ Lady Oracle ~

A few days later, after many dreary excursions and a plethora of successful experiments with a variety of objects, Sy makes an announcement at breakfast.

"Today we visit Lady Oracle."

Ming-huà's heart skips a beat. "When?"

"Now. You can finish your coffee later."

Ming-huà takes a last sip and they are out the door. The wind whips her scarf and as she secures it, she sees a taxi waiting. She looks questioningly at Sy.

"This time we travel in style," he laughs. "No time to lose."

Ming-huà feels a sharp pain in her hump and pauses. "I don't think I'm ready for this."

"You let me throw stoshells at your head but you're too afraid to meet an old lady?"

"She's old?"

"Older than you know."

After they enter the cab, Ming-huà asks him about Lady Oracle.

"She is what you might call a social worker. She owns two apartments in the worst sections of town—Chinatown and Tenderloin. First we go to the Taylor Street apartment in the Tenderloin district."

"What does she do?"

"Like I said, she is a sort of social worker. She uses her apartments as bases of operations."

"What kind of operations?"

"You'll see. Enough questions."

The cab drops them at a run-down neighborhood where the buildings appear not much more than ruins. After walking a couple of blocks, signs of deterioration worsen. The ground is a veritable garbage dump across which every manner of human rubbish is blown about by the wind, where sidewalks are stained, gutters are brimming with trash, and the air itself reeks of malodorous stench. Seedy looking people are scattered about, some walking, some leaning against buildings, all scary to Ming-huà. Her hump is flashing a thousand hostile sensations.

"Not far now," says Scarecrow cheerily.

When they reach Lady Oracle's apartment building, Ming-huà looks at a very bleak exterior of stained concrete defaced by grotesque paint dribbles and obscene graffiti. At least the inside will partly insulate her from the awful sensations and intimidating bystanders. Sy opens the door without knocking and she enters quite willingly. Her first impression is of darkness, cloaking the room in portentous shadows of black and gray.

[54]

A single candle burns on a distant mantlepiece, casting a weak glow that illuminates only the closest objects. She looks at Sy with raised eyebrows.

"That's right, Lady Oracle does not like light."

"She never goes out?"

"Of course she does. But, for whatever reason, when she is in this home, she prefers darkness. Oddly enough, in her other apartment, she prefers bright lights all day and night.

While Ming-huà puzzles over this curious eccentricity, Sy calls out, "Lady Oracle! Are you home?"

A tall figure looms quickly in a doorway, indirect light silhouetting her flowing black hair and flashing eyes. When she flips on the lights, Ming-huà is dazzled by the sight. The woman's bronze skin has a magic sheen, and even the colorful fabric of her resplendent Mongol *deel* cannot hide a svelte musculature underneath. A vital, thirtysomething, very gorgeous face peers intently at the hunchback. The presence of this magnificent woman stuns Ming-huà, and she blurts out, "But you said—" stopping herself in time.

Sy laughs and twirls playfully. "I exaggerated!"

He performs a deep bow and Lady Oracle merely smiles. "Still playing the clown for your wards, Siren Rung?"

"It is a lamentable habit."

Lady Oracle moves gracefully to Ming-huà and takes her hand. "Come in, Ming-huà, you are welcome here."

Only now does Ming-huà notice the abundance of jewelry adorning this intimidating woman. She is speechless and allows Lady Oracle to lead her into another room, much larger and with a bit of sunlight slanting in from a partially shuttered window.

"I am letting in some light for you, my dear, to make you more comfortable in my . . . concrete yurt."

The woman offers Sy and the hunchback chairs. "Tea will arrive in a moment."

Sy moans.

The group remains silent for a short while.

"You are Mongol," says Ming-huà softly.

Lady Oracle seems surprised. "Siren told you?"

"No, he tells me very little. I just know."

"How?"

"I don't know, perhaps the mention of a yurt?"

"Your intuition is correct. I am Mongol."

Sy fidgets and twirls his hands. "Not intuition. Not this one. Her magical hump told her."

A self-possessed young boy brings a tray containing a steaming teapot and cups. He leaves without a word being spoken. Lady Oracle pours tea in two of the cups and looks at Sy inquisitively.

"No, thank you. Too early for me. A shot of whiskey would be nice."

Lady Oracle laughs. "Old habits die hard. How about *airag*?"

"Perfect." He glances in amusement at a puzzled Ming-huà. "Fermented horse milk," he explains.

"Bataar!" she calls. When the boy enters, she speaks in Mongolian and he rushes out, only to quickly return with a bottle of *airag* for Sy.

Lady Oracle says, "You can use the teacup, Siren. No reason to stand on ceremony."

"None at all."

She looks penetratingly at Ming-huà. "Now, dear young lady, I expect you are curious."

"Very."

"Instead of my guessing what you find most curious, I will answer your questions."

Ming-huà hesitates.

"Feel free," prods Lady Oracle.

"I hardly know where to begin," stumbles the hunchback. "Sy brought me here for some reason. As usual with him, I am offered no real explanation. I would like to know what it is."

"I'm afraid it is a test."

"What kind of test?"

"A test of your powers. A test involving real people rather than stones and eggshells. Through me, you will meet many different types of people, and those people are certainly not the most pleasant of people."

"And?'

"And we will see."

"What do you do?" asks Ming-huà after digesting this last, unsatisfying response, but too timid to pursue the subject.

"I used to tell fortunes for a living. They were mostly wrong, but I was paid. Then I met my husband, and I gave up fortune-telling until he died. Now I do not tell fortunes from the past, but rather I try and make futures from the present."

"What did your husband do?"

"He was strong. Magnificent! A great man who could move mountains with his muscles and move multitudes with his words. He was a longshoreman. A union organizer."

"I see. I am sorry."

"You must be curious how he died so young?"

"I admit I am."

"He was murdered."

This unexpected information sets Ming-huà back in her seat. "Oh, I'm so sorry."

"My work is to reach out to his murderers, or people very much like his murderers."

"Yes, Sy told me you are a social worker."

"Oh, no no no, my dear young lady, I am definitely not a social worker."

Ming-huà does not respond. Instead, her hump is receiving the most hauntingly sad vibrations; long, drawn-out chords of great suffering.

"You are in pain, deep pain," whispers Ming-huà, reluctant to offend.

"It is true," replies Lady Oracle.

"If you don't practice social work, what is it you do?"

"Irrelevant. What I have been doing is ineffective. You represent a chance for me to succeed."

"At what?"

"You know, my grandmother Buandelgereen knew your grandparents."

Ming-huà catches her breath. "Really?"

Lady Oracle nods. "Also, your parents."

Ming-huà realizes this is a diversion from the subject at hand, but the revelation astounds her. "How?"

"That was a long time ago, and the story is very very long and involved. Some day when we have fewer pressing issues, I will tell you what I know. I think you are aware your father left manuscripts, very detailed manuscripts, of his parents' quest as well as his own trials and tribulations."

"My mother mentioned something about them," says Ming-huà excitedly. Can I see them?"

"Perhaps, some day. But, for now, we have somewhere to go."

"Can't we stay here a while. I really must know more."

"Not possible," Lady Oracle says firmly.

"Where are we going?"

"To a crack house," says the Mongol woman with a grim smile.

Chapter 4: Trial by Fire

~ First Visit ~

Before she has a chance to make further objections, Ming-huà finds herself tramping down a host of San Francisco's sordid back streets, struggling to keep up with Sy and Lady Oracle. The Mongol woman wields a heavy walking stick which resembles the staff of some Biblical prophet. Ming-huà's hump jars her mind with a succession of painful vibrations that signal danger. At last they reach a stand-alone, dilapidated house. Increasingly powerful waves of anger and desperation cause her hump to rebel against any further agony. She stops in her tracks.

"Come on," says Lady Oracle.

"We're going in there?"

"Of course."

"I'm not sure I can," utters a miserable Ming-huà.

"None of that!" scolds Lady Oracle. "You must. Be brave."

Approaching the front door, an unholy stench of defecation, rotten food, vomit, urine, and a host of other noxious odors taint the air.

"I can't go in there," Ming-huà whispers urgently to Sy.

"You must!" he snaps.

Lady Oracle uses her stick to bang on the door. A small crowd of nasty-looking lowlifes gather around to watch, some laughing, some muttering obscenities, and others issuing warnings to, "Get the fuck outta here, bitches."

Lady Oracle ignores them and keeps banging. Finally, the door is partially opened by a skeletal man with nothing on but a torn T-shirt discolored by a multitude of stains. He is young, but appears to be as ancient as an inmate at Auschwitz. The foul smells roll out the door like a thick fog and envelop all of them in a miasma of reeking stink.

Ming-huà covers her mouth and nose with the scarf and turns to leave, but Sy grabs her arm and pulls her back.

"You again, bitch!" says the half-naked skeleton.

Lady Oracle remains unfazed, and replies placidly, "You told me to return today. You said he would be in today."

"Fuckin'? I did? Fuck me! Who are these two shits?"

"Friends."

"Why're they here?"

"To help."

"Fuck! Help with what?"

"Is Zookeeper in?"

"Yeah."

"Can you call him?"

"Fuckin' bitch! Go on in and find him yourself. I have to take a shit."

When they enter the wretched house, Ming-huà watches the young man go into another room and squat. She hears him grunt, and a runny stream of defecation squirts out onto the floor and splatters against the wall. She feels faint and presses her scarf harder against her nose. As they go from room to room, they must pick their way through piles of trash and debris that cover the floors. Passing a bathroom, she sees the tub is full of rancid, black water with unidentifiable garbage floating on top of the scum. The toilet is backed up to the rim and full of defecation. One room has a baby crib, empty, surrounded by garbage. Occasionally, she sees a person lying on decaying mattresses or on top of mounds of trash. Ming-huà is on the verge of running headlong out of this nightmare when she hears Lady Oracle say, "Ah! There you are, Zookeeper!"

Another young man, just as grubby and thin as the first, rises to meet her. He is covered in tattoos and has a scraggily beard. However, something about him is different than the others. He has a coiled energy, striking features, and a burning, feverish glare that harbors a mixture of extreme viciousness and exquisitely angelic charisma. Even through her scarf, Ming-huà notices he has probably not bathed for months. He catches her looking at him.

"Where'd you dig up the hunchback? She might be pretty but for that beetle-back."

"And you might be handsome but for the fact you're butt-ugly," replies Lady Oracle.

Zookeeper ignores the comment and continues to stare at Ming-huà. "It's got a pretty face if you get past the 'foul bunch-back'd toad' look."

Sy suddenly leaps in the air and pirouettes, freezing in the most dramatic of operatic poses. "Sooo! The young crackhead speaks Shakespeare! Wonder of wonders!"

"Holy shit, Lady Orgasm!" exclaims Zookeeper in a richly modulated voice, gaping wide-eyed at Siren Rung. "You brought two freaks today."

"Yes," she replies, ignoring the insult. "You must be used to freaks by now."

"She speaks who never utters a lie," he replies. "Zookeeper is the keeper of zoos. This zoo is full of exiles from Doctor Moreau's bestiary. I am their keeper. I love all of them, but they must be fed."

"Better and better!" enthuses Sy, rubbing his hands together. "More evidence of an educated derelict."

Zookeeper glares at him contemptuously. "Be careful little man, I am the Zookeeper and you're here at my pleasure."

Lady Oracle abruptly turns her attention from Zookeeper and asks Ming-huà, "What are you feeling now?"

Ming-huà is taken off-guard. "What?"

"Your hump, your hump. What is it telling you?"

"It is telling me I am in a bottomless pit of suffering."

Zookeeper looks at her curiously.

"Yet," says Lady Oracle. "You have not run away. Not from the stench. Not from the desolation. Not from the pain. Not from the suffering. Why haven't you?"

Ming-huà appears perplexed. "That is a good question. I should. I would have before. My hump is burning with a thousand painful sensations, yet I remain. I don't know."

"Is that why you brought hunchback here?" asks Zookeeper. "To observe us derelicts . . . the walking-dead . . . the bestiary?"

"Of course. This is a zoo, correct Zookeeper?"

"Ha-ha! You got me there, Lady Clitoris. Now, did you bring money to pay the entrance fee?"

Lady Oracle silently digs out of her pocket a one-hundred-dollar bill and hands it to him. "As per our agreement."

He takes it, hands shaking. "When rich villains need poor ones, poor ones may make what price they will."

"Lordy!" exclaims Sy. "This boy continues to amaze!"

Lady Oracle turns to Ming-huà. "Tell me what Zookeeper is feeling."

Ming-huà hesitates, but Lady Oracle nods her head and smiles encouragement.

"He is a congealed mass of anger, pain, fear, and . . . something else. It's unclear . . . fury, cruelty, vengeance . . . maybe kindness, compassion? Unclear. He must have spent years compacting his feelings into such a tight ball. Hard to see. Opaque."

While Ming-huà is speaking, she perceives Zookeeper closely examining her with undeniably perceptive and intelligent eyes.

When their eyes meet, Zookeeper laughs and turns his attention back to Lady Oracle. "What the fuck? Are those brilliant observations worth one-hundred-dollars to you, Lady Tits? Jesus! You got fuckin' cheated! Hey, hunchback, it's you who need analysis, not Zookeeper."

"Yes, I am sure I do," says Ming-huà meekly.

This makes him pause, but he quickly tries to recover his bravado. "Look, hunchback, you're curtailed of fair proportion, cheated of feature by dissembling nature. You're deformed, unfinished, sent before your time into this breathing world, half made up."

Tears well in her eyes.

Zookeeper seems stricken. "But look, hunchback, you're not so bad looking. Not at all. Shit, you've got a nice face. The rest of you is nice also."

He turns on Lady Oracle. "Why the fuck did you bring her here? This shithole ain't no place for her. Freak or no freak, she's a different kind of freak." As if to himself, Zookeeper adds, "Very different."

Sy claps his hands and leaps in the air. When he lands, he looks at a surprised Zookeeper and cries, "A wicked conscience mouldeth goblins swift as frenzy thoughts!"

Zookeeper starts to reply, but two seedy looking men skulk into the room and stand threateningly. Each carry knifes. "What about us, Lady What's-Your-Name. Hand over our fuckin' shares."

"The agreement was between she and me," says Zookeeper leering at Lady Oracle. "But my exhibits deserve a fee also. How else does a keeper keep them fed?"

Lady Oracle, with a shake of her magnificent long hair, tosses them ten dollars each.

"Not enough," one of them says.

"More than enough," replies Lady Oracle calmly. "Let's go."

She starts to walk out of the room with her two companions when the men block the door.

"Not enough, bitch."

Sy digs in his pocket and says in his usual supercilious manner. "Let's see, I think I have a couple of quarters here."

A knife is soon pressed against his neck. "Funny man! Look, bitch, hand over or this piece of shit gets his jugular cut."

The other man also brandishes his knife.

Ming-huà is terrified and directs her attention to the men's hands, but before she can act, Sy turns to her and shouts, "No, not yet! This is not the test!"

Confused, she takes a step back. Meanwhile, Lady Oracle has produced two more hundred-dollar bills. "Here you are, gentlemen. Take it. We will leave quietly."

Zookeeper whistles. "Damn! I should have asked for more. Fuck me!"

The two men grab the bills and lower their knifes.

As they are leaving, Ming-huà hears Zookeeper say, "Let witchcraft join with beauty, lust with both! By damn! I've got the hots for that hunchback!"

"Then go fuck her," says one of the men.

By the time she hears these words, Ming-huà and her companions are out the door and moving rapidly down the street toward home.

~ Refractory ~

The next few days pass without incident. Ming-huà no longer takes walks with Sy, and he has given up throwing things at her, as she is always successful. However, he does return late every night after visiting Lady Oracle. He is never drunk, only tipsy from her *airag*, but he makes up for that deficiency by downing any number of whiskeys before turning in for the night. Ming-huà begins to suspect the entire knife incident at the crack house was a set-up. A test to see her reaction. Why did he stop her then? Of course, the three men were in on the conspiracy. That is why they were paid so exorbitantly. Nevertheless, the motives of Lady Oracle and Sy are suspicious, even malevolent. What is their next step? Ming-huà now knows she can at least partly succeed in controlling her reactions to extreme environments. In the past, she never would have been able to enter that crack house, let alone stay for so long. She is becoming hardened. That, she is certain, is their goal. But to what end? Go around the world seeking out evil and making the perpetrators, or parts of them, disappear? How will that end suffering? Will it not create more? Maybe one of those hunters she 'reconfigured' on the island would have invented a cure for cancer if he had lived longer. The suffering of a fawn weighed against the suffering of millions? It makes no sense. The more she thinks, the more confused she becomes. *What of Lady Oracle? What does she know about my parents and grandparents? What is her connection to Sy? So many questions!* She goes to sleep that night determined to force an explanation from Sy the next day before he leaves to meet Lady Oracle. *He must! Or else? Am I truly willing to leave? I will face that bridge when it comes.*

~

Next morning after finishing breakfast, both sit together quietly sipping their coffee. Ming-huà gathers her courage and is about to make her demands when Sy holds up a cautionary hand.

"No need! I know. You want a full explanation of everything I know, annotated and with footnotes. Or else? Well, you never got that far in your thinking. I'll save you the trouble of having to make that decision. This morning you are accompanying me to Lady Oracle's other apartment in Chinatown, where there is abundant light. She will throw some of it on your demands. Satisfied?"

Ming-huà stares at him admiringly. "Yes."

Sy leaps up in his most loose-jointed scarecrow manner. "Then, let's go!"

Ming-huà is not enthusiastic about returning to another run-down, dangerous neighborhood.

"Wait. Could we maybe invite her to come here?"

Scarecrow looks askance at her. "You are the one seeking the information. It's your obligation to go there since Lady Oracle is willing to provide some clarity to your . . . history. The seeker must seek the one who is sought."

Ming-huà reluctantly nods agreement.

Once again they tromp through the helter-skelter crowds and trudge up and down San Francisco streets, this time moving in an unfamiliar direction. Chinatown is bursting with activity. Multitudes of tourists mix with local residents, shopkeepers, and street vendors who cater to them by accentuating stereotypical Chinese humility. Sy leads her off the main artery of Grant Street and down a dizzying array of small side streets and alleys to an apartment building designed in traditional Qing dynasty style. Ming-hua's hump has been busy, but in a very different way than the Tenderloin district. The sensations seem as mysterious and menacing as if she were penetrating the lair of an ancient secret society.

"Scared?" asks Sy as they look up at the facade.

"A little."

"You should have met her grandmother! Whew!" Sy shakes his hand as if it had been burned.

"You knew her grandmother?"

"Of course. In her heyday, carried a rifle strapped to her back. Whew! What a woman!"

"Sy—"

"Shhhhh!" He knocks on the bright red, dragon-carved front door.

A moment passes and Ming-huà blurts, "She's not in. Let's go."

But even as the last words leave her mouth, the door opens and Lady Oracle stands majestically before them.

Ming-huà's hump is instantly alive with unfamiliar vibrations that defy translation.

Lady Oracle's flashing eyes settle on her. "Come in."

The apartment is almost blindingly bright, with an array of huge, spherically-shaped windows pouring fierce sunlight into the rooms. Supplementing this natural radiance, innumerable electric lights and lanterns add to the excess of brilliance.

"Yes, I see your reaction, Ming-huà," says Lady Oracle. "This is my yang to the other apartment's yin. Although, contrary to popular opinion, they are not opposite. When I am here, I am the dark spot in the light yang, and when I am there, I am the light spot in the dark yin."

"I see," says Ming-huà, thinking of nothing better to say.

[65]

They enter a room full of traditional Chinese furniture, scrolls, calligraphy, books, lacquerware, and all manner of bric-a-brac. Pungent incense from an ancestral shrine fills the air.

"Sit and Bataar will bring tea," says Lady Oracle. She turns to Sy, "And you come with me."

Ming-huà is left alone for a long time, amusing herself by looking at all the intriguing objects that fill the room to bursting. A Mongol boy enters holding a tray. When Lady Oracle returns, she takes it saying, "Thank you, Bataar," and sets it on a massive Chinese table. She offers tea. Ming-huà accepts.

"So many beautiful things," says the hunchback. "They take my breath away, but most are Chinese. Aren't you from Mongolia?"

Lady Oracle chuckles. "Yes, but remember, we conquered them. I believe the saying goes, 'to the victors go the spoils.'"

Ming-huà smiles back. "The Yuan dynasty was a long time ago."

"True, but my linage also goes back a long time. However, that is not why you're here. Sy told you I would provide explanations. He is only partly correct. Last time we spoke, you expressed an interest in your past. I will tell you what I can, but reserve the right to be brief and not provide too many details. In some cases, I will provide no details. Where do you want to start?"

"My father."

"A schizophrenic, so humans thought."

"And?"

"A lawyer."

"Lady Oracle, I already know these facts. This will take a very long time if all I get are such short, almost monosyllabic answers."

"It is all you will get."

Ming-huà sighs. *More games, more deflections.* "He was in the war?" she asks.

"Yes."

"Vietnam, I know," says Ming-huà impatiently.

"Yes."

"But something happened to him there?"

"Yes, as war does to young men . . . women also. . . . "

"No, I think this was different."

Lady Oracle pauses and looks at Ming-huà in a new light. "How different?"

"That is what I am asking you."

"Your mother didn't tell you?"

"All she has told me is that Michael Powers was a schizophrenic, a lawyer, and a soldier in Vietnam. He had a first wife who was killed in an auto accident and a son who lives in the East Coast, I don't remember where."

"That's all you know?"

"Yes, mainly."

"That is enough," says Lady Oracle sharply.

"No, it is not enough. What happened to father in Vietnam?"

"There was a battle."

"Yes?"

"His comrades all died."

"And?"

Lady Oracle narrows her eyes. "Did your mother tell you about his voices?"

"No."

"The Precious Object? . . . the Great Warrior?"

"No."

"Then better to leave well enough alone."

"No."

Lady Oracle looks at Ming-huà curiously. "Then how do you know his experiences in war were different from other men?"

"Because my hump does not stop working when I talk with my mother. Every time she mentioned his name, every time she mentioned the war, I felt weird pulsations I have never felt before. Like tremors. Something about him was different. Something happened to him that was different. What was it?"

"He survived. His comrades died."

"Yes, but there is more to it, isn't there?"

"Next question," says Lady Oracle curtly.

"You are unwilling to explain?"

"Yes, for now. Perhaps later in the course of our conversation."

"But—"

"Next!" snaps Lady Oracle.

"All right, my grandfather."

"On your father's side, I presume?"

"Yes, John Powers."

"A businessman. Very bright. And like your father, also a misdiagnosed schizophrenic."

"Really?"

"Go on, ask."

"My mother mentioned something about a quest?"

"Yes."

"To China?"

"Yes, and Mongolia."

Ming-huà's eyes widen. "What was the quest?"

"Your mother did not explain?"

"No."

Lady Oracle sighs deeply, resignedly. "To find someone."

"Who?"

"*Her.*"

"What?"

"*Her.*"

Ming-huà blinks in confusion. "I don't understand. He went on a quest to seek a woman? Was it my grandmother?"

Lady Oracle laughs. "No! The person he sought is a very special person. A very powerful person. A very mysterious person. It was during the quest he met your grandmother on your mother's side."

"My grandmother. . . Child of Buddha?"

"Yes, Chinese. Like your mother, also a hunchback. She helped your grandfather."

"My grandmother was also on the quest?"

"Yes."

Ming-huà buries her face in her hands. "This is all too confusing. Your answers are too short. I need clarification. Explanation. I don't know the correct questions to ask. Please!"

"Your grandfather met a young Chinese pianist—Bai Meiying— on the quest. It was during the Japanese invasion. Later, they married and escaped war-torn China, eventually making it to San Francisco. That is where your father was born."

"And my grandmother?"

[68]

"She stayed in China, in a mental institution, where your mother was born."

Ming-huà shakes her head in frustration. "This is too confusing. It is like some unsolvable puzzle."

"Not at all," says Lady Oracle calmly. To cut through the maze of facts, think like a Mongol."

"How is that?"

"What is the common thread connecting your grandfather, your grandmother, your father, your mother, Bai Meiying, and you?"

"I don't know."

"Yes, you do. Think."

"The quest?"

"Bingo!" cries Lady Oracle.

"What was the quest about?"

"As I told you, to find *her*."

"But who is *her*?"

"Well, to make a long story short, *her* was a small part of . . . well, a larger *Her*, and as it turns out, the larger *Her* was also on a quest. In fact, the larger *Her* still is on a quest."

"To find what?"

"You."

Chapter 5: Trials

~ Tangled Webs ~

Ming-huà stares at Lady Oracle dumbstruck. All she can manage to utter is, "Me?"

"Yes."

Lady Oracle turns to Sy. "Siren, take her home. It is enough today."

"No!" cries Ming-huà. "Please! I need to know more. I . . . cannot . . . fathom. . . . "

"Take her home!" snaps Lady Oracle.

Scarecrow jumps. "Yes! Indeed, you're right. She does need time to think." He looks askance at Lady Oracle. "However, use caution Great Lady. We do not want another broken one."

"Ha! This one will not break!" Without warning, the Mongol woman grabs a small statuette and flings it at Ming-huà's head.

It disappears.

"You see? Even in her muddled state, she will prevail. Even the unexpected will be dealt with. She is tougher than you think, Siren. Now, go!"

Ming-huà stands dazed. "But, I have so many questions!"

Sy takes her hand. "Come, there will be time enough later."

As they step outside, Lady Oracle calls from the doorway, "Questions are mother's milk! Build up your hunger, my teat awaits! Now rest and ponder what lies in wait for you. All will be revealed in good time."

~

Making their way home, Ming-huà feels worse than if she had never visited Lady Oracle. Her mind grasps at straws, trying to decode the paltry hints she had been given. Distressed at her overwhelming confusion, she briefly entertains the idea of turning around and storming into Lady Oracle's apartment demanding answers.

"Don't even think it!" cries Scarecrow. "It is enough for today. Going back will only incur her ire, and I have seen the results of her wrath. No, keep walking!"

Sy reverts to his usual skipping, dancing, parading shenanigans, but Ming-huà will not be distracted from her thoughts and remains grim the entire way home. Once inside, she retires upstairs, but Sy calls as she ascends the staircase, "An hour, in the usual place! We have things to discuss. Perhaps you may find them interesting! I will be waiting, drinking my own mother's milk!"

When she joins Sy, he has already downed any number of whiskeys, but hardly shows any effect. Nonetheless, she soon realizes his tongue is loosened, and sits in anticipation.

"Look, little hunchback, there are things at play here that are far beyond your comprehension. Forces are at play. Forces you cannot imagine."

"Are they dangerous?" she asks, alarmed.

"Well, that depends. Yes and no."

"I don't understand."

"You're caught between two . . . opposing . . . oh, how do I put it? Two opposing powers. So was your father."

"How?"

"Remember what Lady Oracle told you; the one common element in this entangled web is the quest?"

"Yes, I remember."

"Well, the quest is certainly the key."

"What was it?"

"You mean, what is it?"

"Yes, what is it?"

"You see? That is the key, and it is a key I cannot give you. Not on my life."

"Do you know what it is?"

Sy capers about. "Do I know what it is? Of course I know what it is! *Goddess* knows I've been around it long enough!"

"*Goddess*?"

Sy turns serious and puts his finger to his lips. "Shhhhh! Do not mention *Her*. Too soon."

[71]

Ming-huà lets out her breath in frustration. "How am I ever to make any sense of all this when I am forever given hints and innuendos, but never straight answers!"

"Truth is curved, like spacetime."

"Never mind!" she cries in anger. "I'm going back to my room."

"Wait!" he exclaims.

"Either tell me straight out what this is all about, or leave me alone!"

"Okay. Are you mad?"

"What?"

"Are you crazy—do you hear voices?"

"No."

"Do you see things that are not there?"

"I don't think so."

"Is the crack house we visited real?"

"Too real!"

Sy empties his glass in one big gulp. "We are going back."

Ming-huà shudders. "Oh, no! I will not return to that place. Ever!"

"We are returning in two days' time. Meanwhile, we will return to Lady Oracle's house in preparation."

"No."

"Do you want to learn more about your past? About the quest? About your future?"

"Yes."

"Then we will go. There is no turning back."

Ming-huà leans forward and looks deeply into Sy's eyes. "Who is Lady Oracle?"

He laughs. "You mean *what* is Lady Oracle?"

She blinks. "Okay, now please explain."

"On the surface, she is a woman. A woman who never talks about herself. But there is something far deeper behind her physical appearance. She has a secret, a very deep secret, never revealed to any human. I dare not reveal it now, for she always says humans talk so much. Fortune teller? Perhaps, but if so, that is why she tells others' fortunes and never her own. I remember she told me once, 'I have learned that words chattered by most people are nothing more than threads cleverly stitched together in an embroidery to hang on a wall for public consumption. It is intended to display their life's tapestry; but the tapestry is actually created for the purpose of hiding unsightly stains on the wall behind.'"

Ming-huà shakes her head. "Are you telling me she is not human?"

Sy continues. "Yes, in a way. Oh, she is deep. Very deep. But remember, dear hunchback, her mother and your grandmother were friends. Co-conspirators, if you will. Your grandmother Child of Buddha, and Lady Oracle's grandmother Buandelgereen, shared the quest. It is the quest where your answers lie. And to get to those answers, you must follow where Lady Oracle and I lead. You must trust us."

"Sy, I will not go back to that crack house."

His face contorts into a rage she has never before witnessed. Fury envelops his entire form, and his body flashes shock waves that make her hump quake. "You will go back!" he thunders. "By damn, you will, else you will end up a pathetic wretch in some back alley! You will!"

Shrinking back in the chair, Ming-huà stares at him in a mix of amazement and fear. Speechless.

Instantly, his entire demeanor changes, and he reverts to the loose-jointed scarecrow she is familiar with. He freezes in a comical stance and flippantly says, "So, you see, we will go."

She finally gathers enough courage to speak. "You won't hurt me, will you Sy?"

He maintains his pose, but she sees tears roll down his cheeks. "Never! Don't you see, Ming-huà, there is something deeper here that you must not know too soon. Others have been broken. I do not want to see you broken."

"What others?"

Like his scarecrow namesake, every joint in his body seems to liquify and he plops in a chair. "Well, your father for one," he says wearily.

"What? Sy—"

Scarecrow stiffens and holds out an arm as if fending off an attack. "No! I said too much already. Remember what Lady Oracle said, your questions are like mother's milk. She will answer them."

"But when?"

"In her own time. When the time is right. But even Lady Oracle is the lesser she. When that greater one, the one I refer to as *She*, determines the time is right. No sooner."

[73]

"*She?*"

"Shhhhhh! Mustn't go there yet. Suffice to say, keep asking questions, but do what I say, and what Lady Oracle says. It is the only way. Do you believe me?"

"I wish I could, but you scare me. Lady Oracle scares me. But what scares me the most is this *She* who keeps coming up."

"Mum's the word, for now," he says smiling. "All in good time. First, we must return to the crack house."

"Why?"

"That you will discover. Now, will you go?"

Ming-huà's answer is firm. "Yes."

As soon as the word leaves her mouth, she is shocked at having said it.

~ A Nightmare ~

Lying in bed that night, Ming-huà finds it impossible to sleep. Images of that horrible crack house haunt her, and she cannot make herself reconcile her agreement to return with the revulsion she feels at the prospect. What force drives her to these awful decisions against her own will? All along her journey, from the death of those two hunters—to San Francisco—to this apartment—to Lady Oracle's—to a crack house where she would normally never consider entering; some compulsion makes her agree to the unagreeable. Where does this compulsion arise? Does it come from Lady Oracle? From this mysterious *She*? From Scarecrow himself? It is all too much, but all too real. Hump ablaze, she drifts in and out of sleep. Finally, a deep canyon opens beneath and she falls over the edge, plunging deeper and deeper. . . .

~

In freefall, she panics and wildly tries to grab projections from the cliff face, but to no avail. Although the bottom is black, she knows it is rushing up to meet her. Suddenly, she stops hurtling downward and finds herself floating above a sterile, white room where a group of people shuffle back and forth aimlessly. They act in odd ways, some talking to themselves, some with violent tics that snap their heads up and down, back and forth. Their clothes are loose-fitting pajamas. Ming-huà abruptly realizes she is in some sort of asylum. Hovering above the inmates as they pace back and forth, she sees a familiar face. . . .

~

No! She wakes up with a silent scream and labors to get out of bed, half-asleep but fully terrified. Free of the covers, she begins to rant, "Mother mother mother! . . . Crazy, mad, insane!"

Ming-huà runs to Sy's door and bangs as hard as she can. The door opens immediately, as if he had been waiting. Taken aback, she retreats a few steps and shouts, "My mother, Sy! She was crazy! She is crazy! A mad woman!"

Scarecrow swiftly rushes up to her and holds her head in his hands. "No, no, no, Ming-huà. No. She was not. She is not. It was for the sake of your father."

"But I saw her in the mental institute! Don't tell me she wasn't there! My hump tells me the dream is true!"

Sy leads her downstairs and fixes them both hot tea. As they sit, he continues to speak a string of soothing words until her composure returns.

"Now," he says gently. "Are you ready to listen?"

"Yes."

He takes a sip of tea and makes a face. "Awful stuff! Anyway, I can tell you this much: your mother checked herself into that asylum to be with your father."

Ming-huà shakes her head in perplexity.

"You see," continues Sy. "She was a gift, so to speak, from the greater *Her* to your father."

"A gift?"

"Um, yeah."

"What are you talking about? A gift? A slave?"

"No, not that exactly. Not at all. Perhaps a better word to use is not gift, but vessel."

"Vessel? Speak clearly, Sy."

"Yes, I cannot make it clearer. A vessel."

"For what purpose?"

"Isn't it obvious?" Sy tilts his head, waiting.

"No."

"To give birth to you, of course."

Ming-huà lets that statement sink in, but this time she refuses to be shocked into muteness. "Sy," she says as calmly as her taut nerves allow. "I want answers. If the quest is about me, and my mother was used as breeding stock, then it must be important. Correct?"

"Correct."

"So, if I am important, I am entitled to clear, unambiguous answers."

"Agreed."

Ming-huà lets out a deep sigh. "Then tell me, who, or what, is Lady Oracle?"

"Who's on first?"

Ming-huà blinks in confusion.

Sy leaps up and capers about the room. "Who is on first! That's what I asked! Who's on first? Who, of course! Who? That's what I just said! Who's on—"

"Sy, stop!"

He stops and mutters, "Well, you get the picture. Don't you see, little hunchback, you're asking the wrong question of the wrong person."

"Then who should I ask?"

"Who's on first!"

"Sy! I—"

"No, no, just listen. You must ask Lady Oracle, but she will ask the greater *Her* and only then decide which question to answer. Their answers may be circular, but to really get to the bottom, you must return to the crack house."

"But why? Why a crack house? In all this vast world, what's so important about a crack house?"

"It is not the crack house that's important."

Ming-huà snorts in frustration. "Then what is?"

Sy laughs. "Who's on first?"

This time, Ming-huà refrains from getting angry and furrows her brow in thought. *It is code, foolish girl!* she chides herself, searching her mind for a solution. But it won't come. Not yet.

Sy smiles complacently. "Give it time. You'll figure it out. More tea?"

~ Return to Lady Oracle ~

"Sy tells me you have agreed to return to the crack house," says Lady Oracle.

Ming-huà sits nervously with Sy back at Lady Oracle's Chinatown apartment. The lights are ablaze, exacerbating Ming-hua's headache, but she is determined to remain quiet and let this strange Mongol woman take the lead.

"Yes," she says curtly.

There is a drawn-out moment of silence. Lady Oracle seems to be waiting in anticipation. Sy, not as patient as either woman, pipes up.

"Lady Oracle, I think she deserves answers before continuing."

The Mongol raises her eyebrows. "Answers to what?"

"You know very well. I am powerless, and can only give clues. Ming-huà knows about her mother and father—how they met—and is anxious to learn more."

"You are now her advocate?"

He strikes a dramatic pose. "In a manner of speaking."

"Remember what happened to your . . . predecessor . . . in China?"

"Bullet in the head," says Sy nonchalantly.

Ming-huà stiffens.

Lady Oracle quickly interjects, "From a Japanese rifle."

"Yes, but directed by *Him*," says Sy accusingly.

Ming-huà is stung by these insider references that so clearly mark her as an outsider. Not understanding what her two companions are talking about, she can only sit and wait, hoping to discover a few familiar, explanatory shells on the desolate beach of their shared allusions.

Lady Oracle falls silent and gazes at Ming-huà. "Last time you were here," she says. "I told you questions are mother's milk and my teat awaits. I await."

"Both of you refer to *Her*, and now a *Him*. Who . . . or what . . . are they?"

"Voices in your father's head."

Sy coughs and casts a skeptical glance at Lady Oracle.

"I will ask again," says Ming-huà, taking the hint. "Who, or what, are they?"

Lady Oracle smiles appreciatively. "You have grown backbone along with your strengthening powers. *He* is God. *She* is Goddess."

~

"*God* and *Goddess*," repeated Ming-huà reflexively. "Those were his voices?"

"Yes. Your mother didn't tell you?" asks Lady Oracle.

"No. But if those were the voices in his head, what does it signify? As I understand it, schizophrenics hear all sorts of voices and see things that aren't real."

Lady Oracle nods agreement, but does not reply.

Ming-huà looks at her two companions. "Well, what do they signify?"

Sy fidgets and leans forward in his chair. "What if they were more than voices?"

"You mean if they are real?"

Lady Oracle casts a cautionary glance at Sy. "Let's not get ahead of ourselves. All of us here are aware that the belief in supernatural deities, ancient and revered as it is, cannot be more than mere superstition. Suffice it to say your father, or part of him, believed they were real. He was a very conflicted man."

"So, we know he was ill," says Ming-huà. "What about both of you? Do you believe the *God* and *Goddess* in my father's hallucination, or delusion, or whatever you call it, are real?"

"To your father they were real," says Sy.

"I'm asking about your beliefs!" she exclaims.

Lady Oracle rises and stands haughtily. "Ming-huà, reality is a tricky proposition. You ask us to explain the unexplainable. Now, tomorrow we visit the crack house again. It is already arranged. Sy, have her here at ten o'clock in the morning."

"Wait a minute!" cries Ming-huà jumping up from her chair to face the Mongol woman. "You can't just leave it at this! Why why why must we go to this crack house?"

"Dear," says Lady Oracle softly. "Crack usage causes hallucinations and delusions."

"And?"

"And a person who resides there may very well be . . . how do I put it? May very well be pertinent to our discussion."

Ming-huà's face registers a dim awareness. "Zookeeper?"

"Yes."

Chapter 6: Hell Awaits

~ Return to the Crack House ~

Since the unexpected visit of the hunchback girl, Zookeeper's voices, long dormant, have been sparked to life and now plague his every waking moment. To him, it is as if she had disturbed a hive of bees whose angry buzzing foretells existential danger. But in this case, the imminent threat is posed not by flesh and blood enemies, but by a reanimation of the once-lifeless demons in his head, unless . . . unless what? Bees will attack intruders in stinging fury, but what weapon does he possess to defend against such an airy, otherworldly menace as the hunchback? The drug-addled but fiercely loyal exhibits he nurtures in his zoo can swarm and sting any intruders from rival gangs, but this hunchback presents an entirely different challenge. He laughs inwardly at the notion that a fragile snit of a girl can represent such power. Yet, he knows it is a power to rival his own.

On the surface, Zookeeper's life story is not particularly unusual, as life stories go in the Tenderloin district. Father unknown—abandoned by drug-addicted mother—in and out of foster care—routinely abused physically and emotionally—in and out of juvenile hall—in and out of violent clashes with other denizens of the street—in and out of jail where he was subjected to the in and out humiliation of soul-coring rape. Spiritual death by a thousand cuts. Yet, early in his young life, Zookeeper recognized he had one powerful advantage over all the others. That advantage he could not put in words, but it resided in his ability to exercise the skill of a coroner and surgically peel back the layers of forensic clues that reveal the inner minutiae of what makes an individual tick. More than that, he is able to plumb the deepest motivations of people, and for what goal they will kill or die to achieve. As he grew older and more street-wise, he quickly learned the desperate craving for drugs represented a goal that made its addicts especially vulnerable to his power. As a student of history, he calculated his own armies, unlike those of Napoleon and Alexander, would be recruited from the most reviled and wretched of

[79]

outcasts. In this, he felt more a kinship with Hitler and his hypnotic ability to attract psychopaths. A limited pool, he admits to himself, but the sad trajectory of his brutal existence reveals to a scarred mind no other path. Throughout his life, many have referred to him as charismatic, but he knows his power far exceeds that inadequate adjective. Just as his own demons have been reanimated by the hunchback, so he has reanimated the demons in others by substituting his will for theirs. At least, until now. Therein lies the problem; the hunchback! Zookeeper, fully aware of his own power, felt it crash like a wave against the unbending breakwater of the hunchback's own mysterious force and disintegrate harmlessly in spattering fragments. Far from repelling him, that force exerts a fatal attraction that draws him as inexorably as he draws others. *Immovable object?* he wonders. *We shall see.*

Zookeeper is unsure how to categorize the hunchback. She is not an enemy, nor friend, nor snotty bourgeoise female, nor a hypocritical do-gooder, nor a curious onlooker like Lady Oracle. During the hunchback's visit, he felt the psychic probing emanating from her extraordinary hump, projecting its delicate tendrils of awareness into his brain. To his all-perceiving eyes, her hump burned as powerfully as the churning core of a nuclear reactor. An enigma. *Queen Mab?* he wonders, *or parasitic wasp?* More importantly, does she represent a threat? Such questions he ponders from the inner sanctum of the crack house while waiting for her next visit, arranged for whatever reason, by Lady Oracle. This inner sanctum is off-limits to all residents of the house. The door is always locked. Inside, it is as clean and pristine as that of the most assiduous housekeeper—an island of spotless paradise amidst the ocean of filth that surrounds it. Perfumed air freshener and joss sticks mask the all-pervasive stench. Books line its walls, and Zookeeper sits meditatively in an easy chair, sifting the cascade of thoughts and barrage of newly arrived voices that assault his sanity. What puzzles him the most is that the revivified voices triggered by the hunchback's visit are completely different than any of those he experienced in the past. Still distant and growlingly hazy, their rumblings scare him in ways he cannot define. His concentration is directed at the connection between these new voices and the hunchback when he hears a knocking at the sanctum's door.

"Hey! Zookeeper! You in there, motherfucker? We got a juiced-up nigger-boy cravin' apple jack."

Zookeeper calls toward the closed door, "Got cash?"

"Fuck yeah! Wouldn't bother you if he didn't."

"How juiced up?"

"Big time."

"Weapons?"

"Shit, didn't check."

"Fuck you, Angel Cake! Is he inside the fort?"

"Naw, left his cock hangin' outside. He's fuckin' jumpy though."

"Strong boy or weak?"

"Looks fuckin' strong to me."

"Hang, I'll be there. Shit! He wearin' gang colors?"

"Not that I can tell, but, damn Zookeeper, get your ass out here, I got to weasel in my shit. You handle the cash; I handle the blood."

By the time Zookeeper has dispensed with the "client" by accepting cash for crack, he sees three figures approach, one of whom bears a quite distinctive hump. Immediately, his senses are on full alert. He discards his pusher persona and assumes the mantle of Shakespeare to project a defensive shield against non-addict intruders. The Bard almost always works to captivate even the most resistant of them. When they approach near enough for his voice to be heard, he assumes a lavish bow.

"Good morrow, Mistress Oracle!"

"What are you doing out in the fresh air and daylight so early Sir Zookeeper?" she replies. "Aren't you afraid of being desiccated by too much time in the sun?"

"Business. I see you bring your two freaks. Well, two freaks among my other exhibits will cause no particular disturbance. Nature teaches beasts to know their friends."

Again, a small crowd has gathered to make various obscene comments. One skeletal man whose tissue-thin white skin seems so slack his tattoos fairly run down his arms like melting wax shouts, "Shiiiit! Listen to that fucker Zookeeper talk fancy shit. That's dope, motherfucker!"

Zookeeper grins and bows low in recognition. He turns to Ming-huà and says, "Welcome back to my zoo. The animals inside do bite, so don't try to feed them. And definitely don't stick your hand through their cages. You hear?"

Ming-huà submissively nods assent, while Lady Oracle rolls her eyes. "Ming-huà, this boy is just trying to scare you. The only danger in that house is from slipping on rotting garbage and breaking your neck."

Sy laughs and dances a little jig. "Guess I'd better be careful!"

Zookeeper has kept his eyes on Ming-huà, and he feels the tingling pressure of some inexplicable power flowing from her body to his. He shakes it off and leads them into the house. With no intention to show them his inner sanctum, he wades through the trash, past the nervously suspicious stares of his addicts, to an abandoned room where the stench is slightly less overwhelming.

"We can talk here," he says. "Now, what do you want this time?" he asks Lady Oracle.

"Before I tell you, I want you to have this." She jams a folded piece of paper in his shirt pocket.

"What the fuck's that?"

"My address. After our meeting today, you will want to come and talk with me."

"About what?"

"You'll see. Now, you asked what I want. This time I want to ask you some questions about yourself."

Zookeeper gives her a cold stare and his eyes flash hostility. "What the fuck for?"

"What happened to Shakespeare?" chuckles Sy. "Discarded for more pressing business?"

"Shut the fuck up, freak, I'm talkin' to Lady Clitoris here."

While waiting for Lady Oracle to respond, he notices out of the corner of his eye the reactions of the hunchback. She stands awkwardly, clearly uncomfortable and skittish. *This is definitely not her idea*, he thinks. Just as Lady Oracle opens her mouth to speak, the same two men who threatened them before enter the room brandishing the same knives. The stink from their bodies cuts through the already foul-smelling atmosphere.

"Zookeeper, you fuckin' failed to inform us the bitch would come back. Does she have enough bread to pay all of us?"

"I dunno," says Zookeeper. "Don't even know what the fuck she wants." He looks at Lady Oracle. "Well?"

"You will be paid."

[82]

"And my exhibits here? They are my two palace guards, and whew!" He shakes his hand as if it had touched a hot stove. "They get mean when deprived of their daily sustenance. Bring enough coin to keep them happy?"

"Perhaps," says Lady Oracle. "Depends."

"On what, bitch?" asks one of the men.

She glares at him with a fierce smile. "On whether you are good boys."

"Shiiiit! Give us the money first, then we leave you alone," says the other man.

"You have to forgive my friends," says Zookeeper. "They haven't been properly introduced. This is Pepper Spray and Amygdala. I named Amygdala myself because of his emotional nature. Clever, eh?"

"I'm impressed," says Lady Oracle.

"Shit!" barks Pepper Spray. "What about it, Lady Fuck! Prepay or get out. Cash up front in this house. Right, Zookeeper?"

Lady Oracle looks at Zookeeper. He shrugs. "Exhibits got to be fed, appetites appeased, you know? Peace in the zoo is essential for the well-being of our . . . rarer exhibits."

She pulls out five one-hundred-dollar bills and holds them up. "This is yours if you do something for me first."

Amygdala smiles maliciously. "Shit, lady. We can just take the money."

"Let's go!" she says to her two companions, and turns on her heel to leave.

Both men flash their knives and block the door, but Zookeeper holds up his hand. "Wait a minute! She might want something simple." He turns his attention to Lady Oracle and slightly bows. "What the fuck do you want us to do, Mistress Oracle? I mean, you've still not explained why you're here?"

"You have been around a lot of violence, right, Zookeeper?"

"Yeah."

"Also committed quite a bit of your own violence on others, correct?"

Zookeeper snorts. "Hell, yes! Goddamn right I have! War gives the right to the conquerors to impose any condition they please upon the vanquished." He pauses and narrows his eyes suspiciously. "Why do ya ask?"

She nods toward Ming-huà. "I want you to kill this girl."

A collective gasp comes from everyone in the room except Sy and Lady Oracle. Ming-huà lets out a shocked squeal and cringes in terror.

"You're shittin' me!" says Pepper Spray.

Zookeeper tries to recover from his shock. "Why?" he utters.

"That's my business."

"No fuckin' way!" shouts Zookeeper. "What kind of a set-up is this?" He looks out the window. "You're setting us up for the cops!"

Lady Oracle takes out five more one-hundred-dollar bills. "Will a thousand convince you?"

The eyes of the palace guards widen as they greedily ogle the cash.

By this time, Ming-huà is clawing at Sy's arm, crying, begging him to get her away, but he pushes her down.

The men stare at her in confusion.

Lady Oracle waves the money. "Well?"

Zookeeper's brain is suddenly exploding with commands from the new voices. "Do it! Do it!" they scream. "Kill her! Do it!"

Ming-huà is on her knees, begging hysterically. Sy stands above her, harshly squeezing her shoulder to hold her down.

"Do it!" Zookeeper shouts to Pepper Spray and Amygdala. "But don't kill the hunchback! Kill her! Mistress Oracle!" In a momentary flash of insight, Zookeeper knows his words are not his own, but is helpless to stop them. "Kill her! Do it!"

Even with Zookeeper's frantic orders ringing in their ears, his two comrades hesitate. "Just fuckin' give us the money, lady!" cries Pepper Spray.

"Kill her!" commands Zookeeper. "Kill her! There's more where that came from!" Furious at his henchmen's reluctance, he gestures wildly. "Do it! Kill her!"

The two men pause for a brief instant and glance nervously at each other. Then, at some unspoken agreement, rush toward her with their knives, Zookeeper urges them on. "Do it! Do it!" He still does not recognize his own voice, and realizes with horror the demons in his head are forcing their own words out. "Kill her! Do it!"

Lady Oracle stands perfectly still and waits.

Pepper Spray and Amygdala, are upon her, knives gleaming in the light as their blades tear into her body.

Ming-huà screams.

~

A sudden and horrifying silence grips the room in a death-like moment of frozen shock.

Lady Oracle stands tall, unharmed.

Pepper Spray, Amygdala, and Zookeeper stagger in speechless disbelief.

No longer do any of them have arms. Mere stumps emerge from their shoulders. No blood. No pain. No open wounds. The skin as smooth as if they had been born armless.

Not a word is spoken for an agonizingly long moment, then Amygdala screams and runs out of the room, followed by a babbling Pepper Spray. Zookeeper stares in shock at Ming-huà. The voices in his head are quiet. He feels her probing him and he collapses in a chair, stupefied.

"Let's go," says Lady Oracle smoothly.

"But we can't leave them like this!" objects Ming-huà.

"Yes, we must. They are in no danger of dying. It is best if we leave and let them come to terms with their situation."

Lady Oracle motions to Sy, who forcefully lifts Ming-huà by the arm and leads her out of the house.

Zookeeper, still in shock, watches them leave and reaches down to push himself out of the chair when he realizes to his horror that he truly has no arms.

The rest is blank.

~ Zookeeper Faces His Demons ~

Zookeeper remains sitting in the chair, stupefied, unwilling to acknowledge what just happened. Looking around absently, he spots a pack of cigarettes and a lighter on the end table. Instinctively, he reaches for them, and again is confronted with reality. No arms. No hands. No fingers. No sense of touching. Not anything—never to touch a cigarette, a woman, his cock, an enemy, a weapon, a tissue to wipe his ass, change his clothes, pour a drink, nothing! Life without arms unfolds before his horrified imagination, and it appears impossible. Others of his "exhibits" wander in and stare at him with uncomprehending eyes.

"Shit, man!" cries Angel Cake, utterly befuddled. "What the fuck! Shit! What the fuck happened to you, man! Fuckin' shit! I saw Amygdala and Pepper Spray runnin' like hell outta here with no arms, man! Fuckin' insane! What happened? What happened to the two bros? Shit! Fuckin' speak to me, man!"

There can be no response from Zookeeper, whose face reflects severe shock and disbelief. He does not hear or comprehend the questions thrown at him from Angel Cake. One thought, and one thought only, pushes its way through the fog—seek out the hunchback and reverse the process. Make her give him back his arms! Find the hunchback! Where is she? Lady Oracle! He'll take a gun! But he becomes sick knowing he can't even hold a gun, let alone point it. Nonetheless, his only salvation is to go find Lady Oracle and the hunchback. Now! Now!

He reaches for his shirt pocket to retrieve the paper with her address, but again the grim reality hits him.

"Angel Cake! Shit, no time to explain, man! Reach into my shirt pocket and pull out a paper!"

"What?" asks his confused exhibit, whose dull mind is already making its laborious pivot from abstract incredulity to material enrichment—de facto inheritance of the crack house.

"Goddamn it, get it outta my pocket!" He thrusts his chest toward Angel Cake, who pulls out the paper.

"Read it to me!"

Angel Cake reads the address.

"I know that fuckin' street!" cries Zookeeper, now running past a visibly astonished but coldly calculating Angel Cake.

Before he knows it, he is in the street, stumbling awkwardly. With no arms it is difficult, and he often veers and careens wildly. Dimly aware of the stares from passers-by, he makes his way toward Lady Oracle's apartment nearby in the Tenderloin.

~

By the time he stands at Lady Oracle's front door, he is gasping for breath and cursing the horrific exertion required to run and keep his balance. His legs ache, muscles excruciatingly cramp up, and shooting pains rack long neglected parts of his body. Zookeeper's mind continues to reel at the unreality of his situation. He tries to knock, but again the inconceivable reality slaps him in the face. Inflamed to a new level of desperation, he uses his foot to kick the door, but without arms as counterweights, he flies backward and lands heavily on the concrete. For the first time, tears of frustration and helplessness flow in rivulets, blurring his view of the bright San Francisco sky. He is literally a helpless babe, and like a babe teetering on the edge of a well, he loses his balance. Zookeeper free falls into the deep well of anguish, watching the sun-lit rim of the world race away, receding so far only a tiny round patch of blue remains, so distant it is beyond hope of ever reaching again. So lost is he, the figure of Lady Oracle helping him into the apartment does not register. Once inside and sitting in the dark of her "yin apartment", he regains some semblance of reason, and gathers his inner resolve to make the most important plea of his life.

He tries to force a sentence out of his mouth, but the only word he can rasp under his breath is, "Hunchback!"

"What about her?" asks Lady Oracle nonchalantly.

How can she be so calm? he asks himself. *How in the fuck can she be so fuckin' calm!* "Hunchback!" he screams.

"Zookeeper, she is not here."

"You fuckin' bitch! Such goddamn calmness . . . and me. Look at me! At me!"

"I see. Let me get you a drink."

"I can't. . . . "

Lady Oracle smiles. "No problem."

She calls a name. A boy enters the room and she tells him to bring a glass of whiskey, no ice, no water. He nods and returns carrying a tray. "Thank you, Bataar." She picks up the glass and holds it to his mouth.

Zookeeper turns his head away.

"You might as well get used to it," she says smoothly.

"How can you be so fuckin' calm?" he says in wonder, still clearly in shock.

"Tilt your head back."

He does.

Lady Oracle lifts the glass to his lips and gently lets the whiskey trickle into his mouth. He sucks greedily.

"Bataar!" she calls.

"Yes?"

"Another."

And so it goes until Zookeeper is numb enough to sleep.

When he wakes, he is on the couch. How much time has passed is a mystery to him.

Lady Oracle sits across from the couch.

"Well?" she asks. "Can you talk now?"

"The hunchback," he rasps.

"What about her?"

"I need her to replace my arms! Put them back!"

"She can't."

"Bullshit! Where is she?" He looks around wildly.

"Zookeeper, she is not here. You are. You are still in shock, but it is slowly wearing off. Try and remain calm or I will kick you out."

Zookeeper starts to fly at her in a rage until he realizes he is no longer in a position to make any threats.

"Okay, okay. I want to see the hunchback. I want her to return my arms. I don't give a fuck how she does it. Just have her do it!"

"No, Zookeeper, you and I must talk first."

"Go fuck yourself! I want the hunchback!"

"I can put you back out on the street."

"I can call the cops."

Lady Oracle laughs. "That's rich! And tell them what? A crack dealer's arms were somehow removed by a hunchback without leaving any blood or scars? Go ahead."

"I . . . I . . . don't know what the fuck to do. Help me, or if not, I'll do harm to you. Somehow, some way, I'll do you harm."

Lady Oracle shakes her head in pity. "Zookeeper, as your Bard wrote, 'Diseases desperate grown, by desperate appliance are relieved, or not at all.'"

"What do I have to do?"

"Stay here with me for a few days. I have a number of things we need to talk about. You will be looked after by Bataar."

"What about the hunchback?"

"Later."

"I want her now!"

[88]

"You're slipping again, Zookeeper. I cannot help you unless you get past this shock and help me."

"How the fuck can I help you?"

"By talking to me?"

"About?"

"The new voices in your head. Especially one particular new voice."

"These fuckin' voices are driving me batshit crazy! How do you make them stop!

"Bataar!" calls Lady Oracle. "More whiskey!"

Zookeeper tries to rise from the couch, but without arms as counterweights, he slumps back in defeat. "And a fag!" he shouts in helpless rage.

Bataar somehow produces a cigarette as if from thin air, places it between Zookeeper's lips, and lights it. Without being asked, he hovers over Zookeeper, pulling out the cigarette and putting it back. Although just a boy, he performs this service as if he had been a servant for a lifetime.

Zookeeper looks at Bataar quizzically. "Thanks, kid," he says resignedly.

Even as he speaks, a voice emerges as a low, ominous growl deep within his mind. It gets louder. It gets nearer. Its words spoken in the deep timbre of creation. Zookeeper's face is rendered immobile in a mask of trepidation.

"You hear it, don't you?" asks Lady Oracle. "It isn't multiple voices; it is one voice; a composite of all voices."

Zookeeper remains still. The voice reverberates like an approaching locomotive.

"Zookeeper!" shouts Lady Oracle.

He remains frozen in terror.

"You're here, aren't you, *God*?" she says.

Chapter 7: *God*'s History Revealed

~ Ming-huà is Confronted ~

Zookeeper struggles to keep the terrifying voice at bay. Its words dampen his normally radiant spirits. Like rain dousing a campfire, it splutters and sizzles a sort of all-pervasive dreariness. To bring back the light requires reversing the rotation of earth itself. Faced with such impossibility, his psychic core curls up its flowery petals and retreats from the approaching night. Lady Oracle can only watch Zookeeper slip into unconsciousness.

"He is fighting *You*," she says aloud toward the ceiling. "He is strong. Yes, he will do . . . perhaps. Now that he is defanged, the task can begin. Bataar, help me get him into the spare bedroom and tuck him in. I am leaving and will not return for hours. If he wakes, give him the special tea . . . no, better make it decaf coffee. He's definitely not a tea man. If he asks for booze, give him that. So long as he sleeps and does not leave. Understand?"

Bataar nods.

~

Lady Oracle stands resolutely before the front door of the old Victorian house and knocks. When Sy opens it, she pulls him outside and whispers, "How is Ming-huà?"

Sy looks away. "Terrible."

"Good."

"It is according to plan?"

"Yes, now let me see her."

"Are you sure—" Sy starts to object.

"I'm sure." Lady Oracle interrupts, her voice severe.

"In that case, let's meet in the room where Ming-huà feels most comfortable. You know the way. Go ahead and I'll bring her down."

Lady Oracle smiles. "Lots of ghosts in that room."

"Lots. Maybe that's why she feels so comfortable. Friendly ghosts. Kind of comforting."

"I'll heat up some tea."

Sy lets out a long groan. "I'll get her."

Lady Oracle waits for a long time. Although a patient woman, she begins to wonder. Just as she moves toward the door, Sy, returns with an apologetic expression.

"She won't come."

"Why?"

"Doesn't want to see you. Really doesn't want to see me either, but she's stuck with me. But you . . . well, after all, you did sic those druggies on her."

"For the sake of humanity."

"She doesn't know that. She views it as a set-up. A callous exercise. An immoral experiment."

Lady Oracle chuckles. "Of course she does. So much the better. Her resistance is the next hurdle. Bring her down."

"I'm telling you; she won't come."

"Then I'll go to her."

"Door's locked."

"Unlock it."

Sy shakes his head doubtfully. "Okay. I won't be responsible for whatever happens."

"She can do nothing to me."

"I know, but. . . . "

"So?"

"Okay, let's go."

Sy and Lady Oracle ascend the stairs, keys jingling in his hand. When they stand outside Ming-huà's door, Sy knocks.

"Go away!" she calls.

"Ming-huà, open up. Lady Oracle needs to talk with you."

"No! I'm going back to the island. I'm packing now. Don't want to see either of you! Leave!"

Lady Oracle nods.

Sy unlocks the door.

Ming-huà is leaning over her suitcase, packing some clothes. Surprisingly, she does not bother to look up. "I know you have a key. I knew you would unlock the door regardless of my wishes. As you can see, I am serious. The farther I get from the two of you, the better. The non-human animals on my island have more morals than the entire human race. I want to be with them. There's a certain squirrel . . . anyway, nothing you can say—"

"Your mother is on her way."

"What?" cries an astonished Ming-huà.

Even Sy is surprised, and shows his amazement by croaking out in tandem with the hunchback, "What! Really?"

"Your mother will be here tomorrow," says Lady Oracle in an infuriatingly placid tone. "She wants to talk with you, as I do now. There are many things you do not understand."

Ming-huà is speechless and slumps in a nearby chair, waiting.

"Tamara Powers, your globe-trotting mother, has returned from a very long trip, visiting many different places in many different times. She is aware of what happened at the crack house, and wants to speak with you about it."

"What do you mean 'many different places and many different times?" asks Ming-huà. "The last thing she told me was that she traveled to a magic cave from where she would never return. Naturally, I chalked this up to a mother's clumsy way of breaking to a young girl that she was leaving and would never return. Probably with some man, but who knows? I never really questioned it."

"She did go to a magic cave located in a vast desert," says Lady Oracle.

"I never for once believed it was real," murmurs Ming-huà.

"That cave," Lady Oracle continues, "Is why retiring to the desert was out of the question. Your mother, your father, your grandparents, all of us in this room, are in many ways connected to that cave. Now, do you want to hear what I have to say?"

"And those men I mutilated because of you? Are they connected as well, or are they innocent victims?"

"All connected. Do you or do you not want to hear?"

Ming-huà reluctantly nods.

"Then let us go down to the room of ghosts, have tea, and discuss the situation without theatrics."

"Ghosts?" asks Ming-huà.

Lady Oracle shows her teeth. "You know very well."

Ming-huà's silence speaks volumes.

Once they settle in the anteroom, tea is poured and an eerie quiet prevails.

"Well?" says Ming-huà, determined to maintain her frigid disapproval.

"Are you aware of how your mother met your father?"

"She never told me."

"And you were too young when your father died to ask about it," confirms Sy.

"Obviously," says Ming-huà. "What does this have to do with anything?"

"Well," says Lady Oracle. "Your parents' marriage was arranged."

"Arranged? Like in medieval times?"

"Sort of."

Ming-huà shakes her head in frustration. "Just explain it to me. Dispense with the Socratic method."

"True," chimes in Sy. "Humans are hard-wired to respond to a story. You know, once upon a time. . . . " He garnishes his observation with a comedic pose.

"Good idea," says Lady Oracle. She takes a deep breath. "Once upon a time, a *Goddess* instructed *Her* representatives on earth to arrange a marriage between Michael Powers, schizophrenic (and once fated to be *The Son*) with Tamara, daughter of Child of Buddha (now fated to be the mother of *The Daughter*). You are the product. You are *The Daughter*. Brief enough?"

Ming-huà furrows her brow. "Too brief. I don't understand any of it. *Goddess*? The son? The daughter? Magic caves? Really, this is too absurd!"

"Is it more absurd than your ability to remove objects and people from existence and scatter their atoms to the four winds? Is it more absurd than blinking out of existence two hunters? Is it more absurd than leaving three men without arms?"

Ming-huà looks down in silence.

"Is it?"

"No. Tell me more."

[93]

"You are to . . . get together . . . with Zookeeper."

Ming-huà looks horror-stricken. "Are you out of your minds! How can you even suggest such . . . such . . . such an atrocity? Do you think I'm completely stupid! Me? A brood mare? Is the atrocity committed on my mother to be repeated on me?"

"No, not that. Your mother was selected, as was your father. They were happy together."

"Selected!" Ming-huà is laughing hysterically. "I see! Selected by who?"

"By *Goddess*."

"And you are . . . the breeder?" asks Ming-huà sarcastically.

"No. I, like my mother, am the facilitator."

"Facilitator! Is that another word for murderer! Is *facilitator* in the same absurdly euphemistic category as *reconfigure*?"

"This is why your mother is coming. It is to explain. You do want an explanation?"

Ming-huà looks out the window, her eyes misty. "She is my mother."

~ Zookeeper is Confronted ~

When Lady Oracle returns to her apartment, Zookeeper is awake and relatively calm, thanks to the ministrations of Bataar. He sits on the couch, brooding, angry, eyes watery red from being plied with whiskey.

She sits across from him in her favorite chair. Zookeeper stares at her with homicide in his heart.

"No need to make such an ugly face, Zookeeper," she says. "You can't kill me, but I can kill you easily enough. You are a victim, like all the innocent people you victimized. How does it feel?"

"Fuckin' bitch! Mocking me is fucked! Go to hell!"

"Go to Shakespeare."

"What?"

"Go to Shakespeare and respond."

"Fuck you!"

"That is not Shakespeare. Do it properly."

Zookeeper looks at her in wonder. "What kind of a fucked-up bitch are you?"

"Shakespeare, Zookeeper."

[94]

"Fuck!"

"Reconnect, Zookeeper."

He pauses, letting her words percolate. "Oh, I see. Therapy."

"Therapy."

He bares his teeth. "You have a kid, Lady Oracle?"

She tilts her head in mock confusion. "A goat?"

"A child, damn you!"

"No."

"Want one?"

"Perhaps."

"Hear, nature, hear; dear *Goddess*, hear! Suspend thy purpose, if thou didst intend to make this creature fruitful! Into her womb convey sterility! Dry up in her the organs of increase; and from her derogate body never spring a babe to honor her! If she must teem, create her child of spleen; that it may live, and be a thwart disnatured torment to her! Let us stamp wrinkles in her brow of youth; with cadent tears fret channels in her cheeks; turn al her mother's pains and benefits to laughter and contempt; that she may feel how sharper than a serpent's tooth it is to have a thankless child!" Zookeeper ends his soliloquy with a low growl, and continues, "May her child fall into the clutches of a pusher, who will make it an addict and live in its own shit! *Goddess*, may thee remove its arms and legs so its mother will cry in agony!"

"Excellent, Zookeeper!" cries Lady Oracle clapping. "You never disappoint! Deep does your genius go. Now, how much deeper can it go?"

"Deep enough to find a way to get revenge!"

"On me?"

"On that fuckin' hunchback! You wanted her killed, didn't you? Don't tell me you didn't! Pretend as you will, you are afraid of her. That I know!"

"Well then, what do you think of her?"

Zookeeper is rendered speechless.

"What do you think of her?" repeats Lady Oracle.

"She is fuckin' evil! Look at me! Take me to her so she can put my arms back on."

"If she is evil, why should she?"

He has no answer.

"Zookeeper, look at me."

[95]

He does.

"She is not your enemy; she is your salvation."

"What?"

"She is your salvation. She will be you wife. You both will have a child."

"What the fuck are you talking about? That's complete bullshit! If I see the little mutant, I'll kill her!"

"What you don't understand, Zookeeper, is that you also are a mutant."

~

His face darkens. "I may have had . . . certain powers once, now, I'm just a freak, like your little hunchback."

"You just called her a mutant, not a freak."

"Slip of the tongue."

"Do you want to know her name?"

Zookeeper doubles down. "It has a name?"

"Same as you."

"What's her fuckin' name?"

"Ming-huà. Ming-huà Powers."

"What kind of fuckin' name is that? She's a chink bitch, right?"

"It is a quite beautiful and quite rare name, just as she is quite beautiful and quite rare."

"She's rare all right!"

"As are you."

"Hell!"

"Her mother had magical powers."

Zookeeper laughs sarcastically. "My mother had magical powers all right! Magical junkie powers. She would steal my baby teeth for money."

Lady Oracle looks him compassionately. "Zookeeper, your mother did have magical powers, but they were hijacked by drugs. Nonetheless, she unknowingly passed them on to you, just as Ming-huà's mother passed her powers on. Now, you both need the power the other possesses."

"Bullshit! She's the one who took my arms! The only thing I need her for is to put them back!"

"But she will, don't you see?"

[96]

Zookeeper's eyes widen. "She will?"

"In a manner of speaking."

"Shit! I know what that means. Fuck her!"

Lady Oracle smiles. "That is the goal."

"Christ! You people are crazy!"

"Even now the wheels have been set in motion. All we have to do is bring you both together, leave you alone with each other, and you will find that miracles do happen."

"Fuck!"

Lady Oracle groans. "Zookeeper, do you possess a vocabulary of useful words between the glorious poetry of Shakespeare and the gutter variations of fuck?"

Zookeeper is at a loss and fails to dredge up a suitable response.

Lady Oracle stubbornly continues, "Even you have admitted she is pretty."

Zookeeper starts to blurt an obscenity, but hesitates, still smarting from her insult to his carefully built façade of esoteric intelligence. Finally, he says, "Her face maybe, but that fuckin' hump!"

"And your armless body? Who will have you now?"

"Not looking for anyone."

"You have no choice. No way you can care for yourself."

"So, she is to be my nurse?"

"No, she is to be your savior."

Zookeeper shakes his head ruefully. "Not in the market for a savior."

"But, Zookeeper, you are also to be her savior."

He bares his teeth. "You want us to get married and live happily ever after?"

"No, we want you to get married and have a child. It is the child that we are most interested in. Whether you live happily ever after is up to the both of you. Being a savior is not being happy."

Zookeeper began mulling the possibility. First and foremost, what could he gain out of it? A hunchback wife? No bargain. But . . . but. . . .

"Does she have money?"

"You mean an income?"

"Fuckin' right that's what I mean!"

"Yes."

"She has a place to live?"

"Yes."

Zookeeper shakes his head. "Lady Oracle, you gotta understand, this hunchback took off my arms. How am I supposed to forgive her? You fuckin' think we both just trip merrily on our way?"

"Zookeeper, she took off your arms to defend me. Think, boy! She can also defend you."

This possibility opens up an entirely new dimension to Zookeeper's thoughts. Not only could she defend him, she could do more, so much more. She could help him rebuild his drug empire. Who needs an enforcer? Who needs palace guards? With her powers, anything suddenly seems achievable.

"When can we meet?" he asks.

"I'll let you know. In the meantime, you will stay here until arrangements can be made."

Zookeeper feels his power surging back, but that terrible voice still growls menacingly in the background.

Observing the blank look in his face, Lady Oracle asks, "You hear *Him*, don't you?"

"What?"

"You hear a voice, correct?"

"What, you think I'm some sort of schizo?"

"You hear a voice, correct?" she repeats firmly.

"If I do?"

"It is *Him*."

"Who?"

"*Him*."

Zookeeper looks at her askance, but the voice keeps dragging his attention back. He tilts his head sideways and violently shakes it, as one might do if he had water in the ears.

"Zookeeper, you cannot rid yourself of *Him* that way," scolds Lady Oracle.

"Who are you talkin' about? Who is *Him*?"

"*God*."

"Christ! Here we go again with your crazy talk! Why go and talk to me that crazy way?"

Lady Oracle ignores the question. "Do you believe in *God*, Zookeeper?"

"Shit no! *God* has done nothing for me."

"Are you a junkie, Zookeeper?" asks Lady Oracle.

"Used to be. Got smart. Sold it, not snorted it."

"But you were an addict?"

"Goddamn it, told you so! Fuckin' while back, took forever to get myself clean. Went through hell, but I did it."

"Yes, that was due to your power. Remember when you were addicted?"

"Shit, yeah."

"Do you know *God* is also an addict?"

As if a lion had been prodded to fury, the voice from the depths of his mind roars to life; pulling at him, tearing at him, like some monstrosity buried alive trying to claw its way out. Zookeeper closes his eyes, rocking his head side-to-side. "No! Fuckin' voices! Get out! Out!"

Lady Oracle's face is inches from Zookeeper's. "*God* is also an addict, only *His* crack house is the entire world, and *He* wants you to give *Him* a high!"

Tears of frustration are pouring from Zookeeper's eyes. "What the fuck does *He* want! Make *Him* stop!"

"*He* craves suffering, and only the hunchback can make *Him* stop the shouting in your head."

"How?" cries an anguished Zookeeper.

"She can make *Him* disappear, or at least *His* voice, the same way she did your arms. Are you ready to see her?"

"Yes, yes, yes!"

"Bataar!" shouts Lady Oracle.

The lad instantly appears.

"Bring Zookeeper a special whiskey."

Lady Oracle goes into a back room reserved only for herself and sits in a chair behind a massive desk full of papers. She picks up one of the papers and whispers, "Tamara arrives tomorrow. We'll see."

~ Hunchback Converses with Scarecrow ~

Ming-huà wakes up very early the next day at the Victorian house and sits in the kitchen sipping tea. She nervously fidgets with whatever objects are within reach. Her mother is scheduled to arrive sometime in the afternoon. *Why so nervous?* she asks herself. Answering her own question is easy enough: her mother has become an unknown quantity. This business about a magic cave renders her a riddle, an exotic stranger to explore; and exploration of riddles is always dangerous. Nonetheless, mixed in with the nervousness is a deep yearning to reconnect with the loving mother of her childhood. Such conflicting emotions complicate the anticipation. While impatiently mulling these conundrums, Ming-huà also ponders the power she inherited from her mother. According to Lady Oracle's telling, Ming-huà's power flows from her mother, although during her entire childhood, she had not seen any evidence of it. Only the "magic cave" exists as a tantalizing hint of some supernatural ability. She does recall her mother mentioning something about her grandmother in the old days during the war in China. Something about a quest, and her grandmother being a woman possessed of unique powers. Typically, her mother refused to answer questions that would clarify the story. Her mother—always evading the past. *Yet,* Ming-huà remembers, *not just the past; the present also made her restless and jittery.* As a girl, her mother's presence always seemed evanescent, as if the merest wisp of a breeze would carry her away. This maternal, transitory figure was thus made all the more precious to a young Ming-huà.

No less precious now, she thinks. *There are so many questions!* She tries to catalog the plenitude of questions she wants to ask, but her thoughts are sidetracked by the unavoidable catastrophe of her actions at the crack house, not to mention the distressing problem of Zookeeper. *Is that why she comes?* wonders Ming-huà. *To take Lady Oracle's side and convince me to . . . be with that horrible addict, or pusher, or whatever he is? Never! Not even my mother can convince me to take that path!*

While engrossed in these thoughts, Sy bounds into the kitchen, pours himself a cup of coffee, and sits across from her with a wily look on his face.

"Thinking about your mother?"

Ming-huà frowns, still angry with him. "Trying to."

"Remember I mentioned a predecessor?"

"Yes."

"My predecessor's predecessor knew your grandmother in China, during the war."

Ming-huà is breathless. At last she murmurs, "Go on."

"She had the power, in spades."

"Go on."

"She could decipher taps from inside a statue."

"Taps . . . statue?"

"It was called the Precious Object. They found your grandmother Child of Buddha, in a mental institution."

"They?"

"People on the quest, including your father."

"Quest for. . . . "

"*Her*, of course."

"Go on."

"*She* is *Her* is *Goddess* is the Precious Object is. . . . "

"A quest for *Goddess*?"

"Yes and no. Up and down, I can tell you no more. What I can tell you, is that this junkie, Zookeeper, holds a key to something else."

"What else?"

"*God*, of course."

"I don't understand."

"Look, I am only able to give hints, hints I myself do not really understand. Yin and Yang, *God* and *Goddess*, Light and Dark, Male and Female, Suffering and . . . ?"

"Joy?"

"No, not that. Not that simple. Not all is dialectically opposite. Ask your father."

"He is dead."

"Exactly. Death is not a logical opposite."

"Yes, it is. Life and Death."

"No, that is the key. Symmetry broken. As *She* would so often say, 'fate starves at probability's door.'"

"How is the dialectic opposite broken?" asks Ming-huà. "Life and Death. It works."

"No. All before and all after Life is stillness—not Death. Furthermore, all before and all after Life is also motion—also not Death. Stillness and Motion. You see, death is not at all opposite. Perhaps that explains—" he abruptly pauses.

"What?"

"Riddles. Your own mother is a riddle, as was her mother, as was your father, as are you . . . you and Zookeeper."

"Funny, I was just thinking of my mother as a riddle."

Sy leapt in the air. "There! You see? Riddles everywhere. But I do know your grandmother could read the taps."

"And?"

Sy wags his finger. "Ah, ah, ah! Your grandmother is the key to your mother, your mother is the key to you, you are the key to . . . what?"

"I don't know."

"Your own child of course, but only with Zookeeper."

"What? . . . why?"

Sy collapsed back onto the chair. "I do not know. I am only told so much."

"By?"

"*Her.*"

Ming-huà shakes her head in frustration. "Now we're back to the beginning!" She pauses; a light flickers on in her mind. "Or is Lady Oracle *Her*?"

Sy laughs uproariously "No, no! Not at all. Is Beginning and End a dialectic opposite?"

Ming-huà groans and holds her head. "I don't know. It is too much!"

"Would you prefer too little?"

Ming-huà stands and stomps angrily out of the room, calling over her shoulder, "I would prefer to return to my island with my mother and leave the rest of you to your . . . dialectic! And that is precisely what I intend to do!"

Sy watches her bound up the stairs and smiles smugly.

Chapter 8: A Fateful Meeting

~ Mother and Daughter ~

When her mother walks through the front door, Ming-huà's heart skips a beat and she blinks back tears of recognition. At first glance, Tamara Powers looks almost the same but for greyer hair and deeper cracks in her already leathery skin. But on closer inspection, her mother's hunchback seems more pronounced than ever. A cane projects before her, tapping on the hardwood floor as she walks. Ming-huà rushes to her and they both hug in a heartfelt embrace emblematic of two people deeply in love. Lady Oracle and Sy stand aside and let mother and daughter bask in the moment. No words are spoken for many moments. Finally, Lady Oracle coughs and guides Tamara into the anteroom. Bataar follows with the suitcase. Sy conducts the Mongol boy to the guest room, while the others find seats. Ming-huà and Tamara sit in adjoining chairs, refusing to let go of the others' hand, their arms forming a chain between them.

A few words pass between mother and daughter when Lady Oracle turns her attention to Ming-huà and interjects. "Your mother cannot stay long, and we have many things to discuss. I must soon return to my apartment and my . . . guest."

Ming-huà's heart clenches. She feels her mother's hand tighten in her own. "Can we have some time to catch-up?" she asks.

She is surprised when her mother says, "No, daughter, best to face this now rather than later."

"But—" Ming-huà starts to object, but stops when she sees her mother frowning.

"We'll have time later," reassures Tamara. "But now"—she turns to Lady Oracle—"the issue is this young man."

"Yes," agrees the Mongol woman. "Zookeeper is his assumed name. His real name is Matthew Weston. Parents dead. No siblings, as far as we know. You have been informed of the circumstances, correct Tamara?"

[103]

"Correct."

Lady Oracle looks at Ming-huà with a placid expression. "Your daughter here is adamantly opposed to the idea of . . . union."

Ming-huà stiffens in her seat, forcing herself to remain quiet, intent on listening to her mother's response.

"I understand she is opposed," says her mother. She gazes at Ming-huà and squeezes her hand tighter. "Will it surprise you to know the same arrangements were made for me and your father?"

"I have been told something about it," replies Ming-huà.

"Yes, the same arrangements. Exactly the same. Lady Oracle's grandmother, Buandelgereen, acted as the . . . facilitator. The goal, or purpose, or intent, was to have a child. A special child."

"But, Mama! You don't—" again Ming-huà tries to voice an objection, but her mother pulls her hand from her daughter's and holds it up in a cautionary gesture.

"No, just listen." Tamara starts to continue, but pauses when Sy returns and sits quietly. She nods and turns back to face her daughter. "That special child turned out to be you. Now, I am told you have many questions. Not all can be answered, but some can. As I was saying, Buandelgereen came to me with a long, complicated story. The details do not concern us here. Suffice to say, she knew your grandmother, Child of Buddha.

"My grandmother Child of Buddha," Ming-huà repeats in wonder.

"Yes, your grandmother—Child of Buddha—participated in a quest—"

"To find *Her*!" blurts Ming-huà.

"Correct . . . sort of. At the end of Buandelgereen's long story, I was told to marry Michael Powers, an American who supposedly suffered from schizophrenia, but also possessed some unspecified power. Not being a good Chinese girl, I strenuously objected, but Buandelgereen explained the purpose, so I eventually agreed. Long story short, I ended up marrying your father, and here you are."

"Faced with the same decision!" exclaims Ming-huà in disgust.

"Yes."

"Did you love father?" presses Ming-huà.

"Eventually."

"Were you attracted to him?"

"Eventually."

"Well, there's the problem!" snaps Ming-huà. "I don't love Zookeeper, I am not attracted to Zookeeper, he is a disgusting, filthy, horrible person, a drug dealer, and probably much worse. Speaking of worse, the purpose of this . . . union . . . has not been explained to me."

"Suffering," says Lady Oracle.

"What?"

"The world is full of unnecessary suffering. *God* is addicted to suffering. *Goddess . . . Her . . .* wants to cure *Him* of *His* addiction."

Ming-huà is speechless.

"Of course, it is far more complicated, dear," says Tamara, again taking hold of her daughter's hand. "We all speak in metaphors, don't we?"

"You may have married father, but you certainly wouldn't have married this Zookeeper character!" exclaims Ming-huà. "Have you seen him?"

"No."

"Not only is he a bad person, he now has no arms, thanks to me! Would you marry him?"

"If I were responsible for his . . . disability," says Tamara. "Remember, as far as I knew, your father had schizophrenia when I married him."

Ming-huà falls silent for a few moments, then says, "That's different."

"No," says Lady Oracle. "Zookeeper is not what you make him out to be. He is actually a very worthwhile person, and his power makes him a very valuable person. He has lost his way."

Ming-huà laughs derisively. "I should say so! But I am not going to lose my way."

"You have not met *Her*," says Lady Oracle.

"A *Goddess*? You must be joking. Mama, she is joking, right?"

"No, she is not joking. I met *Her*. I would never have agreed to marry your father if I had not."

"Well, I haven't met *Her*, nor do I intend to. Mama, let's go back to the island together and live peacefully and simply! No more San Francisco. This is madness!"

"But, dear," says Tamara. "All of us sitting here are mad—your grandmother was mad, I am mad, and you, dear girl, are the maddest of the lot."

~ Zookeeper Again Faces His Demon ~

The more Zookeeper thinks about Lady Oracle's offer of sacrificing the hunchback's future to him, the more he likes it. All sorts of fantasies pass through his mind, spurred on by the voice howling at him to kill her, or kill himself, or kill someone, anyone! All of those shouted proposals to commit homicide have attracted him. Revenge on the human race is appealing. In his current state, the thought of revenge on any person, regardless of who it is exacted upon, is supremely satisfying. But revenge on those responsible for his current condition elicits the most graphic images. He envisions drawing the hunchback into his good graces, then finding a way to cut off all her limbs, not just her arms. He dreams about torturing Lady Oracle, maybe cutting out her tongue and forcing it down her throat until her smug superior attitude ends in a pathetic death rattle. He relishes pulling the intestines out of the skinny friend of Lady Oracle who dances around and insults with sarcastic humor. These delicious reveries are urged on by the voice—a brother sadist who understands the erotic excitement of inflicting pain and suffering. Lady Oracle has hinted the voice is that of *God*. That idea has him in stitches. How fitting! *God* is addicted to pain and suffering! Who knew? *God* is the greatest sadist in the universe! Zookeeper fancies himself a graduate student in search of a mentor. Steeped in pain himself, he understands how sadism works. This voice, this *God*, sure as hell does. Let the voice rant on; *God* will become Zookeeper's master, and Zookeeper *His* apprentice.

Yet, Zookeeper has an inkling that these sadistic fictions he so relishes are not the true temper of his steel. If the horrific voice be *God*, it is a false *God*. Try as he might, Zookeeper's self-image as the disciple of a sadistic deity is tainted by some deeper skepticism that, if he is honest, arises from more virtuous roots. Such roots have always been his downfall, preventing him from taking that extra step of cruelty that would lead him to triumph over his enemies. It is, paradoxically, a vexatious compassion and annoying empathy that, try as he might, cannot be expunged from his mind. Always these weaknesses of compassion and empathy prevent him from fully implementing actions that he otherwise must perform to succeed. How else could he rise to the top of a streetwise hierarchy? As if he wore an electrified collar, he cannot murder or rape without feeling a painful jolt from his soft core. Often, he faced brutal choices, but in the end, could never pull the trigger or bury a knife in someone's stomach, or rape a pretty junkie in need. He has tried. He has failed. A weakness only the power of projecting his will onto the dull-witted is able to camouflage. Using Shakespeare is merely an amateur's parlor trick when dealing with intelligent people. He intrigues intelligent people long enough to temporarily use them, but can never hold them long enough to truly satisfy a conqueror as, say, Hitler could. Shabby indeed.

Zookeeper aspires to be a vicious killer, leader of an empire, but the soft core of his soul is more angelic than anarchist. Up to now, he has succeeded in clipping the wings of his inner angel, but this latest disaster cries out for him to once and for all pull the wings out by their roots so they never grow back. Unfortunately, deep down he knows he can't. Truth be told, he won't. An infernal beatific soothsayer deep within warns him not to abandon the last chance he might have for redemption. What if the hunchback is truly his chance at salvation? After all, when they first met, Zookeeper's power clearly told him she is good. Very good. And she does have a nice face. No, a beautiful face!

In the midst of these reveries, Bataar enters the room and asks, "Need anything?"

Zookeeper looks at him sideways, his face reflecting distrust and puzzlement. "What do you get outta this, kid? She pays you a lotta bread? Teaches you about sex?"

Bataar's expression does not change; it remains a mask of imperturbability. "Need anything?" he repeats calmly.

"Yeah, pour some whiskey down my gullet, but first come wipe my ass. I gotta shit."

Bataar nods and follows him into the bathroom. In spite of his crude bravado, Zookeeper is sick with embarrassment. He feels humiliation, but also a nagging curiosity at this boy's odd comportment, so much Mother Theresa in one so young—especially a boy. When he was a boy—

"Are you finished," asks Bataar.

"Yeah, Goddamn it! Just do it!"

Bataar ignores his outburst and quietly wipes Zookeeper with placid detachment.

While performing the unpleasant task, the boy is just as unruffled as when he pours a whiskey or helps Zookeeper puff his cigarettes. This puzzles the armless man immensely. Faced with unstinting kindness from others, he feels disoriented and self-doubting. That very kindness triggers the unwanted softness which, in turn, makes him rage even more insistently against it. If he had a psychic scalpel, he would cut out the malignancy.

Back on his comfortable couch, Zookeeper is assailed by the voice to kill Lady Oracle, or Bataar, or himself.

Do it! Do it! screams the voice in his head.

"Shut-up!" Zookeeper bellows in futile rage.

Bataar, apparently unmoved by his distress, calmly puts a cigarette between Zookeeper's lips, then patiently pulls it out after he takes a long drag.

Do it! Do it! the voice keeps insisting.

Zookeeper laughs mirthlessly. "How?" he barks.

Bataar ignores the non-sequitur, somehow knowing it is not directed at him.

As if noticing the Mongol boy for the first time, Zookeeper asks, "Where the fuck is Lady Oracle? I want to talk with her."

"She will soon return," he replies serenely.

"Well," grumbles Zookeeper. "I hope she gets here soon. I want to talk to her. How about that whiskey, kid?"

Do it! Kill her! Do it! It you don't, she will poison you! the voice persists.

"Damn it, shut up!"

~

Lady Oracle strides into the room after her visit with Sy, Ming-huà, and Tamara. Her face is flushed from the long walk, and she abruptly stops before Zookeeper. "Who are you talking to?"

"Bataar."

"You told Bataar to shut up?"

He points to his head. "No. That was directed at the fuckin' voice."

"It is *God*."

"Whatever. I want it to go away."

"We will see Ming-huà soon."

[108]

"Oh, yeah, the hunchback," he says derisively. "My savior."

Bataar pulls out the last stub of Zookeeper's cigarette and crushes it in an ash tray. "Anything else?" he asks.

"No, thanks buddy," says Zookeeper. "Uh, for everything, you know?"

Bataar flashes a rare smile. "Still want whiskey?"

"Naw, thanks. I need to talk with Lady Oracle."

The boy nods and leaves.

~

Lady Oracle and Zookeeper do not speak for a long while. He breaks the silence. "When do I get to see this bitch?"

Lady Oracle shakes her head as if disappointed in an unruly child. "Zookeeper, you needn't keep up this ridiculous vulgarity. It is beneath you. Any man who can recite Shakespeare needn't revert to gutter language. Not only that, your entire behavior is beneath your power."

"What is this power you keep talking about? I mean, I know how to manipulate stupid people, but that's nothing special."

"Oh, Zookeeper, if you only knew! The power you exercise on 'stupid people', as you call them, is merely the tip of an iceberg. The vast bulk of your power remains submerged."

"Ha! I'm just waiting for a Titanic to sink!"

"That's just it, Zookeeper. Your default view of life is one of brutal struggle, violence, and death."

Zookeeper smiles sardonically. "Well, ain't that the way life is? Natural selection, Lady Oracle. This *God* crap you keep talkin' about is a ruse. It's survival of the fittest."

Lady Oracle moves her eyes across his armless stumps. "How are you doing on that score?"

"Winners and losers," he sulks.

"Have you ever felt joy?"

"What's that?"

"Only suffering?"

"More or less. Screwing a woman, jacking off, drinking, there's been moments." He looks at his stumps and his expression reflects seething fury. "Suffering! Is there no pity sitting in the clouds that sees into the bottom of my grief! Suffering is my boon companion. You nailed it. I said I suffer, more or less. Well, lately, more!"

[109]

"What if you could help stop suffering?"

"Not possible."

"True, not all suffering, but what if you could stop unnecessary suffering?"

"Still not possible."

"Let me ask you a question."

"Shoot."

"Do you believe your two friends—Pepper Spray and Amygdala—have caused others to suffer?"

"Sure as shit have."

"Can they cause suffering to others now, without arms?"

Zookeeper scoffs, "Sure as fuck be a hell of a lot more difficult!"

"So, the incident at the crack house, did it prevent greater suffering in the future in exchange for inflicting lesser suffering in the present?"

Zookeeper mulls this over. "I don't know. Can't read the future."

"Yes, you do know. And yes, you can read."

"No."

"Yes. Why do you know? Because you know Pepper Spray and Amygdala. You know what they're capable of with arms, and you know what they are not capable of without them."

"Look, if you so all-fired hot about preventing suffering, why not just kill them? Cut to the chase. Eliminate the middle-man. In the long run, that would have caused less suffering, because I can fuckin' *God* damn assure you, they are suffering now. Just like me. And it's a long, drawn-out suffering, like torture."

He hears his inner voice burst out in a deep, coital moan of pleasure. "Jesus Christ!" he mutters under his breath.

"*God* liked that description," says Lady Oracle.

"Okay, enough of that *God* stuff. It scares the shit outta me. Anyway, you haven't answered my question. Why not just kill them and get it the fuck over with?"

"You know the answer to that."

"Let me guess; bleeding heart."

"No; redemption through suffering."

Zookeeper's face glows with excitement. "Ha! You just contradicted yourself! No redemption without suffering? So how can it be you want to eliminate suffering? That would screw up your whole premise."

"Not at all," says Lady Oracle calmly. "Redemption for those who cause suffering, not those who are the victims of suffering. Eliminate the ability of those who unnecessarily inflict suffering to do it, then you eliminate the need for redemption."

"In other words, if you don't cause suffering, there's no need for redemption?"

"Correct. Suffering by non-intentional, non-directed means—fire, disease, flood, predation, famine—will continue. But what of suffering by intentional, directed means—murder, war, rape—what if that ended?"

"Impossible."

"True, that is what *He* banks on to feed *His* addiction. What if some new, inexplicable power arises that stops intentional, directed suffering?"

Zookeeper laughs mockingly. "By removing the arms of all those millions who inflict suffering on others?"

"Yes, figuratively." Lady Oracle stares at him unblinking.

"You're mad! There will always be at least psychological suffering!"

"That is the next step."

"To what?"

"Erasure of humanity as we know it."

Stunned at this completely absurd statement, Zookeeper looks upon Lady Oracle as a woman needing to be institutionalized. "So, a pathetic ex-junkie with no arms and a kind hunchback with no clue will change humanity? You really are fuckin' crazy!"

"True, but so are you and the hunchback."

Zookeeper hears the voice stirring ominously.

Lady Oracle leans forward like a bird of prey. "Look, Zookeeper, you are an intelligent young mutant with untapped power who has suffered much and, in the process, has abused your mind and body in the most wasteful and tragic of ways. Therefore, you have mutilated the pristine core of your power. Think back, over two hundred thousand years ago. Think! You were there, in the genes of a woman who gave birth in Africa. Out of her womb came the first modern human. Out of Ming-huà's womb will come . . . something similar, and yet something not. After many, many false starts, the birth of this child has been carefully arranged for two generations. Two generations of people considered mad. People who simply needed nurturing and protection from an uncomprehending world bent on destroying them, or burying them in institutions."

Zookeeper chuckles. "All this trouble only to end up creating a third generation of fucked-up crazy! Lady Oracle, you can't eliminate suffering. Give it up. I grew up learning that the hard way. War, violence, cruelty, ignorance, superstition, racism, bigotry, and all the rest. You're going to just sweep all that away? Fuckin' batshit lunacy!"

Lady Oracle stares at him unfazed. "It has already begun. It began many generations ago; it began two hundred thousand years ago."

"Yeah, and only a few hundred thousand generations to go! Fuck, don't you get it?"

"Look around you, Zookeeper. What do you see? Fancy apartments, high-rises, electricity, automobiles, jet airplanes, computers, men on the moon. Which of these miracles of science do you think those first humans, living brutal, savage lives, anticipated? What if you tried to tell them in their own language? I can only imagine the look they would give you."

Zookeeper remains silent, but shakes his head doubtfully.

Lady Oracle continues. "You may be among the first ancestor of a new race of humans."

"But they won't be human anymore," he says.

Lady Oracle says with chilling finality, "No, they won't."

~

Zookeeper decides to stop objecting to these nonsensical notions. He will go along with the madness and use these wackos for his own purposes. Let them indulge in whatever fantasies makes them happy. As long as they feed him, give him booze and cigarettes, wipe his ass, and provide him a place to crash, he'll stick . . . at least until he gets his shot at the hunchback. He is convinced Lady Oracle lies, and the hunchback really has the power to replace his arms.

You are right, she lies! screams his voice. *She lies! Kill her!* Zookeeper shudders and calls Bataar.

He appears from nowhere. "Yes?"

"Get me a whiskey, okay, kid?"

[112]

Bataar hesitates and looks at Lady Oracle. She nods.

Lady Oracle watches Bataar leave to fetch the whiskey and turns to Zookeeper. "It is *God*," she says firmly. "Metaphorically speaking, that voice is *God*, and *He* feels threatened again." Unexpectedly, she claps her hands, looks toward the ceiling, and beams. "Good!"

~ Mother and Daughter Alone ~

Shortly after Lady Oracle finished her meeting at the Victorian house and left to attend the impatient Zookeeper, Sy also retires, trailing the wake of his burdens up the stairs after him. Ming-huà and her mother are left alone to discuss their problems with a privacy only one of them desires. More tea is poured.

Ming-huà takes a sip and, as if afraid to wait and weaken, quickly says, "I won't marry him. I won't have anything to do with him, let alone have a child by him. Nothing you can say will make me. Oh, mama! Let's go back to the island and live a quiet life!"

Tamara stays quiet for a while, then says, "Let me tell you a story. It is the story of a young, beautiful Chinese pianist. Oh, such a pianist! She was asked to marry an American and have a child by him, same as you have been asked."

"I've heard this," Ming-huà says resentfully. "It won't matter."

"Just listen, child. Be patient and let your mother have her say. Now, you can guess the identity of the American in my story; your grandpapa, of course. Like your father, he believed he suffered from schizophrenia. Now, this beautiful Chinese pianist who accompanied him on the quest, Bai Meiying, had great compassion for him, but certainly not love. Not at all. Oh, Ming-huà, it was much worse than that. For this beautiful Chinese pianist, this Meiying, was also a lesbian, and could never see the American as others wished, including him. Your grandpapa wanted her to love him so much! But there could be no possibility of her agreeing to conceive his child. None."

"Mama," says an exasperated Ming-huà. "Grandpapa was no Zookeeper!"

Tamara lifts her eyebrows. "How do you know? You know nothing about him! He heard voices, like your papa. Terrible voices. His mental illness scared Meiying terribly, and made even the idea of marrying him and conceiving his child an impossibility. As a lesbian also, the thought of it made her physically ill. You are not facing that."

"And what about you, mama? What did you have to face when they told you to marry papa and conceive a child?"

"At first, I objected strenuously, but I owed Buandelgereen my very life. Without her, I would have been forced to grow up with your grandmama in China in a mental institution. Still, I initially refused. I was adamant with Buandelgereen. After all, the man was mentally ill. And, although I am not a lesbian like Meiying, the thought of having sex with him petrified me and made me stubbornly unwilling to go along."

"So, what convinced you?"

"*Her.*"

"Is that all?"

"No, there was much much more. But, now is not the time to go into that."

"Magic caves in the desert?"

"Yes."

"Well, mama, I have not met *Her*, have not been in any magic caves, and am confronted with a disgusting man whose violent temperament and brutal ways terrify me. Being schizophrenic would be his least worrisome trait."

"You know, Ming-huà, he looks at you the same way."

"I am not schizophrenic!"

"No, you only removed both his arms, are a hunchback, and possess powers that terrify him as much as his power terrifies you."

"Okay, neither of us are marriageable material."

"Daughter, you must marry him and conceive his child!"

The vehemence of her mother's words startles Ming-huà and she blurts, "Mama! No! Why?"

"Because not to would render all the sacrifice of your parents and grandparents futile!"

"How?"

"Girl, haven't you figured it out? The child you must birth will be like none before it. It's powers, male or female, will far surpass your grandparents, your parents, and yourself. This power has been carefully nurtured and protected. By doing so, it has increased in potency through the generations."

"But—"

"No, daughter! You must go through with this! I will not have all those lives who went before wasted because of your squeamishness, and that includes my own life. Lady Oracle tells me this boy, this Zookeeper, is not who you think he is. Trust me, she knows. He is actually quite remarkable himself. It is your duty to obey, and it is your imperative to find in him the goodness he must possess. Your father, I discovered, was good. A good man. A haunted man, like Zookeeper, but at the core, someone different than the run-of-the-mill person. You will discover Zookeeper to be similarly worthwhile. Besides which, you owe him. Always remember, it was you who took off his arms."

Ming-huà buries her face in her hands and sobs.

Chapter 9: A Fatal Flaw

~ Zookeeper Rebels ~

"It's been three fuckin' days since you told me I would see the hunchback," Zookeeper complains to Lady Oracle. "When do I see her? I mean, shit or get off the pot."

"Her name is Ming-huà. You will see her when I say so."

Zookeeper has a sardonic glint in his eyes. "Got problems with your plan, Lady Oracle?"

"She is not ready."

"Can't blame her. But I'm ready."

"You can help."

"How?"

"Perform major surgery on your personality. Connect with the better part of your soul and jettison the rest. There is a very worthwhile person inside you, let it out. If you do, then the sooner life will get easier, and the sooner your power will fully bloom."

"You keep talkin' about this power of mine. Well, what do you think it is? I mean, shit, it must be a hell of a lot more than I think it is, so, what is it?"

"Do you see this object?" Lady Oracle holds up a stoshell.

"Yeah, I've been wondering about that."

She suddenly throws it at Zookeeper's head. He ducks and it sails harmlessly past.

"Ming-huà would have made it disappear before it hit her. You anticipated the throw and ducked. Two different kinds of power."

"Shiiit! Anyone would have ducked."

"No, I threw it very fast. An average person, even an athlete, would have been hit. You don't know it, but you read my mind and reacted before it was thrown."

"You're telling me I can read minds? That I'm a fuckin' mutant like hunchback?"

"Yes, but you have wasted the power and corrupted it with drugs. It is like a withered muscle, slack and next to useless. It will require intensive therapy to rebuild. Are you willing?"

"First, I want my arms rebuilt!" he shouts.

"That can never be."

"Well then, take your bullshit theories and stick them—" Zookeeper abruptly stops, remembering his plan to go along with their madness until he can reach the hunchback. "Oh, well . . . maybe you're right. I always felt I had a certain power to influence people. Yeah, you're right. Help me." He hopes his words sound sincere enough.

Lady Oracle smiles. "You may be able to read minds, but you are terrible at reading mine. What am I thinking right now?"

"I don't know."

She grabs his shirt front and pulls him forward. "You do! Think! If you cannot tell me, then you are out on the street! No use to me!"

"I don't know!"

Lady Oracle stares deep into his eyes. "Calmly, now. Think."

Images fly through his head. Crazy images. Images of deserts and caves and jungles and iron doors and *Goddess* statues; a mishmash of exotic fragments. None make any sense. But then the fragments suddenly come together like the film of a broken mirror run backwards. He sees Lady Oracle clearly in the mirror.

"You are thinking that I am a liar, a cheat, a thief; a fool who has the audacity to think he can so easily deceive you. You know I am lying about wanting help. You know I want to use you. You know I want to use hunchback."

"Yes," exclaims Lady Oracle. "All that is easily surmised. Now go deeper. Deeper!"

"You know I think you lie about the hunchback's inability to return my arms. You know I have often thought of murdering you, if I could. You know I think you are insane."

"Too easy. Deeper!"

Zookeeper shudders, locked in the embrace of the mesmerizing mirror that is Lady Oracle's mind. "You think I am worthwhile. You think that underneath my façade, I have extraordinary powers which have yet to be freed. You think that I am worth the aggravation and the effort. You

[117]

think my power can be used for good purposes. You think I am destined to be with the hunchback and conceive a child with her."

"And?"

"And you think I will cease to exist if your plan fails."

"Correct."

As if snapping out of a hypnotic trance, Zookeeper quavers and snaps his head to clear it, saying under his breath, "Well then, I must make sure your plan succeeds."

~

After Lady Oracle excuses herself, Zookeeper sits for a while feeling the worst kind of dread. There will be no fooling this lady, no deception. She sees through him as clearly as one sees though a window. Never has he been in such an exposed position; naked and helpless before her searching mind. His one thought now is not that of revenge, or acquiring advantage, or even of comfort, but of flight. He wants to run out the door and flee back to the crack house where he will submit to others and fill his body with enough drugs to find oblivion. That is where he belongs. In reading Lady Oracle's mind, he realizes she is not lying about the hunchback. His arms are gone for good. Now, there is nothing left but the strongest drugs he can find to pour into his body. And then. . . .

"That is not a good idea, Zookeeper," says Lady Oracle who has just returned.

"How did you know. . . . ?" His heads sinks. "Never mind."

"Tomorrow we go to see Ming-huà."

This news stirs no joy in Zookeeper. "What's the point now?"

"Remember? Salvation?"

"I need a whiskey."

"No, not this time. You can wait. If you prefer not to wait so you can fill your body with drugs, the front door is unlocked. If you leave, no one will stop you."

Zookeeper glares fiercely but keeps his mouth shut.

"Tomorrow morning, if you are still here, we leave after breakfast at nine o'clock. If you are gone—" she shrugs.

The next morning, Zookeeper is gone.

Lady Oracle views his absence with her typical nonchalance.

"He'll be back," she remarks.

~ Ming-huà's Decision ~

That night, Sy, Lady Oracle, Tamara, and Ming-huà all sit together in the anteroom of the Victorian house gloomily silent. Outside, the swollen San Francisco fog rolls out of a dark night and presses its wet obesity against the windows. Zookeeper's disappearance has been discussed, but now there seems nothing more to say. Suddenly, Sy jumps up and dances a jig. "Look! I know what you've said, but just let me go get him! Getting him back here will be easy!"

"No, Sy," says Lady Oracle resignedly. "He is gone."

"Only gone if we let him be gone!" exclaims Sy.

Ming-huà notices her mother ignoring Scarecrow and staring at her.

"Dear daughter, you can go back to the island now," says Tamara. "There is nothing holding you here any longer."

"And you, mama?"

"I return to the place from which I came."

"Can I go with you?"

"No, dear."

Ming-huà looks down. "I know that." She thinks of her squirrel friend scolding from his perch in the branches of a Douglas fir.

Lady Oracle stands abruptly. "I must go."

Everyone mumbles their goodbyes and silence again descends on the group. Now Sy slowly rises from his chair and slinks out of the room like a puppet whose strings have been cut.

Tamara watches him leave and turns to Ming-huà. "Well, daughter, this will be our last evening together."

"Oh, mama, must you leave so soon? We haven't had enough time."

Tamara smiles her enigmatic smile. "Time is plastic, bending this way and that, even bending back upon itself. We will visit with each other again, but I must return to my own . . . duties."

Ming-huà wants to ask about the nature of her duties, but some inner warning stops the words before they leave her mouth.

"Duty. . . . " her mother repeats. "I must also go to bed." She chuckles. "Older I get, more easily tired. Goodnight, dear." She kisses her daughter and, on the way out of the room, picks up a stoshell, turning it in her hand as if it was a strange object she had never before seen. "Life is indeed a mystery."

Ming-huà rises and walks her to the foot of the stairs. "Goodnight, mama. Sleep well."

"Thank you, dear."

As Ming-huà watches her mother ascend the stairs, she makes up her mind.

Tamara stops half-way up and looks back at Ming-huà. "Good! You will not regret it!"

Next morning, Ming-huà has already left for the crack house by the time Sy and Tamara meet downstairs for breakfast.

~ At the Crack House ~

Upon his return to the crack house, Zookeeper is greeted rudely by Angel Cake.

"Well, look who the fuckin' cat dragged in!" he exclaims.

Zookeeper ignores the tone. "I need a place to crash."

"Well," says Angel Cake imperiously, "Find a corner with soft garbage to lay on. I have your old sanctum room. Remodeled it, too. Got rid of the fuckin' books. Did that bitch Lady Clitoris give you bread?"

"No."

"Shiiit. What you gonna do?"

"Stay here. Get myself pumped with crack."

"Not if you don't contribute. Go back to that bitch and get money, man, else you ain't welcome. You ain't Zookeeper anymore, you is just kept." Angel Cake laughed at his own joke. "Now *you* is an exhibit!"

Zookeeper stares into space, listening to the voice demanding he kill Angel Cake.

After surveying Zookeeper's two stumps, Angel Cake says, "Guess you in a world of hurt, man. I sympathize, but, shit, we all gotta do what we gotta do to survive. Like you said, survival of the fittest."

"Yeah. What about Pepper Spray and Amygdala?"

"Ain't seen their sorry asses since . . . since when that weird shit went down. Find that hunchback chick?"

"No."

"Find out how she done it?"

"No. Say, man, you got some candy? I'm sorely in need."

Angel Cake's face hardens. "So, you lower yourself down to our level, eh? No, man, not unless you got bread. Tell you what I'll do though, you can crash here a couple days for old times' sake, then you gotta go, unless you put the touch on that bitch woman. Cabbage is always good here.

"Thanks," says Zookeeper sarcastically.

"Hey, man, don't blame me for your troubles. Brought 'em on yourself, man, for letting those freaks in to the sanctuary."

"Yeah."

"Poetic justice, man. Now you're a freak. Now, you're one of them."

These words hit Zookeeper hard, and reverberate like Quasimodo's bells.

"Yeah," he says submissively.

"Go find your corner," dismisses Angel Cake over his shoulder as he walks away.

The stench makes Zookeeper queasy, and he chalks it up to being gone so long breathing fresh air. *Have to get used to it again*, he thinks, and finds himself an unoccupied corner where he lays down on a pile of trash and sleeps.

~

While Angel Cake sits in the sanctum, his feet on the table, peering at a collection of crack chips and rocks, a sky-high junkie whose appearance is that of a somnambulant zombie, knocks feebly on the door.

"What!"

"Someone at th' front," croaks the zombie.

"Ain't th cops?"

"Fuck no, just some hunchback girl."

Angel Cake jumps up. "What?"

"Hunchback girl."

"Shiiiiit!" screeches Angel Cake. "What she want?"

"I dunno . . . ah, go fuck yourself Angel, I'm gone back to my hootch. Ask her yourself, shithead."

Angel Cake is scared. He knows she is the one who took off three guys' arms somehow, some way. Some kind of witch. He hesitates, even considering skipping out the back door, but he hides the rocks and gathers his courage.

"Yeah?" he says at the front door, staring down at the hunchback.

Ming-huà has her scarf pulled over her mouth and nose, and speaks in a muffled voice, "I want to see Zookeeper."

"Shit!" cries Angel Cake anxiously. "You wanna take off his legs now?"

"No. Is he here?" She looks conspicuously at his arms.

"Yeah, yeah," says Angel Cake apprehensively, backing away. "He's here."

Ming-huà feels emboldened by his fear. "Show me."

Angel Cake quickly finds where Zookeeper is sleeping, points him out to the hunchback, and scurries back to his safe room. Ming-huà wants to wait for him to wake up, but the smell is making her sick, so she leans over and calls his name. He does not stir. She calls again. Nothing. Finally, unable to stay longer, she makes a last attempt and shakes him awake. Startled, he tries to rise, but lack of arms is still new, and he flops back like a fish on land. She helps him up and steadies his swaying body.

"Let's go outside and talk," she says urgently, as the stench had by now made her nauseous.

"Can you put my arms back on?" asks Zookeeper with the anticipatory look of a hopeful puppy.

Ming-huà's heart aches for what she has done, but replies simply, "Outside." She hurries him out the front door and down a few blocks where she knows there is a bench. As they walk, she frequently glances at Zookeeper, and realizes he has a nice face, quite handsome actually. His vulnerability has softened his features and make him more appealing, and certainly much less frightening. Nevertheless, on deeper inspection, the incipient lines in his face project the somber mien of a lonely sufferer. Maternal instinct aroused, Ming-huà is stung by pangs of guilty compassion and spiritual empathy. She notices he keeps his eyes lowered to avoid passersby gawking at the sight of an armless man.

The instant they sit, Zookeeper again asks, "Can you put my arms back on?"

"No."

"Why not?" he snaps.

"I don't know why not. I've tried."

"Try again."

"Zookeeper, it doesn't work that way."

"Try!"

"I have. My whole life I have tried."

"So, you've done this to other people before?"

Ming-huà lowers her eyes. "Yes."

"How many fuckin' people are running around out there without arms because of you?"

"Zookeeper, you and your friends are the only ones."

"Then what the fuck do you want with me?"

His harsh words frighten her, but she presses on. "To explain."

"Guilty conscience?"

"Yes."

Zookeeper's voice softens. "Why did you do it?"

"Zookeeper, I was just trying to defend Lady Oracle from being hurt. I'm so sorry. I did not think." Tears roll unimpeded down her cheeks.

Zookeeper seems unmoved. "Look, what do you want? Want me to forgive you? Make you feel better? If you want to feel better, give me some br . . . ah, money, so I can find comfort."

"That's not why I'm here," she says, wiping away the tears.

"Well?"

"I want you to come back with me."

"Hell no! I'm not going back to that crazy-ass woman Lady Oracle!" He shudders and murmurs, "That fuckin' woman scares the hell out of me. She's crazier than you."

"I don't mean back to her place. I mean, come back with me to the house I'm staying at. Let me help you."

He looks at her suspiciously. "Charity?"

Ming-huà ignores his question. "What did Lady Oracle tell you about me?"

"Some shit about us having a kid."

"For what purpose?" Ming-huà asks, though she knows the answer.

"I don't know. Couldn't figure it out. Something about a magical kid who could end suffering . . . just crazy shit like that."

"Yes," sighs Ming-huà. "Crazy to think someone as ugly and misshapen as me could even consider such a thing."

At first, Zookeeper thinks this remark is an invitation to flatter, but his powerful insight tells him she is utterly sincere. In spite of his resistance to gushing "naïve, romantic shit", he sees her for the first time as not a fake, or clueless, but someone possessing a deep and profound goodness of a type he had never dared expect to encounter. But this realization scares rather than inspires him. In response, he forces himself to recall his plans to use her for his own purposes.

"You're not so bad," he says.

Ming-huà smiles sadly. "Thank you."

Zookeeper realizes he said the wrong thing. Her melancholy washes over him with such a sweet sorrow that he is anxious to repair the damage.

"Hunchback, I actually think you are quite beautiful." He locks his eyes on hers. "If I could write the beauty of your eyes, and in fresh numbers number all your graces, the age to come would say, 'This poet lies; such heavenly touches ne'er touch'd earthly faces.'" He is shocked to realize his words are spoken with undeniable sincerity.

Ming-huà, with her own powerful faculty, knows his words come from the heart. She blushes and says, "First things first. My name is Ming-huà. I understand your real name is Matthew Weston. May I call you Matthew?"

He laughs acerbically. "No, no! That name is *verboten*! I am Zookeeper. Forever Zookeeper." He pauses. "Ming-huà. Did I say it right?"

"Yes, perfectly. So, will you?"

"Will I?"

"Come with me."

Zookeeper mulls over his options. A crack house full of junkies and filth, or a nice house with Ming-huà? The decision is a no-brainer.

"Yes, I will. But, Ming-huà, you know I need help with . . . personal things. Do you have anyone who performs that sort of service?"

"I am perfectly willing to—"

"No!" he cries. "Not you! No. I would be too . . . embarrassed."

"But—"

"Absolutely not. If that's the case, then I'm going back to the crack house."

Ming-huà thinks aloud. "Maybe we could borrow Bataar's services."

"That's the ticket! That kid is amazing. I'll feel more comfortable with him wip . . . helping me."

"Then let's go," says Ming-huà cheerfully. "Do you need anything at the crack house?"

"Not a damn thing except distance."

As they walk, Zookeeper feels inexplicably happy. For the first time since he lost his arms, there is some light pulsing dimly through the dark night. He feels his spirits rise Phoenix-like.

In this jocular mood, he quips, "Well, what the hell. You and me are gonna change the world. None of these rubes around us knows they are passing two saviors. Ha ha! What a joke!"

"Zookeeper," says Ming-huà. "I do not believe it is a joke."

"You don't really buy all that shit Lady Oracle is selling, do you?"

Ming-huà suddenly chuckles, taking Zookeeper by surprise.

"What?" he asks.

"There are more things in heaven and earth, Horatio, than are dreamt of in your philosophy."

Zookeeper roars with laughter. "You got me there, hunchback!"

Ming-huà frowns.

Zookeeper stops abruptly. "Oh, shit! You don't mind me calling you that, do you?"

"No, that's not it," she says. "I was just thinking how much you and I both have to learn."

"You got that right. Listen, Ming-huà, what do you get outta this gig really? I mean, I get a place to stay, food, all that shit, but you?"

Ming-huà cannot answer that question, even to herself. She came to Zookeeper with no plan beyond convincing him to return so he can be cared for. But the idea of he and she actually getting together, let alone having a child together, is a thought she will not allow access to her conscious mind as even a remote possibility.

"It is enough that I know you will be cared for," she says.

Again, his insight tells him that Ming-huà's words are reliably true, but his old scars and prejudices will not admit of that possibility. There has to be some angle he is leaving out. Maybe she really wants to have a kid, and he is the only one she could ever hope to have sex with. But when he looks at her face and scans her body, he sees a very beautiful woman, and knows his notion is absurdly fallacious.

[125]

"Ming-huà, do you actually think we should have a baby together for these people?" he asks in the form of disbelief.

Again she blushes, this time all the way down her neck. "Of course not," she whispers.

"What?"

"Of course not."

Zookeeper feels oddly let-down by her response. "Don't get me wrong, I mean, you're pretty and all that, but . . . but the whole idea seems too weird, even for me."

"Yes."

Something in her answers make him uncomfortable. "Come on, Ming-huà, tell me the truth. Could you ever conceive a situation where we could . . . get together?"

"Yes," she says boldly.

This takes Zookeeper as much by surprise as it does her.

"Really?" It is a silly reply, but the best his confused brain can produce.

"Yessss," she says tentatively. "But I think that is one of the reasons why I want you to return with me. If you do not, then neither of us will ever get the answers."

"Answers?"

"We will never see *Her*."

"Oh, come on Ming-huà, now you're sounding like Lady Oracle!"

As they walk, Ming-huà speaks more to herself than to Zookeeper, trying to sort it all out in her mind before they reach the house. "The truth lies very deep in the past, even before my ancestors, my grandfather, my grandmother, my mother, my father, even before them. *She* holds the key. I must see *Her* to understand, just as my parents and grandparents did. I cannot do that without you."

"Why?"

"It is the plan . . . you and I. If not the plan, then no *Her*."

Zookeeper shakes his head. "But that's crazy."

Ming-huà says nothing.

"Ming-huà, look at me. I can barely walk. I can't wipe my own ass or put on my own trousers. Christ! Why do you even look at me?"

"Hush!"

"Okay, okay. Let's change the damn subject. Jesus, how much farther?"

"Not too far. Up that hill."

"Oh, shit, that's fuckin' steep."

"Yes."

"Forget I said that. Where are you from?"

"All over. Mainly from a beautiful island where I lived a beautiful life with. . . . "

"With?"

"Never mind, you'd only laugh at me."

"No, I wouldn't."

"Sometimes you are cruel like that."

Zookeeper falls silent.

After walking a while longer, Zookeeper says, "Let's sit on that bench. I'm pooped."

"Okay."

After they sit for a few moments, he gathers his courage. "Ming-huà, I'm crude and cruel. Actually, can be quite vicious. My mother taught me to be prepared to say or do anything to get what you want. Beg, borrow, steal, kill. You're from a different world." Tears well in his eyes. "I . . . I just don't understand you, or Lady Oracle, or any of this shit. Why me? That's what I can't get through my noggin. Why me?"

"I don't know. Let's find out."

"Tell me more about this *Her* you keep harpin' at."

"Wait till we get to the house. Save your breath. One last big hill and we're there."

"What's that weird guy's name again?"

"Sy." She chuckles. "Sometimes I call him Scarecrow."

"Yeah, fits. What's he gonna think?"

Ming-huà just laughs. "You'll see."

When they reach the front door, Ming-huà finds it locked. She knocks and Sy cracks it open. At once he throws it open wide and hugs Ming-huà. "Thank *Goddess* you're back!" he cries.

Ming-huà looks around. "Where's mama?"

Sy makes a whistling sound. "Gone! Gone while you were away, like the ghost she is. Said to tell you she would be waiting for you at another place and time. A ghost woman!"

After saying these words, he looks over Ming-huà's shoulder and sees a ragged man standing in the doorway. A man with no arms.

Chapter 10: Stormy Weather

~ Greetings and Salutations ~

Zookeeper stares in wonder from his seat on the couch as Sy dances jig after jig, whooping like a madman.

"How'd you do it, Ming-huà?" he shouts. Mohammed to the mountain! All is well! All is well! I'm going to call Lady Oracle. That cagey old fox knew this would happen!"

"Not now, Scarecrow!" scolds Ming-huà. "It's late and we need rest, don't we Zookeeper?"

"Shit! Right now, I need a fuckin' whiskey and a smoke!"

Ming-huà glares.

"Sorry. Old habits die hard. Hey, Scarecrow or Sy or whatever your damn name is, got some whiskey? Prithee?"

Sy places his hand over his heart. "A man after my own heart! Do I have whiskey? Can I dance?"

He rushes to the cabinet and pours a row of shot glasses.

Ming-huà laughs and takes a glass to Zookeeper. He rolls his head back and opens his mouth greedily. She hesitates.

"Give it to me, baby!" he cries. "Straight shot straight down the hatch! Do it!"

She empties the contents into his throat. Zookeeper swallows and smacks his lips. "Ahhhhh!" he bellows in pleasure.

After this ritual has emptied all the shot glasses, Zookeeper is flushed and garrulous. "Hey, Sy good buddy!"

"Yes, my friend?"

"Tell me about this chick Ming-huà keeps talking about . . . this *Her* person."

Sy's demeanor instantly transforms from clown to raging prophet of Biblical proportions. "*She*? *She* is *Goddess*! The Great Deity who dares to challenge *God*! That old addicted bastard of a *God* trembles before *Her*

wrath at *His* abusive ways! And both of you are tiny parts of the Great
Plan, as am I."

Ming-huà, already having some knowledge of this Great Plan and
accustomed to Sy's usual histrionics, remains meekly silent, but
Zookeeper is drunk enough to flap his tongue in derision. "Shit, man!
You're just as crazy as Lady Oracle! Ha, ha! Well, I'll play along. Just
keep the whiskey flowing and ol' Zookeeper will be right there with you,
buddy!"

Embarrassed by Zookeeper's outburst, Ming-huà stares at the
floor.

But Sy leaps backward startling everyone, and shouts in outrage,
"You scum! You dare . . . !?"

He suddenly grabs a small bronze statue from the etagere and
throws it as hard as he can at Zookeeper's head.

Before a shocked Zookeeper has time to react, it disappears inches
from his face.

Stunned silence.

Instantly sober, Zookeeper quickly turns his astonished eyes on
Ming-huà who meets his gaze with a dazed expression.

Sy surveys the scene, relaxed and smiling. He lets the moment
sink in so a shocked Zookeeper can adequately recover his scrambled
senses. After a while, he says in a genial manner, "You see, Zookeeper, it
is best to keep your mockery to yourself, or else next time I will do
something similar without your protector nearby."

Zookeeper's first reaction after his astonishment fades is to
suspect a set-up, but when he sees Ming-huà's face, sad and weary,
looking at him with relief, he knows the truth and it burns deep into his
heart.

"I'm sorry, Zookeeper," she says. "I did not know Scarecrow
would do that. You have had too much to drink, and your lesser self came
out a bit. My Scarecrow friend here is very fond of sudden, unexpected,
and dramatic demonstrations."

"My *God*!" sputters Zookeeper. "You really . . . I mean . . . it
actually . . . Jesus! . . . to see it again! Fuck me!" He looks at Ming-huà in
awe. "Christ! You ain't human girl! Christ almighty!"

"She saved you," says Sy gently. "I would show some respect."

"I . . . I know, Sy. It just takes time to get used to . . . to her power, you know? My *God*, Ming-huà! You are . . . are . . . magnificent! The icy precepts of respect have frozen in my veins!"

"That's better, young man," says Sy. "Shakespeare in a pinch. There is indeed hope for you! Now, it's time to go to work."

"Huh?" grunts Zookeeper.

"It is time to get to work! To be useful to yourself and to the rest of the world, you must learn to use your feet."

"Feet?" Zookeeper shakes his head, thoroughly confused.

"Come over here," says Sy.

Zookeeper stands next to Sy whose computer screen is open and displays a website showing armless people performing a variety of activities one would think impossible without arms.

"You see?" says Sy. "Driving a car, eating, cooking, playing music, writing, painting, dancing, all using only their feet! You can do just about anything!"

Zookeeper experiences his second revelation of the day watching the videos.

"How do I learn?" he asks.

"By doing," replies Sy with a little jig. "However, I have a close friend who was born without arms. He will visit tomorrow and help you get started."

"Why are you doing all this?"

Sy laughs. "Still so suspicious? We must remove your distrust as your arms have been removed—painlessly."

"So I'm part of this Grand Plan you all have, right?"

"Correct."

"I still don't get what my contribution will be, other than"—he looks diffidently at Ming-huà— "sorry babe, sperm."

"If you actually think you know what your contribution will be, you would not be here because you would not be contributing."

Zookeeper wrinkles his brow. "I think I understand what you just said, but it doesn't answer my question. Since I don't know what my contribution will be, why don't you tell me?"

"You won't know until we have completed our journey."

"What journey?" asks Zookeeper.

"Yes, what journey?" echoes Ming-huà.

"Why, the journey we three, maybe four, are gonna take."

"To?"

Sy assumes his best operatic pose. "A quest. Yes, Ming-huà, a quest, like your parents and grandparents. The same quest. A quest to finish the quest."

Ming-huà is struck dumb, but Zookeeper plows ahead. "Where to, goddamn it!"

"To a different place and time."

"What the fuck does that mean?"

"It means, Zookeeper, that we cannot even consider going on this quest until you learn to use your feet. So, the quest starts tomorrow with your first lesson."

Zookeeper wants to object, to curse, to threaten, to stomp out, to throw something, but within his mind, the voice stirs and thunders with ominous vibrations of unmistakable threat. A low, rumbling earthquake warning, *No, no, no, never, never, never. . . .*

Zookeeper turns pale and feels faint.

Sy shouts, "Ignore *Him*! It is only *God* trying to frighten you. Ignore *Him* and embrace your destiny!"

Zookeeper experiences a seismic jerk; some coupling shatters and disconnects the heavy freight of his drug-befuddled, obscene self, releasing it to drift away, freeing his core self, his powerful self, to soar like a runaway train.

"Yes, yes!" he shouts as if he were at some evangelical come-to-Jesus meeting, except the reverse. "Go to hell, *God*!" he shouts. After this emotional release, Zookeeper collapses back on the couch and says in a hoarse voice, "I need whiskey, Scarecrow."

~ Toe Maps ~

The next day Zookeeper spends hours with Ben Solokov, a man born with no arms. Solokov demonstrates amazing dexterity by using his toes for a variety of tasks, and explains how the brain will remap its neural structure to signal organized commands to the toes just as it normally does to the hands and fingers.

"But you were born this way, man!" objects Zookeeper. "You've had your whole life to adjust. Look at me. This shit just happened and I can't even think of making my toes work the way yours do."

Ben shakes his head. "No, you're wrong. I have helped many armless people right after they suffered accidents, and it did not take nearly as long as you think. It just takes practice. It just takes doing, over and over, till the brain remaps. Look, we'll start with simple exercises."

Zookeeper complains, but reluctantly tries, at Solokov's direction, to manipulate his toes in completely novel ways. They are uncooperative. Somewhere, deep within him, a power begins to stir. Dormant for a long time, his stubbornly creative nature asserts itself, and the unused potential of his true capabilities emerge.

"Here, try and pick this up," says Ben. "Do it like this." He curls his toes around the handle of one of Ming-huà's hair brushes, leans his head down, bends his leg at an impossible angle, and combs his hair.

Zookeeper whistles. "Shit, I couldn't do that in a million years!" In spite of his protestations, it is clear he wants to try.

"Oh, yes you can. I've been watching you. Get some practice . . . no not some, practice all the time. It'll take hours, not years. Now, try it."

Zookeeper makes a clumsy attempt. He fails.

"Try again."

He fails again, cursing all the way.

Ben chuckles. "I know how you feel. Again."

And so it goes.

For days.

For weeks.

For months . . . of agonizing progress. But progress he makes. His skills are developed in fits and starts, yet to the amazement of everyone, Zookeeper perseveres with a stoicism that arises from some deep well of inner strength, surprising even himself.

One day, Ben pulls Sy aside. "That kid is amazing. Never seen anyone make such progress so fast."

Sy winks knowingly. "It's his power."

"Power?"

"Yeah, power. Hard to explain, but he's special."

"Well," says Ben. "Don't know about that, but he sure learns quick."

"That's why he's here," quips Sy, who dances a jig in celebration.

"Why is he here?" asks Ben.

[133]

"Ben, that one is not for you to know. Suffice to say, he's here for the same reason the hunchback is here."

"Which is?"

"To save the world."

Ben takes a moment to soak in that statement. "Well, that's a big task. He gonna do it with his toes?"

"Ben, wait and see. That's enough talking. You've been a big help. Someday, historians will write about your role in all this."

"All what?"

"Never mind. Just keep doing what you're doing."

And so he does, with Bataar as his constant companion helping with the most thankless of chores. Day after day. Week after week. Month after month, until Zookeeper can perform most of the daily tasks he needs to function. Then, one day, Ben does not return and Zookeeper is left to his own devices. The next day, Lady Oracle pays a visit.

~ Ming-huà Struggles ~

During the weeks and months that Zookeeper has striven to develop his skills, Ming-huà has undergone an extended internal dialogue, alternately berating herself for continued collaboration with Sy and Lady Oracle to implement the Grand Plan, and justifying her participation in such a potentially violent scheme. In the process, she has suffered a crisis of confidence in her own ability to recognize right from wrong. Wild swings in her mood have characterized this process. Recognizing it for what it is, Sy has left her alone to work it out.

Ming-huà remembers reading about pilots flying over cities during wartime, dropping bombs on thousands of civilians without having to witness the carnage, and she feels equally disengaged from the damage she inflicts. After all, she never sees blood, just a cauterized, clean nothing where there should be gore and intense physical pain. In fact, she may be in a worse position than the pilots, because she actually witnesses the resulting mental anguish caused by her actions. Somehow, this seems worse than the pilots' situation.

Yet . . . yet, on the other hand, the news recently reported a kidnapper being arrested for sexually abusing a little girl. Ming-huà realizes that if she witnessed such an atrocity, she would remove the man's penis, or arms, or legs, without compunction. While dissociating him

[134]

entirely would be horrifying, simply and painlessly erasing his organ seems the epitome of justice. Or is it? Her life is getting more and more complicated, and she fears her moral compass no longer points true north. No human should be in this position. Human? Is she even that? If not, is that good or bad? Ming-huà's default position is to think of her difference as bad. Letting her power be developed and used by others has driven her into a daily crisis of self-doubt and uncertainty. In the course of her seeking assurance, she has undergone an intense period of reading about the legal, religious, and philosophical underpinnings of justice. The subject of vigilantism has particular shaken her.

How can one be judge and jury? What punishment is fair? How can she remove parts of people (or the people themselves) and maintain any sense of justice? What if she is wrong? What if she misinterprets or overreacts or is ignorant of conditions leading up to her irreversible action? Lady Oracle and Sy have given her no guidance in this regard. How can they ask so much of her? After all, she is no dark rider in the night snatching evildoers to punish according to her own justification. . . or whim. What right has she? Justice or vigilantism? Those two men on the island. Gone forever! Their families, wives, children—all to save a fawn! Lesson enough to quit this madness. Or is it? Does the fawn not share the earth with humans? Does the fawn deserve to be tortured by humans without consequences to the torturers simply because it is a different species? Kant argues, as an extension of his categorical imperative, that all people must act in a morally correct manner at all times. Failure to do so must result in "just deserts" and the perpetrator suffer punishment through a sentence proportionate to the crime committed. Is removing arms proportionate to attempted murder? Is complete dissolution proportionate to drowning a fawn? Is it possible *She* has conceived of Ming-huà as some sort of *übermensch*? If so, Ming-huà makes a vow not to end up like the murderer Raskolnikov. But how can she be a murderer if she acts in the defense of others? No, no! It is all too confusing! She is torn between the dictatorship of carved in stone black letter law, and the sensory improvisation of Nature's braille. Back and forth the dialectical underpinnings of her emotional conscience and calculating logic battle, each scoring victories, each suffering defeats. Behind this stormy conflict, her power awaits its liberation, or incarceration. Aware of her internal struggles, Scarecrow also bides his time and awaits the outcome.

[135]

~ Anteroom Discussion ~

Sitting in the anteroom one evening, Ming-huà sips tea while Sy and Zookeeper drink whiskey. Bataar, as always, helps Zookeeper, who has not quite mastered using his feet to lift a cup and drink. He is close, but often spills the liquid while lifting it to his lips, so he insists Bataar help him with whiskey, as it is "too valuable to waste on practice."

Sy sets a mug half full of water on the floor in front of Zookeeper. "Come on, lad!" he booms. "Give it a shot. Got to keep practicing."

Zookeeper is in unusually good spirits. He nods toward Bataar holding a full glass of whiskey and winks. "I'd rather just keep giving shots to my poor, overworked stomach."

"Do it," says Sy with a low warning in his tone.

"All right, all right." Zookeeper wraps both feet around the mug and works it so that his big toe grips the handle. Holding it steady, he carefully lifts his foot over his knee and leans down so his lips can meet the mug being slowly lifted by his foot. Only a little spills as he succeeds in taking a sip. He carefully sets it back on the floor.

"Excellent!" chirps Sy and Ming-huà simultaneously.

"Just before he left, Ben showed me how to open a pop-top beer can with my feet. Once I get this easy shit down, that's my next project."

He gives Bataar the sign, leans his head back, and the Mongol boy carefully pours whiskey down his gullet.

"Aaaahhhh! Hits the spot!"

Sy turns to Bataar. "Pour some whiskey into a beer mug, Bataar. Let's see him do his stuff with a little incentive."

"No, no, no," says Zookeeper. "Not now."

"Yes, yes, yes, now," says Sy. "Do it, Bataar."

The boy fills the mug a quarter full of whiskey and sets it on the floor. Zookeeper sighs, but seems to relish the challenge. As he wraps both feet around the mug and grasps the handle with his big toe, he carefully lifts it over his knee and pauses. "Shit, this fucker is heavy!"

"You can do it," encourages Ming-huà. "Think of the reward."

This time, he doesn't quite make it and the mug is listing to the side where Bataar saves it from spilling the contents.

"Crap!" cries Zookeeper.

Sy waves his arms in dismissal. "Next time. Keep trying. Every day you get better."

"Another shot, would'cha kid?" asks Zookeeper.

Scarecrow turns to Ming-huà. "And how about the weight you've been lifting? Reached your lips yet?"

She assumes a puzzled look, though she assuredly knows what he is driving at. "Sorry?"

"The weight you're carrying. Found a way to lift it and drink from the pure well of serenity?"

"No. I am far behind Zookeeper."

He sets an empty glass before her. "For you, it is not to fill, but to empty."

She looks at it with a knowing suspicion. "Empty what?"

"Your doubts. These concerns of yours have already filled the glass and you are just pouring more on top, so the whole thing is just an overflowing waterfall going down the drain."

"Chinese philosophy, Scarecrow?"

"Absolutely. It is your heritage. Use it. Wasting your time on Immanuel Kant. Read Zhuang Zi."

"I have."

"Read him again. You are not of their world, Ming-huà. You follow your own Way now, your own Dao. Old Lao Zi had it right; 'the Dao that can be spoken is not the eternal Dao'. Ming-huà, I would also argue that the Dao that can be understood is not the eternal Dao. Don't try to understand."

"But Sy, I have to understand. How can I go on if I don't understand?"

"Remember your squirrel back on the island?"

"Of course."

"He understood."

"How can you say that?"

"Didn't he scold you?"

"Yes, for what I did to those two men."

"No, for hesitating to leave the island and fulfill your destiny."

"That's just nonsense. I mean—"

"The fawn also understood. Still does. Still understands. As we speak, she is happily cavorting in the forest, feeling the sun, enjoying the

[137]

abundance of fresh grass, full of bounteous life! And a mother now to boot!"

Ming-huà scrutinizes Scarecrow. "And the two men?"

"They are in everything, living or not. The fundamental constituents of themselves continue on, diffused throughout the world in a billion different ways."

"Cold comfort to their loved ones."

"Hot comfort to Bambi."

"But—"

Sy interrupts harshly. "No more! You're pouring more useless guilt in a glass already full to the brim. Empty it and let the future have room to grow."

"What is my future, Sy? Removing body parts from the human race?"

"No! The opposite! Removing their tumors. That means their viciousness, their sadism, their blind hatred, bigotry, cruelty. In other words, removing injustice!"

"Removing these things from billions of people?"

"You are the start. The beginning. The ancient mother of mothers in Africa two hundred thousand years ago."

~

"Hey!" cries Zookeeper, well into his cups. "What about the father?"

Sy laughs. "Without the father, there is a dead end."

"Okay, well, if Ming-huà can do all that with her fuckin' power, what can I do to contribute to this Grand Plan of saving humanity?"

"We are not saving humanity," says Sy. "We are changing humanity."

"Evolution?"

"If you wish."

Zookeeper is suddenly quite excited. "Well, shit! Tell *Her* to give me the power to put stuff back on . . . I mean, you know, reassemble the parts Ming-huà removes. She removes bits and pieces from bad people so they are punished; then they see the error of their ways and change and become good little humans; then I step in and replace the parts they lost. You know, it's like your fuckin' yin and yang idea. Perfect! Father takes away and Mother gives back . . . or rather, Mother takes away and Father gives back . . . ah, fuck! You get the picture."

Sy chuckles. "I'll pass that suggestion along to *Her*."

"Do it, man! We've got this nailed! Shit, give me another shot, kiddo! Man am I smart or what?"

Ming-huà shakes her head and looks at Sy. "He has a point. The whole thing is absurd, so one additional absurdity won't hurt."

"You and I both know it doesn't work that way," says Sy. "Maybe two hundred thousand more years into the future and. . . . "

"Shit, I'll wait!" cries Zookeeper. "Just keep the whiskey coming and I'll stick around like some old Egyptian mummy."

In spite of the silly banter, Ming-huà remains conflicted. Words alone will not allay her fears. To her dismay, she realizes a definitive answer will never come. With power comes burden, and with burden comes doubt, and with doubt comes wisdom. This, at least, is her hope.

Chapter 11: Announcements

~ News ~

At breakfast one morning, Sy gives his announcement in the most ostentatious manner. He bangs his spoon against a coffee mug and rises. Ming-huà and Zookeeper, accustomed to his eccentricities, await whatever he has to say with aplomb.

After clearing his throat numerous times, Sy assumes a solemn demeanor.

"This announcement is one we have all been waiting for. It is time."

The others wait, but he abruptly sits down.

"Okay, I'll play the game," says Zookeeper. "It's time for what?"

"To leave, of course."

"Okay, I'll keep playing. Where to?"

"A place that is many places and a time that is many times."

Zookeeper roars, "Shiiitttt! Quit fuckin' around, man. Tell me straight. Where are we going?"

Ming-huà speaks softly to Zookeeper. "He won't tell you."

"Why the fuck not?"

Sy leaps up and holds an operatic pose. "She's right, I won't tell you. Why? Because I don't know myself."

"Well, you must know something," insists Zookeeper.

"I do know a little. As I said, we are going to many places; we will go to the American desert, to a cave in Mongolia, to a mental institute in China, to a tunnel in Vietnam, to a cemetery in Rhode Island. Furthermore, we will visit these places at different times in the past and future. Does that satisfy you?"

"Sure . . . if was true," laughs Zookeeper. "Now, where are we really going?"

"We are going into the minds of a thousand people. We are going into the past lives of a thousand people. We are going to the future lives of a thousand people."

"Christ!' Zookeeper grumbles. He looks at Ming-huà. "Do you know what the fuck he's talking about?"

Ming-huà shudders. "Every word he says vibrates in my hump. He speaks the truth." A painful ache encircles her head as if barbed wire was being tightened. The ache quickly penetrates deep inside her brain.

"What truth? We ain't going to all those places!" scoffs Zookeeper.

Sy sits again. "You'll see."

"Where do we go first?" asks Ming-huà.

"You know," he replies.

Again, she shudders. "The desert?"

"Yes."

"My mother. . . . "

"And your father," adds Sy.

"What's the point?" asks Zookeeper, now quite concerned.

"Don't worry, Zookeeper," says Sy. "It will only take a short time to cover thousands of miles, all those countries, and tens of thousands of years past and future. More coffee?"

Ming-hua's headache becomes unbearable. She pushes her coffee cup aside and quietly announces, "I have a bad headache. I must go back to bed with a cold cloth. Sy, when do we leave?"

Scarecrow gives her an enigmatic glance, and says in a clipped voice, "Tomorrow."

"Thank you." She leaves the kitchen abruptly with no further words spoken.

In her wake, Zookeeper looks at Sy quizzically.

In response to his questioning stare, Sy's face darkens. "She suffers. She, who hopes to help ease suffering in others, is herself suffering. We shall see."

"You look worried," says Zookeeper.

"We shall see."

~

The next morning, Ming-huà has disappeared. Sy discovers a note on her bed. It reads: *I am going to the most dangerous parts of town and invite attack. It may take a few days, but I am resolved to avoid using my power regardless of the consequences. I MUST know I can control it, even when provoked. If not, then I will return to the island and live the happy life of a hermit.*

~ The Fatal Test ~

The first night Ming-huà sneaks out of the house and sleeps in an alley with other street people, there is no incident. She carries a bedroll, and those around her appear to be uninterested in this new inhabitant of their own private alley. A few grunts of acknowledgement are all she gets. The stench is bad, but the cold wind of San Francisco lessens the sting. During the day, she wanders the streets, looking for the most dilapidated area. Next night, she has found an even worse looking alley, and again nothing of consequence happens. Ming-huà, frustrated, considers returning to the crack house, but is afraid Sy or Lady Oracle will find her there, so she stays put. *Perhaps I went overboard looking like a homeless person,* she thinks. *Nicer clothes would have invited robbers. Too late now.* So, she continues her wandering and settles into another alley, this one even more disgusting than the other two. This time, the stench is not washed away by the wind, and only two other night crawlers have joined her, both male, both nasty looking characters. It is late afternoon, and the shadows lengthen, cloaking the alley in ominous gloom. Ming-huà is already there, claiming her spot by unrolling her blanket. The two men lean against the opposite wall, their legs stretched out in front, passing a bottle between them. A nearby neon sign pulses like a heartbeat, casting its sickly red glow in rhythmic on-again, off-again regularity through the alley.

Ming-huà feels a gnawing fear in her gut, but she forces herself to stare at the men, almost willing them to accost her. The more they drink, the eviler their words and more threatening their crude laughter. Every time they cast a glance in her direction, they start to bray like donkeys. Now her fear doubles, but she is intent. Suddenly, her hump comes alive with sensations and they are unmistakable; these men mean her great harm. They are drunk and angry, looking to take their pound of flesh from an uncaring world, and her flesh is the most readily available.

Both men shamble over to her. Their figures undulate like shadows at the bottom of a pool. Neither speaks. The stink they project reaches Ming-huà long before they do. Now truly scared, she hunches down to make herself as small as possible and pulls her blanket up around her neck, but they are soon hovering over her. Though they are murky forms, her hump picks up fiery sparks shooting out from the blackness of their souls. Without a word, one leans over and pulls off her blanket, while the other stumbles to the other side and fumbles at the button of her coat. Ming-huà grips the fabric close to her chest and exclaims forcefully but without screaming, "No!"

"Come on, girly!" slurs one of the shadows. His shaky hands jerk her upward.

"Look at this!" cries the other. "A hunchback!"

"Don't matter," slobbers the first. "It's got a pretty face and a wet cunt. Don't give a shit about her back."

Ming-huà gives a sharp kick and momentarily frees herself from their clutches. Now half standing, her back against the wall, she wants to run, but is blocked by the two men. The pulsating red throb from the sign gives the scene an ominous blood-like quality. Reflected in its rhythmic pulse, a knife appears. She feels it pressed against her throat. Both men are now excited, and they renew their fumbling efforts to remove her clothes. Ming-huà briefly struggles, but the blade cuts into her flesh and she stops.

Closing her eyes, she repeats aloud to herself, "Now is the test. Now is the test."

"Shut up, bitch!"

She is jerked fully upright and her pants are pulled down.

Ming-huà whispers, "Now is the test. Now is the test."

She focuses on the pulsing red glow, willing herself not to wish harm to these sad, desperate men.

Increasingly terrified at their frantic efforts, she again closes her eyes. "Now is the test. Now is the test."

They are pulling at her panties. She opens her eyes and is roughly thrown to the ground on her back. One man continues to hold the knife to her throat, the other straddles her, his penis now visible in the throbbing light.

"Now is the test!' she cries, trying to focus on graffiti scrawled in white paint on the opposite wall. Oddly, her hump transmits hunger pangs from a bird perched on the lid of a dumpster squatting in metallic disinterest at the back of the alley.

The man with the knife calls out, "Do it! Do it!"

[143]

Ming-huà feels her legs roughly spread apart.

"Do it! Fuck her good!"

In a flash, the knife is gone.

The hand holding it is gone.

The other man's erect penis and scrotum are gone.

All three figures are frozen in a bizarre tableau of horror. Only the pulsations of light convey movement.

Then, the screams. The blind terror. The running. She is alone.

The light throbs in disregard of the ugly violence that just happened, providing an almost soothing beat to the now incongruously quiet alley.

"*You are The Daughter.*" A voice in her head. Its first appearance. She knows the owner of the voice. Now, she knows she is as insane as the others.

"Is there no escape from this? I do not want to be the daughter, whatever that means."

"*No escape. Go back to Scarecrow and do as Lady Oracle says. You have just wasted your power on two fools.*"

"They were once innocent boys."

"*There is no innocence.*"

"Even in the womb?"

"*Especially in the womb.*"

Ming-huà feels the tears roll down her cheek. "Then there is no escape," she mutters in resignation and defeated acceptance.

"*There is no escape. It is your fate.*"

"No. There is always hope. Lady Oracle told me there is an old saying: fate starves at probability's door."

"*Ha, ha! Yes! You are learning, Daughter. Now, go back, unless you want others to suffer as those two are.*"

~

It is early morning when Ming-huà walks through the front door, to be greeted by Sy, Zookeeper, and Lady Oracle. Her face speaks volumes, and Lady Oracle says simply, "Go to bed. We will leave in two days, after you have a chance to recover. Meanwhile, stay in bed. Food will be brought."

Without replying, Ming-huà slowly ascends the steps to her room.

~ A Conversation ~

Two days come and go. Ming-huà cannot get out of bed. She suffers from a complete breakdown; raging fever; conscience in freefall; unquenchable desire for the liberating painlessness of death. Sy. Lady Oracle, and Bataar all take turns at her bedside. Visiting doctors have no solutions. Zookeeper, now facing his own existential crisis, has withdrawn to an inner sanctuary invulnerable to penetration by anyone. Ming-huà's condition declines with such inexorable rapidity that Sy is obliged to suggest the unthinkable to Lady Oracle one morning. He says, "I fear we must return her to the island or else all is lost."

Lady Oracle glares with imperious severity. "Foolish man! Once back on that island, she will never leave!"

Sy shakes his head sadly. "Then, she dies."

"No! Call Zookeeper. I want to see him."

"Why?"

"He is our only hope."

"But he refuses to come out of his room except to eat."

"I know, but he will not refuse me!"

Sy disappears and returns after a long time with a recalcitrant Zookeeper in tow, whose mood for days has not strayed beyond snarling resentment and silent fear.

As soon as he sits, Lady Oracle admonishes him, her mental finger figuratively wagging at him like a strict mother scolding a naughty child.

"Do you know what will happen to you if Ming-huà leaves?"

"Yeah."

"Then we need your help."

Zookeeper scoffs. "She is practically on her deathbed. What do you want me to do?"

"Get in touch with the one reason we have taken so much trouble with you."

"What's that?"

"The seed of empathy and kindness that has yet to fully germinate in your barren soil."

"I feel so badly for her!"

"No! You are terrified for her and for yourself. You love her and are afraid to learn she does not reciprocate. We know you weep for her, Zookeeper. We know!"

[145]

"What do you want me to do?"

"Go to her."

"And?"

"Go to her. Now."

"If I don't?"

"She will be gone, and so will you."

"Let her go back to her island. That's the best thing for her."

"Even if it means you're on your own?"

"I can manage."

"Well, Zookeeper, that is fine sentiment, but that is not what I mean when I said she will be gone."

Zookeeper feels a sudden and frightening chill. "I'm waiting," he says.

Lady Oracle shakes her head. "You know. If she does not resolve this crisis now, she will die. The power inside her is now beyond her ability to direct, or ours."

"Who says she'll die? Send her back to the island. She can recover there."

Lady Oracle stares at him in heartfelt pity. "She will die, Zookeeper."

His extraordinary power can leave no doubt of her sincerity.

Shaken, he mutters, "What do I say to her?"

"Zookeeper, you will know what to say when you say it."

"I don't—"

"Go!" Lady Oracle commands.

And so he does.

~

"Ming-huà, are you in?"

"Go away, Zookeeper," she says weakly.

"Come on, I want to talk to you. Open the door."

"Leave me alone. Go away!"

"You owe me at least this, Ming-huà. I've already told them to let you return to the island."

"I don't need their approval."

"Then let's go. Let's go together to the island. Take me with you. Gotta be better than this shithole."

The door slowly opens and Zookeeper sees an alarmingly weak Ming-huà stagger back to bed.

"You mean it?" asks Ming-huà, pulling the blanket up to her chin.

"You bet."

"Come in and sit."

Zookeeper sits uncomfortably in a straight back chair.

"Tell me, Zookeeper," begins Ming-huà with a non-sequitur. "What do you think of suffering in the world?"

"You mean, do I think you can help remove it?"

"No, not entirely, but lessen suffering. Can I do it?"

"We can all do it."

"No, Zookeeper! You know what I mean."

"Okay, be more specific."

"Can I lessen suffering in the world by using my power?"

Zookeeper looks down toward his missing arms. "I'm not the one to ask."

"If you had my power, what would you use it for?"

"You know very well what I'd use it for."

"Money."

Zookeeper chuckles. "Not money at all. Power. With power anything is possible, including money."

"Is there no one you would use your power to save, even it didn't benefit you directly?"

"No."

Ming-huà is not deceived. "You lie."

"Really! I have no one!"

"You lie, I tell you. I can see into your soul, Zookeeper."

"Ha! Who would I protect?"

"Me."

This takes him aback. It is true, and he knows she knows it. *Stupid,* he thinks, *to hide it.* "It's true, I would," he admits. "I do care for you."

"Even with what I have done to you?"

"Why ask? You know the answer."

"I want to hear it from you."

"Yes, even with what you have done to me."

"Why?"

"You really want to make this hard, don't you Ming-huà?"

"Sorry, I don't mean to. But it is important to me."

"Because I think I'm falling in love with you."

"I have thought so for a while," sighs Ming-huà. "Is it because of my power? Is it because you can use my power for your own purposes?"

"If you believe that, you're not much of a mind-reader."

"Both of us can read minds, Zookeeper."

"It's true, but in this case, your thoughts are unclear to me. I am certain you just despise me, or feel some sort of pity. But no real feeling for who I am."

"Did you know I can also recite some Shakespeare?" asks Ming-huà playfully.

"No, tell me."

"Love looks not with the eyes, but with the mind."

"Yes," says Zookeeper. "Now finish it."

"I can't remember the rest," admits Ming-huà.

"And therefore is winged Cupid painted blind."

Ming-huà laughs. "Then are we both blind?"

"Maybe," says Zookeeper. "But, seriously Ming-huà, can you love me? I mean, look at me! Look at who I am! Fucked-up junkie with no arms."

"I don't know if I can love you, Zookeeper. But I know I need your help."

"That's a joke," he scoffs. "What can I give you?"

"Grounding."

"Grounding in what?"

"Ugly reality."

"So, that's my role."

"Partly. Tell me, is suffering necessary for life?"

Zookeeper sighs. "That again?"

"Must there be suffering to experience joy?"

"Certainly."

"Then, if I lessen suffering, I lessen joy?"

Zookeeper's demeanor suddenly changes. His face morphs into that of a thoughtful, serious man. "Let me ask you this, did the fawn you saved feel joy after you saved it?"

"Yes, I assume so."

"So, its joy was not lessened?"

"No, but the men—"

"You always return to the fate of those who dispense suffering, never to those who escape it."

"And you? Would you have killed Lady Oracle if I had not removed your arms?"

"No, but I would have let the others do it, encouraged them even, which is worse. Now, let me tell you a little secret. If you had not stopped me, I would be a murderer, would not have met you, and spent the money robbed from a dead woman on more drugs to addict more people and thereby increase suffering many times over. However, by doing to me what I deserved, I am experiencing joy. Why? Because now I can see there is another way in this world . . . and I would not have met you."

"We live in a strange world."

"You possess a strange power." Zookeeper peers into the distance, as if observing some far distant object. "You know, your power is untested. What I mean is, we don't really know whether it is for the ultimate good, the ultimate bad, or just more random gyrations. But if Lady Oracle and Sy are correct, it is not just you and me that are involved here, it's your parents and grandparents too. Not only that, Lady Oracle and Sy, or"—he points skyward—"*She*, are talking about us making sure your powers are passed on, for the good of the human race. Now, I don't know whether it's good for the human race or not, but if your power is not a beneficial adaptation, natural selection will take care of it soon enough. Mr. Darwin was very clear on that point."

Ming-huà looks at him in a new light. "Where did you get your education, Zookeeper? When you're not talking like a drunken sailor, you certainly don't sound like some low-life junkie scrabbling for existence among the world's castoffs."

Zookeeper guffaws. "That's rich! Ming-huà, we're the world's castoffs! Don't you get it? Either your power will work for the greater good and give us an adaptive edge, or we'll be goners. Ground under by a vengeful mob of lesser humans. Question is, will we end up like the Neanderthals? . . . or, I should say, will you end up like the Neanderthals, since I am merely a lesser member of the mob. Or, on the other hand, will they be the Neanderthals and you be the successor species to *Homo sapiens*?"

"I plan to be neither."

Zookeeper shakes his head. "Don't think that will be a choice."

"Stuck with you, am I?"

"Ha! I'm beginning to think you are. Still want to go back to your island?"

"Zookeeper, that is what they assume. That is never what my intention has been."

"But I thought—"

"You thought wrong."

"Then what is your intention?"

"For the time being, to do as they say."

"Locked in your room?"

"For show."

Zookeeper gives a deep snicker. "You're pretty amazing."

"You're pretty amazing yourself. You have learned so quickly how to use your feet. You know, I was wrong about you."

"How so?"

"I assumed—there's that word again—you would be forever angry and bitter. That you would want revenge, or worse, go back to drugs and just give up. But I was wrong."

"Almost did, but you came visiting, remember?"

"Yes, I remember. Now, let's get down to business, Zookeeper."

"Okay."

"I propose we go along with Lady Oracle and Scarecrow. I have become somewhat familiar with these places and times they talk about. The journey will be long and definitely dangerous, but I need you beside me."

"Why?"

"For show."

Zookeeper grunts with displeasure. "So that's all I am to you? For show?"

"Don't be offended, Zookeeper. I use the words in a special way. Will you listen without getting all huffy for a minute?"

He grunts again, this time in accord.

"Once I am ready, they will take us first to the desert. To a cave. A special cave."

"How do you know this? They told you?"

"No, my mama told me."

"I thought she left before you really had a chance to talk."

"We talk in many different ways, Zookeeper. Not always with our voices."

"Um. Okay. What's so special about this cave?"

"Did you know Lady Oracle has a grandmother still living?"

"Well obviously she has a grandmother. I just assumed she was dead."

"No. Her mother is dead, but her grandmother is very much alive, although very old. Yes, she is very very old and lives in one of Lady Oracle's apartments. In fact, she lives in the yin apartment."

"The dark one?"

"Yes. Not just dark. Yin represents everything hard, cold, wet, and feminine."

"Yeah? I've never seen her."

Ming-huà chuckles. "Of course not. Neither have I."

"What about her?"

"Her name is Buandelgereen. Lady Oracle told me she is an old Mongol woman whose powers are beyond even my ability to fathom. She is bedridden now, barely alive, but very very active in other worlds."

"Shit, Ming-huà, this is getting too deep for me. What do you mean *other worlds*?"

"Don't you remember? Lady Oracle said we're traveling to a place that is many places and a time that is many times?"

"Yeah, and I still don't get it. What does it mean?"

"What it says."

Zookeeper groans. "Oh, don't you start with that mystical crap! Just tell me straight out. What does it mean?"

"It means something happened to me after that last incident in the alleyway. I mutilated two men whose fates I will never know. I brought it on them. I asked for it. I thought I could control the power. I couldn't. They paid the price. This devastated me even more than I already was. But, in my depths of pain, *Her* voice came to me. Those men were on a path to harm many more people before they die. Now, they are rendered harmless. Is that good or bad for the world?"

"Well, I've been thinking about that. Suppose you had removed Hitler from the scene before he took power, or even when he was in power. Or Himmler, or any of those guys. What then?"

"No one knows."

"Exactly. It could lead to worse things."

"Yes, I am aware. It could. Now, what if a thousand years in the future, the entire human species has this power?"

"No longer human. Either way, they would have a near-perfect society, or they would wipe themselves out."

"How is that different from today?"

"It ain't."

"Like you said, Zookeeper, natural selection will determine the right or wrong of it. Not us." Ming-hua's voice is reduced to a rasping whisper. "Now we understand each other. Go, please. I need to rest."

~

As Zookeeper takes his leave, his intuitive perception tells him there is a flaw in Ming-huà's thinking—an imperfection or defect she has missed. He can't quite put his finger on it, but he suffers a nagging fear that this failing is potentially catastrophic.

Chapter 12: The Eve of the Journey

~ A Visit to the Past ~

"Before we leave, you must first meet my grandmother," says Lady Oracle two mornings later.

Ming-huà is excited but maintains her poise. "I want to meet her. Mama tells me she is a legend. Almost a deity. Is there something you wish me to say to her?"

"No. It is she who wants to see you before . . . well, before the opportunity passes. She knew your grandmother and your mother."

"Yes, I know."

"She is very old now, well over a hundred, and cannot leave her bed. But her spirit is as strong as ever. You are someone special to her."

"I think I understand," says Ming-huà nervously. She remembers her mama giving brief glimpses into the extraordinarily adventurous past of this woman whose life is so entwined with that of her own. In her day, said Tamara once, Buandelgereen was a veritable Mongol warrior whom even Genghis Khan would envy. This woman warrior used her skills to help protect her grandparents in their quest. "But, is there anything I should refrain from saying?" she asks Lady Oracle.

"She will ask you questions," replies Lady Oracle. "You will have a very hard time understanding because of her frailty. Her voice is barely perceptible. She often unknowingly reverts to speaking Mongolian. I will help you understand the questions."

Ming-huà feels painfully intimidated. "But, really, is there anything I should not say? Any subject I should avoid?"

"Why should you?"

Ming-huà turns quite solemn. "Memories."

"Dear girl, the only threads that hold her together comprise the thinnest, most precarious strands. This threadbare life force is as fragile as the web spun by an ancient spider, and its silken fabric is otherwise known as memories. Without memories, she would blow away at the lightest of breezes. You are her forward memory."

"Forward memory?"

"You are one of those precious remaining threads that hold her together, and she has teased it out of her threadbare soul to cast it forward like a fisherman at the end of day harboring one last hope."

"And Zookeeper?"

"Yet another thread. There are none left to spare. She is now naked to the world."

"Yes, I know. I am The Daughter," says Ming-huà bitterly.

"Don't make light of it. *She* will not be happy."

"Buandelgereen?"

"No. *She*."

"*Goddess*?"

"Yes."

"*She* has spoken to me only once. You may believe in *Her*, but I believe in schizophrenia, and voices in my head lead me to only one conclusion: I suffer from a mental illness."

"Have it your way. You'll see."

"Yes, I'll see. Why else would I be going with you?"

"Oh, I can think of other reasons. Come! It is time!"

~

Flying through the busy San Francisco streets, Lady Oracle seems a woman on a desperate mission, as if Buandelgereen would die before they made it to her bedside. Before she knows it, Ming-huà enters the dark yin apartment and pauses to adjust her eyes. From outside, it seems a normal apartment building with a Chinese facade, but once inside, it somehow mushrooms to appear impossibly cavernous. Yet all that space swallows light, and only the muted glare of sun squeezing through covered windows reveals the clutter on floors and walls. Ancient furniture, faded scrolls, dusty paintings, colorful vases, statues, and assorted bric-a-brac leave almost no space for navigating around. It is the eerie repository of ageless artifacts.

When Ming-huà enters Buandelgereen's room, she can barely perceive the withered body beneath great folds of bedding. Her ancient head is propped on a pillow, white hair in wild disarray, spread out explosively to form a circular halo around the wrinkled face. Her eyes are closed. It seems to Ming-huà that the sheer weight of blankets has crushed the life out of this old woman. Near the bed stands an oxygen tank with mask at the ready. Lady Oracle leans close to her grandmother's ear and whispers something inaudible. Buandelgereen's eyes flutter open. Her lips move, but no one can hear. Again, Lady Oracle leans close, but Buandelgereen suddenly speaks in a surprisingly strong voice.

"Welcome, daughter of hope."

"Thank you."

Ming-hua's hump is awash with conflicting signals. Buandelgereen's mind is a mad swirl of passionate loves, deep regrets, angry grudges, unbending hates, boundless joys, warrior belligerence, and so many other deep emotions that are mixed up and enigmatic. *This woman is powerful*, thinks Ming-huà. *Very powerful. Her portends are confusing and uncertain. What does she really think?*

There is silence while Buandelgereen gathers her strength. Finally, she says, "Granddaughter?"

"Yes?" replies Lady Oracle.

"Have you told this child about the cave?"

"A little. Too much too soon might be overwhelming."

"Come closer, child," says Buandelgereen to Ming-huà. "Closer so I can warn you."

Ming-huà walks to the side of the bed and leans close to Buandelgereen's ear, whispering, "Yes? A warning?"

The old woman's voice is again very frail and hard to understand. "There are ghosts in that cave. Many many ghosts. If you are not careful, they will take you places you do not want to go. *He* has minions there. Terrible demons who will lead you down the wrong pathways. Those bad pathways will take you to different times, past and future. You must always be on your guard."

Ming-huà realizes with shock that Buandelgereen must suffer from dementia. "Who is *He*?"

"*God*, of course."

"Oh."

Buandelgereen's voice again gains strength. "Your grandmother, Child of Buddha, could read the taps."

"From the Precious Object?"

"Exactly. She had a gift."

"So does mother."

[155]

Buandelgereen manages to life her head a bit, and speaks with emphasis, "And so do you, child. So do you. In spades, as Americans like to say. Nonetheless, you are afraid?"

"I am afraid of the consequences."

"Go on."

Ming-huà feels disinclined to humor this old woman who clearly suffers from delusions. "That's all."

"No, that is not all. It is the issue of suffering that bothers you, isn't it?"

"Well, yes, in a way."

The old woman asks for water and Lady Oracle starts to put a glass to her lips when Buandelgereen pushes it away and demands to sit up. Pillows are brought and once in the sitting position, she takes a moment to catch her breath, then says, "Now, we must talk about suffering. What are you worried about?"

Ming-huà is so taken with the apparent insight of Buandelgereen, she speaks truthfully. "Madame, If I use my power, I am afraid I will only make suffering worse, not better. Already, I have caused great suffering."

"How much have you prevented?"

"That's just it, I don't know. I'll never know! It might take a thousand years for some terrible result to occur because of what I did a thousand years earlier."

"We will all be dead in a thousand years, dear. Nonetheless, here is the detail you are forgetting; eventually, you will not be alone. Like all evolutionary adaptations, either this works for the better or it does not, and it will not take a thousand years. In point of fact, the human world has unknowingly seen thousands of intermediates throughout history—ones whose powers are great, but not equal to yours. Some of these intermediates are famous, some not, some lived lives for the good, some not. Most procreated with their own kind, so in this lengthy process of mate selection, became a relatively isolated population. Therefore, over time, genetic drift has accelerated the acquisition of powers you now possess."

"That is precisely what Zookeeper said. Natural selection will decide. Not some deity. Have you considered the possibility that this experiment should end now, and I be allowed to die in peaceful isolation so this 'adaptation' is snuffed out before it does too much harm?"

"Yes. However, believe it or not, there is someone addicted to suffering who will not allow natural selection to do its work."

Ming-huà sighs. "Yes, so I have been told. *God*."

"And, all this time, your parents and grandparents, yourself, have all been, shall I say, protected. All of us around you, and many others in the past, have been protectors."

"Others?"

"There are many. However, the intermediates they protected never reached the evolutionary stage you are now at."

"But what interest do you have in creating this new species of human?"

Buandelgereen coughs and gasps for breath. Lady Oracle quickly turns the dial on the oxygen tank and places a mask to her face. The old woman takes shallow breaths, but holds up her hand indicating they should wait. After a while her breathing stabilizes and the mask is removed. Buandelgereen once more focuses her attention on Ming-Huà.

"You see me as a delusional old woman. You see yourself as having a mental illness. You see your gift—your power—as . . . what? A curse?"

"None of those things are definite in my mind," says Ming-huà. "That is why I stayed. That is why I'm here. To find out the truth of those propositions."

"Are you aware, child, of the number of sociopaths, narcissists, antisocial psychopaths, and serial killers out there?"

"No. Are you?"

"I see a world where they increase every day. I have lived in an age where they controlled much of the world. I see no future for the human race as long as *He* receives the drug *He* so craves."

"I do not believe there is a *He*," says Ming-huà. "You yourself talked about natural selection. There cannot be both."

"What if *He* is simply another term for Nature? Another term for the universe? Or, consider this, *He* and *She* are metaphysical terms for two conflicting schools of thought among those who oversee the protectors. After all, even Einstein—intermediate that he was—used *God* as a metaphor for the natural laws of the universe."

Ming-huà does not reply.

"Don't you see, child, the two are interchangeable. *He* represents all the idols humans have fashioned and nailed as personifications of the mystical unknown to a giant tree. As the tree grows it absorbs the idols, gradually developing gnarled tumors as it engulfs them, their mystical features permanently entombed by the bark itself. For a while perhaps still recognizable by their protruding visages as idols, mind you, but eventually, for all intents and purposes, become a part of the tree; an unnatural part of the natural world. *She* represents One who would tear out the foreign objects before the tumors become fatal, and let the tree revert to being simply a tree. Which is which? Whichever you choose, the underlying truth remains."

With this long speech, Buandelgereen is wheezing for breath. She slumps down a bit and closes her eyes. Again, the oxygen mask is applied, and she does not resist. Again, she raises her hand to signal there is more to come. Everyone waits while she regains her energy. During this interval, Ming-huà's mind is racing ahead to questions she wants to ask. No longer does she see this old Mongol woman as demented. A new vista has been opened to her, and she feels the urgent need to explore it.

Buandelgereen opens her eyes and peers at Ming-huà. "Where were we, dear?"

"Deities and Nature are interchangeable. One is not distinguishable from the other."

"Only to humans, child. Only to humans. On the other hand, perhaps, to that fawn, you are a *Goddess* with supernatural powers."

Lady Oracle speaks for the first time. "She does have supernatural powers."

Buandelgereen holds up an ancient, cautionary finger. "Ah, not at all. Ming-huà's power is as natural as flight to a bird. True, it has been nurtured, but more in the nature of caring for a beloved plant, not bowing in supplication to an unnatural . . . idol. If the concept of *God* is inhaled into consciousness, is *He* not raised to substantive existence by virtue of Nature's myriad neuronal pathways, like the idol in the tree. Do you still hear the voices, girl?"

Ming-huà is startled. "Only once. Not since."

"And what did *She* say?"

"The voice said I am The Daughter and there is no escape from my fate."

"Ah, true, true. But fate starves at Probability's door."

"I know that phrase! That's what I told *Goddess*!" exclaims Ming-huà.

"Who taught you that phrase?"

"My mother."

"I see," whispers Buandelgereen. "And what did *She* say in response?"

"*She* laughed and said I was learning."

"Ha! So like *Her*."

"Does *She* ever give a straight answer?" asks Ming-huà expectantly.

"Never, child. Spacetime is warped, as are *Gods* and *Goddesses*. Their singularities are beyond us."

"What is it you want me to do?" asks Ming-huà with an urgency tinged with frustration.

"To start a world where, figuratively speaking, nobody is without arms except those caused by accident."

"Or a world where, figuratively speaking, everybody is without arms," mutters Ming-huà.

"That is what we will find out," says Buandelgereen. "Now, go. Too tired."

The grand old lady turns her head and closes her eyes to the troublesome present.

~ Aftermath ~

On their way back to the Victorian house, Lady Oracle says, "You and Sy be ready to leave tomorrow morning at nine o'clock. In the meantime, we will both think about what grandmother said."

Ming-huà has a sudden thought. "Before we leave, I want to find out what happened to the other two men whose arms I took off at the crack house."

"Why?"

"I need to know."

"I already know," says Lady Oracle.

"Tell me."

"One is dead, suicide. Jumped from a tenth story window. The other is in a halfway house. Also suicidal, but has help."

Ming-huà feels as if she has been punched in the stomach. "So, this is the brave new world we're building?"

"No, it's the bad old world we're leaving behind," snaps Lady Oracle gruffly. Too gruffly for Ming-huà not to recognize a kernel of doubt. "Be ready tomorrow morning."

~

Morning reveals a bright day, with the San Francisco wind blowing them out of the city southward. Sy drives, Lady Oracle beside him in front. Ming-huà is settled in the back seat jammed in with Zookeeper amongst a pile of suitcases. Ming-huà is distracted, appraising and reappraising her conversation with Buandelgereen. Since the trip began, Zookeeper has remained steadfastly silent. Sy, easily bored, reverts to his natural state—royal jester.

"Look," he chirps. "If I'm going to be betwixt and between two women, I expect some compensation, like conversation maybe."

Neither responds.

"You two belie the stereotype of chattering females. Well, chattering is politically incorrect these days. Wasn't back in my day of medieval concubinage. But today!" He pounds on the steering wheel. "Good *Goddess*! Never met such a pair with x chromosomes that are so mute!" He mutters beneath his breath, "Or however many your kind has."

Neither of the women respond.

"Whew! Still mum! I mean, if you're both so good at reading minds, what is mine telling you both right now?"

"It's telling me you want to get out and walk," says Lady Oracle. "And I will happily let you and do the driving myself."

"Well, that's a good guess, but unfortunately for you, incorrect. How about you, Ming-huà? Want to take a crack at what I'm thinking?"

"You're nervous, scared really."

"What?"

"Nervous and scared."

Sy laughs. "About what?"

"About this trip we're taking. I know your predecessors and their predecessors before them died doing the bidding of . . . whoever is in charge of this experiment. When my mother was a little girl back in China, staying at a mental institute, my grandmother mentioned a Mr. Feng shiren. He—"

[160]

"Not an experiment," interrupts Lady Oracle, clearly wanting to change the subject.

Sy laughs nervously. "Whoa!" He locks Ming-huà's eyes with his in the rear-view mirror. "You're actually partly right, hunchback. But it's the wrong part! I'm not scared or nervous, I'm anxious."

"Same difference," says Ming-huà.

"I beg to differ. Scared and nervous means hesitation. Anxious means the opposite. Speed it up! Let's find out how this will work out! Better than the movies."

"*Goddess*," says Lady Oracle.

"What?" asks Ming-huà.

"I said *Goddess. She's* the one in charge of this . . . quest, not experiment."

"Another quest?"

"What else is life but a series of quests?"

Although Ming-huà is secretly gratified at such a label being placed on this trip (a quest—just like her mama and grandmama embarked upon so long ago), she feigns hard-headed detachment and presses. "Look, if we're on a quest, then we're working together, else it's not a quest. And if we're working together, tell me about this cave in the desert we're heading to."

"Your mother knows all about it," says Lady Oracle matter-of-factly. "She didn't tell you?"

"I've already said my mama told me very little, and what little she did tell me, I didn't understand. Didn't understand your grandmother either."

"My grandmother was vague on purpose. If I tell you, you won't understand. Got to see it to believe it. After all, you already consider yourself mentally ill. When we get to the cave, you will be confronted with either the fact you truly are mentally ill, or . . . something else, a different reality. By the way, have you heard the voice again?"

"No."

"*She's* not ready, which means you're not ready."

"I'm as ready as grandmama was! As mama was!"

"Are you? They were in regular contact with *Her*."

"Please be clear, Lady Oracle. I have doubts about this entire . . . quest idea. I have doubts about the existence of any deity, *God* or *Goddess*, even metaphorically. On the other hand, I cannot ignore my own power. I've tried, but it doesn't work to ignore it. Now I can somewhat control it, which is good. Therefore, I follow along with you on this trip. You may find what you're looking for, but that may be different from what I'm looking for. Know what I mean?"

"Perfectly."

Zookeeper suddenly cries, "Pull over!"

"Why?" asks Sy.

"Gotta pee. All this talk makes me wanna pee. We're in the middle of nowhere. Pull over."

It is late afternoon and the desert stretches to infinity on all sides. Distant mountains cast long shadows.

"All right. Nearest town is still sixty or so miles away," says Lady Oracle.

"That where we're going to stay?" asks Ming-huà.

"One night only, then to the cave."

Sy pulls over and Zookeeper gets out to pee. He walks some distance, and finds a spot behind a little rise. Wearing loose fitting suspenders, his fly already open, Sy slips off a shoe and uses his toes to tug down on a trouser leg to expose his penis. He leans forward and relieves himself, then lets the trouser leg ride up with the tension of the suspenders. Satisfied, he ambles slowly back to the car, but it eats at him to know defecating will be another matter not taken care of so simply. For that he needs help. Always in the past it has been Bataar, but now Ming-huà has volunteered and the thought makes him shudder. A new and unsettling feeling of helplessness has set in all over again, almost as strong as when he first lost his arms. That's why he won't talk. He wants to be invisible, especially to Ming-huà. Anger and depression gnaw at him, and they bear down the hardest when pissing and shitting are necessary.

When they arrive at the nearest town, they check in to a motel and stay in two separate rooms, Sy and Zookeeper in one, Ming-huà and Lady Oracle in the other. Almost immediately, Ming-huà's hump is alive with signals, many of which are echoes of some past guests whose traces still linger.

"Where's a good place to eat?" Sy asks the clerk.

"Restaurant here is closed," she replies. There are a couple of good restaurants in town, and one farther out."

"Which has the best food?"

"Locals prefer the one farther out."

"How far?"

"Few miles."

"What's it called?"

"El Fantasma."

Ming-huà is standing close, and the mention of that name suddenly overwhelms her with a rush of images that obscure awareness of the moment. Flashes of long dead presences burn through her mind. Dizziness and weakness overcome and she sways unsteadily.

"Ming-huà, wake up girl!" exclaims Sy. "We're going to drive a bit more to this El Fantasma place and eat where the locals hang out. You okay?"

"I ain't going," says Zookeeper. "Need shut-eye, but can someone help me get situated in bed?" He looks at Ming-huà.

"I'll stay," says Lady Oracle. "I can help."

Zookeeper casts his gaze on Ming-huà with a bit of hang-dog look in his eyes. "You gonna stay here or go?"

Go! Do not stay. Go! roars a voice in her head. Deafening. Commanding. Not to be denied.

Ming-huà is rattled. "No, I'll go with Sy. I'm pretty hungry."

"Okay," says Zookeeper hesitantly. He would be more comfortable with Ming-huà as a helper, but can offer no plausible reason why Lady Oracle will not be suitable.

~

Sitting next to Sy in the front seat on the way to the restaurant, Ming-huà realizes something that surprises her because she had not thought of it before.

"Sy, you say you are protectors, yet you do not have my . . . I don't know, power or ability."

"Ha! Nor do we have the power of your parents and grandparents!"

"But without these abilities, how do you. . . . "

"Understand? We don't. However, beware Ming-huà, we have other powers unavailable to you."

"I have always suspected that. Can you share what these powers might be?"

[163]

"Ming-huà, you are going to find that out tomorrow when we go to the cave." He gives a shrill cry. "Oh, yes! You will find out! Ah, here's the restaurant."

Even before entering, Ming-huà's hump is a beehive of messages, all swarming in an indistinguishable electric buzz. After they find a booth, menus are delivered by a tired looking waitress clearly unhappy they have arrived so close to closing time.

"This place is full of ghosts," says Ming-huà to Sy.

"I'm not surprised," he retorts enigmatically. "See any you recognize?"

Before she can answer, the waitress returns. "Decide?"

"Tonight's special," says Sy. "And decaf."

"Cream?"

"No."

The waitress looks at Ming-huà, her eyes passing quickly over her hump. "You?"

"Same."

"Drink?"

"Just water."

"Okay."

With menus collected, the waitress turns and quickly calls out, "Two specials!" to the cook without bothering to attach the order to the wheel. She plops down the water and decaf, then disappears into the kitchen.

"Recognize any?" asks Sy.

"Any what?"

"Ghosts."

"Hush!" whispers Ming-huà. "Let me concentrate."

The sullen waitress delivers dishes to a nearby table. Ming-huà fights through strong signals from the woman's unhappy but commonplace mood to focus on a clattering tangle of background noise from previous lives whose shadows must have hovered in this place from some distant past to intersect with her in the present. It is remarkable these echoes from the past remain so strong after so much time (their spirits appear more like ancient parchment than crisp paper to her). It is an unmistakable message they have been waiting to convey for so many years. *Waiting for what?* wonders Ming-huà. *And why?*

[164]

"For you to arrive," says Sy. "But I do not know why."

"I'm still not quite used to your reading my mind, Sy, but the ghosts are here, and strong, and they want me. But what do they want me for?"

"I may be of some help. Your mother and father worked here when you were a baby."

"What! Why didn't you tell me earlier?"

"So you could find out for yourself. Seeing for yourself is better than second-hand reports."

"But mother is still alive. She is no ghost."

"Well, yes she is. You see—"

The sullen waitress brings their food and refills their drinks with the alacrity of a person in a hurry. "That be all?" she asks.

"Yes," Sy and Ming-huà chime in simultaneously.

Both ignore their meals. "Ming-huà," says Sy with gravity, leaning forward in his seat for emphasis. "Your mother exists in many places and many times, even those times when she has already died."

"Are you saying she is dead?"

"I'm saying . . . well, I don't know what I'm saying. It is up to you now."

"What is?"

"To decipher what these ghosts want of you."

This statement makes Ming-huà quiver. The signals are confused, contradictory, weak. However, one word rises clearly above the whispering cacophony of the spirits: cave. All the rest is undecipherable. Nevertheless, the word itself cuts to the core of her fears and insecurities. Somehow, the voices are trying to warn her.

"Sy," she says wearily. "It is something about the cave. These voices, these phantoms and their signals, all these years, are trying to tell me something about the cave. I am afraid."

"Come," says Sy quietly. "Let's go get some sleep, for tomorrow it is the cave you must face."

That night, one very impatient waitress breathes a sigh of relief when the hunchback and Scarecrow leave without eating a bite.

Chapter 13: The Cave

~ Desert Stillness ~

Breakfast that morning is tense, conversation sparse, every mind turned toward their desert destination. Ming-huà's hump becomes strangely silent, merely a low background hum which strikes her as quiet before the storm. But her brain is a different story.

Do not go!

Those words had been repeated in her head all night, spoken by a male voice. A swampy voice. A deep, dank, gritty rumble that fills her mind with a corrosive slag of wet soot and harsh sulfur—a nineteenth century furnace bellowing smoke from a thirteenth century hell. The voice is not of her hump.

"I hear a voice," she announces."

"I think I can tell," says Lady Oracle. "Male or female?"

"Male."

"Probably *God*, although *He* and *She* can switch one to the other. What does *He* say?"

"Not to go."

"Of course!"

"I'm afraid. Yesterday at the restaurant, my hump was crazy alive. Sy will tell you. Wasn't it, Sy?"

"Oh, yes."

"Today, it is silent, but now this voice."

"*He* is nervous," says Sy.

"Where's Zookeeper?" asks Ming-huà.

"In his room," says Sy. "I took care of him. He's eaten and taken care of business."

"Isn't he coming?" asks Ming-huà. "He shouldn't be left alone."

"I offered but . . . best he stays here today," says Lady Oracle.

"But who will take care of him?"

Sy laughs. "That kid is amazing. Said he would be fine until we return. Don't worry, I got him set-up. Left him practicing opening a pop-top can with his toes. Amazing."

"Lady Oracle, I hear the voice," says Ming-huà evenly. "Male. It is *God* trying to talk me out of going to the cave. Correct?"

"More or less."

"This frightens me, but I am also concerned about why you think Zookeeper should stay here. Why? Is my life in danger, or his?"

Lady Oracle frowns. "Let's not get too dramatic, Ming-huà."

"It is not I that am being dramatic. This cave for example, and your unwillingness to explain. . . . "

"Zookeeper's role in this entire affair is unrelated to the cave. Your role, however, is."

"Then tell me what I am about to find."

"Actually, I can't," sighs Lady Oracle.

Ming-huà's hump perceives sincerity.

Do not go!

"The voice scares me, Lady Oracle. It keeps at me. Why can't you tell me?"

"Very simple. Because I don't know myself. This is *Her* doing, and *She* will be the one to decide what happens at the cave, not me."

"You honestly don't know what to expect?"

"Correct."

Do not go!

"That scares me even more."

"Which?" asks Sy. "The voice or the cave?"

Ming-huà shakes her head dolefully. "That is a question I cannot answer . . . yet."

"Are you ready?" asks Lady Oracle.

Ming-huà takes a deep breath. "Yes."

Sy dances ahead to the car. "Whew! Already hot!"

~

The road stretches endlessly in front and behind. Sand and rock extend on all sides; a monotonous landscape only broken in the distance by a necklace of purple hills. Ahead, Ming-huà sees a dust devil swirling madly, locking its frenzied grains of sand in violent bondage, twisting and contorting to form a tortured column spiraling upward, like one of

[167]

Michelangelo's agonized slaves struggling to free himself from the marble. The voice has ceased for the moment, and she enjoys a brief respite from reminders of what she will soon face. No one interrupts the quiet. Even the voluble Sy has nothing to say, but grips the steering wheel and stares straight ahead. Ming-huà nods off for a few minutes, and when she awakes, they are driving on a dirt road spewing plumes of dust behind. Sharp dips and deep rills violently shake the car and cause enough strain on the shock absorbers to trigger a moaning, grinding metallic protest from the suspension system. Still, no one says a word. At last, Sy pulls off what little dirt road there is onto a sandy flat area where a lonely acacia tree leans mournfully in their direction, but casts no shade on the car.

"From here we walk," says Lady Oracle, stepping out and pulling on a wide brim straw hat.

Sy hops from one foot to the other pretending as if the ground is a griddle. "Desert just made for dancing!" he exclaims. From his pocket, he snatches a crumpled little hat and dons it in a grand gesture, though it does nothing to shade his face.

Ming-huà stands next to Lady Oracle and breathes in deeply the scorched air, then adjusts her own straw hat to provide the best angle for shade. "I'm ready," she says.

"Hold on," says Sy, reaching into the car and pulling out his backpack. He checks to make sure the flashlights are packed and there are adequate water bottles. "Okay, let's go! Onward and upward!"

Ming-huà fancies the three of them look like a scene from *Wizard of Oz*, surrealist style. Hunchback Dorothy, Scarecrow Sy, and the odd one out, Lady Oracle, who to Ming-huà is a combination of the Good Witch and the Wizard himself. They start off down what appears to be an animal trail.

Do not go!

The voice again, this time much louder and more desperate. She pushes it aside and concentrates on what might await at the cave. It is her firm intention to not be shocked at whatever happens. For her, it is essential she remain calm and draw from her own resources to deal with whatever occurs. When they reach the mouth of the cave, her hump signals nothing more dramatic than a constant, droning hum. Sy juggles a couple of flashlights while they sit on rocks just inside the entrance, enjoying the cool interior and sipping water. Still, few words are spoken. Lady Oracle and Sy seem to be waiting for something.

But nothing happens.

Ming-huà grabs a flashlight. "I'm going to explore," she says.

"No!" exclaims Lady Oracle. "It is not time."

"For what?"

"I do not know. All I know is that it is not time."

Ming-huà snorts in frustration. "This is crazy!"

Sy stands in front of her. His malleable face changes again, to an expression of firm determination. "You will not go, hunchback."

Before she has time to respond, a shrill cry floods the cavern, sending chills up Ming-huà's neck.

Lady Oracle rises from her seat and says, "Now we can go."

~

Before they can take a step, a figure emerges from the black depths of the cave. It is a young woman, quite beautiful, wearing a backpack and carrying a walking stick. *Her* eyes are luminous, and shine as if *she* had been crying. As *she* approaches, no one moves. Ming-huà consults her hump and draws a complete blank. No messages. No signals. Not even the usual low static. When the woman draws near, it is as if all the air had been sucked from the cave and only *her* breathing keeps them alive. Ming-huà notices *she* has no flashlight, yet *she* had just come from a lightless world. Lady Oracle and Sy remain speechless, evidently waiting for instructions. Now, Ming-huà's hump is suddenly buffeted by a flurry of messages as if her mind had been tossed into a mental wind tunnel. One message resonates clearly through the storm: this is no young woman. This woman is as ancient as the wind itself. *She* looks at Ming-huà and speaks.

"You alone, come with me."

Her few words carry an odd, ethereal quality; a handful of miniscule snow crystals tossed to the wind, leaving in their wake the impression of a glassy film suffused with the cold purity of ice.

Ming-huà looks at Lady Oracle and Sy. Although they remain silent, both nod in acknowledgement of the woman's words.

"Would you hand me a flashlight, Sy?" asks Ming-huà.

Sy dances one of his patented jigs and pretends to point a flashlight in multiple directions. "You won't need it, hunchback dear!"

As Ming-huà opens her mouth to respond, the woman has turned and is heading through the icy film into the black void. Ming-huà takes a deep breath and follows.

She is determined to ask no questions for fear of appearing to this formidable woman a panicky child. Onward they walk in complete darkness, yet fully aware of their surroundings in some manner which is a mystifying wonder to Ming-huà. Miraculously, she sees without seeing; rock walls, rock ceiling, side tunnels, jagged quartz protrusions that erupt downward, reminding Ming-huà of misshapen gargoyle faces fiercely scowling. Still, they walk. They walk down endless corridors and across narrow stone bridges formed naturally by the bottomless gorges that fall away on either side. From the depths of these bottomless pits Ming-huà fancies she hears distant wailing arise in sorrowful lamentations. Still, they walk. After what seems an eternity, the woman finally stops and stands as motionless as the surrounding stone. They remain frozen for such an indeterminate amount of time that Ming-huà momentarily thinks they both have solidified and exist merely as fossils. The only perceptible movement comes from Ming-huà's own hump that vibrates in anticipation.

As if a switch had been flipped, the vibrations stop completely, and by the time Ming-huà casts a startled glace at the woman, *she* has disappeared. A black veil drops, black curtains close, and Ming-huà can see nothing. Now, the fanciful sensation of being fossilized is replaced by the gruesome reality. Ming-huà's racing thoughts slow to long, drawn-out meanderings, then to dim awareness of the barely perceptible thumping of her own heartbeats, until they too are doused.

When she awakes from the black void, she sees faint outlines of unidentifiable shapes, and feels crushing weight from above and resistance from below. She is suspended, her body disoriented and splayed sideways at a peculiar angle. Panic strikes and she tries to move, but in struggling, she feels the weight bearing harder down upon; the more she squirms, the more suffocating the weight. She rubs against cold, corrupted flesh that also moves and shifts in reply to her futile efforts; arms, legs, heads, feet. She hears male deep-throated groans, female agonized sighs, whimpering children, and infants whose cries are little more than pathetic, hoarse squeals. As her struggles become more desperate, the surrounding body parts likewise thrash about, as if she transferred to them sparks of animated life. Somehow, from outside this decayed mass, her disembodied gaze floats above, and she sees mountains of bodies stacked so high they disappear into the sky. Layer upon layer of decaying human flesh; African, Asian, European, American, and more, of every shape, size, and color. So great is the mound that all the victims of the Holocaust comprise but a miniscule stratum. To her utter horror, Ming-huà realizes her struggles to disentangle from the writhing mass is a hopeless endeavor, as every moment new layers of dead are stacked atop the multitudes of existing corpses. With each passing minute, no matter how hard she struggles upward, she is pressed farther down into the lower realms where the endless bodies become liquified.

"Get me out!" she tries to scream. "Get me out!"

But the words are muffled by the press of bodies. Trying to push limbs and torsos and heads away, desperate to find an airhole, her arms are trapped by the sheer bulk, the pressure from above mercilessly pushes her into the ocean of corruption below.

"Get me out!"

Never has she felt such absolute, unthinking, mad panic. Ming-huà tries to remove the bodies entirely by using her power, but nothing happens, only the irreversible downward slide to a deeper hell, not of bodies, but simply an endless ocean of putrefaction.

~

"Well?"

Ming-huà is back in the dark cave, standing unsteadily next to the woman with the backpack whose one-word question has just entered her consciousness. *Her* question had somehow sliced its way through the stifling air to Ming-huà's ears.

Without responding, Ming-huà's knees buckle and she drops to her knees. She wants to answer, but her shaking is intense, and her mouth will not work properly. Words form deep inside, but are twisted out of recognition when they reach her lips.

"Well?" repeats the woman.

Ming-huà takes a few deep breaths and clenches her fists in tight, painful balls, but still the words will not come.

"Well?" echoes the woman.

A sudden feeling of outrage lashes Ming-huà's mind. How can this woman put her through such humiliating horror? How can this woman strip her so bare of humanity and expose the raw animal instinct to survive that lurks in her soul? Finally, after struggling with her rage, she weakly stammers, "How could you?"

"You have been given a glimpse," comes the terse answer.

"Damn you!" Ming-huà blurts with uncharacteristic bile.

The woman assumes a rather tragic expression. "No, child, do not damn me. Damn *Him*. The entire mass of dead humans you experienced all died in great suffering. Furthermore, all those bodies surrounding you died at the hands, directly or indirectly, of their fellow humans; war, murder, torture, genocide, and all the rest. All for the express purpose of satisfying the addiction of *God*."

"I do not believe there is a *God*," says Ming-huà weakly.

"Call it what you will, humans have given it a name. In fact, they have given it multiple names. Those that died of natural causes; disease, old age, flood, fire, and the like, occupy a separate pile. No pile of human or non-human corpses reeks of perverted injustice as the pile in which you found yourself. Humans wreaking havoc on humans (and non-humans). Why? One label is Human Nature, another is Natural Law, another is Evolution and Natural Selection, another is *God*, another Allah, Shiva, Satan, and a multitude of other names circulating among humanity. All are the same."

Ming-huà feels her strength returning, and with it, the old objections. "I have heard this argument before. It is as ancient as the earliest hominins whose brains began to swell. What do you want of me?"

"You can start the long process of changing things. Of scaling back the immensity of this suffering . . . this pile."

Ming-huà has no intention of retreating. "How? By removing arms?" She intends the question to be sarcastic, but it comes out as a plea to have it not be so.

"Yes, to remove arms, figuratively," responds the woman to Ming-huà's surprise.

"With this power to 'reconfigure' as Sy calls it, we would soon kill each other."

"No. Imagine if you had been around to remove Hitler's arms? In his case, the supremely delicious irony."

"Yes, and imagine a world where jealous spouses could remove the arms of their betrayers, real or imagined. Or drunken fathers who remove the arms or legs of a disobedient child. Of course, the potential for

[172]

much worse exists, like the two hunters I murdered. I could go on. This idea is madness."

"Daughter, as this power evolves, so does the human brain. The acts you mention would be performed by the current species. As tools brought power and the abuse of power, so too did the concept of compassion and forgiveness. Thus it will be in the future. Absolute power to all brings absolute compassion to all."

"And if you're wrong?"

"Then large brains are inevitably an evolutionary dead end. Your prediction is true. *Voila!* The stage is cleared."

Still sitting on the ground, Ming-huà is unwilling to stand for fear her shaky legs will not hold her upright. She fingers a rock absently and says, "And if I just return to my island, live a quiet life, and die an anonymous death?"

Sparks flare from the woman. "I can force you down all those side tunnels we passed where you will emerge into the heart of every holocaust, large and small, that have afflicted the human race from the beginning."

Ming-huà trembles. "I have seen enough."

"Enough to do what you know you must?"

"With Zookeeper?"

"For a start."

Ming-huà speaks as if to herself. "And once started, no going back."

"Dear girl," says the woman. "It is already started."

Ming-huà has a sudden thought that quickly transforms into an unanticipated compulsion. "I want to see my father."

"He is a shade."

Ming-huà forces her voice to project unbending insistence. "I want to see my father."

"Why?"

"Did he suffer from schizophrenia?"

"You know he did, at least according to humans."

"And the humans were wrong?"

"Of course."

"Did he have a . . . power like mine?"

"Dear girl, absolutely. But he never came to grips with it, even when guided by it."

"What was his power?"

"Turns out to have been the ability to create you."

~ A Question of Taste ~

This last comment of the woman makes Ming-huà pause, but she is determined to get clear answers she can make sense of.

"Why have you chosen Zookeeper?"

"One of his sperm is the key to a lock that opens the future."

Ming-huà scoffs, "I'm no biologist, but I know enough to understand you are talking about one sperm among millions. How—"

The woman explodes in a burst of sparks burning red trails in the dark. "We know!"

Ming-huà instinctively cowers, but remembers something said to her in the past. She is not even quite sure what it means, but says it anyway. "Fate starves at probability's door."

At this non-sequitur, the woman laughs appreciatively. "You are smart, very smart. It is true, there is uncertainty. All his sperm will have the power to create, but each in its own unique way."

"In other words, it is an uncertainty that could equally give birth to a monster as well as a saint."

"Bluntly, yes. At this stage, anyway."

"Speaking of which, what is to prevent a mutated baby or toddler to simply make everyone disappear unintentionally?"

"You did not. Others will not. The power builds slowly."

"You're losing control of the variables."

"Welcome to the universe," says the woman evenly.

Ming-huà shakes her head. "I have read many cautionary tales."

"Risk is the only path forward for the human species. Look where they are headed now."

During this entire conversation, Ming-huà has been sitting on the ground, arms wrapped around her knees. Now she stands and looks deeply into the eyes of the woman.

"No, I refuse," she says with all the authority she can muster.

As if expecting these words, the woman does not blink. "Do you wish to return to the pile?"

Ming-huà staggers back. "You threaten?"

"Not a threat. That is where you will end up—a victim."

"So, you offer the choice of accepting your theory with the hope
it turns out for the best—keeping in mind the benefit of removing Hitler's
arms—or accepting your theory knowing it may just as easily be an
unparalleled disaster—keeping in mind the horror of removing millions of
arms and legs and bodies of innocent people who happen to be in the
wrong place at the wrong time? Is it to be only the limbs of evil people, or
the limbs of everyone?"

"Correct. Time will tell. And time is running out for the human
race as presently configured; a species sacrificed on the altar of *His*
addiction."

"Sorry, I still do not believe in *Him*. We are a species sacrificed
on the altar of Natural Selection and the unfortunate long-term
inadaptability of big brains."

"That has yet to be determined. This power will change the
equation from the inevitable extinction of humans to the enormous
potential of a new, more peaceful age."

Ming-huà is too weary to argue, and the mention of *Him* jogs her
memory. "I want to see my father."

"You are stubborn."

"I want to see my father."

~

Ming-huà finds herself sitting on a chair in some nondescript,
antiseptic-smelling room painted white and green. One small window in
the door breaks the monotony. All else is sterile and bathed in dull,
fluorescent light. An older man in pajamas sits disconsolately on a
rumpled bed, looking down at the tile floor. Ming-huà recognizes her
father from old photos her mother often shared.

"Father?" she ventures.

He blinks at her, and says nonchalantly, "Hello daughter. You've
grown. Of course, hallucinations can do that. Quite suddenly, for that
matter. How are you?"

Before she can answer, he adds, "Of course, it is my motto that
one must always be polite to hallucinations, especially family ones. I was
even polite to myself when I appeared as a young soldier crashing
perfectly good dinner parties. Anyway, I ask again, how are you?"

"I am well, father."

"So, the future is not as bleak as we sometimes picture it, eh?"

"No."

"How is your mother? Oh, I miss her horribly!"

"She is well. How are you, father?"

"Not well, as you can see. Sacrificed myself for you and your mother. Glad to see she raised you to be a strong young woman."

Ming-huà thanks him, and says, "There is this question of *God* and *Goddess*."

Michael's face reddens. "Are *They* after you too? I had hoped *Their* voices would end with me."

"Not quite, father. Are *They* real?"

"As real as you."

"Am I real?"

"Of course not. And since you're not real, I can tell you. This afternoon, I intend to murder Doctor Wang."

Ming-huà's mother never told her how her father died, and when asked, gave the curt reply, "Heart."

"Father," says an alarmed Ming-huà. "You can't do that."

"Of course I can. And I will. A fitting act of desperation for a total failure."

"You are no failure. Mother and I love you very much."

Michael's eyes tear up. "Yes, yes. Tamara is a remarkable woman. Ha! Look at how well she's taken care of you, hunchback and all. No, I can't continue this way. The ending is already written."

"Change it, father."

"Too late, daughter. Your strong, healthy presence before me, hallucination or not, is proof my decision is correct. You have done perfectly fine without a father."

"Then at least give it an alternate ending."

"Once the deed is done, I can't leave behind two endings to my story."

"Okay," says Ming-huà. "Then just change it."

Michael chuckles. "My girl, I have been pulling your leg. It is already changed. You see, I anticipated your visit"—he leans forward and whispers confidentially—"as I can see into the future. You're not the only one with powers. In fact, this meeting has already been written, the manuscript hidden away. It is all down. Lord how that used to drive the psychiatrists crazy. Literally did."

"What do you mean?"

"I mean, daughter, the book of your life has already been written. The knife I hide in my robe will not harm Doctor Wang. No, the blade will not violate her flesh. It will enter my own heart."

Ming-huà's head reels at the tectonic shocks colliding into her psyche one after the other; the cave, the ancient young woman, the titanic pile of corpses, her father, the sanitorium, his confession of murder, and the intimation of suicide. All that sticks in the miasma of revelations is that her father had the power to see into the future. Even her own future. That was his power!

"Father, how will it end?" she cries.

~

"But he squandered it," says the young woman.

Ming-huà is back in the cave. Minutes, hours, decades might have passed. She is unsure. Her head is spinning with a million thoughts and questions elbowing each other for priority. As a result, she says nothing. The woman continues.

"Your grandfather John and grandmothers Meiying and Child of Buddha prepared the way, and Michael was to be The Son. Unfortunately, the organic severity of his presumed schizophrenia ultimately made him unsuitable."

"And I am suitable?" asks Ming-huà.

"Only if you agree to be suitable."

Ming-huà sighs with the tragic gravitas of a Greek chorus. "I think it will be a total disaster. I see a holocaust of proportions larger than the pile you showed me. It must be in father's writings."

"Ming-huà," says the woman, addressing her by name for the first time. "Your father had the power of prophecy, not you. Have you considered the future if it works? A world where unnecessary suffering caused by unscrupulously evil men and women will be eliminated? A world where *His* addiction to suffering is withered on the vine? A world where heinous acts that cause such unnatural agonies are not tolerated?"

"I have. And I have also considered its opposite."

"One way to find out."

"Natural selection?"

"As always."

"Father's writings?"

[177]

"Gone missing for a long time, but now found. They will be made available to you."

Ming-huà pauses. "Somehow, I don't believe you. Are you the deity my ancestors saw? Are you *Goddess*?"

The woman shoots back. "Are you human?"

~

Ming-huà is escorted in silence back to the cave entrance. Then, without a word, the woman turns and walks back into the gloomy darkness. Sy and Lady Oracle rise from their rock seats to greet Ming-huà.

"Is it decided?" asks Lady Oracle.

"Yes."

"The verdict?"

"I have reluctantly agreed to carry-on, for now anyway. But I reserve the right to quit anytime and return to my island."

Lady Oracle laughs. "No such right exists, my dear."

Sy leaps from boulder to boulder. "She is correct, Ming-huà! Even if you go back, the authorities will follow!"

"Authorities?"

"Once you become known, the chase is on! You—the fox, and them—the hounds!"

Ming-huà looks to Lady Oracle, whose rather cold demeanor conveys the beginnings of a changed relationship.

~ Zookeeper Balks ~

Alone in the motel room, Zookeeper feels increasingly frustrated. Although he agreed to stay behind while they went galivanting off to the cave, their obvious relief at his absence reminds him that his position in this little group is entirely secondary. Do they think of him simply as breeding stock? Is he to be kept on hand but out of the way until his services are needed? At least, in the heyday of the crack house, he occupied a position of power. Here?—an afterthought. Yet, he is fully aware he cannot simply leave and survive in the outside world alone. Trapped. This knowledge, long since understood, has buttressed a renewed sense of impotence now that he is abandoned so readily within the four walls of a cheap motel room.

Zookeeper toys with the idea of leaving just for the satisfaction of imagining them scramble to get him back. However, in his current state of development, he would not get past ten steps before he would be confronted with unmanageable difficulties. He tries to gauge his true feelings toward Ming-huà, and can only come up with respect tinged with a healthy fear of her awesome power. *And love?* he asks himself. That feeling lacks solidity, reality, and appears to him a mystery he has never experienced, an impenetrable fog of confusion and conflict. Truth be told, he knows that being married to her would forever cast in stone his inferior status. He knows quite well it is his ability to get into the heads of others and manipulate them that gives him pleasure and purpose. Just as bad as her superior role, he knows he can never give her the type of sexual pleasure others can. With his limitations, she would soon seek in other men what he cannot provide. He feels resentment, self-loathing, and anger all rise in his gut.

In the midst of these thoughts, his companions return.

~

Sy bursts into the room and waits impatiently while from the open door, Lady Oracle and Ming-huà take their leave by addressing Zookeeper with half-hearted wishes to sleep well before they wearily disappear to their own rooms.

When the door closes behind them, Zookeeper looks at Sy with raised eyebrows. "Well, how'd it go?"

Sy, unlike the others, is wired from the trip and twirls like a Dervish. "As well as could be expected! On to the next step!"

"Which is?"

"Do you need anything?" asks Sy, ignoring Zookeeper's question.

"I will soon."

"Just let me know," chirps Sy.

"Are you going to answer my question?" asks Zookeeper.

"Which is?" asks Sy with a balletic twirl.

"What is the next step?"

Scarecrow stops his clowning and sobers immediately. "Tomorrow we return to the cave."

"With me?"

"Yes."

"And then?"

Sy lets out a deep sigh. "A place has been set aside."

Zookeeper rolls his eyes in disgust. "This is like pulling fuckin' teeth! Set aside for what?"

"You and Ming-huà, of course!"

"Oh crap!" moans Zookeeper. "A special stall for the brood mare?"

Sy leaps about and mimics vigorous masturbation. "And you're the stallion!"

"Fuck you, Sy!" growls Zookeeper.

"No, not me. It's Ming-huà you're to fuck!"

Zookeeper wants to react angrily, but only a chuckle is released from his lips. "*God*, you're a fuckin' idiot!" he jibes.

Sy makes an exaggerated bow. "Thank you, kind sir."

"Now," says Zookeeper, his tone a harbinger of serious words to come. "Once this kid is born—if Ming-huà and I hook up—what happens to me?"

"Easy. You're a husband and a father."

"Who's to marry us, huh? Lady Oracle? You? Is some preacher waiting at the cave?"

"Details," says Sy dismissively. "We are on the verge of changing the destiny of humanity, and you worry about bureaucratic scraps of paper. Don't worry about it!"

Zookeeper glares. "Look, I wasn't born yesterday. If I'm to breed like some damn bull, I want protection. I want compensation." He assumes a malicious smile. "My sperm is valuable, is it not?"

Sy affects shock. "You don't trust us?"

"Not on your life! I've been screwed over a thousand different ways, upside down and inside out. I'll not put myself in a position to be tossed aside without a second thought."

"And humanity?" says Sy tilting his head as if puzzled.

"Fuck humanity!"

Suddenly, shockingly, Sy's jester guise disintegrates and out of the ruins comes a maniacal killer. He thrusts one powerful hand around Zookeeper's neck and viciously pushes him against a table, bending him backwards so violently Zookeeper's vertebrate is in danger of cracking apart. Helpless, the back of his head pressed against the tabletop, Zookeeper is choking to death under Sy's vise-like grip.

"You will do this for the love of humanity! Not sex! Not drugs! Not money! You will do this to facilitate the metamorphosis of humanity from crawling caterpillar to soaring butterfly! True, you are just a grub among billions of grubs! And like human grubs everywhere, you spend your lives navel-gazing at your own pathetic life stories. Love, you fool! Love Ming-huà and what you and she can do together!"

During this tirade, Sy has progressively loosened his grip so as not to kill Zookeeper. Now he releases the neck entirely and stands back.

Zookeeper clumsily tries to rise, but the combination of gasping for air and lack of arms for balance compel him to collapse on the floor in a heap. He wants to cry out, "Bastard!" but only a sad croak is emitted from his scorching throat.

Sy is unmoved. "Who you once were is the type of human I would not object to Ming-huà making disappear, or, as I prefer to say, reconfigure. No loss to the world, but a gain of rich molecules and atoms with which to make other things. You, and others like you, are the hunters and people are the fawns you delight in drowning. Look at you now! Worthy, at least, to continue living and contribute to something better. Are you going to squander your second chance, fool?"

Zookeeper has managed to stand and stumble to the bed where he sits with lowered head. "I want out of this fuckin' madness!"

"No. You will go with us to the cave tomorrow."

"Don't you understand, Scarecrow? I'm scared. Very scared."

"Now we're talking sense," says Sy. "What are you scared of?"

"Her, the child, Lady Oracle, you, everything! You're right, I belong in the trash heap where I came from."

"Nonsense! None of the maudlin self-pity. In terms you understand, go shit. I'll wipe your ass. The earth turns. Then sleep. The earth turns some more. Tomorrow, you will see wonders! The earth will turn more and more."

Sy leans over Zookeeper and gently kisses him on the forehead, then leads him to the bathroom.

[181]

Chapter 14: Lessons In Time And Space

~ Perfect Flaw ~

When they return to the cave next morning, there is no one to greet them. Upon entering, it is as dark, lonely, and bleak as one would expect of an ordinary cave. Lady Oracle has continued to manifest an air of distance from Ming-huà, speaking few words and leaving conversation to Sy. Her replies to questions from Zookeeper are likewise monosyllabic. However, after the group mills around the entrance for some time, she suddenly proclaims, "Come. We travel to the very end."

This time, flashlights are necessary, and Ming-huà sees the cave very differently than the day before when accompanying the young woman. Yesterday, with the young woman, the cave exuded a magical aura and pulsed with hidden warmth. It now appears ordinary and cold. Side tunnels beckon, as before, but Lady Oracle ignores them, passing by without pausing or even a glance. On the other hand, Ming-huà is baffled by their magnetic attraction. They call to her in strange and disturbing ways. Sy helps Zookeeper, whose armless body is sometimes thrown off balance by the uneven, rocky ground. Lady Oracle glides ahead, utterly unconcerned by any distraction.

When they reach the end, there is nothing to be seen but solid rock on three sides. Lady Oracle douses her light and tells the others to do likewise. The silence soon becomes oppressive, yet no one dares speak.

~

"I want to speak with Zookeeper alone," says a woman who has appeared *ex nihilo*. *She* nods towards him and walks away. In a daze, he follows. Just as with Ming-huà, Zookeeper is surprised to find he does not need his flashlight. As he navigates the rocky terrain, he is immediately struck with conflicting emotions. Firstly, that he has been singled out has sent his heart all aflutter with a feeling of importance and purpose. Secondly, he is terrified, for from any angle he looks, he is acutely aware of his vulnerability and insignificance.

She leads him far from the others, and his anxious excitement rises with every step. She leads him to a massive chamber that reveals its dimensions purely from the luminosity pulsing from the core of her being. An alien in an alien land, Zookeeper forcefully represses his accelerating suspense and focuses on controlling his nerves. He has always prided himself on never giving in to the foolish excesses of the mob. Nevertheless, his heart is about to burst from his chest when *she* finally stops and turns to face him. In the glare of *her* presence, his courage falters, and he cannot look at *her* in the eyes. It is just as well.

The woman bursts forth in a glowing blue light. Zookeeper is momentarily blinded, and when he cracks open his eyes, he squints into the intensity to see an image beyond his imagination. *She* sits in the lotus position on a huge, dazzling white flower floating above the ground. *Her* sad, contemplative face gazes from beneath an elaborate crown glimmering a kaleidoscope of colors. A cinder-bright jewel embedded in *her* forehead burns brightly and an intricate necklace lays cradled between *her* bare breasts. *Her* left-hand rests on *her* thigh, the upturned curve of *her* fingers resembling the albino legs of a gracefully dead spider. *Her* right hand is poised in the air, index finger and thumb touching to form an almost perfect circle while the other fingers radiate outward. The hypnotic power of *her* stare makes him quiver.

Unversed in the iconography of this incomprehensible vision, he sinks to his knees, completely overwhelmed. Normally able to handle extraordinary situations that occur in the world of the ordinary, he is incapable of dealing with such supernatural pyrotechnics. Somewhere deep inside, his rational mind fights against the onslaught, but it is overmatched. He closes his eyes against the radiance and awaits whatever will happen next. A voice booms out from the luminous vision but he keeps his eyes tightly shut.

"You are a scrubby crackhead who has dealt in despicable acts. You are smart, but not the smartest. You are good at what you do, but not the best. You can manipulate the weak and vulnerable, but are not in the same league as successful demagogues. You are cruel, but not the cruelest. You are kind, but not the kindest. You are a fool, but not the most foolish. However, Zookeeper, you have something else, something hidden deep within your genes, not yet fully expressed because it lacks the proper analogue. It is for that you quail before Me. Be not afraid."

He feels the words inhabit every cell of his body, vibrating so powerfully that he fears his constituent parts will simply break apart.

"Zookeeper." It is the melodic gentleness of the strange woman's voice. "Open your eyes and calm yourself."

With these soothing words, he cracks open his eyes again and peeks out.

She stands before him, still beautiful, still remarkable, but after the astonishing vision he just experienced, *she* is blessedly normal in a human way. Zookeeper straightens and tries to diminish *her* power by thinking of *her* as another junkie begging for relief. His fantasy is destroyed by *her* next words.

"Zookeeper, it is true you are a walking mediocrity. However, there is that one precious nugget you possess that makes you the most valuable man on the planet."

Zookeeper reddens at this unexpected critique so close on the heels of his comeuppance from the vision.

"Hey!" he exclaims. "I didn't ask—"

She cuts him off with a flick of the wrist, and continues, "However, you do possess that nugget, that valuable nugget tucked deep inside your DNA. As just explained to you, it lacks an analogue to be fully expressible. Ming-huà has that analogue. Upon such a union are species transformed."

"Great," he says weakly.

"In other words," *she* says, ignoring his sarcasm. "In you we have the perfect flaw."

~ Zookeeper Broods ~

"The perfect flaw," Zookeeper repeats as if unable to believe it had been spoken. Nonetheless the words give him renewed energy, he puffs up and continues. "Fuck! It's nice to know I am useful as a mediocre idiot." His face morphs into a cunning smile. "I'll agree to this bullshit if you replace my arms."

"Impossible," says the woman.

"Not for a *Goddess*."

"What you call *Goddess* is illusion. A parlor trick. Natural Law, as always, prevails. What you call *God* . . . and *Goddess* as well, are shiny rocks polished by humans to sparkle, but ultimately boil down to nothing more than physics and chemistry. Humans and their big-brain imaginations collect deities like bower birds collect trinkets."

"Very interesting, but irrelevant," says Zookeeper. "If you can't help me, why should I help you?"

"Dear boy, you have already been helped."

"By removing my arms and making me half a man?"

"You were already half a man. This will make you whole."

Zookeeper knows these debates are utterly useless. He changes tack and probes.

"What will this kid I am supposed to have with Ming-huà be like? I mean, what power will he offer to the world?"

"He?"

"Okay, he or she."

"That is the question."

"How do you know he . . . or she, will be other than a normal person?"

"That is the only thing we know for sure."

Zookeeper shakes his head in defeat. "Shit, I don't know," he mumbles.

"Do you not want to be a new Adam?"

At first, he misses the reference, then picks up on it. "To Ming-huà's Eve? Like she has pointed out before, what if we are creating a race of monsters?"

"Monsters? What do you call humans now? Besides, what have normal humans done for you?"

"Good point."

"Have you ever been in love?"

Zookeeper's eyes grow large. "Funny, I was just thinking about that. Shiiittt! What a stupid question. I've never known what that meant, except as a sort of addiction which destroys people worse than crack cocaine."

"Can you love Ming-huà?"

"Told you, I don't know what that means."

"Can you have sex with her?"

"That I can do. Now you're talkin' my language."

"In exchange for food, drink, lodging, toilet assistance, training, companionship, and all the rest . . . in exchange for those things, having sex with her is all we ask you to do."

"And marriage? I want protection."

"And marriage."

"Well, if you hold up your end of the bargain, I can fuck like a rabbit. You prepared for multiple monsters?"

"We're counting on it."

A dark pall falls across Zookeeper's face. "Are you sure you know what you're doing? Are you prepared to unleash upon the world such potential havoc?"

"No and yes. Fate starves at probability's door."

"Ha! Heard that one before. At least you're an honest *Goddess*!"

"I am no *Goddess*."

"Sure, if you say so."

The young woman points at *her* back. "Zookeeper, *Goddess's* do not carry backpacks."

"What's in it?"

"Cruelty. I pick it up wherever I see it and stuff it in here like trash to dispose of later."

"Awfully small backpack for an awful lot of cruelty."

"It is actually a black hole. Voracious. Always happy for more."

"I can be cruel," laughs Zookeeper. "Will it suck me in?"

She looks at him severely. "Without a burp."

He thinks it best to change direction. "Heavy?" he asks.

"Heavy as *God*."

~

Zookeeper knows he will go along with these people. His options are nil. Besides, he likes Ming-huà, perhaps could even learn to love her, so long as his love is not returned by pity. However, the cunning part of him growls displeasure in the background, and he secretly tells himself to bolt when a propitious opportunity arises—besides, he does not believe his arms cannot be replaced by "these people". *If they are holding out on me, I'll hold out on them*, he reasons.

He turns to the woman and says, "Well, all I have to say is—"

But when he blinks, *she* is gone. Once alone, the ordinariness of their conversation is overtaken by the magic, and again he feels overmatched and inadequate to make any serious decisions. Question is, will these fantastic people do more harm to him than they have done already if he bolts? For all his laborious mining efforts, trust is the gold he has never found in his life, only fool's gold. This corrupted vein pollutes the bedrock of his beliefs and cannot be surgically removed, either by heaven or earth. With a mix of conflicting thoughts, he returns to the group, muttering obscenities the entire way.

~

"We sleep here tonight," announces Lady Oracle.

"And then?" asks Zookeeper.

"And then you and Ming-huà make a baby."

"What?" shout Ming-huà and Zookeeper simultaneously.

"You will make love tonight." She looks at Zookeeper. "Don't worry, a formal marriage will be arranged later. Follow me to the bridal chamber."

"It's too soon!" objects Ming-huà. "I'm not ready! Not here! It's too soon!"

"No shit!" adds Zookeeper.

"No time like the present. Sy is unloading the rest of the gear, but your room is ready. Let me show you."

They reluctantly follow Lady Oracle to a side chamber, and when she steps through the opening, the drab rock walls miraculously transform into a gorgeous bedroom, complete with a magnificent bed, antique furniture, and a massive chandelier bathing it in soft light.

"You see?" says Lady Oracle. "We can perform our own magic."

"But—" Ming-huà starts to renew her objections.

"Not to worry," interrupts Lady Oracle. "Just an illusionists' trick. Nevertheless, it will do." She gazes from Zookeeper to Ming-huà. "You have all night. It must be this night, in this room. Don't worry about oversleeping. No one will bother you."

When Lady Oracle leaves, Ming-huà approaches the objects in the room carefully, putting out her hands to make sure the furniture, including the bed, is solid.

Zookeeper laughs when she pats a chair to test it. "I really thought your hand would just go straight through."

"Hard to believe," marvels Ming-huà. "How do they do it?"

"Good question. I wonder, with their powers, why they need us at all?"

Ming-huà glances at the bed. "Should we do this, Zookeeper?"

He shakes his head. "It's really up to you. I'm afraid my limitations prevent me from . . . you know."

"Yes, I know. Give me a few moments. Just a few moments to collect myself. I was not prepared for this to be . . . so . . . soon."

"Am I that ugly?"

"No! That's not it at all. You're really quite handsome, you know. I am the ugly one." Ming-huà utters these words in the sincerest humility, but she is reeling under the harsh reality of what before had been only speculation. How can she sleep with this man whose past is so horrific and who now presents an armless conundrum? Is she even attracted to him? His face is quite handsome, and his body trim and muscular, but she considers the guilt of what she did to him. . . his arms. And his care? Can she deal with that? The idea of sex with anyone is frightening, let alone this strange, mutilated man. Yet, in the background, she is intrigued by her power and the idea of having a child whose own powers will be unpredictable, but so fascinating to watch develop. Besides, Zookeeper is considered by many to be a freak, like her. However, his image fades into the background when she thinks about having her own child, one to whom she can give unconditional love and, hopefully, receive it in return. Oh, it is all so confusing!

"Hello, Ming-huà! You're drifting. I said you are not ugly. No, not at all. You are actually quite beautiful."

"No, thank you but I know what I am."

"Hell!" exclaims Zookeeper, evidently out of patience. "Are we going to continue chattering these meaningless niceties like . . . snobby prigs? Are we going to have sex or not?"

"That is no way to light a woman's romantic fires."

"Ha, ha! Very good! How about this: graze on my lips, and if those hills be dry, stray lower where the pleasant fountains lie."

Ming-huà blushes in spite of herself, and lets out a dry chuckle, but inside she is an agony of indecision. Disoriented by the suddenness of the situation, she cannot find words and stands awkwardly, fidgeting with her hands. Fully convinced her hump is considered grotesque by others, Ming-huà feels deep embarrassment and self-conscious shame.

Nevertheless, she senses Zookeeper's rising anticipation and finds herself warming to the idea.

His voice becomes gentle. "Have you ever made love before?"

"No."

"Look, Ming-huà, you're going to have to initiate this. Before we start, turn off that damn chandelier. Firstly, I want you to remove my clothes. After that, I will lay on the bed. Then I want you to strip naked and follow your instincts."

"I'm not sure—"

"I will help. Come on, Ming-huà, let's make a remarkable baby that will surprise even these creeps who have put us here. First, let me kiss you." Zookeeper leans down.

Ming-huà moves forward to meet his lips, and experiences a wave of pleasure that becomes a series of delightful tremors as their lips touch again and again.

She unbuttons his shirt, and guided by purely feminine instinct, moves sensuously lower.

~ Next Morning ~

When Zookeeper awakes, Ming-huà is nowhere to be seen. Worse, everything is gone; the bed, chandelier, furniture. He is laying on the ground inside a sleeping bag. Only a kerosene lantern casts a faint, flickering light. He wants to get up, but his armless state makes it difficult to extricate from the mummy-like bag. Zookeeper is happy to stay warm for a while longer, but now he has the urge to pee. To distract his mind, he replays the night with Ming-huà in his head, smiling at the memory and marveling at her perfect instincts and dormant skills. When he made suggestions, she responded willingly, skillfully, and eventually, passionately. But now he begins to worry. What if they have all left? What if he's alone? Abandoned.

"Ming-huà!" he shouts.

Nothing.

"Hey, anybody here?"

Nothing.

"Hello!" he shouts louder.

Nothing.

Now he feels a bit panicky. He kicks off the sleeping bag and struggles to stand. "Hello! Anybody here?"

Nothing. He cannot grab the lantern unless he holds the handle in his teeth.

"Hey! Somebody answer!"

Nothing.

After a number of tries, he manages to clamp the handle of the lantern in his teeth and awkwardly moves toward the main tunnel, cursing to himself the entire way. Once he reaches the main tunnel, he starts to put down the lantern and shout again, when he sees a glowing light in the direction of the cave's end. Like a moth, it calls to him. As he approaches the light, he has no further need of the burdensome lantern, so he sets it on the ground and starts off again. He strains his ears hoping to hear voices, but silence is total and oppressive. As he approaches the end, the light grows in brightness and is now rhythmically pulsing. Again, he tilts his head to hear better.

Tap. Tap. Tap.

Zookeeper hears a series of tapping sounds. Now he feels the full impact of terror, but tries to calm himself by assuming it must be the others performing some weird ritual. Nevertheless, he inches forward until he reaches the mouth of the last chamber. Peeking around the corner he sees his friends staring down at a statue. It is like no statue he has ever seen, glowing like some white-hot furnace. The figurine is made of gold, some kind of goddess, Hindu or Buddhist is Zookeeper's guess. She sits in a meditative pose. The figurine's legs are crossed, hands resting above both knees, right hand facing up, thumb touching forefinger, gracefully curved into a circle. And from inside the statue, he can hear the tapping more clearly.

Tap. Tap. Tap.

Sy and Lady Oracle are standing on either side of Ming-huà, who is kneeling in front of the statue, evidently concentrating on something. Oddly, Sy and Lady Oracle are both looking at Ming-huà, not the figurine.

This frozen tableau lasts a long time. Zookeeper is mesmerized, unwilling to show himself and break the spell. Finally, someone speaks.

"Do you understand what it means, Ming-huà?" asks Lady Oracle.

"Every time I think I have found the pattern, the key, it slips away," she replies.

"Your grandmother could read it like a book," says Sy. "Child of Buddha was the Great Interpreter. None of the rest could decipher it."

"And my mother?"

"I don't think she can," says Lady Oracle.

Sy laughs. "Don't underestimate Tamara! She—"

"Hush!" snaps Ming-huà. Let me listen."

Sy cups a hand to his mouth and whispers to Lady Oracle. "Her pride is at stake."

Zookeeper is not sure what aspect of this scene is more intriguing; the tapping coming from within the statue, or Ming-huà's efforts to decipher it.

While still staring at the figurine, Ming-huà shouts, "Might as well come in, Zookeeper, can't stand there all day."

She sounds like nothing happened last night, he grumbles to himself, somewhat deflated that she is not more . . . more what? Shy? Embarrassed?

"Yes, come on Zookeeper," encourages Lady Oracle. "Join us."

"What is it?" he asks walking up to the group.

Sy jumps and makes a complete spin in the air. "What do you think it is?"

"A statue."

"Bingo! Do you have a more intelligent question?"

Ming-huà abruptly stands and orders them out of the chamber so she can concentrate.

They leave and huddle farther up the tunnel. Waiting.

Tap. Tap. Tap.

Ming-huà focuses all her concentration to detect any slight variation in rhythm. When she picks up on the almost imperceptible variations, she concentrates on minute alterations in tone, texture, and timbre. Gradually, taken as a whole, patterns begin to form. They are tiny, but noticeable. When honing in on these elements, she focuses on variants that gradually emerge like movements in a concerto.

Tap. Tap. Tap.

Soon, meaning begins to emerge from the tapping. It is not as distinct as individual words or sentences, but comes to her as might a figure materialize from the ethereal shape of a cloud. The taps now vibrate in harmony with her hump, amplifying the urgency of whatever dwells inside this statue is communicating.

Tap. Tap. Tap.

What is communicated goes directly to her heart, to the core of her being, and carries with it the weight of first principles. A murky, primordial sense of beginnings infuses the message with meaning predating the invention of language.

The tapping suddenly stops.

"I understand," she whispers.

"Do you?" Lady Oracle is now standing behind Ming-huà.

"I do."

"Care to tell me what it means?"

"You don't know?" asks Ming-huà. "I thought this was a test."

Lady Oracle frowns. "Dear girl, what we are doing here, what we intend to do, our plans, your future, the future of humanity, all of it is twisted and contorted into an incomprehensible multidimensional maze. A fantastic phantasmagoria of ghostly specters, deceptive paths, phantom snares, and deadly pits. In short, I do not."

"Ah," sighs Ming-huà.

"However, I do know what this statue is called. Do you?"

"Well, I think it is some Buddhist or Hindu goddess. I don't really know what it is called. Should I?"

"Indeed you should."

"Why?"

"Because it has crossed paths many times with your grandparents and parents, from China to Vietnam to Mongolia to here."

"What is it called."

"The Precious Object."

"Yes, that name is familiar, something I have heard my mother mention, but it's not clear."

"Now tell me."

"What?"

"What does the tapping mean?"

"No, I will not tell you. I cannot tell you. At least for now."

"I understand."

"What next?" asks Ming-huà.

"Return to San Francisco. Rest a week. Then, to Baltimore."

"Baltimore!" cries Zookeeper. "What the fuck's in Baltimore?"
"A trial by fire," replies Lady Oracle grimly.

Chapter 15: Into The Shadow Of Death

~ Destination Hell ~

Musty Baltimore motel room; dark; dingy corners; broken blinds yellowed with age and grime; blinking neon light hurls spears through the gaps illuminating cockroaches scurrying in disco jerks; wallpaper torn; bed stinking; Ming-huà sits disconsolately in a wooden chair and stares up at Lady Oracle who is making a speech as if she stood on the Senate floor.

"In future, there will be no cruelty and suffering over race, ethnicity, religion, philosophic beliefs, political beliefs, sexual preferences, and so forth. Those foolish biases are to be relegated to the dust-bin of evolutionary history. No one will care whether you are black or white or yellow or red or green. No one will care where you came from, what you worship, how you talk. All the books and novels and films and poems and plays in all the world written about human conflict and suffering will be artifacts of a brutal, dead past. Mutually assured destruction will compel peace and compassion to evolve. After all, upright walking evolved first, then big brains. You will take the first step here in at North Monroe and West Lanvale Street in Baltimore, one of the most dangerous slums the United States has to offer."

Slowly, Ming-huà has come to partially accept the virtuous possibilities her power might bring to the world. She has recently taken to fantasizing about stopping cruel people from committing evil acts and bravely protecting the innocent. She is now certain too many in the world are like that poor fawn on the island, tortured by the wicked few who take delight in sadistic cruelty. Nevertheless, when deep into these musings, her better instincts intervene and insinuate grave doubts that bore like a worm through the sweet pulp of her savior dreams. Whenever she finds herself getting a bit too carried away by the melodrama, she applies the brakes of skepticism. But to her dismay, the thoughts intrude ever more often.

"That is a very nice speech, Lady Oracle, but how does a lone hunchback girl achieve this grand shift in the world's paradigm?"

"A journey of ten thousand miles starts with the first step, which we have already taken by honing your power to be both more powerful and more discriminating. Now we take another step."

Ming-huà looks about the room with distaste, and says, "Given the neighborhood you have chosen to take me, I can guess. However, I want to hear it from you since until now you have evaded my questions. What exactly is the next step?"

"Every night, you will walk out alone, inviting attack. We will see if your skills can cope."

"If not?"

Lady Oracle shrugs. "You will."

"What if I'm pregnant? What if I lose this precious child you are so keen on?"

"You won't. Look, Ming-huà, we must test your ability. Let us say this is a field test. Whoever attacks you will be a predator, a person who has attacked before and will attack again. Your job is to give him whatever punishment is appropriate, what is deserved."

"What is it to be?" asks Ming-huà, tapping on the brakes of sarcasm to slow Lady Oracle's headlong presumptions. "Arms? Legs? Head?"

"In every legal system, the punishment must fit the crime. This is your test. You will decide."

"If I make a mistake? If I maim someone for life because I have a false impression of their intentions or motivations? What then? And how do I live with that?"

"Dear girl, you know the answer to those questions. You simply won't make a mistake. You have the gift of insight into the heart of others, and Zookeeper will accompany you. He is intimately acquainted with the darker side of human nature and human behavior. He will stop you if you are mistaking something for what it is not."

"I thought you said I would be alone!" exclaims Ming-huà.

"You will. Zookeeper will be close by."

"How can he help?"

"He is like your silent guide. If an incident occurs, he will be your advisor. He is familiar with slum dwellers. He can also shout."

"So, a hunchback and an armless man are dropped into the most dangerous area in the country and told to . . . to do what? Entice evil to fight evil?"

"In short, yes."

Ming-huà is in the middle of shaking her head dubiously, when Sy and Zookeeper walk into the room. Scarecrow struggles with multiple bags of take-out food while Zookeeper plops on the bed and bellows, "I'm starving! Had to smell this stuff all the way here."

As Ming-huà surveys the grungy room and the bizarre cast of characters in it, she marvels at the absurdity of it all. *What a paradigm shift for evolution and the world! A timid hunchback girl, a disjointed clown, an armless ex-crackhead, and a good witch overseeing the whole ridiculous business!*

Zookeeper has become quite adept at eating hamburgers with his feet, and he sits contentedly munching on a thick one when Ming-huà asks, "When do we start?"

"Sooner the better," says Sy.

"I agree," says Zookeeper. "I used to thrive in dumps like this, but you all have spoiled me. Sooner we finish, sooner we go back to that nice apartment with unlimited whiskey and the pleasant company of Bataar."

"Tonight?" asks Ming-huà.

"Do you want it to be tonight?" asks Lady Oracle.

"I agree with Zookeeper. Sooner the better, before I get too nervous and fly back to San Francisco."

"Damn!" bursts Zookeeper. "At least let me finish this burger."

"No hurry," says Lady Oracle glancing at the clock on the nightstand. "The bewitching hour is not yet here."

~

Ming-huà, at the suggestion of Zookeeper, has put on a nice dress and carries a distinctive handbag, but he nixes the idea of donning an expensive looking necklace. When she appears surprised at his objection, he calmly points out, "If we go overboard, they'll think you're an undercover cop." Zookeeper is decked out in rags.

Both stand in the middle of the shabby room, hesitant to leave. Finally, Ming-huà says, "Well, let's go. Now or never."

"Yeah," replies Zookeeper. "You have to go first. I'll follow in a couple of minutes. Walk slow. Remember, I'll be close by."

Ming-huà says goodbye to a miserable looking Sy, who with difficulty suppresses the compulsion to be with her for protection, but his hang-dog demeanor clearly conveys the trouble he is having grappling with the urge to follow anyway.

In contrast, Lady Oracle looks on with a stern countenance. Only a certain softness in her gaze reveals the emotions roiling within.

Ming-huà slips out of the motel and walks down the sidewalk as boldly as her nerves will allow. It seems to her every other streetlight is broken, and the few that do work cast a sickly yellow glow that serves only to emphasize malevolent shadows. Every alleyway murmurs obscene invitations to enter. Ming-huà stays her course, hoping Zookeeper is close even if he would be of little use in case of attack. Crossing many blocks, a gentle breeze carries a stench that comes and goes as she passes each alley, and the awful feeling that any minute she will be accosted strains her nerves to the limit, but nothing happens. Eerie silence accompanies her lonely figure, broken only by occasional rustling and stirring sounds that drift from deep within the alleyways. After traversing more blocks, she crosses the street and walks back toward the motel. Still nothing. But the alleys in their black malevolence continue to whisper their enticements. Ming-huà looks around for Zookeeper, but he is nowhere in sight. She reaches the motel, crosses the street again and retraces her steps up the same sidewalk she first took, this time less frightened. After passing four now familiar blocks, she pauses in front of an alley which emits the sound of rustling papers skittering across the pavement. As she tilts her head to hear better, whispering voices emerge from the darkness. Peering in, she can see nothing but a black maw. She scans the street one last time for Zookeeper, still cannot spot him, and takes a deep breath. Without further thought, she plunges into the alley.

Ming-huà takes a few steps when she realizes she cannot see a thing. The noise has stopped, and her hump picks up emanations from the blackness. These sensations are confused and terrible. They do not convey evil intent, but rather intense fear, even terror. As she moves slowly toward the vibrations, a flash of light abruptly shines from behind, illuminating the alley with the suddenness of an electric shock. A frightful scream from the end of the alley shatters the night. Ming-huà quickly turns about and is momentarily blinded.

"It's me," comes a voice. She makes out the figures of Sy and Zookeeper behind the glare.

"Step aside," barks Sy roughly. When she does, he directs the flashlight toward the end of the alley where the scream originated. Two bundles of rags form the vague outline of a pair of figures huddled together. As they approach, the beam reveals two people, one tiny and the other full grown, cowering before them.

"Careful," says Zookeeper. "One of them has a knife."

Closer still and the figures become discernable. Two faces stare out from hooded jackets that rise from under a patchwork of torn blankets; one an adult woman with a skeletal face, the other a child in wide-eyed terror. The woman brandishes a knife but says nothing, while the child quivers against her body.

"Don't worry," says Ming-huà, greatly relieved. "We won't hurt you."

Neither figure responds, remaining motionless and huddled together in their filthy coverlets. The knife blade glints menacingly from Sy's flashlight.

"Say," says Zookeeper. "You know where a guy can get some fuckin' crack around here? We're new to the neighborhood."

The woman shakes her head and raises the knife.

"All right, we're leaving," says Sy. "No problem."

But Ming-huà walks up to the two figures holding out some cash. Still brandishing the knife, the woman snatches it.

"Let's go," says Sy.

Ming-huà remains looking at the woman. "Is this your daughter?" she asks.

In response, the woman waves her knife threateningly.

"Okay, I'm leaving," sighs Ming-huà.

~

"Of course she doesn't trust us!" exclaims Zookeeper back in the motel room. "We, you, could be anybody with evil intentions. She's probably a crackhead herself, or hooked on some other drug of choice. Anyway, as far as she knows, we want her little girl for some child pornography scam, or worse."

"But, the money?" asks Ming-huà.

"To her, probably a ruse to get close. Rule number one in this jungle is never to get close to anyone, especially junkies. No one offers something for nothing in this world."

"My hump still vibrates from their terror," says Ming-huà. "I also sensed real hunger. I'm going out again."

"Now?" asks Zookeeper.

"Yes."

"Enough for tonight," says Lady Oracle. "There's always tomorrow."

"No, I want to go out tonight . . . alone."

"But that's crazy!" exclaims Zookeeper. "Gonna get yourself killed, or raped!"

"Let her go," says Lady Oracle calmly, her gaze never leaving Ming-huà. "Her choice."

"You going back to the same alley?" asks Sy.

"Maybe, maybe not. But I'm going."

"Why the hurry?" asks Zookeeper.

"I don't know," replies Ming-huà.

"Well, shit. If you have to go, now's the time 'cause it's so fuckin' early in the morning. Past the bedtime of most murderers and rapists. Nay, but make haste; the better foot before."

"Geezz, you and your Shakespeare, Zookeeper!" says Sy. "I'll follow you out, Ming-huà."

"No!"

"Why not?"

"I don't know that either. Give me the flashlight."

"But—"

"Enough!" bursts Lady Oracle. "I said let her go! Give her the flashlight!"

With these words ringing in her ears, Ming-huà steps out of the room and heads back to the familiar sidewalk. This time, although her nerves are taut, she is more determined than frightened. The night is damp and chilly, and the first faint light of dawn is still a few hours away. Her destination is a foregone conclusion. With the memory of the two pathetic figures huddling together, and the scream of one still echoing in her mind, Ming-huà feels compelled to return. Her hump vibrates in a mishmash of confusing signals. Suddenly, a spike shoots into her mind and she spots

[199]

two males leaning against a lamppost on the other side of the street. They are watching. As she walks farther down the sidewalk, they saunter parallel with her, keeping their distance but obviously attentive. With these two swaggering males, waves of threat wash through her hump and into her mind, triggering the return of fear. The alley with the two people is fast approaching, but now she is afraid to turn back and face her two followers, or worse, lead them into the alley where there is no hope of escape. Ming-huà searches for a way out, but the streets and intersections are deserted and stretch on in bleak geometry. Only stop lights uselessly cycle red, yellow, and green through the darkness. A cackling laughter now floats through the air from the two men following, reminiscent of the mirthless, malevolent laughter of the hunters drowning the fawn. For some reason, she also laughs.

To her surprise, her own laughter actually emboldens Ming-huà. At that instant, she realizes she is no longer the fragile young woman that lived in solitude on an isolated island for so many years. Somehow, a fundamental change has occurred during her time with Lady Oracle and Sy, one that has made her confident and strong. Fear no longer rules her life. This strength certainly arises in part from her power, but there is something else she cannot quite put her finger on. Perhaps she has made peace with the ordeal to come, perhaps she even looks forward to the challenge. Whatever the answer may be, she reaches the alley, pushes aside her trepidation, and does not hesitate to enter. Before she has taken four steps into the darkness, both men follow close behind, whispering to themselves. Her hump lights up with warnings, but this time, she deflects the fear and continues walking where she hopes the mother and daughter await. She clicks on the flashlight. Behind, the whispering voices grow louder. Ming-huà is shocked to discover she actually wants these two predators to attack, wants to teach them a lesson, wants to. . . .

"Hey, lady," one of the voices says in a normal, husky tone. "You don't wanna go deeper into this here alley. There's a mama bear hangs out in here, and she'll hurt you real bad if you keep goin'"

One of the men flicks on his own flashlight and directs its beam past Ming-huà to the two figures at the end of the alley. She clearly sees the knife gleaming in the light. The scene is being played out again, but with different actors.

Ming-huà turns around to confront the men, and is greeted with two smiling faces, white teeth bursting from the dark cave of their hoods, one short, the other tall.

"Oh," she mumbles.

"What's you doin' here anyhow?" asks the taller one.

"I was just walking," replies Ming-huà, still wary.

"No need to be scared. Julian and me, we're kinda like a neighborhood watch, you know what I mean? We look scary, but . . . well, we just wanna make sure you're okay. Don't see many women . . . leastways respectable women, walkin' around here in the middle of the night. You're quite a sight. Anyways, what you doin' here?"

"Just walking. Well, actually, I saw this woman and her child earlier and couldn't sleep, so I wanted to see if I could help."

They both laugh. The shorter one says, "Ol' Crazy Jasmine here is a bit off, keeps her daughter real close so no one can get near without havin' a knife pulled. Gets her food from dumpster diving and begging in daylight. This here alleyway is her home. You're trespassin', you might say. Yup, she's a real mother bear, sharp claws and all, so I suggest you turn around."

"Can I give her money?"

"Oh! She'll take that all right!" exclaims the taller one.

"Hey, Jasmine!" shouts the short one. "She's got money for you. Don't do nothin' you'll regret."

Silence. Ming-huà looks questioningly at the two men.

"Oh, she don't talk. Go on ahead, but be careful. We'll stick around."

They keep the flashlight on the woman and her daughter. Ming-huà gingerly approaches and holds out a twenty-dollar bill. Crazy Jasmine stares unbelievingly, then lightning quick grabs it while still holding up the knife with her other hand.

When Ming-huà rejoins the two men, they chuckle. "You're a brave woman," says the taller one. "Where you stayin'? From the looks of you, it ain't in no alleyway."

Ming-huà consults her hump and continues to receive vibrations that can only be interpreted as threat. *Something is wrong with this picture,* she thinks. "Lamplighter Motel," she says.

"We'll accompany you there," says the tall one. "Jesus Christ! I still don't get why you're walkin' out here alone like this. You ain't lookin' for drugs or anything like that, are you?"

"No."

The short one takes a stab. "You for sale?"

"No."

He shrugs. "Okay."

Trying to ignore the warning vibrations from her hump, she starts walking with the two men back to the motel. Still on high alert, she suspects they will shove her in every alley they pass.

"What's your name?" asks the short one.

"Ming-huà," she replies. "And yours?"

"I'm Micari and this is Julian."

"Thank you for your concern," she says.

"Ain't nothin'. You know, this is a crazy-ass place to be for a woman like you, even if you are a hunchback, no offense."

"No offense taken. Here we are."

A neon light displaying "Lamplighter Motel" casts a pale glow on the three figures.

Ming-huà pauses, trying to find words, but they do not come.

"Okay, you're good to go," says Micari, looking perplexed.

Ming-huà is still at a loss, considering the peculiar way the evening has unfolded. Somehow, her hump failed tonight, and this failure has thrown her off balance. Having given her wrong information, what if she had acted on it prematurely?

"Thank you both," she says, and watches them walk away, conversing and laughing until they disappear around a corner.

As she walks to the room, Ming-huà finds herself greatly troubled by the entire evening's events. Sy, Lady Oracle, and Zookeeper are all waiting in her room, and when she enters, Zookeeper is the first to speak.

"Well? Left any armless, headless, legless people out there?"

"Don't even joke about that, Zookeeper."

"I assume there were no incidents?" asks Lady Oracle.

"No."

"Tomorrow night you go again," says Lady Oracle, clearly disappointed.

~

Ming-huà sleeps as best she can during the day, but her bumpy journey from doubt to confidence has now shifted back to doubt. How had she so misread Julian and Micari? Far from being threats, they actually protected her. If she cannot rely on the accuracy of her hump, how can she be confident she will not take some irreversibly erroneous step and ruin lives?

She wakes in the glare of the afternoon light to find food ordered by Lady Oracle waiting. Both women eat in silence, broken only by a few monosyllabic niceties. This quiet time suits Ming-huà, whose thoughts of the previous night are rekindled by a disturbing low-key buzz from her hump. Jarring sounds of the inner-city filter into the room; sirens, trash talking passersby, homeless mumbling to themselves, shouts from balconies, a few muffled screams behind windows, loud hip-hop music, and the squeal of tires. *At least there are no gunshots*, thinks Ming-huà glumly. The memory of a certain chatty squirrel runs through her mind, and she is hit with nostalgia for a more serene life on the island, yet her new confidence and independence continue to assert themselves and again she looks forward to testing herself tonight. These back-and-forth emotional swings are noticed by Lady Oracle.

"You're changing," she says bluntly.

"Yes, I know."

"You're like a young butterfly squirming in the cocoon, struggling to burst out and spread your wings. That is part of the process. Back and forth. Does it bother you?"

"The process?"

"Everything is a process, including evolution."

"I'm still human, you know," says Ming-huà.

"Well, that may be a bit of a technical issue," replies Lady Oracle with a sly smile. "You see, we might call *Homo erectus* and *Homo heidelbergensis* and *Homo Neanderthals* and the rest of your ancestors human, but they represent a different species under the same genus— *Homo*. Well, it's the same with *Homo sapiens*."

"Are you saying I'm a different species?"

"Maybe. Does that bother you? It is all part of the process. Rest assured, you are still genus *Homo*, so all is not lost. We may categorize you as *Homo Minghuasis*." Lady Oracle laughs at this last little *bon mot*. "Being of the same genus must be of some comfort to you."

[203]

"Thanks," says Ming-huà sarcastically. She tries to be insulted by this paleontological musing, but is surprised to find herself pleased by the possibility. *Imagine being a different species!* she marvels, throwing in the cautionary, *If it is true.*

"Do you want to go out alone tonight, or do you want Sy or Zookeeper along? You know, on a Saturday night there will be quite a bit more activity."

"Definitely alone."

"Why? You know it is very dangerous out there."

"Because I don't want to be distracted by worrying about someone else. If something bad happens, I want to make sure I don't make any mistakes. I have come so far and—" She abruptly stops, dismissing such a thought as brash.

Lady Oracle smiles but says nothing.

The rest of the day goes quickly, and Ming-huà waits impatiently for night. When it arrives, she leaves the motel and confronts a very different environment.

~

Misty darkness has fully cloaked the neighborhood, the sidewalks are full of people, mainly young males looking for trouble. Female streetwalkers are hailed from cars. Sickly light from sickly streetlamps only serve to punctuate the sickly gloom. Before she walks a block, all eyes are on this Asian-looking hunchback apparition gliding through their accustomed turf. She turns down an offer tossed out from the rolled down window of a battered Chevy. What arrogance drives this malformed bitch to saunter so brazenly without an apparent fear in the world? For some, a curiosity. For some, a challenge. For others, a target.

"Hey, bitch, need some comfort?" says a junkie sidling up to her. "Got what you need. Just say the word."

"No, thanks."

He laughs. "So polite! Baby, hunchbacks turn me on. I can give some for cheap, whatever suits your fancy."

"No, thanks."

Mercifully, he shrugs and moves on. She continues walking. It is odd to Ming-huà, but she feels more confident with each step. So many broken people surround her, maybe her power can be used for good after all. Strangest of all, she feels empowered, almost invulnerable. She has had this feeling before, but each time it returns she forcefully tamps it down, only to have it resurface even stronger. This time, she strolls farther than the previous night and turns down a side street that is as bleak and ominous as anything she has experienced so far. To her astonishment, she finds herself actually wanting to be attacked. A cautionary voice tells her this attitude is going too far, but before she has time to continue this line of thought, a terrific force knocks her off her feet. Stunned, Ming-huà peers up to see her attacker but a brutal kick in her belly makes her vomit. Still trying to clear her senses, she feels hands tear at her clothes. More than two hands, many. She blinks through her pain, but a blunt object slams against her head and she momentarily blacks out. By the time she regains consciousness, her purse has been yanked away and half her clothes are gone. Some hands continue to tear violently at the remainder of her clothes while others clumsily grope her body. All is confusion. Crass voices alternately laugh and curse. She cannot distinguish one figure from another. Her legs are forced apart. Lashing out with all her might, she bursts forth in a torrent of mental rage. All is suddenly quiet. A stunned silence of shocked disbelief, then the attackers scream in unison. Ming-huà scrambles to her feet and covers herself as best she can with torn rags that were once her dress. Unearthly screaming continues to reverberate off the impinging walls and echo back to accentuate the horror. She can now distinguish individual forms.

There are four of them. Two sway precariously on stumps. No legs, no hands. Waving their truncated arms in horror. The other two lay still, bodies without heads, arms, or legs. Torsos only. A gun and four knives glint in the dim light. In horror, Ming-huà scrambles to escape the carnage, screams still ringing behind as she runs.

In her panic, she does not see a figure in the shadows silently watching the entire incident unfold; a knife gleams in one hand, while the other cradles a baby.

Chapter 16: The Purge

~ Collapse ~

Ming-huà has barely stumbled back into the apartment and sputtered an almost incoherent synopsis of the terrible incident when Lady Oracle commands everyone to pack and leave immediately. While she takes care of the bill, the others tumble helter-skelter into their rental car. Sy idles the car, waiting impatiently for Lady Oracle, and when she arrives, he immediately pulls out of the parking lot and speeds off without knowing what direction he is going.

"Slow down," says Lady Oracle calmly. "Now is not a good time for a ticket."

"Where to?" asks Sy.

"Airport."

In the back seat, Ming-huà begins to hyper-ventilate, and Zookeeper does his best to soothe her panic.

"No sweat," Zookeeper says. "All the cops know is that a hunchback was attacked. The fact that there will be no blood or any evidence of a crime being committed will confuse the shit out of them. Besides, how could a hunchback woman take out four kick-ass men?"

Ming-huà moans in agony.

"Now is not the time, Zookeeper" says Lady Oracle.

"Ming-huà, dear girl, try and calm yourself," says Sy. "You acted in self-defense. You did what you had to do. You did what we came here for."

"To kill two men and maim two others?" She barely gets the words out without choking on them.

"Zookeeper is right," says Lady Oracle. "This has been anticipated. I was hoping to keep it not quite so . . . extreme. But we will return to San Francisco and do further work."

"No!" screams Ming-huà. "I'm going back to the island. Enough of this madness! No more!"

"Ming-huà, you defended yourself from being raped and very probably murdered. You did nothing wrong. In fact, you have proven the point, albeit quite dramatically."

"What point?" cries Ming-huà.

"You are not of their kind. Like it or not, you are the next step. All that remains is to learn to exert more control in extreme situations. Just as consciousness, self-awareness of their inevitably mortality, and conscience evolved, humans had to learn to somehow tame them. Thus, legal codes. Your legal code will be imprinted into your brain. Your verdict will be instantaneous and just. It will be passed down even more precisely. Thus, your child."

"Is this enough justification to kill two men and maim two others?"

"Control, Ming-huà. We will work with you so you learn to control your power more . . . well, as I said, more precisely. And you will learn to do it in extreme and fluid situations that leave almost no time for thought. In any case, those four predators will not again prey on innocent people."

"No. I am returning to my island. This has to end. I can't survive this."

"You will have to deal with a child whose powers will likely exceed yours. Or do you want an abortion if you're pregnant?"

"That will be my decision, not yours."

"Granted. Let me ask you this, why do your powers not work on me or Sy?"

"I don't know. Something to do with this *Goddess* business."

"We're here," says Sy stopping in front of the terminal building. "Go on in and get the luggage checked while I park. I assume we all have our open return tickets?"

With a unanimous confirmation, Lady Oracle mutters, "I hope so. It was next to impossible to get them."

Ming-huà has calmed, but the tears will not stop. "So that's why you took such trouble to get open return tickets—you knew this would happen! I'm warning you that when we get back to San Francisco, I'm leaving for the island. No amount of argument will convince me otherwise."

"We shall see," says Lady Oracle grimly.

During this conversation, Zookeeper has kept silent, but his anger now burst out. "Shit! No one in this fuckin' car is thinking of me! It's also my baby that might be cooking in Ming-huà's belly! Mine! If she goes, I go with her! I fuckin' like the idea of being the father of a new species."

Although Ming-huà is clearly distressed at his words, she says, "Of course, you are welcome to come with me."

Zookeeper laughs. "Wonder what those poor cops are thinking now? They're probably shitting their pants."

"Please, no more," pleads Ming-huà.

"Yes, be quiet Zookeeper!" snaps Lady Oracle. "From now on, try being more Shakespeare and less Zookeeper. And speaking of the police, let's go now!"

~

During the flight back to San Francisco, none speaks, each lost in their own thoughts, each confronting their own hopes and fears, all except one. Lady Oracle sits stolidly, an enigmatic smile painted on her face. When eye-contact is made, she smiles even more, much to Ming-huà's consternation. After arriving in San Francisco, they stumble into the mansion bone-weary and loath to say much more than "Goodnight." Next morning at breakfast, Ming-huà repeats her intention to immediately return to the island. Sy starts to protest, but Lady Oracle stops him.

"There is a law in physics," she says, directing her gaze at Ming-huà. "The law states that nothing, or should I say nothingness, is not what it seems. If you construct a perfect vacuum so there are no sub-atomic particles and reduce the temperature to absolute zero, then one presumably has created nothingness. No particles, no motion, no energy, just nothing. However, quantum physics tells us this is impossible due to virtual fluctuations in which particles pop in and out of existence, always leaving at least a little heat or energy remaining out of nothing. To create absolute nothingness would violate Heisenberg's uncertainty principle. Humans, at least, arrived at this elementary level. Okay, so far so good. You, my dear, are the closest to perfect nothingness, the closest to being utterly and completely still and pristinely unmoving. Some argue only *God* can violate this principle of perfect stillness. Or *Goddess*. Only the position and momentum of deities can be measured simultaneously, because they dwell in a realm outside the laws of physics. Call it superstition, faith, or delusion. It is none of these; it is simply a metaphor for that beyond your

[208]

imaginings. Now, listen well. You have a gift no other entity on the planet has. Evolution has crafted you in such a way as to attain almost perfect nothingness. Almost, but for those virtual particles popping in and out of existence, giving you brief glimpses into the thoughts and emotions of others (your father could hear the voices of sidewalks and dogs). When you use your gift, that power of nothingness is projected onto the world. What it touches remains no longer in this existence, other than the tiny constituent particles left behind that disperse into the air. Whether you retreat to your island or not is irrelevant. More importantly, your child will inherit your power in ways we do not know and cannot predict. If you do not learn to use your power, your child will be adrift in a sea of calamity. You must learn! You must immerse yourself in this world! You must hone your power to use for just causes! Failure to take on this responsibility will result in the eventual demise of humanity, bound to disappear in self-inflicted extinction. Worse, they will take countless other species with them. To learn, you must be of the world with all its messiness and chaos and unpredictability. Learn to use your gift, or die as your future child will die, at the hands of an angry, frightened, and ignorant mob."

"I'm pregnant," Ming-huà says in a hollow voice. She stands up nervously and fidgets with clearing her dishes.

Lady Oracle cannot suppress her excitement. "Are you sure?"

"I'm sure."

"But that is excellent news!" Lady Oracle exclaims, her face aglow with pleasure.

"No!" blurts Ming-huà. "I'm no longer sure it is good news. What am I bringing into the world?"

"You are one of the first steps; this child will be the next."

"Yes, but they are steps leading toward what?"

"The future."

"And my parents and grandparents?"

"Precursors," says Lady Oracle curtly.

Ming-huà blinks in anger. "Precursors? Is that all? Did the hell they went through qualify them to be nothing more than useful little steps in your grand progression?"

"But, of course, it is not my grand progression. Evolution, chemistry, natural selection, all lead the way. The steps reside in your genes, not your mind."

[209]

Ming-huà scoffs. "I repeat, steps toward what?"

Lady Oracle stares deeply into Ming-huà's eyes. "Adaptation. Fitness. Salvation"

"Salvation to you, damnation to me."

"No, salvation to life on earth. Damnation to needless suffering."

"And the corpses and half-men I left behind in the past, or those I will leave behind in the future?"

"As I said, damnation to those who cause needless suffering."

"Lady Oracle, I am not up to being the salvation or the damnation of anyone or anything. You are looking for a new species, I am looking for peace and tranquility."

"Ming-huà!" Lady Oracle lashes out. "I am not looking for a new species, I have found a new species! Do you want to squander this golden chance for humankind to advance? Do you want unnecessary suffering and useless devastation to continue? Do you want *Him* to win, the Vengeful Godhead?"

Ming-huà shakes her head dubiously and paces like a caged animal. "So, we are back to this battle between *Goddess* and *God*? Those are figments of a schizophrenic's mind. Fantasies. They drove my father mad. They drove him to suicide. They are not my responsibility."

Lady Oracle draws herself up and assumes an intimidating air. "Then leave! Go! Flee to your isolated island. Isolate yourself. Grow old and die a lonely old woman whose child will be left without direction because you will not know what direction to give."

"I will have Zookeeper," says Ming-huà feebly.

Lady Oracle laughs heartily. "Go! Take him with you! Leave this world behind, trapped in the suffocating mire humans have made of it, and thanks to you, will continue to make of it until it is no more."

"I cannot change the world."

"Foolish girl! You are the change! Tell the first *Homo sapiens* to evolve in Africa they did not change the world."

"Nothing you can say will stop me from leaving," insists Ming-huà. But her words falter, and everyone in the room feels her uncertainties and anxieties wash over them.

"Go," repeats Lady Oracle. "Run to your island and see what peace you find."

[210]

Ming-huà hesitates, and looks at Sy whose face is unspeakably sad, tears running down his cheeks. She turns to Zookeeper who looks on with a grim countenance.

"What should I do?" she asks Zookeeper.

"Do what you think is right."

"But, right for who?" she pleads. "Me? Humanity? You? this child?"

"Yes," replies Zookeeper.

"Zookeeper," she says. "You are the closest of all in this room to the violent world of degenerate humankind. You know their propensities for vile addictions and murderous rages. I owe you the most. I took your arms. I beg you answer me honestly, should I stay?"

He does not waver. "Yes."

Ming-huà reels backward a step as if physically struck. "But . . . I thought . . . why?"

"If there is a chance to change this bullshit world—no, let me be as eloquent as you. If there is a chance to alter the trajectory of our species and create a new age of enlightenment, then I say you should stay and try."

While Ming-huà processes his words, Zookeeper adds in forced levity, "Besides, I ain't no fuckin' hillbilly suited for living in the woods."

Lady Oracle speaks in a low, husky voice. "Correction, Zookeeper. She is not changing the trajectory of your *species*, she is changing the trajectory of your *genus*."

Zookeeper feels the hairs on his head tingle. "What do you mean '*your* species' and '*your* genus'?"

"A figure of speech."

"Look," says Zookeeper brusquely. "Who the fuck are you? Better yet, what the fuck are you?"

"I am no different than you."

"Bullshit! Tell me, tell us, the truth!"

"The only truth lies in nothingness. All else is deception. Your lost arms are dwelling where there is truth."

"Goddamn it! Speak English! None of these fuckin' riddles!"

Lady Oracle smiles. "Get used to them."

"Forget it, Zookeeper," says Ming-huà. "You'll never get a straight answer. I've heard things they didn't want me to know. My mother had conversations with herself about my father, and I listened. She told me things in moments of weakness. I'm starting to remember. I'm beginning to understand."

"Well, shit, I'm not," says Zookeeper. "What do you understand?"

"I understand, or I'm beginning to understand. You're right. I should stay . . . no, I have to stay."

"Because of what I said?"

"No, because of what she is." Ming-huà points at Lady Oracle. "Her grandmother is Buandelgereen, at least that's the story my mother told me. Now, yes, now I'm beginning to understand."

"Shit, Ming-huà, you're starting to scare the shit outta me. What is she?"

Ming-huà speaks as if she had not heard his words. "Sy also. Both of them. The stories are coming back. I always thought my mother never spoke about the past, but now I realize she did. Strange stories about quests and tunnels and caves and iron doors. Names come up from the depths. Names like Feng shiren. Odd names. Storyteller, Nature, Han Tinh, Mountain Man, Tuyet Mai, and so many others. Yes, she talked sometimes as if in her sleep, and I listened. Can't quite put it together yet, but it's coming back slowly."

"Now you know why it is imperative you stay?" asks Lady Oracle.

"Now I know."

~ Resurrection and Return ~

In the months after returning to San Francisco, Ming-huà feels her power growing stronger. Her ability to translate the messages her hump picks up from the environment are growing as well. This growth has given her a sense of euphoria that has all but obliterated the shy, innocent girl who once played with Miss Gladflower. She has even taken a serious interest in further developing her empathic and extra sensory perception abilities, challenging herself to converse with inanimate objects like her father could. Nothing is immune from her attempts to establish communication; sidewalks, trees, rocks, and a host of other entities. Sy and Zookeeper have conspired to throw ever more startling surprises her way when she least expects them. They often travel to the nearby mountains where Lady Oracle challenges her to dissociate a bullet before it hits its target, even though she is not alerted to when it is fired. Her success is hit and miss, but she achieves more hits than misses as time

[212]

passes. Gradually, even when utterly shocked by some elaborate ruse, she succeeds in controlling her power to its maximum effect at minimum damage. Stoshells have become child's play. These are halcyon days for Ming-huà. Since she is not subjected to the dangers of street life, this training period is a confidence-building series of harmless, even enjoyable challenges. Guilt recedes, but it is never completely gone.

One day, Sy gets carried away and creeps up behind her and swings a bat at her head, fully expecting it to dissociate in his hands. However, it lands a hard blow and knocks her to the floor. Stunned, Sy kneels over her crying, "Oh, *God*! Ming-huà, are you okay? What have I done! Are you okay?"

But she does not respond and he calls for help.

Lady Oracle rushes into the room and they lay her on the couch.

"Should I call Altan?" asks Sy.

"No! She is only knocked out. I can feel the knot rising on the back of her head. She'll come around. How did it happen?"

When Sy explains, Lady Oracle laughs. "Live and learn. It is an important lesson. Perhaps she felt your presence and your intent, but ignored it assuming you would not carry through. Or worse, she did not pick any of it up."

"You were right the first time," says Ming-huà a bit groggily. "I knew he was there, but ignored the signs. It is entirely my fault. Ouch! It hurts!"

"Never assume, girl!" scolds Lady Oracle. "You could easily have been killed. Remember: simplicity without flourishes! Threatening signals are to be ignored at your peril."

"But I knew it was only Sy."

"She that increaseth knowledge increaseth sorrow."

"That's fuckin' right!" pipes in Zookeeper. "Can't trust anyone, especially in your position. There's no trust, no faith, no honesty in men; all perjured, all forsworn, all naught, all dissemblers."

Ming-huà vows to never again allow Sy, Zookeeper or anyone else to take her by surprise.

~

As all good things must end, one morning Lady Oracle announces the termination of the training period. After making this curt proclamation, she falls silent.

[213]

"Well?" asks Ming-huà. "What now?"

"You won't like it."

Ming-huà has visions of being transported to the vilest neighborhoods in America, and is afraid to ask more. Zookeeper, however, is not so restrained.

"Come on!" he cries. "Tell us goddammit!"

Lady Oracle laughs. "So impatient!"

"Damn right I'm impatient! I want to know what shithole your gonna to send us to."

Lady Oracle looks at Ming-huà. "And you? Are you also impatient to know what comes next?"

"Somehow I think this is a trap, but yes, I want to know. Tell us."

"Okay, here it is. We wait."

"What? After all this training shit! We wait?"

Lady Oracle nods her head toward Ming-huà. "Look at her. We cannot risk the pregnancy."

"Good," says Ming-huà. "But what about after the baby is born?"

"When that time comes, we'll decide how to proceed. The baby must take first priority. First let us ensure it is born healthy, then let us have time to observe it."

"Maybe you should rephrase that," says an angry Ming-huà. "I agree the baby must take first priority, but not because we must observe it, rather because we must take time to love and nurture it."

"I agree," pops in Zookeeper.

"And so we will, dear boy. This baby will be surrounded by love and something else as well."

"What?"

"Curiosity."

"Ah, yes," says Ming-huà sarcastically. "We must be good little scientists, or guides, or whatever, and always observe the little freak to see just how freakish it might turn out to be."

"No," says Lady Oracle. "This baby will be no freak. And trust me, it will receive ample amounts of what you call love."

~

Back in her room, Ming-huà feels euphoric. Her pregnancy is proceeding well, the baby is to be kept safe, and there are no plans for plunging her into dangerous environments. Her physical surroundings are pleasant, even luxurious. It is in this frame of mind that the low rumble of a threatening voice shakes her out of her complacency with shocking and unnerving suddenness.

You must flee this place! For your baby's sake, you must escape before it is too late!

Before Ming-huà has time to react, a feminine voice exclaims, *Hush! Do not listen to this frightened, pathetic God! He lies to you!*

Abruptly, the voices are gone, leaving a faint echo to mark their passing. Were it not for these echoes, Ming-huà would chalk the voices up to an overactive imagination. However, the words have reverberated their way into her hump, which lights up in a frenzy of warning signals. Which of the two voices to believe? The male? Female? Neither?

The pleasant bath of contentment in which Ming-huà had been luxuriating turns cold and acidic. Worse, she has now experienced the war between *God* and *Goddess* firsthand, which she had always dismissed as the delusional fantasy of her schizophrenic father.

Once again, the solitude and serenity of the island beckons. To divert her mind from these disturbing thoughts, she imagines all the myriad ways this child might reveal its powers to the world.

Chapter 17: The Child

~ Mental Warfare ~

As the due date draws near, Ming-huà has had to face increasingly disturbing phenomena. One unanticipated instance is the non-stop and rapidly accelerating growth of articulate communication by the fetus through Ming-huà's hump and into her brain. Daily, its messages grow more insistent and demanding, and their content more frighteningly sophisticated. Another is the terrifying increase in the frequency and escalating volume of the outraged voices of *God* and *Goddess* as her time approaches. When the voices argue, the fetus becomes upset, and flails about both physically and in the tangled messages it sends. Ming-huà is aware of research indicating the threshold of conscious thinking arises in a normal child at about five months after birth, but she is convinced this fetus is already conscious. Unfortunately, though she is aware the fetus is communicating, it is in an undecipherable language, one that baffles her most determined efforts to crack its code. As she grapples with the colossal implications of this alien life assembling itself within her body, she alternates between immense joy, anticipatory fear, and debilitating depression. In the process of becoming fully formed, the swiftly developing fetus is diverging from Ming-huà's conception of what is recognizably human. Instead, it is becoming more foreign by the minute. This realization scares her most of all. If the mother is indeed a new, emerging species, would not this fetus be of the same kind, and thereby not so strange, so incomprehensible? Yet its burgeoning consciousness invades her hump with hieroglyphic complexity beyond her power to interpret. Her grandmother, Child of Buddha, could interpret the taps from the Precious Object, but this strange. . . .

"What troubles you?" asks Lady Oracle.

They sit together in the anteroom where so many ghosts from the past reside.

"Many things."

[216]

"Such as?"

Ming-huà speaks bitterly. "I do not understand this concept of *Goddess*. I do not understand this concept of *God*. You must tell me truthfully, are They real or am I as sick as my father and grandfather?"

"They are as real as the neural pathways giving Them the power of existence. Please remember, neither your father nor your grandfather were what humans labeled schizophrenic."

Ming-huà glares. "I am asking; are they real or not?"

Lady Oracle blinks placidly in the face of Ming-hua's vehemence. "What else worries you?"

"I give up trying to get a straight answer out of you!" Ming-huà exclaims. "Why should I share my concerns with a Sphinx? All I get in return are riddles . . . and don't tell me life is a riddle!"

"I will."

Ming-huà has to laugh at this farcical response. "Okay, I give up, but I'll tell you anyway because I have no one else to confide in."

She trembles, her lip quivers, and Ming-huà seems on the verge of sobbing, but she collects herself and continues. "It is the fetus within me. I am afraid."

For the first time, Ming-huà sees uncertainty in the eyes of Lady Oracle.

"Why are you afraid?"

"Because this child is so different, so foreign."

"All pregnant mothers have times when they feel that way."

"You don't understand. My hump, the truest guide of my life, tells me this is no ordinary child."

Lady Oracle laughs weakly. "Of course, we know that."

"Again, you mistake my words. This child is not developing in any sense I understand. What I mean is that I was prepared for some recognizable difference, something more in the mold of my own . . . power, if you will. But. . . . "

"You are worried about what it may turn out to be?"

"We chose to not find out whether it is a boy or girl, but the 'it' part of your designation is what worries me. What if the child turns out to be so far beyond . . . beyond our ability to understand and control? Zookeeper may be right, what are we about to loose upon the world?"

[217]

"I understand. I also am worried, to be honest. I fear *God* has somehow intervened—metaphorically speaking."

"What?" Ming-huà cries. "I thought *God* and *Goddess* are no more than 'neural pathways', as you put it. Are you saying this child is not natural?"

"No, that is not what I'm saying. The child is completely natural, but evolution is capable of great leaps in short periods of time. However, mutations are random and unpredictable. We can only hope for the best. You know, it may be the child will turn out far less advanced than we have speculated."

Ming-huà contemplates this thought for only a moment. "No, no, that is not it. Not what is inside me. No. This person, or whatever label you want to attach, is definitely not inferior."

"All of us are afraid of what we do not understand, even me. My own abilities are not insubstantial, but I too have felt emanations, tremors, that indicate something is happening none of us anticipated. We can only hope it is for the best."

"The voices in my head, *Goddess* in particular, have grown more and more cruel and vindictive. *She* lashes *God* with invective that would curl your hair, and *He* returns *Her* attacks with even more venom. They upset the fetus."

Lady Oracle nods. "Yes, the stakes are very high. Higher than I imagined."

"What if this child is far more advanced than me? I will not be a mother, but a burden."

"You leave out a crucial piece of the puzzle."

"What?"

Lady Oracle replies a bit self-consciously. "I am not one to romanticize, but love must be the glue that bonds you to this child, and this child to you."

Ming-huà smiles. "Love? I never thought I would hear you say that particular emotion was anything other than a human defect to be tolerated but not praised."

"Shows how even your sensitive hump can mislead."

"But what if love is not in the DNA of this child. Love, after all, is personal and can be lacerating. It has the capability of hindering a broader and more objective view of the universe."

[218]

"You are wrong. Love need not be personal. *Goddess*, for example, loves without loving. Thus, *Her* quest to end suffering."

"So! *She* is real!"

"Of course, haven't I made that clear? You must understand, *She* exists as a convenient metaphor."

Zookeeper enters the room followed by Bataar. "Make what clear?" he asks. "Metaphors are supposed to clarify, not obfuscate!"

"Do you love Ming-huà?" asks Lady Oracle.

"Yes, every day more and more."

"And how do you feel about this baby?"

"I feel great! Why?"

"Why do you feel great?" pursues Lady Oracle.

"Because, it will be my kid . . . well, half me."

"What if this child does not have the same emotions, the same feelings, as other children?"

"What do you mean?"

Lady Oracle bears down. "Well, what if this child is so far beyond your ability to understand that it sees you as . . . lesser."

"Christ, is that all! Fuckin' kid had better be superior to me or I'll kick its ass!"

Lady Oracle and Ming-huà exchange glances.

"Zookeeper," says Ming-huà. "You have powerful empathic abilities. Have you felt any . . . I don't know, disturbing emanations from this pregnancy?"

"Are you joking? No. What is this, anyway? Why the questions?"

Lady Oracle coughs. "Well, Ming-huà is simply having the usual maternal doubts about how perfect the child will be."

"That all? With my genes and Ming-huà's mixed together, the kid will be more than perfect!"

"Thus spake Zarathustra!" cries Sy who has been listening from the doorway.

~ Dream or Foreshadowing? ~

Ming-huà tries to sleep that night, but wearisome doubts, endless questions, and a subtle but pervasive uneasiness make it difficult. Finally, she drifts off, and is in that alpha state between consciousness and sleep when the fetus comes alive with explosive energy. Like a highly intelligent octopus, its tentacles curl and twist and wrap themselves into and around her entire body, particularly exploring the cavernous realm of her hump. She feels the tentacles coil and squeeze in acrobatic contortions to penetrate the most secret of her labyrinthine recesses. Cherished secrets are revealed to the probing of this obsessively inquisitive fetus, whose keen intelligence seems to operate over the entirety of its cephalopod-like body. Ming-huà finds herself in labor, the baby clawing to get out, tentacles emerging from her vagina and gripping her thighs to pull its body through the birth canal. She wakes screaming and soaked in sweat. Letting her heart slow its throbbing, she waits to see if anyone has heard her cries. Silence. This preternatural quiet is terribly disturbing, as it is an imperturbable backdrop to the lingering image of an alien life being born into the world. She feels her mind slipping. A terrible compulsion to run away, as fast as her legs can carry her, takes hold of her mind, and only with the greatest effort does she conquer this impulse and remain in bed, dreading the thought of carrying through with the pregnancy. As if to place a capstone on her madness, a bright light suddenly pervades the room, and she stares in amazement at a wondrous scene.

Goddess sits in the lotus position on a huge, dazzling white flower floating above the bed. *Her* sad, contemplative face gazes from beneath an elaborate crown glimmering a kaleidoscope of colors. A cinder-bright jewel embedded in *Her* forehead burns brightly and an intricate necklace lays cradled between *Her* bare breasts. *Her* left-hand rests on *Her* thigh, the upturned curve of *Her* fingers resembling the albino legs of a gracefully dead spider. *Her* right-hand poises in the air, index finger and thumb touching to form an almost perfect circle while the other fingers radiate outward. Ming-huà stares in speechless disbelief.

Her first words are automatic. "You are not real."

"Yet here I am."

"Go away! Isn't Your voice enough? You drove my father mad. Go!"

"I will if you will it."

"I do!"

Goddess smiles down at *Her* own body. *"Yet here I am."*

"Do You want to drive me mad also?" Ming-huà's words are a pleading whimper. She is on the verge of hysteria.

"You fear this child, but need not."

[220]

"I am terrified of this child. My mind is going. You are driving me mad! Let me go!"

You are free to go anytime, but the child will remain with you. Even after birth, the child will always be connected to you. The umbilical cord that connects you both is not of the physical type. It is far more powerful.

"The child will be a monster!" screams Ming-huà.

There is only one monster, and He is not of you or your kind. However, He wants you to abort and you are yielding to His machinations.

"Why does *He* want me to abort?"

You know the answer to that.

"I don't know! I don't know anything! I know I want to be free of this . . . thing inside me.

That is not possible. The only way to make this child a monster is to do what is essential for every monster to be monstrous. Withdraw you love. Abandonment.

"So be it! I cannot survive this way! It is killing me!"

You are killing you.

"I am so tired. Tired of being a freak. Tired of being alone. Tired of having my best friend be a squirrel. Tired of always being *the other*!"

Foolish girl! All of you, all humans, are the other! To all the rest of life on earth, humans are the destroyer others! Do you not realize the millions that have gone before you who have suffered far more? Freaks burned alive, solitary despair ending in suicide, imaginary friends the only recourse to stave off the soul-destroyers, the pain! The suffering! Is it so terrible that humans must either move on or disappear and take all with them? You are that vehicle, that hope, yet you sob for your own suffering. Here you are crying amidst the luxury of your surroundings.

"But what is within me, what is growing in me, is monstrous!"

Because you had a dream? A dream sent by Him! Are you so weak of mind that you believe dreams?

"You are a dream! You are the monstrous one!"

The room bursts into a flaming inferno, blinding in its intensity, scarlet with the rage of a firestorm conscious of its own destructive aim. Ming-huà feels her body melt away like wax, leaving in its place only the fetus exposed to the lapping flames, smiling, seeming to revel in their searing intensity. Only tendrils of smoke and ash remain of her body, yet the child remains indestructible.

~

Next morning, Ming-huà awakes with the empty feeling of a hollowed-out husk. Perhaps the *Goddess's* flames really did burn away her flesh and bone. All that remains of Ming-huà is the kernel of life that is growing within, impervious to Armageddon.

But it is still there! She thinks with a start, the kick definite, directed, and painful.

As she doubles over, a flood of untranslatable messages overwhelms her hump and flood into her brain. Strange words coat the ache from the kick like a syrupy tonic, relieving the discomfort as if apologizing for the hurt caused. Ming-huà is puzzled and frustrated at her inability to understand what this creature is trying to communicate.

Hours later, Sy comes to check on Ming-huà. He knocks. No answer. Repeatedly he knocks. No answer. Alarmed, he gingerly opens the door and calls her name. No response. When at last he enters the room, he immediately sees Ming-huà crouching in the corner, trembling uncontrollably. Sy rushes to her and kneels to put his arms about her shaking body, but she pushes him away automatically, no emotion apparent.

"What is it, Ming-huà?" he asks.

No response. Her eyes are glazed. To Sy, she seems disconnected from the present moment, dwelling in some other place and time. Now Sy is frantic and without leaving her side, calls for Lady Oracle to come. Zookeeper is the first to appear. He looks at her in shocked silence.

"Get Lady Oracle fast!" exclaims Sy.

But Zookeeper is glued in place. "What's wrong with her?" he asks.

"Just go!" snaps Sy.

When Zookeeper disappears, he puts his hands on both sides of her face and turns her head toward him. "Ming-huà!" he shouts.

No response. All he sees is a blank stare, body trembling. He gently slaps her. "Ming-huà!"

No response.

Zookeeper returns. "She's coming," he says, then adds, "What's wrong with her?"

"Not sure," replies Sy, still staring into her eyes.

Lady Oracle arrives, sizes up the situation, and orders everyone out. After they leave, she tries talking to the hunchback, but has the same

[222]

luck as Sy. With a worried sigh, she sits next to Ming-huà and leans her back against the wall. She takes the quivering hand and waits.

Hours pass. Just as she is about to give up, Lady Oracle notices a change in Ming-huà's expression. The vacant emptiness slowly fades to a growing awareness.

"Ming-huà?" Lady Oracle says. "Are you back? You've been scaring us."

Nothing.

"Ming-huà?"

Still nothing, just an open, wondering curiosity in the eyes. Lady Oracle feels the hairs on the back of her neck stand up.

"Ming-huà?"

Book II: Pythia and Tara

Chapter 18: Struggle for Control

~ Ming-huà Sinks Deeper ~

Ming-huà has lain in bed for two days, nursed by a tag-team of Lady Oracle and Sy, with Zookeeper continuously watching over her to make sure she is never alone. Her reactions to the tending of her bodily functions are strangely automatic, accepted without comment, and her caretakers are amazed at the lack of embarrassment the young hunchback they know would normally display at the necessity for such intrusive tasks. She has not spoken, but everyone notices the unmistakable change, though none can explain what it is, except for the feverish, luminous eyes that stare at them with otherworldly attention. Zookeeper describes her stare as akin to an intensely curious dog looking at cats for the first time. When spoken to, she alertly turns toward the sound and peers at the speaker as if puzzling out what the noise means.

Zookeeper, with his heightened sensibilities, is aware Lady Oracle and Sy are frightened, but they are unwilling to allow him a glimpse into their growing concerns, and that reticence particularly applies to Ming-huà. He fears their anxiety is like a doctor aware the fetus's head is perilously facing the wrong direction, but intent on keeping the news from the suffering mother. Even so, Zookeeper is not as worried about the status of the fetus as he is the odd, unnatural expression on Ming-huà's face. Although her features outwardly reflect the same beautiful young woman, some indescribable transformation has animated the subcutaneous elasticity of her features so that he no longer looks at Ming-huà, but a different person.

As he sits up with her on the morning of the third day, suddenly, out of nowhere, Ming-huà says in a crisp, clear, unfamiliar voice, "We must go out tonight."

Zookeeper is so taken aback, he can only mumble, "What?"

[224]

"Tonight. We must go."

"Why?"

But the vacant gaze returns, dropping over her face as if a veil had fallen. No amount of encouragement by Zookeeper brings her back. He rushes to get Lady Oracle, and when they return, the same peculiar look, alert and inquisitive stares at them.

"I must go out tonight."

"Why?" asks Lady Oracle.

"I must."

"Ming-huà, we cannot risk your pregnancy. Due date is too near."

"We will be fine. It must be done."

"Who is speaking?" asks Lady Oracle.

"Who do you think?"

"I don't know."

"Ming-huà, of course. Have you forgotten me so quickly?"

Sy has entered and now speaks. "Excuse me, but you are so different, Ming-huà. We hardly recognize you."

"How can you not recognize a pregnant hunchback?"

Sy is at a loss.

"Now," says Ming-huà. "I have to go out tonight, and I want Sy to accompany me."

"Why?" asks Lady Oracle.

"I need a witness."

"I mean, why do you have to go out tonight?"

"Too many reasons and not enough time."

"Try."

Ming-huà sighs in frustration. "In your terms, to save people."

"I need to know who I'm talking to," insists Lady Oracle.

"Are you not Lady Oracle?" Ming-huà shoots back.

Momentarily confused, she answers, "Yes."

"Are you not the one who put this hunchback through so much in order to stop suffering?"

"Are you not the hunchback?" asks a surprised Lady Oracle.

"Of course, we've established that."

Sy breaks in. "Sorry, you don't talk like the Ming-huà I know."

"You are Sy, the magical buffoon. Scarecrow."

"Yes."

[225]

"Then you know less than your reputation suggests."

"I suppose so. However, question is, who do you intend to save?"

"All of you."

After uttering these startling words, Ming-huà closes her eyes and appears to sleep. The others quietly slip out.

~

Gathered in the anteroom downstairs, Sy, Lady Oracle, and Zookeeper are meeting.

"It is not her, it's the fetus," says Lady Oracle.

"That's fuckin stupid!" says Zookeeper. "No fetus can think, let alone take over someone."

"This one can," says Sy. "How else do you explain it?"

"She's delusional," insists Zookeeper. "Too much strain."

"No, she is not delusional," says Lady Oracle. "But she is in danger."

"Of?" asks Zookeeper.

Lady Oracle shakes her head. "That I do not know."

"So, do we let her go tonight?"

"A late term pregnant woman out on the streets to save an unknown person whose life she imagines is in danger?" says Sy.

"She said it was to save all of us," corrects Zookeeper.

"Whether us or someone else, we must not let her go."

"Absolutely, we let her go . . . or whoever is controlling her now," says Lady Oracle to everyone's surprise. "This is neither overactive imagination nor delusion. There is foresight. There is purpose. There is learning going on at an incredibly rapid pace."

But even as these words leave her mouth, Ming-huà enters the room and announces somewhat apologetically, "Sorry, I haven't been feeling well. I have been dreaming."

"Ming-huà?" says Sy.

"Of course, who else would it be?"

"How do you feel?"

"Strange dream. I dreamed about Miss Gladflower. I dreamed about where I sent her. No, that's not quite right. I dreamed I was where I sent her."

Lady Oracle responds cautiously. "You have been . . . gone, for a while."

"Gone?"

"Well, out of it a bit."

"I know . . . sort of. I have felt it. Can't remember much, except something terrified me, and then I'm here."

"Where were you when you were with Miss Gladflower?" asks Lady Oracle.

"That is the strangest thing of all."

"Tell us," says Sy.

But once again the transformation occurs, even quicker this time. Its instantaneous arrival takes everyone aback.

"I must go tonight." She stares at Sy. "You will go with me. The other . . . the armless one"—she turns her attention to Zookeeper—"can also come if so inclined. She is attached to the one whose arms are unattached."

"I'll go!" cries Zookeeper.

"I know," says Ming-huà.

Lady Oracle and Sy exchange glances.

Ming-huà notices. "No need to be worried and look at each other so. Now that it is settled, we are going to rest now. Meet us at eleven o'clock here and we will go. As the birth date is close, we need rest before tonight."

All stare in wide-eyed wonder at these pronouncements. Sy is startled to see a flicker or two of the old Ming-huà as one might catch a glimpse of movement through thick vegetation. Before anyone responds, the hunchback is gone, leaving them to gape at one another. Lady Oracle finally breaks the silence.

"We?"

~ Back on the Street ~

Rocket had become a devotee of curb stomping since early adolescence. When he discovered the Nazi SS and Gestapo used this method of inflicting maximum pain, he reveled in its exquisite bloodline. Ironically, he himself was almost a victim of this same torture and its method of internal decapitation, but a gang brother saved him at the last moment. Now, he gleefully seizes any excuse to use it on others, particularly those of a darker skin color. To make his point, he has engraved a swastika on the soles of his boots. Tonight, he has targeted a black business owner who openly cursed at him during the morning rush hour while Rocket stood outside his store spouting racist rhetoric to a small collection of cheering skinheads and jeering black passersby. (In truth, he did not actually hear cursing by the store owner, but he is sure the man is guilty because he gave Rocket a disapproving scowl.) The store, a small consignment shop, has a very prominent neon sign which is familiar to Rocket as a convenient landmark to meet and transact quick drug deals. He knows when the shop closes, so he now waits down the sidewalk where the owner will pass on his way to a nearby parking garage. Rocket has carefully chosen the alley where he will force the owner into at gun point. A curb-like concrete lip runs along the base of the walls that will serve nicely for his purpose. As always, he has played the scene over and over in his mind, relishing its outcome and the anguish it will cause. Paralysis, he decides, will be the best outcome, as death is too final and the suffering too short. The amount of force he will use when he stomps on the back of the man's head and neck is the exciting part of the ritual, as too much or too little will not produce a satisfactory result.

He waits across the street until the neon light is extinguished. Now his excitement grows and he twitches in anticipation. The owner is middle-aged, somewhat stooped and weary-looking, his gait more shuffling than walking. He pauses to pull the heavy collar of his overcoat around his neck and moves on. Rocket follows, his nerves tingling, his mouth watering. Once he gets the man in the alley, that coat will have to go, he decides. Rocket wants a clear view of the neck and the exposed teeth biting down on edge of the curb. The alley is now a few steps away, so he picks up his pace and fondles the pistol grip nestled against his ribs. Just as he is about to rush up and push the man into the alley, a pedestrian appears walking toward them. Disappointed, Rocket decides to wait until the interloper has passed, then grab the man and pull him back to the dark place of execution. As he slows to let the pedestrian pass, the store owner moves slowly beyond the alley, much to Rocket's consternation. In the glow of a street light, he sees that the approaching pedestrian is a strangely formed woman. Looking closer, he sees she is Asian, and to his disgust, a hunchback. Revolted, he looks down at his feet as she draws alongside. But instead of continuing past, the hunchback stops and looks up at him. He is startled by the luminous beauty of her face and the accusatory, piercing eyes that turn him cold.

"You don't want to do what you are planning," she says.

Shocked, he automatically assumes his best vicious scowl and says, "Mind you own fuckin' business bitch."

"This is my business," she replies.

He grins and spits in her face. "If you know what's good for you bitch, you'll keep walkin' 'till you're out of my sight." He glances at the store owner, who pauses and looks around at he and the woman. "Go on!" he growls at the hunchback. "Get the fuck outta here!"

"No."

Once again, he checks his intended victim who still stands motionless, waiting for something. Good.

Rocket pushes the hunchback away and pulls his gun. "Look, bitch, I'll shoot! Get the fuck out!"

Now the target is slowly walking up to them, hesitantly but steadily. He clearly does not see the gun. The hunchback won't move.

"Is there a problem here?" asks the man from a safe distance.

Rocket makes a split-second decision to abort his mission, but the man sidles a bit closer and says, "Are you in trouble, lady? I know this man and he is not one to fool with. You must come away from him. I'll walk with you."

Infuriated by this impertinence, Rocket rushes up to the man and jabs the barrel of the gun into his stomach. The man yells, but Rocket strikes him across the face and pushes him toward the alley.

"Stop!"

Rocket hears the hunchback, but he ignores her and knocks the man to the ground just inside the alley. Too close to the street, but he no longer cares. He leans over with his gun to the man's head and orders him to bite the curb.

"Stop, or you will regret it!" shouts the hunchback, but Rocket's blood is up, and he savagely kicks the man and orders him to lay on his stomach. When the man does not respond, he kicks again. By now, the man is gasping for breath and issues muffled cries for help. Rocket kicks again, and the store owner's head is now on the curb staring up in terror. Rocket presses the barrel of his gun into the man's forehead and screams at him to turn over and bite the concrete edge. He hears the hunchback screaming warnings, but is far too inflamed to pay any attention. The man turns over, his neck still disappointingly covered by the collar of the coat, but Rocket can see his teeth bared against the concrete. Grinning in satisfaction, he lifts his foot to stomp.

The next thing Rocket knows, he is lying on his back on the sidewalk. Confused, he tries to get up, but realizes something is wrong. Terribly wrong. It finally comes to him that he only has one leg. Terrified, he grabs for his gun but discovers his hand is also gone, only the stump of a wrist waves helplessly in the night air. His screams reverberate up and down the street. The store owner draws himself to a sitting position and stares in disbelief at his attacker. He looks at the dark figure of the hunchback, who quickly disappears into the night, then painfully stands and makes his way toward the parking garage, not noticing an armless man pass him on the sidewalk heading toward the still screaming Rocket.

~

By the time Zookeeper reaches the shrieking man lying on the ground, a few onlookers have come to look. Rocket's eyes bulge in terror and he flails about, shouting, "My leg! My hand!"

Zookeeper is alternately sickened and fascinated. No blood. No sign of violence. Just stumps. Just like him. A gun with no barrel sits on the pavement beside the stricken figure. He catches a glimpse through the swelling crowd of Sy rushing Ming-huà away.

"What happened?" asks an onlooker.

"Don't know," says a newcomer. "Just heard the screams and came to see. Guy has no leg and no hand. Weird. Look at him! Wavin' that stump and screaming like it just happened! No blood. Must be high on some bad shit."

"Yeah, weird. Anyone call the cops?"

"Yeah," says another. "Damn, he's still shouting bloody murder about his hand and leg. It's like it just happened, but there ain't no blood. Weird as shit."

"Yeah."

"No matter what you say, I'll bet there's a wheelchair or crutches laying around here somewhere," claims Zookeeper. He now feels the stares intensify at his own armless figure.

An onlooker edges up and scrutinizes Zookeeper. "Was you involved in this mess?" he asks.

"Naw, just came when I seen the rubberneckers. Still think there's a wheelchair and crutches around somewhere. How else to explain it?"

"Yeah," comes a different voice. "Got to be. Guess you'd know, eh, bud?"

As the words are spoken, Zookeeper hears a police siren, so he turns and walks quickly back from where he came. His mind reels in the face of undeniable, dreadful evidence of Ming-huà's power. But now the question is who controls it?

~ Birth ~

By the time Zookeeper arrives back at the mansion, Sy and Lady Oracle have seen Ming-huà to bed and are meeting in the anteroom.

"How is she?" he asks.

Lady Oracle shakes her head. "It is odd. Sy told me about the incident. He wisely spirited Ming-huà away before the police arrived on the scene. After she came here, she would not speak or answer any questions. So, I was about to give up asking when she surprised me. She said, 'We must sleep. Now we know. Not sure what happened with the gun. Enough of this until after.' Then she went to bed, and when I checked on her, she was fast asleep."

"Did she say anything on the way here, Sy?" asks Zookeeper.

"Not a word."

"What about the pregnancy? Is she in pain?"

Lady Oracle sighs. "Not that I can tell, but. . . . "

"But?"

"But there is something, something I don't quite understand."

"Now what?" asks Zookeeper.

"Now we wait," says Lady Oracle.

"And hope the police do not show up asking questions," adds Sy.

"Fuckin' A," says Zookeeper. "The world don't have an abundance of pregnant hunchbacks to track down."

~

The next month passes without incident. Zookeeper often wanders downtown to the area where the confrontation occurred in order to put his ear to the ground and pick up any useful information. He is alarmed at a number of things. Firstly, the police have been asking a lot of questions. Secondly, the neighborhood is aflame with rumors of the supernatural, of a loose demon, a witch, some sort of blood drinking Dracula, a zombie killer, and all sorts of similar superstitious claptrap spouted by the fearful and the ignorant. Some of the more rational theorize the existence of a serial killer who has perfected a way to torture without spilling blood. In any case, these rumors have found their way into the press, which is putting more pressure on the police to find answers. Already, they have connected what happened to Zookeeper and his crack house friends to the recent incident involving Rocket. "It is only a matter of time before they come calling," he warns Lady Oracle and Sy. "*God* knows whether they have managed to connect what happened in Baltimore to here. If so, we're in a fuckin' world of hurt."

"Yes, unfortunately it is inevitable," says Lady Oracle. "But even if they put two and two together, they still have nothing on which to base a criminal charge. How can a hunchback girl kill and maim in such a manner, at a distance, without there being blood?"

"Perhaps," says Sy. "But put nothing past the government. They may want to take her, test her, experiment on her."

Lady Oracle laughs. "You have been watching too many movies, Sy! Don't be ridiculous. Nevertheless, we will lay low, make sure the birth goes smoothly, and then see where to go from there."

"Probably the best we can do for the time being," says Sy with a shrug.

Zookeeper downs a whiskey using his feet. He smacks his lips and says serenely, "Long as the kid is safe."

The others do not respond, but Lady Oracle finally breaks the silence by announcing she is returning to her *yang* house. On the way, she mulls over the situation and decides things are not too bad. For one, she is intent on using a trusted midwife for the delivery. For another, she is comforted that in spite of the alarming emanations from the fetus, Ming-huà is healthy and otherwise shows no sign of complications. Nevertheless, a nagging uncertainty leaves her anxious and more troubled than she would ever let on to Sy or Zookeeper. When she settles into her *yang* house with pajamas and a cup of hot tea, she calls to *Goddess*, but there is no response. Occasionally she finds herself longing for her grandmother Buandelgereen from whom she has always found comfort and reassurance. But, to her great sorrow, the old woman has recently sunk into a state of incoherence.

"*Goddess*!" she cries out in frustration. There is no answer. Wait and see, she tells herself. Be patient.

A couple of weeks later, Ming-huà experiences labor pains and the midwife is called when her water breaks. Since the incident with Rocket, she has not spoken.

~

Lady Oracle, Sy, and Zookeeper wait nervously in the anteroom. Other than brief snippets of small talk, they are silent. Zookeeper sips a beer with his feet, Lady Oracle and Sy drink cold tea. All periodically glance at the doorway. They have seen the midwife a few times, bustling back and forth to the kitchen and bathroom, but her face registers no emotion other than tight-lipped solemnity.

Sy breaks the tense atmosphere and says, "Zookeeper, you can read people, what is she thinking?"

"Who?"

"The midwife, of course."

Zookeeper looks perplexed. "Yeah, all I get is a weird mix of determination, confusion, and . . . I think . . . fear. But the signals are a mishmash."

"Great."

"Can we hear the baby cry from here?" asks Zookeeper.

"Depends," says Lady Oracle absently.

The conversation again drops off into silent anticipation, but the hours stretch on. Finally, the midwife enters the room. Her face is blank, as one in shock. Everyone jumps up, faces full of expectation. The midwife sits and leans back, staring blankly up at the ceiling.

"Well?" asks Lady Oracle.

The question falls on deaf ears.

"I'm going up to see her," says Zookeeper, but he remains standing.

The midwife sighs and looks at all of them. "Sit down," she says.

They obediently sit, now genuinely concerned. For a long time, the midwife is quiet, seemingly collecting her thoughts.

"Tell us," says Lady Oracle. "Is it bad?"

Gathering her strength, the midwife replies. "I do not know what to say. The birth was long, but basically uneventful. Ming-huà made no sound, not even a groan or a grunt. It was as if a corpse were giving birth. Then the child's crown appeared. I cannot explain it, but the room was utterly silent, as if time stopped. I checked the clock and noted the time,

[233]

surprised to see the second hand still moving. When the baby was clear, I cut the umbilical cord as normal and began the Apgar check." She shivers and asks for a glass of wine. Sy gives her the glass and she takes a few swallows, then continues. "Anyway, the Apgar check. All was perfectly normal, yet all was also perfectly abnormal. Never have I seen such a thing."

"Is it a boy or girl?" interjects Zookeeper.

"A girl, but. . . . "

"But?"

She continues to shiver and downs more wine. "Let me finish. Ming-huà, as I said, did not and still has not uttered a sound. As for the baby, appearance is normal healthy, heartbeat is one hundred beats per minute, which is good, but the baby's response to stimulus elicited behavior I have never seen; a kind of bemused patience. The baby's activity was far more advanced than a newborn, and appeared calculated and cognitively deliberate. Lastly, the baby would not cry. Not a sound. She is not deaf, that I know. But she did not cry or utter a sound."

"What did she do?" asks Sy.

"Stared at me as might a curious scientist; as if she performed the Apgar test on me, rather than vice versa."

"What is the significance of the baby not crying?" asks Zookeeper.

"Well, normally I would say it is of no real significance," says the midwife. "But in this case, a combination of the baby not crying, and its apparent cognitive abilities make it very different. But even that does not explain it. I sensed something from this baby, something I never before sensed . . . she is thinking, analyzing, evaluating, whatever you want to call it. It sends chills up my spine. The baby follows my movements with intense interest, which is not necessarily unusual, but . . . oh, I don't know how to explain it. You will see for yourselves. I put the baby in Ming-huà's arms, and she held it close by instinct, but exhibited no bonding signs, no cooing, no smiles."

"And the baby?" asks Lady Oracle.

The midwife shivers again. "The baby seems interested only in the surroundings, not the mother."

"Is she a hunchback?" asks Zookeeper.

The woman stiffens and assumes her most officious tone. "Ah, yes. I checked carefully for signs of *Kyphosis* and saw a hump that will be

[234]

more pronounced than her mother's." She falls silent, evidently rethinking her answer. "Well, it is different from the mother, and I'll leave it at that."

"Oh, *God*," murmurs Zookeeper.

Lady Oracle jumps out of her seat. "Never say that in my presence!" she shouts.

"Okay, okay. Just a figure of speech. Thank *Goddess*! How's that? Anyway, I don't give a rat's ass if she's got two heads, she's my kid."

Lady Oracle glares and turns to the midwife. "I assume we can see her now?"

"Yes. My job is done here. I should go."

"You don't want to see her and say goodbye?" asks Sy.

The midwife shivers again, as if squirming out of clingy wet clothes. "No, I am going." She puts down her wine glass and stands. "Thank you. No need to show me out. You know where to send payment." With that, she is gone.

All three look at each other wordlessly, then ascend the stairs to see Ming-huà and the baby.

Chapter 19: Human Child?

~ First Impressions ~

When the three enter Ming-huà's room, they are astonished to see the baby staring at them with an open, intelligent gaze. Ming-huà herself has a vacant look. All three feel an electric presence in the air that tingles the body and sets the teeth on edge. Zookeeper is the first to approach and he leans over to kiss the baby. When in the middle of doing so, the baby's eyes scan where his arms should be and smiles. This expression is so deliberate and unnerving, Zookeeper straightens up and looks at Ming-huà, whose eyes continue to stare vacantly.

"Ming-huà, dear, how are you?" asks Lady Oracle.

The baby seems to follow the question and turns to look at her mother.

Ming-huà says, "Fine."

"You have a healthy baby girl," says Sy.

"No," replies Ming-huà in a flat voice. "The world has a healthy new . . . inhabitant."

"We often talked about a name, and came up with a lot of boy's and girl's names, but could never decide. What do you think now, Ming-huà? Any ideas?"

To everyone's unspoken amazement, the baby is following the conversation with her eyes, evidently intent on the discussion.

Tears run down Ming-huà's cheeks. "How about Miss Gladflower?"

Zookeeper is agitated. "Come on, Ming-huà, be serious. What name do you like?"

"It is not my choice," she replies.

"No, it's both of our choices," says Zookeeper.

Ming-huà laughs humorlessly. "No, it is neither of our choices. It is hers'." She gazes down at the baby, who looks up at her in silent agreement.

Zookeeper feels the power of the child, and he glances at Sy and Lady Oracle who are both looking at the baby in grim fascination.

"Well, I'm not—"

Zookeeper starts to speak, but Ming-huà suddenly bursts forth in a loud voice, "Pythia!"

"What?" asks Zookeeper, clearly confused.

"Pythia is her name."

Zookeeper is at a loss. "How . . . where did that come from?"

"Where do you think?"

Zookeeper looks at the baby and frowns. "Well . . . okay, what does it mean?"

"I don't know," says Ming-huà. "Ask her." She gestures toward Lady Oracle, but the woman's face has turned white and remains unmoving as stone.

Zookeeper asks, "What does it mean?"

No answer, so he turns to Sy. "What does it mean?"

Before he can respond, Lady Oracle suddenly and completely unexpectedly breaks into raucous laughter; her jollity bears the unmistakable sound of relief.

"What?" he asks again.

Lady Oracle takes a break from her mirth and stares at Ming-huà with a new appreciation. "This child arises from the rotting corpse of a snake," she says, adding quickly, "Figuratively, of course."

Pythia smiles approvingly.

Zookeeper still looks confused. "Google it," says Lady Oracle. "Evidently, this child does not need Google."

Zookeeper turns to Ming-huà. "How do you feel babe? Are you tired?"

Ming-huà returns his look with a faint smile. "Yes, I think the worst is over for me. She borrowed my substance, my power, my soul, if you will, but has now returned it. I can feel it coming back like a battery being recharged. She no longer needs it. But even she will need my milk. Even she."

"What do we have, Ming-huà?" asks Zookeeper.

"To be determined," replies his wife. "But whatever she is, she is not something the world has ever seen."

"Nor are you, Ming-huà," says Lady Oracle. "Nor are you."

"Perhaps, but from now on, we are the helpless babies."

"Indeed," says Lady Oracle. "Oracle has arrived to replace Oracle. The more the snake rots, the more powerful she becomes, figuratively, of course."

"What is all this snake shit?" asks Zookeeper.

"Pythia will make this all very clear, very quickly. Congratulations to the father and to the mother."

"If humans let her live," says Sy.

"Still obsessed with the movies?" asks Lady Oracle.

"Yes, the longest movie ever made; the navel-gazing history of the human race. It is very informative."

Lady Oracle nods. "I fear you are right. Caution is the name of the game now."

As the last word leaves Lady Oracle's mouth, a loud knocking on the front door startles them all. Sy goes downstairs and opens it. Two men in civilian clothes flash their badges.

"Police detectives. May we come in and ask a few questions?"

~ Cloud ~

"What is your business, may I ask?" says Sy.

"Just routine checking," says the taller man. "Does a hunchback live here?"

"Yes, why?"

"We have reason to believe she may have been a witness to a crime."

"Crime? Where?"

"Another part of town. Your name?"

"Sy."

The shorter man jots the name in his notebook and looks up, "Sy what?"

"Sy Rung."

"What is the hunchback's name?"

"Look, she just delivered a baby and is resting. Can these questions be asked some other time?"

"She is returned from the hospital?"

"She had the baby here."

The taller man lifts an eyebrow. "Here?"

[238]

"Yes, by a midwife."

"Her name?" repeats the shorter one.

"Ming-huà. Ming-huà Powers . . . uh, now married, so her name is Ming-huà Weston."

"May we see her? It will only take a few minutes."

"No, that is out of the question. She is resting perhaps later."

"Look, Mr. Rung, we will only ask a few questions. In and out. It is important, as the crime she witnessed is very serious. It resulted in multiple deaths and mutilations"

"Yes, most certainly officers," says Lady Oracle coming down the stairs.

Sy looks at her in amazement. "But—"

"No, it's okay. You won't be long, officers? She is very tired."

"We are detectives ma'am," says the taller one. "And no, we will be as brief as possible. You are?"

"Judith Ganbaatar."

The shorter detective jots it down.

"Follow me, please," says Lady Oracle.

Sy watches them ascend the staircase in wonder.

Zookeeper waits at the top of the stairs and nods to the detectives.

"You are?" asks the taller one.

"Matthew Weston. Please be brief."

The shorter detective looks long and hard at Zookeeper and his stumps. He writes a great deal in his notebook.

"Sorry about your . . . condition, Mr. Weston," says the taller one. "May I ask how you lost your arms?"

"Oh, birth defect, but thank you."

When they enter Ming-huà's bedroom, the infant is propped up on a pillow, observing them with riveted eyes; the detectives note a disturbingly intelligent curiosity apparent in the stare. They bow to Ming-huà, introduce themselves, and apologize for the inconvenience. She nods heavily, showing little interest in their presence.

They ask whether she was present at the location they specify on the night of the attack. She again nods.

When they ask if she observed anything unusual on that night, she shakes her head, then nods hesitantly.

"What did you see?" asks the taller detective.

[239]

"A man being accosted, but then I left as I was afraid to get involved," she says.

"Why were you out on the street at such a time of night?" asks the short one.

"Research."

"Research?"

"Yes, I'm researching high crime areas to gather data."

"Are you writing a book?"

"Perhaps."

As they ask questions, the detectives notice the infant following the conversation as intently as might an interested adult. More and more they look at the infant rather than Ming-huà. Slowly, they begin to fall into a lethargy and their questions are drawn out and become indistinct and unfocused. The short detective stops taking notes, even when Ming-huà responds to a question. It is as if they are in a haze. Confused, they give their apologies and back out of the room.

"We have what we need," says the tall one.

"Yes, thank you," adds the shorter, absently tucking his notebook in a pocket.

They leave in a muddle and drive away.

~

After watching them leave, Sy closes the front door and turns to Lady Oracle.

"How did you know?"

She shrugs. "Isn't it obvious? Pythia is now in charge."

"An infant less than an hour old?"

"A formality."

Zookeeper joins them. He glances toward the upstairs. "She's asleep. What do you mean, Pythia is now in charge?"

Lady Oracle wears a smug grin. "What is the current inane saying? It is what it is."

"Yeah, well I'm the father and I'll be goddamn if she knows more than I do about surviving on the street. If she shows her hand too soon, there'll be hell to pay."

"I know," nods Lady Oracle. "I agree. We should lay low for years until she is old enough to venture out alone. Unfortunately, Pythia will have her own ideas on the subject."

"Christ," mutters Zookeeper. "What have we done?"

"We have done nothing. Chemistry, biology, genetics, natural selection, all are causes, all are implicated."

"I saw an old horror show on T.V. once," says Zookeeper. "This little kid had the power to turn people into animals, or part animals. He even turned some guy he didn't like into a jack-in-the-box. I mean, is this the shit we're going to be dealing with, 'cause if it is, I'm outta here."

Lady Oracle laughs. "You and Sy are alike—you've both seen too many movies. This is not make-believe. It's real, and the implications are real."

"Yeah, too fuckin' real for my taste," says Zookeeper. "What if I scold the kid for doing somethin' wrong or dangerous, is she gonna remove my legs? Or will it be my head like those poor bastards in the street that Ming-huà took care of?"

"I don't think you have to worry about that, Zookeeper," says Ming-huà from the doorway. She is holding the baby who stares at them calmly.

As Zookeeper hurries up to lean over the child, he cries, "Holy shit! You shouldn't be up!"

Lady Oracle remains calm and asks Ming-huà, "Why don't we have to worry?"

"Ahhhhh!" screams Zookeeper.

Everyone's eyes stare in wonder. They see the baby touching her index finger to Zookeeper's forehead. He seems frozen in place.

When the finger is removed, the spell seems broken.

"You understand?" asks Ming-huà.

"I think so," replies Zookeeper in a somewhat bewildered tone. "I mean, she speaks no language but her meaning emerges like a goddamn bolt of lightning from the fuckin' sky."

"Please," says Ming-huà. "Language. You are now a father."

~ Safe Refuge ~

Over the next few weeks, other detectives visit the mansion. Ming-huà continues to give vague answers, and her ever-present baby smiles on in apparent satisfaction. One day, Lady Oracle makes an announcement.

"It is time to leave."

[241]

Ming-huà nods approval, evidently confirming what she already knows. The others express no surprise. Lady Oracle feels it necessary to explain anyway.

"There is mounting suspicion by the police that Ming-huà is somehow involved in these strange encounters where people are bloodlessly left without limbs. We know the federal government has been contacted. Soon, more will come and the vague answers will be more difficult to satisfy."

Pythia lifts a finger as if to give the plan her blessing. She has not yet spoken a word, but everyone intuitively understands what she wants. This odd communication is now accepted, and speculation about its origin and composition has died down.

"Where to?" asks Zookeeper.

"Ah, that has been quite the conundrum," replies Lady Oracle. "Do we go far away, over the sea, or do we stay in this country? After all, Pythia is a citizen of the world."

"I would think we want her in the safest place possible," says Sy.

"So would I," says Lady Oracle. "But the emanations are ambiguous, and *Goddess* has not been in touch for a long time, despite my best efforts to reach *Her*."

"Perhaps *She* is no longer needed?" suggests Sy.

"No, that is not the case," says Lady Oracle. "Something else is going on, some power struggle that is occurring in other planes or dimensions that we are unaware of. For the time being, decisions lay with us . . . and her." Lady Oracle gestures toward Pythia.

Each in their own way tries to penetrate the mind of this child, and each finds an opaque cloud of impenetrable brainwaves occasionally punctuated by the flash of some insight piercing the fog. When this happens, each feels as though they are the recipient of a revelation.

~ Refuge, Training, or Exile ~

Lady Oracle spends the next few days attempting to receive guidance from sources that have, by unspoken agreement, been collectively shortened to the code word *Goddess*. It is evident to all that the final determination of where to go would be cataclysmic if proven wrong. However, evidently *Goddess* had dropped out of the universe, leaving Lady Oracle to spend many nights pondering the choices with Sy,

Zookeeper, and Ming-huà. Pythia seems oddly silent on the resolution of this most auspicious of decisions. It seems the extreme alternatives are to either plunge into the maelstrom and travel to some dangerous neighborhood in a different state and nurture Pythia's power, or play it safe and find a quiet location in which to become invisible exiles while she grows older. Due to this indecision, they delay departure. But this delay has consequences.

Two new detectives stand in the doorway.

"Can I help you?" asks Sy.

"This is a follow-up visit from the last few our colleagues have made, Mr. Rung. Some questions have popped up that we would like answers to. May we come in?"

"Sure." Sy leads them to the anteroom. "Have a seat. Can I offer you gentlemen some tea or coffee?"

Both wave him off. "Mr. Rung, there is a man living here, Mr. Weston, who has no arms, correct?"

"Yes."

"How did he lose them?"

"I . . . shall I call him?"

"Please."

When Zookeeper arrives, the detectives stand and nod.

"Take a load off," says Zookeeper. "What can I do ya for?"

One detective flips open his notebook, the other leans forward and asks, "How did you lose your arms, Mr. Weston?"

"I told you people a hundred times; I don't know. Just woke up and my arms were gone."

"Why did you originally tell us it was a birth defect?"

"Again, for the hundredth time, I didn't wanna get involved."

"You were in some sort of fight, correct?"

"Yeah, some guys I know were hassling the two ladies that live here, so I stepped in to try and stop it, and bam! No arms. Have no idea how it happened."

"It was in a crack house?"

"Yeah."

"Why were the two ladies there, you wife and Judith Ganbaatar?"

"Here we go again," grumbles Zookeeper. "One more time: they told me later they were doing community service, reaching out to

[243]

crackheads and trying to help. Found that out afterward. They took me in, thank *God*. The rest is history."

"Do you believe your wife had something to do with you and your friends—"

"Not friends, just . . . business associates."

"Okay, do you believe your wife had something to do with you and your business associates losing their limbs?"

Zookeeper laughs. "Of course not! How could someone just take off limbs like that, clean and all, no blood. And a small hunchback girl to boot! No."

"Do you find it odd that a hunchback that matches the description of your wife was also involved in people losing not only their limbs, but their lives? In fact, we have records indicating she was present in three different places, one on the east coast, where people ended up losing limbs. Do you find that coincidental?"

Zookeeper shrugs. "Has to be. My wife and Ms. Ganbaatar have been working together to help disadvantaged people in rough neighborhoods. Shit happens."

"Yes, but shit does not happen in the manner in which these events have gone down. People do not just lose their limbs, blood or no blood, unless someone or something caused it."

"How do I know?" says Zookeeper. "All I know is that my wife is just a normal woman who cares about people and who would not harm a fly. Shit, I mean how in the fuck could she remove these limbs without leaving a bloody mess?"

"That's what we're trying to find out."

"You want me to call her? She's upstairs with the baby."

"No, but we are going to have to request you, your wife, Mr. Grafton, and Ms. Ganbaatar come to this address tomorrow where we can discuss what they witnessed in more detail." He hands Sy a card.

"Speaking of which, is Ms. Ganbaatar here?"

"Out shopping," says Sy.

"No problem," says the detective. "Just make sure you all come in tomorrow, okay? It's very important to our investigation."

"Is anyone being charged with something?" asks Zookeeper.

"No, no, we just need to clarify a few facts."

"Such as?" asks Sy.

"Such as why we can't find your wife's name on any database, including social security. Same goes for Ms. Ganbaatar."

"Oh, that's easy to explain," says Sy.

"Tomorrow, Mr. Rung, Mr. Weston."

"Just for kicks, since we're only witnesses, what if we don't show up?" asks Zookeeper.

"Well, all of you are persons of interest in this investigation of mutilations and murders. Subpoenas and warrants would be next. However, we are confident you will cooperate. After all, you told us you are in the business of helping people. Good day."

~

"That's done it," says Lady Oracle watching the detectives' car drive away. "We go to the cave."

Zookeeper whistles. "Shiiittt! That weird ass fuckin' place. Too much spooky shit for me. Can't we go somewhere else? Hawaii maybe?"

Ignoring Zookeeper, Sy looks severely at Lady Oracle. "But, have you heard from *Goddess*?"

"No."

"Then when we get there, it may be just a cave. No *Goddess*, no magic. No magic, no magic cave. No magic cave . . . then what? Cops will be looking. Zookeeper, use that street smart empathetic power of yours and tell us what you think."

"About what?"

"About whether they suspect Ming-huà of being responsible somehow, or whether they really just see her as a witness."

"That's fuckin' easy to answer, man. They suspect her, and right now they're just trying to figure out how it was done."

Sy turns to Lady Oracle. "How about we leave the country?"

"Impossible. First, to allay your concerns, Zookeeper, we check in to a motel near the cave. In the morning we take Ming-huà there. You stay in the motel and wait."

"No way!" snaps Zookeeper. "I go where Ming-huà goes!"

"No. We take Ming-huà to the cave and hope. Maybe Pythia will give us a clue whether it's the right decision. Maybe *Goddess* is only communicating with her now, I don't know. But regardless, we go to the cave and, if all goes well, send Ming-huà and Pythia on a long trip up one of the magical side tunnels. *Goddess* willing, she goes up one of those

[245]

tunnels to somewhere else, to some other time, and we return to San Francisco to face the police and tell them she unexpectedly left for parts unknown. She knows where to find us when she returns."

Sy shakes his head doubtfully but says nothing. Zookeeper, however, is agitated and chimes in. "I'll go with Ming-huà and Pythia wherever they go! Don't matter what you say."

Lady Oracle glares. "You will not go. You will stay in the motel until we return."

Zookeeper is cowed, and says falteringly, "But, why? I mean, what if she and Pythia don't return?"

"That is entirely up to *Her*," says Lady Oracle.

"Ming-huà?"

"No." Lady Oracle points upward. "*Her*."

"Zookeeper has a point," says Sy. "What if she doesn't return? In that case, everything for naught."

"No, no," replies Lady Oracle. "Wherever she goes, the change is come one way or the other. No turning back for humanity."

~

Two days later, after a long drive and a night in the motel, they say goodbye to Zookeeper and are on the dirt road heading for the cave. Ming-huà sits in the back seat with Pythia, whose baby face is smiling in apparent satisfaction. On the other hand, Ming-huà appears exhausted. Sy drives, with Lady Oracle in the passenger seat.

Sy looks in the rearview mirror and nods toward the baby. "She looks happy. Seems like she approves of our destination."

Ming-huà absently strokes Pythia's chubby arm. "She drains me of my own thoughts, my own power. Seems like she's using me as some sort of organic battery, or charger, but I can feel the energy draining from my every cell."

Lady Oracle looks on in alarm. "Probably just the late nights and early mornings. New mothers are always fatigued."

"I miss Zookeeper already," says Ming-huà as if surprised at her own reaction.

"Don't think about him," says Lady Oracle. "There are more important considerations now."

Ming-huà does not respond.

Chapter 20: Cave Redux

~ Crisis in the Desert ~

Among the last things Ming-huà remembers, she had been standing just inside the cave opening holding Pythia and listening to Lady Oracle speak words in a language she did not understand. At some point, she recalls being directed to a side tunnel. Now she stares in wonder at an unfamiliar scene while Pythia, still cradled in her arms, laughs with delight. No cave, no Lady Oracle, none of the others. Just her staring like a fool and Pythia laughing.

They stand on a sandy rise gazing in wonder at an outspreading sea. Dark clouds roil overhead, but there is no rain. Angry waves crash into the jagged basaltic reef, driven by a terrific wind that whips the ocean into a frenzy of foam and thunder. When Ming-huà looks behind, she sees a range of volcanic mountains, the largest caldera in the center and smaller ones tapering off on either side. Vegetation is abundant and thick, but abruptly vanishes near the top of the peaks to reveal naked, brownish/blackish cones belching pillars of smoke and steam into the fierce atmosphere. Though the ferocious wind bites painfully and forces her to lean into it so she does not fall backward, yet Pythia seems in a frenzy of joyous agitation. Bolts of lightning flash in the distance, and from her vantage point, Ming-huà imagines them to be sizzling hot irons boiling the surface. She sees heavy rainfall on the horizon moving toward the island, and she scans the tree line for a path to escape the savaged beach. She spots an opening and hastily takes it.

Just before the rain hits, she and Pythia come upon a house, snug and tight and beautiful, that reveals itself in all its charm before them in a clearing dotted with flowers. Ming-huà is enchanted by it, but Pythia communicates the necessity to quickly enter and make themselves comfortable, as it evidently exists solely for them. Ming-huà is aware this is all illusion, so she shrugs off all doubts and enters. It is two stories, full of antique furniture, and well stocked with food. For the first time, Pythia seems fatigued, so Ming-huà puts her to bed in a second story room brightly decorated with a menagerie of strange objects and a crib sitting invitingly in the corner. When she turns to leave, Pythia opens her eyes and smiles from the crib at her mother's incorrect assumption that she is tired. In fact, the child is fully awake and makes it clear she is merely waiting for the morning when Ming-huà will return her to the shore. After that?

Finding a comfy chair in a downstairs room very much like the one in her old, beloved cottage, Ming-huà sits and meditates on the extraordinary events she has experienced since her departure from that dear island so long ago. Now she finds herself on a very different island, assaulted by a storm that howls and rages as if wanting to tear her world apart. Yet, Pythia lays quietly upstairs, seemingly at home in this maelstrom. What does it mean? Is this wild place a metaphor for Pythia's power? Surely its primordial rumblings dwarf in ferocity the genial surroundings of Ming-huà's old island with its affable squirrels and pleasant surroundings. She feels a slight pressure on her lap and looks down to find Miss Gladflower staring up at her as if questioning where she had been all this time. *Is this where all the missing parts go?* she wonders. *All the people and all the things we have dismissed or ignored or. . . .*

No. This line of thought will lead her nowhere. She reminds herself she is really back in the cave in the California desert and all this is illusion. Nevertheless, the illusion must mean something. Someone is trying to give her clues . . . a secret . . . a key. A deep weariness settles over her and she forces herself to check on Pythia who appears to be smiling in her sleep. Ming-huà trundles into the adjoining bedroom and collapses on the bed to quickly fall into a deep slumber. Visions come in short vignettes. Her father stands at the foot of her bed, and next to him is a young soldier, hollow-eyed, holding a gun. Her grandmother replaces them, bars between her and Ming-huà, her face twisted in despair. Others, less familiar, dance around her bed in some bizarre St. Vitus's machinations. Soldiers, ants, country women, some legless. The others fade away leaving only the ones without legs. Ming-huà is panic stricken that she is responsible for their condition. Names seep out of the cloud of haze in which these people swirl; Tuyet Mai, Han Tinh. These names repeat over and over, triggering some primal memory that is deeply disturbing. With a sudden jerk, Ming-huà awakens and blinks at a bright morning sun through the window. She rushes to check on Pythia, who greets her with shining eyes, opened wide in anticipation. For the first time, she speaks to Ming-huà clearly and articulately in her head. The word is unmistakable.

Beach.

Momentarily stunned, Ming-huà says, "Let me feed you first, sweet girl."

Beach. Once again, the word reverberates deep in her mind.

"No, first you must eat. You need to grow strong and healthy."

Beach! The command will brook no opposition.

Now resigned to carry this insistent child to the beach, Ming-huà slips on a loose-fitting dress that allows ample room for hump in back and post-partum belly in front. When she steps outside with Pythia cradled on her hip, the sky blazes in cobalt intensity. The wind is a moderate series of refreshing gusts, and the vegetation a cornucopia of scents, intensified by the drenching brought the previous night by the storm. All in all, it is a gorgeous day, but one Ming-huà takes no notice of, for a profound and growing dread clouds her mind the closer the two approach the ocean. On the other hand, Pythia's laughter becomes more joyous. As the path nears the sandy beach, Ming-huà feels an almost unbearable urge to turn around and run, but Pythia's euphoria compels her onward.

At last, Ming-huà steps onto the sand and stares in dazed silence at the scene before her. Up and down the beach, as far as the eye can see, are littered body parts of all races and genders. Arms, legs, heads, torsos, feet, hands, all glistening in the sun. And when Ming-huà looks at the ocean, the breakers are depositing more and more limbs as if regurgitating undigested food. In fact, beyond the breakers, the sea is choked with the awful dismembered remains of people. Bile rises in her gorge and she leans over to vomit, but Pythia looks at the carnage and intensifies her laughter. She violently squirms to be let down, and when Ming-huà can hold her no longer, she places her carefully on the sand. Pythia crawls with startling dexterity from one body part to another, examining them as might a forensic scientist. Ming-huà stays close to make sure Pythia does not get too close to the crashing waves and their cargo of limbs. Suddenly, the child stops at a torso and abruptly stops laughing. She seems to be waiting. Ming-huà picks her way through the littered beach and stands close, also waiting, but for what she does not know.

Slowly detached arms and legs move toward the torso. Soon, hands and feet also make their way across the sand toward the same destination. Lastly, a head slides closer. Before her astonished eyes, the parts attach themselves to the torso, and a complete human being forms in the sand. It stands and stares in naked serenity at Ming-huà. Gradually, the openness is replaced by a look of accusation.

Ming-huà cannot breathe while frozen in the glare of this assembled marvel. Pythia sits at its feet gazing up curiously.

It is Lady Oracle.

As Ming-huà stares in wonder, she does not notice another body assembling some distance off. Pythia notices, and has turned to gaze at the sight. When complete, a tall male stands unmoving, his eyes locked onto those of Pythia. He moves toward the baby and enters Ming-huà's field of vision. She jumps in fright and turns to Lady Oracle for an explanation, but none is forthcoming, so she returns her attention to the man. As he approaches, she realizes the extent of his towering height, raw musculature, and the intense mien of his swarthy face. Hardly giving her a glance, he reaches down and picks up Pythia as one would a tiny stuffed toy. Unsmiling, yet gentle, he looks at the little girl reverentially, then speaks to Lady Oracle in a strange tongue.

Mongol, concludes Ming-huà.

While he speaks in a rather growly, slow pace, his words wrap around her like a comfortable fog. Dizzy from staring and listening, his entire being projects a hallucinatory effect, so she closes her eyes to keep from being sick.

~ A New Companion ~

"This is Altan, your new companion," says Lady Oracle.

The words are a shock. Ming-huà shakes her head to clear her confusing thoughts, and finds she is standing back in the cave, Pythia on her hip. How she has ended up back here is a complete mystery. Sy looks on attentively. When she follows Lady Oracle's eyes, she sees the giant man walking toward them, his face a granitic enigma. Stranger still, each eye is comprised of two different colors, one-half bluish-emerald and one-half goldish-brown. Unable to tear her gaze from him, she stands like a fool, desperately trying to organize her thoughts.

"New companion?" she manages to utter at last.

[250]

"Yes," says Lady Oracle. "Do not let his heterochromia bother you. It is from birth." She chuckles. "Your new companion has yin and yang for eyes."

"What does that mean?"

"What?"

"What does new companion mean?"

"It means you are to go with him."

This answer bowls her over, and she asks in a stunned voice, "Why? What about you and Sy? What about Zookeeper?"

"Forget us."

Ming-huà feels faint and sits on a large rock. She stammers, "How can I forget you? How can I forget Zookeeper? He is my husband!"

"He no longer exists."

"I . . . what? . . . what do you mean he no longer exists?"

"To you, from this moment on, the only persons on earth that exist are yourself, Pythia, and Altan."

Ming-huà can hardly get hold of any cogent thought. "I want to see Zookeeper," she says vaguely, not knowing even why she says it.

"I told you he no longer exists."

"He's dead? You don't mean he's dead, do you?"

Lady Oracle laughs. "No, of course not. I mean Altan will be taking you and Pythia to many different places."

"You're kidding! Is he some sort of bodyguard?"

"If you want to look at it that way, but he will be much more than a bodyguard. Much more."

Ming-huà sets her jaw and says coldly, "I still want to see Zookeeper, my husband, father of my child."

"Not possible."

"Why not?"

"Because Altan is taking you with him."

"Where?"

"Deeper into the cave."

Ming-huà's eyes widen. "And then?"

"And then you will be in a different place, sort of like the island you just dreamed about."

"Terrible dream," shudders Ming-huà. "Did *She* bring it to me? It was really more like a hallucination than a dream."

[251]

"Well," says Sy. "Your lineage certainly is chock full of hallucinating . . . relatives."

During this conversation, Altan has stood stolidly aloof, his striking features focused almost exclusively on Pythia, and Pythia's on him. They appear to be communicating without speaking, and eventually Ming-huà notices.

"Excuse me, Mr. Altan," she says abruptly. "What is your background?"

"My background?" His voice is a guttural rumble, a sort of Tuvan throat music all its own. Ugly to an untutored ear, but soon familiarity makes it mesmerizingly beautiful.

"Yes, your background."

"Ahab is Ahab," he says with an ironic smile.

"What an odd thing to say."

Lady Oracle breaks in. "You and Altan will have plenty of time to get to know each other." She looks at Altan. "You need to leave now."

He bows.

As if spurred to action by Lady Oracle's words, Pythia vehemently fusses and squirms, so much so that Ming-huà sets her on the ground and stands unmoving. "I'm not going anywhere until I know more."

Altan suddenly scoops up Pythia and strides deeper into the cave.

"Wait!" cries Ming-huà.

"Go with him," commands Lady Oracle. She holds out a flashlight.

Ming-huà starts to protest.

"Go with him or you won't see Pythia for a very long time."

Ming-huà lets out a shriek, grabs the flashlight, and rushes after Altan, following Pythia's laughter into the darkness.

When she catches up, he turns to look, his face illuminated by the light. Ming-huà stares into the half-blue, half gold eyes.

"Do not let my yin and yang eyes worry you," he says. "They are only parts of my parts, pieces of my pieces, fragments of my fragments."

"I dreamed you were pieced together bit by bit," she says. "A composite being. Yet, you do not look like some sort of Frankenstein's monster. Dreams are so bizarre."

He bellows with laughter. "Indeed, they are! I am born of a mother, same as you."

"And *her*!" Ming-huà exclaims, nodding toward Pythia now quietly settled in Altan's arms.

"Well, there you are partly right and partly wrong."

"What do you mean? Remember, I was there when she was born. No parts need to have been added after leaving my womb."

"No, you're right, not after."

"What are you trying to say?" asks Ming-huà.

"Careful, you'll trip if you keep talking. We're almost there."

"Where?"

"Another good question—the answer you will soon discover."

"Please tell me now."

"Just the beginning of her education. First Kigali, then Auschwitz."

Ming-huà freezes in her tracks. "No, no, no, no, no. . . . "

"Yes."

"The baby!"

"She will be safe. I am your companion now."

"How do you know she'll be safe?"

Altan smiles broadly. "As you said, it is all just a dream."

"Then what is the point?"

"To see."

"What?"

Altan looks down at the smiling Pythia. "Her response."

"She's just a baby."

"No, she is as old as the hominin species . . . older even."

"You obviously weren't there when I gave birth to Pythia. She was almost exactly nine months old. A normal birth. Now—"

Altan begins singing throat music over her words as they walk; the deep, guttural sounds reverberating in waves from the cave walls. Immediately, Pythia, still in his arms, begins laughing even more infectiously, evidently basking in the tonal vibrations emanating from Altan's throat.

They take a side tunnel and Ming-huà's flashlight goes dark.

The next moment she squints in the glare of a bright sun.

They stand on a road where hundreds of people are struggling, pleading, screaming.

Black men with machetes. Dozens of them.

[253]

The crazed men with machetes are hacking the people screaming for mercy; men, women, and children. Hundreds of them. Hacking them to death.

Ming-huà's hump is overwhelmed with the terror and she drops to her knees, faint, nauseous, trying to scream at Altan to take them out of this terrible place. Chaos clouds her mind and her powers are useless against such mass slaughter. It is as if her hump has short-circuited.

Pythia's laughing has turned to wide-eyed fascination. Gradually, her fascination turns to distaste. She lets out a primal screech, clearly terrified . . . or outraged.

Every man swinging a machete is suddenly without arms. Every one of them, arms gone, no blood, machetes scattered on the ground. An eerie silence falls over the bloody scene as victims and perpetrators look on in disbelief. To Ming-huà, it is like there are a hundred black Zookeepers, but she knows she could never pull this off on such a scale. Stoshells, yes. A few people, yes. Not this. She stares at Pythia in astonishment. The stunned silence of the mob last only a few moments.

Then the cacophonous wailing commences and carries on without abatement, the armless men running aimlessly around in mad shock as if insanity afflicted all of them simultaneously; the surviving victims ignoring them and screaming for their loved ones who have been chopped to pieces. No one thinks to look at the three strange observers to this grisly spectacle. A hunchback, a giant, and a baby. No one notices the threesome turn around and hike back down the road toward Kigali where the nightmare continues to unfold as they walk. When they reach the outskirts of the city, more men without arms are wailing and blindly rushing in mad circles, sometimes falling over their victims who lie dead or moaning on the ground. Machetes lie everywhere amidst the dead and dying, their blades gleaming in the sun. Onlookers pour into the area, staring dumbstruck at the armless wretches, none willing to touch the machetes.

Ming-huà blinks uncomprehendingly, holding out her arms to take Pythia from Altan who has held her the entire time.

"Not yet," he says. "One more stop."

"This is a dream, right?" asks Ming-huà, her arms still extended.

"Absolutely." Altan speeds up, unwilling to surrender Pythia. "Education *is* a dream, to many."

"Where to next?" asks Ming-huà, struggling to catch up. "Not Auschwitz? Please, not Auschwitz! I have seen enough!"

"But *she* hasn't," says Altan nodding toward Pythia.

Ming-huà doubles over in pain.

A blackness renders her blind.

When she opens her eyes, a different horror unfolds before her.

Smoke. Ash. A Great Wailing.

A sign becomes visible through the gloom.

It is an obscene tattoo carved into the flesh of humanity.

~ Arbeit Macht Frei ~

Ming-huà staggers back a few steps and sees Pythia staring with total concentration. She now looks to be about ten years old. Ming-huà is disoriented by the preposterous aging of her daughter and trembles in shock. How can so many years have passed without her knowing? Smoke still spews from the ovens. Ash still falls from the sky. The Great Wailing still continues. A line of forlorn people, women and children and babies, are moving in mechanical hopelessness toward the place where smoke and ash spew in turbulent columns. These angry black vapors permeate the sky and cast a sickly reddish hue from the clogged sun. Suddenly they stop in amazement. The Nazi guards that threatened them every step of the way are now like statues, staring numbly into space. No arms, no legs. Just torsos, looking absurd as if dwarfs crawled into voluminous uniforms. Inmates mill around in confusion, unsure what to do or where to go. They gingerly approach the limbless Nazis who teeter like puny statues that have just been unearthed from centuries of entombment. Their unbelieving mouths emit primal howls and pathetic whimpers of shock. Pythia, the ten-year-old, stares and smiles, nodding encouragement to the liberated inmates. She glows with satisfaction.

Altan nods in approval and sets off along the railroad tracks, under the sign, and outside the camp. Ming-huà follows numbly and soon the little band fades from view.

On they travel from one ghastly brutality to another, the result always the same—mutilated perpetrators and stunned onlookers. Interspersing the horror, an endless series of lectures, demonstrations, and assessments by strangely aloof instructors. And then, something happens to end the repetitious drone.

~

"Do you see now?" asks Lady Oracle.

Ming-huà is back in the cave. Pythia stands beside Altan.

"Today is her sixteenth birthday in human terms," he announces proudly. "Few have passed through these dimensions."

"You have guided her well, Altan," says Lady Oracle, who looks quite older. "Her formal education is complete. Though she is now sixteen, only a few years have passed here. Even so, the wait has been difficult."

"But . . . but. . . . " Ming-huà stammers.

"It will come back to you. Don't worry, it will all come back to you. Pythia excelled in her lessons with Altan's help all these years. For now, Pythia is ready to leave the cave and deal with the people who have been hunting her while all of you were away." She looks at Pythia. "Correct?"

"Absolutely."

"Good then. We can start."

Ming-huà is too stunned to comprehend the meaning of Lady Oracle's words. Instinctively, she scrutinizes Pythia with such intensity that one might surmise an attempt to compress years of lost memories to grasp mere moments of found ones. But the memories will not come. What stands before her is a stranger, an enigma; a young hunchbacked girl endowed with exquisite beauty unsullied by the barely perceptible curvature of her spine. No, Ming-huà decides incredulously, it is a curve that adds to her daughter's extraordinary presence rather than subtracts. Emanations from Pythia's hump had always overwhelmed Ming-huà's own natural powers, and the force behind them continues to render her mother a rather ordinary, if not mundane, run-of-the-mill person. Ming-huà is fully aware this young girl possesses abilities that dwarf her own, and she can now only stand muttering in astonishment, "Sixteen. . . . "

As she stares, Ming-huà feels old and sapped of her fledgling sense of power and purpose. Like a vampire, the daughter has drained the mother of vital energy. Ming-huà wearily recalls telling Zookeeper with pride not too long ago that her hump is where she deposits cruelty to dispose of, like a black hole that can never regurgitate its meal. But now she is painfully aware of her limitations. Dealing with cruelty and suffering on the scale of genocide is too much for her, but not too much for her daughter. This is a wondrous but terrifying realization.

~ Where the Lost Years? ~

A defeated Ming-huà now spends her time trying to account for the lost years of Pythia's childhood. Other than snippets of episodic memory, she has no recollection of being with her daughter all that time, and suspects the girl had been removed from her care and taken away to some unfathomable place for years until the girl turned sixteen. Lady Oracle, Sy, and Altan refuse to answer her questions other than hinting Ming-huà has suffered amnesia from an unspecified trauma. They try to soften the blow by assuring her the memories will return. But it is clear the torch has been passed from mother to daughter, and Ming-huà, in her emotional depletion, is perfectly amenable to being shuffled aside. Her job is done. Yet, the regrets are painfully real, and the lost chance at motherhood is an almost unbearable burden. Her relationship with her daughter is now as superfluous as might be some distant ancestor whose only reminder of once existing consists of a faded portrait on a castle wall. Where was Pythia all those years? The question is like an agonizing burn that will not heal. Now, there is little left for her. She wearily looks forward to spending the time she has remaining on that comfy island pondering the mystery of lost years and commiserating with Zookeeper and her chatty, non-human friends.

Chapter 21: Into The World

~ First Steps ~

"Hunted!" Ming-huà blurts, suddenly shaken from her hypnotic reverie by the recollection of Lady Oracle's word. Pythia remains motionless, letting her mother's telepathic probes explore at their own leisurely pace and convey their soothing waves of affection. She is fully aware how weak her mother's power is compared to her own, and how deeply Ming-huà feels the pain of others, but years of witnessing human pathologies play themselves out on grand scales have made her patient with such a slight frailties.

Pythia sends a silent message to her mother. "Not to worry, all is as it should be."

Lady Oracle, not privy to this hump-to-hump communication, tries to explain, but soon gives up in the face of severe complications in conveying such a long story, and the fact they must quit the cave as its purpose, evidently, has been served.

"Oh, never mind all this right now!" cries Lady Oracle. "Although many years have passed in the places you have visited, not that much time has passed outside·this cave. More importantly, we must all be off to our new lodgings. Once we are there, in more comfortable surroundings, I will fill you in on everything. In the meantime, Ming-huà, while we're in the car, I can try and catch you up."

"Where are we going?" sighs Ming-huà.

"Not far. Still in the desert. A very nice house. One that will do quite nicely for the time being." She looks around the cave and shudders. "Off we go now!"

Once in the car, driven by Sy, the story tumbles out of Lady Oracle's mouth in a very disjointed manner, leaving Ming-huà thoroughly confused and full of many more questions than before. It almost seems the story is being told with intentional elusiveness. As part of her education, explains Lady Oracle, Ming-huà, Pythia, and Altan found themselves in a time trap, orchestrated, no doubt, by the instructors. Although the

[258]

adventures they encountered were elaborate simulations, time itself continued in unpredictable jerks and starts. A few years lost, a few years gained, until the gains overwhelmed the losses. After a decade of enduring this maze of lessons, they sensed the end drew nearer when her graduation ceremony, figuratively speaking, would be held. Altan, being a resourceful guide, managed to navigate them through this process until they returned safely.

"But why don't I remember any of this?" cries Ming-huà. "Why did I never experience this strange education when I was young?"

"Because, dear, you are not . . . how do I put this . . . you are not configured like Pythia and Altan."

"What does that mean?"

"We are not sure."

"But—" Ming-huà starts to object.

"Anyway," interjects Lady Oracle. "In the meantime, while you were gone, the police in the here and now have pieced together a theory of how so many people turned up limbless and/or dead. Agencies of the government too numerous to count, have been harassing me, Sy, and Zookeeper for the last year or so, determined to understand how a small hunchbacked girl could leave such carnage in her wake. Even the FBI is involved. Finally, the investigations petered out somewhat, as they have never been able to locate their strange 'person of interest.' Nevertheless, if they ever find you, I don't know what will happen, but it won't be good."

By the time Sy drives up to the house, Ming-huà feels too exhausted and confused to ask the multitude of questions raised by Lady Oracle's bizarre explanation. Arriving late at night, they pass through an iron gate that automatically closes behind and enter the intricately-carved front door. Even Pythia seems tired, so she and her mother are shown to their rooms on the second floor.

"Tomorrow we must talk," says Ming-huà to Pythia before they separate to their own rooms. "But tonight, I think, sleep is the most important thing."

"I agree," replies Pythia. Ming-huà is startled to realize this is the first time her daughter has used her actual voice rather than clairvoyant channels. It is a deep, yet feminine purr that jolts the senses with its sensual timbre. Within moments of retiring to bed, Ming-huà is asleep, and not even chaotic thoughts or dreams and nightmares disturb her slumber.

Altan arrives a few hours later to find Pythia waiting. They talk until early morning. What do they discuss? Mainly, how a burgeoning new species must navigate a brutal world dominated by *Homo sapiens*; an intelligent and savage population primarily focused on inflicting domestic abuses against its own kind. More dangerously, humans will hurl their destructive powers onto any peacemaker with superior adaptive traits that comes along to try and break the endless cycles of violence and suffering. Altan tells Pythia she represents a profound challenge to modern humans who have never had to face such an existential threat. Pythia and Altan speculate about how possible it may be for a single individual, mutant or not, to thwart the human propensity for cruelty and aggression so craved by an addicted, metaphorical *God*, and replace unnecessary misery with a more benign reality. If that means replacing one species with a more adaptive one, then so be it. Question is; how best to achieve this transformation?

Pythia has bloomed into quite a stunning female. The strikingly potent genes of her great-grandparents John Powers and Child of Buddha; her grandparents Michael Powers and Tamara; and her parents Ming-huà and Zookeeper; are the powerful rivers converging like great tributaries to form the vast ocean of her being. There are, of course, serious dangers. Michael Powers, for example, was misdiagnosed with schizophrenia, and he paid the price by committing suicide. But she feels his presence, as she does all of them, and the extraordinary power they have conferred flows like molten steel through her veins. However, along with their powers flow the cautionary tales of their trials and tribulations.

Nevertheless, her virtual tours of awe-inspiring human intellectual achievements and concomitantly spectacular human directed barbarities during her education have led her to the inescapable conclusion that only one goal must drive every action of her unique existence: survival and procreation.

"And to survive here," agrees Altan, "is to blend in. But to procreate with the correct mate or mates is far more problematic. We do not know how susceptible your genes are to dilution."

"Or to amplification," adds Pythia.

After a short pause, she continues, "Could I have stopped the Holocaust?"

Altan shakes his head. "Perhaps, but how many crazed dictators and serial abusers would you neutralize before they found a way to eliminate you? One of you is not enough."

"Then what is the critical mass necessary to ensure a future for my kind?"

"That is an unknown. We will not see it in our lifetime." He slaps his knee. "First things first. Blend in and then procreate. I'm not sure you can reasonably be expected to achieve the first, let alone the second."

Pythia smiles. "Perhaps you underestimate me."

"Perhaps you underestimate them. They are exquisitely attuned to difference, to otherness, which to most of them translates into a direct, immediate and irreconcilable threat. And for their kind, threats are to be confronted and destroyed."

"Fair enough. Where does one go to blend in?"

"For a sixteen-year-old human girl? High school. But that would be a foolish waste of time for you. It is my suggestion you take a variety of intelligence tests and curriculum content tests, then with the results surely to be beyond brilliant, get admitted to a good university. What would you want to major in?"

"Everything."

"Impossible. Humor them and pick one or two."

"No problem. What would be the best choices to help me blend in?"

Altan rubs his chin. "Physics and neuroscience, for obvious reasons. If you find a mate, we want him to be of the highest order intelligence."

"My father does not possess that."

"True, true. Another mutant or someone with extraordinary abilities outside academia would also be appropriate. There are many intermediates in the human world."

"Crack dealers?" she laughs.

"You never know. Are you excited to begin?"

But Pythia has stopped listening and speaks as if to herself. "Music is essential. I must learn to play the piano as homage to my great grandmother Bai Meiying."

Altan raises his eyebrows. "Excellent."

She returns her attention to the topic. "What university should I attend?"

"Berkeley, of course."

"Why there?"

Again, Altan cracks a sly smile. "Close to San Francisco. We will reoccupy Lady Oracle's Yin and Yang apartments as well as that quite beautiful old mansion that still remains at our disposal while you matriculate. Other than clairvoyancy, you will not need to exercise your more . . . forceful powers."

"And mother?"

"She would have been comfortable in the old Victorian house, but she insists on returning to her little island paradise."

"Father?"

Altan screws up his eyes. "Zookeeper is a different ball of wax. We are working on that. Probably the old Victorian house where Bataar can attend to his needs. But you father is stubborn. He may follow your mother to the island. We shall see. He is quite angry at his fate, but is adapting to his disability and is becoming reconciled to his limits. My guess is that he will follow your mother to the island."

Pythia laughs. "From what I have heard of Zookeeper, he will be bored. He must truly love her."

"He does."

"Romantic love is still a mystery to me, though I have seen virtual libraries full of such novels and films. I wonder if the ability to fall in love on a personal level is within the power of my mutant genes?"

Altan shakes his head. "That is another unknown."

Pythia stares intently into his eyes. "Why not you as a mate?"

He squirms. "Not possible."

"Strange, I cannot read your mind. I've always wondered why I can't read your mind. All I get is hieroglyphic gibberish. Why is it not possible to be my mate?"

"I am configured differently."

Now it is Pythia's turn to smile. "I see. You are the son of a certain *Goddess*, or perhaps an alien with some cosmic agenda?"

"I am configured differently."

"Is that why I cannot read your mind?"

"Yes." Altan waves his hand to signal a change in direction. "Now remember, species do not generally procreate with other species. Nevertheless, though you are supremely advanced, you are physiologically similar enough to mate with humans, so it should work. After all, *Homo sapiens* mated with *Homo neanderthalensis*."

"I see. Let us hope they are the *neanderthals* and not us!" she exclaims coyly.

"Oh, no worries there, my dear! They are! You are the next step, if you step carefully."

Pythia says, "Am I a *neanderthal* compared to you?"

"Quite the contrary. I am not of the genus *Homo* at all."

~ At University ~

With her admittance to Berkeley, Pythia takes her first steps on campus. She is now almost seventeen (in Earth years), and classes start early. Since her return to here-and-now reality, she has already assiduously studied all academic disciplines. As Altan anticipated, learning for Pythia is like breathing, and during those many years he helped guide her education, every breath tucked away in her voracious mind the most advanced principles of physics, chemistry, biology, cosmology, astronomy, history, literature, and a host of other intellectual realms. Compared to her own education in these subjects, even the most advanced human knowledge remains at an extremely rudimentary level. While Berkeley caters to a certain academic regimen, she quickly learns that most human knowledge acquisition consists of navel-gazing, pettifogging personal interests, and a partly formed mental reality crushed and flattened between their ears in vice-like ignorance; most of them seemingly devoid of sentience beyond self-absorption. Perpetually positioning themselves before mirrors, every wrinkle is noticed and obsessed over. In other words, other than a gifted few, they exhibit an almost total lack of awareness—even among the so-called intelligentsia—of universal, non-human existence.

On this first day of classes, Pythia is surrounded by hordes of animated students lugging an assortment of scholastic paraphernalia, streaming to their destination like harvester ants—not transporting sliced leaves, but the husks of thick books and metallically antiseptic laptop computers. Yet it is the non-human world making its living within this protected campus environment that she is most drawn to. Human chatter, both verbal and via telepathy, is tiresome, but the diversity of vegetation and non-human animals that dot the grounds stir in her a profound sense of oneness with the natural world. On the other hand, she feels a lamentable sense of separateness from the humans who have distanced themselves from the natural world surrounding them. Never has she felt so different. However, Altan's words of warning reverberate in her head, and she rather clumsily assumes the demeanor most likely to blend in. Once she takes a seat in the lecture hall, a wave of pity sweeps over her as she picks up the cumulative stress of the students. Most are talkative, yet all are secretly sizing up the others and measuring their own worth against the perceived competitors that fill the hall. Pythia wonders how different this environment might be if every one of them possessed her powers? How different might she herself be if the others possessed such powers? Would there be more or less competition? More downright violence, both physical and mental? More suffering or less? Stopping genocide or violent crime is one thing, but stopping inner turmoil, enervating depression, and personal anguish is another. Her existence seems a great experiment that will either advance the precepts of peace and goodwill, or wreck them altogether. An unexpected flush of compassion causes her to look around at these young faces and she feels the unfamiliar sting of guilt about their futures residing in the tender shoots of her pity. Perhaps there is more of Ming-huà in her than she imagined.

A young professor, hale and hearty, strides to the podium and begins his lecture, but Pythia is not listening. Instead, she is ruminating on the future consequences of this power she possesses. If natural selection is the great sculptor of successful adaptations, then those members of a species with such power must by necessity evolve a broader capacity for compassion and forgiveness, otherwise the experiment will end quickly in mass slaughter. Perhaps the proportion of hawks to doves will tilt in the more peaceful direction. Mutually assured destruction is a powerful incentive to lessen conflict. Breaking from these thoughts, she quickly listens to a short segment of the professor's words and is immediately aware he is teaching her nothing she does not already know. Her inclination is to leave, but this is the first class session and she is intent on blending in, so she stays and continues her musings. However, her reverie is often interrupted by the intrusive interior thoughts of many students.

Pythia is amazed how important it is for *Homo sapien* young people to spend so much time agonizing over self-awareness, self-identity, physical looks, and other forms of wasteful trivialities. Perhaps an evolutionary step forward is also a step that necessarily creates more distance between the purely personal and purely rational based objectivity. Many of humanity's greatest geniuses were more interested in humanity as a unified whole than in humans as individual bits and pieces prone to splintering. Splinters can hurt. Splinters can get infected. Splinters must be removed.

A couple of months later, after sitting through all her various scheduled lectures without paying attention, a day comes when Pythia, as is her routine, lingers after class to ruminate on the future of her species. As usual, she remains seated while the lecture hall empties. In this instance, her puzzling over the mundanity of human anxieties has segued to worries about her mother. She knows Ming-huà is depressed and her powers diminished, and is aware this is a toll that has been exacted unwillingly by the birth of Pythia herself. This unfortunate situation leads her to wonder if there is too much of *Homo sapiens* in her mother. After all, signs of human vulnerability, extreme emotion, violence-induced trauma, and lacerating guilt evidently have driven Ming-huà to self-imposed exile on a distant island, isolated both literally and figuratively. Pythia recalls Altan labeling others as "intermediates", just as her mother must be, though more advanced. Now that Ming-huà is no longer at her side, Pythia feels quite lonely, a feeling evidently not evolved out of her kind as yet.

Such emotional human remnants as loneliness that may persist in her blood Pythia considers inherited weakness, yet her attitude toward *Homo sapiens*, while superior, is also unequivocally compassionate. It is true, one result of her horrific tour in the cave of past human genocides and atrocities, is that she has come to the conclusion that to end human suffering and the abhorrent suffering humans inflict on others, humans themselves must end. However, if they are to be replaced, let it happen compassionately, gently, over time, without the ugly necessity of a brutal accession struggle. Still, she is also fully aware that the tiny spark of her own existence can be easily extinguished by the overwhelming background mass of *Homo sapiens*. How to spread her DNA against this overwhelming background? It is certain she cannot be too exacting or severe in her choice of mates. *Too bad Altan—*

[265]

"Hello. Do you need help?"

Pythia's deep concentration is broken by a youngish man standing in the aisle and leaning over the back of a seat looking at her sitting in the shadows at the row's end. She is angry at letting herself be surprised, but responds politely.

"No, thank you."

"I just returned to retrieve my notes when I noticed you sitting here."

Now she recognizes the professor whose lecture she just ignored.

"Ah, I see," she says non-committedly.

"Are you in my class?" he asks.

"Yes."

He chuckles and says, "Quantum mechanics can be the devil of a topic. You would not be the first student bedeviled by its bizarre maths and mind-twisting implications."

"It is quite elementary." The words have escaped before she remembers Altan's admonition to blend in. Such a response is not well conceived to further that goal. It is obvious he is taken aback.

"Well," he says rather defensively. "It is, after all, only a second-year quantum mechanics course, but nonetheless does baffle many students."

Pythia now weighs her words more carefully, and can come up with nothing better than, "Yes, that is true."

He is clearly interested in this very young-looking student. Always on the alert for a dyed-in-the-wool genius, he continues, "Yet you say it is elementary. I take it you understand everything so far?"

Pythia is somewhat piqued at his persistence (and the implication in his tone that she really does not understand everything) so she says, "Professor Paine, I assure you my understanding is complete."

"Ah, *touché*! Your name is. . . ?"

"Pythia Powers."

His eyes widen. "So, it's you!"

She gives him a quizzical look.

"You are the student who not only has perfect scores, but even goes beyond your answers with explanatory extensions as if I was the student and you the teacher. I often wrote an invitation on the papers to visit me during office hours, but. . . . " he throws up his hands.

[266]

"Sorry I create more work for you," says Pythia.

He ignores her comment. "Yet, I get the impression, complete as your work is, that you constrain yourself from going further . . . deeper."

"Perhaps."

Jared Paine stares openly at this young prodigy for long moments as if she is an exotic bird, then says, "Will you visit me during office hours tomorrow? There are a number of questions I would like to ask, if you would be so kind."

Pythia is not sure her being so open with this professor is suitable for blending in. "I'll try," she says unconvincingly.

"No, really. You must come. I insist. Shall we say eleven o'clock tomorrow morning in my office?"

Which answer blends better, yes or no, she wonders. The words pop out. "If you insist."

"Excellent!" he cries. "I have a lecture in a few minutes, but I'll see you tomorrow."

As he rushes off, Pythia curses herself for getting into this fix, and vows to play dumb from now on.

~

The next morning, she knocks on the professor's office door. Quickly, she hears, "Come in!" and enters to find him unabashedly leaning forward on his desk in anticipation.

"Welcome, Pythia. Have a seat."

She eyes him critically. Last night in more contemplative moments, she explored the potential of this intelligent male to be a mate. She came to no firm conclusion, but she fully intends to keep open the prospect.

"Thank you."

They look at each other briefly. Jared is suddenly and quite unexpectedly nonplussed. Something about this girl belies her youth. She is no naïve little undergraduate student anxious to please. There is an agelessness about her that—

"You said you had questions, I believe?" she asks, startling him out of his musings.

"Yes, yes." Jared's mind seems locked in a sort of haze which confuses him even more as he is used to talking with authority to young students. He tries to focus and, in the meantime, finds himself fiddling with some papers to gain time. In desperation, he grabs at a feeble lifeline and says, "Tell me about yourself."

Pythia silently laughs at his inner turmoil, so clearly conveyed through her hump. She has the mischievous inclination of suddenly dissociating the papers he absently shuffles in his hands, but vows to be good.

"Nothing to tell. Just a typical college student." *Blend in. . . .*

At last, Jared has a nucleus on which to build an intelligible conversation. "Based on what I have seen, you are definitely not a typical student. I have been thinking about our conversation yesterday and wondered if you would like to try more advanced material?"

"I don't know."

"What would you say if I give you a graduate level problem to solve right now? Just one."

"Well. . . . " Her word trails off, delightfully amused at the thoughts going through his head.

He rummages through some papers and pulls out a sheet. "Here is a problem I just gave to my graduate students. Would you like to try?"

Pythia knows she ought to accept the offer and then plead frustrated ignorance once she looks at the problem, but she senses his motives are honorable and his curiosity genuine. Besides, she feels an unbecoming but perverse desire to show off. She feigns a sigh and holds out her hand. When he releases it to her, their eyes briefly meet again and he blinks in pain at some transmission of vital energy that momentarily jolts him like a strong dose of static electricity. By the time he regains his equilibrium, she is holding up her solution to the problem.

"Do you have one that is more difficult?" she asks innocently.

"You found the solutions already?"

"They are obvious. Here is the answer to the first part of the question about how the scattering amplitude is related to the differential scattering cross-section under the Sommerfeld Radiation Condition equation. And here is the answer to the second part using the Born Approximation."

When he takes the papers from her hand, he feels the same shock and again looks at her wonderingly, then turns his attention to her answers.

While he peruses the solutions, she says, "Rather trivial, don't you think?" She quickly grimaces at this superfluous tag line and rushes to add,

"Sorry if that offended." She searches his mind for resentment, but he is genuinely impressed and more than intrigued. *That will do*, she thinks.

Concentrating on her solutions, he keeps murmuring, "Good, good, very good."

Finally, Jared looks up as wide-eyed as a kid. "Where did you learn this? I took the liberty of looking at your transcripts and they contain no information on your early schooling."

"Self-taught."

For the first time, he registers clear disbelief. "Impossible!" he blurts. "You must have had a tutor, a mentor."

Pythia reads his conflicting thoughts and detects the first hint of suspicion as well as disbelief. This realization nudges her to adopt a more cautionary position. "Yes, yes, of course I have had tutors. The strength of my knowledge is quite feeble, however. It lacks depth. That is why I am here to learn from masters like yourself."

This is Pythia's initial frank intercourse with a normal human outside her circle. She finds Jared distinctly inferior in some ways, but like a highly intelligent dog, extremely compelling and eminently pettable. She has just given him a first pet. He responds as expected.

"Well," he says. "I am impressed. Very impressed. I believe you are wasting such talents in a second-year quantum mechanics course. The problem is, if it is a problem, that your skills are similarly stellar in all your classes, regardless of subject matter."

"Why is that a problem?" (Pythia already knows, of course, but must force herself to appear unaware of a person's thoughts before they speak.)

"I want to invite you to join my graduate research team. In the beginning, it would be an unpaid position—hence, I fear you already are working with some other professor whose budget is more flexible than mine."

Pythia ponders whether accepting the offer would further the goal of blending in. As for Doctor Paine being a potential mate, she is cognizant of the difficulties involved in professors and students fraternizing. Nevertheless, there should be alternate male material in the form of graduate students.

"I would be honored."

"Good! It is unfortunately too late in the semester to transfer out of my current 'elementary' course, but you will, I hope, be more challenged around my research team. Can you come after office hours on Thursday? If so, I will walk you to my lab and introduce you to my graduate students."

With this, Pythia decides to burnish her humility skills. "Certainly. I am grateful for the opportunity. You know, there are many child prodigies that are ten- or eleven-years-old attending universities. I am truly nothing special."

Jared cannot decide whether she is being sincere, or assuming an attitude of false modesty, but he is convinced the power he feels emanating from her mind is somehow unique. *Time will tell,* he thinks.

"Yes, indeed Professor Paine, time will tell," says Pythia, unable to refrain from this last bit of whimsy. With this, she smiles and leaves.

Chapter 22: Freefall

~ Doctor Jared Paine ~

Jared Paine watches the door close behind this remarkable young woman, and his first inclination is to dismiss her last few words about child prodigies. Initially, he was willing to give her sincerity the benefit of the doubt, but upon further reflection, he concludes she is falsely modest at best, and lying at worst. Jared knows child prodigies very well. From the age of four, he himself displayed a brilliance, particularly in math, that has continued his entire life. *No,* he thinks. *This girl is different. Something about her is unique, something I feel, something I must know more about.*

No doubt the surge of electricity he felt when they exchanged papers has rattled the self-confidence he has always possessed in dealing with students, even brilliant ones. Moreover, during the entire interview, he felt an odd sensation, as if his very brain was being probed. And her final verbalization of his silent thought! As a good scientist, he scrolls through all rational explanations; perhaps he unknowingly spoke his thought aloud; perhaps it was a coincidence; maybe a reasonable guess on her part? Any might be true, but it added to the allure of her personality.

Jared Paine is single, and has never found the opposite sex particularly alluring. Neither is he homosexual. Instead, he has always found the mysteries of the universe far more fascinating and worthy of his time. All his time. Young and handsome, his self-image is almost totally devoid of any element involving the concerns of a sexual being. Many women have attempted to draw him away from his single-minded track of investigating and solving the most complex riddles of the cosmos, but all have failed. He certainly received no privileged or entitled upbringing that would have bound him so tightly to academic excellence. Somehow, his genius rose Phoenix-like from the damp ashes of a humble, rather depressing small midwestern town. His parents were working class folks, confused and uncertain about how to raise such a genius son, so their solution was to let him be and concentrate on holding together their own rather precarious financial and emotional lives. Fortunately, an elementary school English teacher and a high school Physics teacher took him under their wings and found outside help bright enough to guide his voracious appetite for learning. He already had graduated from university by the time he reached twenty. *BUT I HAD TUTORS!* he bellows inwardly when his thoughts replay the conversation with Pythia. Although she said tutors helped her along the way, he now begins wondering whether she told the truth. The more he thinks about her, the more he feels diminished. *She threw me a couple of bones about her "feeble knowledge" and needing a master with deeper knowledge. I don't think any of that is true,* he reflects peevishly.

~

Now, after retiring to his small apartment near Berkeley at the end of the day, Jared sits alone sipping wine and continuing to muse about Pythia. The residue of her presence remains in his mind; a perturbation that has rearranged the settled constellations of his comfortable, but monastic life. Jared is quite aware of the fact that he has only met her once, so the data are insufficient for such wild thoughts to be flying recklessly about in his head. Still, try as he might, he cannot quite convince himself to apply the usually potent cautionary creed of all physicists: insufficient data is perilous data. Conclusions based on insufficient data can be fatal to one's career. However, the more he thinks about it, the more he is certain Pythia presents a puzzle worthy of his time, worthy to take her place among the other puzzles he is working on, certainly worthy of pursuing additional data. In the midst of these mental peregrinations, he is surprised to discover he finds her quite beautiful, hump and all, and more intriguingly, her beauty is inexplicably different from any young woman he has ever known. Despite her tender age, she seems more sage than sorority, more worldly wise than naively impulsive. In fact, that is one of the more fascinating aspects of her personality—she appears far older and more mature than her years warrant, as one might expect a young survivor of Auschwitz or a victim of some similar catastrophic trauma to be. There is, in her, a touch of some melancholy burden underpinning the brilliant prodigy—perhaps a trauma? Abusive past? Or something altogether different? A sequestered personal trauma such as cancer or tragic accident is framed in the survivor's mind differently than trauma arising from involvement in some epic, world-shattering event. Confined personal traumas inflate pain to an outlandish degree, unbounded by the presence of others who have been untouched by the experience. However, world-shattering, tectonic catastrophes broaden the awareness that one shares pain with a multitude of others, and effectively reduces that same suffering to the recognition of personal insignificance.

Jared takes another sip of wine and laughs inwardly. "Bewitched," he says to the air. "Modern quantum physicist succumbs to medieval witchcraft." With this amusing riposte, his mind wanders off to the contemplation of consciousness and its relationship to quantum mechanics. How can ethereal thoughts and ideas arise from the behavior of matter; from mere collections of quarks and electrons? What is the physical nature of a force such as love or hate? Can thoughts alone operate on matter? Surely not. A physical push or pull is necessary to affect the behavior of matter! So why did he feel an actual physical jolt in his brain when they exchanged papers? His reaction at the time seemed to him akin to the retraction of a snail into its shell when touched. Puzzles!

But the hour is late and Jared has classes tomorrow. He puts aside these disturbing thoughts and leisurely finishes his wine as he reviews the next day's curriculum and research goals.

~

When Jared awakes the following morning, he busies himself with breakfast. No dreams had come to him, and the chilled air brings with it a more balanced, reasoned view of Pythia. Coffee clears his mind, and he chastises himself for the romantic puffery he indulged in the previous evening. *Must have been the wine,* he muses. *She is a very smart student, no more and no less. Let's see how she does with the research team.* With this dismissal, he turns his attention to other matters.

However, as Thursday's office hours approach, Pythia increasingly intrudes into his thoughts, much to his chagrin. Nevertheless, even as he grouses about this irritant, an unmistakable excitement creeps in, and he finds himself unwilling to fight against such unaccustomed arousal. No matter how hard he has tried to bury himself in work, his anticipation has grown. In frustration, he surrenders to the feeling and indulges in choreographing the meeting like an adolescent boy on the eve of his first date. In moments of self-reflection, Jared feels sheepish about his "foolish romanticism", and mocks himself for giving in to such rubbish. Truth is, Doctor Paine, stuck in his *homo sapiens* weaknesses, unknowingly aspires to be what Pythia already is. He is a chimpanzee in a rainstorm dimly aware of the advantages possessed by more technologically advanced humans sitting in dry houses eating bananas.

When Pythia enters his office, that same disorienting sense of being in the presence of someone wholly unique again takes over, and he is once more unprepared for the force she projects onto his otherwise stable mental state. Nevertheless, Jared is determined to maintain a professional demeanor, one that is appropriate for a professor toward his student (especially if the student is of the opposite sex).

"Hello again, Pythia."

"Hello."

"Before I take you to the lab, I wanted to chat a bit more."

"Okay."

Jared takes a deep breath. "Although this is a quantum mechanics course, I wonder what you know about General Relativity?"

Pythia knows where this is going, and she feels comfortable following where he leads, at least for the time being.

"Quite a lot."

"May I ask a difficult question regarding General Relativity?"

"Of course."

Jared settles back in his chair, appearing calm in spite of his nerves. "Why does zero-point energy of the vacuum not cause a large cosmological constant?"

Pythia knows the answer, but is aware this an unsolved problem in physics. Red lights go off in her head, and she knows she must proceed with utmost caution.

"Wow, that is a tough one. As far as I know, it hasn't been solved yet."

Jared nods in agreement, but a niggling doubt suggests she is not being entirely truthful. How he can doubt the words of this young student is beyond his understanding, but the feeling will not go away.

"But you have some ideas?" he prods.

Pythia has read his mind and is aware of his suspicions. On the one hand, she wants to show off her knowledge to this professor and give him further food for thought. She has chosen to play along with these little intellectual games to size up his suitability as a mate. On the other hand, blending in is essential, according to Altan. Safety first, then procreation, then, perhaps, action. Still, she cannot resist leaving him a few more crumbs to ponder.

"I have some ideas, but they are not fully formed."

"May I ask what they are?"

"Give me a chance to put them into a more cogent form and I will be happy to share."

"No problem. I am amazed you have any thoughts at all on the problem. I don't believe you have taken a General Relativity course?" He waits. Her move.

"True."

"You are just interested? Study on your own?"

Now Pythia is becoming perturbed at his persistent probing. *Fine,* she thinks. *You asked for it.* "Yes, Professor Paine, I have researched the subject on my own, and the field equations are not too difficult. As we all know, they have serious limitations. Is there a reason you are asking these questions?"

"Well, my research does involve a great deal of General Relativity, and many of my postdoc research students find it far more difficult than you make it sound."

Pythia shrugs.

"String theory? Any background?"

"Uninteresting. On the wrong track. Some interesting maths, but on the whole, from a physics point of view, a waste of time. No, I'm not very interested in going down that rabbit hole except for historical interest."

Jared is stunned at this sweeping condemnation. "Historical interest! That *is* a mouthful! My string theorist colleagues would be either outraged or amused."

Pythia shrugs again.

"Are you this way in all your subjects?"

"What way?"

"Cocky . . . not that is necessarily a bad thing in science, if you have the chops to back it up."

"I am here to learn."

Jared claps his hands. "Well, with that, let's go to the lab and get you acquainted with your lab mates."

As they walk together, Jared is shaken anew by the depths of her mind in spite of his flippant comments. Now, more convinced then ever that Pyhia Powers is something more than meets the eye, he begins to view her as a fascinating and unique asset—one to watch with care and treat with utmost deference so as not to lose her to another researcher. Little does he know (and much to her amusement) she is reading his thoughts and has viewed him in somewhat the same light as he sees her, but for different purposes. While Jared may not be unique, or the next step in hominin evolution, Pythia increasingly sees him as potentially her first sexual partner. As for any child that would be produced . . . well, she assumes Lady Oracle, Sy, and Altan will deal with that situation when it arrives. Motherhood, to her, is a technical detail, and if the child is anything like her, it will inevitably be independent of needing such an obsolete caretaker. Tender feelings for all life on earth will be the hallmark of her species, transcending the merely personal that *Homo sapiens* are so obsessed with. Her world view spans the universe while his kind is inevitably bound by these narrow human obsessions. Yet, in a primitive way, his dedication to research over socialization is encouraging. Nonetheless, Pythia sees spread before him a career filled with accolades, and, she is sure, a desire for a wife and children. On the other hand, spread before her unrolls a never-ending quest to perpetuate the survival and prosperity of a new species that will ultimately avert, with luck, the inevitable destruction of the planet and all its diverse life forms by the uncontrolled excesses of *Homo sapiens*. This is the passion that directs her passionless actions. While Pythia follows Jared, she is reminded of a famous writer's observation that passion is analogous to the nature of a seed, and finds nourishment within, tending to a predominance directing all currents toward itself, and making the whole of life its tributary.

Jared introduces Pythia to his research assistants and gives her a quick synopsis of the hypothesis they are testing. She finds the subject prosaic and searches the minds of her lab partners for signs of useful scientific knowledge. Finding none, she focuses on their interpersonal relationships, which she views as part of the process of collecting additional data to help her blend in. While Pythia is acclimating herself to the lab environment, Jared has been observing her interactions with immense curiosity. As he watches her talk with the others, he feels, not for the first time, a strong sexual attraction. Her physical beauty has finally

[276]

caught up to her intellectual splendor in his eyes. To his continuing surprise, her hump forms an exquisite curve that enhances the exotic nature of her figure. Still, he slaps down these erotic urgings with the harsh reminder that she is not yet eighteen. But, in moments of reverie, he allows his mind to wander ahead a few years.

~ Mosquitoes ~

Months pass, the term ends, and summer has arrived. Pythia has been careful not to overplay her hand and exhibit any extraordinary genius. She has followed the direction of the lab manager Sean Colby diligently, but without imagination or initiative. Her goal has been to quietly perform routine grunt work while processing valuable information on how people interact socially and in the workforce. It never fails to surprise her how much humans stress "becoming", and "finding themselves". Jewish students struggle with their cultural baggage, African American students struggle with prejudice and pride, transgender students struggle with sexual identity, and so on and so forth, *ad infinitum*. To Pythia, these are distinctions without a difference. Humans are like dogs allowing fleas to dictate their lives. Non-human animals seem to move through their lives without the need for all these human superfluities. In their obsessions with "becoming", *Homo sapiens* lash out at the world for economic power, prestige, religious dominance, political hegemony, and the like. Such lashing out inflicts on the rest of life on earth what a whip in the hands of a sadistic overseer does to the flesh on the back of a slave. Pythia often contemplates the fact that her evolved point of view might, by ignorant human standards, be a step backward toward the perspective of non-human animals. This, of course, she rejects, and views her more universal perspective as an evolutionary correction. Not uncaring, but instead more inclusive caring.

"What are you thinking?" asks Jared. He and Pythia are walking with a couple of their lab colleagues at the end of a day's work. They have reached a small stream flowing through the campus, and have paused to chat before each takes their own path home.

"Nothing," says Pythia.

Jared waves his hand in front of his face in irritation. "Damn, the mosquitoes are out in force tonight."

"Yeah, I've already been bitten a bunch of times," says Sean Colby.

The others agree, and as gnats and mosquitoes form visible clouds around their heads, they start to break up. Jared is also ready to depart when he notices there are no insects around Pythia's head.

"Mosquito repellant?" he asks.

Distracted by her own thoughts, she does not pick up his question, and responds. "What?"

"I said, did you think ahead and apply mosquito repellant? I notice you seem to be free of the little suckers."

"No, I just blink them away," she says carelessly.

"You mean ignore them?"

"No, just send them . . . elsewhere."

Jared is confused and stares at her. When a mosquito or gnat gets close to her skin, it disappears. He blinks to confirm what he sees is real. It is.

"I don't understand," he says.

Pythia realizes her mistake. "I'm just kidding," she says, finding the need to backtrack. "I really did apply mosquito repellant."

"Ah," replies Jared doubtfully. He peers closer and now sees the insects alighting on her skin. "Seems to be wearing off," he says.

"Yes, they are starting to bother me. Well, I'm off. See you tomorrow!" With this, she walks off at a brisk pace, leaving Jared to grapple with the evidence of his own eyes. *Could be a trick of the light*, he thinks. With no other plausible explanation, he turns his attention to her behavior at the lab. In this case, she is performing far below his expectations. Her passive role would ordinarily be perfectly explainable by her youth and inexperience compared to his postdoc students, but he knows she is not a normal student. Something is holding her back, he concludes. But this leads to a host of other questions, not the least of which is the mystery of what is holding her back. *If only she was older*, he thinks. *Can't take her on a date, but there's always office hours*. Having access to her records, he knows she will turn eighteen in a few weeks. Even so, a thirty-something professor dating an eighteen-year-old girl would raise not a few eyebrows. Jared Paine has no intention of ruining his career, but on the other hand. . . .

~ Office Hours Again ~

In order to explore his concerns and satisfy his scruples further, Jared is waiting to meet Pythia for office hours one afternoon late in the semester. To his dismay, the sexual arousal she induces in him is growing more intense. Fantasies of making love with her have intensified, and his determination to block them has weakened. Nevertheless, he has risked calling for a meeting with her alone in order to try and get to the bottom of why she is performing at a mediocre level in the lab. After carefully examining his motives to meet her alone, he persuades himself they are honorable professional concerns rather than personal.

~

The instant Pythia enters his office, her hump picks up the cognitive dissonance plaguing his mind. Before their conversation begins, for example, she is pricked by a very clear and intense desire on his part to see her naked. It is a fleeting thought, but a powerful one. This does not displease her, and she tucks the knowledge away for future use. One of the advantages of being among the first individual to branch off into a new species is that the physiognomy of the old species is not so different as to be sexually unattractive. Jared Paine is a good-looking man; a healthy specimen to experience intercourse with for the first time.

"Hello Pythia, have a seat."

"Thank you."

Jared clears his throat nervously. "I wanted to talk with you a little about the lab."

"Yes?"

"Are you happy there?"

"Yes, why do you ask?"

Jared, now feeling a bit more comfortable, leans back in his chair. "It just seems you are not fully using your substantial talents. Is Sean holding you back?"

"Not at all."

"Is there something else holding you back?"

Though she knows precisely his meaning and the fears behind it, she feigns ignorance. "Not that I'm aware of. How do you mean?"

"I mean, you seem hesitant to fully engage, make suggestions, come up with new ideas, contribute your own point of view and analyses."

[279]

Pythia hesitates, then seems to come to a decision. "The breakthrough you are hoping to make with this research, your hypothesis, is, well, flawed. I can only do what is asked and wait for you and your team to discover the errors."

Jared's face turns red, then white. He remains speechless for a few shocked moments.

Pythia waits quietly.

"What do you mean?" he sputters feebly.

"Vacuum energy is orders of magnitude weaker than predicted for different reasons than you have hypothesized."

Jared feels faint. "You know?"

"Of course."

In words he barely recognizes are coming from his mouth, Jared asks in stupefaction, "Who are you?"

"As a friend once said, 'Ahab is Ahab'."

Jared rubs his forehead and sits marshalling his reasoning mind. Nevertheless, his pique gets the better of him. "Pythia, or whatever your real name is, I need you to tell me why we are on the wrong track."

"I will simplify." She balances her notebook on her knees and begins writing equations. After filling a few pages, she hands them to Jared.

Again, he feels an electric shock when he takes hold of them. He scans the papers, narrows his eyes in frustration, and starts again with the utmost concentration. When he reaches the end, he drops the papers on his desk and looks at her in frightened perplexity.

"I don't understand them," he says.

"I know."

"How do you know?"

"Your thoughts are tangled, a mixture of anger and disbelief. I cannot expect you to understand."

He grabs one of the papers and waves it in the air. "But it is gibberish to me! Some terms I don't even recognize as part of physics or math!"

"I am aware."

"What? You can read my thoughts?"

"They are simple enough."

[280]

Pythia is fully aware she is throwing all caution to the wind. Altan's warning is a distant echo now. Somehow, these past few months of leafy serenity above ground have concealed an explosive growth of roots boring deep into the rocks and soil below. They have smashed through the hardpan installed by the deistic masters that control Lady Oracle, Sy, and Altan. In short, Pythia has come to realize she is fully independent of the behavioral demands of metaphorical *Gods*, *Goddesses*, or any plethora of minor deities. Her natural inclination is toward action rather than subterfuge.

With this last insult, Jared's face burns red and he flares in rage. "Who the hell do you think you are?"

Pythia remains silent, gazing steadily at him until the brief squall passes.

"Okay," says Jared, forcing himself to be calm. "Do you work for the government? Some sort of secret program? NASA? FBI? CIA? Tell me who you are working for. Or are you. . . . ?"

"Am I what?" Pythia, superior as she is, still is young enough to enjoy the pleasure of cat paws toying with mouse lives.

"I don't know . . . an alien? . . . from the future? . . . Christ! I can't believe I'm even saying these things!"

"I am none of those things," she says evenly.

He loosens a bit. "Well, that's a relief. So tell me, why Berkeley? Why these low-level classes? Why bother with my little lab with its doomed research hypothesis? Why?"

"At first, it was important for me to blend in, but now, I am searching for appropriate mates."

Jared's mouth drops open. He shakes his head and laughs a little crazily. "Well, with statements like that, you're doing one hell of a job not blending in!"

"As it stands now, with you at least, I am less interested in blending in than exploring relationship opportunities. As I indicated, I am looking for mates."

Paine looks duly shocked. "Mates? Plural?"

Pythia is fully aware of the human male's fragile ego, primitive perspective about female sexuality, and obsession with personal property rights. "One as extraordinary as yourself will suffice," she says.

For the time being, she adds in her mind.

[281]

Chapter 23: Secrets Revealed

~ Fallout ~

"Pythia!" cries Jared in horror. "Mates? Really, are you some robot or stereotypical alien, or . . . I don't know what! I hardly know where to begin. First, your knowledge is beyond my understanding, but I know enough to consider you an invaluable asset to science. Second, as for mating, you're only seventeen!"

"Yet, when I first entered your office, you clearly expressed the strong thought that you wanted to see me naked."

Jared's face flushes red as a beet. "I . . . I . . . that is irrelevant. You really can read minds?"

"Yes. For your peace of mind, I will soon be eighteen."

Jared stands and paces nervously. "Pythia, you have to tell me who you are. I need to know. It is incumbent on me to inform people . . . powerful and influential people, what you are capable of."

"Yes, I know that is in your mind, but it will not be possible to let you do that."

"And if I do?"

"I will feign ignorance."

"I . . . I. . . . " Jared splutters. "As far as I know, Pythia, you are escaped from some asylum. For heaven's sake, tell me! You know the government will be interested, Pythia. There is too much here to let pass."

"Professor Paine, I know your thoughts. There is a little larceny in your heart. If I cooperate in your lab, you might forego mentioning my talents, particularly to the government, eh? Am I right?"

Jared is again dumbstruck, and has a terrible feeling of impotence before the power of this person. A great, helpless resentment grips his mind.

"Damn you! Who are you?"

"Pythia Powers, hunchback."

He lets out a tremendous sigh. "Regardless of your threats, I will speak out. Science demands it. Now, tell me who you really are and where you're really from."

"Professor Paine, none of what you say will matter to me beyond your consideration of me as a mate, a lover." She holds up a dismissive hand. "After I turn eighteen, of course. Or do you prefer nineteen?"

"Why this interest in a mate? I have to say, your attitude toward the subject is hardly flattering to me, or any male for that matter."

"Yes, *Homo sapiens* males," she says with a touch of contempt, or pity, he is not quite sure.

Jared tilts his head in an exaggerated manner. "Are you not *Homo sapiens* yourself?"

Pythia stares at him in an odd way. "You are thinking now that I am suffering from delusions of grandeur, perhaps schizophrenic delusions, not unusual in brilliant people. Here, you are catastrophically wrong. My grandfather Michael Powers . . . well, that is a different story for a different time."

"So, at least it is now established you have a grandfather. Since I cannot keep my thoughts secret from you, it is true I have considered the possibility you are suffering from delusions, possibly schizophrenia. Are you?"

"What I am 'suffering from' is very much beyond your understanding right now. Just as you did not recognize many terms in my equations regarding vacuum energy, you would not recognize the terms of my own existence. Suffice to say, I am looking for mates, and I have found you."

"I ask again, do you believe you are not from the species *Homo sapiens*?"

"That is a trick question. One I am not inclined to answer. Now that you at least partially understand me, I will leave. I'm afraid I must also leave your lab. However, I will remain at Berkeley and take classes as usual next semester. I am easily found."

"Blending in?"

Pythia smiles and nods. Without another word, she walks out, and in her wake, leaves a mystified, angry, and fearfully conflicted professor who stares at the closed door in a fog of absurd speculations.

~

Jared eventually stops staring into space like a fool and hurriedly rummages through the papers on his desk, trying to find the equations she had written. They are gone. He is sure he did not return them, and is equally sure she did not take them from his desk. *Another mystery!* he moans inwardly. But fast upon this uneasy reflection comes a distinct memory. *The mosquitoes!*

With this epiphany, Jared cancels his classes for the day and sequesters himself in the confines of his apartment to concentrate on putting himself back together and commanding his rational mind to resume control. *It seems more likely she's delusional than some supernatural or extraterrestrial explanation*, he reasons. *If I report her condition, she will simply deny and deflect. But what if I do my own investigation? Start with the data on file with Berkeley, contact her parents, maybe interview them. There's the ticket! Better a low-key background check. More data, more basis for action.*

As much as Jared attempts to organize his thoughts and mentally rough out his next steps, the mosquitoes keep disrupting his concentration. In exasperation, he shakes his head and focuses on the essentials. First, locate her parents. Second, visit them. Third, go from there. Period! He toys with the idea of taking a leave of absence, but it is close to summer break so he has some time to perform his detective work.

The next day, Jared has obtained the telephone numbers of Pythia's parents from student records. He dials the mother, Ming-huà Powers. Disconnected. Next, he dials father, Matthew Weston. (He notes with interest that Pythia has taken her mother's maiden name.) Disconnected. Somehow, he is not surprised. Email addresses are also invalid. He checks the physical addresses and finds they are fictitious. Dead ends. During the following weeks, he checks online sites that assist in finding people as well as every search engine, social media, mental institution, court records, government watch, traffic violations, felonies, weapons permits, occupational registries, ancestry sites, bankruptcies, even obituaries. Nothing. All dead ends.

Far from allowing such setbacks to discourage him, Jared is confirmed in his belief there is a rational explanation for the profound mystery surrounding Pythia Powers. His inclination is tending towards some sort of government involvement, perhaps she is involved in undercover work. Also left open is the possibility of a delusional personality abandoned by family. He has eliminated aliens; a path that if taken, would certainly lead into a deep pit where only crackpots reside. Another far-fetched possibility is that she is involved in some bizarre government experiment. However, none of these theories hold up under his professionally tempered scrutiny. Nevertheless, the scientist's stubborn pursuit of truth drives him on. *But those damn mosquitoes! And the disappearing equations! Damn!*

Jared might have gone on indefinitely pursuing the invisible, but one late morning he is summoned to the administration building. When he arrives imbued with equal measures of trepidation and curiosity, two men introduce themselves as investigators for the FBI and ask to speak in a private room. After entering and closing the door, they sit stone-faced behind a long table. One of the investigators openly turns on a tape recorder. "Do you mind?"

"No."

"Have a seat, please."

"Thank you."

"Sorry for the intrusion," says the one who is evidently senior. "We have been asking a number of your colleagues some questions pertaining to a student of yours, and now we would like to ask you."

"Yes?"

"Her name, as far as we can ascertain, is Pythia Powers. Berkeley has kindly provided us with her records."

"Yes?"

"Her mother, Ming-huà Powers, was a witness many years ago to a rather odd incident. Take a look."

The agent hands Jared a binder. Opening it, he finds numerous old San Francisco newspaper articles about victims inexplicably losing their arms at a presumed crime scene. He scans the clippings and looks up.

The agent hands him a second binder, this time with articles from Baltimore about a similar incident where people lost more than just their arms. In both instances, the bloodless nature of the mutilations could not be explained.

"Are you sensitive to graphic pictures, Professor Paine?"

"Not particularly."

A third binder is handed him, this with official police photographs. Multiple men are shown in an alley with missing body parts, including heads. There is no blood. Jared murmurs, "Oh, my *God*, these are awful. What happened to them?"

Shaking his head in horror, Jared returns the binders and waits. The agent ignores Jared's question and continues in a clipped, professional manner.

"We have recently received new evidence so the case has been reopened. Since your student's mother was a witness to both the San Francisco and Baltimore incidents, we wish to speak with her. Unfortunately, she has disappeared, so we want to talk with her daughter and hopefully find her mother's whereabouts."

"Yes, I can see that," says Jared reddening. "Why not just ask the daughter, Pythia Powers? What do you want of me?"

"Before approaching Ms. Powers, we have asked her professors to inform us if any of you have noticed peculiarities or areas of concern regarding the girl."

"I see."

"Have you?"

Jared feels faint. In no way did he ever foresee this eventuality. His heart pounding in an agony of indecision, he stalls.

"Is she involved in some crime?"

"No, not that we know of."

"Her mother?"

The two men glance at each other. The one who has not yet spoken now looks at Jared and says, "A witness only, as far as we know."

"Then I'm not sure why you're asking me these questions."

"They are harmless enough," says the same man. "We're just trying to find her mother."

"But why ask about peculiarities?"

"Professor Paine, if you are unwilling to answer our questions, please tell us now."

Jared pales. "I am willing, I am willing. Well, to answer your question, she is a very very smart girl. That is the only peculiarity I have noticed." Jared assumes his best poker face, but inside his stomach is churning. *I just lied to the FBI*, he thinks.

"Has she ever mentioned her mother to you?"

"No."

"Have you met her during your office hours?"

"A few times."

"Anything she said or did that strike you as different?"

"How do you mean?"

The first agent says rather sharply, "I am sure you understand the word different, professor. Anything out of the ordinary, other than her brains, that you noticed?"

"No."

"Did you ever notice anything missing at the end of your meetings?"

"Missing, like she stole something?"

"No, like it was there and then it was gone."

Worse and worse, frets Jared. He hesitates, then speaks with as much confidence as he can muster. "No."

Again, the two agents exchange glances, making him even more nervous. Jared now feels certain they know he is lying. A strong urge to backtrack and tell the truth almost overcomes him, but he is in too deep. Even if he corrects the record, how are they now to believe what he has seen and suspects? They would think him either a liar or crazy.

"Professor Paine, are you sure you noticed nothing at all unusual other than her academic skills? Anything at all?"

"Absolutely not." When will they stop asking these questions? After answering each one with a lie, Jared feels increasingly trapped, panicky, and angry. He feels compelled to elaborate. "I mean, we only talked about her classes, assignments, working in the lab, that sort of thing."

"We know she has been working in your lab."

"No longer."

"Why not?"

"I don't know. Summer break. She had other projects and interests. It happens all the time with lab assistants."

"She is a bit young to be working in your lab with graduate students and post-docs, isn't she?"

Jared is afraid he will soon fall apart, but continues with what he prays is a steady voice. "Yes, indeed. But, as I said, she is an extraordinary student. Very advanced."

"Anything else?"

"No." He worries he spoke the word too quickly.

Both agents rise. "Thank you, Professor Paine. Here are our cards. If you think of anything, please call. Call anytime, day or night."

"Yes, okay. I can go?"

They both nod and gesture toward the door.

Jared walks very carefully out of the room, not wanting to appear in a hurry. His mind is whirling with a host of questions and suppositions. His nerves are jittery and he goes over the interview many times, cursing at himself for lying. *Why didn't I just tell the truth?* he keeps asking. No answer comes. Now, he wants to get as far away from Pythia Powers as possible. Stop his search, stop talking with her, stop any and all communication. *I'm in enough hot water as it is*, he thinks resentfully.

~ Enter Pythia ~

Jared is walking to his car with laptop case swinging by his side. His mind turns down a thousand different alleyways, all leading nowhere except to the fact he is torn between fears of entanglement (particularly in unsavory criminal investigations) and scientific exhilaration that Pythia, his discovery, is so utterly unique. He begins to question the basis of his anxieties and too-hasty decision to flee from her. After all, he has no involvement in covering up any crimes. Evidently, they are only after Pythia's mother as a witness. Besides, there are confidentiality issues he can fall back on, if things get a little hot. But Pythia herself! The driving questions remain unanswered. Who is she? What is she? Where did she come from? Should he go to her after time has passed and the FBI have long departed? What would he say? If he plays his cards right, and she cooperates with him, a Nobel prize might be in the offing. But, ah! There is this nonsense about being a mate. But she is attractive. And the mosquitoes! The equations!

In this rather feverish state, Jared does not notice someone walking parallel to him. After a while, the person closes the gap and is so close they are touching shoulders, so startling Jared he abruptly stops. He turns to give a disapproving look to this rude individual when, to his amazement, he sees it is Pythia. He is momentarily speechless, and before he can gather his composure, she laughs.

"Don't be concerned," she says cheerfully. "You did the right thing. I will speak with them and dispel any concerns regarding your . . . involvement."

"Damn it, Pythia! I could be fired for this, or worse if the FBI wants to push it."

"If you feel this way, why didn't you simply tell them the truth?"

By this time, Jared has jettisoned his disbelief in her clairvoyant powers and assumes she knows everything he is thinking. "Since you can read my mind, you should know the answer to that, although *God* knows I don't! That is a damn good question. What is the truth, Pythia? You have never, well, what I mean is that you have never told me what the truth about you is! Why I stick my neck out for a person who will not be honest with me is . . . ridiculous! It's just plain stupid! Now look, I have put myself in harm's way for you, so the least you can do is tell me the truth."

"You humans—I mean we humans—are perpetually in search of truth, which in fact is as pliable as potter's clay."

"Christ! No armchair philosophy now, Pythia." He looks around anxiously. "We're probably being followed by the FBI as we speak."

"In point of fact we are, so let us lead them to somewhere more comfortable. I know a nice little restaurant which serves excellent tea and we can talk."

"Christ!" Jared mutters again, but reluctantly follows, one hand planted firmly in his trouser pocket to hide his nervousness and convey nonchalance, the other gripping the laptop handle with white-knuckle force.

Once seated and tea served, Pythia proceeds in what Jared considers an infuriatingly calm voice.

"Professor Paine, I understand you have been shaken by your experience, but your unwillingness to give information will serve you well in future."

"Oh, really? How nice. What good does that do me now?"

Pythia reads in his mind a troubling kernel of weakness. This takes her a bit by surprise, but she reassures herself by giving him the benefit of the doubt. After all, he is well out of his comfy academic element. She asks somewhat sarcastically, "Is your fear of outside consequences overcoming your scientific curiosity? If so, Galileo would be disappointed."

Evidently taken aback, Jared knows it does no good to lie. "Why ask a question you already know the answer to? Of course I am afraid. And as for my scientific curiosity, you have given me precious little

[289]

information to go on, and if I am fired because of this, I cannot do proper science anyway."

Her eyes drill into his soul. "I am your science," she says.

Again, he is taken off guard. "What do you mean?"

"I mean there is much more to me that you can even imagine."

"Oh, don't worry on that score, I have been imagining you and your . . . uniqueness, for a very long time."

"Professor, you haven't scratched the surface."

"Tell me."

"No. At least, not yet. There are things that must first be settled."

"Such as?"

"I know you will instinctively recoil when you hear, so let us leave it for the time being. I must think further. It is possible I have made a mistake. A very grave error, which I do not want to compound."

"Goddamn it, Pythia!" he cries, then catches himself and exercises damage control. "Didn't know you made mistakes."

"A major mistake in adaptation can end this experiment in evolution."

"You talk in riddles."

"That propensity is apparently in my genes."

"No more riddles. Tell me who you are. Tell me everything. If not, I swear I'll go to the FBI."

"Yes, yes, I see this was a mistake. Professor Paine, go to the FBI if you wish. There is nothing amiss. There is no deep criminal mystery here. They are simply looking for my mother who witnessed some terrible incidents. I will gladly inform them where she can be found. It is you I am disappointed in. However well I can read minds, reading character is a much deeper mystery."

Jared stares off into space, feeling an inexplicable tinge of guilt and shame. But as he looks, he sees two familiar figures enter the restaurant. Immediately, his emotions swing to near panic.

"It's them!" he whispers to Pythia.

"Yes, I know. They followed us here and have been waiting patiently outside. I don't need to read their minds to know they are tired of waiting. Invite them to join us."

"What?"

"Invite them!"

Stunned by the power of her command, he hails the two agents. As they approach, Jared gestures toward two empty chairs. "Have a seat," he says as nonchalantly as he can.

"Hello again," says the older agent smiling. "Long time no see."

"Yes, I just unexpectedly ran into Pythia and we opted to have tea."

"I see that."

Jared introduces them to Pythia.

She smiles sweetly. "Professor Paine tells me you are searching for my mother. Is that correct?"

"Indeed, it is."

"Well, that is simple enough. She is living with my father on an island off the coast of Washington State. What do you want of her?"

"She witnessed some nasty business years ago. Actually, she witnessed two rather violent incidents. People were killed. New evidence has recently emerged causing us to reopen the case."

"New evidence?" In asking this question, Pythia probes their minds to learn about this new evidence. Once she finds out what she is seeking, her interest in these men melts away.

"Yes, but we cannot divulge that information," says the younger agent. "Do you know anything about the incidents she witnessed? Did she talk about them to you?"

"There were more than one?"

"Yes. As I just said, there were two, each a continent apart."

"And a third as well," injects the senior partner.

"No, mother never told me. However, I do know she will want to cooperate with the FBI. Do you have paper? If so, I will write her address and telephone number."

The younger agent hands her a dog-eared notebook. "You can write it in this."

Meanwhile, the older agent asks, "Have you ever noticed anything unusual about your mother?"

"Unusual?"

"Yeah."

"Like what?"

"We were hoping you could tell us."

"I mean, what do you mean by unusual?"

"Oh, anything. Unusual abilities. Unusual powers, that sort of thing."

Pythia laughs. "Not at all. Only the power to make me feel awful if I was naughty."

"Miss Powers, let me be honest. We have reason to believe your mother saw something that we have not yet been able to explain."

"Oh?"

"Would you mind looking at some crime scene photos for us?"

"Here?"

"Well, we can go to our offices if you wish."

"No, here is good. Much more relaxing, don't you think?"

"Are you at all squeamish, Miss Powers?" asks the older agent sharply. "The pictures are quite graphic."

"I don't think so."

The younger agent gives her the binders. As Pythia leafs through the pages, the older agent says, "This is what your mother witnessed. What we do not understand is why there is no blood, no signs of violence. The survivors swear they had all of their limbs before the incidents. Either they are lying, or there is something very odd going on here."

"And you think my mother saw what caused this?"

"Well, yes, that is our hope."

"But didn't you already interview her?"

"Yes."

"And what did she say?"

"She knew nothing about how it happened."

"Do you think her story will have changed now?"

"As I said, new evidence has emerged. Maybe her memory will be jogged."

"This is terrible," Pythia says returning the binders. "I hope she is able to help solve the mystery."

"So do we. Here are our cards, Miss Powers. If you think of anything, please call us."

"Of course."

"Thank you. We may be in touch with both of you in the future."

They nod to Jared and leave.

Chapter 24: A Suitable Mate?

~ Sinking Deeper ~

After the two agents are out of sight, Jared turns to Pythia angrily. "You lied again!"

"How so?"

"You played dumb that entire time. What is your game?"

"I gave them the information they requested, did I not?"

"But the rest of it—all make believe innocence."

Pythia frowns. "I sense those around us are getting too curious. Let us leave and I will answer those questions I can."

"No, you go your way and I go mine. I'm done. From now on, you are on your own. I'm a physicist, not a detective."

Jared pays and joins Pythia waiting outside. "Okay," says Jared. "I'm going home. Tomorrow, I have work to do. I'm serious. Much as I want to help you, I don't want to get more involved than I already am."

"Foolish man!" snaps Pythia. "You are not helping me! It is I that am helping you. I am giving you an opportunity that no scientist has ever had. Your thoughts tell me you are a scared boy, in over his head. Are you really so weak and so blind?"

"Maybe I am, but I do not intend to let you drag me into a situation I don't even understand, especially if it involves the FBI."

"Perhaps you will understand this; take a look at your laptop."

Jared looks down and sees it disappear in an instant. He is left grasping thin air and watching dumbfounded as Pythia walks briskly away. Pedestrians swirl around him muttering angrily while he stands statue-like, his mind a chaotic miasma of disordered thoughts.

That night, his mental tribulations continue, and sleep will not come. In the morning, over coffee, his intentions begin to turn. Distance in time and space from the shock of dealing with FBI agents has a calming effect, and Jared weighs the consequences of walking away from Pythia for good. While her presence has been disruptive, to say the least, he knows she has brought an oddly exhilarating immediacy to his life.

[293]

Certainly, he ponders between sips, *my career has been as satisfying as one could hope for, but assuming she is right about my research . . . damn! Of course she's right! Where does that leave me? It leaves me access to perhaps the most significant scientific development in history. And to chuck that once-in-a-lifetime opportunity overboard merely to continue a placid existence? Who is she really? What are her true powers? She hints there are many more . . . good God! . . . mosquitoes and equations and now a laptop! Gone in a blink! Turn my back on that? What sort of gargantuan fool would I be to do such a thing? Then there is the mating business. To mate? She is beautiful, but how can one be married to a person who can read your mind . . . and God knows what else!*

These thoughts and the possibilities they engender make him dizzy. Eventually, they drive him to a bold decision he would never have considered even a few days ago. This bold move becomes an on-again, off-again proposition for a few harried days, but finally. . . .

~

One late afternoon, Doctor Jared Paine stands in front of Pythia Powers' apartment, hesitating momentarily before he takes the plunge and lifts his hand to knock. Just as his knuckles are about to strike the door, it opens and Pythia stares at him in all her glory. She looks gorgeous, to him, clothed in a long, understated dress, her eyes lustrous with an air of amusement creasing the corners.

"Hello Professor Paine," she says brightly, without any hint of surprise.

"You have been expecting me, I suppose," he says a bit morosely, his hand still raised in preparation to knock.

"Of course. I once questioned your character, but your presence here is quite reassuring. Come in."

A sudden desire to see her naked again pops into his consciousness, and he quickly tries to suppress it before she notices. Too late.

"If all goes well," she says as she leads him to a small living room. "You will see me naked soon enough."

"This is impossible," he bellows. "Reading minds is like a form of rape."

"You're the one who wants me naked—but I will desist from verbal observations of your thoughts. Although, I have to admit, I cannot

[294]

resist one more comment; you are fascinated to know what my hump looks like unclothed."

Jared reddens even more, but holds his tongue.

"Wine?" she asks.

"Yes, that would be nice."

"Red or white?"

Jared laughs. "You already know."

"Red it is."

He accepts the wine and takes a rather long swig. "I guess you also know why I'm here?"

Pythia looks at him sympathetically and says, "Professor Paine, although I can read minds, more often than not only a few thoughts rise to clarity above the low-level gabbling which is non-stop and basically undecipherable to me. From now on, just speak what you have to say and there should be no confusion. As I said, no more verbalization of your mental cognitions on my part. Please recall what I also said; words are transparent, but character is opaque. Now, let's start over. "Why are you here?"

Jared flashes a mischievous smile. "To get my laptop back."

"Unfortunately, that is impossible."

"One way street, eh?"

"Correct."

"Did you really make it disappear, or are you a master hypnotist? Tell the truth or I'll be well on my way to Bedlam."

"I really made it disappear, at least in the current dimensions we occupy."

Jared's eyes widen. "Your mother! Those poor men! Can it be?"

"It can and is. Those 'poor' men, by the way, were rapists and murderers."

"Yes, perhaps, but you can't just go around killing people and removing their limbs."

Pythia remains silent.

"How is it done? I mean, tell me the physics of it."

"Even I do not fully understand. For sixteen years, I was taught knowledge far beyond humans, yet that was never explained to my satisfaction. Some concepts are beyond even me."

"Beyond humans? Are you not human?"

Pythia shrugs. "Depends on your definition of human."

"Okay, I'll be more precise. Are you a member of species *Homo sapiens*?"

"If I tell you, I fear you will feel insulted."

Jared swallows nervously. "Just tell me. I am a scientist after all."

"No, I am not of your species . . . or perhaps better to say, not entirely of your species."

"And this business of a mate? How would that work?"

"At this stage of the evolutionary process, reproduction with a member of *Homo sapiens* is possible."

"How nice and romantic! Look, Pythia, my interest in you is purely scientific."

"That is why you want to see me naked? Careful, I can read minds, professor. Your statement is not entirely accurate."

"Christ! This is impossible! Can we get back to science? I want to understand what you understand. I want to learn how your powers work. You are research enough for a hundred physicists for a hundred years."

For the first time, Pythia looks at him with sadness in her eyes. "Professor Paine, you cannot understand what I understand, not even in a hundred years."

"Why is that?" huffs Jared. "Are you so advanced that a Ph.D in physics will never understand?"

"Correct."

"But, that's absurd!"

Pythia is tempted to use the *Homo neanderthal-Homo sapiens* analogy, but thinks better of it. "Be that as it may, it is so."

"In other words, I can be no help to you as a scientist; only as a lying co-conspirator with the FBI?"

"Not entirely true."

"Don't tell me; it's the whole mating thing again."

Pythia abruptly stands and holds out a heavy marble bookend. "Here, take this and stand on the other side of the room."

"Why?"

"Please, just do it."

Jared moves to the far wall and waits, weighing the heft of the bookend, wondering what this alien hunchback is up to now. While waiting, he feels an increasingly exhilarating excitement complemented by a new appreciation of her beauty. This appreciation is not born of any normal sexual attraction he is aware of, but of some undiscovered sensation somewhat analogous to physically perceiving the presence of other dimensions. The impression conveyed is a bone-chilling but breathtaking awareness of complete alienation from earthly reality.

"Throw it," she says.

"What?"

"Throw it at me!"

He tosses it underhand to her.

She catches it and tosses it back. "No, no! Throw it at my head as hard as you can! Try and hit me. Try and hurt me."

Jared hesitates.

"Do it!" she commands.

"No," he objects. "If I hit you, it could be fatal. Don't be ridiculous!"

"I told you to do it! You are the presumed scientist. Here is your experiment. Are you that weak?"

"I don't want to hurt you! I have a strong arm. Used to be a pitcher in high school."

"I understand. Now, throw it as hard as you can. Now!"

Jared throws the object at a much-slower speed than he is capable of.

Pythia disgustedly catches it in one hand and tosses it back. "For the last time, as hard as you can!"

Jared reaches back and flings it as hard as he can at her body, trying to avoid her head. It disappears in mid-flight.

Before he has time to close his astonished mouth, she tosses him the matching bookend. "Again! Harder! At my head!"

He winds up and throws all his weight into the pitch using her head as a target.

Again, it vanishes.

"I don't believe it," mutters a shocked Jared. "I can't believe it! Hypnosis, or some parlor trick! Has to be."

"No, Professor Paine, no parlor trick. In reading your mind, I can tell you are struggling to make sense of the nonsensical. Nevertheless, it is true. What you just saw is real."

"Where did they go?"

Pythia spreads her arms. "Atoms and molecules disbursed into the environment. For all intents and purposes, gone, but for their constituent particles. This, at any rate, is the simplest answer. Other dimensions are involved, but I prefer not to go there."

"Like the mosquitoes? Like the equations? Like my laptop? Like those men in the photographs? Right?"

"Yes."

"Pythia, you need to tell me everything, from the beginning, so I can understand all this."

"You will not understand. I want you as a mate, not a disciple."

"Don't think of me as a disciple, think of me as a student. Role reversal!"

Pythia laughs. "Charming. Professors should not sleep with their students. Especially young students, like you."

"Pythia, I'm older than you, by a lot."

This time, it is Pythia that appears confused. "I'm not sure about that. Remember I mentioned being taught for sixteen years?"

"Yes."

"Well, I don't think they were the kind of years that pass here."

"Here?"

"You see, impossible to explain and impossible for you to understand. Let me ask you this: you are a physicist, correct?"

"Correct."

"And modern string theory posits multiple dimensions, correct?"

"Correct."

"Now, here is the crucial point: can you visualize (or even really comprehend) a fifth or sixth or tenth dimension?"

"The math—"

"No! Not the maths. Can you visualize it? Comprehend it beyond the equations?"

"Well, no."

"And even the equations are unknown to you."

"Well, there are those who—"

"No. I guarantee you and your colleagues do not know, and in fact are on the wrong track. You are a prisoner of the four dimensions your brains evolved to experience. No amount of abstract knowledge or imagination will ever truly free you from this four-dimensional

[298]

incarceration no matter how hard you try. Now do you see what I mean? You cannot visualize multiple dimensions, you cannot comprehend multiple dimensions, and you do not even have the math correct."

"And you can. . . . "

"Yes, I can visualize some multiple dimensions, I can comprehend them, I can enter them, I can experience them, and I know the underlying maths. In your frame of reference I am now eighteen."

"But you just said you're not sure."

"Yes, but that uncertainty is the great grey area of my life. I believe those sixteen years were much much longer, and they passed in some space unconnected to the here and now on earth. However, I simply do not know for sure; perhaps a hundred years or more, perhaps less."

"Then who taught you?"

"That is as far as we can go, Jared."

"First time you called me that. Now I feel extremely young compared to you. You really want a thirty-something *Homo sapiens* male to mate with a potentially ancient female of unknown origin? A female of a different species?"

Pythia assumes a sly smile. "I understand many males prefer exotic relationships, exotic sex. And you?"

"Damn it, you ask that question to get me thinking and probe my mind. I can feel you rummaging around. Get out!"

"Okay, I am out, but I saw enough to know you are definitely a *Homo sapiens* male, one who has abstained from sex for far too long."

"Regardless of what you say, I am still a scientist. Simply being a stud service for you is unacceptable. What do I get out of this mating business?"

"Oh, Jared, you get to father a new species. Your genes are serviceable and will act as a substrate for mine."

"That will go down as the most bizarre pick-up line in history."

"Think of what worlds will open before you!"

"As an inferior slave?"

"No, that is not in the consciousness of our kind. You are thinking like a monkey. Inferiority is a *Homo sapiens* concept. You will be by my side if you make the decision to go forward."

"Go forward? How do you mean?"

"I mean, you will be my interpreter of the intricacies and eccentricities of your species, just as Zookeeper was my mother's interpreter. There are many places to go, many injustices to prevent, and much suffering to be addressed."

Jared is too overwhelmed to take it all in, so he says simply, "I can't understand why I am chosen for this."

"One important caveat you must remember and accept."

"What is that?"

"While you will be the first mate, there will of necessity be others."

Jared nods. "I'm not so stupid that I didn't figure that out. If I agree, what next? Hop in bed?"

"One asset possessed by *Homo sapiens* is their endless penchant for expressing humor at precise moments. No. Next step is to meet those who have guided me."

"Introduction to the parents for approval?"

"Something like that. Be here next Tuesday at ten and we will leave for San Francisco."

"I don't . . . okay, I'll be here."

"Meanwhile," says Pythia with a wry smile. "I have to find a couple of new bookends."

~ A Meeting ~

With this exchange ringing in his ears, Jared returns home for the next few days to contemplate what had just happened. He feels a mix of emotions so alien as to force a reevaluation of who he is, who he thought he was, and who he will be in future. To his surprise, in the course of this reflection, he experiences tremendous liberation from a cluster of benevolent tyrannies that had surreptitiously driven his life to this point; career, prestige, self-importance, and a cavalier attitude toward the roiling swarm of life surrounding him. Now, with his surrender to Pythia's authentic superiority in both intellectual ascendence and spatial manipulation, he floats free of human-induced gravitational warping that so grounded him, and the feeling is one of emancipation. Jared inwardly acknowledges Pythia's powers, but stubbornly rejects her insistence that he will be unable to understand. Given enough time to be with her, he is confident she will be proven wrong if he can only apply his native intelligence assiduously and with single-minded dedication. *She will underestimate me at her own risk*, he thinks. Jared is cognizant of the fact she is using him to propagate, but he will also use her to unveil the mysteries that now seem beyond understanding. Yet, even in these moments of hopeful confidence, he realizes her ability to read his mind will trump any conspiratorial efforts he undertakes to steal secrets. Still, he disposes of this inconvenient thought by vowing to deal with it when the time comes.

Nevertheless, in spite of all his doubts and trepidations, a newly acquired exhilaration propels him to embrace this opportunity to embark on an entirely fresh start in life. He pictures himself marrying Pythia, quit teaching, give up his research, and follow her on whatever grand quest she has in store for them. In this process, he begins constructing a multitude of outlandish hypotheses. Can she make a bullet disappear before it strikes? What if someone shoots her from behind, very far away? How would one go about arresting and incarcerating such a being? How will her powers be received by the civilized world? Yes, yes, he gets more excited as he ponders the chance to explore these imponderables. How would his own species stop her from propagating and driving *Homo sapiens* to extinction? Ah, here is the existential question: does he help her eliminate his own species? That ultimate test he will also have to set aside and deal with only when, or if, that time comes.

~

"So, you are Professor Paine?" says Lady Oracle holding out her hand in greeting. She is standing in the foyer of the old Victorian house in San Francisco with Sy and Altan at her side.

As introductions proceed, Jared's impression of these people is one of astonishment. Lady Oracle is a giantess of mythological appearance. Sy is the prototypical jester. And Altan is a somber, granite-like figure of impenetrable countenance. After a few moments of light conversation, they retire to an expansive, exquisitely decorated living room with large bay windows admitting great swaths of late morning sunlight.

After providing coffee to Jared, Lady Oracle says, "I understand you know about Pythia's powers?"

"Yes."

"And are you not concerned?"

"Concerned about what?"

"Your safety, your sanity, your reputation, your sense of self, your sense of worth, your career, your relationship with such a being, your future, the future of your species . . . I could go on, but you get the drift."

"Yes, I am concerned about all of those. But, before we go on, may I ask about the three of you"—he looks in turn at Sy and Altan, then back to Lady Oracle— "what is the nature of your relationship to Pythia?"

"Consider us her guardians."

"Okay, but do you also possess her powers?"

"No."

"So you are, excuse the expression, normal human beings?"

"For your purposes, yes."

"For my purposes?"

Lady Oracle does not respond, instead passing him a plate of almond cookies. He waves it away distractedly.

After waiting in vain for a response, Jared says, "Look, I really don't know what my role is in all this, other than contributing sperm. What is my . . . well, I guess I would ask, what is my job description?"

Sy jumps in. "You, sir, will serve a very similar role as myself! You will be the interface between Pythia and the rest of humanity." He suddenly strikes a comical pose. "You may not have my panache, but your native intelligence and scientific background will serve you, and her, well."

Jared cannot help scoffing. "Like an intelligent dog?"

"No," says Altan in a severe tone that compels Jared's attention. "You are to be her husband, father to the next generation."

Sy turns another twist in the air. "Like Thetis and Peleus!"

Jared looks at him blankly.

Sy continues his physical peregrinations as he explains.

"Thetis was *Goddess*, a nereid, a sea-nymph—they are always beautiful—and Peleus a mortal man, King of the Myrmidons (Greeks, if you will). Pythia is Thetis and you are Peleus. When they got together and had sex, Voila! Out came Achilles, immortal but for his heel."

Jared chuckles skeptically. "So, I am King of the Greeks!"

"No, the point is, you will be a highly respected man, and if you play your cards right, King of Science!"

In spite of Jared's outward resistance and vocal sarcasm, the excitement he is suppressing builds to the point of a veritable explosion of anticipation. Only his strict scientific inclination to outwardly exhibit stoic skepticism keeps him from jumping up and down like a child on Christmas morning.

Pythia, silent up to this point, feels her hump awash with the subterranean surge of his elation.

"Jared is aware of these points, Sy," she says. "Like any good scientist, he simply seeks explanations and clarifications of unexplained phenomena. I appreciate that about him."

The others fall silent. This fact does not go unnoticed by Jared, but Pythia quickly quashes his surmise as to why.

"No, Jared, it is not that they are subservient to me. In fact, if this new species is to mean anything, it is that all life and non-life are equal in the complex weave of the universe. The merely personal must be selected out, or else the destructive nature of humans will unravel the tapestry, and all will suffer."

Lady Oracle nods and says softly, "Correct, Pythia. From the time of your great-grandparents John and Meiying, through your grandparents Michael and Tamara, to your parents Ming-huà and Zookeeper, the chart of their trajectories has been drawn by the one humans know as *Goddess*. Sole intent: reduce unnecessary suffering and save the future for all."

"Who then is this *Goddess*?" asks Jared.

Altan speaks in the deep baritone of conviction. "You may as well ask who is the rock you stand on, who is the air you breathe, and who is the water you drink."

"*Goddess* is such an ancient concept," says Jared. "A bit out-of-date, isn't it?"

"It is a useful concept," replies Lady Oracle. "An archetype that strikes a chord in the human psyche. Pythia's other great-grandmother, Child of Buddha, understood. She could read meaning in the enigmatic sounds of the Oracle by listening to the Precious Object."

"I'm sorry, I cannot keep up," says Jared. "These names are all strange and mysterious to me. It will take time to understand these allusions. While I don't yet understand the past, I can understand the future. What comes next?"

"Next," says Lady Oracle. "You will combine business with pleasure. You and Pythia will take a trip together . . . a sort of honeymoon, without the ritual wedding humans so love—and sometimes come to hate."

"No wedding?" says a surprised Jared.

"Such an event would draw too much attention," replies Lady Oracle.

"From?"

"For one, your peers. But, more importantly, the government. Paperwork leaves such an obvious trail."

"Where are we going on this trip?" asks Jared nervously.

"Before I reveal that, Pythia and the rest of us have agreed you must first meet her parents."

Jared nods and says, "Who live on a small island off the coast of Washington State, correct?"

"Correct," says Pythia as she passes him a plate of almond cookies. "Take one, it's good."

~ Another Meeting ~

A couple of weeks after Jared Paine's discussion with Pythia's "guardians" at the San Francisco mansion, Ming-huà and Zookeeper are standing at a window watching the path leading to their little island house. Finally, they see Pythia and Jared approaching in the distance. A squirrel chatters at the intruders, eliciting a smile from Ming-huà at the power of genetic dispositions. "Like mother like daughter," she observes aloud. "We do drive our little friend to distraction."

"Christ!" cries Zookeeper following her gaze. "She's gotten to be almost as pretty as you!"

Ming-huà laughs. "The professor isn't so bad looking either. Supposed to be very smart for good measure."

"You mean smart for a *Homo sapien* like me?" grumbles Zookeeper. "At least the fucker has both arms."

"He'll be full of questions," says Ming-huà, ignoring this ever-touchy sore point. "Pythia tells me she has put off giving him many answers, but we're in for it—and I suspect it will be story-telling time."

"Yup. Bet that fancy professor doesn't even smoke pot. As the Bard said, "How sometimes Nature will betray its folly, its tenderness, and make itself a pastime to harder bosoms."

"Remember, Zookeeper, he's a physicist, not an English major."

"Yeah, yeah."

When welcoming them inside, Zookeeper notices Jared casting quick, nervous glances at his armless shoulders. Once everyone is seated with glasses of lemonade, Zookeeper is amused to watch Jared's surprise at the dexterity with which he drinks using his feet.

"Before we get too settled in," says Ming-huà. "I want to ask whether Professor Paine knows how my husband lost his arms."

"He does, mother," says Pythia.

Jared leans forward in his chair. "No need for formalities, Mrs. Powers. Please call me Jared."

"Does Jared know how my husband came about the name Zookeeper?"

"He knows that also."

"I see. Good. Jared, I believe you have more questions of us than we of you?"

"Perhaps," says Jared.

Now Pythia leans forward. "Before we start with that, mother, I am interested to know how the meeting with the FBI went."

Ming-huà gives a deep sigh. "I'm afraid they left with more questions than answers. Being FBI, they are naturally suspicious. I remain a 'person of interest'."

Jared remains tight-lipped during these remarks, but Pythia speaks up.

"Jared knows you are responsible for the unfortunate results of those incidents, mother, so perhaps you can enlighten him on the details so he does not think he's hobnobbing with a gang of murderers."

Ming-huà recites the details, fully aware they are all taking a risk by allowing this man access to her secrets. Nonetheless, he has been chosen by Pythia, and Pythia is no fool. Besides, Ming-huà keeps in mind her own marriage to Zookeeper, not only a *Homo sapien*, but a crack cocaine dealer to boot. Genetics and natural selection are full of truly wondrous surprises.

At the end of her long recitation, she looks lovingly, but sadly, at Zookeeper. "So you see, Jared, these powers must be used, if ever, with the greatest care, else suffering is increased, not diminished, and justice becomes injustice."

"Yes, unintended consequences," says Jared.

"Indeed."

Jared directs his attention to Zookeeper. "How do you cope with being married to such a . . . person as Ming-huà Powers?"

Zookeeper flashes a sly smile. "Can't hide much, so the trick is not to have anything to hide. You might think that's a burden, but it's really the opposite. My hiding-lying-frying-dying days are over. All that was required to gain my freedom was to sacrifice my arms. It has proven to be a good trade. Couldn't get a better deal anywhere on the street."

Chapter 25: Preparation

~ A Vision Before Sex ~

Pythia and Jared have stayed in Ming-huà's tiny guest room for two days and plan to spend an additional week. Although never explicitly stated, this would be their honeymoon—a chance to conceive in uninterrupted peace. That first night of sex is indelibly stamped on Jared's memory, for it consisted of contradictory elements; part ecstasy, part horror, part love, part fear, part lust, and part revulsion.

When they retired to their room that night, Pythia disrobed as calmly as if preparing for a routine bath. As she did so, Jared sat on the edge of the bed, watching, breathing heavily, anticipation mixed with dread, and to his embarrassment, causing him to perspire. When completely naked, she unabashedly faced him, giving him time to explore her body in every minute detail. Jared held himself together, but his flesh quivered uncontrollably. He fought against his basest impulses. To his disgust, he experienced a compulsion to violently rape, which he resisted. Always in his mind was her hump. The hump. He knew she teased him with the magnificent vision of her frontal nudity, taunting him to wait until she would deign to turn around. Taunting. Never had his cock been so focused and his mind so scrambled. Finally, she turned. . . .

~

At first, the hump appeared to Jared as the loveliest curve he had ever seen. Pythia's perfect skin, the color of rich, creamy coffee, covered a divinely graceful slope fairly pulsing with a strange glow. Yet, the hump disconcertingly seemed fashioned from the purest marble, forcing the softness of that rich, creamy coffee to co-exist with the hardness of that cold marble, together radiating a comprehensiveness, a repository of all-that-is and all-that-will-be. As he stared in wonder, a complex web of reddish veins emerged faintly from the cream color and cascaded across the hump, rising from the marble like an intricate swarm of living tentacles. This moving web coalesced, broke apart, and merged again, moving in a sort of purposeful dance, until patterns became distinguishable and meaning began to reveal itself. Figures appeared, life was breathed into their world by the pulsing veins, and a story unfolded before his eyes.

In the beginning, Jared was unable to interpret the meaning of these shape-shifting patterns, so he stood and moved very close, leaning his head down to only a few millimeters from her hump. A faint sheen of sweat covered her skin, appearing like a mist slightly distorting the figures that moved beneath. He squinted through the mist at the seemingly infinite matrix of veins crisscrossing the hump. The closer he looked, the more creases and crevices appeared, channeling the moisture of her body so they became glistening rivulets in a delta. Now Jared could make out villages near the rivulets. Closer yet and he saw individual huts and houses clumped in small groupings. To his astonishment and horror, Jared perceived an entire world in Pythia's hump, a miraculous miniature world. He knew his eyes must be possessed by some *God* or *Goddess*, for the miniature world constantly moved, swirling in chaotic activity. Time seemed suspended and his questions hung motionless in the heavy air as the scenes unfolded on the landscape of her flesh. . . .

~

Spread before him were two villages, evidently Asian in nature. In one of the villages, there appeared to be a marriage festival underway. Now, a strange familiarity was planted in Jared's mind's eye, for he could see and understand the events that led to the celebration as if he were a participant. An intermediary had made the necessary introductions, and the elders of both families had already agreed to the match. A fortune teller had been consulted to insure approval not only by the living but also by the Gods and ancestors. An auspicious day had been selected from the lunar calendar for the first meeting of the parents. Gifts of rice, alcohol, fruit and flowers were exchanged amid much bowing, grinning, and scrutinizing.

The bride had served candied fruit, tea and cookies, and the groom had provided the traditional engagement gift of gold earrings, silk scarf, and other jewelry. Candles burned profusely on the altar of the ancestors at the bride's house, and decorations of green boughs, palm fronds, and flowers were displayed in abundance. A great feast had been attended by both families at which time the date of the wedding was announced according to a careful scrutiny of the horoscopes.

Now Jared could see the wedding procession itself. He squinted hard to distinguish the faces of the bride and groom and their entourage, but he could not quite make out individual faces. The wedding procession wound through the village, comprised of the bride, groom, kinfolk, and other celebrants anxious to enjoy the food and drink. The crowd danced from the bride's house to that of the groom. The old women in the procession walked slowly and solemnly. Others in the procession swayed to the melody of mandolin and lute players. A few men, having consumed too much rice wine, twirled and stumbled as they marched along.

The groom's house had been enlarged by removing the front wall and constructing a thatch and bamboo overhang to accommodate the guests. Brightly colored banners hung from the bamboo frame showing Chinese characters wishing the bride and groom good luck, prosperity, and many children. Women busied themselves in back of the house under another extension which served as a temporary kitchen. Smoke and steam rose in black and white swirls above the pots, and the atmosphere crackled with the hustle and bustle of women cutting, chopping, boiling, steaming, stirring, tossing, and cleaning.

The intermediary, a man with a wispy beard and a permanent, knowing laugh that conspicuously displayed his wisdom and life-loving character, had consumed more rice wine than anyone else and wove recklessly in front of the procession. Multicolored parasols carried by the groom's assistants glistened and twirled in the sunlight, like gaudy wheels turning endlessly on the wagons of an emperor's baggage caravan. One of the members of the procession, best friend of the groom, tossed his parasol in the air and it tumbled end over end and back into his waiting hand. Younger women followed in beautiful *ao dais*. The older women, dressed in black, provided a solemn border encasing the coy girls. Jared's eyes creased in a broad smile as he anticipated his own wedding to Pythia.

Close by, in the village square, an argument broke out between two men over the price of a water buffalo. An arbitrator arrived to mediate the dispute. Anger flashed between the two men and the threat of violence charged the air. Jared saw the arbitrator quite clearly—he resembled Sy. In the course of mediation one of the men complained that the other man had hit him on the left side of his face causing a cut and swelling, ruining his good looks. At the end of his plea, the arbitrator smiled and suggested in a wry manner that the perpetrator should be allowed to hit the victim on the right side of his face "to restore balance and harmony" to the victim's good looks. Everyone laughed and eventually even the victim smiled. The dispute settled promptly. After successfully mediating the dispute, the arbitrator returned to his house, its interior walls covered in books. Buddhist canon, Confucian ethics, and Daoist mysticism. Even a section, Jared noticed, of illustrated erotic classics. *Sy always has a twinkle in his eye*, he thought.

But even as he thought these things, Jared closed his eyes against a blur of movement so as not to get dizzy and nauseous. When he opened his eyes, he saw a husband and wife working together in the rice fields outside the village, their backs soaked in sweat, legs covered in mud. Two of their older children, a teenaged boy and his younger sister, helped them harvest the rice. Jared noticed that their grandmother remained in the village, caring for the two youngest children in a thatched home with an earthen floor. A baby slept in the wooden bed and a toddler laughed and giggled while playing with a jackfruit. This poor peasant family owned only a few *mou* of paddies, growing vegetables and fruit for household consumption and, when not working in the fields, they collected reeds to make into baskets and hats.

Jared saw that the husband and wife worked well together and with good humor. He somehow knew they were literate. Very unusual for poor peasants. He sensed that they would become well-off landowners before the grass grew over their heads. As they worked in the fields under the blazing sun, their faces were obscured by the shade of their conical hats, but Jared felt he knew them. Then the husband made a joke, pointed upward toward the sky, and they both followed his upraised finger to look up at the heavens. Grinning broadly, both of them stared upward, directly at Jared, squinting as if he was the sun pouring down upon their bodies. Startled, Jared rocked backward in a spasm of shock. He knew these two people were the bride and groom of the wedding ceremony he had seen earlier and realized in wonder that he was watching the progression of familiar lives in unfamiliar time and space.

Another whirl of movement. More dizziness. Again, Jared closed his eyes. Opening them impatiently he saw the woman in the field, now as an old woman sitting on the front porch of a prosperous-looking wood and tile house. Surrounded by other women, friends, and family, she watched children play in the village square. The women ate almond cookies and drank tea, laughing and cracking jokes at the expense of the village men. The old woman scolded her daughter, telling her to shoo the children away from playing under a great banyan tree rising above the village square so that the spirits of the ancestors could enjoy the shade undisturbed. Jared knew that the woman's laughing husband had died years earlier of disease and that the sadness associated with his death lingered at the edges of her happiness.

The villagers were all in good spirits, celebrating another year in the wheel of life.

~

And yet again the wheeling movement, but this time more severe. Jared's stomach dropping from under him. This time, he instinctively did not want to open his eyes, afraid of what he would see. But he did. He saw a second village, similar to the first, but it looked darker, poorer. The spirits of the village were disturbed and restless. This village seemed more familiar to Jared, more real, and very frightening.

The fields lay fallow and unproductive, neglect rending the paddies helpless against the encroaching forest. Fruit groves, their trees nothing more than desiccated corpses, were left untended. What little fruit there was undulated with armies of ants gorging and staggering like drunken dancers in a wedding procession gone bad.

Armed men gathered in the village square near the twisted metal helix of a resting machine, sunlight gleaming off their rifles, periodically flashing painfully in Jared's eyes. No tall and sheltering banyan tree in sight. The anger and fright of the men spread to the villagers who hid with their children in the stifling heat of closed houses, stinking ditches, and oppressive tunnels.

Distrust and factionalism had long ago fragmented these villagers into smaller and smaller groups until parents no longer trusted their own children. The young and strong had either left to fight in the war, or had fled the village for the allure of easy money, or were dead.

Boys had become men. Men had either been killed or were killing; either lying on their backs, being reabsorbed by the earth or standing above those lying on their backs, taunting the will of the Gods. Girls had become women. Women no longer observing the ancient rituals; either lying on the backs with their legs spread accepting the male cock-demons of lust and hatred, or standing above those lying on their backs, counting money.

[311]

Older, powerful men, no longer observing right relationships, gorging themselves on the banquet of weaker people's misfortunes, eating the flayed skin of their own children and grandchildren. Old women wailed and rocked in vain, the pride discarded and disregarded.

Using bamboo sticks to draw their plans in the sand, the leaders of the armed men in the village square displayed dark, livid faces and furiously debated how to attack the men huddled in a stone fortress outside their village. As a ragtag group of common soldiers leaned forward on their haunches and listened, Jared could see that among them stood a few female warriors with bold breasts and broad hips. One couple in particular caught his attention, a man tightly holding the hand of a woman squatting next to him, both armed. The man made a joke and pointed upward, and as they both laughed nervously, they looked up at the sky directly into the eyes of Jared Paine. He saw what he knew; that these two were the same couple who had been married in the first village. But they now looked poor and starving, their eyes dark. Sorrow, anger, and hatred hung over and around them, and he knew they worried about their children and their mother whom they had left in the tunnels. An arc of fear passed between them, and their attempts at humor did not straighten the curve of their backs, square the slump of their shoulders, or lift the weight from their hearts.

Again the dizzying movement amidst the fog and rain and mist. Thunder rumbled across the ground, and Jared did not know if the noise came from Pythia's hump or from the suspended world around him. Then he saw a ferocious battle with men and women carrying dead and wounded on their backs, their clothing soaked red with blood. Hatred, confusion, fear, pain, and death surrounded the soldiers, the villagers, and the non-human animals cowering in the jungle. Suddenly, in the middle of the carnage, a young woman, a hunchback, walked among the living and the dead. Miraculously, the blood disappeared and the weapons vanished. As in a film run backwards, the victims all left the battlefield and returned to their villages. There were celebrations to be held. The livid red veins that had been telling the story faded until the rich cream color returned and the marble cold returned and Jared stood back as Pythia again turned to face him.

Jared staggered back to sit on the bed, all the while looking incredulously at Pythia. "What did I just see?"

[312]

"You saw one slice of space and time that my ancestors, and your ancestors, and all of humanity's ancestors experienced. I am full of billions of such stories. I'm afraid you will have to accommodate yourself to the unrepressed tales that will unfold from the depths of my hump to play themselves out on the surface. I can feel them moving, like hordes of ants, probing in long filaments, circling back, always changing, forming and re-forming the stories. So many stories, human and non-human, all in constant flux."

~ Sex ~

Looking back on that night, Jared recalls a feeling of utter terror followed by inexpressible joy. On that night, never had Pythia seemed so alien, so un-human. Having sex with this unimaginably unique being filled him with the intense desire to run, to escape this nightmare as fast as possible. Again, the frightening thought of what was he getting himself into dominated his anxiety. Far from being sexually aroused, he experienced the terrifying prospect of having sex with something on the order of a jellyfish or a shape-shifting octopus.

He remembers fondly how Pythia read his mind and quickly moved to reassure. She sat next to him and held his hand.

"You have seen much, Jared, something no other human has seen, and I know you are shocked. But remember, our DNA is compatible. We can successfully mate and have healthy children."

"Please stop using the word 'mate', Pythia."

"What word should I use?"

"Love. Make love. Hell, even to say 'have sex' is better than 'mate'. It is very hard for me to look at you and see all the incredible differences between us, and then want to make love . . . or have sex, with an alien."

"I am certainly not an alien."

"You are to me."

"Jared, please disrobe."

"I'm not sure I can."

"Please. I want to show you something."

Jared complied, and in the process began to get excited, especially seeing Pythia in all her stunning nudity, as she watched him with riveting curiosity."

When he was fully naked, his cock was stiff. Pythia, now on her knees, first massaged it with her hand, causing Jared's body to rigidly tense in anticipation. Next, she put his cock gently in her mouth and slowly sucked in a rhythmic up and down motion. Just before he climaxed, she lay on the edge of the bed and maneuvered his quivering member into her vagina. Jared was as pliable as a child, and as her vagina enveloped his cock, he could no longer abstain and thrust as deeply as possible, culminating in an explosive orgasm. As if an invisible barrier had been torn down, Jared made love to Pythia multiple times that glorious night, until both were exhausted witnesses to the early morning sunrise. Jared knows on looking back at that first night that he had never felt more complete and fulfilled in his life.

~

In the days that follow, they continue their love making, and openly discuss the details and explore the possibilities before and after each session. However, eventually their time in the little house is drawing to a close. The nearer it comes to leave, the more frantic their sex. One thing Pythia never does during their love making is to turn her naked back to him and reveal her hump again, which she knows is alive with the movement of numberless stories. Once was enough, she thinks. He must not see it a second time. That sharing will be reserved for her kind.

Chapter 26: To Work

~ Alarming News ~

On the day of their departure, Pythia and Jared have packed and are finishing their coffee while engaged in conveying final farewells to Ming-huà and Zookeeper.

"Give our best to Sy, Altan, and Lady Oracle," says Ming-huà.

Just as the words have left her mouth, Pythia stands and looks at the front door.

"Come in!" she calls.

Jared heard no knocking, but he is now conditioned to accept such telepathic irregularities.

Sy appears a few moments later, having been some steps from the door when Pythia sensed his arrival. As is his style, he makes a grand sweeping entrance, doffing his floppy hat and bowing low.

"Scarecrow!" exclaims Ming-huà. "So good to see you!"

"Yeah, likewise," adds a smiling Zookeeper. "How's the ol' jester business these days? Not yet ready to contribute your skull to Hamlet so he can spout a depressing soliloquy?"

"Ha, ha!" laughs Sy. "My skull is still surrounded by all that yucky wet stuff. It sloshes this way and that, making me seasick most of the time, but I never vomit into the wind."

With this typical Sy diversion, he stops in his tracks and looking at Ming-huà says, "Well, you ready to go?"

"Your presence is unexpected even to me," says Pythia.

"Always expect the unexpected, my dear! I am here to chaperone you and your lover back to San Francisco."

"Why the need?" asks Jared, piqued at the insinuation.

"So, I can brief you on the way. Vacation is over. Time to go to work. You won't stay in San Francisco longer than it takes a fly to avoid the swatter."

"Where to from San Francisco?" asks Pythia.

"Long story," replies Sy. "I can tell you about that when we're on the road." He looks at Jared. "You too, youngster."

Again, Jared feels a grating, odd-man-out irrelevance and remains silent.

"Anyway," continues Sy. "Where to from San Francisco, you ask? Well, let me put it to you this way: I don't know."

Ming-huà chuckles. "Lady Oracle leaving you out of the loop again, Scarecrow?"

He assumes a tragic face. "Yes."

"Tough being just a fuckin' messenger," says a cocky Zookeeper. "Sucks, doesn't it?"

Sy looks directly at Pythia. "Speaking of sucking, I assume you enjoyed your . . . vacation?"

Jared's face glows red, but Pythia merely laughs. "Indeed. Sorry it has to end, but I look forward to starting work."

"Work?" asks Jared, his face still flushed. "What work?"

"Work," says Sy in confirmation. "*She* expects great things from Pythia."

Zookeeper glances at Ming-huà, searching for any sign of resentment at her daughter's ascendency, but she returns his look and laughs. "Don't worry sweet one, I'm very happy to be put out to pasture. Especially here, with you. Pythia has the mentality for it. I am merely a stepping stone, and glad of it."

"Mother," says Pythia. "You are much more than a stepping stone. Same with you, father. Without either of you, there is void, there is no hope."

"Well said!' cries Sy. "Now, let's go or we'll miss the boat."

~

On the way to San Francisco, Sy is stubbornly uncommunicative about what is most important. He tells jokes. He prattles on about extraneous matters, but he avoids the substantive topic of what comes next for Pythia and Jared.

"I thought you were supposed to brief us on the way," says Pythia. "Do you really have no idea?"

"None."

Pythia detects a sadness, or regret, or some dissatisfaction in his tone. She steals a glance at Jared, but he is staring out the car window in blissful ignorance of what is coming. At this moment, she asks herself if she loves him the way humans always define the word. The answer is a resounding "No". She is immune to the lure of the personal, and instead views Jared as a tiny part of the greater whole—the human species—for which she feels a deep empathy and an even deeper sadness at their limitations and the catastrophic future that awaits them. Oh, she tried on that first night with Jared to view love as *Homo sapiens* seem to. To make herself more stereotypically attractive to a human male, she experimented with lipstick and make-up, but ultimately recoiled at such preening as a human would if they tried to mimic a dog or cat by licking their own skin. She washed it all off in disgust. Even so, Pythia feels deeply gratified at the way things turned out, and will, from now on, closely monitor her body for signs of pregnancy. Sy gives her an odd look in the rear-view mirror, but quickly averts his eyes, giving Pythia reason to be anxious about this upcoming meeting with Lady Oracle. Nevertheless, her powers have barely been tested, and her muscles coil like a caged leopard, ready for the bolted door to be opened. In fact, that is precisely what Lady Oracle says when they are comfortably ensconced in the anteroom of the San Francisco Victorian mansion.

"Are you ready to be let free of all artificial restraints?" Lady Oracle asks.

"More than ready."

"Yes," says Lady Oracle looking askance at Jared. "You have already flaunted your independence."

"To good purpose," says Pythia.

"We shall see."

Jared squirms.

Altan, stoic and stony-faced as always, notices his discomfort and comes to Jared's defense. "Jared will be the father. Although not possessed of Pythia's powers, he is a good man, intelligent, and will, I believe, be a loyal and devoted friend. There will come a time when he will be tested." At this statement, Altan looks at Jared and says sternly, "You will be torn by loyalties that may present unspeakable choices to a human being. Let science and reason guide you, as they have done up to now."

Jared replies firmly. "As I have always tried to do. If I had not adhered my entire life to the two touchstones you mentioned, I dare say I would not be here now."

[317]

Sy jumps up and twirls. "Well said!"

Lady Oracle is unmoved. "We shall see."

Even as these words are leaving her mouth, Pythia is gazing proudly at Jared as if her favorite dog just won the Grand National. At least, this is how Jared himself interprets her look, and as evidence of his evolving view of himself and his place in the world, he is not dissatisfied with Pythia's attitude. Sometimes, it still shocks him to realize how far he has come in depending upon Pythia's good graces and craving her reinforcing pats. He has willingly stopped flailing and dog-paddling in the great sea of her being. Now he is happy to float on his back and wait to be called forth from the mesmerizing feel of her gentle waves lapping against his body.

Lady Oracle looks around regally and says, "I know you are ready for this task. In any case, you will be traveling abroad, but will still be close. Staying in this country is out of the question due to the questions that would be raised. At the place you are going, you will be exercising your powers in an environment not unlike what *Homo sapiens* ancestors dealt with—Nature red in tooth ad claw, to paraphrase Mr. Tennyson."

"I understand."

"Neither we, nor you, really understand the extent of your powers. Your mother was tested, and she displayed, in a limited way, what these powers can do. But, in Ming-huà's case, the result of her actions devastated her gentle nature and almost destroyed her physically. You are different, but the extent of that difference is a major unknown. You are familiar with human trafficking, I presume?"

"Of course."

"If you agree, we would like to send you to Tijuana, Mexico, a notorious center for human trafficking and one of the most dangerous cities on the planet. You will know what to do once you get there. Jared can go with you if he is willing, but in any case, Altan will also be there watching over the. . . . "

Lady Oracle lapses into silence.

"Experiment!" exclaims Jared in disgust.

"No, I think 'test run' is a better description," replies Lady Oracle placidly.

[318]

"It's out of the question," says Jared. "It's far too dangerous. I mean, for *God*'s sake, she might already be pregnant! Did you think of that?"

Before Lady Oracle can respond, Pythia says, "No, it is fine, Jared, but thank you for your concern. It will not be dangerous for me."

"How do you know that? Is this how you intend to start a new species? By killing off one of its first individuals? And perhaps an unborn child to boot?"

Lady Oracle continues calmly, "*Her* goals are twofold: reduce suffering and elevate genus *Homo* to a new level."

"*Her?*" asks Jared.

"Who others before you have called *Goddess*."

"Yes, I've heard the name. A term of convenience, I presume?"

"In a manner of speaking. Purely metaphorical."

"Who, or what, is this *Goddess?*" demands Jared.

"That is beyond your purview."

Pythia looks sympathetically at Jared and tries to take the sting out of Lady Oracle's admonishment. "My great-grandparents, my grandparents, my mother, have all dealt with this entity before. As Lady Oracle said, the term is only metaphorical. I will give you the details later."

"Pythia," says Lady Oracle. "You know what you have to do. Can your powers carry you through the furnace of natural selection at its most extreme?"

"I am confident," says Pythia.

"I'm not," objects Jared. He is struggling with the more selfish notion of living in the most crime-ridden sections of Tijuana. "Remember, I don't have your powers."

Altan nods agreement. "True. Best you stay here."

Instantly, Jared feels guilty, and tries to backtrack. "Well, I didn't mean I wouldn't go, just that it will be difficult."

"I agree with Altan, I think you should stay here," says Pythia. "If you stay here, I won't have to worry about you."

"Your decision, Jared," says Lady Oracle. "But you don't have much time to decide. Pythia and Altan leave day after tomorrow."

He does not hesitate, but bursts out defiantly, "Then, in that case, I'm going. No arguments!"

[319]

Jared feels a bit foolish after this outburst, but he takes comfort in the lack of pushback by anyone in the room. Perhaps, just perhaps, he will have more influence than they currently give him credit for. After all, a physicist must surely be more useful for survival purposes than an uneducated layman.

To his dismay, Pythia says in a scolding tone, "Such thoughts are quite foolish, Jared. You should know better."

~ Arrival in Mexico ~

Lady Oracle had chosen their destination with great care. Pythia and Jared will check-in to a seedy motel called Motel Vargas in the most notorious part of Tijuana—Zona Norte, otherwise called the Hong Kong district. Altan will be an independent agent, always lurking nearby in case of need. During her deliberations, Lady Oracle considered many foreign countries with bad reputations, Tijuana itself ranks as one of the most dangerous cities in the world, and Zona Norte is the most dangerous of all. Human sex trafficking surpasses drugs as the most profitable income for organized crime cartels. Six-year-old girls to seventeen- and eighteen-year old's can be sold multiple times a day, whereas crack cocaine, for example, can only be sold once, then must be replenished. As Lady Oracle pointed out before they departed for Mexico, "There is today more slavery than ever in human history. The utterly vile, hopeless, shattered lives endured by millions of girls worldwide is suffering at its most potent and tragic. They are imprisoned for years, or even their entire lives, in a hellish existence, forced to serve as sexual slaves, abused and polluted multiple times every day by predatory adults—men and women. Only one percent of these innocent victims are ever saved. Most end up hollow shells, zombie-like, bodies without minds. Now, imagine if these girls had the powers that Pythia possesses. Imagine if everyone had such powers!"

"A bloodbath!" exclaimed Jared. "It would never work."

"Perhaps," said Lady Oracle. "But just as likely: peace by mutually assured destruction." She glances at Pythia. "And, of course, undergirded by advanced intelligence combined with enhanced empathy."

~

Once in Tijuana, Pythia and Jared check-in to the Motel Vargas and peruse the sparse, dirty, bleak room; he with dismay, she with satisfaction.

"Perfect," says Pythia.

"For what, a cockroach?"

"Jared, it provides some degree of anonymity. There is a large Asian population here in Tijuana. I have Asian blood, my skin is dark, and hopefully, I will—"

"Blend in," interjects Jared morosely. "I've heard it before."

"I will be fine."

"Until you're kidnapped and raped."

"Jared, you know I will not allow myself to be raped. You must not underestimate my powers, nor should you underestimate my intelligence. You have done so in the past and been burned."

"Maybe, but you do not possess this kind of intelligence; the streetwise kind, the kind you need to survive out there."

Pythia snorts dismissively. "Why do you think my father was chosen to mate with mother? Zookeeper's streetwise, raw survival-savvy genes are within me."

"Yeah, and look what happened to him."

"Yes, but not by the actions of his vicious comrades, but by mother herself."

Jared assumes his sarcastic face. "Are you planning to remove a lot of arms? Legs? Heads?"

Pythia's expression hardens. "If necessary to free these girls from the hell they are in. Unfortunately, I have to do this undetected. My hump will mark me as unusual, which although something I can use to my advantage, is also something that will stand out to witnesses, and worse, to the police."

"Aren't they all corrupt? I've heard they are in the pockets of the cartels."

"Not all. And another consideration is that Tijuana is right on the border with the U.S., so word will spread north, if I am not careful."

"Bottom line is that I am to sit around this disgusting room and wait? I'll be sick with worry."

"I'll be in touch, Altan will be in touch, and if I become incommunicado, that means I am succeeding."

"Or dead."

Pythia shakes her head. "You're incorrigible. Enjoy the sights. Catch up on the latest in physics. Be a tourist."

[321]

"You're the latest in physics and I can't even catch up with you! And as for being a tourist—this isn't exactly Paris."

"Jared, I can't deal with this now. Do your best. Remember, you had the chance to stay in San Francisco."

"True, I'm here because I've actually fallen in love with you, even though that particular concept is not in your vocabulary—or rather, in your genes. Anyway, you're right. Let's take a taxi to a nicer part of town and have a good dinner."

"Yes, okay. A last supper, if you will. Tomorrow, Jared, I'm on the street and we may not see each other for some time."

~ On the Street ~

The next morning, Pythia dresses in worn, drab clothes, the type that might be worn by a poor person. Her goal is to look somewhat desperate and lost. She chooses Maria as the most common, nondescript name, and wears only earrings, much to her disgust and discomfort. Lack of Spanish speaking ability is a handicap, but she has her story ready, and most people in Tijuana speak English, particularly the predators. She asks herself in a supercilious mood how a *Homo sapiens* woman would act in order to fit into *Neanderthal* society. Dumb down, be inarticulate, let physicality dominate over intellect, at all times act submissive, pliable, and naïve, avoid eye contact, and appear easily frightened. She knows eliminating intelligence from the eyes and body language is most difficult. Nevertheless, donning this coarse persona, she ventures out at dusk, completely confident of her plan, much to the worried chagrin of Jared (whose feelings of helplessness reach their peak when the door closes emphatically behind her).

Disappointingly, the first two evenings of street walking are relatively uneventful but for ubiquitous vendors selling their cheap wares; ubiquitous street children selling ubiquitous pieces of stale Chiclets gum from ubiquitous trays for a quarter each; ubiquitous *mariachi* performers grinding out songs for five dollars each to a small smattering of nervous tourists; and ubiquitous taco stand vendors selling ubiquitous tacos to beer guzzling, tattoo-covered locals (mostly males at nighttime).

While on the street these first two days, communication from her hump devolves into a background noise totally devoid of meaning. She does spy Altan at his undercover best, stern and intimidating, getting his shoes shined by one of a ubiquitous number of shoeshine boys. Yet, like the buzzing of a troublesome gnat, she knows someone is following her, their distinctive, discordant hum always registering just above the baseline drone of white noise. Pythia can only describe this person's signature psychic chord as purely and unrelentingly sinister. When picking up his unique signal, she scans the crowds, but can never locate him, even at night when the streets have thinned. During this late-night thinning, Pythia encounters mostly pimps obsequiously escorting wealthier customers to their prostitute victims or drug exchanges between two or more people flitting past as nervous hands quickly swap money for fixes. Police patrol cars cruise like sharks among the little fish, ignoring all illegalities with supreme disinterest. Still, even in this less densely populated environment, he is there, honed in on her, biding his time, watching.

During these two uneventful nights (but for the stalker), Pythia performs her role masterfully. She wanders the streets doe-eyed, confused, hesitant, frightened. She plants her seeds by asking random locals where she can find a job, or how to get in touch with a *coyote*, or where she might find money for her family. Always, she knows her stalker will find out later what she said, what she asked for, whether she was a familiar face, if she had been seen before, perhaps undercover? She can tell her stalker is cautious, clever, and, by the tone of his thoughts, utterly ruthless. Good! Little does he know she is stalking him. The only difficulty is in losing him before she returns to the motel. He must not know where she stays. Only when positive he does not follow will she join a relieved Jared in the sordid little room.

~

Now it is the third evening and Pythia sets out as usual. She wears the same clothes and assumes the same rather pathetic demeanor. She passes by Altan eating tacos at a little stand. Neither betray any sign of recognition. As she continues her walk, some locals recognize her, and she even receives an occasional nod from some prostitutes leaning languidly against walls and doorways, their short skirts barely covering their sexually charged, protruding buttocks. She pauses near one of them to read the woman's thoughts, which are a mix of curiosity about Pythia's hump, pity for the deformity, admiration for her beauty in spite of the hump, and fear that this hunchback might be a future competitor who will take up residence on her turf and attract customers with a penchant for exotic sex.

[323]

In the middle of this clairvoyant eavesdropping, Pythia is jolted by sudden and powerful signals that *he* is near. Again, she casually scans the faces, but again no identification is made, which puzzles her. Darkness is now complete, and she instinctively moves away from the lights and people. Now her senses are on full alert, for her hump tells her the predator is approaching what he believes is a sacrificial goat, tethered by the foolishness of innocence and a female's vulnerability. As Pythia pauses at the edge of a dark alley (just as her mother did years ago to attract the same species of hunter), a figure approaches. Passing under a streetlight, the figure is illuminated in the sickly glow, and Pythia sees a rather large woman, clearly a prostitute, displaying big hair, big breasts, a big bottom, and caked-on make-up. For a moment, she feels a slight let-down, but she nevertheless tunes her sensors fully onto this woman and is blinded by conflicting signals that jam the normal clarity of her telepathic receptors.

"*Hola cariño,*" comes the woman's voice. "*Necesitas ayuda?*"

"I don't speak Spanish. I'm Chinese. My father brought me here, but went back to China."

"Why didn't he take you, *cariño?*" asks the woman in almost perfect English.

"We fought. I'm alone."

"Where are you from?"

"Michoacan. My father had a store."

"Oh, *cariño*, you do need help. *Popre bebè!*"

Pythia feigns nervousness and cringes back. "No, not really."

"Oh, *cariño*, I think you do. Are you lost?"

"I'm trying to find work."

"Here? In Zona Norte? Near a dark alley? *Cariño*, you must truly be lost in the head, or have suicide on the mind. You can be attacked here. Murdered. Raped." The woman leans forward for a closer look. "Are you loco?"

"No."

"*¿Cómo te llamas?*"

"What?"

"Your name, *cariño*. What is your name?"

"Maria."

"Ah! Not very Chinese!"

"My real name is Meiying." Pythia smiles to herself.

"Come on, Maria or Meiying or whatever your name is. Come with me and I'll take you to a safe place for girls."

"Where?"

"A shelter run by a good priest. You will be safe there. Maybe you can even find work."

During this entire conversation, Pythia struggles to solve some unspoken mystery about the woman; an incongruous aspect of her that for some reason she can not pin down. Then, in a flash, it comes to her with the violence of a slap in the face.

This is a man!

She lets slip an intake of breath.

"What's wrong, *cariño?*"

Pythia makes a snap decision to be honest and see where this leads.

"You're a man!"

The woman's voice changes to a low snarl. "Well, you're smarter than you look."

He removes his wig and smiles broadly. "Actually, I am from the *policía.* Undercover. Let me help you."

Pythia knows it is a lie, but now positions herself to capture the prey.

"Oh, thank you, sir. I am so scared. I don't know where to turn. Please help me."

"Just come with me to my car and I'll drive you to the station. From there, you can eat and obtain counseling. It's okay. Come on, Maria, and we'll get you fixed up."

She follows meekly, feigning timidity, but inwardly celebrates the closing of the trap.

Chapter 27: Into the Snake Pit

~ First Blood ~

As the two approach his parked vehicle, Pythia sees it is a van with no windows in the cargo area. A man is standing beside the driver's door smoking, listening to popular songs on the radio. Her hump, supercharged by both men's coiled hostility, soon picks up a cacophony of subdued moaning and sobbing from inside the van. She does not react as the sound is inaudible to anyone standing outside. Instead, she meekly follows her stalker. When they reach the van, he opens the back doors and roughly motions her to enter. Now, the crying and moaning can be clearly heard, and she backs up.

"What are you doing?" she cries. "Aren't we going to the police station?"

He laughs viciously, saying, "Don't worry. These are just *prostitutas* on their way to jail. Get in!"

Pythia resists and tries to run (not too hard), but he violently picks her up and throws her in with the others. She offers minimal resistance and finds herself on the floor of the van looking up in the dim light at benches lining both walls, occupied by young girls and children leaning forward in despair, crying, trembling, and hugging each other in abject terror. The doors slam shut behind and the lock snaps loudly. Pythia, still on the floor, pulls out a small flashlight and quickly darts it around the tear-streaked faces. In the brief time she has the light on, she sees a sad collection: little girls of six or seven up to teenagers who look to be around sixteen. No one speaks, though the crying continues. Pythia, now seated with her arms around her knees, concentrates. She is determined to play the victim for as long as possible, at least until she can free the maximum number of girls and disable the maximum number of their tormentors.

Some of the girls stop crying and look curiously at Pythia. It is not her hunch back they wonder at, but her preternatural calm. All of them are aware what their kidnapping means (except the youngest girls), and this hunchback girl must be either *loco*, or too naïve to understand. When her

[326]

flashlight was on, Pythia had seen one girl of about ten hugging her younger sibling and whispering assurances to the sobbing, shuddering little one. It was a heartbreaking scene, and one which makes Pythia's blood boil. She is sorely tempted to make these evil men disappear, then make the doors disappear and free these tragic, innocent victims. But, the belly of the beast awaits.

One of the older girls, one of the curious ones, says to Pythia, "*De donde eres, hermana?*"

Pythia looks up into the dark where the words came from. "*No hablo español.*"

"English?" comes the voice.

"Yes."

"I thought so. You look different."

"Part Chinese."

"Ah, that explains it," says the girl impressively. "Rogelio finally got me. Looks like he also got you. How did he trick you?"

"The usual."

"Not me. Not the usual. I don't fall for that crap. He just held a knife to my throat when I let my guard down. Bastard!"

"Who is he?" asks Pythia.

"*El Diablo.* Works for one of these fucking cartels. An animal he is. He has been wanting to rape me for a long time. Now he will get his fucking chance."

"*Y un centenar de hombres más también,*" says another girl from the dark.

"Yes, a hundred others will try. I'll fight back!"

"What's your name?" asks Pythia.

"Luciana. Yours?"

"Maria."

Pythia hears a broken sob from Luciana, one the brave girl quickly stifles.

"Don't worry, Luciana, I'll fight with you."

~

After traveling a short distance, the van comes to a stop and the women and girls get out and see in front of them a large, industrial-type building. It looms darkly against the glowing lights from the city, and appears for all intents and purposes to be abandoned. A group of armed men line the concrete walkway to the building, where the girls are taken up flights of stairs and deposited in various rooms, unfurnished but for filthy mattresses on the concrete floors. Pythia becomes separated from Luciana, and ends up being escorted to a room on the higher levels where three other young girls stand shivering in tattered nightdresses. Two look to be no more than fifteen, and one appears to be about twelve. One of the armed men pushes Pythia into the room and orders her to disrobe and put her clothes in a cardboard box. She understands his gestures and stands in her underwear, covering herself as best she can. He openly gawks, then laughs and he hands her a skimpy nightgown to wear.

"*Jorobada! Ganar mucho dinero!*" he brays in the voice of a donkey. "*Aiee! Quiero follarla!*"

"I don't understand," she says.

He looks at her stupidly. "*No hablo español, jorobada?*"

"No," she says, but cannot resist adding, "Are you fond of your body parts, señor?"

"*¿Qué?*"

The older girl says, "*Dijo que Eres bien paracido. Supongo que las chicas te quieren.*"

The man stares at the older girl, trying to determine if she is engaged in impermissible mockery. She maintains a poker face, so he leans closer to Pythia, slitting eyes in an effort to intimidate. She smells a revolting combination of male sweat and rotten fish emanating from his body, and tucks away in her mind what particularly punishment he will receive for his brutality. Nevertheless, outwardly she plays along and looks appropriately frightened. He laughs again and leers at her one last time, then turns and leaves, closing and locking the door behind.

Pythia turns to the older girl. "Do you speak English?"

"Yes."

"What did you say to him?"

"I told him you said he was handsome and must be attractive to all the girls."

Pythia can't help laughing. "Why did you tell him that?"

"Look, girl, he is one of the meanest of the bunch. If you push him, he will find a way to make you suffer."

"We'll see about that," Pythia says under her breath. "Thank you. What is your name?"

"Elena. What is yours?"

"Maria."

"Where are you from?"

"Well, that is a long story. Let's just say my father is Chinese and we lived in Michoacan until he abandoned me and went back to China."

"So you're stuck here?"

"Yes."

"Well, you're really stuck now, sister. We are slaves and our lives are living hells. That is why I lied to him. You have to learn to survive here. The man you just insulted, Mateo, would happily stick a broken bottle up your vagina and twist."

"Thanks for the warning. What happens next?"

"Sleep, then have rice and beans for breakfast, then start servicing customers."

"If I refuse?"

Elena shakes her head. "Then I cannot help you."

Pythia changes tack. "How long have you been here?"

Elena trembles and the tears gush forth. "Years. It doesn't matter. He didn't get my younger sister. I protected her and let myself get caught so she could run. Thank *God*. But oh, Maria, now I am so hollow. There is nothing left. Something inside of me is broken, both down there and up here. When the evil ones have fucked me a thousand times, and a thousand times more, I will die, or be killed, or kill myself. It doesn't matter. *Mi hermana está a salvo*. My sister is safe. Soon, you will see for yourself, Maria. Men are spiders and we are the flies caught in their web."

Pythia looks at her curiously. "You sound very sad, but also very smart, Elena. Why haven't you found a way to escape?"

"I have, many times, but either these terrible men found me, or the *policia* found me and returned me to them. Every time I was beaten and fucked, again and again, worse and worse, until I gave up. I tell you, there is nothing left, Maria."

"The *policia*?"

"Bastards!" Elena cries. Then as if remembering herself, adds gruffly, "Go to sleep. You will need it to survive."

"One last question. How did you learn to speak such good English?"

"Before I was taken here, I studied hard. I wanted to be a teacher and make a difference for my people. Now, go to sleep."

"You will make a difference, I promise."

"No. You will see, Maria. Now sleep!"

~ Contemplating Chess ~

Pythia certainly does not sleep. Instead, she stays awake and applies her prodigious intelligence to anticipating a series of possible moves and countermoves, much as a chess master would do. For every move she contemplates to help these girls, a major limiting factor makes success difficult. Her default position is to not allow any man to violate her body. This correlates to protecting her Queen. This gambit severely limits other moves, but having sex with these genetically deficient, mentally warped, and physically polluted males would be like a human forced to have sex with walruses. How to protect the Queen while making the moves necessary to checkmate these evil men? For a brief moment, she calculates the odds of her already being pregnant by Jared. So far, her period is late, but not late enough to be sure. If she is pregnant, having sex with these monsters will not lead to that disaster, but there is still the disgust factor. If she swallows her revulsion and goes along with having sex, what is gained? Time. Time to do what? Of course, time to find the head of this vile cartel. Then what? cut off the head, either literally or figuratively. How to find the head? Play along and ask. If she asks, they cannot keep the name or names of the heads out of their thoughts. From there, work her way to the top. One complication is how to play along without having sex? Another is that these men think in Spanish, so how to find the names? No matter, she has just solved these two problems. Once she reaches the top and is poised to declare "mate", that is when she will reap maximum pleasure.

And so it goes throughout the night until morning arrives and she is ready to proceed with a plan. There are, however, uncertainties to be dealt with, so she must remain flexible. Her first target is Rogelio, who she assumes is a pawn, or perhaps a knight. Anyway, he must be somewhat advanced in the hierarchy of evil, given his apparent reputation and the way the other men took his orders. This morning, she is still working out some of the details, particularly the question of precision. The trick will be to ascertain how finely she can adjust her power to make things disappear. Can she surgically remove something without casting suspicion on herself, or will she damage the gross anatomy too clumsily? This will be quite interesting, she thinks. *Can I achieve such refinement under stressful conditions? We'll see soon enough.*

~ Slight Error ~

The first day of her captivity turns out to be a disappointment. After eating their meager breakfast of rice and beans, Mateo appears with three men. Pythia uses her telepathic powers to determine two of the men are wealthier Americans, and one is Mexican, middle-class by the look of his clothes. Mateo is disgustingly obsequious toward the men, but glares at the girls with an unmistakable message to cooperate or else. Already the twelve-year-old, whose name is Margarita but called *mija* by the girls, is crying and whimpering, while the others try to console her. Mateo scowls at their behavior and orders them to line up in front of the customers, and snarls, "*Tira!*"

"Take off your clothes, Maria," says Elena under her breath. Mateo hears, but allows her to interpret.

Standing naked, the girls whimper as the men inspect their bodies, turning them this way and that, probing them in the most private places.

When Pythia is ordered to turn around and face backward by one of the men, an American, he takes one look at her hump, steps back and shakes his head. "No, no. No good! Ugly!"

Mateo shows his teeth. "No, *amigo*, pretty. Very pretty *jorobada*!"

"No!" exclaims the man, then says in bad Spanish, "*Muy malo!*"

"Want another?" asks Mateo in bad English.

"*Si,*" says the man, turning to the twelve-year-old. "This one. *Muy bonita!*"

Mateo pulls Margarita forward and hands her to him, saying, "*Si, la hijita es muy bonita!*" She cries out, but there is no one to help. The American pulls her out of the room, saying, "Quit your crying little girl," he says vexingly. "I'll make you feel better." He winks at the other American and adds, "And she'll make me feel better, eh, Bud?" Pythia is frozen, agonized that she has to stick to her plan or else lose everything.

Mateo now turns to the Mexican, still undecided. He gestures toward Pythia. "*Ella es la major follodora!*"

Elena, on her way out with the other American who chose her, says over her shoulder, "Maria, you see? You see? Mateo told the man you are the best fucker."

"Shut-up, bitch!" says the American, jerking her elbow. "I have a little surprise waiting for smart ass wetbacks like you."

But Mateo's efforts are to no avail. The Mexican choses Juana, the other girl, and Pythia is left standing alone, naked, inwardly shaking with rage but outwardly meek and trembling, using all her energy to keep from erasing these men from the face of the earth. Mateo returns alone, fuming. He slaps Pythia hard across the face, but she has read his mind and avoids the worst of the impact. She pretends to fall down in pain and fear, which clearly give him pleasure.

"*Estúpita! Estúpita jorobada!*" He spits on her and stomps out.

This procedure occurred three more times that day, with the three girls always being chosen over Pythia. Late that night, when all are in the room, Pythia is struck at how subdued and broken they are. Eyes glazed, no affect, weary hopelessness and pain. Elena finally looks at Pythia.

"You're so lucky! I wish I had a hump! That bastard American liked to hurt me."

"Your luck will change soon, Elena. Trust me. Stay strong. Tell the others."

The second day is very different

~

The routine is much the same, but this time there are only two men in the morning, one American and one German. The American picks Elena, but the German hones in on Pythia as soon as he sees her hump. Pythia reads his mind and is revolted at the poisonous images. He is attracted to filth, and in seeking filth, he seeks filthy sex. The more bizarre, the better. Pythia is disgusted, but she has her plan, and now it can be implemented.

As soon as she turns to reveal her back, she receives a flood of pornographic messages and images from his overheated brain. When she turns back to face him, he cries in heavily accented English, "This one! This one, definitely!"

Mateo smiles his oily smile. "*Muy bien, señor. Muy bien!*"

Pythia does not react and follows the German submissively, much to Mateo's relief. They enter a stinking room with a stained mattress on the floor. The walls are crisscrossed with spidery cracks and the reddish paint is chipped. There is no window. Pythia stands and waits. He tries to kiss her, and when she resists, he turns her around and fondles her hump. She turns back and says, "Strip, please." When he begins to remove his clothes, she finally uses her power.

At first the man looks confused, then frantically tears at his pants and underwear. "*Irgendwas stimmt nicht!*" he shouts in pain.

He starts to shake and runs out of the room with his pants half-down. "*Was ist los?*" he cries as he stumbles out.

Pythia laughs in relief. She will soon learn if it worked. From the bathroom down the hall, she hears a scream. If all has gone well, he has peed a bloody stream. She has removed his urethra from the prostrate gland to the tip of his penis. To urinate in future, an incision must be made to divert the urine to a bag. No more erections. No more rape. She listens with pleasure to the hubbub in the hallway which continues to attract a crowd. After the German is sent away to fend for himself, Pythia's captors have no explanation for what happened, so she is left unpunished.

On the third morning at breakfast, Elena tells her one of the girls who witnessed the German as he hopped around in the hallway claims he had only half a penis. Pythia is confident she removed his urethra, but must have inadvertently also amputated half his penis. A slight error. At first, this news does not trouble her, but she would have to be more careful in future. To remain incognito, she must limit damage to internal structures, where the obvious cannot be seen and raise unwelcome suspicions. In any case, she needs to move fast, as she can't keep mutilating these men indefinitely without exposing herself to danger. How to get past Mateo and confront Rogelio without falling into these traps?

Events will not allow her to tarry. Soon after breakfast, Mateo enters with three men, and she again finds herself standing naked for their inspection. Mateo seems particularly glum and distracted, which Pythia assumes is a holdover from the previous night's incident. To her relief, none of them choose Margarita, but the ugliest of the bunch, an overweight American stinking of pot and stale beer, picks her. When he sees her hump, he says, "I like ugly. But this one is ugly-pretty. Never had one of them before. You like to fuck, honey?"

His breath is nauseating, and Pythia turns to Elena and asks her to interpret so Mateo will clearly understand. She then locks eyes with Mateo and says, "I won't fuck this bastard. Go tell Rogelio I want to talk to him. Tell him I know what happened to the German last night."

When Elena finishes interpreting, Mateo is thrown into a rage. Without a word, he punches Pythia in the stomach, knocking the wind out of her. She falls to the ground and he kicks her in the ribs, screaming all the while, "*La maldita perra! La maldita perra!*"

He turns to the fat American deferentially. "You want another? I get you another. Better. *Mucho mejor!*"

But the fat American is smiling cruelly. "No, I want this one. This one. By *God*, she's fuckin' ugly-pretty and feisty. I like 'em feisty!"

"No, se*ñor*, I get you another."

"I'll pay double for this one."

Mateo stops objecting, his eyes wide with greed. "Okay, *señor*, okay. I bring her to you in other room."

"Hell no! I'll carry the bitch myself." He jerks Pythia to her feet and wraps his arms around her, lifting her off her feet. "Show me the way!"

Pythia does not struggle, instead spending energy calculating her next move. *Now I've done it!* she thinks. *What to do now?*

A host of possibilities race through her mind on the way to the room. All of them involve extreme action. None of them are attractive. None of them will get her where she wants to go. Think harder. . . .

~ Correction ~

The fat American carries her into the room and throws her on the filthy mattress. As he stands over her, he undresses to show off his enormous stomach and pornographic tattoos. She cannot see his penis beneath the rolls of fat, and decides to simply repeat yesterday's surgery, only this time with more precision. Once it is done, she waits impatiently for him to notice the effect. At first, he stands over her and demands she put her mouth over his cock.

"What cock?" she asks innocently.

He gives her a puzzled look, then his face morphs into alarm. Reaching down to pull back the fat, his flaccid penis looks sadly like a tiny twig protruding from a hillside. Alarm turns into fear. "What the fuck?" he exclaims. Now fear turns into panic and he runs out of the room, shouting, "I'll be back. Something . . . is wrong. Goddamn it! Something . . . oh, shit!"

Pythia smiles in satisfaction to hear the same screams from the bathroom and the commotion in the hallway as yesterday, but this time she knows she did not accidentally remove half his penis. Correction made. Now, she waits. She does not have to wait long. Mateo appears and orders her back to her room. He is sweating and muttering obscenities under his breath while the shouting, cursing, and screaming continues in the background.

Pythia hesitates at the doorway to scrutinize the fat American now moaning and whimpering, surrounded by hopelessly confused cartel men. Mateo violently shoves her into the hallway, and Pythia stumbles, almost falling, then rights herself and turns to face him. He stops and stares with a mixture of hatred and fear in his bulging eyes.

"Tell Rogelio, or whoever your boss is, I want to see him."

Mateo lifts his arm to strike, but hesitates when she raises her hand in warning and continues, "You will not touch me unless you want the same thing to happen to you. Get me your boss. Now!"

She senses his brain awash in a swelter of conflicting emotions, but he lowers his arm and they walk to her room where he leaves her without another word, locking the door behind. Now she dons her nightgown and settles in to wait. To her surprise, none of her roommates return, and night comes without any other visitors. She is not given food, and remains in the dark until morning, both literally and figuratively. Although surprised, Pythia remains unfazed by these unforeseen circumstances. Knowing full well she can use her powers to leave whenever it suits, she is prepared to be patient. Nevertheless, her intellectual curiosity is aroused, and the hour pass in contemplation of how her predicament will resolve itself. Finally, a few hours before dawn, she falls asleep, ready for whatever eventuality presents itself at sunrise.

While sleeping, a dream comes to her that portends evil doings. In the dream, she is on a rocky precipice looking down at throngs of humans far below in a broad valley. They are all looking up at her and shouting in extreme agitation, but she cannot distinguish the words, which could either be calling for her destruction or hailing her presence. She raises her arm in regal acknowledgement and is met with a hail of rocks thrown by the frenzied mob. Now covered in blood, she wonders, *How can they throw the rocks so high? There must be great pent-up fury in them to be able to reach me way up here. They are mere dots, yet the rocks keep coming.* She tries to use her power to make the rocks disappear, but they only grow in numbers, tearing through her body until nothing remains.

Upon waking from this nightmare, the second day of her isolation begins. By the afternoon, she is becoming restless, not to say hungry. If this continues a change in plan will be necessary. Not long after this thought, a man she does not recognize enters the room with a tray of food.

"Eat," he says.

"You speak English?"

"Yes."

"Where is Mateo?"

The man's face is a blank. She reads his mind, but it is little more than a void, empty of useful information. Only his snake and dragon tattoos seem to have life.

"Don't know," he says lethargically.

"My roommates?"

"Don't know. Eat." He leaves and locks the door behind.

After finishing her food, the door again opens and another man she does not recognize enters. His English is much better than Mateo's. "A man, a customer, has asked for you," he says. "Your reputation is already spread to the street. Some men like *demonio* bitches." Baring his teeth in an animal snarl, he continues, "This man paid big money for you. Rogelio says for you to fuck him, and if all goes well, he will then see you. If not, if you refuse, if something happens to this man, you will be killed without delay."

"I want to see Rogelio first."

"Shut-up, take off your clothes, and wait." He collects the food tray and leaves.

Now Pythia feels trapped. If she refuses to have sex, or harms this man, her plans will be ruined. After all, it is the head she seeks, not the tail. Refusing sex or mutilating the customer would result in either forcing her to institute a bloodbath in order to free all the girls, creating a terrible mess with the authorities, or she would have to quietly escape and leave them to their fate. While still absorbed in these thoughts, Mateo opens the door. He glares at her with hatred in his eyes, but now tinged with fear. Close behind follows a tall, dark man. Pythia at once recognizes Altan, but refrains from registering any emotion.

"*Aquí está ella, amigo,*" says Mateo. "*Inspeccionar su cuerpo.*"

"*No hay necesidad,*" replies Altan in perfect Spanish. "No need to inspect her body," he adds in English for Pythia's sake.

"*Bien, entonces ven conmigo.*"

Staring at Pythia, Altan says, "No, this room is fine." Turning to Mateo, he repeats in Spanish, "*No. Esta habitación está bien para mi.*"

"*Pero, señor—*" Mateo starts to say.

"Leave! *Déjanos en paz!*" commands Altan in a tone that will not be questioned.

Mateo slouches out.

His demeanor unchanged after Mateo leaves, Altan asks, "How are you?"

"Fine." Pythia feels renewed confidence as she looks into those hypnotic gold and blue eyes.

"Tell me."

She fills him in on the details of her capture, her stay, and her goal.

After listening without interruption, Altan says, "Good. I will tell them you serviced me very well. Watch out for Rogelio. His is vicious, but very clever, in a feral sort of way. Also, he is not the head."

"The neck?' Pythia asks with a smile.

"Yes, but if you must sever the neck, at least it will slow them down."

"I have a plan to go through the neck and get to the head."

"Good. I'll wait a while and leave. Before I forget, Jared sends his love."

Pythia shakes her head. "*Homo sapiens* males, so unstable! His small, personal love would be better served if he loves all of them."

"Humans?"

"Yes, like the girls here. Sad little creatures, all of them, who we must put down gently when the time comes."

"*If* the time comes," cautions Altan. "By the way, are you pregnant?"

"Yes, I believe so."

Chapter 28: Off The Rails

~ Prelude to Disaster ~

After hearing Pythia's announcement, Altan sits cross-legged on the floor and waits silently, the usual stoic expression carved on his features. Pythia looks at him curiously. With humans, she is perfectly at ease even when being bombarded by their scattered and emotionally charged brainwaves. But Altan (as well as Lady Oracle and Sy) are vastly different. First and foremost, their status as beings somehow superior has never been questioned, either by her mother or by herself. Second, she cannot read their minds as she can with humans, and whenever an attempt is made, it is met with an impenetrable fog, a sort of cosmic microwave background that blocks any possible view of creation. Third, she has no doubt (though she has rarely tried) they are immune to her other powers, including, as Sy calls it, reconfiguring objects. More notably, Pythia is certain they have mysterious powers far beyond those she possesses.

Whenever Pythia tries to categorize them as, say, advanced beings or *Gods* and *Goddesses*, she is met with a dismissal of such childish concepts. So here she is, completely naked in front of Altan, at the heart of a violent cartel with many lives on the line, and he sits across from her with no more conscious awareness than if he was surrounded by an infinite sea of sand; aware, perhaps, of the total environment, but utterly disinterested in the fate of the individual grains comprising it. She wonders what secret powers he, Sy, and Lady Oracle possess, surely as far surpassing her ability to understand, as she is far beyond the ability of humans to understand her.

"Altan," she says, interrupting his meditation. "What do you truly think of *Homo sapiens*?"

"Cobbled together intermediates blinded by the glare of nascent intelligence. Unfinished."

"And me?"

"A step."

"And you?"

Here, he actually smiles. "Another step."

"Is there an end to the steps?"

"Yes and no. Extinction or adaptation."

"Some humans are trying to take another step. Multiculturalism and environmentalism are attempts."

Altan nods sympathetically. "Some aspire to multiculturalism, but even those few are utterly incapable of conceiving it beyond their own species, blindly denying equal weight to the cultures of elephants, ants, termites, sparrows, Douglas fir, lobsters, and all the others; choosing instead to devour them (and themselves) in an all-consuming predilection for unrestrained gluttony. Environmentalists are a sad lot, aware they are too few too late, shouting words that will not be heard above the inane howl of bickering voices."

"True, but there *are* some."

"Yes, the ones who make handprints on cave walls for us to marvel at and see the seeds of a viable, creative future for their genus. However, in their current state, the navel-gazers, hand-wringers, and hand-claspers of the world are like canaries in a mine. Problem is, when they croak, no one heeds. Rather, from a more historical or cosmic perspective, the navel-gazers, hand-wringers, and hand-drawers of the world are actually the prey on which more brutally primitive forces feast, twisting their fears and prophecies of doom into wealth and power, accelerating the demise of their own species and countless others. This is where you come in."

"Is the knowledge given me over those sixteen years all of your knowledge?"

"Not possible."

"Sounds like me talking to Jared."

He shrugs. "It is time for me to go. Now that you are pregnant, you must be extra careful."

"I am in no danger of being killed."

"Perhaps, but you do not take my meaning. You must be extra careful and not draw too much attention to yourself."

"Then why have you put me in this situation?"

"There are others above me. *She* is weary of fighting *His* addiction. *She* wants you tested sooner rather than later."

[339]

"Why?"

"If you and your progeny take too long, by then most of *Her* other joys on this planet will be driven to extinction. Even *She* is capable of impatience."

"Well, isn't *She* just a metaphor?"

"True. What lurks behind the metaphor is not for you to know. Not yet."

"To extend the metaphor, isn't *She* supposed to be timeless?"

"No such thing. Metaphors have their limits." He abruptly stands. "Goodbye."

Altan nods in her direction with a conspiratorial wink, and leaves.

Pythia quickly puts on her nightgown and waits.

~

By mid-afternoon, Pythia has received no visitors. Just as she begins to wonder, the door opens and Mateo shoves in her three roommates, each looking haggard and defeated. Only Elena's eyes briefly light up at the sight of Pythia, but little Margarita, evidently in pain, hobbles to her mattress and rests in the arms of Juana, who herself stares into space with a hollow expression. Mateo, a satisfied smirk on his face, turns to leave.

"Where is Rogelio!" demands Pythia.

Mateo guffaws. "Who? Never heard of him, *jorobada*."

"I did my part of the bargain!" exclaims Pythia. "Where is he?"

"*Yo no hablo inglés*," replies Mateo, who abruptly leaves and locks the door behind.

Pythia is left fuming, her patience at an end. She sees Elena looking at her expectantly, and hears twelve-year-old Margarita moaning in Juana's arms. She recalls Altan's cautionary advice, but the volatile mix of vestigial genes still containing the roots of human emotion, including anger at injustice, and revenge against those who perpetrate it, now express themselves in full force. You are right, Altan, *even a Goddess can be driven beyond endurance!*

An hour later, Mateo returns, accompanied by four brutal-looking men, and orders only Pythia to disrobe. Still furious, she forces herself to bide her time and strips, hoping the men will be disgusted by her hump and leave. This time, Mateo steps back and lets the men speak for themselves. Pythia has read their minds and now knows they are all cartel thugs. The spokesman, a tall, heavily bearded Mexican with multiple piercings and covered in tattoos, speaks for all of them.

"So, you are the famous hunchback *demonio*. We are all going to fuck you. This will help soften you up so you are good to our paying customers. After this, bitch, you will be nice to them, or we will return and fuck you to death." He grabs her arm and pulls her into the hallway.

"Do not fight us, bitch! Do exactly what we command."

Mateo trails after the four men with a gleeful sneer. They take her into the "fucking" room. She sees the same soiled mattress, still wet with multiple stains. Same cracked walls, but seemingly more so. Same chipped red paint, but revealing even more ugly concrete beneath.

But not the same Pythia.

She twirls around, assumes a wild, crazed expression, and starts chanting loudly in gibberish. The men pause and look at each other uncertainly, taken off guard by this sorceresses' mad incantations. She dances before them as if possessed. The leader boldly steps forward to twist her arm.

"*Esta la maldita perra está actuando!* This fucking bitch is acting, *amigos*! Hold her down! *Sostenia abajo!*"

As soon as his fingers grip her arm, Pythia howls like a wolf. Instantly his hand, up to the wrist, disappears. He freezes in horror, raising a stump in front of his stricken face. No blood, no pain, no hand. His companions are also struck dumb. An eerie silence momentarily pervades the room. Then, all hell breaks loose. The handless man screams and runs out the door, the others following, shouting obscenities and yelling threats. Pythia picks up bits and pieces of their rants. They will return with guns! They will kill this fucking bitch! This *demonio*!

Pythia knows she must leave before this debacle gets worse. How to free the captive girls, possibly dozens in multiple rooms, with cartel men surely arriving in droves? Faced with this dilemma, she starts to act when Rogelio suddenly appears in the doorway. He calmly walks in, boldly, arrogantly, and supremely confident of his position and ability to turn the situation to his favor. Pythia immediately notices he carries no weapon.

"*Cariño*," he purrs. "I am impressed. Your magic is powerful. Is it mass hypnosis?"

She is surprised at his sophistication.

[341]

"Yes," she lies.

"Then I can kill you now, with my bare hands, if all you have is hypnosis. I cannot be hypnotized—too dangerous. Foolish, superstitious *peons* can, but not me. So, I will now break your neck, unless you prove to me your magic is real and not a trick."

Pythia remembers her mother told her once, "A definitive answer will never come. With power comes burden, and with burden come doubt, and with doubt comes wisdom."

Rogelio moves toward her, a confident grin still lining his cruel face.

"Stop!" exclaims Pythia. "Look at your ring."

He stops and holds up his hands, displaying multiple rings. "Which one, *cariño*?"

As he speaks, they all vanish. The color drains from his face and for the first time his eyes reflect fear.

"All of them, as you see," says Pythia.

"What kind of bullshit is this?" he blusters. "More tricks?" His eyes narrow to slits and he assumes his most intimidating face. "Put them back!"

"No can do. Once gone, always gone."

"Put them back or I kill you now."

"Take one step toward me and you lose your fingers. Take another step after that and you lose your penis and scrotum. After that. . . . "

Rogelio stares in disbelief, then Pythia watches in fascination as his expression melts into a broad smile. She reads his thoughts and waits for the inevitable.

"Ha, ha! *Cariño*, your tricks are very good! Work with us! We can make you very rich. I can put you in charge of this operation, then you can treat the girls good, eh? One word from me and you're in with some of the richest, most powerful men in Mexico. One word, and you're rich."

Pythia remains stone-faced. "First, you will release the girls here."

"Release them?"

"Yes."

Rogelio's face is flushed with wrath and he takes a step forward.

"Stop!" cries Pythia. "Look at your hands!"

Stunned by her command, he raises both hands and sees the ring fingers missing.

He lets out a stifled scream and sputters, "How can this be?"

"It is."

"You will die for this! I promise you! You're dead, bitch!"

He pauses to calculate the effect of his words, but there is no effect; Pythia remains pitilessly unmoved.

"No, no! I didn't mean it! Oh, *God*! Put them back! Please!"

"If you are not anxious to lose more body parts, release the girls."

"I can't!" he wails.

"Why?"

"They'll kill me!"

"Who?"

"All of them. My bosses!"

"Write down the names of your bosses and give me the list. That is the only reason I removed just your ring fingers—so you can still write."

"You don't understand. If I do, I'm dead."

"Well, you can rest easy, I have already read your mind and now know who they are."

"You can read minds?"

"Of course."

Rogelio again assumes a calculating demeanor. "What am I thinking right now?"

"You are afraid of me, but also admire me. You want to fuck me and make me your silent partner so you—not me, of course—can rule an empire. Your thoughts are a bit chaotic, but that is the gist."

Rogelio sags back into speechless incredulity.

"Now, release the girls and give them each ten thousand *pesos* so they can escape this hellhole."

"What? Ten thousand *pesos*?" Now his eyes are pleading. "No! I can't! My own men will not allow it! They have guns!"

"Tell them there is to be a raid by the *Federales* and DEA that will be worse than Tlaxcala. Tell them anything, but make it happen!"

"Yes, yes, maybe. Oh, *God*! What are you?"

"A next step."

"¿*Que*?"

"Just do it. Give them, and me, back our clothes, plus ten thousand pesos for each of them, and you will be rid of me. If you don't, I will remove you piece by piece until only your head and torso remain. No arms,

[343]

no legs, no penis, but you will still live. My offer is generous, for I would happily reduce you to an utterly helpless lump of flesh."

"Okay, but then you replace my fingers."

"You have no bargaining power, Rogelio. Besides, I cannot. As I said, once gone, always gone."

"Oh, *God*!" he simpers.

"By the way," says Pythia as he starts to back out of the room submissively. "I can read your mind, remember? Much of your crying and whining is faked. I know you intend to have your men shoot me from concealed locations. Any man with a weapon will vanish forever, and you will be left to account for their disappearances to your bosses. Also, I hardly think you will be foolish enough to report this to the *policia*. Who would believe such a fantastic story, particularly by a leader of an illegal sex trafficking cartel? Go and make the arrangements."

Rogelio listens to this speech with the gaping air of a village idiot. His brain cannot cope with the avalanche of *demonia* miracles he has witnessed, and his feet seem glued to the floor.

"Go, or I will start removing parts of you now."

Rogelio quickly leaves, his mind desiccated, curled-up like a dead spider.

~ Denouement ~

As for Pythia, this temporary victory is, to her, a permanent defeat. Yes, she will have freed these girl-slaves and humbled their oppressors, but at what cost? Foremost in her mind is that it still might not work. She has made threats she is uncertain can be enforced. A distant shooter with a high-powered rifle might succeed. Pythia is uncomfortably aware she is blind to the limits of her power, a flaw that must be rectified. This real experience has been qualitatively different than the simulations administered during her sixteen-year tutorial. Worse, within a month or so, the cartel will be back in business, and Pythia is under no illusion that even some of the girls she has saved will return to slavery out of desperation. What has been gained? Nevertheless, the path has been laid and she must carry through with it.

She returns to her roommates who are huddled together in fear.

"We heard shouting, Maria!" cries Elena. "Horrible things are being said by the men. What is happening?"

"If all goes well—" Pythia starts to say.

A box is thrown into the room with their clothes. The person throwing it scrambles away as if afraid to linger. As she dresses, her mind is roaming the facility, searching for any clues or hints that an ambush is being prepared. Nearby thoughts are cacophonous, but relatively distinct, however, the more distant the person, the more unclear their designs. She casts a psychokinetic demand that all weapons vanish as far and indiscriminately wide as her dominion permits. There is no confirming message, no tangible proof of how far or successful her command has extended. She will walk the hallways and leave the building vulnerable to any who have escaped the decree and possess the means to shoot her in the back.

Eventually, the girls are assembled in the hallways, excitedly talking and shaking with fear and anticipation. Elena stands next to Pythia, and soon Luciana runs up.

"Maria, what is happening? I hear rumors! What is it?"

Pythia gives her a brief hug. "If all goes well, Luciana, you will soon be free. But we have to get out of here first."

Pythia leads the group past a gauntlet of fierce looking men. To her great relief, none of them carry weapons. Rogelio himself stands at the entrance door next to a table on which sits a box. Pythia makes eye contact and he nods. She orders the girls to take the money from Rogelio and leave immediately, adding, "Go to your families, and if you have none, go with girls who do." Elena interprets and the girls all squeal with pleasure and excitement. Pythia takes up the rear, and when all the girls have left, only Elena and Luciana remain.

"Go!" exclaims Pythia to the two. "Hurry!"

"We will wait outside for you, Maria."

"No! I have business with Rogelio. It may turn out bad. Now, go before it is too late!"

Reluctantly, the two take the money from Rogelio and leave. Pythia hears him laugh. "I also have magic, *cariño*."

Pythia hears two shots, a scream, and another shot. Her brain erupts in primal outrage, which she turns on Rogelio.

"Your two friends are dead, *cariño*. Do your worst to me, I am dead anyway. My men have orders to kill me. You can go to hell where those two whores are waiting!"

Pythia draws back and in a fury is about to carry through with her threat and remove Rogelio's body piece by piece, but before she can act, Altan strides through the door. The cartel men move to intercept, but one warning look from Pythia causes them to retreat.

"It is your shooter who is dead, *señor*," says Altan calmly. "Or more accurately, gone where your rings and your fingers have gone. The two girls live."

An astonished growl intermixed with curses stream from Rogelio's mouth.

Pythia listens grimly, and without hesitation, in front of the horrified cartel men, removes Rogelio's arms, legs, and penis, deaf to his pleas for mercy.

The terrified men stampede toward the exits as fast as they can run.

As she and Altan leave and walk far enough away that Rogelio's screams fade to a distant echo, Pythia turns to him and says, "I thought you might possess such powers, but I did not think you would intervene."

"I didn't," he says calmly. "The shots you heard were ineffective because your command to eliminate all weapons, although weak when it reached the killer, still caused the rifle to misfire, presumably because some part disappeared or was altered. It made noises, but the bullets never reached the intended targets. The scream was from the man just before he . . . went missing."

"So you *did* intervene."

"No, wrong again. The instant you heard the shots, you knew what was happening and unconsciously willed the killer to vanish. I did nothing, except be the bearer of bad news to Rogelio."

"Now what?"

"Now *you* will disappear, from this country at least. Much has been learned. Natural selection and genetic expression are complicated. Some of the unknowns have been eliminated. However, one big unknown remains."

"Which is?"

"What this baby of yours will be like. Jared, by the way, will be a very happy human to see you again."

"*Homo sapien* males," says Pythia wonderingly.

~ A Postscript ~

When she returns to the waiting arms of Jared in the Motel Vargas, Pythia debriefs him with as many details as she thinks are adequate, but leaves out much that would have interested him. She feels residual animosity towards males, and it takes a bit of time to retune her receptivity to Jared's more benign and intelligent type of male. Altan has lingered with her and is preparing to leave when Pythia asks him to wait.

"There remains the question of who really leads this cartel. They are still out there. If we leave them alone, all of this is for naught."

"No, Pythia," says Altan. "You have already exposed yourself to enough danger, not just of your physical well-being, but of your . . . unusual abilities. The cartel men will talk, word will get out about a crazy woman with magical powers, but no one will listen. I guarantee the *policia* will not want to hear about supernatural goings-on, nor will any other government agency. Rogelio will be dead by now, killed by his own men, whether he wanted them to or not. However, if you pursue the leaders, there is no way you can avoid too much exposure. You are still very vulnerable, Pythia, whether you know it or not. Because of this event, we obtained clues in a real situation as to how far your power can be projected. It is not limitless. A determined effort by professionals, government or otherwise, will certainly guarantee your demise. Your species, Pythia, is as vulnerable as those first *Homo sapiens* facing predators, including other, more established and aggressive hominins. It is no different today. You would be an unacceptable threat if your capabilities are known. Early *Homo sapiens* survived because of their relative isolation from others. You do not have that luxury."

"Is this advice or a command?"

"Neither. It is a fact."

Chapter 29: No Escape

~ Back to San Francisco ~

Upon their return to San Francisco, Pythia and Jared settle into the old Victorian house for a few days before going separate ways. It is agreed by all that Jared must return to his duties at Berkeley, while Pythia will lay low with her mother until the baby is born. There must be no hospital birth, as no one is quite sure how the child will turn out post-partum. Will he or she be more *Homo-sapiens*-like, or more similar to Pythia, or perhaps yet another step beyond Ming-huà and Pythia to some unknowable creature altogether? Lady Oracle is adamant that Pythia's genetic changes must be allowed to progress naturally, without undue manipulation.

"What do you mean by 'undue manipulation'?" asks Jared.

"Ming-huà and Pythia are the products of saltation," says Lady Oracle.

"I'm a physicist, not a geneticist. What is saltation?"

Sy puts on his serious face. "It is a sudden, huge mutational change causing speciation to occur in a single-step."

"I thought large-scale mutations are always fatal," says Jared. "Besides, isn't saltation an argument used by crazy Creationists?"

"It is an argument they use, but like their other arguments, has no relationship to reality. Saltation is not always fatal. Ming-huà and Pythia, no doubt, are the result of polyploidy, where triploid or even tetraploid or hexaploidy chromosomes occur. This phenomenon is seen in many plants, but also in animals. It leads to sympatric evolution, as you can see from Pythia's pregnancy. As such, there exist vast unexpressed segments of Pythia's genome. These will likely manifest, for good or ill, in the next few generations of offspring. The eventual selectively stable outcome of such rapid sympatric evolution is far too uncertain to predict."

"And sympatric evolution is?"

"The evolution of new species from surviving ancestral species while both inhabit the same geographical region."

"Then, doesn't this show in their medical records? I mean, wouldn't this make the medical journals?"

"Ah!" exclaims Sy. "Here's the deal: neither have *any* medical records."

"None?"

"None. Both were birthed by midwives, carefully chosen midwives. No documentation."

"Intentional?"

Lady Oracle interjects. "Perhaps. That is what I meant by 'undue manipulation'."

Pythia rubs her stomach. "So you see, Jared, none of us know what this baby will be like, just as none knew what I would be like. The process—saltation—is still operating, as far as we know."

"And this *Goddess* everyone talks about?"

"That subject is not to be discussed," says Lady Oracle sternly.

Jared shakes his head and feels an obligation to push back. "Can't we have tests run? I mean, this is important to medical science." A budding defensiveness toward his own species prods Jared to voice this obviously bad idea.

Lady Oracle glares. "Jared, do not even suggest such a thing. Do you realize what that would mean?"

"Yeah, actually I do. You're right. But I want to be there when the baby is born. I am the father, after all."

"And you will. However, for now, especially after the events in Mexico, Pythia needs to lay low, have a healthy baby in private, and then we will see. You need to continue teaching at Berkeley as usual."

"I wonder. . . . " muses Pythia.

"What?" asks Sy.

"I wonder how long the gestation period will be for this one?"

"Yes," says Lady Oracle. "We all have been wondering."

Jared appears puzzled. "All of this saltation and polyploidy business sounds plausible for simple organisms, but they still must continue to obey the laws of physics. Reading minds, telepathy and clairvoyance, not to speak of psychokinesis, are not possible as evidenced by the laws of physics."

"The known laws of physics, Jared," says Pythia. "The equations I wrote for you, and then destroyed, go a long way in quantitatively explaining the phenomena. This is why your String Theory is wrong, but tangentially on the right track. So far, you humans have achieved the analogous progress of chimpanzees stripping branches to catch termites. The concept of a space shuttle is utterly beyond their ability to grasp, no matter how smart the chimp."

"Gee, thanks. Or should I just grunt?"

"Same difference," says Pythia coldly.

This comment strikes a raw nerve in the young physicist, but he tucks it away to add to a lengthening list of resentments. Ever skeptical of hypotheses and theories without adequate evidence, his native brilliance tells him something is not quite right in their biological explanations. Notwithstanding their speculative certainty, he silently vows to seek a second opinion from a colleague specializing in genetics. He feels Pythia's probing, but ignores it. Instead, he flashes in his mind the old line from *Hamlet* for her to read: *Something is rotten in the state of Denmark.* Never has he felt his *Homo sapiens* humanity with more immediacy, and his remoteness from Pythia so great.

For her part, Pythia is dealing with her own doubts. Her ancestral human genes have expressed themselves in the form of guilt. Although she has told no one, when she was in the process of dismembering Rogelio, a flash of agony from his brain penetrated quite painfully into her conscience. He was thinking of his old mother, who he loved deeply, and how his death would impact her life, causing untold emotional and financial devastation. His last thoughts, as far as she knows, were of his loving mother. Such intrusions of the merely personal are disturbing, though she is aware conscience is essential to the judicious use of her powers. Nonetheless, she must not allow herself to use those powers for tribalistic, unduly emotional purposes.

On top of these uncertainties, she has picked-up Jared's own conflicted thoughts, and can see no easy way to allay his fears and suspicions, for she herself finds Lady Oracle, Sy, and Altan to be disconcertingly opaque. Overlaying all of this, she is excruciatingly aware of how critical this baby will be to her ultimate success or failure in nurturing the next generation of her kind. Her mother's more cautious, human-like introversion and easily bruised conscience are not weaknesses Pythia has inherited, but she too, as with the first humans, is not entirely comfortable with such new capacities. Like early humans, she must satisfy herself with outlining hands in caves before setting out to dominate the world. However, like those early ancestors, she is fully capable of using her own tools to bring down game and skin them for food and shelter from the cold.

~ The Island Again ~

The anxieties besetting Pythia fade quickly when she is again with her mother and Zookeeper on their peaceful little island. No doubt, distance from Lady Oracle, Sy, and Altan contribute to her sense of lightness, and the focus of attention now must lie with the growing fetus. Jared too, upon returning to Berkeley, is distracted by his professional duties and the demands of his students. An aura of unreality hovers over the mundane routines of teaching and research, for his experiences with Pythia seem a fantastic dream in which he continues to be enmeshed. Nevertheless, he calls and texts her often, and her presence is never far from mind. He has conducted superficial research confirming some of what he had been told about Pythia's genetic make-up, but has put off conferring with his genetics colleague for fear of how to pose outrageous suppositions without appearing to be wacky. Both have submerged their unspoken resentments into other areas, and the physical distance has strengthened their bond.

~

Now that Pythia is happily free from anticipating Jared's fragile human ego, along with addressing his quirks and too often expressed anxieties, she is absorbed in probing the limits of her powers. Mexico taught her a valuable lesson. There are vast areas of her capabilities that remain unexplored and untested. After all, early *Homo sapiens* had large brains, but continued using stones and spears for thousands of years. In consequence, she has enlisted her parents' help, and Zookeeper particularly, is keen to assist. Although he loves Ming-huà dearly, and is generally satisfied with his life on the island, restlessness often plagues him and the high-octane life of a crack cocaine dealer is sometimes looked at with nostalgic longing. Pythia's experiments will bring some excitement to his quiet, woodland life.

Most days of the week the two of them (often joined by Ming-huà) tromp through the forest, with Zookeeper moving farther and farther away from Pythia to test the geographic extent of her clairvoyance and telepathy.

[351]

If she concentrates, she can hear the hum of human brain chatter all the way into town, but she has learned that she can train her hump and mind to filter the thoughts of others as one might tune a radio. Like an octopus, she can figuratively change colors and mental shapes to confuse an antagonist. But her greatest concern is to be injured or killed by an ambush from someone far away with a powerful rifle. Can she pick up the signal with enough time to make the bullet disappear? What if there are ten shooters? Or more? Certainly, she is only too aware that any determined effort to kill her would succeed, but precautions must be essential to her survival. Of greater interest is the extent she can make things disappear in quantity. So far, if the objects are in close enough range, she can make a sweeping command to destroy all of them. This ability, again, is similar to another aquatic organism: the squid and its jet-shooting ink. As she practices, her capacities for greater and greater accuracy and precision improve. She is determined to make as great a leap as possible away from stones and spears onward to computers and particle accelerators without the need for thousands of years incubation time. But what about this baby? Will it continue the line? Will it progress, slip backwards, or evolve sideways into the role of a supreme monster? . . . for monsters lurk not in the hearts of sharks or lions or, for that matter, in mythical creatures, but in the neural networks of advanced intelligence where malevolent monstrosities are created and given life by the madness of greed and *hubris*.

Whenever Pythia is overly enraptured by such lofty concerns, Zookeeper is always at hand to gleefully burst her bubbles, even if she is a member of a superior species. One day, while out experimenting with ways to fine-tune his daughter's clairvoyant powers, Zookeeper decides to place himself over a mile away, not to test her clairvoyance itself, but to determine whether she can reverse the process and implant thoughts in his head without the use of hypnosis. The results of his clever test turn out quite differently than either could anticipate.

The idea is for Pythia to write down what Zookeeper is thinking after he mentally conjures a list of questions concerning topics unknown to her beforehand. They synchronize their watches and choose a time to begin the test (Zookeeper keeps his watch pinned to the leg of his trousers for easy visible access). Here is his list of questions and the answers she should provide:

1. What am I thinking of at this moment? If you know, respond with the specifics.
2. If you know the specifics, tell me what I am doing at this moment and respond.
3. If you know what I am doing at this moment, tell me how I am feeling and respond.
4. If you know how I am feeling now, tell me how I am feeling at this moment and respond.
5. If you know how I am feeling now, make my feeling a part of your own feeling and tell me how are you are feeling now and respond.
6. Now make me feel how you are feeling and use your power to make me feel better.

Of course, the key to the entire series of questions and their correct responses is that Zookeeper has with him a bottle of whisky unbeknownst to Pythia. Zookeeper's list of correct answers Pythia should have come up with are: 1. I (Zookeeper) am thinking about drinking whiskey of a particular brand and proof. 2. I am drinking the whiskey. 3. I am feeling high from the whiskey. 4. I am drunk. 5. You (Pythia) are also drunk (because you have absorbed my altered brain waves). 6. Since we are both drunk and sober, Zookeeper and Pythia, use your Pythia power to make me sober.

Unfortunately, when comparing notes afterward, Pythia had become drunk and could not make Zookeeper sober. Thus, she aced numbers one through five, but failed number six. This ability to actually experience other people's physical condition as if it was her own is a revelation to both of them. For Zookeeper, it is a "really cool" demonstration of yet another power she can use in her arsenal to rid the world of all the "fuckin' idiots". For Pythia, it brings with it an alarming capacity for empathy that might end up undermining her emotional distance from humans and hold her captive to their tribal instabilities and slavish deference to the merely personal. It seems evident the more she strives to deepen and broaden her powers, the more powerful they become, revealing previously unsuspected nooks and crannies. Nonetheless, as is her wont, she issues a cautionary warning to a euphoric father.

[353]

"Zookeeper, I know you are fond of Shakespeare. With these powers I may be able to destroy many 'fuckin' idiots' as you call them, but Shakespeare said, 'The evil that men do lives after them; the good is oft interred with their bones.' If I simply destroy those humans I deem to be evil, they will have no opportunity to change for the good, and the evil not only continues on, but strengthens and spreads."

"True, true. But to also paraphrase the Bard, 'Well, if Fortune be a woman, she is a good wench for this gear. Come not between the Dragon and her wrath.' You are a damn good wench for rebuking this species and using your Dragon's breath to burn the bastards down and fertilize the scorched earth with their ashes for future Phoenixes like yourself to rise."

Pythia looks admiringly at Zookeeper. "You are quite the poet, but remember, it was my kind that took your arms."

"Best thing that ever happened to me. Your mother did me a favor; she let the light into my heart through these two stumps." His face darkens. "You know, I hear you were close in Mexico to being ash yourself. Can't lose you, or the little one in your belly. Build on your power, Pythia, so the bastards can't snuff you without moving heaven and earth. In my experience, if you are considered a threat, the threatened, if stronger, will destroy you. Natural selection. Keep getting stronger. I'm fuckin' worried you'll need every goddamn bit of it."

"Well, let's hope we do not reach that point, Zookeeper. You are my father. You succeeded in surviving on the street by being circumspect, not by charging into oblivion like a crazed bull. The human race is not evil, it simply does not know how to use the power it has without destroying everything around it. The good they do is too often interred with their bones, and the evil they do continues on and keeps growing with their technology, swamping any hope for their future (and the future of all the others with whom they share the planet)."

Zookeeper lowers his voice. "Between you and me, I'm worried about your mother."

"Oh?"

"Yeah. The FBI keeps calling on the phone and she never returns their calls. I think they are on her trail again. Remember how they said new evidence had turned up?"

"Yes," says an alarmed Pythia.

[354]

"Well, I don't know what it is, but she did leave a trail on both ends of the continent, and you have now left another trail in Mexico. Without the explanation for how I lost these arms, I'm also a prime witness. Damn it, Pythia, I'm worried."

"Do not underestimate mother, Zookeeper, she knows what she is doing."

"Your mother is very sensitive, and she carries a lot of guilt over what happened to me and the others. I know she really doesn't care about herself, but her goal now is to protect you."

"Yes, I see that, but keep in mind, Zookeeper, we do not carry the same attachment only to those closest to us in DNA. We, for better or worse, feel an attachment to all DNA rather than merely those who either propagated us or who we propagated. Kinship and lineage have not the same narrow obsession for us. Ever mindful are we of kinship and lineage with the universe. All things share the same atoms and sub-atomic particles. All are of a common kinship and lineage."

"I know, your mother has also told me that. But the idea is hard for me to swallow. I mean, I don't think it's true. I would hope your mother feels closer to me than a ringworm."

Pythia does not respond to this remark, as it is prototypically human, and yet not entirely without merit. Nevertheless, she knows many *Homo sapiens* who do far more harm to the natural world than ringworms. Question is, do *Homo sapiens* as a species do far more harm to the natural world than any other species? The answer is undeniable. Given free rein to continue their trajectory, humans will soil their own bed so thoroughly that it will be too late to save most lifeforms, their own included. Pythia and her recent ancestors offer both hope and devastation. People like Jared and Zookeeper must inevitably fall by the wayside, but will their replacement species do better?

"Pythia!" cries Zookeeper. "Come back to earth. Do you think Ming-huà feels closer to me than a ringworm?"

Homo sapiens will never fully understand and accept this concept, so Pythia takes the path of least resistance. "Of course, don't be absurd."

"And you?"

"You are my father, of course."

"Jesus fuckin' Christ! Why doesn't that answer comfort me?"

[355]

"Be comforted, father. If my kind survives, you will be revered. Enough today. Let's return home."

"Righto. Have to shit anyway."

Pythia tries an experiment. "Father, do you feel a deep kinship to that tree?" She points to a venerable Douglas fir.

"Hell no. But I do feel a deep kinship to whiskey. Let's go."

~ A Bad Day ~

A few days later, during a sunny afternoon, Ming-huà and Pythia are together in the kitchen chatting about the baby. Suddenly, both sit upright, make eye contact, and wait for the inevitable.

"I'll get it," says Pythia.

She hovers by the door, waiting for a knock. It comes. Casting a last glance at her mother she opens it. Standing on the doorstep are the same two FBI agents who interviewed her at Berkeley. Between them fidgets a small, wizened woman whose burned-out demeanor and haggard face appear ancient, though she is much younger. Reading her mind, Pythia instantly knows who she is and feels her stomach drop.

"Good afternoon Ms. Powers, Agent Saunders. It's good to see you again."

"Yes, good afternoon."

The other agent nods. "Agent Dunlap, ma'am, if you recall. Good to see you."

Pythia continues holding open the door but not inviting them in. "Yes," she says. "I remember you. Good afternoon." Her eyes fall on the woman who is scratching her arm vigorously. *Drugs have excavated her soul*, thinks Pythia.

Agent Saunders says, "And this is Jasmine Walker. Is your mother home?"

Ming-huà steps into view. "Yes. Can I help you?"

"May we come in and ask a few questions?"

"Of course."

As they enter, Dunlap asks, "Is your husband home?"

"No. He's gone to the mainland."

The agents trade glances as they stand awkwardly in the living room.

"Please have a seat," says Ming-huà.

[356]

Once everyone is seated, Agent Saunders looks at Ming-huà. "Mrs. Powers, do you recognize Ms. Walker here?"

Ming-huà blinks. "No."

Pythia's hump buzzes with the clipped and focused thoughts of the two agents. They are well trained, disciplined sharks gliding beneath the surface and drawn to her mother with hopeful expectations. Yet, she also senses uncertainty. There is no blood in the water—yet.

Agent Dunlap speaks in a soft-spoken monotone, betraying no undue emotion. "Jasmine—Ms. Walker—was a witness in Baltimore on the night those men were somehow dismembered. As you know, there is no explanation as to how this dismemberment was accomplished. The two survivors claim you had something to do with it. Up to now, only yourself and those two survivors were witnesses, as far as we knew, until now. Not long ago, Ms. Walker has come forward as an eye witness."

"Ain't true, sonny boy!" exclaims Jasmine. "They offered a reward for information." Her words are jittery, her face a hard mask of bitterness and animal cunning. "I need the goddamn money."

Dunlap continues in the same tone. "We have two other witnesses who saw you the night before the incident give money to Ms. Walker. In those days she lived in a particular alleyway. Her nickname in the neighborhood was 'Crazy Jasmine' and she had the reputation for defending herself with a knife. The two witnesses have said they warned you away from her. If you recall, she . . . oh . . . had a child."

Jasmine cries out, "She's gone! Gone! Dead, poor thing! I killed her 'cause of my addiction, which I've given up. I'm clean now, swear it!" She looks enthusiastically at Ming-huà. "You were nice, lady. You give me money. Me and Yolanda could eat next day 'cause of you. That's why I followed you when I seen you the next night. Why you out there, girl? Anyways, I followed you to ask for more money."

Both Pythia and Ming-huà are fully aware that Jasmine has no idea how those men ended up the way they did, but she does believe Ming-huà is a witch—a witch with money and devilish powers. They realize her testimony would be worthless in a trial. They also know the agents are hoping Ming-huà will make some incriminating statement, but are also plagued with doubts about what that statement could be. After all, how could a small, hunchbacked woman make men's limbs simply disappear without any sign of blood? But then, there is the California incident, and

[357]

just recently some sketchy reports from Mexico with the same pattern. They still operate in the dark. *No blood*, thinks Pythia, *but plenty of turbulence on the surface to attract attention.*

After Jasmine finishes her statement, Ming-huà nods and looks at the agents, "What does this have to do with me?"

Saunders replies, "Ms. Walker thinks you are responsible for what happened to those men."

"As I have already told you many times, I have no idea what happened to those men, or to be more precise, how it happened to those men."

Dunlap asks, "Why were you out on such a dangerous street two nights in a row?"

"I have also answered that question many times. I could not sleep. I have a soft spot for the homeless. My hump has made me sensitive to the disadvantaged and abused."

"Mrs. Powers, we know your husband is without arms. We know he was present at a crack house in San Francisco when others also lost their arms, the same as those men in Baltimore. You were also present at the San Francisco incident."

"For the same reason, charity work. I've now repeated this multiple times. Sirs, I wish I could help, I really do. I have nightmares. Could these incidences be caused by some sort of government test of weapons, perhaps by the military?"

"You tell 'em, honey!" exclaims Jasmine, still scratching her raw arms.

Dunlap continues unperturbed. "No ma'am. Ms. Walker says you were being physically attacked when the dismemberment occurred."

"Correct."

"You were angry?"

"No, terrified."

Dunlap coughs. "Did you . . . ah . . . want your attackers to . . . ah . . . die or lose body parts? I mean, in your terrorized state?"

"What a silly question. As I said, I was terrified. Revenge played no role in my terror."

"You did not . . . like . . . form a mental picture of them dismembered or dead?"

"No. I just wanted them to stop and leave me alone."

"Did you notice anything at all just before the men, ah, suffered their injuries?"

"Again, I have already said no to that question many times, and the answer is still no. In spite of what you say, I have come to believe the government or military is testing some horrible new technology on the weakest members of society."

Agent Saunders ignores her last statement and asks, "Have either of you been to Mexico recently?" He glances at Pythia.

"I have," says Pythia.

"Why?"

"Research."

"Into?"

"I want to continue my mother's outreach work with disadvantaged people. Not only do I share my mother's condition, my father was once involved in drugs. I need field data to finish a paper I'm working on."

"At Berkeley?"

"Partly."

"For Doctor Paine?"

"No."

"Does the paper involve drugs?"

"Yes, and their effects on poor women."

"How about sex trafficking?"

"Same idea."

After more questions of this nature, the two agents leave with Jasmine in tow, still scratching. But her last words to Ming-huà are, "You, lady, are a good witch, devil or no, you're a good witch. Give 'em hell! You can take the fuckin' arms and legs off every goddamn man out there as far as I care!"

~

Once alone, Ming-huà and Pythia sit quietly, communicating via telepathy. Zookeeper soon joins them.

"Soon as I heard the bastards, I high-tailed it out the back door and waited in the woods till they left. Took them long enough. Is it bad?"

"Bad enough," says Ming-huà despondently.

"Not that bad," says Pythia. "They have no real evidence that any jury would listen to or believe. They don't believe it themselves."

"It's not that, daughter. It's that we will be given no peace. Eventually, they will come for both of us—maybe not to arrest, but under some obscure statute about national security. They already have put together two plus two, but are in the dark about the mechanism by which these men were . . . disarmed."

"Yup," says Zookeeper. "They don't give a rat's ass about the victims. All they care about is that mechanism, as you call it. It's fuckin' driving them crazy how the perpetrator achieved the unachievable. There's your fuckin' national security issue right there."

"Well, I see no point in running," says Pythia. "They'll find us eventually, and by running will assume we are the guilty ones—we are the mechanism Zookeeper and you refer to."

"You're right," says Ming-huà. "Stay here with us until the baby is born, then we'll see."

"I have a feeling Lady Oracle, Sy, and Altan will have something to say about this," says Zookeeper grimly. "Maybe go back to that haunted-ass cave?"

Ming-huà's face hardens. "The cave! My mother and father were born and died and were reborn many times in that mystical place where time and space get twisted and folded in a thousand different shapes. It is a carnival house of mirrors, easy to enter, hard to get out."

Pythia nods agreement. "All of us have had our own experiences in that place. Sixteen years, mother!"

Tears fill Ming-huà's eyes. "Lost to us in the amnesia-causing cracks and crevices of unknowable dimensions."

"Yet, that is where I learned things outside the scope of this simpler world."

"Where'd you go?" asks a curious Zookeeper.

Pythia pauses, then says, "Nowhere and everywhere. I witnessed the vilest deeds of men, and worse, their governments. I acquired the highest levels of knowledge beyond the known laws of physics, chemistry, and biology. While in those spaces, my powers and practices were safely nurtured. I plumbed the terrible ability to destroy. Is not the cave a perfect metaphor for my life? I became unchained from my ancestors, cast out by the vagaries of genetics; cast out of Plato's illusory world, and into the light of a multi-dimensional reality. These *Homo-sapiens* cave-dwellers have been born blind, but even so, will drag their chains behind them outside the cave and grope for me amongst the forms of am unfamiliar new world. They will fail. They must fail."

"Fuckin' A!" enthuses Zookeeper. "Let's drink on it!"

Chapter 30: Labor

~ Approaching Birth ~

The rigors of his work have left Jared with little time to dwell on his separation from Pythia. But as her pregnancy progresses, he is once again compelled to look more deeply into this notion of sympatric evolution and saltation. His fiancé, the mother of his child is, after all, a different species. Try as he might, with all his scientific training and intellectual curiosity, he cannot wrap his head around this undeniable revelation. Much as he believes he loves Pythia for herself, the nugget that glitters in his eyes and propels his enthusiasm past cautionary doubts is her scientific knowledge and the ability to wield unimaginable powers. He has thoroughly rejected the notion that he, or any other intelligent scientist, cannot comprehend the cognitive depths of her kind. He and the other intellectual inheritors of Darwin, Newton, Einstein, and so many others, are surely sufficiently brilliant to pass muster. Excited as he is about a next step for humanity, he quite sincerely believes any collection of people larger than two, possessing Pythia's powers, will wreak havoc on each other and the world in general. Nevertheless, this experiment of evolution is embryonic, and he agrees with Pythia, Lady Oracle, and the others not to jeopardize its success too early. As for his own species, while confident the behavior and motivations of highly educated, scientifically-minded contemporaries would be benevolent, he is, sadly, pessimistic about humanity in general.

Thus, Jared finds himself a bit hoisted on his own petard. Can he have it both ways, or will circumstances compel him to turn against the woman he loves, not to speak of his own child? *My child!* he thinks. *How can it be I will father an alien species?* Absurd, but at the same time his quick mind revels in the possibilities.

"You wanted to ask some questions?" asks his colleague, Professor Frank Rutledge, calling Jared back to the immediate present.

[362]

At Jared's request, the two men sit in a small coffee shop on campus.

"Yes, thank you for coming. I want your opinion on a couple of genetics questions."

"Which are?"

"Well, it involves"—he checks his notes—"sympatric evolution, saltation, and polyploidy."

Professor Rutledge, an old academician in the rumpled tradition of Einstein, runs his hand through a shock of unruly gray hair, and chuckles. "Each of those topics fills multiple libraries with research papers alone. What triggers this interest? Especially by a physicist!"

"Oh, a group of grad students in my lab were debating, more like speculating really, tossing about outrageous ideas of how humans might evolve quickly, in a generation or two."

"Young people today are pretty pessimistic about good ol' *Homo sapiens*, eh? Sounds like your group was grabbing at straws."

"Well, that's my question. Is it feasible for a species like ours, through the process of saltation, or polyploidy, or whatever, to evolve dramatically in one or two generations, enough to constitute a separate species?"

"Yes, if you're fond of science fiction!"

"So, it's impossible?"

Rutledge turns serious. "Well, it is orders of magnitude unlikely."

"But possible?" Jared's heart quickens.

"Look, Jared, take polyploidy for instance. For most vertebrate species, an extra chromosome is a death sentence. As for humans, we can barely tolerate the presence of even one extra chromosome out of a total set of twenty-three."

"I'm not hearing the word impossible, Frank."

"Let me be clear; saltation, or multimutational leaps, and polyploidy in the case of vertebrates are exceedingly rare, and for humans, almost always fatal."

"Again, I hear the word rare. I do not hear the word impossible."

Frank sighs. "It's true that a number of studies on dramatic, very rapid chromosomal rearrangements have occurred, including between chimpanzees and humans; chromosome 2 fusion is only one of many cases. Human and chimp lineages diverged seven to eight million years ago. Mechanisms of speciation are hotly debated and technical. However, to take another example, the pelvis of *Australopithecus afarensis*—Lucy—is dated about 3.5 million years ago, and is very similar in configuration to a modern human pelvis and drastically different from a chimp. There are theories out there for very rapid speciation, especially during periods of environmental stress. Some argue that multimutational leaps with a beneficial effect are nonnegligible and could be an important mechanism for rapid evolution. Saltational evolution might contribute to the history of life, contradicting the old saw, '*Natura non facit saltus*'."

"So, saltation could lead to sympatric evolution?"

"Yes, it's possible, and is not necessarily all that rare in plants and the lower order animals."

"And the differences—these leaps—in the new species could be significant?"

Frank laughs and shakes his head. "Within reason. One or two multimutational generations would not turn us from earthbound bipeds to flying mammals."

Jared is unwilling to propose absurd examples of saltational leaps, such as clairvoyance, psychokinesis, or telepathy. "Great, thanks Frank. Do you have some papers on this subject I might read up on?"

"Sure, I'll email a list with links."

"Perfect."

Later, after studying the papers recommended by Professor Rutledge, Jared comes to the tentative conclusion that Ming-huà's and Pythia's supernatural (to modern science) abilities are the result of intentional genetic manipulation, not through natural processes. By who or what? Of course, he reasons, it must be Lady Oracle, Sy, and Altan and their predecessors. They are the only logical choices. For whatever reason, they are guiding this process, but it evidently is not a certain outcome. Clearly, there are elements of chance, miscalculation, and danger. *What if this baby is a monster who we will all live to fear?* He wonders. *Science fiction indeed! But, at the same time, would this monster possess the type of intelligence exhibited by Ming-huà and Pythia? Surely, empathy must evolve alongside such destructive potential, or the entire experiment will be a short-lived failure!*

Rarely does sex enter into his musings, but Professor Jared Paine retains vivid, deep, and powerful memories of intercourse with Pythia.

When inside her, a swaddling electrifying pulse seems to make him glow, not with release of sexual energy, but with an indescribable feeling of enhanced energy and far-reaching cognitive awareness. That energy is unity; unity with the entire universe; unity with its underlying laws; unity with its beating soul.

"Nonsense!" he scolds himself. "Romance novel dreck!"

Yet, he cannot help shuddering with a contradictory mix of intense exhilaration and apocalyptic dread at the birth of this child.

~ Nearer ~

One day, during the seventh month of her pregnancy, Pythia is out walking with her mother on their favorite path through the forest. They communicate on multiple levels, verbal and telepathic. Birds, squirrels, and other denizens of the forest join in their deepest communicative levels. Even the low, patient respiration of the great trees is felt, making the forest quiver to their breathings as if benevolent earthquakes gently stir the air.

Pythia suddenly stops and feels her stomach.

"What?" asks a concerned Ming-huà.

Pythia's face is flushed and radiant. "I heard the baby!"

"And?"

"It said, *I am become*."

"Pythia, is the—"

"Oh!" Pythia cries. "Again, the child says, *I am become*."

Both women look at each other expectantly.

"Now quiet," says Pythia.

"I wonder," says Ming-huà. "Daughter, do you think this will be the usual nine months gestation?"

"I don't know."

"Do you feel any pain?"

"No, but my hump seems to be sharing emanations from the outside world with another lodger, just moved in." She pauses and smiles. "Quite harmoniously."

Ming-huà says, "I have picked up nothing yet."

"Curious," says Pythia. "With this announcement of *I am become*, we most likely will be hearing much more, and very soon."

"I trust it is not of the same character as Mr. Oppenheimer's portentous quote from the *Bhagavad Gita*."

Pythia picks up a fallen madrone leaf and holds it in front of her eyes. "I hope not, mother. I hope not."

"You know where the key to wisdom lies, daughter?"

"Yes. Not in ballooning destructive powers, but in the growth of cerebral executive function and diminishment of limbic dictatorship."

"Yes. We will soon enough see in which direction this child is headed."

Pythia continues to gaze at the dead leaf. "I believe we will see sooner rather than later. What revelations will follow *I am become*?"

She is correct about the sooner part of her prediction. Two weeks after the first message, another is added. *I am become. Becoming, I am become.* Pythia and her mother spend hours pondering its meaning, trying to read the runes, as great-grandmother Child of Buddha read the taps from the Precious Object.

Zookeeper, in his own inimitable way, cuts to the chase. "Shit! It's obvious! If you know ol' Will Shakespeare, you know what it means. The kid is saying, 'I am now conscious, and my consciousness is growing.'"

Ming-huà and Pythia secretly grin at each other. Of course, they had already thought of this, but both agree some deeper meaning lurks in the words.

"You may be right, Zookeeper," observes Pythia.

"Damn right I'm right!"

Ming-huà cannot resist a jab. "Never known you not to be right, husband."

"Hey, self-love, my lady, is not so vile a sin as self-neglecting."

"Humph! The empty vessel makes the loudest sound!"

Zookeeper looks up and howls like a wolf.

Ming-huà and Pythia, via their humps, privately agree there is no reason to keep pushing it, so both fall quiet. Nonetheless, each is troubled by their inability to crack the code latent in this child's message. They will wait.

More communications come, each more puzzling than the previous, until the ninth month arrives. The child seems to be descending into a sort of cognitive incomprehensibility. Ming-huà and Pythia are alarmed and spend many more hours trying to decipher the child's increasingly obscure messages. Yet, in spite of intensifying chatter from the womb, the due date passes without any indication that labor is close.

Weeks pass after the due date, and a deepening concern has brought Jared, Lady Oracle, Sy, and Altan. Jared stays with Pythia, Ming-huà, and Zookeeper while the others take up quarters in town. Now, the messages are coming fast and furious, with great efforts expended by all to render them comprehensible. But those efforts have failed, and a pall settles over the house. Everyone fears something has gone terribly wrong. Perhaps lethally wrong.

~ Birth ~

Over a month past her due date, Pythia's water finally breaks and she soon feels the first painful rumblings. Starting like a flash of lightning, followed by the sharp crack of thunder, she is gripped by a contraction. Searing pain seizes her pelvic area. The household is abuzz with concerned activity and the old trusted midwife, enigmatic and somber, is hastily summoned, arriving hours later in a jeep driven by Altan. Lady Oracle instructs Jared to wait outside as there is no guarantee he will be safe. When her contractions increase, incessant chatter from the womb floods Pythia's senses, filling the ever-shortening spaces between clinching pain and spookily alien words. Fragmented sentences rush into her brain as if the child is speaking in tongues, demonic in their bellicosity. Against this cacophonous birth-cry, Pythia is engulfed in agony as she struggles to endure the pain. Occasionally breaking through this miasma of sound and fury, she hears the midwife (normally calm as the eye of a storm) cry out, "Oh my God!" and fears the worst.

Meanwhile, Ming-huà tries to read Pythia's mind, but when she does, a tornado of concentrated pain acts as a complete barrier to any meaningful contact. To her immense frustration, there is no way to determine how the birth is progressing. Lady Oracle and Altan wait with their usual stoicism, but Sy cannot help fidgeting and periodically goes outside to perform his bizarre version of calisthenics. Zookeeper is nowhere to be seen, sitting against a nearby tree, rocking and mumbling to himself that Pythia must be okay. Jared, on the other hand, is a white-knuckled ball of anxiety. He is reluctant to speak, and when he does, it is in monosyllabic generalities. He is engaged in an inner war, alternating between scientific anticipation and paternal apprehension.

Poor Pythia! This agonizing ordeal seems endless. Throughout the day and into the next morning, she is subjected to the most intense suffering. The midwife, her face contorted in exhausted disbelief, struggles to maintain her professional demeanor and not run screaming out of the house. Adamant in her refusal to answer questions, she is witnessing something astonishing. The extreme dilation of the cervix and violent distortions of the abdomen are beyond anything she has witnessed in the past. There are forces at play unknown to any physician or practitioner of her profession. In spite of her best efforts, still the baby will not come. Nonetheless, Pythia has it much worse. The child continues its unholy incantations as liturgical accompaniment to Pythia's weakening efforts to force the issue. By midday, Pythia no longer has the strength to scream, and violently jerks to the waves of contractions in mute surrender. Night comes with no relief, and the midwife assembles the waiting group.

"I have never seen anything like this," she announces grimly. "There are things I have seen and heard that defy any words of explanation. I am afraid mother and child will die. Call an ambulance and take her to a hospital. Helicopter her to the mainland as quickly as possible. This situation, this birth, presents elements I am no longer prepared to deal with."

Jared takes out his cellphone, but Lady Oracle puts her hand atop his.

"No. That is not possible."

Jared's face contorts in anger. "The hell it isn't! Let go of my hand!"

Lady Oracle looks at him with a withering glare, drawing herself to her full height. "Put the phone away."

"They may die!"

"No, neither will die."

"How do you know? How can you be so goddamn sure?"

Lady Oracle turns her gaze to the midwife. "You had best go back to her, the child is coming now."

Jared blinks in confusion as the midwife rushes out of the room to verify this astonishing statement. From the birthing room, her voice rings loud and clear.

"Yes! Yes! Good! The baby is crowning! Push! Push! You're almost there! Oh my *God*! Oh my *God*!"

Jared unthinkingly puts his phone back in his pocket and trembles as he waits for the proverbial cry of a newborn.

~

But no crying is heard. In fact, an eerie silence emanates from the room and hangs threateningly over the group as they wait. Finally, the midwife emerges, exhaustion and wonderment animate in her worn face.

"The child is born," she rasps. "Healthy. A girl. But. . . well, a girl, I think."

"You think?" asks Jared.

"Well, yes, it's a girl, but. . . . "

Her face takes on a deathly pale hue.

Jared rushes past her into the birthing room. The others follow slowly, cautiously. Zookeeper silently trails everyone, still mumbling prayers to himself.

When he first sets eyes on Pythia, Jared fears she is dead. She lies on her back, eyes closed, blood drained from her face. To his relief, Jared does see her chest rise and fall, but his attention is immediately diverted to the baby, who has a large head, bright eyes, and is already sitting upright, leaning against the headboard. He almost expects the baby to greet him in words. This vision so startles him, he takes a step back, bumping into Lady Oracle.

"It's fine, Jared," she says. "Just go slowly."

"You act as if she's going to strike out like some snake . . . she's a baby, not a cobra." After saying these words, Jared nevertheless holds back, awkwardly remaining at a distance.

Lady Oracle nods to Altan, who gingerly approaches the baby. As he is about to gently lift her up, Pythia suddenly sits up and cries, "No!"

Startled, he draws back.

"I am now fully become, but still becoming," says Pythia, her eyes feverish. "Leave me with this one and wait."

"Pythia," calls Jared in the voice of a scared child. "Is that you? Are you okay?"

"I am becoming," she replies firmly. "Leave me with this one and wait."

"The child is speaking through her," says Lady Oracle.

Pythia gazes into every face. "Leave me with this one and wait. Still becoming."

Ming-huà speaks up authoritatively. "Pythia tells me that we must wait. Let's leave them for a while."

[369]

Jared lingers as the others leave. He hesitates, then takes a step toward the baby.

"No, Jared!" cries Pythia, frantically waving him away. Having used up her remaining reserves of energy in this outburst, she collapses back and whispers hoarsely, "Please go."

Jared is frightened and quickly leaves, his heart sinking at prospects for the future.

"My *God*, what have we done?" he exclaims to the others upon joining them.

To his utter shock, Lady Oracle laughs, evidently greatly relieved. "All is well, all is well. We have done what is necessary, and necessity's child is in the other room."

"Yes, I agree," says the ever-composed Altan.

"As do I," adds Sy.

Jared, somewhat encouraged, looks to Ming-huà. She returns a reassuring smile. "Yes, Jared, all is well."

"What is all this becoming business?" asks Zookeeper, speaking for the first time.

"It is business," says Altan.

Sy, on an impulse, leaps in the air and twirls gleefully. "She is in the becoming business! As we speak, she is become and becoming! Soon to be a multinational corporation!"

"When will she stop?" asks Jared, put out by Sy's supercilious buffoonery.

"Never," replies Lady Oracle.

Jared laughs nervously. "For a moment, I thought Pythia was afraid the baby would harm me . . . you know, make me. . . you know."

Lady Oracle observes gravely, "Jared, you must confront the reality that this child is not like other children. You must proceed cautiously. Her kind is not wired to have the same parental connection as *Homo sapiens*."

"You mean she might have harmed me?"

"No. But while she is in the process of becoming, you must also become someone you are not used to being. Follow Pythia's lead and do not try and overrule her, as human males sometimes have a tendency to do, even physicist males."

"Especially physicist males," says Jared. "But what happens if I do try and . . . express myself?"

"Take my word for it, old man!" cries Zookeeper, glancing at Ming-huà. "If you push too hard with these ones, you're fuckin' toast!"

Lady Oracle shrugs. "Genetics, gene expression, are notoriously complicated affairs. We must all be patient."

"That is not a particular strength of us humans," says Jared.

"Then you must try and be more than human," says Altan.

Meanwhile, the midwife, having donned her coat, says, "I am returning to the mainland. You know where to send payment." She shudders. "I will fulfill my end of the bargain by keeping this quiet, but whatever has transpired in that room, whatever came out of the mother is, well, not entirely as expected."

"What do you mean?" asks Jared.

Lady Oracle swiftly interjects, "Thank you, Ms. Coleman. Altan will drive you back to town."

"No, first I want to know what you meant!" demands Jared.

Ms. Coleman shifts her eyes from Lady Oracle to Jared. "What I meant is that, internally, the mother, Pythia, is anatomically different. At first I didn't notice, but—"

"Thank you, Ms. Coleman," repeats Lady Oracle forcefully. "You will find payment transferred to your account by the time you return to the mainland."

Ms. Coleman blinks, hesitates, then follows Altan out of the house.

"Wait a minute!" cries Jared. He follows her to the jeep. "How is she different?"

But Ms. Coleman is already seated in the passenger seat, and closes the door. Altan pauses before getting behind the wheel and looks sympathetically at Jared. "Minor differences, Jared, minor. Remember, she is not the same species as you. Minor differences." He hops in and drives away.

Chapter 31: Terra Incognita

~ Becoming ~

Confounding expectations after emerging into the world, especially given the uninhibited flow of esoteric chatter from the womb, the baby rarely asserts her presence. Mesmerizingly liquid, shining eyes, a large head, prominent hump, and relentless concentration when presented with any novelty, abstract or spatial, characterizes her. However, in spite of this intense but unobtrusive persona, the child carries on a nonstop exchange of information with her mother. When asked what the child has most recently said or thought, Pythia is uncharacteristically non-responsive, even with Ming-huà. Choosing a name for the newborn presents Pythia and Jared with their first parental test of wills. He wants a solid, non-controversial American name, the better to "blend in" as he says. Pythia, on the other hand, is equally adamant about letting the child pick, which Jared believes is impossible for one so young, even if she is of a different species. Unfortunately, the debate has continued for a long time since the girl has given no hint of her preference (even though Pythia has repeatedly posed the question). Finally, on one early morning the child responds telepathically after Pythia again asks the question.

I know you as mother. You are Pythia.

Yes.

I am Tara.

Ah! replies Pythia, her heart racing with delight. *That is a name that honors your ancestor Child of Buddha, my great-grandmother. She could understand the riddles of the Precious Object.*

I am aware.

When Pythia presents Jared with this name, he grits his teeth and stifles a sarcastic comment, only saying, "That's a *Goddess*, right?" in as neutral a tone as he can muster.

"Yes, but it is much more, certainly in the history of my kind. It started with great-grandmother Child of Buddha in war torn China. In fact, even earlier than that, in the misery of a mental institution."

"Yes, I have heard this story in bits and pieces from you and your mother."

Jared, a kind and generous man, nonetheless feels excluded from any traditional role as father of this child, different species or not. He is the outsider looking in. Worse, he is the inferior outsider, without the facility to join in the communication between Pythia and the child—his own child. An ugly core of resentment already existing in nascent form, begins to grow into alienation and mistrust. *Thank God we are not married*, he thinks for the first time. *An alien child who views me as a sub-species is an impossibility to conceive! I don't think I can endure it.* Still, he struggles against these depressing thoughts and forces himself to focus on two circumstances that do make it endurable: sex and science. When having intercourse with Pythia, Jared completely loses himself in the preternatural forces available to her, and for those brief moments, can share (at least partially) in the extraordinary power of her inexplicably potent abilities.

"Remember, Jared, I can read your mind and am aware of the struggles you are having. Unfortunately, I can do nothing to help lessen the reality of the situation. Soon, Tara and I will travel to the cave, just as I did years ago. Many of your years will pass before you see her again, and by then she will be, in your terms, an adolescent. I cannot prevent this from happening, nor can you."

"Okay, but what happens in the cave during all those years?"

"Many things happen, but not in the cave. It is not possible to explain to most humans, although as a brilliant physicist, you can at least project your knowledge of multiple dimensions into otherwise impossible to believe scenarios. My grandfather Michael Powers experienced the cave many times, and he was judged insane, finally committing suicide in an institution."

Up to this point, Jared has listened with a jaundiced ear, having heard about the impossibility of humans to understand, but now his professional interest is piqued. It is just such a moment he has been waiting for, and he jumps at the chance.

"Okay, Pythia, you mention multiple dimensions. As you know, we low-life *Homo sapiens* physicists have certainly been entertaining the possibility for a long time, and not just string theory. Explain how this works."

"Jared, you wouldn't—"

"Goddamn it! Here's a sheet of paper, explain!"

"Jared—"

"No excuses! Look, Pythia, if we're going to make this work, you need to give me something. I am not a complete idiot."

Pythia takes the sheet and goes to the kitchen table. "I'll need more paper."

Provided with more, she begins scrawling equations, page after page of equations. As Jared stands behind her and watches, his face drops and he feels a tightening in his heart.

"Here are some of the simpler field equations, incomplete and elementary, but they will give you the idea."

Jared sits and leafs through them. It is an exercise in futility. He does not even recognize the notations. "This may as well be written in hieroglyphics," he says. "These notations are completely unknown to me."

"Yes, alien. Each includes an entire substrate of other field equations, and these, even taken together, are totally inadequate to give a complete quantitative picture. Furthermore, you face an insurmountable obstacle."

"Which is?" he asks.

"Can you visualize a fifth or ninth dimension as easily and concretely as you can visualize the three spatial dimensions you evolved to comprehend?"

"No," he says, defeated. "Can't you teach me?"

"You know the answer to that. I can read it in your mind now. It is access in the physical world to what these equations represent mathematically that I can do this."

She makes the papers disappear.

"Protecting your superiority?" he asks bitterly.

"Quite the contrary. Protecting you from yourselves and all the others that inhabit this planet."

Never has Jared felt more miserable. He can't even nurse his resentment in privacy as he can feel her mind probing his. It is certainly true that he is as deficient as *Homo Neanderthalensis* is to *Homo sapiens*. *Maybe worse*, he thinks despondently. *As a beloved dog to a human. How can I be a father to Tara, who will also view me in this light?* Pythia offers no words of solace, for to her, harsh reality is something Jared must learn to deal with. Natural selection is not a nurturing master.

As a consequence of being "put in my place" as he called it, Jared puts off his sulking and decides to be quiet and learn as much as possible, when possible. He will view Tara as a fascinating study, and do his best to use the feeble tools at his disposal to communicate with her. *At least, superior as she is, she must surely appreciate affection*, he thinks. *Hell, even a human appreciates the affectionate loyalty of a dog.* These thoughts, once lacerating, no longer carry the same sting, and Jared falls into the habit of trying to shrug off his lowly position with self-deprecating humor. Nevertheless, an unpleasant seed of resentment still exists that occasionally germinates and pokes above ground. When this happens, Jared wonders if he is capable of betraying all of them to the proper authorities. But given the clairvoyant capacities of Ming-huà, Pythia—and my *God*, now there is Tara!—he quickly represses such traitorous thoughts. It is during these perilous musings that he is not sure what any of them would do if they find out what he is sometimes thinking—so unthinkable he banishes such ideas from his brain. Resigned to the situation, Jared satisfies himself with watching Tara (whose features are so striking and her responses to stimuli so remarkable that he spends hours simply gazing); talking to her (she responds in alien words he does not understand); and learning from Pythia the latest communiqués (as he calls them) from the baby, translated into English for his benefit. Although he knows his daughter is of a different order, his resentment is tempered by a natural father's love and an acute scientific opportunity to observe phenomena no other human on the planet has the opportunity to do.

~

Against this domestic backdrop, Tara daily extends her vast abilities to explore the world in ways utterly inaccessible to humans. After spending a little more time with Ming-huà and Zookeeper, Pythia and Jared move back to San Francisco; he to his apartment in Berkeley to resume teaching, she to the old Victorian house. Lady Oracle, Sy, and Altan quietly return to their respective abodes and wait. Pythia is aware of what they are waiting for. In a short while, Tara and she will return to the

[375]

cave just as she and Ming-huà did so long ago. Then there will be sixteen or so human years while they both journey to times and places unimaginable. It does pain her a little to realize there may be the great forgetting that so distressed Ming-huà, removing her memory of that time with her daughter, but it is necessary. Ming-huà and Lady Oracle have prepared her for this trial. On the other hand, she does feel a pang for Jared who, like Zookeeper before him, will be left with his own vast blank for all those years.

Even before experiencing the cave, Tara's development is remarkably rapid, much faster than Pythia when she was a baby. By six months, she is walking and by one year is talking like an adult. Not once has she cried, and not once has the curious attentiveness to her surroundings wavered. Jared is delighted, as he now can speak with his daughter, but Pythia is increasingly unsettled. There is an edge to Tara that cuts a bit too deep; a rather hard attitude which expresses itself too often for comfort. She practices making inanimate objects disappear, but is clearly anxious to use her power to "make the world a better place, like you and grandmother have done."

One foggy morning, mother and daughter are relaxing in the anteroom. Pythia is on the laptop and Tara, as is often the case, stares at her intently. They have been communicating via telepathy, but Pythia looks up from her computer and asks aloud, "Did you enjoy your father's visit this weekend?"

"Yes, he is funny, but rather dull."

"Dull?"

"Yes. His mind works very slowly and he misses a lot."

"Such as?"

"A spider in the corner of the ceiling near his chair. He did not notice, even when it made a meal of a fly. The sound of hissing while eating and also the quickening respiration after the meal went unnoticed by him. I know father is human, and cannot sense things as we do, but he really should take more notice of what is around him, even in his own three spatial dimensions. He misses so much."

"You know your father is different from us. He notices other things."

"Such as?"

"Oh, little things."

"For example?"

"Well, he is a well-known physicist. They are excellent observers."

"Mother, you understand physics far better than he. What else?"

"He notices you. He often talks about how you are so smart and so observant. Not too long ago, when we bathed you together, he paid particular attention to your hump and how it glowed and told amazing stories across the skin. He said he could watch for hours but you would be too wrinkly. Not only that, he has said you are precocious, even for ones of your kind."

"Yes, of course, compared to him. Furthermore, he doesn't know any of *our kind* except you and grandmother."

"That is not generous, Tara. Do you feel this superior to the spider?"

"That is different."

"How?"

"The spider has skills I lack, father does not."

"He produces sperm, you cannot. What's more, his sperm helped create you."

This makes Tara pause. After a moment, she responds with her patented answer to confounding matters. "Excuse me. I am become and still becoming."

"Soon, we will travel to the cave. However, Tara, you must develop your empathy and compassion for humans."

"All of them?"

"Yes."

"Yet, you and grandmother killed some of them."

"That was out of necessity."

"When do you recognize necessity?"

"If you are raised properly, and *become* properly, you will know."

"But killing is bad."

"Yes, killing can be bad."

"When?"

"Was the spider bad for killing the fly?"

"No. That was necessity, am I correct?"

"Yes."

"But you did not need the humans you killed to survive. After all, you did not eat them."

"No, but they were killed in order for *others* to survive."

"If we are to eventually replace humans, are they not like the flies to the spider?"

"No. That is not the same. That is a destructive attitude. Would you have us kill all competitors, human and non-human?"

"Nooo," says Tara doubtfully. "We could protect humans in special places, even though we occupy the same niche—just like humans protect lions and elephants."

"Humans will fight to prevent that."

"Then by necessity we must kill them."

"No, that is wrong."

"Why?"

Pythia senses Tara's deep puzzlement, but before she responds, her daughter continues, "Is it because humans are sentient? After all, we compete against other sentient animals, do we not?"

"Lions and elephants are sentient. Do we kill them?"

"Nooo. Killing is wrong . . . but evidently only sometimes; I mean out of necessity, whatever that entails."

"Consider killing always wrong unless it is a last resort to protect innocent creatures from intentional harm."

"Like grandmother and the fawn?"

"Well, yes, but she has since regretted her actions against the hunters. She has since improved her skills and knows she need not have taken such drastic action."

"You mean like just removing a hand?"

"Yes."

"I can remove as much or as little as I want."

"Yes, but you must always use your powers for good purposes."

Tara furrows her brow. "Mother, do we have a religion? After all, human religions and secular moral codes say killing is wrong, yet those same moral and religious codes also say killing is sometimes moral and virtuous. Also, massive amounts of killing has been done in their names, and the killing is still happening now. So, do we have a religion?"

"No. Harmonious relationship with the universe and all its inhabitants is our belief, not our religion."

[378]

"I do not quite understand."

"You will know with more *becoming*."

"But, mother, then please explain *God* and *Goddess*."

"No. Enough for today. Soon, you will learn everything, as I did. Perhaps the cave will take you where you want to go, but it will also certainly take you places you do not. *God* and *Goddess*, for the present, are beyond you. After all, by human measurement, you are only approaching three of their years. Not understanding is a form of understanding."

Tara nods. "I am becoming."

~

Conversations such as this make Pythia uneasy. She recalls being much more compliant at Tara's age. Where might this rash attitude lead? When discussing this with her gentle mother, Ming-huà is much less concerned and much more forgiving of Tara's youthful struggles to understand. But Pythia argues that if Tara is free to develop her own moral code, there is no telling where that will lead, to which Ming-huà replies, "Exactly."

So, Pythia is left to wonder at the irony. She is more aggressive than her mother, willing to take far more risks, yet she is also less tolerant of her daughter, who apparently is willing to take even greater risks. Still, she monitors her daughter's mind carefully, hoping the constant telepathic intrusions do not make the child resentful and rebellious. No telling how that rebellion would play itself out, but leftover alleles from emotionally aggressive humans still lurk in her genome. Pythia remembers the last thoughts of a dismembered Rogelio for his aging mother, and regrets the long-term futility of exercising her powers on such a negligible, local level. True, some were saved, but at the expense of others. And for what? She knows nothing fundamentally changed afterwards. Although she learned much from the incident, it became apparent that only hard-wired empathic sympathy for all life forms will save her kind from their own self-destruction. Yet, on the other hand, the inevitability of her specie's success will mean the eventual end of *Homo sapiens*. How can one species take over from another without necessitating massive suffering? Perhaps Tara, albeit young, is smarter than all of them. Perhaps she will crack the code and solve a vexing puzzle: when does the necessity to do good by inflicting suffering on the bad start, and when does it stop? Oddly, since the nasty incident in Mexico (even with all her cosmological knowledge), she has been forced to confront another thorny question: should one with unique powers help those who suffer agonies by fighting against those who inflict the agonies, yet do so with the knowledge that those who inflict agonies are themselves in agony? Does the exercise of power simply stack more agony upon agony? Will replacing humans make a positive difference to this small planet, or will it be made worse? Her sixteen years in the thrall of the cave raised these conundrums by exposing her to vast simulations of world-shattering historical events, but in the end provided no real answers. What is the key to prevent her kind from overly employing their powers to eliminate unnecessary suffering and surreptitiously replace *Homo sapiens*, only to end up destroying themselves and others at an even faster pace? Even humans, cognitively inferior as they are, have produced wise men and women who realize only empathy and compassion will break the cycles of violence, made ever more virulent by technology. But extrinsic realization is not the same as intrinsic imperative. Have Tara's genes overridden or replaced enough primitive human limbic emotions to ensure a future for her own emerging species?

~ A Preparatory Visit ~

Lady Oracle, Sy, and Altan visit one spring day to discuss the upcoming journey to the cave. At his insistence, Jared is on hand to participate and ask questions.

Upon their arrival, Lady Oracle takes Pythia's arm as they walk to the living room and asks, "How is she progressing?"

"Very well."

Tara, trailing behind, adds, "I am becoming."

Lady Oracle turns her attention to the child. "Tara, Sy is going to take you for a long walk while we talk."

"Yes, I know," says Tara. "I hate all the noise from my hump when I walk the streets, but I know you all want to talk freely." She looks at Sy, wags her finger and speaks in a mock scolding tone. "But Sy, the walk must be long to minimize my telepathic snooping, for I can snoop from a very long distance. Sy, you must do what you can to distract me from all the chattering humans, and you must also jam my sensors so I can't receive any thoughts of those that remain here. We must protect their privacy and my sanity." She glances at Lady Oracle. "Correct?"

"Correct," says Lady Oracle matter-of-factly.

Sy takes her hand but she tugs at it and pauses in the doorway. "Before we go, I know what you are all thinking. You are thinking I am ahead of mother when she was my age."

"Correct, in some ways," says Lady Oracle. "There is a word the ancient Greeks coined, which may be appropriate for you to carefully pay attention to."

"Yes, I know. *Hubris*. I will reread *The Iliad* to refresh my memory. You fear I have too much *hubris*?"

"Yes."

"Sweetie, all of the adults in this room, not just you, have too much hubris," says Jared frowning. "It may take down our species, don't let it take down yours."

"Yes, thank you, father. But I will heed Lady Oracle's words. I am still becoming."

~

When Tara is well gone with Sy, everyone settles in for the upcoming discussion. Tara's absence seems to have cleared a heavy atmosphere from the room. Only Jared, as always when he converses with these people, is uncomfortably aware of his lower status and lack of ability to participate telepathically.

"We all must verbalize our thoughts so Jared can understand," says Pythia after reading his thoughts.

Of course, the others had already silently agreed, but Lady Oracle says, "Yes, absolutely. Jared is the father."

Stung by this clumsy remark, Jared is nonetheless grateful for the gesture.

"Jared, let us start with you, since my remark causes you some pain," declares Lady Oracle. "I am afraid these next sixteen or so other-dimension years will be very trying. You are aware you will not see nor be in contact with Pythia or Tara for a few Earth years?"

Jared is ready for this question and raises his chin proudly. "I am ready. I do have my own life, my own work, you know."

Lady Oracle is relentless. "And you are also aware the students you teach, and their children, and their children's children, will eventually be, shall we say, replaced, as well as your research?"

"You know, Lady Oracle, we *Homo sapiens* can still lead full lives, but without education there is no life, only bleak ignorance. You haven't taken over yet, you know."

"Yes, it is true. This evolutionary experiment may fail, but if it does, I'm not sure you full appreciate what 'bleak' really means in that case."

"I'm not sure that would be inevitable."

"As sure as the existence of billions of habitable planets in the universe that are now . . . bleak."

Jared falls silent.

"But we are not here to discuss that. You know Pythia will not remember her time with Tara for all those years?"

"So I have been told, though I do not know why."

Lady Oracle turns her attention to Pythia. "And you realize you will not be allowed to direct or help Tara in any way when she encounters what she will encounter?"

"Yes."

Lady Oracle continues officiously. "You must leave her to her own devices, unless a disaster occurs, in which case you may have no alternative but to act."

Jared is alarmed. "What kind of disaster would justify Pythia's intervention?"

"Pythia will know if the time comes."

"And speaking of time, is it true she and Tara will be traveling back and forth in time?" asks Jared, his scientific curiosity aroused.

Lady Oracle laughs. "Oh, not to worry, Jared. No laws of physics will be broken. Think of the whole experience as a dream."

"A long dream!" exclaims Jared, letting his frustration get the better of him. "Sixteen years worth of dream!"

"Jared, you well know Pythia and Tara are capable of traveling in ways not yet known to your kind."

"I don't 'well know' if you don't tell me."

"I can tell you this," says Lady Oracle. "We are being watched by the FBI."

"What?"

"Yes, by a variety of methods, including drones and wiretaps. Fortunately, they cannot wiretap our minds. However, you deserve to know."

"But, they need warrants!"

Lady Oracle nods.

"Which means they must show probable cause."

She nods again.

"How long?"

"Months."

"But, they'll follow you to the cave."

"They may see some of us go in, but they will not see any of us come out."

"Unless they wait for sixteen years."

Lady Oracle nods once more, then says, "Actually, many fewer in Earth years. Nonetheless, during all that time, you will be innocently teaching."

This last statement has a curious effect on Jared. On the one hand, he feels relieved at returning to his old life without the constant stress of dealing with earth-shattering events, but on the other hand, he knows he will sorely miss the hair-raising euphoria of being so near to those same earth-shattering events.

It is his turn to nod.

Chapter 32: Official Interest

~ On the Edge ~

Pythia has just given Jared a final hug and walks with little Tara and big Altan into the cave. She turns as the darkness is about to swallow them and waves to Lady Oracle, Sy, and Jared standing in the sunlight, waving back. Via telepathy, Lady Oracle is speaking. *As you know, we are being watched. So foolish they are. See you in a few human years. Let's see how patient they are.* Pythia suffers a sharp pang of regret at these soon-to-be lost years, and wishes she could remain to deal with the on-coming law enforcement scrutiny that is sure to follow. Even more painful, she already feels a compulsion to find a new mate to diversify her progeny, but that also will have to wait. But these thoughts are interrupted as Tara is excited to begin the journey and tugs on her mother's hand. Altan, with no need for light, fairly glides across the uneven ground in front, his walking stick plowing the path as if he was Charon parting the waves with his oar. After a short while, he pauses and waits. Soon, a woman's siren voice floats from the black void.

"Welcome little Tara. A long human time ago, I once asked your great-great-grandfather John Powers when he was a young man how one justifies a life without cruelty, and therefore without the distilled beauty of cruelty. What do you say to that question?"

Tara stares into the dark, her bright eyes glowing from some inner source. "The spider's web is intricately beautiful, the taste of captured flies exquisite. Is that what you mean?"

"Is that what *you* mean?" replies the woman, whose lovely form in all its glory is now visible by some inner light, similar to Pythia's.

Tara blinks. "I am still becoming."

"Come," says the woman. "Speaking of your great-great-grandfather, we will eventually visit him when he was a young man in a human war. But first, you have, in human terms, many years of *becoming* ahead of you."

"Like school?"

"Yes and no. Definitely not like any school you know. It will be very hard, but not as hard as what will come thereafter."

"I look forward to it. Who are you?"

"Who do you think I am?"

"A teacher."

"Yes and no."

"An alien intelligence from some advanced civilization?"

"Yes and no."

Tara looks at Altan. "Do you know who *she* is?"

He shrugs but does not answer.

"Mother, do you?"

"Yes and no," says Pythia smiling.

"Then tell me what you do know. Who is *she*?"

"I do not know. I have never known, though we have met many times. Your grandparents and great-grandparents and great-great-grandparents did not know either."

"But they are old, or dead, and *she* is young and beautiful."

"Yes. There you are—your first riddle," says Pythia.

The beautiful woman seems to emit a stronger radiance pulsing from *her* entire body. "Almost right, Pythia," *she* says. "Tara's first riddle was my question about cruelty."

"Did I get it right after all?" asks Tara excitedly.

"Yes and no. Now we must go deeper into the cave. There are many paths to many places and many times. Eventually, you will see all the ancestors your mother mentioned, and many more as well."

After they walk farther into the darkness, the beautiful lady points *her* finger and a side tunnel is suddenly bathed in light.

"Go there."

Tara gives her mother's hand a pull, and preceded by Altan, they enter. The path is well-remembered by Pythia, and when they emerge into the destination, she smiles at Tara's intake of breath, just as she had done eons ago.

As Altan leads mother and daughter forward, the tunnel's dark eye blinks out behind, he gives a preview of Tara's first, introductory courses on topics such as the physics of accessing and manipulating multiple dimensions, navigating standard and non-standard singularities, hypermutability, hominin accelerated regions, evolutionary rescue, and so forth. . . .

Thus begins the beginning years of her journey—her *education*.

~ On the Trail ~

A week after Pythia, Tara, and Altan disappeared into the cave, an FBI agent in his mid-thirties is perusing the latest intelligence reports about the movements of two targeted 'persons of interest'—Ming-huà Powers and Pythia Powers. He notes that the mother remains quietly ensconced on her island with the armless husband, but the daughter, with her child and an accomplice, entered a certain cave but never came out. This particular cave is of the greatest interest to Agent Lance Romellian. It is at his insistence that a number of unsolved cases with similar patterns have been bundled together and reopened. All have the unique characteristic of some mysterious phenomena that caused victims to lose life and limbs without a trace of violent means employed to effectuate their dismemberment. In fact, these cases have absorbed Romellian's attention on and off for almost a decade. When he was a youngster, his old uncle Emile Ruska, told him fascinating tales of epic quests, mysterious characters, bizarre mentally ill hallucinations, and magical caves. Ruska, a career police detective before he retired, framed his stories as tall tales, but Lance always suspected he hid something from his young nephew. Years ago, as a young field agent working in a regional office of the FBI, Lance received information about strange goings-on in the California desert, and out of curiosity he obtained his uncle's old records. To his surprise, the notes contained many real-life details his uncle had previously told him were fanciful tall tales.

Although as a young agent he did some preliminary research into his uncle's old case files, nothing came of it and his interest faded until a baffling series of recent unsolved incidents kept crossing his desk, all of which bore certain similarities to Ruska's old cases. Eventually, after many hours of field work investigating these incidents, the same inexplicable characteristics kept popping up. One event occurred on an island off the coast of Washington state in which two hunters vanished without a trace, with no explanation for their disappearance yet discovered. Another occurrence took place in San Francisco at a crack house where a number of individuals lost their limbs, also with no resolution and no signs of violence. Yet another transpired in Baltimore, with the same reports of bodies dismembered and no evidence of violence used. Then there was the skinhead incident, and now, vague reports from Mexico involving a sex trafficking ring have surfaced. In every case, a hunchback woman was present. In three of the cases, it turned out to be Ming-huà Powers. It now appears her daughter, Pythia, may have been involved in the Mexico case. The feasibility of it being coincidental the two hunchbacks would be present in all five incidents strains credulity (not to mention Ming-huà Powers being married to one of the men who lost their arms at the crack house). When further investigation led the FBI to trace their movements to periodic visits to a cave in the desert, Lance quickly discovered it was the same as the "magical cave" in his uncle's stories. As a consequence of these revelations, Romellian is hooked, and connecting Ruska's old, cold cases to the new ones has become an obsession. Convinced that some dire conspiracy is afoot, he has assigned multiple agents and other valuable resources to investigate. However, up to now no definitive evidence has been found implicating the two women that would pass muster in a courtroom.

When he received information that the 'persons of interest' and their accomplices entered the infamous cave a few days ago, he ordered his team to hold back and record all movements in and out. Now, he sits at a conference table in San Francisco listening to reports that continue to defy reason.

"Yes," says Agent Duffy. "They all went to the cave, but only three went in—Pythia Powers and her child, accompanied by a man named Altan. We are still trying to find a last name for him."

"And you're sure these three never came out?"

"Correct. We watched via drone and long-range scopes for hours. Then we set up a nighttime camera with ultraviolet lens. Nothing. For three days and nights, nothing."

"And you never violated our perimeter red zone?"

"Never. Didn't go near the cave."

"Then, unless there is an exit we are unaware of, they must still be in there."

"Correct."

The room fell silent.

"What do you want to do, Lance?" asks Agent Lorenz. "Should we go in?"

"Surveillance still in place?"

"Yup."

"Let's let it ride for a while. All previous investigations, including both on-site inspections and historical records, indicate there is only one way in, and it is also the only way out. They can't stay in there forever. Keep watching for a few more days."

~

Lance decides to take advantage of this hiatus by paying a visit to his old uncle Emile Ruska, ancient but still alive in an assisted living facility. *Time to dredge up those old 'tall tales' and evaluate them in a new light*, he thinks.

When Lance arrives at the facility, he is met by the old man in the lobby, and with few words they retire straightaway to his room. Lance is surprised at his uncle's alertness. Although now confined to a wheelchair, Emile's mind is attentive and openly curious about the purpose of his nephew's visit. After the obligatory preliminaries, Lance gets down to business. First, he briefs Emile on the current status of the cases. Emile listens with his full attention, only lifting his eyebrows in surprise at Lance's description of the dismemberments. When finished with his briefing, Lance leans forward in his chair expectantly.

"Uncle, I have reviewed your old files on Michael Powers and Tamara Chu, aka Tamara Powers. There are certain facts of which I am aware. I know Michael and Tamara were married and had a child—Minghuà Powers. I know Tamara was originally from China. I know she was a hunchback. I know Michael Powers was diagnosed with schizophrenia and committed suicide in an institution in San Francisco. I know Michael Powers was a suspect in the deaths of three psychiatrists who were employed at that institution. I also know you never had enough evidence to charge him, but after he escaped, you did track him down in the desert near the mysterious cave you told me about many years ago. But there are gaping holes in your notes, and a lot of odd references to things that . . . well, that made no sense. Am I more or less correct so far?"

"Less," says Emile in his aged, fragile voice. "What you just checked-off as a summary of the Powers' case is equivalent to describing the oceans of the world as being comprised of salt water and leaving it at that. How deep do you want to go?"

"All the way."

"Impossible."

"I have the time."

Emile laughs. "If you have three lifetimes to spare, it still wouldn't be enough!" This exclamation induces a brief coughing fit.

When his uncle recovers, Lance says, "Try."

"No. I probably don't have three months left to live, let alone three years. Tell you what, nephew, why don't you ask me questions. Play Socrates for a while, and pretend this pathetic little room in this pitiful little facility is the full expanse of the Athenian agora."

"Okay. In the course of your investigations, did you ever run into anything like these bizarre dismemberments I described?"

"No. As you mentioned, Michael Powers was a schizophrenic—so they claimed—but the only dismemberment was of his mind by the voices of *God* and *Goddess*."

"*God* and *Goddess*? For real? I mean, that's what he believed?"

Emile nods.

"What did they say?"

"They constantly argued. *Goddess*, according to Mr. Powers, enlisted his help in breaking *God's* addiction."

"Addiction? Addiction to what?"

"Suffering."

"Suffering?"

"Son, you can't keep repeating my words with your mouth agape. Yes, suffering." Emile finished with a well-worn smile that was part enigmatic and part amused.

"I don't understand," says Lance. "But I guess that's why he ended up in an institution. Schizophrenia is nasty."

Emile's smile is suddenly replaced by a somber frown. "Lance," he says. "I do not believe he suffered from schizophrenia."

"Really? What was wrong with him?"

"Something else, Lance, something I could never put in my official reports."

"What?"

Emile shakes his gray head. "I saw things, Lance, many many things I cannot explain. Things that cannot be explained. I also did things. They were also things I could not describe in my official reports." He shudders. "Things that may have consequences far into the future."

"Like the cave?"

"That's the tip of the iceberg."

"Not following you."

"Those dead psychiatrists—something strange in every death. Tamara Chu, or I should say Tamara Powers—"

"The hunchback? Mother of Ming-huà Powers?"

Emile nods. "That's not all, not by a long shot. Everyone associated with Michael Powers was strange. Inexplicable. Same goes for Tamara. For example, there was Buandelgereen, a formidable Mongol woman, but much more than that, she was a . . . a . . . well shit, a woman with powers unfathomable. What's more, she was connected to individuals, or aliens, or whatever they were, whose powers evidently far exceeded hers."

Lance's face is flushed with excitement, and he exclaims, "She's Lady Oracle's grandmother!"

"Don't know, Lance, that's your bailiwick. Then there was that damn cave and the young woman, and the—" he abruptly stops and lowers his head as if exhausted. "Even I got sucked into their—ah—too much, too much."

"Just a couple more questions if you're up to it, Emile."

Emile rallies and injects what little energy he has left. "Go ahead."

"In your experience with these people, did you see any evidence of extra sensory perception, or clairvoyance, or telepathy . . . anything like that?"

"Lance," says Emile pointedly, revived by the topic. "That's all there was. Hardly anything I saw would fall under the heading of normal. That type of communication, or ability, was everywhere with them. At first, I thought it was some kind of con or mass hypnosis, but now I am convinced otherwise. Furthermore, I'm convinced Michael Powers, or someone using him, got into the minds of those psychiatrists and somehow manipulated or orchestrated their deaths. Proof?—no. Evidence?—no. At least not any evidence that a sane person would believe. I. . . . "—Emile's voice trails off to a whisper—". . . think there is something new in the world. Is it dangerous? . . . maybe, maybe not." He gives a deep sigh and closes his eyes.

"I agree that something very odd is going on here, Emile," says Lance, eager to squeeze what he can from his fading uncle. "All these events, these bizarre incidents, these inexplicable occurrences, are coming from these people. Who are they? What's their game? What are their motivations? Do you have any guesses?"

Emile, worn down, feebly waves a dismissive hand. "Wrong questions."

"What are the right questions?"

"There's only one."

"Which is?"

"*What* are they?"

Lance looks at his uncle sympathetically. "Not sure what you mean."

Lance must lean close to Emile's mouth to hear his reply. "If you go in the cave, watch out for the young woman, *she's* not . . . oh, hell. I've said enough for you to think I'm a crazy old man. Go now. I'm tired. Find out for your own damn self. *Goddess* will have something up *Her* sleeve. You might even be dragged off to Vietnam like I was."

"What?" exclaims Lance.

The old man manages a wan smile and waves his hand signaling the conversation is over. "You'll see."

~

On his way back to the office, Lance's head is abuzz with questions. Of course, he dismisses his uncle's obvious delusions (Young woman? *Goddess*? Aliens? Vietnam?) and also dismisses Emile's overly dramatic embroidering of the 'persons of interest' and their accomplices by ascribing to them supernatural capabilities, but he does hone in on possible motives. Why dismember people? Oher than the missing hunters, all the victims were involved in criminal activities. Are they targeting competitors? Turf wars? Over what? Why attack psychiatrists? So far, the dots are so random, connecting them leads only to more inexplicable motives. What unseen operation is going on in that cave? International drug cartel? Human trafficking? Hostile foreign power testing experimental technologies on unsuspecting Americans? Domestic terrorists? Rogue geniuses out to . . . to what? Eliminate injustices?

Threats? Some weird variation of the Unibomber's *modus operandi*? What kind of threats? These conjectures represent a menu of the most likely conjectures, but none of them make much logical sense. Lance leans toward a hostile foreign power being responsible, but that is also a shot in the dark. Motivations? Motives? Goals? It is all too confusing. However, because of the potential gravity of the situation, he is imbued with a renewed sense of mission. If this group represents a threat to the United States, he will spare no effort to expose it to his superiors. Lance Romellian has a well-earned reputation for obdurate doggedness, and he will spare no effort to get to the bottom of this peril, for he increasingly convinces himself there is a deep malevolence afoot.

~ Deeper into Disbelief ~

A few days later, Lance is standing in front of the cave entrance with two fellow agents and a forest service guide. The agents are decked out in hiking gear, listening politely to the guide, Edward Golden, give a brief history of the cave. When Golden gets to the past few decades, his crisp, fact-filled geology lecture shifts to a rambling grab bag of unsubstantiated speculation, gossip, mysticism, superstition, and local ghost stories.

"White Thunder, an old Native American guide who worked over thirty years for the Forest Service, was the most superstitious of the lot," says Golden. "He never went into the cave, and even refused to accompany an investigating police officer. Said it was haunted. Poor 'ol White Thunder got himself written-up for insubordination. Didn't matter. He claimed the cop went in alone, and when he came out, the guy was not the same person."

"What was the name of the cop?" asks Lance.

"Dunno. That was a long time ago."

"Do you have a problem going in?"

"Not really. To tell the truth, I've never been in."

Lance is surprised. "Why?"

"No reason to, I guess. Almost nobody comes out here anymore. You know, back then, when all this ghost stuff was in the air, I guess there was a search for some crazy guy who escaped from a mental institution. Rumor around here is that he was a serial killer. Lot of activity. Someone found him hiding here. But no one comes here now. Even before the hullabaloo it was pretty much deserted, but now you can't pay people to come."

"Why?"

"Oh, stories."

"Stories?"

"Ghosts, aliens, demons, you name it."

"Well, let's go, gentlemen," says Lance.

All four men point their flashlights and enter the cave. "Remember," says Lance. "Look for any possible exit route. I am informed there are multiple side tunnels, and farther down, a bit of a chasm, so let's be methodical. Duane, you take the first side tunnel, Carl the next, and I'll cover the third. When you have finished, return to the main tunnel and wait for my whistle to meet up and continue the next section."

"What about me?" asks Edward.

"Please stay in the main tunnel. When we enter the next section of side tunnels, you'll be there to make sure no one needs help."

"Okay."

The men move forward, and soon only Lance and Edward remain on the main path. A third side tunnel appears, and Lance says, "That's me. Stick here and wait until all of us meet up, then we can move on."

"Yeah, no problem."

When he first enters, the opening is quite large and comfortably accommodates his height without bending over. As he moves forward, the walls start to close in and the shaft narrows. Now, the rock ceiling is only a few inches above his head. Lance spots a seam that might lead to another spur, but it is a dead end, and when he turns his light back down the shaft, a woman's face is shockingly illuminated. He instinctively bellows, "Oh, shit!"

After recovering his composure, Lance is staring into the eyes of a very beautiful young woman bearing a small backpack, *her* lovely face strikingly framed by a stocking cap. *She* smiles, *her* features expressing a natural, open kindness that caresses him with an almost physical wave of benevolence.

"Hello," *she* says.

"Hello," replies Lance, feeling slightly ridiculous. "What are you doing here?" he stammers.

Her grin flashes a set of perfect teeth. "Exploring, and you?"

Lance fumbles for his FBI identification and shines the light on it. "Investigating," he says.

"Investigating what?" *Her* voice a velvet balm.

Lance is struck by *her* remarkable tranquility. "Oh, missing persons, you might say. Have you seen anyone?"

She shakes her head slowly, hypnotically, never moving *her* brilliant eyes from his. "A cave, some bats, nothing too exciting. I was just on my way out."

"So you didn't see any people at all?"

"People? I hope not. Like I told your uncle Emile many years ago, I was told this cave is pristine. I'm surprised to see you, just as I was surprised to see him."

Lance staggers back a step and tries to process this extraordinary statement. "I don't understand," is all he can manage.

She continues to fix *her* eyes on his. "You must be very careful, Lance. There are shadows in the darkness blacker than black."

Before he finishes stammering, "Who are you?", *she* is gone. He shines his flashlight backwards and forwards, but sees nothing. Shaken to his core, he mechanically trudges to the end of the shaft where he is met by a solid rock wall. Questions swarm chaotically. He vividly recalls Emile's last few words about the "young woman" expressed as a warning. At the time, he dismissed their importance, ascribing them to a tired old man. *How can it be?* he keeps asking himself. *There must be an explanation. Who would have believed. . . ?* But none of these questions have answers, so in the fragmented state of his thoughts, all Lance can do is repeat over and over in his mind, *What the hell is going on here?* Standing at the rock terminus, he calls out, "Come back!" in sheer frustration.

By the time he returns to the main path and joins Edward, he has somewhat reestablished a calmer, more reasoned outlook. *Must be a distant relative*, he thinks. *She may be the key to this . . . this what? Who knows!*

"Hello," says Edward as Lance approaches. "See anything?"

"Before I answer that, did you see anyone come out or go into the shaft I just inspected?"

"No, why?"

"Did you see anyone at all?"

"No."

"Well, did you see anything interesting, any sounds, anything at all suspicious?"

"Nothing. What's this about? What did you see?"

"Nothing," says Lance.

They are soon joined by Duane and Carl. Both agents report seeing nothing of interest in their assigned tunnels. Lance orders them to move on to the next section of the cave, hoping he will run into the young woman again.

After Duane and Carl dutifully enter their respective shafts, Edward and Lance reach his second.

"My turn again," says Lance. "Same procedure, okay?"

"Sure."

"Keep your eyes on the entrance to this one. Even if you only see a shadow, or aren't sure, let me know when we get together again."

"Look, what's up? Did you see something in the last one?"

"No, just want to be certain."

Edward shakes his head doubtfully. "Okay, if you say so."

Lance enters the side shaft, gripping his flashlight in tense anticipation. This one is a bit roomier than the first, and he is assiduous in probing for hidden exits and suspicious seams in the rock. After a while, he has gone almost twice as far as the first, and still no appearance. He reaches the end. Nothing. A solid rock wall. Just to see what will happen, he uses his free hand to push on it. From behind comes the familiar voice.

"My, my, you are conscientious. However, I wouldn't do that. Be careful what you wish for, Lance."

He spins around and is blinded by the same gorgeous face.

"Who are you?" he exclaims before *she* can disappear again.

"You know, Lance, your uncle Emile helped us many years ago. In fact, he was a very great help. Perhaps you are similarly inclined?"

"Help you with what?"

"One never knows. May I ask you, Mr. Romellion, how do you justify a life without cruelty, and also therefore without the distilled beauty of cruelty?"

"Look, I'm with the FBI. Your cooperation is essential if you want to avoid trouble. Please answer my question. Who are you?"

"I am not a who."

"Okay, then what are you?"

"I am not a what."

"Look, whoever or whatever you are, give me some straight answers. We are looking—"

Before he can finish, *she* holds up a cautionary hand and looks at him as one might gaze lovingly at a cute puppy. "Spacetime is curved. Answers are also curved."

Lance forges ahead. "Do you know Pythia Powers?"

The young woman's expression remains unchanged, and *she* ignores his question. "In this cave, space and time are so radically curved, you will end up either back at the beginning, or even worse, before the beginning. Return to catching, as you call them, 'the bad guys', and leave this quixotic compulsion alone."

"Or else?"

"There is no 'else'. Lance, this is no threat, nor is it a warning. Others are more in need of your dedication."

"But if I remember correctly, even you said your people might need my help."

"My people are not people, nor are they mine. If you are needed, it will be to save many of your own people. And if that is the case, you will be summoned, and you will remember these words."

In a flash of multicolored lights, *she* vanishes, leaving Lance Romellian, rational FBI agent, utterly shaken. Returning in a fog to the main path, he mechanically tells Edward and the others that he saw nothing. He considers calling off the search, but a stubborn contrarian attitude compels him to doggedly continue past the next few sections. However, after inspecting a series of side tunnels, nothing is discovered. In a state of fatigued disappointment, the team reaches the narrow rock bridge which spans a deep crevasse plunging into the depths on either side. Once safely across, Lance feels a tingling on his skin and the electric tug of hair on the nape of his neck. The side tunnel he draws this time is enormous, almost as huge as the main cavern. Now deep into it, his flashlight seems hopelessly dim against the inky blackness, which has a strange sticky texture, like trying to shine a light through tar. Lance feels the frightening sensation of drowning. Up to this point, he has been able to push aside these bizarre encounters with an elusive apparition, but now his mind suddenly seems to abandon its defenses and plunges him into a state of complete disorientation. This rudderless drift is so powerful, it causes him to dizzily fall to his knees and drop the useless flashlight.

Lance feels *her* hand upon his shoulder, and a cascading warmth suffuses through his body, rendering his muscles a jelly-like quagmire and his body a puppet whose strings have been cut.

"You seek the unseekable to find the unfindable. Let me help you," *she* says gently.

A gentle squeeze and his mobility returns.

"Follow me."

Lance picks up the flashlight and follows the perfect stealth of *her* movement through the black bog. When they reach the end, *her* pointed finger illuminates yet another solid rock wall.

"Now you may place your hands on the stone and push," *she* says.

Still dazed, Lance braces his body and pushes against the rock wall. Nothing happens.

"Lance," says the young woman. "Gather your strength and that famous determination of yours and push."

He does.

What happens next will haunt him through the remaining years of his life.

Chapter 33: Time After Time

~ Lance's Delirium ~

Lance remembers pushing against unyielding rock, then suddenly plunging downward in terrifying freefall. As if falling in a vacuum, he feels no onrushing air, and in a dreamlike instant, finds himself standing on a hill overlooking a silent throng of thousands. As far as the eye can see, none of them possess a complete set of limbs. Some are legless, some armless, some without hands, some without feet. At first, they silently stare up at him with emotionless expressions. Commencing from the back of the crowd, a rolling wave of piteous wailing spreads to the front, then rebounds back to create an unearthly collision. The crowd surges up the hill, surrounding him, jostling him, exhorting him, begging him; their dismembered bodies a scene from the hell of Hieronymus Bosch. Lance, to his horror, assumes the mob will tear off his own limbs, but a stunning realization strikes him: all these people are criminals, guilty of the cruelest, most heinous crimes. Rapists, murderers, war profiteers, torturers, abusers, all of them corrupt to their cores. In an instant, they vanish, and left standing alone in front of Lance is the young woman.

"You have been given a glimpse."

Lance remains speechless, trembling in shock and fear.

She stares at him, *her* gaze a tonic that restores his composure. He takes deep breaths to try and control his runaway emotions.

"You have been given a glimpse," *she* repeats.

"Of what?" he manages.

"Of what is to come."

"But, all those people . . . what happened to them? . . . all maimed? How? . . . Why?"

"Agent Lance Romellian, they are the ones you seek, are they not?"

"Criminals?"

"As you call them. Murderers. Rapists. Torturers, and the rest."

"Then they are all criminals?"

"As you call them. Humanity has many many varieties of what you call criminals. Should they all be punished?"

"Yes, after given fair trials."

She looks deep into his eyes and he feels *her* probing his mind. "Are you prepared to go on trial?"

"For what?"

"Crimes against all living things on earth. Crimes against Earth itself."

"I don't understand. What trial? Where?"

"Human laws are not as severe, nor as just as the natural laws of the universe. 'Nature red in tooth and claw', one of you once said. Lance, your entire species is on trial. Those dismembered people are merely guilty of crimes against other people. You call them criminals and you hunt them down. Now, at the bar of justice stands humanity itself, accused of heinous crimes against all life on Earth, and against the planet itself. Should all humans be punished, as you said criminals should be?"

"No, not all humans are guilty."

"Based on whose law?"

"Human law . . . I don't know, I'm talking to a dream, or a hallucination, or something."

"Is there a law that supersedes human law?"

"No, not for humans anyway."

The young woman laughs. "Wrong, foolish man. Deception upon deception. Natural selection is the pitiless law of the universe. Ant laws, elephant laws, human laws, shark laws, all bow before it. Adapt or become extinct. Now, adapt to this: you are in this cave to seek those who are your successors. Do not be afraid, do not persecute. They are not your enemies. Remember my words."

"I do not understand."

Lance instantly totters on stumps for legs. Horrified, he tries to use his arms for balance, but he has no arms. A terrible scream reverberates through the cave. In agony, his eyes look at the young woman pleading for mercy.

"You have been found wanting," *she* says, still looking at him lovingly.

Again, Lance screams.

Even as the echoes of his agony continue to reverberate, he is again whole. Speechless, he looks at *her* wonderingly. "What happened?"

"You have been given a glimpse," *she* says.

"Of what?"

But *she* is gone.

In *her* place, the cave seems ominous, cramped and claustrophobic. Lance feels sick and panicky. Solid rock is all his flashlight illuminates. His mind is as dark as the cave. Out of some primal habit, he pushes against the fear, but it is unyielding. A change has occurred. The world is now different. Lance's assumptions, once as solid as these rocks, have evaporated, leaving a void that seems unfillable. Only two frightful connections to the familiar world he inhabits remain: missing limbs and successors.

But those connections carry with them a terrible implication, one he now sets his mind to challenge. In the depths of his ingrained allegiance to track down "the bad guys", contrariness remains a burning ember, making him more convinced than ever of the sacred nature of this case, and redoubling his determination to solve it. Yet, somewhere, somehow, niggling doubts undermine the certainty of his intransigent mindset. Too many strange people and bizarre events litter the case, including his own encounter in the cave. Later, eating dinner at the restaurant El Fantasma with his colleagues, Lance does not tell the others of his strange encounter.

"Well boss, this one fizzled out," says Carl. "What next?"

"Back to the office and keep digging."

~

After he returns to San Francisco, Lance throws himself back into other cases, but the memory of the young woman and those dismembered bodies will not let him sleep. In the midst of his ruminations, one name keeps popping up: Professor Jared Paine. Lance knows his team has gotten nowhere with Judith Ganbaatar and Sy Grafton, but the professor seems a different animal. His answers to difficult questions ring hollow, as if he is struggling to conceal facts he is uncomfortable concealing. Lance decides to interview this Berkeley physicist again, and he sets about to concoct a strategy most designed to succeed with the egghead professor. Oddly enough, he decides his own uncomfortable encounter with the young woman in the cave and the inexplicable hallucination might provide him with leverage.

~ An Unusual Interview ~

In order to provide a less threatening environment, Lance has chosen to conduct the interview in the professor's own turf, so the two men sit in Jared's office at Berkeley.

"Have a seat, Agent Romellian," greets Jared with a gesture toward the most comfortable chair. "What can I tell you I have not already said?"

"This time, Professor Paine, I am going to start by doing most of the talking."

"Suits me," says Jared. In spite of the agent's rather brusque attitude, Jared likes what he sees in Lance, which ironically makes him even more wary. (He has seen too many movies of the "good cop, bad cop" variety.) Since he left Pythia and Tara at the cave, he tried to find renewed interest in his work, but it no longer provides the same appeal, and his passion for research has cooled to the point of disinterest. Going through the motions is now routine, but just as he has reconciled himself to a monotonous life, this FBI agent shows up to zap him with a bolt of danger, and remind him how far he has fallen into a lackadaisical sluggishness.

Lance suspects none of this. He sees Professor Paine as the only "normal" person in the entire case; one he feels confident fruitful connections can be made.

"My team and I recently visited the cave," Lance says. "And I'll be honest, I saw some pretty disturbing things."

Jared tenses, his senses on full alert.

Lance perceives this, and continues in an open, friendly manner. "The last time you were interviewed, you indicated you do not know what happened to the others in the cave, correct?"

"That's right."

"Well, I think I can see now why you're unwilling to talk."

Jared starts to object, but Lance holds up his hand. "No, no, just wait. Let me explain. In my opinion, you have seen the same things I saw in the cave. Assuming that's the case, I need you to tell me about it, particularly the young woman."

"Young woman? Not sure what you mean?"

[401]

"I think you do, but it doesn't matter right now. Let me make my point. Evidently, this young woman has certain powers . . . maybe hypnosis, maybe not, but I can tell you *she* is connected to your friends, and they are connected to these cases involving dismemberments. You seem like a square fellow, and you definitely do not strike me as a man who would willingly associate with such . . . unusual people, unless there is a very good reason. I do not want to think that reason involves criminal activity.

"So," continues Lance. "Since my cave visit, I am now aware of circumstances similar to what you have been dealing with. In other words, professor, I am prepared to listen to anything you have to say, no matter how unbelievable, because now I am inclined to believe it."

"I doubt you would believe," says Jared.

"Oh yes, professor, I would. While in that cave, somehow I saw multitudes of people without limbs. That vision was surely brought to me by the young woman . . . a young woman I know you have met before. What's more, it seems *she* considers those multitudes criminals, and the kicker is that they are us."

"Us?"

"The human race."

Jared does not respond, but Lance perceives the first signs of hesitation, so he hastens to exploit the opening.

"Professor, I know what I saw, but I don't know how I saw it. What I do know is that we are dealing with something extraordinary. I am going to have to consider this a terrorist threat, unless I am given evidence to the contrary."

"I don't know how I can be of help," says a shaken Jared, his words halting and tentative.

"For a physics professor, you are demonstrating a surprising lack of interest in the details of what I just told you. Not a single question about what I experienced?"

Jared flashes an agonized grimace, but quickly suppresses it with a wan smile.

"Okay. What did you experience?"

Jared prefaces his reply by saying, "Look, professor, I'm on your side, unless you are knowingly conspiring with terrorists."

"Certainly not. You were about to tell me about what you experienced."

Lance spends the next few minutes explaining in great detail what happened in the cave. He notices Jared is listening intently, his face emotionless, but his eyes alive in anticipation. When he finishes, Lance looks expectantly at Jared. To his disappointment, the professor remains stolidly silent, except to say, "I see."

"You remain disinterested?" asks Lance peevishly.

"If you suspect me of being a terrorist, the less I say the better."

"Are your friends terrorists?"

"Don't be ridiculous. Assuredly not."

"How do you know?"

"I know. They are certainly extraordinary people, but not terrorists."

Finally, Lance senses a crack in the professor's façade, so he again pounces. "How are they extraordinary?"

"Well . . . " Jared stumbles. "They can do things others cannot."

"Such as?"

"'They are very charismatic."

"Come on, professor, you can do better than that. Can they remove limbs from people?"

"No," replies Jared too quickly.

"Well, what do you mean?"

"It's almost as if they can make you believe you see things that aren't really there . . . I mean, they have, as you pointed out, a kind of hypnotic power."

"Hypnosis?"

"Sort of."

Jared is hopeful this tact will satisfy the agent, as most people crave simplistic answers to complicated questions. But Lance will have none of it.

"I might agree with you, professor, but for the fact that real limbs have actually gone missing, including heads. That, sir, is murder. No hypnosis was involved in those incidents. Are these people developing some sort of new weapon?"

"No! I don't know anything about missing body parts."

"I think you do. I think you are protecting these 'extraordinary' people."

"Agent Romellian, what if you're not dealing with people?"

Lance snorts, but inside he is quivering with anticipation. "What do you mean?"

But Jared again backtracks from the precipice. "Maybe they're zombies," he says with a heavy dose of sarcasm.

Lance is again thwarted but he tries unsuccessfully to not let it show. "This is no joke! People have been crippled and killed, Professor Paine, in a manner that defies reason, not to speak of your laws of physics. As a physicist, you should be far more curious about how these atrocities were performed, yet I see that you are sitting in front of an FBI agent displaying a very uncooperative attitude. That, sir, is a very dangerous thing to do. Consider very carefully about where you are going with this." Romellian knows he is losing his advantage so he tightens the screw with threats. "My next move is to put you under oath as a suspicious person. Perjury is a serious crime, especially if done in furtherance of a felony. Conspiracy leaves you open to far more serious charges. You have a lot to lose here."

Jared's heart flutters and sputters in the face of these threats. He remains quiet for some time, his mind racing to construct a response that will not implicate him or betray those he is closest to.

"Let me posit to you, Agent Romellian, an interesting hypothetical. Keep in mind this is strictly a hypothetical musing, and any similarity to real persons or events is purely coincidental."

"Okay."

"Suppose, from a cosmological perspective (not a narrow human one), humanity is no longer fit to continue as a species—at least in the Darwinian sense. How do you think the human race might disappear?"

"Purely hypothetical, you say?" asks Lance, his eyebrows raised in a display of amused awareness of the professor's ploy.

"Of course."

"Well, I suspect it would be the usual—some catastrophe like nuclear war, terrorist designed virus, or some such."

"So your conjecture assumes the extinction of our species would come about by humans themselves?"

Lance hesitates. "Naturally, it could also be an asteroid or comet, a pandemic, or something like that."

"Do you think humans will become extinct?"

"Sure, at some point in the future."

"When?"

Lance chuckles. "Your guess is as good as mine. Look, what's your point?"

"Guess."

"Don't have a clue."

"Humor me. It might lead you somewhere."

"Okay. A couple thousand years . . . I don't know . . . ten thousand years."

Jared nods as he would to a student during a Socratic seminar. "Good. Now, what if that process of extinction was speeded up?"

"By?"

"Never mind that. Just suppose the process was speeded up; would that help or hurt the planet?"

"Sounds like the kind of question a terrorist would ask."

"Humor me a little more. Think of it as a scientific hypothesis."

"I don't know. Help, I suppose."

"If you were an advanced race of aliens and wanted to speed up the process—for the sake of the planet, how would you do it?"

"Why would aliens care?"

"We'll get to that. How would you do it?"

Lance, now intrigued, forges ahead with the game. "Probably simply cull humans by killing them."

"That would not be easy, especially if you want to avoid killing other living things. Collateral damage would be tremendous. Also, as you—the aliens—are empathetic to all life, you want to avoid pain and suffering, or at least keep it to a minimum."

Lance flashes a crooked smile. "Like removing a few limbs for instance?"

Jared waves his hand in dismissal. No, no. This is purely hypothetical."

"Okay," says Lance. "So I want to take out the human race without causing suffering?"

"Yeah. So how do you do it?"

"Kill them painlessly, I guess."

Jared laughs. "Are you familiar with the practice used by biologists to eliminate a destructive or dangerous pest?"

"Maybe, but go ahead and enlighten me."

"Instead of trying to kill them all by using pesticides, which causes tremendous collateral damage, you introduce a sterile variant of either gender and let them mate with those in the wild thereby eliminating the ability to reproduce offspring. No muss, no fuss."

"Okay, so?"

"Well, if you're an advanced alien civilization, you introduce mutants, strains more adapted to long-term survival, who can still mate with the *Homo sapiens* strain, and if their offspring turn out to be fitter, then over time—voila!—a new species emerges."

"You're telling me your friends are aliens?"

"I didn't say that! You accused me of being disinterested. Here I have given you a hypothetical that is interesting."

"How does that hypothetical tie-in with people mysteriously losing their limbs?"

"It doesn't! I told you this is idle speculation. Do with it what you want."

Lance pauses for a moment, then says, "Okay, let's explore this hypothetical of yours. Why would an advanced civilization want to drive humans to extinction? Conquest?"

Jared laughs. "Spoken like a human. If you were my student, I would give you an F. You didn't listen. This advanced species is interested in Earth in the same way we humans might be interested in preserving a place of beauty and diversity such as the Grand Canyon, the Amazon rain forest, or the Great Barrier Reef. Not aggressive conquest, but empathetic stewardship."

"By removing limbs from people?"

Jared shakes his head in frustration. "You are a one-track machine. Linear thinking personified. You know, there are more control settings than on and off."

"Okay, I'll bite. Hypothetically, of course, if I'm human and I know about these mutants, I would want to eliminate them so I can have children and perpetuate my kind."

Jared wags his finger accusingly. "You mean perpetuate your own genes—it's only natural."

"Ha! There are billions of us and only a handful of your so-called mutants. They would never have a chance to get established."

"Perhaps, thanks to dedicated civil servants like yourself labeling them as terrorists, as unwelcome interlopers who, instead of making the planet a better place, represent an existential threat. You would hunt them down. Grand Inquisitors, all of you." Jared adds a softening touch. "At least from a certain perspective."

"You want to eliminate humans?"

Jared snorts. "You keep putting words in my mouth. I never said any such thing."

"Your friends?"

"Don't be ridiculous. Of course not."

"Yeah," says Lance sarcastically. "Just idle speculation, right?"

"Correct."

Lance assumes his hard-ass face. "Doc, I am now even more convinced I have to interview you under penalty of perjury. Your 'speculation' is, of course, fanciful regarding aliens and such, but I do understand cults and suicidal terrorists. In other words, I am inclined to believe you know all about these maimings and murders. Being an accomplice to murder will give you multiple years in prison, which is plenty of time to spin more speculative yarns."

Jared struggles to retain his composure, but Lance notices his flushed face and the fear in his eyes. Given other circumstances, he would derive satisfaction from forcing such a response, but now the agent's own face reflects deep-seated ambivalence.

"Any further questions?" asks Jared.

"Not for now, but make yourself available in the future. We are not done with you, professor."

~ Jared Debates Himself ~

Following the interview with Agent Romellian, Jared's equanimity is shaken, and the mundane normalcy of daily life in which he had just begun to acclimate, is suddenly and uncomfortably disrupted. Again, the ugly possibility of losing his job, his career, his research, and his reputation, not to speak of his freedom, has returned in spades. Over the next few weeks, a familiar cycle sets in of guilt, self-doubt, recrimination at his own cowardice, self-pity, and a plethora of associated variations on each theme. His dilemma is often turned in anger against Pythia, whose intrusion into his tranquil life now represents a horrible trap ensnaring him into both her agenda and the complicating arrival of Tara (who, after all, carries his own genes). As a consequence, self-doubt and a growing sense of impotence eat at his once unassailable confidence, and alarming bouts of depression increasingly darken his days.

At home, he stares into his scotch and water and more than once asks himself aloud, "Should I cooperate? After all, I am a member of the species they want to replace."

When attempting to rationalize this path of cooperation, he unwillingly turns devil's advocate and reverses the argument, positing the probable benefit to all life on Earth if humans are out of the picture. Over and over, he questions his love for Pythia and the future of his daughter Tara. Over and over, he waffles, pulled this way and that. Such soul searching has brought Jared face-to-face with a mostly unexplored emotional wilderness deep inside, where the pathless way now makes him realize what he previously thought were phantom creatures fit only for ignorant, shallow thinkers have suddenly turned out to be very real.

Yet, for all his feeble rationalizations and self-pitying angst, in the end Jared decides against cooperation with the FBI. He wearily accepts the fact his character may be vacillating, but the final resolve to not collaborate is ultimately based on the glaring fact that no further actions giving rise to the investigatory level of criminal activity will happen for another few years. With Pythia and Tara gone for those years, time is on his side, if not glory. He can wait.

Chapter 34: Ancient Adolescence

~ A New World ~

Out from a long-neglected cave in the California desert emerged an unlikely trio. First to step into the hot sun is a tall man whose craggy face and flinty head seems incongruously appropriated by a human body to sit stonily atop its shoulders, gaze locked forward on its pedestal as if cut from the granitic cave itself. Next, a middle-aged woman, a hunchback, walks stolidly ahead, confident in her strides and never looking back at the black yaw from where she came. Last, an adolescent girl, also a hunchback, moves effortlessly with a marvelous grace and athletic svelteness that compliments her radiantly beautiful face, her eyes shining brighter than the sun. As they walk, the young one fairly glides across the uneven, rocky ground, her head turning this way and that as if determined to soak in every detail of the surrounding desert. When the little group reach the shoulder of a dirt road, they are greeted by a loose-limbed man looking every bit a real scarecrow, jerking from foot to foot and in the process stirring up clouds of parched dust. Scarecrow rests a hand on the hood of the car and kicks his heels at the sight of the approaching figures.

If a hidden observer watched this group, he or she, if perceptive, might see past the glaring oddities of their bodies and recognize in the physiognomy of their more subtle facial and corporeal characteristics a deeper, more profound departure from the look and feel of normal human beings. On closer inspection, each exhibits slight but clear departures separating them from the familiar. It has been said one could dress a Neanderthal in contemporary clothes and he or she would be almost indistinguishable from modern humans—almost, but for the more primitive features impervious to disguise. Here is the opposite case. Rather than a more primitive demeanor, these figures seem more advanced, and our observer would certainly notice a difference, an otherness, that is both alien, troubling to the eye, and superior.

Sy, hopping about by the car, shouts to the approaching threesome, "Hello! Welcome back to planet Earth! How fare the wanderers?"

In the lead, Altan waves but is otherwise stoically quiet. The two women smile, and when close enough, Pythia says, "Hello yourself. Our trip was. . . . " and she finishes the thought telepathically.

Sy opens a side door. "Hop in, we are driving straight through to San Francisco. Are you tired?"

Tara speaks for the first time. "Not at all. I have been waiting for this."

"Anxious, eh?" asks Sy.

The girl exudes a level-headed maturity far beyond her years. "Not the correct word."

"What's a better one?" asks her mother Pythia.

"Curious. That is the right word. Curious."

"About?"

"The world. Reality. Humans. Earth. All of it. Enough school. Enough virtual exercises. Now it is real."

"Ah, humans," says Sy. "Now there's a topic!"

"They cause much suffering," says Tara.

"Yes, but they also are the victims of much suffering, mostly self-inflicted," sighs Pythia.

"Indeed," says Tara. "I have been made fully aware of their penchant for inflicting intentional and unintentional harm. I have been taught well."

"I assume Jared does not know we are returned?" asks Pythia.

"Not yet," replies Sy. "He's still plugging away at Berkeley."

Being the last to enter the car, Tara pauses and looks at a large boulder. In an instant, she makes it disappear. "Would that I could make such universal pain vanish as easily," she says.

Altan speaks in a low, patient tone. "You will have many opportunities, but throughout your lifetime they will be insignificant in the larger scheme of things. Your mother has been miserly in procreating. You must do more."

Pythia speaks up defensively. "I have been gone for many human years; much of my prime fertility time."

Receiving no response, she adds, "But well spent assisting with Tara's education." She sighs, "Sixteen base-dimension years."

"Yes," agrees Altan. "But here, in Earth time, only a few paltry years have passed. Now we must avoid trouble and make up for lost time."

Sy laughs. "Ah, yes! Avoiding trouble indeed! The first year of your absence, FBI agents were a nuisance, but now they have evidently given up."

Altan shakes his head. "If that boulder is any indication, they will soon be back on the case."

After the group settles into the car, Sy pulls onto the dirt road and sings telepathically in a key incapable of being replicated by humans. He accelerates, leaving behind the dissipating molecules and atoms that once comprised a now obliterated boulder. From the outside, it appears the four figures in the car are silently absorbed in their own thoughts, but their brains are alight with inaudible discussion and the invisible threads of shared stories.

~

One fine Spring morning, a week after Tara has returned, Lady Oracle and Pythia sit with her in the anteroom of the San Francisco mansion. The mood is upbeat, but also laden with a sense of urgency.

"As you are aware," says Lady Oracle. "Your task from this point on is twofold: eliminate as much suffering as possible, and have children—enough to assure continuity and a wider gene pool. Question now is where to start?"

Tara turns to Pythia. "Speaking of procreation mother, does father know you and I are back?"

Pythia blinks, her face reddening. "Not yet. I am debating my own course of action. Do I resume our relationship and have other children with him or do I find different mates? Human males are notoriously jealous, and I am hesitant to set your father off. His character is not the strongest, and he might report all of us to the governmental authorities if he feels betrayed."

"Would he insist on monogamy?" asks Tara.

"I'm afraid so, though I don't know for sure."

"Perhaps if you explained?"

"Dear Tara, humans are not rational. Emotions are their triumph and their downfall."

"While at school, one of my mentors had little use for them. He often liked to pronounce in his professorially amused manner, 'The human juxtaposition of amygdala angst and cerebral cunning results in an unfortunate disorder analogous to a creature that must continuously shit, piss, spit, and blow its nose all at the same time. That lovely planet chokes from the excess excretions of such a species.'"

"Be that as it may," says Lady Oracle chuckling in spite of herself. "We must help them at the same time we replace them. That is always a tricky proposition."

"Which leads us back to our original question; what next?" says Pythia.

"Well," says Lady Oracle. "My own opinion is that you return to the arms of Professor Jared Paine and have more children. We don't need a renewal of snooping by the FBI. Tara will go in search of a mate, or mates, and at the same time, see what she can do to prevent this species from doing more harm. We all agree that Tara's powers are superior to your own, Pythia, as well as her grandmother's. It seems the potency of the genes is increasing."

"So is the danger," says Altan who has just entered the room.

"Is it so much greater than before?" asks Lady Oracle.

"Yes."

"Why?"

"Because—and Pythia will confirm this—Tara's powers are so much stronger than seen to date, she as yet cannot control them sufficiently. Even an unconscious whim and they are unleashed. We learned this while she was receiving her advanced education. The greatest mentors could only partially succeed in showing her how to manage these forces. A host of simulations confirmed this peculiarity. Sooner or later, Tara will consciously or unconsciously let loose with actions that cannot be reversed."

"I see," says Lady Oracle somberly.

"With practice, she will learn," says Pythia.

"Yes, but what will she practice on?" asks Altan. "Humans? In that case, trouble is sure to follow."

"What do you say, Tara?" asks Lady Oracle.

"I say you must send me to the most dangerous place on the planet, a place where human iniquity is at its worst. In that setting, I will be away from this rich country and in a more free-flowing environment where mistakes will only affect those who act malevolently."

"And a mate?"

"Well, if I go to the right place, there will be plenty to choose from."

"Yes, and a high probability they would be criminals, mentally deficient, psychopaths, you name it," says Pythia.

"Mother, Ming-huà mated with Zookeeper, remember? Your own father was a crack dealer who had unique talents. Mixing his genes with grandmother's worked for you, it will work for me, if it comes to that."

Altan pours a cup of tea and sits with a long sigh, his face still troubled. "Tara will have no difficulty attracting mates, that is certain. Her reproductive system is healthy. The problem is a strong tendency toward human-style emotional responses, and efforts by mentors to teach her how to suppress them have not been one hundred percent successful. No doubt irrepressible *Homo sapiens* genes are the culprits, but it is worrisome."

"How far-reaching is her power?" asks Lady Oracle.

"That is another problem," says Altan. "Unlike Ming-huà and Pythia, she seems unable to totally moderate her responses to emotional stimuli."

"Which means?"

"Trouble."

"You did not answer my question. How far-reaching is her power?" repeats Lady Oracle.

"Which means, for all we know, she could destroy an entire region if her amygdala and associated pathways are over-stimulated."

"A town? A city?" presses Lady Oracle.

Altan shrugs. "It is all in the report, but a short synopsis will suffice. All the simulations she underwent would point to the possibility of such a large . . . result. Torture, rape, war, abuse, murder, even less severe government and private actions which were unjust, caused a strong reaction that often culminated in the destruction of the good with the bad."

"Resulting in?"

"Widespread dissociation. She is more reactive than either her mother or grandmother. Tara has a tendency to 'throw out the baby with the bath' as the saying goes."

[413]

"However—" Tara starts to speak, but Altan cuts her off with a raised hand.

"Nevertheless, we know that reality is comprised of a far more complex set of variables. Simulations can only go so far. We just don't know for sure how she will respond in extremis."

"An example from one of the simulations would be helpful for Lady Oracle to understand more clearly," says Pythia.

"Which would you use?" asks Altan.

"Unit 731," replies Pythia.

"Okay, yes. Tara was placed in a Japanese-operated biological and chemical warfare research and development unit during World War Two. It was called the Kamo Detachment and was directed by a psychopath, General Shiro Ishii. This *Homo sapien* monster performed lethal human experimentation in Northeast China, and fed his bloodlust by later establishing a network of torture facilities in other parts of the country. Ishii's unit was responsible for some of the most notorious war crimes carried out by Imperial Japan. In addition to torturing and killing over two hundred to three hundred thousand people while testing biological warfare agents, about ten thousand prisoners died horrible deaths from experiments inside Unit 731 itself. After experiencing the horrific and sadistic murder of thousands of men, women, children, and babies, Tara lashed out and completely obliterated every Japanese soldier under the command of Ishii, saving the most extreme punishment for Ishii himself."

"How many soldiers?"

"About ten thousand."

Lady Oracle sits back, stunned. Pythia looks at the floor, and Tara stares straight ahead.

"Of course," says Altan. "This was a simulation. Reality will be something quite different and the consequences far more unpredictable."

"Nevertheless. . . . " stammers Lady Oracle.

Tara addresses the group telepathically. *All of this is a matter of record,* she admits. *However, from an emotional standpoint I am far less prone to overreaction than humans. After each simulation, I was thoroughly debriefed and severely warned of the implications if I acted so rashly in real life. Later simulations were much better . . . I mean, I was able to control my reactions far more successfully. Is that not true, Altan?*

[414]

It is true, replies Altan. *But you still possess a power far beyond Ming-huà and Pythia, and it can be a very blunt instrument indeed. Many of the Japanese you obliterated were good men actively working to oppose, or at least minimize, the atrocities.*

Lady Oracle sets down her teacup and speaks in a raised voice. "I am still inclined to send Tara to one of the most violent cities in the world. Perhaps Ciudad Guayana in Venezuela, Pietermaritzburg or Nyanga in South Africa . . . maybe outside Juba in South Sudan. All far from the United States, all dangerous, all with a sizeable chunk of violent humanity at its worst. But now, in light of your report, I am not sure."

"Send me," says Tara. "I need the most difficult of assignments to truly test myself."

"And finding mates?" asks Pythia.

"Grandmother found Zookeeper. Extraordinary violence can result in extraordinarily heroic people of peace."

"True," says Altan. "Nevertheless, you would be perpetually in great danger. Your powers do not make you invincible, you know."

"Precisely why I want to go to one of these places."

"Will you accompany her, Altan?" asks Pythia. "After all, you were with me in Mexico when I needed you."

"What if there is a blow-up?" asks Lady Oracle.

"Well, at least it would occur far away," says Altan. "Don't think the FBI would be interested, but the CIA is a different story, and if they cross-check with other agencies, then we have even more trouble."

"Perhaps we should call this off and let Tara concentrate on finding mates," says Lady Oracle.

Altan surprises everyone with his response. "No, I think we should do it. Dangerous as this is, it is also a golden opportunity."

"To do what?" asks Pythia.

"To find out whether this entire effort will have a chance to succeed or fail."

~ Into the Wild ~

Tara has been in Nyanga, South Africa for only two days, holed up in a filthy apartment on the second floor of a ravaged building, and already dozens of people in the township have been murdered. In addition, over forty innocent women and children have been raped, tortured, and sold into slavery over the same time period. Gangs wreak havoc among the population, killing themselves over drug territory, as well as killing and raping untold others simply because they can. During this mayhem, Tara has accustomed herself to the gunfire and screams at night. Not once has she used her power, for she has vowed that she will abstain from precipitate action until she makes a few friends and gets the feel of the horrific situation that prevails here. The human ability to inflict immense suffering as shown by numerous simulations she had to endure during her educational period are here confirmed in reality. To understand better, she must get out and find friends, or guides, that will help her navigate this violent and ugly landscape of human degradation. She knows there are good people out there, people that are fighting against the violence, and is in no way anxious to precipitously use her power to unknowingly destroy the good with the bad, as she did in the simulations. Tara is determined to render her *Homo sapiens* genes as unexpressed as possible. Following Altan's suggestion, she surreptitiously took possession of the squalid apartment late at night to maximize anonymity. After seeing she had settled in, Altan left, merely informing her he would be nearby. Now, after two days, it is time to venture out. Moving quickly down the stairwell, she steps out into the South African sun to a chorus of chants and whoops from a group of young men and women watching a soccer game on a shattered concrete foundation where once stood a condemned building.

"Told you!" shouts a boy to the general group. "I told you someone come last night!"

"She? A hunchback? My, my! Look at it!" says a heavy woman with her hand on her hip and a cigarette in her mouth.

"She be Chinese," observes another. "Or some shit like that."

A strongly built young man whose eyes flashed intelligence speaks up. "Don't be foolish Amahle! She might be any number of Asian races."

Tara zeros in on the bright young man. Boldly striding up to him, she says, "Thank you. Your observation is accurate, but I do have Chinese blood in me."

"You sound like an American," he says. The others crowd around staring with naked curiosity.

"Oh, this shit will be good," says another.

"Hunchbacks be bad luck!" cries an ancient lady in a cracking voice from the periphery.

"I am American," says Tara. "And in case you're wondering, I am here because I got kicked out of the States."

"Why not go to China?" asks the young man.

"Because I hear this is one of the most dangerous places in the world."

This answer amazes the listeners, and murmurings ripple through the crowd.

"You what?" he asks incredulously. "You must either be kidding, or you're one of those volunteers that do charity work."

"I am not kidding, and I am not here to do charity work."

"Then why are you here, girl?" asks one of the women. The crowd is getting bigger.

"To relieve your suffering."

This statement results in stunned silence, then laughter.

"You *are* one of those charity workers!" says the young man.

"No. I am here to eliminate the gangs that are causing so much trouble."

This causes even more laughter. Someone shouts from the crowd, "You will be dead by tonight, bitch!'

"Who said that?" asks the young man.

No one responds, but it is apparent the young man has a certain level of respect.

Tara ignores the shouter and says to the young man, "What is your name?"

He flashes a winsome smile. "Name's Siyabonga Ndlovu. And you?"

"Tara."

"Tara what?"

"Tara Powers."

"You are definitely crazy, Tara Powers."

"How do I get in touch with the gangs?" she asks as serenely as if asking for directions to a store.

Instantly a great hubbub arises.

"You be dead before that!" shouts someone.

"Dead as dead can be," adds another.

"She be police!"

"A fuckin' undercover spy!"

Amidst the uproar, Siyabonga retains his composure and is clearly intrigued. "Why you want to do such a crazy thing? Huh? Drugs? You need good meth?"

"I have my reasons, and those reasons do not involve drugs."

"Everything involve drugs, crazy lady!" cries a young woman in disgust. "They be the death of us all!"

Siyabonga stares into Tara's eyes. "What's in it for the gangs if they agree to meet? You a journalist?"

"What is in it for them is survival," says Tara evenly.

This outlandish remark sets off a new round of hoots and jeering laughter.

"Hunchback be crazy!"

"Hunchback be dead!"

"Hunch lady be a witch!"

But Siyabonga does not join in. He looks at her curiously. "I can introduce you to the Mongrels, but it might be a death sentence for you."

"I'll take the risk."

Siyabonga shrugs. "Oh, shit, you must be journalist look for Pulitzer Prize or somethin'. I'll get you a meeting, but it be your funeral. Don't look for me to get you out."

Tara nods and starts to walk away, calling over her shoulder, "I'm in Apartment 2D. Let me know when and where. I'll be there."

More intrigued than ever, Siyabonga shouts at her back, "Your funeral!"

Tara feels light-hearted at such good luck as to meet someone like Siyabonga. She even mulls over whether he is mating material. While thus engaged, she strolls along the streets and alleyways of Nyanga, finding herself in a maze of tumbledown huts cobbled together by wood, aluminum, metal, cardboard, and any other material suitable for providing some semblance of shelter. The huts in this shantytown sprout like multicolored mushrooms from concrete and dirt surfaces. No tree is in sight. Leaving the shantytown, she walks down the main thoroughfares, passing ubiquitous street vendors, tiny neighborhood stores with giant Coca-Cola signs, prostitutes, and half-naked men adorned with acres of tattoos, almost all depicting graphic sex, obscenities, and brutal violence.

Amid this desolate sea of humanity, her hump buzzes with deluge of inner shrieks of rage, fear, lust, drugged-out hallucinations, murder, rape, robbery, and most of all despair and confusion. Fear undulates beneath it all like a vast, poisonous underground lake of toxic sludge. Unlike her grandmother, and to a certain extent her mother, Tara is unfazed by the waves of suffering and pain. This distant objectivity strikes her as counterintuitive, given her reputation for excess emotional affect. It is this detachment that supports her confidence. Perhaps. . . .

"Hey, lady!" shouts a street vendor. "Buy some *bobotie*?"

Tara stops and stares at a heavy, middle-aged woman stirring an odd mixture of curry, eggs, milk, dried fruit, and a sprinkling of various herbs and spices.

"Sure," she says to the woman, taking a seat on a much-abused wooden stool by the stand. While the vendor prepares the dish, Tara picks up on flashes of curiosity and thwarted intelligence that lies trapped in the iron cage of paternalism, female subservience, and the soul-destroying rot of constant apprehension.

"You are curious about me?" asks Tara off-handedly.

The woman shrugs.

"I am a newcomer here," continues Tara. Her hump senses an uptick of curiosity, but the woman remains silent.

"How long have you run this stand?" asks Tara.

"Too long," the woman says briskly.

"How long?" presses Tara.

The woman eyes her suspiciously and hands her the completed dish. "A few years. Business is bad."

Tara takes a bite. "Good."

Silence but for the woman's eyes roaming passersby for potential customers.

"What's your name?" asks Tara.

"Thandolwethu, but you're a foreigner. You can call me Daisy."

"I prefer Thandolwethu."

She shrugs, feigning disinterest, but Tara knows an incipient intelligence, curious and battered as it is, stirs.

"Like I said, I'm new here," says Tara.

"Look, honey, that not be my problem."

"No, your problem is your son, Mpho, whose life is messed up. He's in with a gang and drugs and violence. You have tried everything, but he ignores you. He has a gun, gang brothers, drugs, and you suspect he has committed horrible acts, but don't want to believe it."

Thandolwethu drops her wooden stirring spoon and eyes Tara with fear and distrust.

"You the police!" she cries. "Go away! My son a good boy. He has done no wrong!"

"Do you want to save your son?"

"Go away! Bother someone else."

"I am not police, not security, not army, not a charity worker. You believe your son is a member of the Vura gang. A couple of weeks ago he moved in with the gang and only returns for food and clothes. Vura has killed and raped many people, and other gangs like the Vato want to kill Vura members like your son. Help me."

Thandolwethu stares incredulously at Tara, her expression one of numb horror. "You a *kêrel*! That, or you a demon! What you want?"

"I'll tell you when the time comes, but I am neither police nor demon. I can help you. I want to meet other mothers of gang members. I'll leave you for now. Soon, you will hear of me and I will come to you for help. Your cooperation will help me save Mpho, is it a deal?"

The vendor nods as if in a stupor, but Tara knows she is undergoing terrible psychological turmoil. *The human capacity for suffering is limitless*, she thinks sadly.

"Remember, I'll let you know I need you when the time comes," says Tara in response to the nod. Taking the last bite of *bobotie*, Tara thanks the woman and starts back to the apartment. Her mind is awhirl. She has only been out a few hours and already met victims and perpetrators. *They are everywhere.*

Chapter 35: Demonstrations and Devilry

~ First Meeting ~

A day later, Tara is informed by Siyabonga that The Americans gang will meet with her in "the White House", which turns out to be a nondescript shack amidst a sea of similarly haphazard shacks. All the way from the apartment building to the destination, Siyabonga has given her a crash course in what protocol to use during the meeting. "No guarantees you'll come out alive," he says good-naturedly, "but follow my advice, crazy Lady Hunchback, and you have a chance."

"I understand," she says. "Eye contact, calm demeanor, no judgments, walk in their shoes . . . got it."

"Don't forget, they'll be smoking *tik* for a high, and followed up with Mandrax for a downer. Their moods can change in an instant, from friendly to vicious. Got it?"

"*Tik?*"

"Meth amphetamine."

"Oh, got it."

Now they stand outside the plywood green door waiting to be invited in. Siyabonga has a smug smile on his handsome face. Tara reads his mind and fully understands he is curious, but not about to interfere if she gets in trouble. Murder, mayhem, rape, or cooperation—any outcome is possible, but the thought of violence against Tara makes his stomach churn. Also, she notices there is some block in his mind, some space that she cannot enter, and the anomaly puzzles her greatly. Perhaps this Siyabonga does have some extraordinary genes, like Zookeeper. A mate? More and more possible. He is certainly intriguing. The thought of following in her grandmother's footsteps by choosing the genes of a sturdy gangster-type pleases her. Survivor material. Better than mating with that weak-willed academician like mother did, she concludes.

Her musings are interrupted when a tall, skinny man covered in tattoos comes out of the door and exchanges greetings with Siyabonga.

"Is this the hunch bitch?" he asks, looking Tara up and down.

[421]

"This is her. She is called Tara." Siyabonga turns to Tara and says, "This is Kungawo, but just call him Chris."

"I prefer Kungawo," says Tara.

"I prefer Chris," says Kungawo with a sneer.

"Hello, Chris," she says, reading a mind that is utterly ruthless and full of tamped-down rage. *He wants to rape me*, she realizes. *And cut my hump open to see what happens.* But this knowledge is dismissed as irrelevant, as Tara is completely confident in her powers to defend.

Kungawo waves them into the dark shack, filled with smoke from meth and crowded with stinking gang members, all practically naked, their tattoos shining in the dull glare of an exposed light bulb hanging from the ceiling. Although the stench is awful, she has endured far worse in simulations. When her eyes grow accustomed to the gloom, she sees a line of smiling faces, white teeth shining, eyes rolling in their heads, some staring dumbly at her like an exotic animal on display, the rest are clearly high on tik.

"So," comes a deep voice from the shadows. "You have come to save us."

Siyabonga says with great deference, "This is the hunchback I told you about, great Thato." He does not bother introducing a lowly female to this apparent leader. "It is true, this hunchback has said she wants to meet so that she can save you."

"And she no charity bitch?"

"No. At least, that's what she say."

"Better not be," grumbles Thato. He takes another hit and leans back. "Sit down, hunchback, take a hit."

"No, thank you."

"So, you gonna save us, huh? From what hunchback?"

"From yourselves."

"What the fuck do that mean?" asks Kungawo, following up the question with a giggle.

Tara glances at another gang member who appears to be so out of it he is not following anything. She reads one of his tattoos aloud. "I cry to drink more blood." She then gambles and mimics Kungawo's voice. "What the fuck do that mean?"

Instead of a violent reaction, Thato laughs uproariously. "She got you their bru. Got you fuckin' good."

She reads another tattoo. "Evil deep, grave deep."

"Okay, okay, enough is enough," says Thato. "What you want? Huh? What you want?" He takes another hit but this time leans forward into her face.

"I want you to stop the killing and raping, and make peace with other gangs so they will do the same."

A cacophony of laughter, curses, and threats rain down on her.

"We rape you first, then kill you, hunch!" cries a slurred voice.

Guns appear and are waved about. "Anyone not like us, we kill!" shouts another.

"Heh, hunch! Your *poes* same as a normal bitch? Huh? Or is it more like. . . . " The rest is unintelligible.

"We cut your *poes* open, then the hump on your back and see!" cries Kungawo, wild-eyed and flashing gang gestures.

Knifes are brandished, gleaming malevolently. The taunting continues at a fever pitch. All await Thato's permission to tear her apart.

Tara sits motionless, unmoved, stone-faced.

"Well hunch," says Thato after quieting the uproar. "You can help by sucking our *piels* to start. Then . . . we see."

Tara shakes her head as if disappointed in the unruly behavior of a group of children, and says calmly, "If you want you *piels*, which I assume means penises, you will stop killing and raping."

Now the laughter abruptly ceases and all eyes are aglow with bloodlust in anticipation of this outrage being revenged. Tara's hump lights up with a miasma of horror scenes pouring from each man's overheated brains, all fantasizing how they will make her suffer.

Thato gazes at the faces with a stern countenance befitting his regal status and announces, "Which bru wants her first?"

Kungawo leaps up and barks out in uncontrolled excitement, "I do! I carve her hump, then her *poe*." His knife streaks in a dazzling arc toward her face.

In the blink of an eye, his knife is gone. Kungawo stares in disbelief at his empty hand.

Stunned silence cloaks the room, and Kungawo mutters, "Must be bad *tik*."

Thato laughs uneasily. "Who next, now that Chris fail the task?"

[423]

A chorus of yips from volunteers rocks the shack like a pack of hyenas, knives and guns wave impatiently, posturing chests heave outward, hands flail in gang-gesture preening, threats of dismemberment assault Tara from all directions, but she remains motionless and says not a word.

"You put on brave face, bitch!" cries Thato, his eyes glistening. "All these brus take their *ballas* and *piels* and they gonna fill your *poes* till your hump full up, then we cut that off for trophy! Ha, ha! I give rocks about you being brave. Have at it, brothers!"

But before they can lunge, every knife and gun disappears. Again, stunned silence and the room fairly pulses with heavy breathing.

"Witch!" come astonished cries.

"Demon bitch!"

"Kill her! Kill her!" starts the chant, but this time no one is willing to be the first.

Thato stares with open-mouth wonder. At last, a lanky youth wild with drug-induced rage, growls savagely and with outstretched hands lunges for Tara's throat. Instantly, his right hand is gone. Shrieking horribly, he waves his stump in wild circles. In the face of this devilry, all cringe back except Thato, who leans even closer to Tara, conspicuously sniffing the air.

"She the devil? Demon? Witch?" he cries. "No, I not sniff such demon-scent. It be bad *tik*! We all be under spell of bad *tik*! Not real!"

Thato grabs the wrist of the man with the missing hand and examines the bloodless stump, his lips compressed in confused concentration, trying to find the flaw in the impossible trick she has pulled.

"How you do this?" he asks. "A spell?"

"Never mind how I do it. I can remove any body part I wish from all of you. Will you now listen to me?"

A deathly quiet falls over the room. Beneath the naked bulb, tendrils of meth haze swirl like ghost sharks through the air.

Tara sits straight and looks at every man in turn. "I can start with your penises . . . your *piels*. Which one of you is first?"

Although Tara is outwardly serene and confident, inside she is experiencing a mix of arrogant delight at the extent of her power, and smug satisfaction at the extent of these male hoodlum's powerlessness. Nonetheless, an inner recrimination from her training tugs at her

[424]

awareness that such human sentiments as the arrogance of power and satisfaction at the suffering of others are ultimately counterproductive, if not destructive. However, she is in too deep now to backtrack. Plowing forward is her only option.

"Well," she taunts. "I'm waiting."

Some gang members run out of the room, and only a handful remain, too proud to ingloriously flee from the threats of a mere woman. Yet all of them, she knows, are very afraid.

Thato feels it incumbent on himself to speak, and in consequence struggles to project unintimidated bravado.

"I don't know how you do what you do," he says. "However you do it, I think tomorrow it will be a dream, and bru John Mokoena have his hand back. When we know is a dream, we come for you and you have no place to hide."

"And when tomorrow comes, and John is still without a hand?"

"Then we make a deal. You work with us and take share of money from drugs and protection. You get rich, treated like queen. Good deal for you."

"No. The Americans will give up murder and rape and protection and all the rest. Declare peace. Raise your families in peace. Die in peace."

"Peace!" spits Thato. "Lady Hunch, you not know what it is here. You that stupid? I live under apartheid, now is worse. Us that are Cape Coloreds be the lowest of the low. There is no peace, only killing others before you killed. No work. No jobs. No money. No families. No peace. Nothing exists except us in the bruhood. You understand?"

"Others in the world live in poverty and do not kill and rape and steal. You rape little boys and girls and kill them, torture them! If I were not who I am, I would remove the hands and *piels* of all of you. Then there would be no murder using guns and knives, and no rape using *piels*."

Thato smiles thinly. "No one have that power. If you did, you be president, you be dictator of the world. Nobody have that power. If you can do it, bitch, then do it! I not believe it real. Tomorrow be new day. Chris have hand back and you be hunted down and made to suffer more than you can think!"

Tara reads his mind and sees nothing but savagery. What sits before her is an unrepentant beast who would gnaw off his own leg to seek revenge on his captor. So be it. . . .

~ Aftermath ~

As she returns to the apartment, dusk is darkening the sky and Siyabonga walks beside her in deferential awe. He has not yet found words to address her and simply focuses his energy on taking one step after the other, toiling to process the meaning of what he just witnessed.

"Did you have to do that to Thato?"

"Would he have done what I asked?"

"Probably not, but to remove his hands and penis! We left him screaming like some butchered pig. It be horrible. How you do it?"

"That is not for you to know."

"But he is right, huh? Tomorrow he have back his hands and penis? Chris have back his hand? Right?"

"Wrong."

"But you can make it happen?"

"No, once done, it is done."

"Shit!" Siyabonga blurts in astonishment. "What are you. Not human, for sure. Are you a demon?"

"No."

"Witch?"

"No."

"Well, are you human, or some alien come to fuck with us?"

"I am neither *Homo sapiens* nor an alien. I have been born on Earth of a mother and father just like you."

"You are not like me! Or anyone else! How you do it?"

"Siyabonga, what will happen to the gang now?"

He ponders for a while, then says, "Like a hive lose the queen, there be battle for top spot."

"More killing?"

He nods. "More killing."

"Then I keep going. Sooner or later, it will sink in."

"What?"

"Violence, killing, raping, robbing, all are bad things and all must stop. Surely you understand that?"

"So, you hurt them to stop the violence?"

"If that is what it takes to protect the infants, the children, the mothers, the young women; in other words, the innocents."

[426]

Siyabonga shakes his head in bewilderment. "The innocents? Are they such things?"

"What do you mean?"

"Well, many mothers are whores or beat their children, some selling them for money. The children carry guns and live to be old enough to kill. The young women hope to catch the eye of a high-ranking gang member to prostitute herself and have some money and protection. The infants . . . they are born with the mark and will die the same way. Evil deep, grave deep."

Tara laughs. "You are all very foolish infants yourselves. I—"

Without warning, gunshots shatter the quiet. Siyabonga jumps to the ground. When the firing stops, he gathers his wits and looks up at Tara, still standing and staring at him in amusement.

"You can get up, Siyabonga, they will bother us no more."

"They?"

"Gang members just tried to kill me in ambush. I was expecting it. The atoms and molecules comprising the bullets have disbursed to enrich more peaceful objects."

Siyabonga shutters. "And the shooters?"

Tara frowns and walks on. After a short while in silence, she turns to her companion. "Word will get out of these events, Siyabonga. I need someone to assist me in moving forward. I need something like a secretary, a guide, an interpreter, and an all-around . . . what do the gangs call it? A lieutenant. I need a loyal lieutenant. I can pay well. Are you interested?"

Siyabonga's teeth are still chattering as he says dejectedly, "Miss Powers, I cannot stop bullets. I would be dead within hours."

"Ah! Then we may spread the word that anyone killing you will suffer the same fate as Thato, these gunmen, or worse. Attempting to kill you would be the same as attempting to kill me. Would that work?"

Siyabonga looks at the ground and contemplates the odds. "I need to talk to my mother first," he says awkwardly.

"Your mother!"

Tara believes she may have found that deep, dark hidden spot which even her telepathic skills cannot penetrate. The mother. All mothers. *Goddess*.

By the time they reach the apartment, word has preceded them; a small crowd lines the sidewalk in front of the building. The excited chattering quickly stops and the atmosphere turns eerily quiet when she and Siyabonga come into view. Tara scans for assassins, but picks up only a constant level of life-long, visceral fear and morbid curiosity. But among the psychological wreckage, she registers a few anonymous sparks of hope among the crowd. One face comes into focus: Thandolwethu, the vendor. She stands heavily with a small group of other women, and Tara quickly surmises they are all mothers. When their eyes meet, Thandolwethu briefly nods and looks down as if performing some sort of homage. Tara calls to her.

"Thandolwethu! I want a meeting of mothers, especially mothers of gang members. Tomorrow. Where can we meet?"

The vendor stares at her with hesitation and doubt. She looks about at the eyes now on her, and she says nothing.

"Where can we meet?" insists Tara.

Another woman, older, and according to Tara's hump, bearing far more psychological scars, calls out, "In the graveyard!"

"The graveyard?"

"There is a large pavilion, under canvas. We can meet there. What time tomorrow?"

"Seven o'clock!" replies Tara. "As many as possible. Mothers of sons in every gang are welcome!"

"No!" says the old woman. "Dinnertime at eight o'clock!"

"Okay, four o'clock! Does that work?"

"Yes," says the old woman.

Tara looks at Thandolwethu, who nods in the affirmative.

When Tara enters the lobby of the apartment building, she pauses to look at Siyabonga. "Well, how about your mother? Will she be there?"

He smiles. "My mother? Oh, yes, she be there."

Siyabonga says this in a manner that implies he bears a secret. When she probes his mind, she runs into the same blank wall preventing her from entering into his thoughts. This anomaly deepens her perplexity as she climbs the stairs and wearily lays down on the couch.

I am killing and maiming to lessen the suffering of these violent and ignorant creatures, whose destiny is to be replaced and ultimately driven extinct, she thinks. *Well, perhaps the right characterization is not that they will be driven extinct, but their genome will eventually be diluted to extinction. Save a few of them in the short run while we replace all of them in the long? A contradiction. In response to this inconsistency, one of my mentors said, "Exactly! You finally have it!" Have what? I asked. "Think on it. Do not complicate the simplicity."* Tara fluffs up her hair in exasperation. *Homo sapiens, in and of themselves, are no more complicated than other living things, except for their penchant for imaginative navel-gazing. Their motivations are simple, their science primitive, their superstitions elaborate, their self-absorption endless, and their belief technology will save them. Madness!"* She stares at the stained wall opposite the couch. *Yet, there is something here, something I cannot put my finger on, that is disturbing. What is it? Of course, it is that black box of Siyabonga's that makes me wonder. He himself is as simple as the others. Why this one anomaly? The mother, the mother. The mothers.*

Tara ponders the experiences of her own mother and grandmother when they had to use their powers against *Homo sapiens*. Certainly they were similar to what she is currently facing. What is niggling at her mind and causing her to relive her training? Is it something she has forgotten? A point she missed? It will take thousands of years to totally replace humans, yet a major mistake now would recalibrate the early trajectory and lead to catastrophic failure. Almost ten billion *Homo sapiens* and . . . and . . . so few of us. So few.

~ Prelude ~

The next day, Tara remains in her apartment until she must leave for the meeting at the cemetery. In the meantime, Altan, dressed in shabby clothes, sneaks his way into her room to have a brief word.

"I have heard much gossip on the street about your exploits yesterday. Separating what is true and what is false, as with most things human, is impossible. One point is certain: you have wasted no time in making yourself a target. Tell me precisely what happened."

Tara recounts the events in detail.

Altan listens without interruption. When she finishes, he shakes his head. "You really left their leader that way?"

"Yes."

"This is why we chose a little-known crime-infested region in South Africa . . . little known in the United States anyway. Even here, no one in authority will believe these gang members. However, I must say, you are applying salve on the surface of a far deeper, festering sore."

"Yes, your thoughts tell me the source of these abominations lie not with teenaged gang members, but with corrupt authority itself."

Altan sighs. "Ah, and the undeveloped cortex which renders them grasping for fulfillment, yet so gullible that they are left grasping at straws. Such is the human condition worldwide. Alas, it is more than that—it is the unbridled desires, profound ignorance, self-delusion, and broken dreams of humans themselves that makes them cling to demagogues, dictators, corrupt business leaders, and all the rest."

"What to do?"

"If nothing else, your kind, by a display of such supernatural power, will attract many intelligent males eager to learn your secrets, and even have their sons and daughters mate with such powerful ones. Natural selection, dear Tara."

"Altan!" Tara chides, "Am I no more than a baby-making machine?"

He laughs. "Almost correct. You are a species-making machine! Remember, your first priority is mating, not saving a few vulnerable individuals in a sea of desperate multitudes."

"I thought we are here to reduce suffering as much as we can."

"Reduce, not eliminate. More importantly, learn, not preach."

"How to reduce if I don't use my powers?"

Altan pulls a sardonic face. "You don't. In exchange for a gift of life which is poised tenuously on the razor's edge of survival, the universe demands to be paid in the slices it removes. Such is the currency of the Natural World."

Chapter 36: Slices

~ A Meeting of Mothers ~

When Tara arrives with high hopes at the cemetery and steps under the canvas-covered pavilion, she is greatly disappointed. A smattering of women, some young, the others mostly middle-aged and old, huddle in small groups whispering among themselves. Tara sees that not only are their numbers paltry, but those that are waiting are restless and have begun to mutter about leaving. She looks for Thandolwethu, but the vendor is nowhere to be seen. As Tara approaches, the women fall silent and look at her expectantly. She steps up on a wooden platform and begins to speak.

"Thank you all for coming. My name is Tara Powers. I am not going to make a speech. We all know what the problem is, and we are here to do what we can to organize support for you mothers who have endured this gang violence for too long. How many of you have sons in a gang?"

A few women reluctantly raise their hands, then quickly put them down when others remain motionless.

Tara scans the women's thoughts and receives confirmation that all of them are indeed mothers of gang members. Some, she perceives, have lost their sons to the violence. A few have lost their small children in cross-fires or to gang rape and murder. All of them are terrified, both of the gangs and of Tara herself. She feels a renewed sense of commitment to her course of action. It is imperative she help these unfortunate women.

"I know every one of you has sons in gangs, or children who have been killed by gangs. Do you want to help stop the violence?"

Some women shuffle their feet but no one responds. Finally, a voice from the back of the group speaks haltingly.

"Lady, we do have charity workers and relief organizations that have offered to help. What more can we do?"

"Do you feel the charity workers and relief organizations are succeeding?"

Again, no one responds. More shuffling of feet. Some start moving away.

From the side comes a male voice shouting a resounding, "No!"

Tara turns and sees Siyabonga striding up with Thandolwethu and a larger gathering of women following behind. This group is mixed, young, middle-aged, older, white, black, and Cape Coloreds. While reading their minds as best she can, Tara comes across a striking woman, tall and attractive, walking next to Siyabonga. Here, she encounters a blank, a block that will not allow entry of her telepathic powers. It immediately occurs to Tara that this imposing woman is Siyabonga's mother. As she is processing their arrival, Siyabonga slips up next to her and whispers in her ear, "My mother, Kholwa, will speak. Her name means 'believe' in Zulu. Believe, and follow her lead. Later, we will explain."

As fast as he appeared, he disappears through the crowd of women. Kholwa is already standing on the stage boldly looking out at the women. Tara steps back and listens.

"Women of Cape Flats! Mothers of those taken in by the evil ones!" She points at Tara. "Look hard at this woman! She entered the lion's den and bearded the lion! He is declawed and fangless. Why? Because of her! Do any of you doubt?"

A voice shouts, "We have heard she can make things disappear!"

"Yes!" calls another. "Body parts!"

Yet another grumbles, "Thato was a son also. Now he is a lump of useless flesh!"

Kholwa raises her arms for silence and the crowd obeys. "Our great African proverb says, the best way to eat an elephant in your path is to cut him up into little pieces. The cutting is begun, now we must take advantage of this woman's presence."

"She is a witch!" shouts a heavy-set woman near the front, her hands on hips in an aggressive posture. "Killing does not promote peace."

"Yet, Thato lives," says Kholwa.

"No!" cries the woman. "He was once a brave man before he became a slab of meat!" cries the woman. She points accusingly at Tara. "Because of her!"

"You are mistaken!" exclaims Kholwa. "He was once a murderer and rapist before he became a slab of meat! Now he can do no more harm." She also points at Tara. "Because of her!"

[432]

"Who made him a slab of meat?" asks a brash young woman, brushing away her tears. "I want to thank that person. Gangs killed my brother. He was a sweet boy. I am glad Thato is now a slab of meat. He can't hurt anyone now. But who made him that way?"

Kholwa looks at Tara. "Speak to our mothers and tell them what you want them to do."

Tara steps forward and speaks forcefully. "I want you to organize together and cooperate as a tight-knit group to oppose gangs and the violence they perpetrate on innocents, including your own sons. I am sure none of your sons were raised to be murderers and rapists, yet that is what the gangs and the big people who profit off the gangs would make of them. You must not make them heroes by giving in to the gang threats. Your individual weaknesses and unconditional love for your children are how they draw their strength. Your sons are victims who must be understood for who they are and what makes them join gangs. Were they not once just sweet little babies? Sweet little boys? Are your families to be ruled by fear? By vicious men who see your sons as nothing more than fodder for their own gain?"

Questions begin to fly.

"But, how do we organize?"

"What do we do?"

"The gangs are too strong!"

"Can you really make things disappear?"

Kholwa again steps forward, and Tara tries to probe her mind, but finds to her chagrin that Siyabonga's mother continues to be unreadable. "We organize starting now, at this spot. Once a week we will meet here and tell our stories. Some of our youths are in the Mongrels, some in The Americans, others in the Numbers, and so on. We tell our stories to each other and gradually there will be an understanding that all gangs are the same and all gangs must be stopped."

"Tell stories? What good will that do?" comes a voice.

"It will teach us that we are not alone. It will teach us that we are not powerless. It will teach us that our suffering is not caused by this gang or that gang, but from the blood-soaked soil in which they grow. Do you agree, Tara Powers?"

Tara feels a mind probing her own, and a dawning awareness starts to stir, a shocking awareness. Before she answers, she stares deeply

[433]

into Kholwa's eyes and finds a connection. *You are one of us! Grandmother and mother and myself are not alone!*

Of course not, says Kholwa telepathically. *Many seeds have been planted. But we now know your power is greater by far than the rest of us. Now, speak to them.*

Tara physically staggers backward a few steps with this astonishing revelation. She quickly composes herself and raises her voice so late arrivals in the back can hear. "We are more powerful than the gangs. We are more powerful than those you call in Afrikaans *hoë ome*—the bigwigs—the corrupt police and politicians that make the gangs possible. If we work together, we are their mothers and sisters and grandmothers. We gave these boys and men flesh and bone they use to harm others. Now, we must take back their flesh and bone from the gangs and root out those that have profited from the gangs!"

"So true!" comes a male voice. "And you, dear lady, have courageously removed some of their flesh and bone so they cannot hurt others!"

Tara sees it is Siyabonga and begins to speak, but he continues in a voice full of passion. "I have witnessed it! This woman, Tara Powers, is capable of great things. Even the gang members are terrified of her. I'm not afraid to say so."

"What kind of things?" asks the young woman.

"She performs magic and makes their arms and legs disappear!" cries a middle-aged woman. "My son told me. He is a brave boy, but he stuttered in fear when he told me. I have never seen him like that."

"Witchcraft!" comes the cracking voice of the heavy-set woman in the front, hands still firmly planted on hips.

A collective gasp rises from the crowd.

The young woman angrily raises her voice above the murmurings. "If it is witchcraft, then it is welcome. If this woman can make the gangs fear her, she has great power. I don't care where it comes from, as long as it makes them stop. I am pregnant, and—"

"The police will be interested," loudly grumbles the heavy-set woman, cutting her off.

Tara scolds herself for letting this dialogue go on too long. She waves her arms to quiet the crowd and says, "I did nothing to the gang members. They fear me because I do not fear them. Whatever happened to them was brought about themselves, after I left."

"But Siyabonga said he witnessed it!" shouts a large woman balancing a baby on her hip toward the rear. "What about that?"

Siyabonga jumps forward. "No! I said I witnessed the fear she caused them. That is all! It is her power to make them afraid. That is her secret! What they do afterward is up to them. Not witchcraft, it is a miracle." He holds his arms out and looks up toward the sky. "It is a miracle *God* has sent us this woman!"

Or Goddess! Kholwa's sardonic words ring in Tara's mind.

~ Revelations ~

When the meeting breaks up, the mothers are requested by Tara and Kholwa to meet at the same time next week. Everyone is to bring a friend, and plans will then be made to move on to the next step. Tara accepts Kholwa's invitation to have dinner at her house and discuss "important matters". Siyabonga accompanies them. On the way, several shots are fired, and Tara's companions flinch and duck low. They hear a nearby cry of shock, then another, then quiet.

"Damn!" cries Siyabonga. "Again? Sooner or later. . . . "

"Not to worry," says Tara calmly. "I have removed their guns."

Siyabonga looks at her in amazement. "And the bullets?"

Tara looks skyward and waves her hand. "Poof! Gone. Their atoms and molecules are now available for more productive uses."

"And the shooters?" asks Kholwa. "Have you done with them what you did before?"

"Not to worry," replies Tara with a chuckle. "They are fine. Probably a bit confused, though."

"Let us pick up the pace," says Kholwa hastily. "We must talk in privacy . . . too dangerous out here."

When the little group reaches Kholwa's house, it is after eight o'clock at night. Siyabonga helps his mother hurriedly throw together a few dishes of *chakalaka* and *pap*, and they sit at an old, well-worn table.

"It is late," says Tara. "Sorry for the trouble."

"No trouble," replies Kholwa. "This is normal dinner time in South Africa. Now, you must tell us everything. How you came by your powers. Where you are from. Others like you. Everything!"

[435]

"First," says Tara. "How many like you are here?"

"None that we know personally," replies Siyabonga. "But there are hints of others. We were afraid to show ourselves, that is, until you arrived. Your powers are unbelievable!"

And your own powers? asks Tara telepathically.

Weak, compared to you.

Tara pushes forward a salt shaker. *Can you make it disappear?*

Heavens no! exclaims Kholwa and Siyabonga simultaneously.

Try.

Both make an effort, but have no success.

"You see?" says Kholwa aloud. "We are but sad intermediates, far below your level. We had no idea ones like you exist!"

"Nor I you. I want to speak with certain individuals about this information that has been kept from me."

"We have been guided by a young woman who is far beyond us," says Kholwa. "*She* came to me before I had Siyabonga."

"Who is *she*?" asks Tara.

"We don't know *her* name, but *she* is someone impossible to describe."

"Yes," agrees Tara. "I know *her*. She goes by many names. *Goddess* is one of them. Referring to her simply as *she* is another. Precious Object is another. My ancestors have passed this information on to me, and I have met *her* myself. You are right, *she* is impossible to describe."

Kholwa and Siyabonga stare incredulously. "They are all the same person?"

"Yes, if you want to refer to *her* as a person," says Tara. "However, I see now there is much that has not been passed on to me."

Kholwa and Siyabonga look at Tara questioningly.

"But that is neither here nor there," she says, diverting the topic. "Tell me about the local situation. What is being said about me?"

"Well," says Siyabonga. "Mother knows more than I about the women, but the men are all over the board. You know, this is a patriarchal society. Most men are uncomfortable with a woman possessing powers stronger than theirs. At this point, most deny you are anything other than a glorified charity woman, which translates in their male minds to a reassuringly weak woman up against an impossible task. One who will end up either dead or chased out of the area. However, I know some men who are not sure, and I can see fear in their eyes and in their thoughts."

"As for the women," says Kholwa. "You have raised their hopes, though most are fatalistic about your chances. Still, you have lit a spark. Some, on the other hand, are loyal to their sons and the gang to which their sons belong. These mothers fear something bad might happen to them, like what happened to Thato."

Suddenly, from the darkness outside, a voice chants in a low, ominous cadence, "Hey, bitches, you all goin' to die. You all goin' to die, bitches. Hey, bitches, you all goin' to die. You all—"

The words stop as abruptly as they started.

"What happened?" asks Siyabonga, eyes wide in fear.

"Oh," says Tara matter-of-factly. "One less larynx in the world."

"What. . . . ?" murmurs Siyabonga.

"Whoever that person was, he will not be making any more speeches or chanting any more threats."

Kholwa looks at Tara sadly. "Can you bring it back?"

"No."

"Then he will be permanently mute?"

"Pretty much so."

"So sad. I wonder if I know the boy," murmurs Kholwa.

Siyabonga whistles a low dirge. "This is a very extreme solution, Tara. What if in future he changes and wants to run for National Assembly in order to stop the gangs?"

Tara shrugs. "His lack of a voice will be more powerful than his voice. I know you both think this is harsh, but how else to get through to them? We must focus our attention on the species as a whole organism, and consider the individual a cell. What do humans do to cancer cells?"

"Cancer cells can't think," says Siyabonga.

"Which, of course, would make them even more dangerous."

"Thank *Goddess* you are on our side," says Kholwa.

"Our side is the future," replies Tara. "Unless we make a terrible mistake, in which case we will be forgotten. This lovely planet and all its inhabitants, plant and animal, are at stake."

"Yes, but are we making a mistake now?" asks Siyabonga. "Shouldn't we keep your powers a secret?"

Tara stares openly at him, not in response to his question, but to consider his fitness to be a mate. As an intermediate, he would perfectly fit the bill.

"Perhaps," she says. "But it is unlikely the secret could be kept for very long."

Siyabonga sighs. "For better or worse, the secret is out now."

"Not necessarily," says Tara. "My grandmother Ming-huà and mother Pythia did the same thing to bad people, and they got away with it."

"Okay, but how many arms and legs can be removed before the cure is worse than the disease?" asks Siyabonga haltingly.

"Do you consider yourself fully human?" asks Tara abruptly.

Caught off-guard, Siyabonga looks blankly at his mother.

Kholwa grimaces. "His father was fully human."

"How about your own father and mother, Kholwa?"

"My own father was all too human, just like Siyabonga's," says Kholwa with fire in her eyes.

"Abuse?"

Kholwa rubs her forehead. "Yes. Terrible."

"And your mother?"

"I think she was more than human. She protected me at the cost of her own—"

Siyabonga takes his mother's hand, "Best not to dredge up old wounds, mother."

Tara presses. "But my question is whether your mother demonstrated any unique powers? Powers like you and Siyabonga possess."

"Perhaps . . . I don't know. She died quite young."

Siyabonga slams his fist on the table. "Yes, at the hands of my grandfather! And my own father! Oh, he was not much better, if not worse!"

Kholwa squeezes her son's hand. "I made a poor choice." She turns toward Tara. "Siyabonga's father was in a gang, you know. When I started with him, he was sweet. They brutalized him. I raised Siyabonga to never turn out like his father and grandfather."

Siyabonga says, "Mother, this is why we must help Tara."

"I agree," responds Kholwa. "But if she continues to disable gang members this way, the government will eventually get involved." She looks at Tara. "You have no idea the corruption. They would consider you a threat."

"They would be right."

"You will become a target, not just of gangs, but the entire government apparatus. The truly good are always a target. Ask the Grand Inquisitor."

"Seems to be a very common problem throughout the human world," says Tara grimly. She pushes back her chair and stands. "I mut go. It's late."

"Will we see you tomorrow?" asks Siyabonga.

Tara scans his mind and picks up sexual interest on his part, an interest he has clearly allowed her access to. This breakthrough she views with pleasure, but her thoughts soon turn to a different topic.

"Where is the nearest national wildlife park?"

"Why?" asks Kholwa.

"I need to visit some of the species humans are in the process of destroying."

As they all move toward the door, Siyabonga says, "My head is spinning. Are we going too fast? I mean, you have only been here a few days, and. . . . " He shrugs for lack of words.

"My grandmother and mother did similar things in Washington State, San Francisco, Baltimore, and Mexico. Their actions relieved a miniscule amount of suffering, but caused some as well. The difference is material. Those who were on the receiving end of their powers were the perpetrators of violence, and those whose suffering was relieved by their powers were the victims. Imagine a world where a million or more of us, well, even a few thousand, can bring an end to human devastation. It could be the dawn of a new age, if we can manage to replace them with a minimum of suffering and pain."

"However, we have to survive to get there," says Siyabonga.

Tara steps out the door and pauses on the lighted porch. A glowing bulb shines on her face, revealing a luminous smile. "We will," she says.

As Tara is about to leave, she receives a flow of information telepathically from Kholwa.

There are many wildlife reserves near Cape Town, but I recommend Sanbona Wildlife Reserve. Rhino, elephant, lion, leopard, and buffalo are there, and it is no zoo. It is big. Siyabonga will help you. This last offer contains no small amount of sly innuendo.

~ Animal Minds ~

Though a native South African, Siyabonga is a city boy, and it is Tara that leads the way by foot into the reserve. The endless series of simulations she underwent during her education required extensive hiking, and now she strides confidently across the scrub landscape, breathing deeply the clean air of non-human terrain. She has eschewed any hint of safari luxury, and both she and Siyabonga are utterly on their own in the vast open space of the reserve. For a day and a half, her hump has been alighting with multitudinous signals from non-human animals desperate for food or water and terrified of being prey or missing out on finding prey. All are driven *in extremis*, but the nature of their drives are fundamental and distinct from the artificial maze of human navel-gazing complexity. She longs to establish contact, as her grandmother Ming-huà could do with the fellow inhabitants of her island, and begins to resent the presence of Siyabonga, viewing him as a distraction.

"Why are you walking so fast, Tara?" huffs Siyabonga, struggling to keep up. "What are you looking for?"

"Confirmation."

"Of what?"

"Of the fact that the goal is worth the effort."

Hours later, they ascend a hill and look down at a sprawling valley floor. In the distance they see black dots that flow gracefully one moment, and move in leaping bounds the next.

"Gazelle?" asks Siyabonga.

Tara laughs. "You are the African! Really, Siyabonga, you must learn to identify your neighbors. They are springbok."

"Aren't they the same thing?"

"Springbok are members of the gazelle tribe, just as your genes might identify you as a member of the Zulu tribe. At least your human genes."

"The question you asked me about whether I consider myself human has me wondering. Am I human, or am I something else? What do you think?"

"I think I see a pride of lions in the vicinity, and they seem to be stirring with those springboks around. We must hurry!"

"Wait!" cries Siyabonga at Tara's back as she sprints down the slope. "There are lions down there?"

But Tara is already half-way down the hill, so Siyabonga unenthusiastically trots to try and not fall farther behind.

I wonder if she can read their minds? he thinks as he runs.

No, they are too far away, she responds telepathically. *Hurry up!*

Siyabonga can now see the lions clearly, and Tara is headed almost straight for them. Instinctively, his motivation is to stay close, driven mainly by her ability to make things disappear, so he picks up the pace in the hopes of closing the distance between them.

Sorry, Siyabonga, if you are attacked, I cannot help. It is a sort of prime directive. We are replacing Homo sapiens, *not* Panthera leos. *Non-human animals are not to be interfered with.*

"Shit!" cries Siyabonga aloud.

Quiet or you will draw their attention!

Shit!

In spite of his fear, Siyabonga watches this strangely beautiful hunchback, who possesses otherworldly suppleness and athleticism, gracefully fly across the scrubby ground. Her strong body sings a siren call to his libido as no other has ever done. While in the thrall of his fantasies, he does not notice a lioness crouching in the shrubs watching him intently.

Watch out! shouts Tara in his head. *Stop daydreaming! Roll off my naked body and look around! This will be your last orgasm if you don't pay attention!*

Siyabonga curses at himself for not blocking the intruding mind of his companion, but his erotic musings are quickly put aside when he sees the lioness approach. His first instinct is to run, but he knows enough to resist the temptation. Looking around for Tara, she is nowhere to be seen, so he begins to slowly back away from the lioness, whose eyes now bore into him with ferocious intensity. Now he feels real fear, and panicked, he calls for Tara.

Help!

[441]

He hears her response. *Hold your ground, face the lion, wave your arms, look big, clap, make noise, but do not turn and run!*

Siyabonga sees Tara enter his line of sight on the periphery. She is cautiously walking toward the lioness. But now, other curious pride members, all female, start appearing. In spite of Siyabonga's frantic efforts to bluff, the lions ignore him and have turned their full attention on Tara. It seems to him, for a brief moment, they are exchanging important information with her, then the lions saunter away. Tara stands rigidly, watching them melt back into the swirling dust and savannah grass, a tawny landscape to match their tawny coats. To Siyabonga's great surprise, Tara begins to follow them.

Stay where you are! he hears her command in his head. *I will return after the hunt!*

Siyabonga is astonished. Does she really intend to participate? He stands on tiptoe and strains to see, but his vision is blocked by clouds of dust rising above the scrub. Occasionally, a springbok's head bobs above the vegetation and haze as it leaps in terror from the attackers. Eventually, the swirls of dust become more distant, then dissipate entirely. All is quiet until the low rumble of a male lion throttles the atmosphere, literally shaking the ground beneath his feet.

Tara! Are you okay? He sends forth the question, but there is no reply. *Tara! Answer!*

Nothing.

Just as he is about to search, she suddenly appears from a great distance, a tiny figure amidst the immensity of the vast killing ground.

Siyabonga waves his arms and shouts, "I'm here!"

Tara waves back and moves swiftly in his direction. When she finally reaches him, she says impassively, "Let's camp here."

After they finish setting up, they each sit on the fallen branches of a dying *baobab* tree and eat silently. Siyabonga tries to speak telepathically, but Tara has made her mind opaque. She seems entranced by the outspreading silhouette of another, bizarre-shaped *baobab* against the starry sky. Her face reflects unspeakable sadness.

"What are you thinking?" he asks aloud.

"Desperation is a terrible thing," she says with pain in her voice. "Our friends are barely surviving, and their desperation tears at my heart."

"Yes, I see your point," says Siyabonga. "Humans, I believe, are the most desperate of all."

"Much of their desperation is self-inflicted," replies Tara dismissively.

"But, Tara, you must admit, many other species wage war upon themselves—and in the process bring great devastation. Take, for example, ants waging organized war on ants, chimpanzees waging organized war on chimpanzees. Are they not just as responsible?"

"No," says Tara firmly.

"Why not?"

"When you return to Nyanga, look around, open your eyes, not only to the humans and their gangs, but the mountains of machines, electronic contrivances, concrete dwellings, pollution, trash, and so forth, all accumulated on the backs of their fellow creatures, plant and animal. To live and die for food or water is essential. To live and die for politics, religion, prejudice, racism, power, is a recipe for disaster. Throw in science and technology, and you have the perfect planet-destroying species, not sharks, but humans. You see, humans are not just killing themselves; that would be of little consequence. But a planet is at stake, Siyabonga, one my mentors tell me is a wonder and worth saving. Allowing Armageddon to be inflicted on this celestial marvel by such a species is not an option."

"Your mentors?"

"Never mind. Let's sleep. My powers fade when I am too tired. But we must be careful not to let the fire go out. My friends are still hungry."

In the distance a male lion roars his evening declaration; an ominous tremor in the air that shakes the leaves on nearby bushes.

"By all means," says Siyabonga. "By all means."

[443]

Chapter 37: Back to Fundamentals

~ *Baobab* Love ~

Tara cannot sleep and stands gazing at the same *baobab* tree that so fascinated her earlier, now a deeper black against the moon-lit sky. Enveloped in this dark African night, accompanied by the echoing sounds of hunters and hunted, she is jarred from her musings by the forceful intrusion of Siyabonga's lust. He has waited long enough watching her stare at the sky, and his imagination has taken him to a place from where he is unwilling to return. Flames from the dying campfire light up Tara's figure and he boldly undresses her in his mind, inviting her to see what he envisions. She does not respond, and when she finally breaks her skyward attention and tosses more wood on the fire, he says, "Can't sleep?"

"No."

"Nor can I."

After a long pause, he asks telepathically, *Will you lay with me?*

Your fantasies do not give justice to my figure, she replies. *My hump is made insignificant in your imagination. That is insulting.*

Then show me the error of my ways.

Tara removes her clothes, the campfire making her skin glow against the blackness. She senses Siyabonga's rising desire. Locking eyes with him, she says, "Now, observe carefully."

Slowly she turns around, displaying for him the full view of her hump. He watches in astonishment as the images of two naked people emerge, intricately raised on her skin as though embossed in *bas relief,* and begin moving as they perform an erotic dance. Varied sexual positions are enacted, many new and wonderful to Siyabonga. When climax is achieved by the two figures, and Siyabonga is himself ready to explode, she again faces him and says telepathically, *You see, Siyabonga? My hump is far more beautiful than your imagination could invent.*

Yes, yes!

Would you like to duplicate the movements of the two lovers you have just seen?

Yes, yes!

Then remove your clothes and let me see your own beautiful body.

Just as Siyabonga is moaning from the explosion of his orgasm, the horrifying screech of an animal caught only meters away in the jaws some predator shatters the moment. Instinctively, he withdraws in the middle of coming, rolling off Tara in fright. She quickly stands and claps her hands to her ears, trying to keep out the unbearable pain of the quarry that has driven like a shiv into her brain. Siyabonga's semen drips down her inner thighs, shining thickly in the fire light.

"I'm sorry, I'm sorry," Siyabonga repeats.

Tara does not immediately respond, waiting until the searing pain stops and the sudden stillness of death mercifully arrives. Her eyes are tightly shut to block out Siyabonga's illuminated form. His vital, living body mocks the agony of the prey, still fighting desperately against the inevitable. Finally, the spark of life expires. She opens her eyes and sees Siyabonga pulling on his trousers. He stops and looks at her apologetically.

Is it ended?

Yes.

I am so sorry. I was startled.

I know. Tara shakes her head in disbelief. *Even I was taken by surprise. My lapse is a complement to the incredible power you displayed when inside me.*

You were magnificent . . . until I spoiled it.

So were you.

"What now?" he asks aloud. "Will we continue?"

Tara chuckles. "You will be an excellent mate."

"What?"

"Don't worry about it, Siyabonga, it is an inside joke."

Another death-cry, this one more distant, pierces the night.

"Is this existence better than what humans have?" asks Siyabonga as he wraps his arms around his body and shivers in an exaggerated manner. "Surely the savagery of kill or be killed is not preferable to civilization, no matter how flawed it may be."

"You might be right, Siyabonga, if humans were civilized. Do you find it clean out here in the bush?"

"Clean?"

"Clean."

[445]

"No."

Tara looks at him with fresh eyes. "Think again, Siyabonga. If we are to be lovers, you must understand where my thoughts lie. It is far cleaner out here than Cape Town, New York, San Francisco, or any human area of habitation on the planet. *Homo sapiens* represent the worst of both worlds; they are not fully civilized and not fully savage. Caught betwixt and between, they do not know what to do with their own abstract-laden consciousness. The savage part destroys and the civilized part corrupts. The stage they have reached is the most dangerous known, not only to their own species, but to all other species, and ultimately, to the planet itself."

"Can they grow out of it?"

"Look carefully, my beloved mate. Look at yourself, your mother and grandmother, me, my mother and grandmother, and others like us. Look carefully, for you are looking at how humans will, as you say, grow out of it."

"By replacing them?"

"Exactly. They will grow out of it by becoming extinct."

Tara, still naked, receives strong signals from Siyabonga's libido.

I see you are ready for more?

God, yes!

Correction; Goddess yes!

"Yes, you are right!" cries Siyabonga aloud. "*Goddess*, yes!"

"Only this time, my lovely mate, stay inside me to the end and you will be rewarded."

~ Morning After ~

Awaking to the rising sun spreading its fiercely bright rays across the African landscape, exposing in its glare the sprawling yellow grass and alien-looking *baobab* trees, Tara breathes deeply and glances at Siyabonga sleeping soundly beside her. She feels quite content. One of her goals is now reached, and the other objectives, though more difficult, are challenges she feels renewed strength to face. Her friends the lions and springboks have filled her with the wonder of timeless struggle and tragic beauty. She would stay out here longer, much longer, rather than return to the filth and brutal perversion of human cities, but that is not an option. Nevertheless, she is in no hurry, and hesitates to wake her newfound mate. Tara decides to let him sleep, and takes a walk to explore. After covering only a short distance, she comes across the carcass of a dead Bushpig, the victim of last night's deadly attack. There are few remains. Scavenger birds hover nearby, waiting for the bipedal interloper to go away.

Her mind wanders to earlier years, during her period of education and the horrifying simulations. Is the violent death of this Bushpig more savage than the Japanese torture camp of Unit 731? More savage than carpet bombings or Hiroshima or genocide? More savage than fouling the entire planet with . . . ?

"Enough!" she shouts to the wind. *Focus on the next step.*

~

Behind, she hears footsteps and turns to see Siyabonga walking toward her. Again, she failed to sense his presence and chalks it up to the power he has to block intrusive minds. This both pleases and displeases her, for it gives him a certain equality she is not accustomed to outside her family and mentors. *If we have the power to block others from our thoughts, does that not make us doubly dangerous?* she wonders. While Siyabonga approaches, she quickly reviews her lessons to find the answer to this problem. But her search abruptly ends with more intrusive outside thoughts pushing it aside, unleashed again by Siyabonga's sexual desire.

Let us make love again, Tara. I am so . . . I need you.

Here?

Anywhere! But we must do it now or I will die.

Then you must die, because I will not be on my back among these thorns!

Siyabonga laughs heartily and shouts, "Then be on top! Your two skin-figures did it every which way!"

Much more of this and we will soon outnumber the humans, says Tara craftily.

"So much the better!"

With this, Siyabonga rushes up and takes her in his arms. Their clothes fly off and she has soon wrapped her legs around him and guides his full erection inside. When both have climaxed, they put on their clothes in silent contentment and return to the campsite.

"That was wonderful", sighs Siyabonga for lack of anything better to say.

"Yes, it was," agrees Tara. "Now, we must go farther into the reserve."

"Why?"

"I am looking for something."

"What?"

"I don't know. Something is telling me inside my head to keep going." She pulls on her pack. "You may return. I must go a bit farther."

"How far?"

"I told you, I don't know. I'll only know when I get there."

Siyabonga shakes his head. "I'm going with you."

Tara glares at him severely. It is a commanding expression, one that will not be disregarded. She follows up this look with words shouted telepathically. *No! You must return and I must go on alone. No questions! I will see you when I get back. By that time, I am sure I will have more information on how to proceed. Go!*

I will go, but you must tell me what you find when you return, he replies in a wounded tone.

Tara walks away, her mind bombarded with the same message to keep moving toward the southwest.

~ *She* ~

Hours pass as Tara hikes farther into the bowels of the reserve. The landscape changes to a more desert environment with bare rocks replacing scrub. She passes elephants and giraffes, but remains focused and single-minded on her journey. Although the inner words have stopped urging her onward, a different, deeper compulsion presses her forward. It is late afternoon and the shadows have lengthened. Tara skirts the base of a boulder-strewn hill and, while passing through a narrow gorge between two steep walls, she confronts a solitary figure standing silently in her path. It is a beautiful young woman wearing a backpack, smiling as if an eagerly expected guest has just arrived. Tara immediately recognizes *her*, and the hunchback's heart races at the memory of their first meeting, many many years ago.

"Welcome, Little Tara," *she* says. "A long human time ago, I once asked your great-great grandfather John Powers when he was a young man how one justifies a life without cruelty, and therefore without the distilled beauty of cruelty. Now that you are older, what do you say to that question?"

[448]

Tara stares into *her* depthless eyes, her own glowing from some inner source. "My answer is the same, *Goddess*. The spider's web is intricately beautiful, the taste of captured flies exquisite."

She laughs appreciatively. "As do Bushpigs. Long ago, on that same first meeting, I promised you a visit to your great-great-grandfather when he was a young man on a quest during a human war. And, of course, if we join him on that quest, we will find your revered great-great-grandmother, Child of Buddha. But first you have, how to say, a bone to pick?"

"Why was I not told?"

"Of the others?"

"Yes."

"Those of us who care about this planet are not of one mind. Our differences have a poor, but apt analogy to human war—but our war is of the mind, not the body. Your great-great-grandfather John, your great-grandfather Michael, and your great-great-grandmother Child of Buddha, were the victims of early . . . unfortunate mistakes. They were among the earliest who experienced the first faint echoes of telepathy and clairvoyance. As a result, their muddled creation of *God* and *Goddess* was the twisted product of the human brain's complex pathways. Your ancestors, who possessed the initial fragile seeds of your power, packaged all of the stereotypical components of evil versus good, dark versus light, female versus male, and so forth, into a phantasmagorical distortion of what *God* and *Goddess* represent. These phantom angels and demons settled in your ancestor's minds and waged a great conflict, resulting in the disorientation of their fragile mental states, and inducing horrific hallucinations and delusions. Of course, humans misinterpreted these visions as schizophrenia and locked some of them away. Consequently, untold suffering afflicted the first of your kind, who were too soon exposed to the white-hot prejudices and black-box ignorance of *Home sapiens*."

"What is the nature of these differences?" asks Tara.

"For the time being, I will forego explanation. Soon, you will see for yourself when we reach the cave."

"The cave?"

She smiles. "Isn't there always a cave?"

"So it seems. Does this one also lead . . . elsewhere?"

"Oh, yes. Come with me."

The two figures walk side-by-side, communicating mentally. When they reach the entrance to the cave, they pause and the young woman looks at Tara.

Your question is why I am referred to as Goddess?

It seems curious to me, given the superstitious nature of human religions.

You are right to be curious. I have appeared in that form due to the odd notions humans have of what a Goddess looks like. It is a confused mishmash of attributes, all with the express purpose of inspiring awe, just as God takes many forms in human mythology to achieve the same effect. Your ancestors saw me in this form, for it was made to look so by their own distorted imaginations. When I spoke to them, my voice was transformed, in their minds, to sound **very much like this.** *When I appeared before them, what they beheld in their minds was this:*

Tara sees before her a wondrous transformation. The lovely young woman with the backpack now sits in the lotus position on a huge, dazzling white flower floating above the ground. *Her* sad, contemplative face gazes from beneath an elaborate crown glimmering a kaleidoscope of colors. A cinder-bright jewel is embedded in *her* forehead, burning brightly, and an intricate necklace lies cradled between *her* bare breasts. *Her* left hand rests on *her* thigh, the upturned curve of her fingers resembling the albino legs of a gracefully dead spider. *Her* right hand poises in the air, index finger and thumb touching to form an almost perfect circle while the other fingers radiate outward.

You are so beautiful! So radiant! enthuses Tara.

But oh! How they made us argue!

Us?

Yes, the prototype of all male gods into God, and the prototype of all female goddesses into Goddess. You see, they became the distilled and distorted versions of the two minds I spoke of earlier.

And you argued about?

Everything, but mainly the suffering inflicted on all living things and the pleasure it gave the male God—his drug of choice.

I don't understand.

The *Goddess* persona changes back to the beautiful young woman with a backpack. *She* continues, now speaking in *her* normal voice.

"Listen well. This is how we argued in the mind of your great-grandfather Michael Powers who had seen so much human-caused destruction in the rainforests of Vietnam. The beginning of the debate concerned the appearance of a Great Warrior—a female soldier ant—whom *Goddess* claimed equal to that of human warriors. *God* speaks first:

'Ants, Goddess? Gibberish?'

'I carry a nightmare to him—a special nightmare. Look at how his eyelids flutter so.'

'He has had many nightmares—even invites them to dinner. One more doesn't matter. He will just pull up another chair. You do not need My help. What is the real reason You called Me here?'

'His nightmare is for You. Hear Me. I will speak of human war loose in Nature's nursery, a place in which are wrapped the sexual organs of the planet. Of infinite varieties of sperm and egg, pistil and stamen, codes of life, precious reservoirs of diversity. I will speak of the tropical rainforest under whose canopy came the soldiers and the farmers, the metal and the muscle, gouging great scars between the bamboo ribs of the Mother.'

'I have humored You long enough. Get to the point.'

'Hatred and technology tearing through Her girth, violating Her fruited ovaries, eviscerating the twisted helices where She conceives their future. I will speak of a small battle that took place during a small war.'

'Stop pontificating, Mad Mother! You once stood tall amid the blood of the sacrificed. Now You have reverted to an adolescent girl sneaking peeks at the dirty little book of war under the thick covers of My ascendancy. Ants? Gibberish? Pretentious drivel! Melodramatic mush!'

'Pretentious? You dare speak of pretension? What about, 'In the Beginning God created the Heaven and Earth' or 'O Keshava, what are the signs of the man of steady wisdom, one who as attained God-consciousness' or 'Allah sendeth astray whomsoever He willeth, and guideth aright whomsoever He willeth. He is the Sublime, the Wise'? You have carried pretension to a higher level than I. And as for melodrama; have You ever known a dream, or a nightmare, that was not melodramatic?'

'There is skillful, understated pretension and there is clumsy, overwrought pretension: writhing snakes, multiple arms, serpentine hair, and Your stuttering serpent tongue, so creepy crawly to My femme phobias, not to mention Your fertile fleshly flab and sour milk from Your sagging breasts. Really, Great Mother, pull Yourself together.'

'Your mocking abuse is tiresome.'

[451]

'I'm not—'

'Then listen. Since Evolution invented sex and Our divorce was final, the children have suffered. You speak of pretension. Human war and hunger for blind worship are the ultimate pretensions.'

'Spoken like a starving deity. I have better things to do than listen to Your bilge. You complain about worship because they stopped worshipping You. Old deities never die, They just fade away. Your mortal's nightmare is Your business, not Mine. And as for Evolution, do not mention that desecration again!'

'The truth hurts, Dear God. A pimple on the end of Your nose. A humiliating exposure of Your adolescent—'

'Do not say it! . . . Anyway, it is all Your fault!'

'I want You to hear this story and I will not be put off by Your making Everything My Fault.'"

The young woman finishes and looks meaningfully at Tara. "These were the type of conflicts that plagued the minds of your great-great-grandfather, your great-grandfather, and others of their kind. These internal battles drove them and the others to what humans considered madness. They paid the price for being among the first. You are currently well stabilized, from a genetic point of view. Your battles are now entirely external. You have been educated and mentored. What happens from here forward is up to you and your kind. To survive and flourish is dependent upon an infinite number of variables which no entity can predict."

"Altan seems upset with me."

"You have acted with cruelty against the cruel. Altan understands."

"But where do I stop?"

"When it is time."

"If I overstep, as I did in the simulations?"

"Variables. Uncontrollable. Too many. You are now the spider and they are the flies."

Tara is silent.

She gestures toward the inside of the cave. "Go in."

"How far?"

That is up to you. Go. I will not be here when you return.

But I have so many questions. I need guidance.

Does the spider need guidance on how to build a web? Does the spider need guidance on how to eat a fly?

~ Another Cave ~

As Tara moves deeper into the cave, light from the entrance fades, quickly blinking out to become absolute blackness. Nonetheless, she presses on. While walking, she occasionally stumbles, but her athletic prowess allows her to recover and keep moving forward. A light in the distance draws her, and when she reaches a narrow opening in the rocks from where the shafts of light originate, she steps through. On the other side, she finds herself in a small, poorly lit room. Trash is strewn everywhere, and in the corner, on a greasy mattress, sits what looks to be a broken mannikin. Squinting into the shadowy corner, she makes out a head and legs, but something is wrong with the arms. Looking closer, she sees someone has removed the hands. The mannikin is crying. While trying to make sese of what she is seeing, an older woman enters the room with a bowl and begins carefully feeding the mannikin with a spoon. However, the mannikin refuses to eat and keeps turning its head to look down at a toy in its lap.

"Thato, son, you must eat. This will make you strong."

Tara now understands the scene unfolding in front of her.

"Thato, boy, eat. Please."

But the ex-gang leader turns his head away from the proffered food and keeps gently stroking the toy with his wrists. Stepping closer, Tara sees it is a hand-crafted warthog made with discarded flip flops—a common toy for African youngsters.

"Ain't no man no longer," he says. "Mama, you know what she did! No more reason to live. Got my good-luck toy here. Just a boy again. No good. Not a man."

"Son, you got to eat. No good crying like this. You'll die. Eat some, for me."

"No good. Brus in the gang already cut me out. Got a new leader. I'm useless. No good."

The mother flashes a grim stare straight at Tara without seeing her. "They gonna take care of that woman! Take care of her good for what she did."

"Too late, mama. Too late."

"Son, you got to eat. For me, you got to eat."

[453]

Tara watched this pathetic scene for a few more minutes, her emotions not registering regret, but rather sadness that Thato's own actions made it necessary to do what she did. Probing the mother's brain, she reads only a deep well of ignorance and superstition, embroidered with the twin poisons of alcoholism and helpless rage.

Altan appears and joins her in watching the unfortunate Thato.

"You do not feel guilt for what you did to him?"

"No," replies Tara curtly.

"Or her?"

"No."

"Yet, you are sad?"

"Yes. It is like one feels about a once playful puppy who now has rabies and must be destroyed. In this case, I did not destroy, but merely disabled."

"But, what of the others?"

"Others?"

"Those less overtly violent, aside from those who murder and rape; what about those who lie, cheat, defraud, manipulate, bully, abuse, and a host of other unpleasant traits that cumulatively wreak havoc?"

"Those are the animal traits they have inherited. Are we to mutilate or kill them all?"

Altan laughs. "Good. Good."

Tara continues. "All animal societies have dominance hierarchies. Obviously, *Homo sapiens* are no exception. To fight against that is folly."

"Good. Good."

"But, Altan, will we who succeed them have a dominance hierarchy as well?"

Before Altan replies, a primal scream reverberates through the room. It is the terrible, hopeless wail of Thato.

"Get out!" he shouts at his mother. "Leave me alone!"

After she leaves sobbing to return to her bottle, he moans and holds up his handless wrists, the more to fuel his self-pitying despair.

Altan turns and looks at Tara. "As with all alphas, the fall is precipitous, agonizing, and pitiable to watch."

"But us, Altan. What about us?"

"Hierarchies are detrimental to cooperation. For non-human animals, this is a given, but their hierarchical structures have minimal impact on the larger environment. Human non-cooperation, combined with advanced technological expertise, is non-sustainable. This is the crucial stage intelligent life on Earth has reached. Your kind represents a narrow window of escape for hominins, and failure to evolve through it to a more cooperative civilization spells doom."

"But what guarantee is there that we will be more cooperative than humans? After all, we still possess many of their genes. Won't we end up destroying ourselves as well?"

"No guarantees in this universe except the laws of physics. However, a new species with the individual power to read minds"—Altan holds up his hand and raises his voice for emphasis—"and in addition the ability to reconfigure molecular structure using mental projection to exploit multidimensional spacetime manifolds—" he pauses to let his words sink in, then continues using an admonitory tone. "Well, all of these capacities carry with them an element of mutually-assured destruction. That is a clumsy, short-term deterrent. The key is a concurrent evolutionary leap which expands and deepens the capacity for empathy—not for the individual alone, but for all life forms, and the planet itself. If this compassion is inadequately expressed, failure is inevitable. If it is adequately expressed, then. . . . "

"But can we prevail? Can we reproduce enough to tip the balance?"

"Your new species must be given a chance to survive when it is most vulnerable—at its beginnings. You and your recent ancestors are the vulnerable first individuals. Whether you survive and flourish is still up in the air. As your powers become better known, they will fight back, especially those at the top of the hierarchy."

Tara turns to look at Thato. "Then I should stop using my powers to help these people?"

When she turns back to receive the answer, he is gone, as is the room itself.

In its place stretches a great field of grass. In the distance, she sees a huge building rise majestically. It is a massive, two-story concrete structure complex, with sprawling tile roofs and wrap-around verandas, accentuated with dozens of concrete arches and Romanesque columns. Were it not for the obvious age of the buildings and the holes and indentations where bullets and shrapnel had gouged innumerable scars, it resembles a medieval fortress; an enormous fortification constructed to protect the ostensibly insane against the terrible sanity of the outside world.

Tara keeps walking, across the field, into the main building, and through a maze of stairways and hallways, until she reaches an imposing wall with an iron door blocking the way. She looks through the iron bars of a small window, then pushes open the heavy door and is greeted with a dark, dismal tunnel that passes for a hallway. Sounds come to her ear— strange, plaintive wails and stifled shrieks—all evidently female. Her hump fairly bursts with the intense pain from the eerie nature of the space. Every step she takes is accompanied by a new light illuminating what lurks behind the cell bars; eyes, faces, and hands that, to Tara, make the inmates look like dismembered ghosts. Low moans and purring sounds emanate from the cells, punctuated by occasional laughter, shrieks, and sobs. The stench is unbearable.

A Chinese man materializes and says to Tara, "There is one woman I want you to see. We keep her locked up because she has so often attempted suicide. We call her Child of Buddha. She is your great-great-grandmother. And this man"—he gestures to another figure just arrived— "is your great-great-grandfather, John Powers."

"Is she violent?" asks John of the Chinese man, unaware of Tara's presence. Both are now staring intently at a particular cell.

"No, I am not violent," comes a soft voice from behind the bars.

Tara is just able to probe her great-great-grandmother's mind before everything disappears. *Now I realize how grievously she and my other ancestors have suffered,* she thinks. *But, why am I shown this?*

You are shown this in order to show you this, comes the reply.

With these words ringing in her mind, Tara retraces her steps and exits the cave to start the long journey back to Cape Town.

~ Return ~

Two days later, Tara arrives in Nyanga and learns that Siyabonga and his mother have been shot. She rushes to the hospital and asks a nurse at the front desk about their status.

"Are you a relative?" asks the nurse.

"No, a friend."

The nurse's eyes flit to Tara's hump. "You cannot see them unless I receive the family's permission."

"Just tell me their condition."

"Siyabonga's wound is serious, but not life threatening. Kholwa is in intensive care."

"I would like to see Siyabonga please."

"You can't hon."

Tara reads hesitation in the nurse's mind. "Would you kindly ask him if I can visit?"

"Sit over there and I'll try to get to it."

Within a half hour, Tara is given permission to visit Siyabonga. She finds him in a second floor ward lying in bed, bandaged, with an IV in his arm. When she pulls aside the curtain enclosing his bed, his eyes light up, then dim when he remembers. "How is mama?" he asks quickly.

"I don't know, they won't let me see her."

"Oh."

"What happened?"

Let us speak with our minds, he says telepathically. *Best no one hears.*

Speak.

Had to be the Mongrels. Could have been The Americans. Could have been any of the gangs. We are enemies to all of them. Shot mama and I while we were returning home.

Did you not pick up their presence? Their intent?

No. They were clever. They distracted our mental attention by a diversion.

How?

A group of them approached and flashed gang signals, threatening us and cursing at us. The shooters were hidden and shot us from behind.

Which gang.

That's the thing. Some I recognized, and I know they are from different gangs. Must be some sort of cease-fire until we are eliminated. After we were shot and I was lying on the ground, I did pick up disappointment that you were not with us. You were the main target. Then I lost consciousness. Go see mama and come back.

Yes, I will try.

Siyabonga grasps her hand. *When you go back to your apartment, be careful.*

Tara says grimly, *My powers are greater than yours and Kholwa's. We will see.*

Will you seek revenge?

That is a human trait. We will see. Do you want me to?

Yes, but not for revenge. If we let them neutralize us, there is no hope for the future.

Some would argue that not seeking revenge is the only hope for the future.

Do you not understand the phrase 'let them neutralize us?' Revenge is not the issue.

What is the issue?

Survival of our kind.

We will see.

Please come back after you see mama! I need to know she will be okay.

Yes.

Even as she approached Kholwa's ward, Tara knows she is dead. When one tries to read a dead person's brain, there is a deep chasm of dark, blank nothingness. Such is the case with Kholwa. Without going a step farther, she returns to Siyabonga.

"You need not tell me," he says as she approaches his bed. "I know. My powers are not that weak."

"I am sorry."

Siyabonga stares at her, tears rolling down his cheeks. "I will help you neutralize."

"If that is what I decide, then you may help. They tell me you will recover, but it will take time. I have an idea about how you might best be of assistance. We will talk later. Now, I return to the apartment."

Tara stops speaking and looks at Siyabonga significantly. *I have just announced where I am going. We will see if there are spies in here.*

Yes, yes. Good. My heart aches for mama. Use me. Use me however you wish.

Not revenge?

Siyabonga breaks into a sob. *Yes, revenge. Perhaps there is too much human in me still.*

Yes.

With that, Tara departs the hospital and boards a bus that will take her close to her apartment. On the way, her mind is awash with contradictory thoughts on how best to go forward. If she declares all-out war on the gangs, her identity will certainly be discovered by the authorities, and the scale of her difficulties will exponentially increase. If she does nothing, the gangs will be even more bold, probably leading to another attempt to murder Siyabonga. *Goddess knows there are few enough of us as it is, even if he is only an intermediate.* It is the middle road that she and her kind always seem forced to take. Deep rooted genetic predisposition to empathy and compassion will not allow for complete non-intervention on behalf of the victims, but survival cunning demands staying far enough under *Homo sapiens'* radar to give adequate time for procreation. Altan had it right—razor's edge.

After leaving the bus, Tara is on full alert while walking to her apartment, but there is no incident, so she settles in for a good night's sleep. Laying in bed, her thoughts take on a life of their own, and she tosses and turns, pondering on what to do tomorrow and all the days after. Sirens fill the night air. Mischief, as always, is astir. She knows there will be a desultory investigation of the shootings of Siyabonga and Kholwa, which will lead nowhere; partly due to corruption, partly due to jails already full to bursting, partly due to the futility of locking up these gang members so they fall into the clutches of The Numbers to turn them even more violent. It is all such a vicious cycle, with no end in sight. More killings, more rapes, more drugs, more everything bad. *At this point,* thinks Tara. *Many humans would give up and join the fray, inflicting violence directly or indirectly with the idea that their individual actions would not make a difference. Those that do fight against it, are soon worn down or overwhelmed by the enormity of the task.* But her genetic makeup will allow no such resignation, and her power makes the odds far more favorable than for good-hearted humans. *If that is the case,* she thinks, *then I must use this power for good, within reason. My mistake in the Unit 731 simulation taught me well. Surgical precision must be my guiding principle. I bearded the lion once; I can do it again.*

These conflicting thoughts eventually pass, and she falls into the sleep of the innocents. Her last thoughts of Kholwa are of sadness, not guilt. For Tara, it is like the loss of a loyal dog.

Chapter 38: Confrontations and Consequences

~ Visit to Siyabonga ~

In the morning, Tara makes a stop at the hospital to visit Siyabonga and communicate her plan telepathically. This time, she tells him, she will walk into the headquarters of the Mongrels unannounced. What happens afterward . . . happens. Nonetheless, she explains, she is determined to either convince them to cease their violent behaviors against others, or punish them, come what may. Although in pain, Siyabonga insists on accompanying her.

"No," Tara says aloud. "You will be a hindrance. Your wound has not healed. You will stay."

He smiles. *I'm not too worried about you, but I really want to see their faces when you appear on their home turf.*

I see. Will my visit have any effect?

No, but it would still be worth it to see!

If it will have no effect, why should I bother?

I said it would still be worth it.

How?

If you save only one. . . .

Tara sighs. *For every one saved, thousands are born and bred to violence, inflicted either physically or psychologically or both.*

Frustrated, Siyabonga speaks aloud. "One becomes the many. Not bothering with them is not an option to those of us who are the victims of their brutalities. Would you save a dog trapped in a burning house? After all, one dog is of no consequence to all dogs. No. You would save the dog simply to prevent unnecessary suffering, regardless of its global impact. Am I right?"

A nearby patient, hearing Siyabonga's words, snorts in disgust. "Bullshit, bru! Why save the dog and risk getting all burnt up? It's just a dog!"

"Dog has feelings," says Siyabonga.

[460]

"Shiiiittt! Dog's a dog. Ain't nothin' but a dog."

Siyabonga looks more closely and sees gang tattoos adorning this patient's arms. He glances at Tara as if to say, 'listen to this', and directs his words to the gangster, "Well, would you save a person trapped in a burning house?"

"Depends."

"On what?"

"If that person be a bru."

"You mean, if they are in your gang?"

"Shit, you finally get it. No one else means shit."

"Your mama?"

"Hell no! She dead, and good riddance! Drunken whore!"

Silence for a long while. Finally, Siyabonga points at Tara and asks, "You recognize this woman?"

"'Course. She a witch." He lowers his voice to a murmur. "And she gonna pay her dues soon enough."

"You're not afraid of her?"

"Hell, no." He sits up in bed and spreads his arms invitingly. "Do your best, bitch!"

Tara stares at him curiously. "What if I took off one of your arms?"

"Then I shoot you with the other."

"If I took off the other arm?"

"Then I stomp you good with my feet."

"And if I take off your legs?"

"I find a way to kill you. Count on it, bitch. I hear you two flappin' lips and talking quiet like. You against us. People don't like us, they die. You will die."

Tara walks up to his bed with a menacing scowl and says, "What if I just make you disappear now?"

This time, he cowers back and says nothing.

"You are just a boy, a little boy," she says. "All talk, but wants to live. All talk, but wants to be loved. Silly boy, I would save you if you were trapped in a burning house."

His face registers a pouting intransigence. "Save yourself, bitch. You gonna die."

[461]

Tara recognizes the words are empty boasts, and her hump is abuzz with the conflict raging within his mind between the will to survive and his duty as a gang member. Reluctantly, she delves deeper into this ravaged soul and finds even more disturbing impulses. This young patient had been raped numerous times by a gang captain for botching a murder job. He had been ordered to kill a man, but not being a killer, could not do it. As punishment, he was condemned to be raped first by the captain, and then by other gang members. Afraid to resist, he willingly allowed himself to be continuously brutalized until he became, what the gang calls, "a woman". This means he is treated as nothing more than a domestic slave— wash clothes, bring food, clean dishes, be a runner, and so forth. Tara knows that, as with so many others, his humiliation exemplifies a broken spirit living constantly in fear from his fellow gang members, but required to show no fear toward outsiders. The one primary display of fealty always required of him is gang-sanctioned bluster. Drugs are his only solace. Never has he experienced any human emotion directed his way other than hatred or fear or contempt or violence. Never has he felt any emotion toward others except for hatred or fear or contempt or violence. His world is the size of a grave, and the shovelfuls of dirt keep raining down.

Strangely enough, contact with this sad young man makes Tara even more determined to boldly walk into the belly of the beast and confront the leaders of the Mongrels, armed with the only language they understand—raw power driven by ruthless violence. Tara knows this is a game they cannot win, but she nonetheless decides to wait a couple of days to visit their headquarters. It is certain word will be out about her return, so she will let them wonder what will come next. In the meantime, she plans to lay low and meet again with Altan. She departs from the hospital with Siyabonga's pleas to join her trailing after.

Next day, she meets Altan at the Iziko South African Museum, far away from the snooping eyes at the Flats.

~

Sitting on a bench in front of a display of ancient fossils, the two stare at the exhibits while communicating telepathically.

You are certain this is a good idea? asks Altan in his usual monotone after Tara tells him her plan.

The time has come.

[462]

This improvisational action indicates decreased activation in your dorsolateral prefrontal cortex and increase in medial prefrontal cortex, which is fine. However, the newly evolved corpus quadrittourium exhibits extreme stimulation. With these indicators, you still feel this course of action is wise?

Tara does not hesitate. *Absolutely. I have already taken that into consideration.*

In that case, I have to make arrangements to get you out of the country immediately afterward.

If I do that, what happens to Siyabonga and the others?

He shrugs. *Left to the wolves.*

Then I should stay.

Can't stay forever.

Then what should I do?

You decide, Tara. This is part of your real-world training ground. No simulations here. None of us knows where this will lead.

Tara sets her jaw and shakes her head. *The decision is made. I'll make the necessary arrangements.*

Yes, but I may not take advantage of them right away.

Altan raises an eyebrow, but makes no reply.

Have you heard from mama? asks Tara after a long pause.

Indeed. She ran into some trouble and is now back in the sights of the FBI.

Tara jerks in alarm. *What happened?*

It is over, and all is well—for now. However, complications continue. At this point, know that she and your father are together, safe, and well. Concentrate on your upcoming confrontation with this gang. You will need all your wits about you when the dominoes start to fall. Keep in mind what I said about your brain. As I said, no one knows what the future holds for your species, if there is a future.

~ Into the Den ~

By the time Tara reaches the house which serves as headquarters of the Mongrels, she has already attracted a crowd. Gang members, their women, curiosity-seekers, all have grown in number when she stands at the front door of the run-down, graffiti-covered structure. So many ugly sentiments from the mob that are flooding her hump, she closes it to further

[463]

assault but for the most drastic of threats. Two guards stand between her and the door, and in response to one of them shouting a code word, it opens and a hand waves her in. Looking around for a last glimpse of the crowd, smirks are all she sees when the door closes behind. After stepping inside, she is confronted by a dozen or so gang members crowding the entrance hall. Oddly, no one says a word, only the usual weapons, obscene gestures and aggressive postures are exhibited, but all performed as in a silent movie. Tara senses they are waiting for a signal to attack, and makes an instantaneous decision to strike first. Just as a shouted command is given from some back room, Tara acts. In a flash, all their weapons disappear. Amidst the confusion and outrage, four of the most fearlessly brutal rush at her from all sides. In the blink of an eye, these men also vanish into thin air, immediately causing a panic to strike the remaining "brus" who claw and pummel themselves in a stampede to escape. Tara watches them pour out the front door, leaving the house empty but for one soul hiding somewhere and projecting the most terrified tangle of disjointed thoughts. She calmly checks every room. Trash and drug paraphernalia are strewn everywhere. It is dark, but finally she hones in on waves of terror emanating from a closet. Without hesitation, she dissociates any weapons that might be trained on the door, and cautiously opens it.

Just as she does, she hears police sirens pulling up outside, and at the same time, stares at a curled-up figure cowering in the corner of the closet. As she suspected from the sensations, it is a girl, probably a gang slave, shivering uncontrollably. Tara smiles to convey no evil intent, and quickly turns and strides to the front door in time to confront a host of police officers barking at her to raise her hands over her head. When she does, they throw her to the floor, cuff her, and shove her out the front door and into a patrol car.

Tara now faces a dilemma. Does she simply make the cuffs and the car disappear and walk away? Does she allow herself to be taken to a holding cell? A slight smile hovers on her lips; an appreciation of the delicious irony of police being called for help by a vicious gang. While in this predicament, she thinks of a way to move forward. So comfortable is she with this plan, she sits back and allows the police to do as they will.

~

Subsequently, the police do as they will. Tara is flung into a holding cell, interrogated numerous times, and deprived of sleep by hourly

[464]

visits designed to harass. In response to their questions about disappearing gang members, Tara claims no knowledge, other than hazarding a suggestion that drug-induced delusions by gang members must be the answer. Where they will find the four missing men, she has no idea. After all, everyone knows one cannot make people simply disappear into the air, with no bodies to be found, and no evidence of violence anywhere. The police are stymied. Testimony from the eyewitnesses make no sense, and they are forced to conclude Tara might be on to something about the effect of drugs. Nevertheless, it is hard for the police to explain the extreme fear exhibited by these hardened men, who have killed and raped indiscriminately and brutally, but whose trauma caused by this humpback girl appears real and unrehearsed. Still, they keep Tara a few days until finally, unable to detain her longer, subject her to one more interview. She enters the interrogation room confidently, only to find a surprise waiting— a most unpleasant surprise.

~ International Intrigue ~

Agent Lance Romellion sits behind a long table when Tara enters. He looks up and smiles pleasantly. On either side of him sit two South African detectives.

"Hello, Tara Powers," says Romellion. "I am agent Lance Romellion of the FBI. Last time I saw you was quite a few years ago. It is truly amazing how quickly you have grown. Not natural, I would say. You were a little girl then, when you disappeared with your mother into a cave far from here in the California desert. Do you remember?"

Tara quickly reads his mind and is somewhat comforted by the crux of his thoughts, which are characterized by deep suspicion mixed with a healthy dose of uncertainty. "You must be close to a desk job by now, Agent Romellion."

"And I planned to, except something came up with your mother Pythia after all these years. Now, you couldn't pay me enough to retire."

"You have questions?"

Romellion opens a thick folder and shuffles through the papers. "I see you have already answered the most obvious questions put to you by my South African colleagues. Do you have anything to add before I begin?"

"No."

[465]

"Well then, my first question is simple: how do you make things disappear?"

"I can't."

"How do you make limbs disappear?"

"I can't."

"How do you make people disappear?"

"I can't."

"Then explain to me how your grandmother Ming-huà Powers, your mother Pythia Powers, and yourself are always present when there are bizarre reports of a hunchback making objects, limbs, and people disappear?"

Tara shakes her head. "I don't know."

"You have no explanation?"

"No, except to say such powers are certainly not possible. You may wish to redirect your investigation to more productive areas. In any case, isn't South Africa outside your jurisdiction?"

Romellion waves a hand in dismissal of the question. "You say such powers are not possible?"

"Of course not."

"If they are not possible, how do you, your mother, and your grandmother do it?"

"Do what?"

"Make things disappear?"

"We can't. That is not possible."

Tara reads his next question and blinks.

Romellion glares at her and pauses for effect, not aware his question is already known. "Not possible for humans, perhaps. Are you human, Ms. Powers?"

The two South African detectives squirm in their seats and look wonderingly at Lance Romellion, but remain silent.

Tara laughs and says, "Last I checked in the mirror, Agent Romellion, I was human. I believe I still am."

Romellion suddenly jerks his hand from beneath the table and throws an object at Tara's head. She ducks, but not in time, and it strikes her on the side of the face. She cries out in feign surprise, for, of course, she knew what was coming before he threw it.

A moment of astonished shock by the two South Africa detectives is followed by Tara holding up a soft whiffle ball that had bounced off her head onto the table.

"Is this some novel FBI form of interrogation?" she asks angrily.

Romellion's face turns red, but he maintains his poise. "Just making sure. Sorry for the little demonstration. You're not hurt, I hope?"

"Only my respect for the FBI."

Romellion loses his placid demeanor. "We know you and yours can perform some sort of trickery! The reports are unambiguous; too numerous to indicate otherwise!"

Tara scans his brain and finds no evidence her father, Jared Paine, is an informer. Relieved, she says, "So, your great theory is that I am not human?"

"Something like that."

"An alien?"

"Perhaps."

Tara spreads her arms wide. "As you can see. . . . "

"Ms. Powers, or whoever you are, we know you, your mother, your grandmother, and possibly others, have some sort of inexplicable abilities. The federal government is most interested in these abilities. Others in our agency see this as an important national security issue."

"You see three hunchbacked women as a threat to the United States?"

"Perhaps."

Tara looks at the two South African detectives. "Am I considered a threat to your country?"

"Not at this point," says the senior agent, flashing a toothy grin.

"I am glad trying to curb gang violence is not considered a threat to South Africa. Apparently, your country is far more enlightened than law enforcement in the United States, since I assume you consider me a human being."

In spite of themselves, the two South Africans find these words flattering, and secretly enjoy the FBI agent being taken down a peg. "We consider you a human," says the senior agent. "And since we have no evidence to detain you any longer, you will be released today, unless, that is, our FBI colleague has any further questions?"

[467]

Romellion grimly shakes his head and adds a last warning. "Be assured, Ms. Powers, we will continue our investigation."

"I'm sure you will, Agent Romellion, but your efforts will be for naught if you insist on pursuing such absurd theories."

As she is being escorted out of the room by the South African detectives, she reads Romellion's thoughts, which are akin to the grinding of one's teeth in frustration.

~

Once released, Tara learns to her dismay that one of the gang members she dissociated was street vendor Thandolwethu's son, Mpho. Given the relatively lackadaisical nature of the South African police, rather than leaving the country, she decides to stay in Nyanga and see what happens. But first, she must visit Thandolwethu. The vendor's stand is gone and it takes some digging to discover where she lives. Siyabonga gives her a lead, and after a few days, she finds the tumble-down shack in which the vendor has taken to bed, alone and utterly bereft by the death of her son. One evening, concealed by the night, Tara decides to visit.

She knocks on a poorly-hung plywood door but there is no answer. Her hump picks up a sorrowful dirge from inside, so she pushes open the door and steps into the darkness. Moaning drifts to her ears and she follows the sound, finding Thandolwethu laying in bed. The stench is horrible, and rotten food lies scattered on the floor. Tara carefully steps to the side of the bed and looks down in pity at this once-powerful woman, now as emaciated and brittle as a concentration camp inmate. Her breathing is erratic, and Tara quickly realizes Thandolwethu should be in hospital.

"Thandolwethu," she whispers.

No response, but an intake of breath that makes the body shudder.

"Thandolwethu, it is Tara."

Now the body stiffens and the eyes flutter open.

"Thandolwethu, I am sorry about your son."

Tears roll down the cheek and dampen the already filthy sheet. Still, there is no verbal response but for soft moaning. Tara can actually feel her anterior cingulate vigorously pulse with sensory input.

"Thandolwethu."

"Go away, witch," come the words, rasping and weak, but ripe with pent-up anger.

"Thandolwethu, you must eat."

[468]

"Go away!" Now the words are gasped louder. "You a devil-woman. You kill my son. Go!"

Thandolwethu's mind, although clouded with grief, is clear in its single-minded hatred of Tara. Like a beacon shining through the fog, her animosity bores squarely into Tara's heart so intensely, it burns.

My presence here is useless, Tara thinks. *Best to leave her to her grief.*

But she knows Thandolwethu has no one to care for her, and without proper attention, she will surely die. This would be akin to abandoning a sick animal, and the thought is anathema to Tara's genetic predisposition. With such compulsion in mind, she begins to clean-up the rubbish and prepare a pot of soup.

"Go away," says Thandolwethu, her voice stronger, but her conviction weaker.

Tara ignores the entreaties and continues to tidy up. With the soup heating on a battered stovetop, she begins to wash the dishes.

"You a witch," says Thandolwethu, softening. "Why you kill my son?"

Tara is uncertain how to respond. Finally, while her arms are elbow-deep in soapy water scrubbing a pot, she replies, "You know."

This seems to take Thandolwethu aback. "What you mean?" she asks hesitantly.

"You know. Now, I am going to give you some nice, hot soup, which I hope you will eat."

Tears flowing in streams, Thandolwethu says, "How he die?"

"Painlessly."

"How?"

Tara shakes her head and concentrates on stirring the pot.

"How?"

"Painlessly, I promise you."

Thandolwethu pauses, then says, "My boy was good. Damn drugs do him in. He not a bad boy. I know. Sweet, sweet baby before the drugs. Why you kill him?"

"Here," says Tara walking to the bed with a bowl of soup. She sets it on a side table. "Sit up and eat. I'll help you."

"Why you not tell me?"

"Eat first."

Thandolwethu is stubborn, desperate to hold on to her hate, but failing in the face of her own natural kindness. Still, she takes a sip from the spoon held by Tara.

"Why you do this? Guilty?"

"That is an emotion I'm not too familiar with. I do this because you are suffering."

"You kill my boy, but you do this for me. You be a strange woman. Some say a witch. If not, you be strange."

"So I've been told."

"You really a witch?"

"No."

"Then what are you?"

"I am the beginning of the end."

"What?"

Tara wipes a drop of soup from Thandolwethu's chin, then asks, "What do you think of Siyabonga?"

Thandolwethu cracks a smile in spite of herself. "You sweet on him?"

"He seems suitable."

Thandolwethu peers at Tara. "You odd."

"Here, take another sip. Okay, good. Now, what about Siyabonga?"

"He a good boy. Strange too." Her eyes widen. "Like you."

"How is he strange?"

"Like you."

"How like me?"

"Maybe he a witch too. I don't know. Good boy, but strange. You both come from same egg, I think. Good boy. Lone-wolf boy. Quiet-like; eyes see, ears hear, heart aches, mouth quiet."

"Do the girls like him?"

"Flies to honey."

"So, he has many girlfriends?"

"Lots and lots want the boy, but they always be disappointed."

"How so?"

"Tara girl, love, like rain, don't choose the grass on which it falls. His grass look green, but his roots hate water. I told you, he a loner boy. Don't think like others. Yes, you and him be strange in like ways. Maybe

[470]

he be a witch too. Strange boy. No girls get close, far as I know. 'Cept maybe you?"

"Have some more soup."

"No. Tired. You go now. Can't forget you kill my boy. But somehow, you good. Can't get it straight. Can't make my mind up to hate, but you remind me of my boy. You go."

She closes her eyes and turns away.

Tara finishes up and heads back to her apartment full of conflicting ideas and feeling a need to talk with Altan. References to her mother's troubles have her worried and deeply curious. Sy, Lady Oracle, Ming-huà, Zookeeper, Jared, Pythia—none answer their phones, and they are too far away for telepathy. By the time she reaches her apartment, Altan is waiting.

Tara fills him in on her short incarceration and FBI interview. As usual, he remains impassive.

"Altan, what's going on with mother?"

Even his stony face softens to an expression of sorrowful anxiety. "Well, here's what happened."

Chapter 39: Time of Reckoning

~ Pythia Encounters Trouble ~

Altan settles back in the couch and begins his story. "Weeks ago, in Berkeley, Pythia was with Jared. It was late at night. They had just finished eating at a restaurant and were walking to their car when three men attacked them with knives. Pythia dissociated the knives, but two of the muggers wrestled Jared to the ground, and another knife appeared from somewhere. When she dealt with that, the third attacker pulled a gun and shot Jared. In response, Pythia made him disappear, and the remaining two fled."

Altan pauses.

"Is Jared dead?" asks Tara.

"No. In hospital."

"Condition?"

"Flesh wound. Will recover."

"Yes, okay," says Tara. "This has happened before. It could not be helped, right?"

"Unfortunately," sighs Altan. "By the time Pythia made the attacker disappear, bystanders had arrived, and one of them filmed the entire confrontation on their phone. It ended up in the hands of the police, and eventually, of course, the FBI. All of us are now under the microscope of the federal government and all its extensive apparatus. A host of Lance Romellions will soon be set loose."

"That explains his little visit the other day. Is Pythia in jail?"

"No, after all, she was one of the victims. However, the dissociation is captured on film."

"Then propagation must be our priority."

Altan shrugs. "Yes. Are you pregnant?"

"I believe I am carrying a child."

"Siyabonga?"

"Yes."

"Good. It now becomes imperative to protect the child."

"Yes, but with federal government scrutiny now focused on all of us, how do we escape the inevitable conclusion that we are . . . different? Romellion already thinks we are aliens who pose a threat to the United States."

"There is still hope. After all, the video may be characterized as faulty, since obviously such things are physical impossibilities. Pythia, of course, will continue to deny any knowledge, but that story is running thin. Nevertheless, our friend Romellion and his colleagues believe they are on to something extraordinary, and this will add fuel to the fire."

"And they would be right," sighs Tara.

"Indeed."

"How do we proceed?"

Altan looks at her askance. "Tara, you are now far enough along the road to make that determination yourself. Certainly, your distant *Homo sapien* ancestors had to make their own way among all the other competing hominins they were in the process of replacing, not to speak of all the non-human predators."

"Your thoughts tell me you are leaving."

"Yes."

"Forever?"

"No, but I will be unavailable for some time."

"Without benefit of your counsel, I fear I will fail terribly!"

"You are no longer alone. Sy, Lady Oracle, Ming-huà, Zookeeper, Pythia, Jared, and now Siyabonga, will all be with you. Remember, there are a lot of intermediates out there. You will find them useful."

"Should we all go to the cave and lay low?"

Altan shrugs in his maddening way. *The universe is ruled by uncertainty.*

~

The next day, Thandolwethu is found murdered, stabbed to death by vengeance-seeking gang members. Her blood had been used to spell out, "traitor to her son" on the wall of her room. Tara, at her apartment and unaware of this development, is visited by Siyabonga just released from hospital. Wincing in pain, he sits on her couch and accepts a cup of tea before speaking. After taking a few sips, he looks forlornly at Tara.

"Thandolwethu is dead," he says quietly. "Murdered."

[473]

"Yes," replies Tara. "When you arrived, your thoughts were very clear. I'm so sorry to hear such news."

"I've been wondering," he says. "Are we responsible?"

"Yes. This news has made it clear I must not stay."

"Why?" he asks in surprise.

Tara looks down and speaks telepathically. *Relieving suffering has created more suffering. Gangs continue. Leaders are replaced. Governments remain corrupt. We remove corrupt leaders and they are succeeded by more corrupt leaders. Our simulations always came out the same way. By our actions, some people are saved, some people are killed. Innocents are murdered. The primitive brain structures of* Homo sapiens *ensure this continuation, regardless of what we do. There is only one way out, and that is up. Out with* Homo sapiens *and up the evolutionary ladder.*

Siyabonga nods dejectedly, but remains silent.

"I am carrying your child," announces Tara bluntly.

His sad face instantly transforms into an expression of joy.

"So soon? You know so soon?"

"I know."

"There is a future!" he cries aloud.

"Yes, and it must be preserved."

"But . . . I mean, now I must go with you!"

"Siyabonga, immigrating to the United States is complex and extremely difficult, if not impossible these days."

"I'll get a visa," he proclaims.

"How?"

'Multiple entry. Looked into this before. I have a friend in the ministry. Costs money, but I can do it. I must do it!"

Tara ponders. "Yes, I also have friends who are quite adept at these arrangements. Perhaps it can work."

"Yes, absolutely!" He gives her a wry grin. "We must be diligent in making more babies—for the cause."

"Of course. For the cause."

"Soooo, perhaps now might be—"

"No, Siyabonga. Firstly, I am with child, and our kind possess altered gestation rules. Secondly, your wound has not healed, and sex would exacerbate the problem. Thirdly, I sense the need to hurry away from this place, or you will be killed like the others. I will give you enough

[474]

money to move to Cape Town. There, you can pursue obtaining a visa in peace."

"Not to worry, I have always been on decent terms with the gangs."

"Nonsense. Your mother is dead and you have a bullet wound. Don't be foolish. You may once have been on good terms, but now you are a target as much as your mother and Thandolwethu."

Siyabonga has no response, but his heartbeat is quickened by the thought of being with Tara in the United States.

"In fact," she says with some urgency. "We should leave tonight."

"Well, first I have to go home and pack some stuff."

Tara cranes her neck as if listening to sounds beyond the walls. "No," she says ominously. "You stay here with me until we leave together. They smell blood and they are waiting out there. You will never make it home."

Siyabonga looks stricken. *Are you sure?*

I am sure. They are gathering, anxious for blood. Pumped up with drugs. They want to skin you alive. Only their fear of me prevents them from breaking in here now and slaughtering both of us. I have no desire to make more disappear.

~ Flight ~

Tara and Siyabonga remain in the apartment until early morning. While it is still dark, they bundle up and slip out the rear of the building. Tara is on full alert, but her hump registers no threats, so like thieves in the night, they make their way through a maze of streets and alleyways until well out of Nyanga's most dangerous areas. Eventually, they make it to a well-lit thoroughfare and sit at a bus stop to wait. Few words are exchanged; each is lost in their own thoughts. Suddenly, Tara straightens and touches both temples.

"What?" asks an alarmed Siyabonga.

Quiet!

What is it?

They are here.

Weapons?

Many.

[475]

Now Siyabonga sees shadowy figures moving in the distance. *What do we do?* he asks nervously.

Wait for the bus. Tara is determined to avoid using her powers, but if the bus does not soon arrive, she may have no choice. As usual, it is already behind schedule. Her hump now lights up with alarming sensations, and she tenses, her power on alert, as taut as a finger poised on a trigger.

With terrifying suddenness, a burst of gunfire echoes down the street. The shooting comes in spurts, followed by cries of pain and shouting. Sorting a host of confusing inputs, Tara finally realizes the shots are not aimed at her and Siyabonga. Evidently, it is some sort of gang war; turf, or drugs, or revenge, or all together seem to be the causes. To the great relief of Tara and Siyabonga, the shooting stops just as the bus pulls up to the bench. They quickly board and rush to sit in a vacant rear seat.

That was close, says Siyabonga.

Yes. Thankfully, I did not have to use my powers. That is for Thandolwethu's memory.

And my mother's, adds Siyabonga.

Truly spoken.

"We are safe. Our baby is safe," says Siyabonga aloud.

"Not yet. Not at all."

"What do you mean?"

Now, none of us are safe, no matter where we go.

With these cautionary words, the unusual pair sit back and contemplate whatever the future will bring. Cape Town awaits.

~ Night and Day ~

Cape Town is a busy city, and Tara finds it necessary to mute the raucous crowds and sputtering traffic bombarding her hump. By partially closing the damper, she is able to extinguish the most flammable of sparks that threaten to ignite her weary brain. The city oozes with ogling white tourists and preening black scammers grinning ivory scams. Tara is now fully satiated with the heaviness of human folly, and seeks quiet seclusion in the soundproof bowels of a large hotel. Harmless hum of air conditioning supplants the tiresome screech of human limbic excess During the next few days, while Siyabonga is out in search of a visa (he is ensconced in an adjoining room) she has her meals delivered, all the while

[476]

longing for the company of her own kind. Altan does not appear, but has left her an account in a U.S. bank with ample funds for whatever she and Siyabonga might need. Now back in touch with her mother, Tara closely follows events in the States while luxuriating in this serene interlude.

It is while in the midst of such fleeting serenity that one day a call from the front desk intrudes.

"Yes?"

"Ms. Powers?"

"Yes."

"There is a woman in the lobby asking for you."

"Her name?"

A pause while the clerk evidently reads a note. "Her name is Busisine Okoro."

"Please tell her I am unavailable."

"I'm afraid she is quite insistent. Also, she has with her a young man in a wheelchair."

Tara sighs, and still holding the phone, flings open the air-tight compartments of her clairvoyant mind, and sees the handless Thato parked beside his mother, who impatiently waits for Tara to appear in the lobby with the anticipation of a crouching lioness stalking a gazelle. Tara briefly fantasizes about making both of them disappear and leave her in peace. However, this being impossible, she says into the phone, "I'll be right down." Throwing on an appropriate wrap, she treks downstairs, eschewing the elevator to give herself more time to gather her mental resources.

Three steps into the lobby, and Tara hears, "There be the demon!" shouted from the far side. The epithet "Demon! Demon! Demon!" echoes in her ears as she approaches the woman. In times such as this, Tara finds herself lapsing into a fervent desire that *Homo sapiens* simply vanish, so life on earth can get on with the natural process of living without the incessant demolition of peace by human emotional outbursts. Nevertheless, her heightened empathic neuronal structures forbid paying such a steep price for the joy of attaining a measure of tranquility.

"Demon woman!" shouts Busisine, mother of the unfortunate Thato, who slumps in a wheelchair next to her. "Demon woman, you put back Thato's hands and maleness! Put back what you take away!"

[477]

Tara looks at Thato and sees a mere shell of a person. This once-dominant, vigorous, violent Alpha is now but a pathetic shadow who gazes into her eyes with the dimness of a dying animal.

"Mrs. Okoro, I am not responsible for what happened to your son. I cannot put back what I did not take away."

"Demon! You mean you won't! What I do with him this way? He will die. Die 'cause of you! It be on you!"

By now, a crowd has gathered and the manager called.

"Madame," he addresses Busisine. "You must please leave the lobby. Discuss with this lady outside, or go somewhere else please."

While Busisine is berating him, Siyabonga suddenly appears, and Busisime immediately spots him, becoming further agitated. "Traitor!" she screams. "The demon's slave! Traitor!"

Slouched in his wheelchair, terrified of Tara's power, even Thato shows a spark of anger, but remains silent.

Siyabonga walks toward the screaming woman, pausing briefly at Tara's beckoning to surreptitiously accept a roll of proffered bills from behind her back. He boldly walks up to Busisine, speaking Afrikaans the entire way in a soothing voice. Somehow, he succeeds in quieting her, and while still talking, pushes Thato's wheelchair slowly through the lobby onto the sidewalk outside. Tara follows at a distance and listens to Siyabonga chatter in Afrikaans, eventually placating Busisime enough for her to retire from the battlefield, pushing Thato with one hand while holding a wad of two-hundred Rand notes given her by Siyabonga clutched in the other. After they disappear into the swarm of Cape Town's bustling masses, Tara and Siyabonga retire to her room and share a bottle of wine.

"Any luck on the visa front?" she asks.

"Not yet. Working on it."

"Need additional assistance?"

Siyabonga knows she means money. "Soon, I think. I'll let you know."

Siyabonga reads a certain level of sadness troubling Tara's mind. *Why so sad?*
I feel a sort of bittersweet melancholy.
For?
For my own kind.

[478]

Siyabonga, wounded, declares aloud. "I'm only an intermediate, but I'm here for you."

"Yes, and I am grateful. But, being constantly surrounded by humans is a grind. Those that are not outwardly violent inwardly seem to suffer perpetual conflict."

"Is it not the nature of things?"

"To a degree, but humans amplify the struggles with their incessant abstractions and narcissistic navel-gazing."

"Will we create a better world?"

"One would hope."

Siyabonga breaks into his wonderfully luminescent smile. "We will! For our child and all future children, we must!"

Tara, less placid than Siyabonga about the future, nods and changes the subject.

"Siyabonga, there is the issue of the FBI."

"What about them?"

"Even now, there is an agent watching us day and night."

"So? We have done nothing wrong. You have been exonerated by the South African police. What can they do?"

"In the name of national security, they can do much."

"Such as?"

"Set us up; kidnap us; imprison us; exile us; all sorts of things." She shudders. "Even experiment on us."

"But with your powers, that can't happen!"

"Siyabonga, a lion is no match for a man with a gun, but a man with a gun is no match for a hundred lions."

Siyabonga stares glumly at his empty glass.

"Have more wine," says Tara with a twinkle in her eyes. "There are more of us than just one."

Siyabonga gives a wan smile, then looks at Tara with a face configured to project serious intent.

"Tara, do you love me?"

She has been waiting for this. *Can you not read my mind?*

Only partially. Remember, I am a mere intermediate. Your depths are beyond my reach.

[479]

Love for a single individual to the exclusion of all others, human, non-human, or otherwise, is antithetical to our genetic make-up. Therefore, I love you to the same extent as my love of the whole.

But can't you have a preference of one over another?

Certainly, a preference for certain markings on a dog or certain personalities of a human is unavoidable. However, preference is not the same as irrational loyalty, uncritical servitude, fierce tribal identification, and so forth.

Siyabonga is flummoxed and so resorts to a joke. "But you love me as you do, with a preference for my markings?"

"Indeed I do. You have lovely markings."

With this, Siyabonga lifts his glass in toast to the rather tenuous preferential niche he has been placed. No matter what she says, he takes great comfort and joy in the fact she carries their child.

And what kind of child will it be? he carelessly wonders.

Tara, always alert, does not let the unintentionally public thought pass.

"He or she will be wondrous!"

~ Breakaway ~

Two weeks pass, and Tara can in good conscience no longer delay her return to the States. Siyabonga is near to success in obtaining a visa, but is still tangled in last minute red tape. Even after greasing palms, final approval may be weeks away. Consequently, Tara feels a vague disappointment that he will not join her, but her thoughts are focused quite strongly on the child growing in her womb.

Will he or she truly be wondrous? she ponders. *It seems our powers incrementally increase with every new generation. Will this child be more powerful than me, as I am more powerful than mother? Is there a point at which too much power becomes unsustainable? If empathy is diminished even a whit, and power is increased a whit, will a cataclysm ensue? Ah! Such questions must be in the "we'll see" category!*

~

As Tara makes her affectionate farewells to Siyabonga and boards the plane, she is aware an FBI agent shadows her, evidently with no concern for concealment, or even subtlety. She reads his mind, but finds little more than an unaware automaton doing his duty without knowing

[480]

why or what it is about. Tara reviews the options her powers give her over humans, yet, in the end, how feeble they become when actually exercised! For instance, she can make this agent disappear from his seat, thereby eliminating one troublesome presence, but creating chaos on the plane and initiating a dozen more agents to take his place. Thus it will be for many generations, her kind isolated in a sea of humans. *It seems incumbent on us,* she thinks, *not to make them physically disappear, but replace them in positions of power, where power seems the only force humans are inclined to submit. In other words, use our powers to peacefully grasp the reins of government and industry, not dissociate the innumerable cogs that grease their wheels. After all,* Homo sapiens *gained dominance not by slaughtering their hominin competitors, but by cerebral cunning. It behooves us to move stealthily among humans and use our powers to gradually take over their decision-making positions. Ah! But sooner or later, they will catch on, and then. . . .*

Tara increasingly turns to these musings when alone. Certainly, such conundrums were raised by her mentors and tutors during the years of education, but real-world experience has brought their ideas back to the forefront. It seems to her that efforts to stop unnecessary pain only shifts the suffering rather than eliminating it. She is more convinced than ever that *Homo sapiens* are a lost cause, and that the only hope for the planet is their extinction. But there is the rub. . . .

Plagued by these nettlesome thoughts during long and dreary layovers, her musings are finally interrupted by the plane's approach to San Francisco International Airport. Tara sets aside her existential meanderings and renews her frustration with the primitive state of aeronautical engineering and its underlying crude physics which have given rise to the design of the lumbering plane as it descends. After passing through customs, Tara is happily reunited with Pythia and Jared, now fully recovered. Pythia's first telepathic words are, *We are being followed.* Tara responds with, *Likewise.* With many hugs and greetings exchanged, Jared drives them to the mansion where Lady Oracle and Sy await. On the way, Tara bombards her mother with questions, but Pythia is evasive, her unspoken hesitancy directed pointedly at the unsuspecting Jared.

Is there a problem with Jared? asks an alarmed Tara.

Yes.

An informer?

[481]

No. We'll talk later.

With this brief exchange, Tara must be satisfied, but she does feel somewhat relieved.

Upon arriving at the familiar Victorian mansion, Tara greets Lady Oracle and Sy, unpacks, and joins the group downstairs. She spends a great deal of time reporting to the group about her South African experience with gangs, Siyabonga, her pregnancy, and a host of other matters. Questions fly, and the time approaches one o'clock in the morning. While involved in this lengthy discussion, Tara periodically scans Jared's mind and encounters a troubling pattern of conflicting emotions and a deep well of depression. Although his thoughts are disordered and disorienting, he cannot mask the bottomless pain originating from somewhere beyond her reach. This insight is certainly concerning, but to her great relief there are no signs of betrayal or diminished love for Pythia or herself. With these ruminations, she goes to bed and falls into a deep sleep.

Dreams.

~

It is centuries in the future. Although long dead, Tara, ghostlike, sweeps across the planet observing the conditions below. By now, her kind control the mechanisms of global power. Intermediates are ubiquitous, and pockets of *Homo sapiens* still exist in isolated communities. War has become obsolete, and the overall world population is greatly diminished, relieving the immense pressure that had so threatened the environment. Slowly, the natural world and its diverse inhabitants are recovering. Religions are essentially non-existent but for the few *Homo sapiens* still practicing their rituals. Global government is ruled by Tara's descendants by means of a complex web of telepathic and clairvoyant communication. Technology is minimal, and artificial intelligence has given way to organic, carbon-based cognitive advancements. Crime is reduced to manageable limits. To Tara, all her efforts have borne fruit, and as she soars above this utopia, her heart is full of joy.

However, a sudden darkness spreads across the globe, and the scene dramatically changes. Instead of a utopian zeitgeist, the world is controlled by a dictatorial cabal of the most powerful of Tara's descendants. Intermediates are treated as mentally deficient, and *Homo sapiens* are relegated to a slave class, their numbers kept artificially high. Interbreeding is outlawed and its precepts strictly enforced. Technology is

[482]

everywhere and ruthlessly used to maintain the status quo, releasing the new ruling class to use their extraordinary mental powers for increasingly debased sensual pleasures. The natural world is reduced to a private garden cultivated only by the most powerful. Mass extinctions have accelerated and the planet is cloaked in despair and desolation. War is a thing of the past, and crime is not tolerated. With specter of this horrific future, Tara awakens in a panicked sweat.

Which is it to be? she wonders.

Unable to get back to sleep, she goes downstairs and finds Lady Oracle sipping tea, as if waiting for Tara to show up.

"Nightmare?" she asks.

"Sort of."

"Your mind is troubled," says Lady Oracle as a statement of fact.

"Yes."

"About?"

"The old story—suffering. Our future. Their future."

Lady Oracle assumes a severe face. "All of these issues are complex and intrinsically unknowable. Do you have the answers?"

"No. Do you?"

"Unknowable is unknowable."

"What *do* we know?"

"Your unborn child must be protected."

"True, but what kind of world will he or she be born into? To be different is to suffer."

"To be different is the future."

"But what future?"

Lady Oracle frowns. "Unknowable."

Tara is piqued by her rather cold attitude. She changes tack.

"Tell me about father's problem."

"Jared is facing a crisis."

"How so?"

"He is deeply depressed, sees himself as a useless appendage of Pythia. We are all worried."

"Is he still working?"

"Yes, but he has given up his research, and his classes have been cut. Also, the FBI continues to harass. Rumors among his colleagues are affecting his career, but even his career he sees as a sham. Our knowledge

[483]

is so far beyond his comprehension, he feels doubly useless, both in his personal life and his professional life."

"Suicidal?"

"Yes."

Tara shakes her head. "Another example of our failure to minimize suffering. In fact, it seems the more we try to reduce it, the more we cause."

"Is this what is troubling you?"

"Among other things."

Lady Oracle sighs. "Tara, you are losing sight of the larger picture. If *Homo sapiens* are not replaced, the amount of suffering and destruction will be incalculable . . . not just to humans, but to all life on Earth."

"Yes, of course I understand that."

"Yet you continue to question."

"Yes."

Lady Oracle smoothes the wrinkles in the tablecloth. "I cannot comfort you. The precipice on which you stand is fragile."

Tara stares intently into Lady Oracle's eyes. "Who are you, really?"

"I am you."

"Nonsense."

"That is the only answer you will get."

"Will this child have powers beyond mine?"

"I do not know. Time will tell."

"And if it does have greater powers, who is to control it?"

Lady Oracle smiles. "Did you learn nothing during your education?"

"Apparently not. Who will control the child?"

"The child itself."

~ Jared Paine Makes A Decision ~

Since the assault in Berkeley when Pythia dissociated the mugger, Jared has struggled with his sanity. Watching the man disappear, he felt a deep connection to the attacker and a disturbing disconnect from Pythia. Although the man intended to kill him, Jared cannot help feeling a closer kinship to him, and an increasingly insurmountable distance from the mother of his child. This feeling has grown over time, in spite of his best efforts to repress it. All his insecurities about the value of his work, his manhood, his character, have been shattered. For a time, his love of Pythia and fascination for her superior knowledge blinded him, and he could cope with his human insignificance compared to the super-race of which Pythia is a member. But that awful evening, when he depended upon Pythia to save his skin, the attack stripped his last vestige of self-worth. *I'm little more than a chimpanzee to her,* he thinks. *A clever primate who is useful experimentally, but with no real purpose in a world rapidly on a path to the extinction of my own species.*

Still deeply in love with Pythia (as a dog to its master, he thinks), and tied by parent-child genetics to his daughter Tara (to whom he also considers himself inferior), Jared sees no way forward. His only question is whether to tell everything to the FBI in exchange for assurances Pythia, Tara, and the others be left alone. He has been as careful as possible to build an impenetrable wall around these feelings. Now, he knows it will be impossible to continue keeping such thoughts secret from their prying minds much longer.

Many times, he had picked up the phone to call Lance Romellion, then opted out at the last minute. Now, on a particularly bright, sunny day, he is resolved to act. With no surviving parents, no siblings, and an alien species as his only child, he is at peace with his decision. He reaches for his recorder, clicks it on, and begins describing the long and fantastic history of his relationship with Pythia and her kind. After Professor Jared Paine unburdens his heart, he leaves his office, and many hours later drives his car into a sheer rock wall a few miles from the cave where he watched his daughter disappear as a toddler and return years later as a "monster".

~

UC Berkeley is the first to be officially notified of Doctor Paine's death. Next of kin are contacted, including a distant uncle, but it is a fellow professor who alerts the school to contact Pythia Powers. Local authorities suspect suicide, so the professor's recorded message is turned over to the authorities. Within hours, Agent Romellion is at the morgue. As he stares down at the remains, a host of questions present themselves, but fortunately, to Romellion, many of those questions have been answered just in time. His next stop is a certain Victorian style mansion in San Francisco.

Chapter 40: On the Run

~ Magic, Mysticism, and Mystery ~

When Lance Romellion and two fellow agents arrive at the top of the hill where they intend to confront a group of "alien cultists", as described by some smart-ass in an internal memo, they find no trace of the Victorian house they have come to visit. An empty lot greets their astonished eyes. Where once stood a magnificent mansion, now a barren field is spread before them, dotted by a few plastic grocery bags skittering about in the San Francisco wind.

Romellion, armed with information as yet unknown to the other agents, exclaims in disbelief, "A house existed at this spot yesterday! Also, there were elaborate gardens and a pond. Now . . . nothing. He was telling the truth."

"Who?" asks Agent Aquilar.

"Never mind," replies Romellion with a dismissive wave.

"You sure this is the right address?" asks Agent Chandler.

Romellion's mind is spinning. "Of course!" he snaps. "It's been under surveillance for weeks."

"Where's the agent on duty last night?" asks Aquilar.

"Budget cuts," replies Lance through gritted teeth. "He was to knock off at midnight unless there was any unusual activity. No such report was received. The agent is probably home sleeping like a baby. Still, better have the office call him just to make sure he continues to walk the Earth."

"How can an entire house disappear in a few hours?" asks Chandler incredulously. "This must be the wrong address."

"No, goddamn it!" cries Lance. "This is the correct address, and I think I know how this happened."

"How?"

Lance again waves his hand in angry dismissal. "Not now. The explanation is a long one, and a fantastic one. It is a story hardly to be believed, but here we are."

[486]

He straightens and barks out orders. "You two canvas the area. Talk with the neighbors. Take careful notes of what any other witnesses say. I'll send a car back here to collect both of you later. Also, search the grounds for any evidence—papers, books, writings, receipts, objects, anything—before the wind gets to them. Call if you have questions or find something that needs immediate attention. Right now, I have a few calls to make. I think we can finally get Quantico interested in this. We're going to need more resources."

Lance heads back to the car, mumbling, "*God* knows if they'll believe me—or him."

On the way back to his office, the long narrative of Professor Paine scrolls through Romellion's mind. The professor's story is fantastic, hardly believable, and knowing his superiors, suicide will speak against its veracity. On the other hand, being a physics professor at Berkeley might help. As for himself, Lance Romellion is fully prepared to believe every word of Professor Paine's incredible story, suicide or no suicide. In fact, to Lance, that desperate act adds credence to Paine's claims. After all, Lance himself has seen evidence supporting such a tale, including his own contact with the strange young woman at the cave. Oddly, the full implication of Paine's account—if true—is obscured by the immediacy of the chase. For a long time, Romellion has not questioned the fact that his quarry are bad people whose goal is to destroy humanity. In his heart, he is inclined to see them as terrorists, but whether they are human or not, niggling, uncomfortable doubts have crept into his calculations.

~

Lance spends the next few weeks frantically haranguing FBI headquarters, alerting them to the danger of these "Magician Terrorists" as he has informally labeled the case. Much to his chagrin, Romellion's warnings are pigeonholed, until one day, through sheer tenacity, he succeeds in piquing the interest of an assistant director of the Counterterrorism Division of the National Security Branch. Lance is directed to fly to Washington and meet with Assistant Director Walter Monroe. In the meantime, the disappearance of the mansion remains a mystery—no witnesses, no physical evidence, no evidence of demolition, nothing. Worse, the main persons of interest—Ms. Judith Ganbaatar, aka Lady Oracle, Mr. Sy Grafton, aka Scarecrow, Ms. Pythia Powers, Ms. Tara Powers, and unnamed others—have seemingly dropped off the face of the earth. Field agents in the State of Washington visited Ms. Ming-huà Powers and Mr. Matthew Weston, aka Zookeeper, on the island of their residence, but obtained no information as to the whereabouts of any person of interest.

"Helen!" Lance calls his secretary into his office. "I'm leaving for Washington D.C. in three days. Collect every scrap of evidence on the Magician Terrorists case. Make copies of everything, including tapes, notes, pictures . . . you get it?"

"Yes, but it'll take time."

"Fine, make time. Just get it done and give me the copies each day so I can organize them as we go."

"Can do, but—"

"No buts, Helen. Do it."

After she leaves, Lance Romellion begins to ponder the thorny issue of how he will make a formal presentation of the case. From what angle should he approach the interpretation of the evidence? Usually, all possible theories are laid out and the available clues are categorized to isolate the most likely candidate. But here, to even suggest supernatural capabilities, new species, or alien interference, would incite deep skepticism, if not derision. He remembers how Professor Paine pointed out in his last message that, "Extraordinary claims require extraordinary evidence." The question in Romellion's mind is whether the evidence in his possession will be extraordinary enough to overcome more mundane, and certainly more rational explanations.

God damn it, it is! he thinks.

But this resolution is weakened by frustrating doubts that linger on the far periphery of a standard criminal case. Doubts he cannot put his finger on. Perhaps his hesitation arises from the words of that young woman at the cave when she said, "Remember my words."

Yes, those words. . . .

~ The Meeting ~

Assistant Director Walter Monroe sits across from Lance Romellion, patiently waiting for the California field agent to organize his presentation materials in neat stacks. Words of greeting have already been exchanged, and during this brief period of small talk, Lance now recollects meeting Monroe and his granddaughter at an FBI social in San Francisco a few years earlier. After politely mentioning this tidbit, he launches into his presentation. Monroe has a somewhat bemused expression on his face. Arms extended outward and resting on the table, fingers entwined, he observes with an experienced eye the rather grim demeanor of Romellion. Already in possession of unverified reports describing mysterious disappearances, bizarre maimings, missing bodies, and preposterous eye-witness testimony, Monroe admits the case contains an unusual mixture of incidents rife with curious, inexplicable details. Evidently, credible witnesses have observed these fantastic events, and even more peculiar, swear they have been perpetrated by female hunchbacks. A sketchy and highly suspect video even exists of one of these alleged incidents. Monroe's morning has been a long slog through boring financial reports and expense accounts, so he is ready for a break, especially to learn more about such a bizarre case. He is not, however, quite prepared for what is to come.

~

"A house vanishing in thin air!" cries Walter when Romellion reaches the end of his presentation with the introduction of this last absurdity.

To this point, Monroe has listened in silence to outrageous reports of people's arms, legs, and heads simply disappearing, leaving no trace of blood or any other fluids associated with such butchery. Even entire bodies supposedly vanished in front of witnesses. Worse, these events have taken place in a wide diversity of seemingly random locations—San Francisco, Berkeley, Baltimore, Tijuana, even including spotty reports out of South Africa. Monroe has patiently listened to Romellion describe the one important thread that connects them all, which is the presence of female hunchbacks. Romellion has placed great importance on the Jared Paine suicide tapes, but Monroe's unspoken reaction is to doubt their veracity, the contents striking him as being narrated by an individual suffering from clinical depression, or perhaps a schizophrenic spouting delusional fantasies. But an entire house disappearing? This seems a step too far. After a series of clarifying inquiries, Monroe raises the point Lance Romellion has been dreading.

"What is your theory of the case?"

Lance hesitates for a moment, then plunges into the deep water.

"I believe there are only three possibilities. First, these people are the earliest individuals of an advanced species. Second, they are aliens. Third, they are humans being manipulated by aliens."

Monroe sits back, an enigmatic smile fluttering on his lips, but his eyes aflame with an intensely critical glare.

"In other words, you have no rational theory," he says.

"These incidents have no rational explanation," replies Romellion. "Rational, at least, as I take your meaning of the word."

"Does not the moniker you have given this case—Magical Terrorists—denote a rational explanation, which is simple terrorism?"

"Not really."

Monroe leans forward. "I mean, Agent Romellion, is there a fourth theory? One that can explain these incidents in a manner more suited to the FBI than to NASA or Isaac Asimov?"

"I have tried but cannot find a realistic explanation without the three options I have laid out for you."

"I suggest you come up with one. I am not about to authorize additional resources for such outlandish theories."

"Director Monroe, we have explored more conventional theories such as magic, mirrors, hypnosis, mass hypnosis, hysteria, mass hysteria, drugs, and so forth. None of them fit."

Monroe pounces. "Drugs! There you are! How about the use of hallucinogens by these terrorists to cause a distorted view of reality planted in the minds of victims and witnesses?"

"Doesn't work. Verifiably armless, legless, headless men who hours earlier possessed a full complement of limbs are not hallucinations. Certainly that is not due to mass hypnosis. Same with the disappearing house. All of these reports have been confirmed numerous times by objective investigators."

Director Monroe narrows his eyes but does not speak right away. Agent Romellion folds his hands and respectfully waits.

"All right, Lance, this is what I want you to do. First, develop some plausible theory not involving this supernatural crap. With that, I can reasonably justify embedding the more far-out ideas as alternate possibilities. That should be enough to get you a few additional resources. Call me directly if you obtain further information on these . . . magical terrorists. I don't care how much you have to stretch a rational theory so it can at least be viewed as having some validity, especially if you toss in some bullshit like Chinese or Russian secret experimental programs. Put it all in a formal request specifying what additional resources you require so we can start processing it. Just do it. Kapish?"

"Yeah."

"When can you get it to me?"

"By tomorrow afternoon."

"Good. Once I receive it and confirm it's kosher, I'll approve the request."

~

Although not entirely satisfied with the interview, Lance is at least grateful to receive additional aid. In spite of this, he is disappointed in Monroe's attitude and concludes that the director and others at the top will not take the actual threat seriously, preferring to dismiss any "far-out" hypotheticals in favor of a more conventional theory which, no doubt, will lead nowhere. If the reports about the incredible power of these people (or whatever they are) pan out, Lance fears they will be too formidable for half-measures, and any counterstrike by the FBI will be too late. Burdened by such misgivings, he returns to California more determined than ever to expose whatever evil is afoot.

~

Meanwhile, Lance Romellion would be surprised to learn that Walter Monroe is far more inclined to take his "far-out" theories seriously than he is willing to openly convey. Monroe is aware that Romellion is a capable and experienced field agent with a stellar record. Although unwilling to outwardly express sympathy for Lance's "crap" theories, he is by nature prone to give them more consideration than would his colleagues, and, in fact, considers them quite within the realm of possibility. As a boy, Monroe had always been fascinated by science fiction novels and reports of alien visitations. When in college, he dabbled in astrophysics, and took seriously credible reports of unidentified flying objects. Now, even as a mature man and a highly respected director of FBI, these interests have never left him. Nonetheless, maturity has made him cautious, and he has made it a policy to keep these youthful interests private. Now in his sixties, with an imposing mane of silver hair and a lanky frame of six-foot-three-inches, he thinks this case might contain implications far more important than all others he has encountered combined. His boyhood enthusiasms have lain dormant like dry tinder awaiting a spark. From the reports given him by Lance Romellion, he believes this spellbinding case might provide that spark, but one, he fears, that has the frightening potential to erupt into an existential conflagration. However, always circumspect, his instincts tell him to proceed extremely carefully, to remain openly skeptical, and to stay on top of developments every step of the way. Whether these individuals are truly epic evolutionary advancements or alien-directed agents, he fully intends to find a way to establish communication, enlist them as allies if possible, or, at least, to signal cooperation and obtain some benefit to the country from their astonishing capabilities should the reports turn out to be true.

Although his natural bias is inclined toward peaceful, mutually beneficial interaction, Monroe is fully prepared to use whatever force is necessary to protect national security. In the meantime, he will keep Agent Romellion on a relatively long leash, letting him go far afield to pursue his theories with the tenacious vigor Lance's reputation is built upon. Walter Monroe is happy to play the Hollywood version of a wooden-headed, clueless boss.

Walter lives alone in an unassuming house in an unassuming neighborhood in an unassuming suburb of Falls Church. A widower, his daily routine is habitual; any deviation from said routine leads to frustration and no small amount of dissembling. When he returns home the evening after meeting Romellion, he changes into comfortable clothes, pulls on warm slippers, mixes a vodka tonic, settles in his old recliner, and nurses his drink while ruminating on the day. This evening he has taken the unusual step of bringing home a file containing the more interesting sections of Romellion's report. As he shuffles through the papers and photographs, his fascination increases with every piece of evidence that reveals impossible events and the curious circumstances that surround them. It quickly dawns on him that his earlier fears are confirmed, and that the stakes here are of the highest order. Even so, a jolt of excitement runs through his body at the implications.

An alien invasion seems utterly absurd, but there is something going on here that is more . . . insidious? . . . bizarre? . . . whatever it is, it certainly appears to be happening . . . against all reason, it is genuinely happening. Certainly, the evidence does not point to some highly organized, massive operation by aliens, their agents, or any other such entities. Chinese or Russian secret operations are likewise ridiculous. Why are these female hunchbacks always present at the scene of such grimy little crimes involving drug addicts, gangs, and assorted thugs? Surely, this is no grand attack on humanity. No, definitely something more subtle is going on . . . something more interesting . . . something perhaps even more disturbing.

Suddenly, Walter's plump tabby hisses loudly and races across the floor in a frenzied panic, disappearing under the couch. Startled, Walter scans the room but sees no cause for such extreme behavior.

"What's wrong, Molly?" he says.

Being an experienced law enforcement officer, Walter always pays attention to his pets. Ignore your barking dog or inexplicably skittish cat at your peril.

"Molly, it's okay. Come on out, kitty."

The cat does not appear, so Walter sighs and checks all the rooms and windows in the house.

Everything appears normal.

Satisfied nothing is amiss, he returns to his chair, puts the file back on his lap, opens it and starts to read, but his concentration is interrupted by a female voice floating from across the room.

"You are right to listen to Molly."

"Who are you?" he blurts stupidly as he stares at a beautiful young woman sitting quite contentedly on one of his armchairs.

"I am who you will make of me."

Walter stands and takes a step forward, but *her* powerful presence causes him to stop. Feeling awkward and foolish, the file dangling in his hand, he struggles to gather his thoughts.

Finally, he manages to say, "I don't know you."

"Yes, you do."

"No. Who are you? Why are you here?"

She makes a graceful gesture for him to return to his seat, and against his own inclination, obeys *her* will.

"Okay," he says after sitting. "Who are you?"

"One who cares for you, and who also cares for those you pursue."

"I don't understand."

Her eyes focus on the file now on his lap.

Walter's eyes widen, reflecting a dawning comprehension.

[493]

"You are with them?"

"Them?"

"Yes. The hunchbacks."

"I am with all life on Earth."

Normally, such words would elicit his contempt for their affectation, but somehow the manner in which *she* says them is absolutely sincere, and peculiarly intimidating. His only defense is to turn to sarcasm.

"That's a tall order. Does that include mosquitoes?"

"As a mosquito is to you, you are a mosquito to others."

This response takes him aback, but it also alerts him to the uniquely challenging nature this woman presents. He suspects one of two possibilities: either his drink has been drugged, or he is asleep and dreaming. In either case, he'll play along.

"Am I a mosquito to you?"

"You are less than a mosquito and more than a human to me."

Walter's brain feels sluggish, but *her* answer carries a sting that stimulates him.

"You look like a human to me," he says. "In fact, you are quite a beautiful human."

"And you are an ugly mosquito."

Walter's face flushes red as he remembers the photographs in Romellion's file of all those lost limbs. "Are you going to swat me?"

"Is not that what you would do to a mosquito?"

"I'm not a mosquito," he says, aware how weak he sounds.

"Yet, you view many of your fellow humans as mosquitoes to be swatted. Is that not true?"

"No." Another weak response.

"Then why pursue those who are superior to you?"

Walter's expression flashes momentary fear, but then is quickly controlled. "You're one of them, aren't you?"

"Them?"

Violating one of his unspoken rules governing the need for calm, self-control at all times, he cries, "The hunchbacks! The aliens! . . . or whatever they are! You're one of them!"

The young woman stands and turns around. "Do you see a hunched back?"

Walter is momentarily speechless. *She* sits back down and crosses *her* legs, waiting.

"But," stutters Walter. "Ahhh, I mean . . . well . . . you must be directing them. Where are you from? Who are you?"

She stares at him unblinking but does not speak.

"I know. I know what you want. You want me to drop this investigation. Well, your presence here has achieved the opposite. If you consider me . . . or humans . . . the same as mosquitoes, then that tells me you are the ones that need to be swatted!"

She smiles in a manner that makes him squirm.

"Well?" he says.

She does not respond.

"Are you going to just sit there? You must have come here for a reason. We will hunt you down, whoever you are."

Molly suddenly appears from under the couch and jumps on the visitor's lap, purring loudly. The young woman strokes the cat while staring at Walter in a manner that makes him regret his aggressive attitude. His tone softens.

"How you got in here, I don't know. What your goal is, I don't know. If you are some sort of superior being with superior powers, I'm listening. You will find I am not unreasonable. Can we not talk about this in a rational way and find some common ground? I'm willing if you are."

She is gone.

Molly remains on the empty chair.

Walter is stunned.

His racing thoughts a tangled jumble.

"Bloody hell!" he exclaims.

Chapter 41: Shelter from the Storm

~ Oasis ~

By the time Romellion has finished his meeting with Monroe in Washington, every member of the "Magician Terrorists" have already arrived at an exceptionally isolated location in Mongolia. The route taken is one not available to *Homo sapiens*, at least not in any spacetime accessible to them. Unfettered by the limited capacity of humans to connect with dimensional pathways, the extraordinary group had earlier returned to the California desert where the starting point of their journey waited quietly in a familiar cave. Before departing the city, anxious to leave behind no trace of their existence, they left an empty lot where once stood a lovely San Francisco mansion. Once gathered at the cave entrance, the same beautiful young woman who later was to pay a spectral visit to Walter Monroe guided them to a side tunnel that connected to the Mongolian desert. Tara, unhappy that Siyabonga did not obtain a visa in time to join them, left instructions for him to follow later. Just before plunging into the black tunnel, Lady Oracle said to Tara, "Be prepared to meet a host of those who went before you."

"Yes, dear," added Pythia. "If you listen, their words will prove to be very instructive."

~

Now they are all crowded in a small, dark room with no windows. Sy turns on his flashlight and they find themselves facing a massive iron door. With surprising ease, Lady Oracle pushes it open, and they walk single-file into another room where a ladder leads upward to a trap door in the ceiling. Pythia is the first up the ladder, followed by the others. When they have all emerged, they are standing in yet another room, this one above ground with ample windows. It appears to be a bedroom nicely decorated with Chinese furniture, expensive porcelains, and magnificent scrolls. Tara and Pythia both comment on the welcome brightness, and Sy immediately breaks into a lively jig.

[496]

"At last!" he exclaims. "I will again see my dead brother, who is even crazier than me!"

Lady Oracle nods. "We will all see our lost friends soon enough."

She leads them out of the bedroom into a large foyer.

"Here is where the Precious Object once sat," she says reverently. "Your ancestors sacrificed much to get this far. Bai Meiying, John Powers, Child of Buddha, my own beloved Buandelgereen—"

"Don't forget Feng Shiren!" cries Sy, hopping from one foot to the other.

"Of course. He and so many others."

"I've read so much about them from the writings of Michael Powers," says Tara.

"Yes, dear," says Pythia. "You have met them only through simulations and the written word. Here, it will be different."

"Let us get settled," says Lady Oracle. "Queequeg, Mongol descendant of Ishmael, the famous host of your ancestor John Powers and his little group of pilgrims—truly strange names—will see you to your rooms."

Even as she utters these words, Queequeg enters and bows stiffly to the assembled group. He is an old man garbed in traditional clothes with a long wispy beard, leathery face and a stooped bearing, almost resembling a hunchback in appearance. He speaks in a high-pitched, mesmerizingly soprano voice. "I trust, as your host for the time you spend at this modest retreat, I will do honor to my revered great-grandfather. This gathering is an unexpected pleasure, and those from the past who dwell here are pleased to have your company."

With these welcoming words, the group is shown around the compound, complete with dormitories, a cafeteria, a library, temples, meditation rooms, and assorted other structures, all constructed in Ming Dynasty architectural style. Afterward, they are given the afternoon to settle into their accommodations. Tara and Pythia, both without their mates, soon find each other in the empty cafeteria sipping tea which Queequeg had prepared earlier in anticipation of supper.

"You have been here before, mother?" asks Tara.

"No, but I have heard so much about it. Clearly, the situation in the world requires our temporary absence until things cool down."

Pythia glances at Tara's stomach. "How is the pregnancy?"

[497]

"All seems well. I've had a chance to walk around the grounds. It is beautiful here. And those mountains surrounding us! Gorgeous!"

Pythia nods. "Yes. The Flaming Cliffs. One of the many reasons my mentors told me the planet must be saved." Her eyes gaze into the distance and speaks as if to herself. "So many stories about the old days, the war, our great grandparents . . . have you been visited by any of their specters?"

"No. And you?"

"Not yet. They are quiet. Perhaps tomorrow."

Mother and daughter, comfortable in each other's presence, sip their tea in silent contentment.

Soon, Sy comes tripping in. He spots the women, rushes up to their table, swings his leg over the back of an empty chair, and plops down.

"Tea?" asks Pythia.

He waves his hand. "No, no! Coffee! Great little invention of humans! I'll wait for breakfast." Sy casts his eyes toward the kitchen. "Our Mongol friend with the strange name is hard at work. You two hungry?"

Both women shrug. "A bit," says Tara.

"Have to feed that baby," he says. "We need to speed up this changing of the guard business."

"Sy," says Pythia. "Have you come across any specters yet?"

He slumps dramatically. "No, but I'm anxious."

"Feng Shiren?"

"Indeed. Soul of my soul. His job was much harder than mine."

"How so?" asks Tara.

"He had to deal with some of the very first of your kind." His face darkens. "Although there were a lot of intermediates then, and even before then, unfortunately they . . . ah! . . . forget it. Anyway, Feng Shiren had to do his job in the middle of a war protecting his charges while ignorant humans erroneously ascribed schizophrenia to many of those early mutational anomalies." He shudders. "Imagine."

"It seems hard enough now," says Tara. "By the way, Sy, how many intermediates are out there?"

Again, his face darkens. "More than you can guess. Some have been causing problems for a very very long time. Mistakes were made. Unfortunately, even today, some are taking the wrong path."

"How so?"

"Using their nascent power for bad purposes, just as the earlier ones did."

Tara's eyes widen. "I did not know there were, and are, so many. Did you, mother?"

Pythia looks uncomfortable. *Yes, but those errors are being corrected,* she says telepathically. *That is why you must take care of this baby.*

True mother, but you also are still young enough to have more babies.

Question is to find a mate. We'll see.

Do you miss father much?

Yes. At heart he was a good human.

Sy jumps in with a verbal burst of passion. "This is why it is essential you both procreate more! Your babies must increase in numbers, the more there are, the more powerful each generation becomes. They will perfect the tools necessary to expand and control their burgeoning powers. Problem is all the trouble caused by intermediates, past and present. Rogue intermediates are worse than *Homo sapiens*!"

"So, we are outnumbered by intermediates?" asks Tara.

"Yes."

Lady Oracle arrives to catch the tail end of the conversation.

"Speaking of intermediates," she says. "Siyabonga is on his way."

This news is received by Tara with mixed feelings. Lady Oracle immediately picks up on her subdued response.

"You are not happy?"

"Yes. I like Siyabonga, and he will be a good mate in future, both in procreating and in being a good father, even to those children who turn out far more powerful than he. Certainly, not all intermediates are bad."

"Far from it."

"I just hope this baby works out."

"Why wouldn't it?" asks Pythia, a bit alarmed.

"Well," ponders Tara. "Jared, my own father, was not an intermediate. I'm fairly sure Grandfather Zookeeper is not an intermediate. What will be the result of the mixing of my genes and those of an intermediate?"

"We will see," says Lady Oracle.

"Will this child be more powerful even that I?" asks Tara.

[499]

"We will see."

"I'm a little worried."

"I know," replies Lady Oracle.

"The child will be fine," adds Pythia. "As you know, my clairvoyant power is one of my strong points, and I foresee . . . struggle, but happiness as well."

"What if it's a freak?" insists Tara.

Lady Oracle takes her hánd and gives it a gentle squeeze. "We will see. Right now, your job is to make sure this child is born healthy."

After listening to this conversation, Sy's face becomes even more gloomy than before. Now, he can hold it no longer.

"True! True! The health of this child is most important! The future is in doubt even as we speak. Look around! We are holed up in the same isolated compound where our ancestors had to hide over a century ago. Tara, Pythia, both of you are in a terribly tenuous position. If things go wrong, which they easily can, then there is no hope. Every one of your kind that is born is a crucial step to the viability of this new species. Humans are far from stupid, and their irrational fears and superstitions make them dangerous indeed. Our only hope lies with your ability to procreate and use your powers wisely."

He sighs deeply and continues. "Right now, while we hide here in the safety of this oasis, there are intermediates out there causing trouble, creating chaos, manipulating humans to perform horrendous acts. The only solution is to have more babies with powers far greater than theirs, like you two. Pythia, Tara, you must concentrate on procreating, difficult as that may be. I understand suitable mates are problematic. Just look at Jared Paine for example. It was too much for him. But, at the same time, I see your mating with Siyabonga as a good thing. Yes, he is an intermediate, but one of the good kind rather than the bad. I, for one, look forward with great anticipation to the product of this union!"

Silence reigns as Sy's words sink in.

"Now," he says in a lighter tone. "Have breakfast, then go out and learn from the specters that have been awaiting your arrival."

~ Moving Among the Ghosts ~

After breakfast, mother and daughter go for a stroll around the grounds. They speak to each other via telepathy. It is apparent they are waiting for something to happen. Pythia describes the history of the compound, its walls, its buildings, iron doors, and a host of other topics to pass the time.

"Do you suppose they will communicate with us soon?" asks Tara.

"In their own time, dear," replies Pythia. "Specters will not be rushed. The world of shades is a strange one. As strange to us as we are to humans."

Just as Pythia finishes her thought, they hear a voice calling in the distance.

"Come to the tunnel building!"

"It's Sy," says Tara.

Simultaneously, they both receive the same message telepathically. *Come to the tunnel building!*

Rushing to the building, they pass through its elaborately carved Chinese door and see in the middle of the large foyer a wooden stand painted with red varnish. Upon the stand sits the Precious Object.

Tap. Tap. Tap.

A chill runs down Tara's back. She has heard about such taps coming from within the Precious Object. Her great-great-grandmother Child of Buddha could interpret them. But, to Tara, they are not only undecipherable, but their funereal cadence seem to foretell an ominous portent of disaster.

"That frightens me," says Tara.

No, dear, says Pythia in her head. *Take it from your mother. These taps are not ominous, they are just . . . a mystery.*

Both women stand motionless before the Precious Object and listen to the monotonous taps, neither knowing what they mean.

"I'm going to walk outside, mother," says Tara. "I feel a bit dizzy."

"Take it slow," cautions Pythia. "I'm going to stay here a while longer."

Tara steps out into the sunlight and strolls down the meandering paths of the compound, past Chinese-style pagodas and lovely dormitories, until she reaches the expansive garden area, where she spots Queequeg and a fellow Mongol digging around long rows of arbors heavily laden bean plants. She waves, but they do not notice, so she continues her leisurely excursion. Tara's thoughts flit from one topic to another, and she soon wearies of the disjointed montage.

I'll focus on one issue, she tells herself. *Will it be this child in my womb? Siyabonga's arrival? My powers, so dormant in this peaceful retreat, yet so insistent to be exercised? The surprising extent of so many intermediates?*

She decides to direct her attention to the imminent arrival of Siyabonga, but just as the image of his lovely African face smiles at her, a light breeze sweeps by the sleeve of her blouse, momentarily conferring the sensation of a person gently tugging at her arm. Just for an electrifying instant, her entire being feels wrapped in a cocoon of peace and well-being. The breeze sweeps on ahead, making the leaves of a nearby Sycamore tree flutter in excited recognition of its touch. There, the little breeze pauses, as if waiting.

Tara walks to the Sycamore and steps into the breeze as one might enter the refreshing cool of a light mist. Under those trembling leaves, shimmering in the sunlight stands Child of Buddha, great-great-grandmother of Tara.

The specter glimmers as if gathering energy to speak, and finally intones in a crystalline voice, "You cannot interpret the taps, child?"

"No, great-great-grandmother."

The specter seems to vibrate—perhaps a laugh? Tara surmises.

"I was merely an intermediate when I stayed here with our little group of pilgrims so long ago," says the specter. "Odd. All of us were odd. Yet, somehow I could understand the taps where the others could not."

"What did they say?"

"Oh, child, the secret my beloved comrades never understood—or myself either for the longest time—is that it says nothing."

"Nothing?"

Again, the rippling vibrations from which emerge the delicate voice.

"Nothing. It is a sort of drumhead which echoes mental waves that bang into it—a tuning fork, if you will, that emits its own resonance proportionate to the violence of the force of thoughts striking it."

"Whose thoughts?"

"Why, *God* and *Goddess* of course."

"*God* and *Goddess*?"

[502]

"Code words for beings far different."

"What do you mean?"

"Those that have been guiding the development of your kind have been embroiled in sharp differences of opinion; two camps advocating opposite approaches to saving this lovely Earth. Their heated disagreements, filtered through the rather violent brain structures and neural pathways of your great-great-grandfather John Powers, and your great grandfather Michael Powers, ultimately expressed themselves in the overstrained human part of their brains as an arguing *God* and *Goddess*. Unfortunately, those voices were misinterpreted by *Homo sapiens* psychiatrists (who have primitive clinical and diagnostic skills) as evidence of schizophrenia. Result: tragedy."

"Was Michael Powers an intermediate?"

"Of course. Same as his father John Powers, same as his wife Bai Meiying, and, of course, same as me. Now we are known as Progenitors."

"Are they with you in the land of shades?"

The specter falls silent, still rippling, but far gentler than before. When Tara looks up, she notices the leaves of the Sycamore fluttering less and less energetically as the breeze dies away.

"Yes, they are with me," comes the reply as if uttered from a great distance. "The others will come to you."

Tara hastens to ask, "Those who my ancestors designated as *God* and *Goddess* . . . will they come?"

Tara senses a response, but it is too faint to make out. After the air becomes still, she lingers, pondering Child of Buddha's words. It strikes her that the byzantine, confusing passages of Michael Powers's writings are beginning to make sense—his presumed schizophrenic voices now less baffling.

So, she thinks. *God and Goddess were really just the impassioned debates of two opposing viewpoints by those who are guiding us. And those viewpoints were misinterpreted and distorted into mythological conflicts by the emotional and mental abnormalities my ancestors were so encumbered by . . . and so ignorant of! They could not know what was happening to them. Such must have been the fate of early hominins when self-reflective consciousness and incipient language dawned upon their burgeoning brains. All heard voices for the first time. The voices savaged them by articulating anger, fear, revenge, guilt, love, hatred, and all the other personal trivialities that so enslaves them to this day. They are all schizophrenics!*

~ Pythia Lingers ~

While Tara is encountering Child of Buddha, Pythia has remained in the foyer where the Precious Object continues its enigmatic tapping. For whatever reason, these taps have so mesmerized her the idea of leaving is out of the question. Something she cannot ignore tells her to wait—for what, she does not know. Lady Oracle and Sy have popped in at different times, but her monosyllabic replies to their questions nudged them back out the door. Alone with the Precious Object, the taps continue monotonously, and Pythia's mind wanders. She revisits her years of education and has a sudden notion that greater engagement with humans is needed. To be more precise, a greater display of her powers should be directed against them. Why not simply disable the leaders of countries who oppress the people? Why have empathy for these supremely arrogant humans who, after all, are the ones ultimately responsible for making so many the victims of their despotism? In fact, the same goes for any human in a position of influence who uses their power to cause unnecessary suffering. Pythia is sympathetic to her daughter's more aggressive approach. With this thought, she notices the tapping increase in rapidity and intensity.

"Ah! So, my thoughts affect you?" she blurts.

Tap. Tap. Tap.

"What are you trying to tell me?"

Tap. Tap. Tap.

"Should we simply eliminate those that are most responsible for suffering in the world?"

Tap. Tap. Tap.

"Is that yes? Is that no?"

As she concentrates on listening more closely, she begins to perceive subtle variations in the rhythm and timbre of the taps. As others before her, the actual meaning behind the tapping eludes even her superior mental abilities. Beyond the fluctuations, she cannot find a way to probe deeper. Certainly, she has attempted to use her telepathic power from the beginning, but it has proven to be useless. When she tries, she encounters an opaque fog, impenetrable to her psychic efforts.

"What if we simply dissociate this problem human species altogether without waiting to dilute their genome out of existence?" she chides.

Now the tapping comes fast and furious.

TapTapTap. . . .

Another turn of the screw. "Why not simply cut to the chase and eliminate all humans in one fell swoop?"

Suddenly, the tapping ceases.

Silence.

Pythia feels a terrible weight pressing down upon her. "Well?"

Nothing.

"How am I to interpret what you are trying to tell me?" she insists.

To her surprise, a voice comes from behind.

"Your inquiries are unanswerable."

Pythia whirls around to see the familiar figure of the beautiful young woman whose appearances always result in more questions than answers.

"Then there are no answers?" she asks.

"Of course not."

"If that is the case, what does the tapping mean?"

"The meaning of the tapping lies in the questions, not the answers. To each who listens, a different sender inside does the tapping."

"Yes, I read my grandfather Michael Powers' manuscripts. To him, there were three inside."

"Yes. Those three were created . . . fashioned if you will, from the mind of Michael Powers. If one were to look inside now, they would be not be the same, they would be fashioned from a different mind."

"But isn't it useless if no answers are ever given?"

"You know better than that. Truth lies in doubt, not certainty."

"I don't know better than that! Though Heisenberg thought so, we know there is a deeper reality."

"Deeper is not deepest."

Pythia squares her shoulders and speaks quite firmly. "I am coming to believe the ending of *Homo sapiens* should come sooner rather than later."

"You also know better than that."

"No, I don't. *Homo sapiens* indeed!" She recalls her time in Mexico dealing with the gang of human traffickers and grimaces. "Their minds resemble an ant mentality—but hive restlessness rather than superorganism, unitary wholeness. *Homo sapiens* and their primitive thought processes! Ugh! First, out scurry their scouts, probing restlessly and with the appearance of harmless curiosity for signs of weakness, signs of enemies, signs of prey, signs of domination, signs of us-ness, signs of them-ness. Once returned with such information, these scouts pass on their little packets of intelligence to soldiers who follow the scent trails back to the intended targets where the victims are torn into little pieces and returned to the densely packed colony. There, workers churn the dismembered parts into gooey sustenance, such as it is. In such a savage state, the human brain is stuck."

"Patience will set you free."

"In the meantime, the planet may be irreparably damaged."

"Nature abhors impatience."

Pythia sighs deeply, wilting before the relentless stare of this creature. When she tries to use her telepathic and clairvoyant powers, a sharp pain blinds her and she immediately stops. She surrenders her argument in self-defense. "Of course, you are right. There are not enough of us. Even so—"

Pythia sees the young woman is no longer there. On reflection, she is not at all surprised at the sudden departure of this most mysterious of beings. Nor is she surprised at the usual ambiguity of *her* answers. By nature more prone to action than non-action, Pythia is certain this inclination is frowned upon by those that guide. Even so, she knows she has an ally in her daughter. What a difference they could make if their combined powers are unleashed by the mentors and unrestrained by themselves. Still, the numbers of their kind don't add up. Rash action would be foolish. Procreate, procreate, procreate.

Tap. Tap. Tap.

Chapter 42: Procreation

~ Michael Powers Appears ~

Days pass without further contact with apparitions until one late night, when Pythia and Tara walk arm-in-arm in the moonlight enjoying the cool air, both sense a person lurking in the dark. This time, it is not a breeze that alerts them of some specter's presence, but a palpable feeling of being watched.

Mother, is your hump flashing a message?

Yes. Someone is here.

I also feel it.

"Come out!" calls Pythia.

A figure materializes out of the dark. Its outline seems alive with an electric glow that skitters nervously around the edges, giving its dark silhouette the impression of being on fire.

"It is I," says the figure.

"Who?" demands Pythia, more forcefully than she intends.

"Your grandfather."

"Michael Powers?!" exclaims Tara, more in the form of a statement than a question.

"Yes, and I am your great grandfather, Tara."

Tara is breathless with excitement. "I have read all of your writings! You are the lens through which we have learned our past."

"Being dead is helpful. It gives one an objectivity lacking in those enslaved within the boundaries of life. I wish I had written the gibberish I did after I had died, but, *c'est la vie!*" The electric spiders scurrying across his form seem enlivened by the joke.

"I have always wondered," says Tara, somewhat hesitantly. "How did those psychiatrists who mistakenly diagnosed you with schizophrenia really die? I mean, one right after the other—all three."

"Leakage."

"What?"

"Leakage. Just as you and your mother are able to tap into multi-dimensional spacetime, so could I, except as an intermediate, on a more

[507]

limited scale. As such, I was unable to control such incipient power—of course I didn't even know what it was—so the tremendous gift of clairvoyance and telepathy became warped by the twisted human part of my brain. This internal conflict—the voices, which I construed as *God* and *Goddess*; the delusions; the other hallucinations—drove me to assume I was insane, and this fantasy world eventually emerged to be interpreted by other humans as the projection of a confused, schizophrenic mind. Unfortunately, this toxic blending of human and non-human incongruity leaked out to infect the brains of my treating psychiatrists. For that, I am sorry. When all is said and done, only the loves of my life—mother of mothers Bai Meiying, Diane my first wife, the perceptive Child of Buddha, and her daughter Tamara—truly understood."

"So, the psychiatrists' deaths *were* inadvertently caused by you," says Pythia. "I always wondered."

"Yes, their deaths were caused by me. Such powers, when new and unknown, can cause chaos and calamity. So many intermediates in the past, and those out there among the living now, are unconsciously exercising their powers for good or ill. They are like dumb brutes given the gift—or curse—of abstract thought without comprehending its destructive possibilities."

"But you were different," objects Tara. "You fought to understand it. You were good."

"Perhaps, Tara. That is what I would like to think. Nonetheless I killed. I killed directly and I killed indirectly."

"The deaths of the psychiatrists were not your fault," says Pythia. "You could not have known."

"I'm not speaking of the psychiatrists," replies the specter.

"Then. . . . ?" Tara's question trails off.

"The war, my dear. I killed in the war. I killed good men, not cruel sociopaths or rapists or murderers."

"I see."

"Do you remember, Tara, during your training, you killed thousands who were directly or indirectly involved in the Unit 731 Japanese genocide simulation? Many of those you eliminated were good. Fortunately, that was a simulation. Vietnam was real."

Tara looks down. "Yes, yes I see."

"Given the results of that simulation, do you still want to simply eliminate *Homo sapiens* wholesale . . . if you could?"

"Well, I have given much thought to that question. If the goal is to eliminate unnecessary suffering, why not simply eliminate those who have such devastating capacity to suffer themselves, and to cause immense suffering to others? Non-human animals both suffer and cause suffering, but do not possess the capacity to destroy the planet in the process of undertaking either."

The specter of Michael Powers ripples, giving the appearance of laughter. "Is the goal to eliminate unnecessary suffering or to save the planet?"

"Both," says Pythia.

"Is it? Are you sure?" asks the specter.

"We possess great powers compared to humans, but empathy is also deeply embedded in our genome," says Tara.

"Is it?" The specter ripples even more, and neither woman is able to determine the meaning of its oddly ambiguous replies or agitated appearance. Before they have a chance to enquire further, the ghost of Michael Powers fades away, its figure still rippling in a manner impossible to interpret.

After this encounter, mother and daughter walk their separate ways, yet mentally they remain connected and of one mind. In spite of these ghostly contacts, they agree that after Tara's child is born, more needs to be done to speed the process of replacing the human race. Procreation is, of course, important, but both also believe their powers should be used more liberally for good. Time is running short for the planet and its diminishing diversity of life. After ensuring the viability of this child, they must send it off alone for education by the mentors, then act.

~ Rebellion ~

Months have passed during which the specters have periodically appeared, their presence fleeting, their words few, and their impact powerful. Tara and Pythia have often expanded on their discussions about the wisdom of embarking on a more proactive strategy designed to hasten the departure of *Homo sapiens*. One day, when Tara is very near her due date, the subject comes up over tea with Lady Oracle and Sy. As both mother and daughter expected, the response is prompt and unambiguous.

"I have known what both of you think for some time, but hoped the child would disabuse you of this notion," chides Lady Oracle. "No! No!" she continues. "That path will lead to complications far beyond our abilities to control."

"What complications, for example?" asks Pythia.

Lady Oracle's face reddens in controlled anger. "You are fully aware. It is obvious. Draw attention to yourselves precipitously and, well, disaster will result."

"What disaster?"

"To put it bluntly, they will kill you, or, at the very least, imprison you."

Tara scoffs. "What prison could hold us? What weapons could we not disable?"

"Now you're being foolish!" Sy interjects. "They can overwhelm you! Your powers are not without limit. The range of your power is constrained by distance and geography. You must sleep. You get tired. You make mistakes. There are so many ways things can go wrong with so few of you!"

"Not if we play them off, one against the other," says Pythia.

"What of empathy?" demands Lady Oracle. "Are you simply going to blink them all out of existence? That, my dears, is impossible!"

"Not at all. Would we all agree that some humans—for example, those in power and responsible for great suffering—can be, at the very least, disarmed, disabled, or otherwise neutralized?"

"Will you dissociate every member of the FBI?" asks Sy. "Every head of state? Every gang leader? Every abusive father or mother? Every criminal? Where do you start and where do you stop?"

"It took *Homo sapiens* thousands of years to emerge as the sole hominin species," says Pythia. "Do you propose we wait for thousands of years?"

"A false choice," says Lady Oracle. "There is such a thing as decades, or hundreds of years."

"In the meantime, what happens to the planet? How many of our fellow living beings, plant and animal, will be gone forever? How much suffering will they endure in the agony of slow extinction?"

"And if you fail?" asks Sy.

[510]

"Failure is to not act. What did it take for the first hominins to cast the first spear or hurl the first rock? Had they waited, the planet might not be in the dire position it is in today."

"Precisely my point," says Lady Oracle.

"No. Today is the reverse of then. Today, hesitation will spell doom for all of us, predator and prey, intelligent or purely instinctual."

Lady Oracle and Sy look at each other. They have been fully aware this inevitable turn of events would come sooner rather than later. They do what all parents, guardians, and mentors do when the time has come—withdraw.

And hope for the best.

~ Birth ~

Following this conversation, no one mentions the topic again; all are content to concentrate on the birth of this child.

This child!

To them, this child represents another crucial step in the direction of a new world. What will its powers be? Siyabonga has now joined the group, and his fiercely proud fatherly optimism is fused onto Tara's motherly concerns, resulting in a tamping down of her worries. He is confident the combination of his intermediate genes with her superior ones will produce a being the likes of which the world has never seen. To Siyabonga, it is fitting that part of the child's genome will be African— cradle of all hominin species—and its temperament certain to be a true tamer of lions. Tara, less sanguine, frets about unknown powers that will swamp them all. She has told no one of the communication already directed at her in the boldest possible manner from the fetus. It seems to her this new life is already far superior to humans in intellect, and probably also superior to herself! Others, by necessity, are unaware of this supposition. But she! From the depths of her womb comes the messages. Communications delivered in strangeness upon strangeness, wonder upon wonder. Yet she, the mother, finds them unfathomable and frightening. Even with Pythia, her own mother, she cannot share. As a result, some time ago she obstinately drew the blinds on the window of her mind. In fact, this fetus, this child, practically this adult, is draining her as if greedily sucking every atom of Tara's powers to fuel its own violently growing needs.

"This child will be amazing!" exclaims Siyabonga one night while lying beside Tara with his ear to her bulging stomach.

"What makes you say that?" asks Tara rather wearily, knowing she will hear the same boyishly laudatory comments she has heard many times during the past month.

"Just listen to the rumbling! Great thoughts are percolating in the mind of this child. I try to connect by telepathy, but he or she is too profound to fathom. It's like trying to penetrate a thick fog."

"Hopefully the fog is not an indication of idiocy," she chides.

"Don't even say that!" cries Siyabonga, sitting up abruptly and giving her a stern look. "It's bad luck."

"Tch!" scolds Tara. "Human superstitions, Siyabonga. Get rid of your African notions of luck and monsters. Inkanyamba is not real, although this child will look somewhat like an eel when it emerges."

"Hey, don't tempt fate by mentioning Inkanyamba. May not be real, but sure be scary as hell."

"What if this child turns out to be scary?"

"What do you mean?"

"I mean, what if this child has powers far beyond yours or mine?"

"Great! Have at it! More power the better. More power, more good can be done . . . I mean, more power, the sooner we can eliminate all this terrible oppression and suffering." He looks at her askance. "Isn't that true?"

"Perhaps. That's one way to look at it."

"Hey, what's wrong with you. You're supposed to be the mother. You know, defending your chicks and all that. What's this all about?"

"Siyabonga, we are not wedded to the merely personal. One of our great dissimilarities from *Homo sapiens* is that we are able to see a broader picture, a more global perspective, not a narrow, provincial one all tied in with the destructive notion of family right or wrong, or us versus them."

"Yeah, yeah I get that. But, damn it, you're its mother."

"So I am, and you're its father, and both of us are related to all life on Earth in equal measure. Should we not view all life on Earth as a human mother might view her children?"

Siyabonga puzzles over this for a moment. "I guess." He quickly brightens. "Hey, I'm just an intermediate, remember? You have to give me some leeway for being stupid."

[512]

"Hopefully, this child will give both of us leeway," says Tara glumly.

"What is this, pre-partum depression?" reproaches Siyabonga with a little chuckle to take the edge off.

"Go to sleep," says Tara sharply.

As the words leave her mouth, she doubles over in pain.

~

A shiny new baby boy teeters on unsure legs, amniotic fluid and vernix caseosa not yet washed off. He has been placed on a table where he miraculously makes tentative efforts to stand, his shaky efforts eerily similar to a newborn gazelle. Although he occasionally falls, after a short period of struggle he is standing, albeit wobbling on rubbery legs. Tara lies exhausted, her breathing shallow, her unbelieving eyes fixated on this child struggling to stand and walk as if he instinctively understands predators lurk nearby. He has no prominent hump, but the shape of his back is strikingly unique. It is as if he has a hominin shape with a tortoise back; a thick carapace-type shell rises from the base of his neck to the small of his back, and covers the entire dorsal width, shoulder blade to shoulder blade and top to bottom, down to his waist. And like a tortoise, this thick layer is composed of interlocking dermal plates, but formed of tough, leathery flesh rather than keratin. When the others enter the room and stare incredulously at this astounding vision, they look to the midwife for an explanation. As usual, the mysterious woman makes no comments and offers no answers to unspoken questions. Sphinx-like, she patiently waits until the child appears ready to be cleaned up. Meanwhile, the infant sways on his feet, legs spread apart for balance, staring back at them with large, luminous eyes. He takes a tentative step, then another to the edge of the table.

"Oh!" cries Tara in fright.

The others rush forward as a group, but the child seems to smile and take a step back. This freezes them in their tracks, for to touch him seems a dreadful error.

Finally, Siyabonga breaks the tension. "Look at this child! A wonder! Standing already! He has the fierce look of a warrior. His shield is on his back, his spears are hurled from his eyes, his legs a wonder of strength and resilience. A warrior!"

[513]

The child blinks at Siyabonga and suddenly the young African father is gone.

"No!" exclaims Lady Oracle.

The others are aghast.

Just as suddenly, Siyabonga reappears, looking none the worse for wear. Deathly silence falls over the room Finally, Siyabonga breaks the tension. "Look at this child! A wonder! Standing already! He has the fierce look of a warrior. His shield is on his back, his spears are hurled from his eyes, his legs a wonder of strength and resilience. A warrior!"

Sy peers at Siyabonga in amazement. "Where have you been?"

"What?"

"You were gone, now you are back, but slightly out of sync with time. Where were you?"

"You're crazy. I've been here the entire time."

"No, Siyabonga," says an awestruck Sy.

Siyabonga's eyes grow large. "I've been here!"

"No, you haven't," confirms Lady Oracle in a stunned tone.

The child ignores the talking, turns his head toward his mother, and holds out a hand.

"It is what I feared," whispers Tara shrinking back as if the touch would be fatal.

BOOK III: ABASSI

Chapter 43: A Reckoning

~ Crisis ~

Four years have passed since the child was born.

Siyabonga has named him Abassi, the creator *God* of the Efig, Ibibio, and Annang people of Africa. He is the giver of life, death, and justice.

Abassi has spent his time either outwitting artificial intelligence for amusement, gardening, or taking solitary walks far into the desert, sometimes for days, as he is not subject to the limitations imposed on any other hominin at his stage of development. Even his remarkable mother and grandmother had to be chaperoned at such a young age. Physically, the boy had grown unimaginably fast, but an even more dramatic change soon occurred. Days after he reached the age of four, he went missing for six months, driving his mother Tara wild with anxiety, but eliciting only a calming smile and a few reassuring words from Lady Oracle. Upon returning from wherever he had gone, his body now resembles the svelte, well-muscled figure of an athletic adolescent boy. While his physique is striking, the great dermal plates rising from his back impress the observer with absolute certainty that this person's anatomy is constructed very differently from normal human architecture. Yet the dermal plates, instead of appearing to be a misshapen infirmity, strike one as being the seat of great strength and power.

Abassi has uttered no sound during all these four years; not primitive grunt or complex exposition, nor verbal or telepathic communication, to anyone but his mother. Chronologically, he is a child in earth years, but intellectually and emotionally he is decidedly far more advanced than his mother and grandmother.

Lady Oracle and Sy have withdrawn, keeping a wary eye on his progress only from the shadows. Days and months hold no monotony for the group because Abassi regularly performs some miraculous act which

[515]

never fails to astound. His powers seem limitless. Members of the group know they are his laboratory rats, and as such, are experimented on by Abassi without compunction. He tests his fledgling power by dissociating them, then bringing them back after various lengths of time have passed. He scours their brains with utter thoroughness, even when they are unwilling victims of his intrusions. When asked questions, or told to explain himself, he merely stares without seeing as if they are squirrels chattering incessantly at a person absorbed in their own thoughts.

Most notable and alarming of all, Tara is shriveling little by little in the glare of his demands; his mother being the only one with whom he communicates. Evidently unconcerned about the deleterious effects on her health, he continuously drains her of her own life force to satisfy his insatiable curiosity at the cognitive workings and extra-normal capabilities of her kind.

In the first few years of Abassi's existence, Siyabonga was beside himself with frustration at being excluded from his son's conscious awareness. Many times, he confronted Abassi and loudly demanded to be recognized, when in the blink of an eye, found himself dissociated and returned sometime later in the future. Like a dog repeatedly punished, he sulked in wounded silence. But as he watches his beloved Tara's health fail, he spends hours urging her to tell him what Abassi is saying and what he is thinking. However, Tara refuses to enlighten him (or anyone for that matter) the nature of any communication with her son.

Pythia is also deeply concerned about her daughter's health. Consequently, she has tried to explore Abassi's mind, but like everyone else who has made the attempt, she has failed. The boy's brain is impervious to psychic probing, and in her desperation, Pythia has turned to the specters for guidance. But no ghost or apparition, no human or non-human, has any answers. In fact, as the days and weeks and years drag on, a sort of fatalistic surrender has settled over the compound. Everything has come to revolve around Abassi with no end in sight. Meanwhile, Tara continues her decline. Until one day, that is, when this astonishing entity decides to speak openly.

~

Everyone is eating dinner together in the cafeteria. Queequeg and his Mongol helpers have cooked a particularly lavish feast, and now the assembled friends lean back in their chairs and sip tea. As usual, Abassi sits apart, eyes closed as if in deep meditation. For the others, the conversation is sparse, covering rather trivial topics. Tara, looking very pale and weak, has only nibbled at her food, in spite of Queequeg's exhortations to eat more. Typically, when at table, the subject of her health and Abassi's latest activities are avoided, particularly when he is present. Today is no different until Tara suddenly gives out a slight moan.

"Are you okay?" asks Siyabonga.

"I'm fine."

"No, you are not," says the estimable Lady Oracle with authority. "It is obvious you are not. What is it?"

"Nothing."

Sy jumps up, casting a quick sideways glance at Abassi. "We are all worried about you, Tara. What can we do?"

"Yes, dear, tell us," adds Pythia.

Before she has a chance to respond, her chair is empty. The others join Sy in standing as they stare in surprise at the place where Tara used to be. Eventually, all slowly turn their attention to Abassi.

"Have no fear," he says in an otherworldly, sonorous voice.

Each member of the group has just heard the first words, the first sound, from this remarkable creature, and the effect is electric. Stunned silence is followed by Siyabonga's impassioned cry, "Where is she?"

"I am afraid my demands upon mother were necessary up to the present, but now I have no further need and sent her to a place of rest where she can recover her health."

"Where?" croaks Lady Oracle.

"A place of rest."

Siyabonga, clearly agitated and at the same time wary, asks in a trembling voice, "When will she return?"

"When it is time."

Lady Oracle regains her composure and comes forth with a non-sequitur, "You know, Abassi, it is time for your education."

"I have already received it."

"What?" exclaims Pythia.

"I have already been. It is unnecessary to expend sixteen human years as was the case with you and mother. The past is now the present, and I am ready."

"For what?" asks Sy.

[517]

"To make the species *Homo sapiens* aware of their fate."

"But . . . it is too soon!" cries Lady Oracle.

Abassi does not deign to glance her way. "I will be leaving shortly," he announces.

"And your mother?" insists Siyabonga.

"She will return before my departure. Afterwards, she and grandmother, must continue reproducing."

"Is she in good health?" asks Pythia.

"Of course. Already she is recovering her strength."

"How do you know?" asks Sy.

"I know."

Lady Oracle sits back down, stupefied, and after the others do likewise, says in as calm a tone as she can muster, "How do you propose to notify humans of their fate?"

"The simplicity of their brains dictates the simplicity of my announcement to them."

"Do you have empathy for them?" asks Sy with a crooked smile.

At this pointed question, Abassi's face undergoes a dramatic transformation, and the solemn visage melts into a look of the most abject anguish. This exquisite metamorphosis, obvious to all in its sincerity, impacts his listeners far more than his unprecedented behavior to this point.

"I do," he says. "To the deepest chords of my being, I grieve a requiem to what might have been."

"And a symphony to what will be?" asks Sy.

"The symphony is unfinished," replies Abassi.

"And the requiem?" asks Lady Oracle.

"Finished."

With this ominous pronouncement, Abassi again falls silent and closes his eyes. The others veritably tiptoe out of the cafeteria and, as if some invisible thread is tugging them, filter one-by-one into the building where the Precious Object is housed. Only Pythia is not present, having chosen to remain a few moments longer quietly observing her grandson for clues to his perplexing behavior. No one speaks until they are inside, gathered around the statue. As if expecting to hear something from the *Goddess*, they are disappointed to discover that it greets them with a stolidly inert gaze. Of all members of the group, Lady Oracle seems the

[518]

most lost. She stares at the *Goddess* statue as an ancient Greek petitioner might stand before the Delphic Oracle, waiting for an answer, any answer, to her plea for guidance.

But no answer comes.

"It appears we have been abandoned," she says wearily.

Pythia, who has arrived just in time to hear these words, rises to the defense of her grandson. "I think not. We must have confidence in Abassi."

"What do you mean?" asks Lady Oracle.

"I mean, I have been closely watching him. In my opinion, the mentors have spoken loud and clear."

"How so?" asks Sy.

"I don't know," admits Pythia. "But I think Abassi will not bother to dawdle in the gutters with drug addicts and slave traffickers to relieve tiny pockets of suffering. He has no need of such hands-on training. He will go directly to the once impregnable centers of power. How else to make the species *Homo sapiens* aware of their fate'?"

"Maybe, but then what?"

"Then the world is turned upside-down."

With this statement, a jarring noise reverberates throughout the room.

Tap. Tap. Tap.

~ Tara Returns, Abassi Leads Them Back ~

Weeks have now passed, and the Sphinx-like Abassi remains lost in the depths of his own unfathomable musings. The others are left to speculate. No word from on high has come to disperse the fog, no pause in the tapping from the Precious Object has led to a Eureka moment of understanding. Only the disquieting silence of uncertainty and powerlessness prevails. Lady Oracle has sunk into despair, and Sy increasingly seeks comfort in the company of his favorite apparition— Feng Shiren. Siyabonga pines for his wife, and shuffles about with a permanent hang-dog frown. Meanwhile, Pythia frets about her daughter and longs for her return. All the inmates of the compound now view it as more a prison than a comfortable retreat. Permeating this wilting atmosphere, Abassi's attentions are like a sauna's steam, quietly coiling into every nook and cranny of their lives.

What is he thinking?—the question that is on everyone's mind. All know Abassi can read their thoughts but will never disclose his own intimate feelings, instead choosing to play the role of mysterious hermit. It is at this gloomy juncture that Tara reappears. Her return is as sudden as her departure, and it manifests under the exact same circumstances— dinner in the cafeteria. In fact, she pops back into existence by appearing in precisely the same chair she had disappeared from. After a startled reaction, and many exclamations of surprise piled on top of each other, a fatally confused cacophony ensues. Tara blinks a few times, then raises her hand for quiet.

"I am fine. My health is returned, my powers undiminished. I am ready to take the next step."

Tears welling in his eyes, Siyabonga walks to her side and puts his hand lovingly on her shoulder. "Wife," he says. "You are a sight for a poor African's eyes."

Smiling at these words, she turns her attention to her son, who sits in his accustomed mode of detached meditation. To the astonishment of all, Abassi meets her gaze, breaks into a broad smile, and rushes to her side, grasping her hand in an affectionate gesture of deep regard.

"I'm so happy, mother."

"It is time, is it not?" she asks.

"It is."

"When do we go back through the iron door?" asks Lady Oracle, awkwardly trying to accommodate herself to the harsh reality of a severely lowered status.

"Tomorrow."

"Where will we live?" asks Pythia. "Lady Oracle's apartments are long occupied by others, and the mansion is no longer there."

"Yes, it is," says Abassi.

"But . . . how?" stammers Sy.

"The lot has remained vacant these years. After all, it is owned by, well, shall we say agents of the mentors. I simply returned the house to its proper location."

"How could you know? . . . I mean, how could you possibly know all the details?" asks Sy, genuinely amazed. "Dissociation is far easier. I mean, a close approximation is good enough." He twists his head and prances about, arms flung wide. "Ask a certain German whose urethra

Pythia thought she surgically removed. Ah! Enough of that! How do you do it?"

Abassi narrows his eyes. "True, but as you pointed out, mother and grandmother have already been on the path to more precise dissociative techniques. Nonetheless, from my perspective, reconstitution is quite simple. The mansion's configuration remained all this time, down to the last wastebasket and geranium. All I had to do was tap into the discrete reality it already possesses to dissociate, and reverse engineer, if you will. Multidimensional spacetime is a most useful tool."

"Reaching into the past to undo something is forbidden to us," says Pythia. "Yet, you. . . . "

Her words trail off in wonder.

"I am what I am," says Abassi. For the first time, he looks at Queequeg standing inconspicuously off to the side. "Like your ancestor Ishmael once said to another little gathering here, 'Ahab is Ahab'."

"If the mansion is back, why wait until tomorrow?" asks Lady Oracle.

"Because I have to speak with what you call the Precious Object."

"You understand it?" asks Lady Oracle, again made aware of her increasingly superfluous presence.

"Not to worry," replies Abassi. "Your value is undiminished. We will soon need you."

"We?' says Sy. "Who is included in 'we'?"

"You," says Abassi.

"And me, your own father?" asks a subdued Siyabonga, his hand still resting on Tara's shoulder.

"You are a key. You and mother must continue to procreate." He again cracks a broad smile. "I am anxious to welcome brothers and sisters. And to further this end"—he gazes warmly at Pythia—"grandmother must find a new mate. All of you have been dilatory while lounging in the comforts of this retreat. Numbers do matter."

Sy laughs. "You can live with others like yourself? Is the Earth big enough?"

Abassi's stare bores into him. "I cannot live without them. As for the Earth, when my siblings arrive, it will never seem so big."

~

[521]

The next day, Abassi closets himself with the Precious Object, ordering the others to stay away. No one can take their minds off what is being discussed in that room. Repeated attempts at telepathy and clairvoyance are futile. All day, Abassi does not emerge, leading to a certain nervousness about what is to come. What is he being told by the statue? Who is speaking to him through the object? Are the mentors even involved? Who directs the mentors? What, or who, is actually the Precious Object? All are questions that remain unanswered and open to worried speculation. When Abassi finally emerges late at night, he calls the group together and reconfirms tomorrow's early departure time. When questions are directed his way, he merely stares vacantly as if occupying some other realm that lies beyond reach.

The next morning, everyone lines up at the hatch leading down to the room containing the iron door. Conversation is at a minimum. Since it has been years since they left their home in California, curiosity at what changes they will find is intense. Pythia and Tara are wondering about the FBI and whether Ming-huà and Zookeeper are happily excluded from further government intrusions. Siyabonga dwells on Abassi's plans and how they will affect his beloved Africa. Lady Oracle and Sy are in a quandary as to who their bosses actually are, and to what extent they should take their lead from Abassi. All are anxious to leave the compound, so give hurried thanks to Queequeg and his Mongol staff.

"When you return, we will be waiting with open arms," says Queequeg as each individual pops down the ladder. When he closes the door, a sense of finality pervades the group. Once gathered in front of the iron door, Abassi gestures to Lady Oracle, who opens it to let the others pass, then follows and closes it behind her.

~ Back to the Mansion ~

As usual, the trip to the desert cave is instantaneous, leaving no time to adapt when they set foot outside the entrance and into the bright California sunlight. All except Abassi are surprised to be greeted by Altan himself, so long absent from their thoughts. After giving each other a nod of recognition, Abassi and Altan lead the others to a waiting van. Hours later, they enter the San Francisco mansion and gather in the dining room for a meal and spirited conversation. Reverting to his usual habit of seclusion, Abassi has eaten only a little, and now retires to bed with nothing more than an inaudible chirp. Attention now turns to Altan.

"Tell us, Altan, what do you know about the situation?" asks Lady Oracle.

"The situation?"

"Yes, I mean, what is to happen? Are we to follow Abassi? Who is now directing us? To whom do I ask for guidance?"

"So many questions!" laughs Altan.

"Yes, we all have questions," says Sy. He dances a little jig. "Right now, I don't know whether we're coming or going."

"I see you have been with your friendly ghost Feng Shiren," says Altan dryly.

Sy increases the drama of his movements, mimicking Chinese opera as taught him by Shiren. "He was the King of Masks," says Sy. "But right now, I don't know who is behind what mask. You must enlighten us!"

"There are masks behind masks," says Altan. "Even I do not know which is real and which is not. Too many layers. I simply follow orders."

"And your orders are?" asks Pythia.

"To meet you at the cave and drive you here," says Altan with an apologetic smile.

"A mask!" cries Sy. "You can do better than that! Tell us truly where we stand. This experiment is spiraling out of control, or so it seems."

"Is it?" asks Altan. "How so?"

Lady Oracle takes up the cause. "Sy and I are in the dark. All of us are in the dark, except Abassi. We appear to have been bypassed. Things are moving too quickly. His powers have evolved too quickly to be controlled. As I said, everything is out of control."

"Quite the contrary," says Altan. "As far as I can tell, things are moving fast for good reason."

"What reason?" asks Pythia. "He is my grandson, after all. I have a right to know."

Altan looks at Tara. "Ask her."

Now all eyes turn to Tara.

"Yes, it is true, Abassi has communicated with me. There are many things he has said that I cannot reveal."

[523]

"Even to me?" exclaims Siyabonga.

"Yes, even to you."

"Like what?"

"That I cannot say. As you heard, he wants us to have more children."

Siyabonga scoffs. "I already knew that!"

Tara gives a sigh of impatience. "My son has remarkable powers, that is true. But they have come at a price. He bears a deep wound . . . an aching wound that has festered from the beginning. He was born with it. It is a wound waiting in anticipation of being inflicted; an empty grave waiting to be filled. I don't know. . . . "

Lady Oracle again jumps in. "Tara, this is very serious. What does he plan? Who are his mentors? Does he even have any mentors?" She shudders. "Does he plan to wipe out the entire race of *Homo sapiens* in one great Armageddon?"

"No, he does not. But what he is planning to do, even I have not been informed. All I know is that his powers are far greater than ours, including his cognitive skills." She hesitates, then says, "He tells me things I do not understand. Even we are like chimpanzees to him, let alone humans, who are far, far below his level."

Siyabonga's eyes are wide. "What must he think of me!"

Tara shakes her head. "No, no, you are all getting the wrong impression. He is capable of deep love, not in the human sense of the word, but in the cosmic sense of the word. All things, to him, are sacred. Humans water a plant and fertilize it to keep it healthy, but trim the dead and dying leaves and stems to insure the overall health of the plant itself. So he views humans."

"And us?" asks Sy, his scarecrow head tilted at an impossible angle sideways.

"And us," admits Tara.

A grim hush falls over the group.

Finally breaking the stillness, Pythia says in amazement, "So even we are as loyal dogs to him."

"And as such," says Tara. "We must follow."

Chapter 44: Into the World

~ Lance Romellion Makes a Visit ~

On an otherwise uneventful Saturday, Lance Romellion is jotting notes at home concerning a recent case when he hears a news report on T.V. which causes him to whip his head up and lean forward in astonishment. Evidently, a Victorian-style mansion that had mysteriously disappeared has now mysteriously reappeared. The reporter, standing in front of the building, is interviewing a breathless witness who reports it coalescing from thin air the previous night. Looking like a homeless person, the witness explains he was sleeping nearby when he heard a low rumbling that made his hair stand on end. In front of his eyes (it was a full moon) he saw the mansion rise from an empty lot as if by magic. His explanation is that it is the work of some sort of demons, long known to haunt this part of San Francisco, especially the older buildings. Romellion is intimately familiar with that building and its history, and is certain no demons were responsible for its reappearance.

Without waiting for the end of the report, Lance races to his car and drives to see for himself. When he arrives, he gets out and stands erect, still holding the car door open, staring in awe. He finds it hard to believe his own eyes. Not only is the mansion exactly as it used to be, but the elaborate landscaping is also identical. In his mind's eye, Lance can picture how utterly desolate the vacant lot looked when he last visited the site. Back then, in spite of forensic investigators scouring the grounds for any signs of the missing building and its contents, nothing was found. Nor were any of the inhabitants ever located. Since none had been charged with a crime, his hands were tied and the investigation languished . . . until now. His mind races to decide what step to take next. Should he just go up to the door and knock? Call back-up? Should he wait for more information so as not to spook the residents? It has been years since they disappeared. Why are they back now? Romellion has a premonition that something important is about to happen, otherwise they would not show themselves so brazenly. To his dismay, he remembers that Walter Monroe has retired.

In fact, he retired quite soon after their meeting in Washington. At the time, unpleasant rumors were murmured about his mental health. Now, Lance wonders if Monroe is still alive. Did Monroe brief his replacement about this case? What does the current director know? If there was once an interest in pursuing Lance's wild speculations, the non-activity of the past few years certainly appears to have squelched any possible desire to proceed with the investigation. While lost in these thoughts, he suddenly notices a curtain rustle upstairs, hears a window bang close, sees a moving shadow, and the house itself seems to breathe out some unspecified malevolence. Or is it malevolence? If not malevolence, the ambiance is certainly alien in nature. Such a disturbing sensation coincides with Lance's predisposed tendency to think of an otherworldly involvement in this case, and by extension, in the disappearance and reappearance of this house. A deep, abiding panic briefly immobilizes his body. He feels deeply in his bones that something fantastic dwells in that mansion. Something new. Something powerful. Very very powerful.

Once his legs unfreeze, he immediately jumps back in the car and drives straight to the office with no other thought than to get as far away as possible from the terrible emanations pouring out of that house.

~

When he reaches his office, a few agents and secretaries are keeping themselves moderately busy, though they liven up when their boss enters, evidently in quite a lather. Lance makes a beeline for his private office, waving off curious questions about his unexpected presence. Once ensconced behind his desk, he sits with no definite idea of what to do. Doubts plague him, but he finally puts together a rather pathetic little plan. First, he will remain quiet until he has obtained more information regarding what is going on at the mansion from local authorities. Second, he will obtain some of that information by personally returning without notifying his staff. In his mind, much will depend on secrecy. Local police may be in the area, and he prefers to make his presence as inconspicuous as possible. He cannot count on search warrants or bugs. This simple two step plan is as far as he is willing to project going forward. What he does afterward will depend upon his reception by the residents of the mansion. Romellion girds himself to visit early next morning—a Sunday. With this resolution, he walks out of the office to the puzzled looks of his co-workers. Again, he swats away questions with a wave of his arm.

[526]

Next morning, when Lance again pulls up to the mansion, he is relieved to see a small group of curious on-lookers walking away shaking their heads. Mercifully, the sidewalk is empty and now would be the perfect time to approach the front door. However, try as he might, Lance cannot make himself leave the shelter of the car.

"Stupid!" he says to himself. "This is ridiculous! I'm a damn fool of an FBI agent! Move!"

But no amount of cursing or self-deprecating insults motivate him to move. For all intents and purposes, he is frozen in place as if stricken with paralysis.

While in this immoveable state, the passenger door suddenly opens and a strangely shaped figure squeezes in, closing the door behind.

"Hello, Agent Romellion," comes a deceptively soft voice, yet paradoxically replete with the timbre of great underlying power.

Lance's immediate reaction is to demand the intruder get out, then force him out if necessary, but something in the man's demeanor and the imposing musculature of his rather alien-like body advises against such a move. In fact, on closer inspection, the features of this person seem a bizarre mix of a creature very young and very old at the same time. The massive shape of his back marks him as barely human-looking.

"Who are you?" he demands in a voice far weaker than he desires.

"Not important," says the stranger magisterially. "I know who you are, why you are here, what are your fears, and everything else you have ever done or thought."

Lance is overwhelmed by this all-encompassing statement, and struggles to come up with an authoritative response. None comes.

"I think," continues the intruder. "It would be best if you return to your job and concentrate on catching, as you call them, the bad guys. There are no bad guys here."

"I don't know that," says Lance, starting to regain his composure.

"I know you don't. However, that is neither here nor there."

"What do you want?"

"To speak with your superiors in Washington."

Lance cannot help but laugh. "You're either joking or you're mad!"

"Neither."

"Look, I don't know your name! I don't know anything about you. What's more, I don't know why you're in this car. Are you connected to the people in that house?"

"I am Abassi. I am very different from you and your kind. I am in this car to instruct you to arrange a meeting with your superiors in Washington. I am connected to the people in that house. Now, will you do as I ask?"

"Hell no! For all I know, you're a terrorist!"

"I know you do not believe that, or at least you think it is a vanishingly small probability. I know you are unsure what to believe about these strange incidents of missing limbs and hunchbacked women. I know your theories. I know who you spoke with in Washington years ago. I know right now you are without a clue how to proceed. Would you like a demonstration that might give you clarity on how we might move this discussion along? One that might interest you and which will go a long way toward explaining who I am?"

"Sure," says Lance, an uncertain quiver in his tone.

"Look at your right hand."

Lance looks.

No hand. Just a stump protruding past his cuff.

Too shocked to speak, his lips move, but no sound is emitted. Dragging his attention from the horror of his stump, he looks with astonishment into Abassi's eyes and hears the tremendous roaring of a lion in his head. Now, he breaks. He fumbles for the handle of the door, but it is also gone. When he looks though the windshield, he sees what looks like an African savannah. Pressed against the side window is a curious early hominin, as much ape-like as human-like. Lance wants to scream, but his rigorous training kicks in. He breathes deeply, exerting an iron determination to control his terror, and forces a smile.

"Hypnosis," he says, voice far too shaky for his liking.

"When you are ready, call me," says Abassi.

"How? I don't have your number."

"Just call me."

"No need. I'm driving back to my office, with you or without you."

"That might be difficult."

Lance fumbles with his good hand for the keys.

No steering wheel. No ignition. Both hands now gone.

Outside, the hominin has been joined by others. Lance feels his gorge rise. Swallowing the acidic bile, he looks pleadingly at Abassi.

The man is gone.

Now the hominins are banging on the car.

Lance is convinced this is illusory, caused by hypnosis. With the engine off and the windows closed, the heat rapidly builds. He starts to sweat profusely, closes his eyes, raps the dashboard with the stumps of his wrists, opens his eyes. . . .

. . . same scene, but it has now become intolerably hot. The hominins have left off hitting the car and are simply staring at him.

Lance calls out, "Abassi!"

No response.

Now he is screaming. "Abassi! Abassi! Help me!"

Sweat pours. The stumps of his wrists wave before his delirious eyes. "Abassi! For *God's* sake, help me!"

~ Refractory Period ~

In the blink of an eye, Lance finds himself continuing to sit in his car, but all is normal. The motor is running and the air conditioner is turned on high. Outside, the mansion peers down at him as if waiting patiently, Feeling the cool air on his still moist face, Romellion hurriedly lifts his arms to see if the hands are reattached, and with the exception of the little finger on the left, they appear normal.

"I kept that one off so you will give up this idea that I have simply hypnotized you," says Abassi, once again sitting in the passenger seat.

Lance is speechless.

"Now," continues Abassi. "Are you going to introduce me to your superiors in Washington?"

"What are you?" stammers Lance.

"Beside the point. The question I asked remains suspended in the air."

"Well, yes. I will . . . but, will you repeat this type of demonstration to them? If not, I will appear a fool."

"Do it immediately and I will ensure you are not compromised."

"Are you an alien?" blurts Lance.

"No."

[529]

"Are you . . . I mean, where do you come from?"

"A womb."

"One of the hunchback women?"

Abassi nods.

"Then . . . I mean, who are they? Are they aliens?"

"You seem stuck on this notion of aliens. They are no more aliens than you. They are simply aliens to you."

"Then where did you get these powers?"

"I'm sorry to say, without malice, that you are in the position of a chimpanzee asking a human where he got his cognitive and language abilities. If I explain, you will have no hope of understanding."

"Evolution?"

"Yes, as far as you comprehend it."

"Can't be. Evolution doesn't work that fast."

Abassi sighs. "Ergo, my words: *as far as you comprehend it*."

"The physicist Jared Paine, is that why. . . . ?"

"Partly."

Lance stares at his hand with the missing finger. "What do you intend?"

"I will explain to your superiors. However, I assure you my intentions are peaceful." Abassi laughs heartily. "In your terms, think of me as Jane Goodall and you *Homo sapiens* as the chimps. Did she intend harm?"

"No, but you are not Jane Goodall and we are not chimps."

"Oh, how wrong you are."

Lance reddens and feels foolish, but asks, "Can you replace my finger?"

"Can, but won't. Not until I see your superiors. Remember, I will know immediately if the FBI plans any untoward action." He glances at Lance's hand. "That would be unfortunate for all involved."

"I still don't understand how—"

"Just make the arrangements, Lance," interjects Abassi. "No more questions. And in the meantime, leave us alone."

"What if they don't believe me?"

"They won't."

"Then how. . . . ?"

[530]

"As one of your great philosophers wrote, *the Moving Finger writes, and having writ. . . .* " Abassi raises an eyebrow invitingly.

"*Moves on,*" says Lance.

"You are a highly intelligent species," says Abassi. "But there is always higher . . . and higher above that . . . and higher still; so it goes, on and on."

"You will be seen as a threat."

"Yes, you are correct. So, go ahead and display; throw your sticks. It is to be expected."

Lance is quiet for a while, then says, "There is always an end game. This makes no sense unless there's an end game. What is your end game?"

"Just make the arrangements, Lance."

Abassi exits the car and walks slowly to the house, where the front door is opened before he reaches it, and without breaking stride he disappears within.

Lance is left still sitting behind the wheel, staring at the smooth skin where his finger used to be. Finally, he drives away, watching the house recede in the distance. Before he returns home, he stops at a corner grocery and picks up a random bag of chips. When he pays, he conspicuously uses his left and to hold out a five-dollar bill, searching the clerk's eyes for recognition The man seems too polite to comment, so Lance holds up the hand.

"Old war wound," he says.

"Oh, I was wondering," replies the clerk. "Thank you for your service."

With this upsetting confirmation, Lance arrives home and immediately pours a stiff drink. After taking a few swigs, he starts scrolling through his mind who to contact in Washington, and what he can tell them that will be convincing enough to make them agree to meet this Abassi, this person unknown.

If he is a person.

The alcohol relaxes him somewhat, and he begins to think more coherently about the ramifications of what he has just experienced. Periodically, he raises his hand to check whether the finger is still missing, and that the whole incident was not just a bad dream. Despite what Abassi told him, Lance does not believe evolution has anything to do with either the hunchback women, or Abassi himself. He is convinced they are aliens. With that determination made, his path forward is made clearer. No need to unduly complicate the matter by hypothesizing about foreign intrigue, terrorism, crazy mutants cooked up by Frankenstein doctors, and other such nonsense. Only alien visitation makes sense. Of course, there are unanswered questions, such as why these creatures are so similar to human beings in their physiognomy, but he will leave that to the experts. His conundrum is how to approach the current directors in Washington with a credible enough story to overcome the foregone conclusion that his tale will be met with extreme skepticism. *Unless*, he thinks. *Unless Walter Monroe did brief his successors!* Question is, how to find him if he is still among the living.

Excited by this idea, Lance immediately starts calling old friends in Washington, and eventually reaches Stanislaus Carmone, a retired agent who used to be close to Monroe. After numerous rings, Carmone answers, and Lance plies him with questions. Through Carmone, he learns not only that Walter Monroe is still alive, but that he and Stanislaus often get together at Walter's home in Alexandria. Two days later, Lance is flying to Washington with an appointment to meet Monroe as soon as he lands at Reagan National Airport. He hurries off the plane and rushes to Walter's home, where the old agent is waiting.

"Well well," says Walter upon opening the front door in response to Lance's knock. "Didn't expect to see you again after all these years. Come in and sit down. Drink?"

"Thanks, yes. Vodka tonic. You've probably guessed why I'm here."

"About that bizarre case involving hunchbacked women and missing limbs?"

"Yep."

"It's been a while. Anything new?"

"Before I tell you, I need to know what you told the higher-ups after we had our little meeting."

"Well, there's no reason to sit on it now. I passed on your information, your concerns, and your theory of the case."

"And?"

Walter's eyes sparkle. "You will be surprised, Lance. Not only were they interested, they jumped all over it. That surprised me so much I asked whether they had other information corroborating your story, you know, any information that would support your theory."

"What'd they say?"

"Mind you own business." Walter leans forward in his chair. "Now, what do you have?"

"You won't believe it."

"Yes, I will. I had my own little experience with . . . well, with whatever it is behind these happenings. Now, tell me."

"I will, but first tell me how high up did it go?"

"Don't know for sure. I know it reached the deputy director, but after that. . . . " he shrugs.

"What is his name?"

"Harold Burton."

"Too bad," sighs Romellion. "There's a different deputy director now."

"That's unfortunate. I've been out of the loop for some time. Now enough pissing around. Tell me what you've got!"

Lance brings him up to date in great detail. Walter listens intently, often softly whistling in amazement. The capper is when Lance shows Walter his missing finger. After refreshing their drinks, Lance adds a few more details and ends his briefing.

Monroe is stunned and sits without speaking, taking sips of his drink and shaking his head.

"Walter, this needs to go higher than the deputy director. What are my chances of meeting with the director himself, and the chief of staff?"

"Nil, unless you have already briefed someone who can pass you up the ladder. What evidence can you bring?"

Lance holds up his hand.

Walter shakes his head. "No good. Going to take more than that. You said this Abassi's intentions are peaceful, and he'll demonstrate his power so you're not left holding an empty bag?"

"He said so."

"Well, I believe you when you say these people are aliens. As I said, I had my own experience."

"Which was?"

This time, it is Walter's turn to brief Lance. When finished, both men are left mute in recognition of the situation's enormous implications, and the explosion such a revelation will cause.

Finally, Walter says, "I see nothing for it but to meet first with the deputy director. Don't know him personally, but I still have enough clout to get you in to see him."

"Thanks."

Walter shuts his eyes for a moment. "I remember something, Lance. There is a code name for this investigation. It was sent on to some super-secret group . . . maybe CIA, don't know. I'll bet if I mention it, all hell will break loose."

"Is it Magical Terrorists?"

"Oh, no. It is something far more impressive than that."

"What is it?"

"Armageddon."

Lance shivers. "They know something we don't."

"Until now."

~ A Surprising Meeting ~

Romellion decides to stay in Walter's spare bedroom for another couple of days while his host makes the requisite phone calls. Finally, after extending his stay yet one more day, Walter greets him at the dinner table the night before Lance's scheduled departure. Up to this point, Monroe had been closeted in his office making call after call, which Lance could only hear indistinctly through the door. At the moment Lance picks up the sandwich he had just prepared, Walter breezes into the room sporting a wide grin and rubbing his hands together gleefully. The sandwich is stopped in its upward trajectory and is suspended inches from Lance's mouth as he looks questioningly at his friend.

"Okay, it's arranged! Tomorrow morning, nine o'clock." He pauses waiting for Lance's response, which comes quickly.

"With the deputy director?"

"No! That's the thing. Not only with the deputy director, but also the director, his chief of staff, and a top level mucky-muck from CIA."

Down falls the sandwich. "Wow! How'd this come about so fast?"

"Armageddon, my boy. Armageddon! Magic word that worked like a charm."

Lance's face turns white. "Walter, what if it is exactly that?"

Walter ponders a moment, his excitement doused. "I doubt it, otherwise something would have hit the fan with those hunchbacks long ago. My guess is the intelligence community knows just enough to be concerned. Most of these bureaucrats haven't the imagination to go beyond business as usual; no, they'll go on chasing after the usual suspects. Ten to one they think the Chinese or Russians are up to no good."

Both men are silent, Walter's hasty analysis falling rather flat. To break the impasse, Lance says, "CIA, huh?"

"Yeah."

And with this, the floodgates are open and the two men embark on a spirited dialogue full of speculation and surmise. That night, the vodka and gin flow freely at Walter Monroe's house.

~

The next morning both are slightly hung-over, sitting uneasily at a vast conference table in FBI headquarters. No one has yet joined them, and Lance squirms in his chair, feeling small and childlike as he tortures a paper clip. He glances at his older friend, who also fidgets nervously. A blank legal pad and extra pens rest with geometric precision in front of each, with water glasses also placed in fussy perpendicular. Lance picks up a pen and begins to doodle. Meanwhile, Walter peruses a long row of portraits displaying the genial smiles of past directors looking down as if amused by his discomfort. At last, after what seems an interminable wait, the director bustles in with a cluster of equally energetic aides trailing behind. Moments later, a smaller group arrives, presumably CIA people. Everyone stands, introductions are made, heads nod, and all participants find a seat, with the exception of a pair of aides who remain standing behind both the FBI director and the chief CIA officer. After a few minutes of collegial bantering, Director John Rochelle pushes back his rolling chair and forms a tent with his fingertips.

"Okay, Agent Romellion," he announces. "You're on. Tell us what this is all about."

Lance takes a deep breath, then plunges into a detailed description of recent developments in the case. For fear of revealing something he is not supposed to know, he does not refer to its code name. During his entire presentation, not a sound escapes the lips of any in the room. Even when he holds up his left hand to display the missing finger, no questions are asked, and no surprise or shock is expressed. When he finishes with a synopsis of his theory of the case, quiet reigns as if all the listeners have been ordered to exhibit emotionless deportments. Now Walter adds a brief description of his own experiences pertaining to the investigation. Again, the room remains silent during his discourse. Reaching the end, Walter simply folds his hands and lays them on the table.

"Thank you, gentlemen," says Rochelle. "Any other details you wish to add before we continue?"

Both men shake their heads, so Rochelle resumes. "Permit me to be the first to speak. I assume all other rational explanations have been explored, such as hypnosis, terrorism, and foreign intervention?"

"Absolutely," says Lance.

Rochelle looks around the table, and receiving no comments, turns his attention to Lance and Walter. "Well, gentlemen, you may be surprised to know we are in full agreement with your theory of the case. Well, almost full. We are not so sure of the aliens part. In fact, we are already in possession of most of the facts you have presented. In short, Armageddon is now the top priority of every intelligence agency of this government. Has been for a while now. Be that as it may, the one significant fact that makes this meeting so crucial, is that you have communicated directly with this Abassi fellow, about whom we know very little. His wanting to meet with us here in Washington is a major breakthrough. Now, let's open the floor for discussion."

Paul Brecknell of the CIA raises the issue of security. A lengthy discussion ensues, including the presumed geographical reach and projective limitations of such destructive powers possessed by the *strangers* (no one is quite yet prepared to say the word *aliens*). A liaison from the White House suggests holding the meeting with Abassi at an isolated location, thereby shielding the highest-ranking leaders of government from immediate harm.

"I'm afraid," says Rochelle. "That contingency will be of little use, from what we currently know. Of course, security will be heightened, and fully armed teams standing by at the slightest sign of trouble or provocation. But, based on the CIA's report from South Africa, it is not clear we would fare any better than the armed gang members who are now either gone forever, or dismembered for life."

[536]

"We have a little more firepower than a bunch of African thugs," says a voice dryly.

Lance coughs and holds up his left hand. "Remember, gentlemen, I saw with my own eyes the power Abassi possesses. He removed both my hands, and then replaced them, minus this finger. This is a person, or a stranger, or an alien, or whatever we call him, who we don't want to rile."

"If he is an alien," adds Walter. "Any sign of government sponsored aggression may be disastrous."

"I agree," says the White House liaison. "If we can ally ourselves with this group, we'll get the jump on the Chinese and Russians."

"They may already be talking to someone in those countries as we speak," adds another person.

"Christ," mutters Walter.

As the discussion devolves into scattered conversations among various factions at the table, Rochelle interrupts the cacophony by raising his voice. "Gentlemen! None of us understand the full gravity of what we are facing. Let's have this meeting with Abassi as soon as possible, right here, at this very table. Stakes are high. If I am hearing correctly, we are in agreement that we must meet with this fellow. Let the chips fall where they may, at least we will have achieved some clarity. Are we agreed?"

Having obtained a unanimous agreement, a date is set aside for the following week. Complete secrecy is deemed mandatory. Agent Lance Romellion is given his instructions and sent on his way. When he and Walter leave the room, at a signal from Rochelle, a tall man enters.

"Hello, Altan," says Rochelle.

"Hello."

Chapter 45: Deadlock Broken

~ Consequences ~

Coincidentally, a few days before he is scheduled to leave for his meeting in Washington, Abassi learns that Tara is again pregnant, and Ming-huà, in spite of her advanced years, may be. This news gives him pleasure. Things are moving rapidly now, and all agree the seeding process must accelerate. Pythia has yet to find a replacement male for Jared Paine, so a little conference is called. The group meets in the famous anteroom of the mansion, and Lady Oracle is asked to start things off. Only Siyabonga has not been invited.

"Since you have yet to find a male, Pythia, we have wondered at the possibility of mating with Siyabonga. His intermediate genes are obviously excellent, and the resulting child will strengthen the line."

Pythia glances at Tara.

"I think it is a great idea," says Tara. "We must hasten to birth more of our kind, especially those like Abassi. Nonetheless, his mating with mother may be too much for him." Tara looks squarely at Pythia. "How do you feel about the suggestion?"

"I have no objection," says Pythia. "But Siyabonga, being an intermediate, has his share of human characteristics, and seems to prefer monogamy."

"Not so sure about that," says Tara. "He is definitely quite attached to me, but he is also aware of our ultimate goal. Let me talk to him."

"Good," says Lady Oracle. "Now, Abassi, you already know my objections to this Washington meeting. You have yet to explain—and I cannot access your mind—how going to Washington will help our cause. What do you hope to accomplish?"

"Let me try to explain as simply as possible," replies Abassi with a patronizing sigh. "We have a narrow window of opportunity. Your objection, Lady Oracle, is that I move too quickly. Actually, delay will put

[538]

us in a far graver position. Humans will come to view us not only as threats, but monsters who will destroy their lives. On the other hand, if we strike now by explaining who we are, in terms they would understand, they will see us as allies in the improvement of their stock. Alternatively, if they are not quite that enlightened, their government leaders will see us as potential allies in their never ending tribal conflicts."

"They are dumb, but not that dumb," objects Sy. "They will understand interbreeding with us will dilute, and eventually overwhelm their genome. I'm sure they will figure out this will mean the end of their species."

Abassi shakes his head. "You don't understand. The brightest among them will stand in line to breed with us. Remember, humans are primitive in their view of the cosmos, and consequently they place great value in their own children, often to the exclusion of all other children, and by extension, all other lifeforms. The bright ones would see this as an opportunity to breed superchildren, with the accompanying benefits flowing mainly to themselves as parents. We must use this provincial human attitude that places so much investment in the merely personal."

"Won't this be a bit much for them to swallow in one pill?" asks Pythia.

"To be honest," says Abassi. "This plan has emanated from a place beyond even me, and certainly far beyond all of you as well. Implementation has already begun."

"What?' cries Lady Oracle. "How?'

"Altan."

With this, a commotion ensues, and every person in the room aggressively presses their demand for an explanation. When he is not immediately forthcoming, exclamations of shock and anger swell, assailing Abassi from all sides. After waiting for the proper moment, he raises his hand for silence.

"I will explain. Altan has spent a great deal of time gaining the trust of those in power, both in the FBI and beyond. As a plant, his job has been to guide decision-makers in the direction of viewing us as aliens. Using his presumed inside knowledge of details they could confirm, he eventually persuaded them of his credibility, gradually leading them to conclude we are here for peaceful purposes. To spice the cake, so to speak, he has focused on the added incentive that cooperation will be beneficial to the security and dominance of the United States. Of course, they are a suspicious bunch, and are both cautious and highly skeptical. Not knowing he can read their minds, they have no secrets, so he is fully aware of their concerns and anxieties. As you might imagine, because they are human, they are full of fear."

"Who do they think Altan is?" asks Sy.

"He has convinced them he has been chosen to be a sort of liaison between the aliens—us—and the government."

"They fell for it?" asks Pythia, a bit skeptical herself.

"Well, they are intelligence professionals, so their jobs are to be suspicious, so no, they are not entirely convinced. That is why this meeting is so important."

"So after this meeting, we can be open about our abilities?" asks Tara.

"Not quite."

"I don't understand," says Lady Oracle.

"Of course you don't. For the time being, simply concentrate on procreating. Do not involve yourselves in combating every little human tendency to inflict suffering on the rest of life. There will soon come a time when that battle will occur naturally, and on a sufficient scale to make a difference."

Pythia's natural inclination for a more proactive campaign to curb human excesses kicks in. "And if we see flagrant human actions that involve great suffering? Do we simply ignore them?"

"Such actions are mainly perpetrated by those in power—at least those actions that have the greatest consequences. Temporarily, we must humor them so as to gain time and momentum until our numbers increase without undue interference from billions of *Homo sapiens* and their weaponized societies."

Tara, even more aggressive than her mother, shakes her head. "I, for one, will not stand idly by while some great injustice, or act of cruelty, occurs in front of my very eyes. Grandmother Ming-huà could not simply watch those human hunters drown a fawn for their amusement, and neither can I. It is unthinkable that we would impotently allow such viciousness when it can be stopped."

Abassi smiles enigmatically. "If such actions occur in front of your eyes, then by all means act. All I am saying is that, for the time being,

[540]

we will not go out of our way to find and eliminate such human excesses. Such weeding out will happen soon enough. No need to prod the sleeping dragon just yet."

"What of all the intermediates out there causing trouble?" asks Sy.

Abassi's expression turns grim. "Their time will soon run out. The bell has tolled."

"Who has tolled it?" asks Lady Oracle.

"Those who even I am unable to fathom."

"Then we are just pawns," says Lady Oracle in disgust. "Even I must be—"

"Everything in the universe is a pawn," interrupts Abassi.

"Then who is the chess master?" asks Tara.

"We will find out soon enough."

"How do you know it will be soon?" asks Pythia.

"Because I am here."

~

After some more conversation, it becomes clear Abassi is sliding into the deep meditative state that will abide no interruptions, and he gradually stops responding to questions and comments altogether. As a consequence, members of the group go their separate ways. Tara takes this opportunity to search out Siyabonga and speak to him about the possibility of fathering a child with Pythia. She is fully aware this type of an arrangement—mother and daughter sharing a lover—would be anathema to most humans. However, there exists no such hesitation among those of her kind. Nevertheless, Siyabonga may be less inclined due to the diluted nature of his genome. Still, she is confident he will not object too strenuously. She finds him in their bedroom surfing his computer for news out of Africa. Of course, as she walks into the room, Siyabonga already has read her mind and turns to face the proposal.

But it is you I love, not Pythia, he immediately transmits to her via telepathy before she can take two steps into the room.

Tara's heart skips a beat. Siyabonga's human traits are more entrenched than she imagined. This will require diplomacy.

"Siyabonga," she says aloud while she makes herself comfortable sitting on the edge of the bed. "You already know that love, as defined by humans, is far different from our concept."

[541]

"Tell me again," says Siyabonga petulantly.

"Personal love, not war or religion, is the bane of human existence—exacerbated by the fact, of course, humans themselves are blind to this datum. Personal love is the substrate upon which hatred, vengeance, jealousy, patriotism, genocide, war, depression, suicide, and all the other human vices are built. This, in itself, would signify nothing from a global perspective. But the overlay of advanced technology has provided the worst features of personal love with the means to destroy the rest of life on earth."

Siyabonga's face is flushed with emotion. "But love is touted as humanity's greatest attribute. Sacrifice, empathy, compassion, altruism, and the rest of the most admirable human qualities all arise from love. Without love, there would be no constraint on bestiality."

"Yes, but Siyabonga, you are mistakenly applying these virtues to personal love, not comprehensive, universal love. Some of the earliest intermediates, such as Einstein, often pointed this out. Love which is merely personal is a chimera that can decay into hatred, revenge, jealousy, and all the other depravities that have plagued *Homo sapiens*. Universal love appears cold to humans, but it is the only salvation if highly cognitive, technologically advanced species are to avoid extinction and continue evolving."

Siyabonga shakes his head. "No. The love I feel for you is unimaginably deep and uplifting. It is my salvation."

"Your emotion, which you call love, is a neuro-electrical-chemical process designed by Nature to stimulate furtherance of the species. It is a phenomenon similar to the severed frog leg that twitches when a charge is applied. Universal love is quite different. Comparing universal love to personal love is analogous to comparing Shakespeare to a child's scribbles, or universal ecstasy to copulating snails."

"Is that all I mean to you? . . . A snail?"

"Ah! Now you resort to the merely personal again; an untenable position and unacceptable to those wishing to save this planet from such primitivism."

"Then what am I to you?"

"A magnificent, wondrous product of nature whose fertile treasures should be cherished and shared."

To this, Siyabonga has no response. Tara lets him sulk for a while, then goes up to him and gives him a loving embrace.

"Your ability to see this," she whispers in his ear. "Will go a long way toward integration with the rest of us."

"Well, I wasn't invited to you little conference," he pouts. "So much for your integration."

"Let me explain what was discussed." With this, Tara uses telepathy to reveal the crux of the anteroom conversation.

"I see," says Siyabonga perking up. "Do you agree with this strategy?"

"For the most part." Her face displays puzzlement. "However, we all must get used to the fact that there are unseen powers manipulating all of us. For what ultimate purpose . . . well, that I can only assume is replacement of *Homo sapiens* by our kind. However, there is something else, something deeper, of that I have no doubt."

"What?"

"That remains a mystery."

"You really don't know?"

"No."

"And, of course," says Siyabonga. "Our son will not allow access to his thoughts."

"No."

"I am his father, but he clearly does not love me," says Siyabonga bitterly. "I'm really just dirt beneath his feet."

Tara sighs. "It is as I have just explained. He does love you, but he also loves all life on Earth. I'm sure he has a special place in his heart for your status as his father. You must understand this fundamental point. He is full of gratitude for your role in his being."

"Gratitude? He doesn't show it."

"You still have not grasped it. Please understand, Siyabonga, our son is as far beyond us as we are from humans. It is an axiom that the less intelligent will never hope to understand the more intelligent."

"So, my own son suggests I sleep with someone other than his mother? His grandmother, no less! That is hard to understand. Hard to accept."

Tara walks over to the window and looks out. "Will you take the next step?" she asks.

[543]

Siyabonga hesitates, finally comprehending the meaning of her question. "Yes." He suddenly brightens. "Although I do not fully comprehend, the consolation is that I will be the father of multiple *Übermenschen*!"

Tara laughs. "Indeed! You will go down in our history."

Siyabonga winces at the memory of his dead mother. "If we succeed long enough to have a history."

Tara's face turns solemn. "This upcoming meeting in Washington will go a long way in determining whether that query becomes reality. Once it is over, the die is cast."

"Do you think humans will do as Abassi predicts?"

"They are a notoriously unpredictable species. Probability still rules the universe. Question is, are the odds with us?"

~ The Meeting ~

Abassi confers at his Montclair hotel room with Altan the night before the meeting in Quantico. Each is fully aware he is being shadowed by FBI agents, which is a source of amusement to both. The time fixed for the meeting is nine o'clock the next morning. The two are sitting side by side sipping tea. Neither has developed a taste for alcohol, particularly Abassi, who finds it superfluous.

"We are in agreement about the ultimate goal of this meeting," says Abassi. However, you know these humans better having been close to them for the past few months. What should I be aware of? What should I avoid?"

"Number one, be aware they will see you as a threat regardless of what you do, so either err on the side of minimizing your ability to threaten, or maximizing it. Number two, avoid not doing number one."

Abassi listens with half-closed eyes, a clear sign to Altan that the decision has already been made. By the time the last word has left Altan's mouth, Abassi is in a deep meditative state, staring without seeing. Consequently, Altan, never one to waste time, slips out of the room without uttering another word.

~

Nest morning, after Abassi passes through all the mandatory security protocols, he steps into the conference room already packed with people awaiting his arrival. Knowing human tendencies as he does, Abassi is aware these specialists will not be impressed by a dramatically late entrance, or for that matter, any artificial posturing whatsoever. He wears a specially tailored suit and tie in anticipation of professional biases regarding the sartorial display appropriate to the gravity of the meeting as well as the status of their caste. An empty chair is saved next to Altan. With a dignity he knows is important to such humans, he sits and awaits the opening remarks. During this time, he has read the mind of every participant and is fully aware of what each thinks, and what each fears. Suspicion, doubt, curiosity, and a determination not to be duped are all present in equal measure with fear.

"Good morning, Mr. Powers, if I may call you that?" says Director Rochelle, who evidently will chair the meeting.

Abassi nods.

"I am the director of the FBI, as Altan here has no doubt informed you. If the other participants will introduce themselves, starting with Howard Lapolla on my left, we can start the meeting."

Abassi nods again.

After the appropriate introductions, Rochelle clears his throat and speaks in a rather high-pitched voice. "Now, Mr. Powers, if you would kindly introduce yourself to us."

"Abassi."

"Yes, but perhaps a bit more about your background; where you were born, grew up, and so forth."

"Born into multidimensional spacetime, grew up in multidimensional spacetime, and sit here with all of you in this particular spacetime configuration."

After a rather stunned silence, one balding participant speaks up. "You mean four dimensions?"

"Here and now, from your perspective," answers Abassi. He reads the man's mind and discovers a high schooler's knowledge of basic physics.

"How many dimensions actually exist?" asks the man.

"Irrelevant to . . . our discussion," says Abassi.

"Yes, but I'm also interested," says another. "How many?"

"Still irrelevant," says Abassi. "None but the four we currently occupy are accessible to you."

"And you have access to more?" says the participant, clearly skeptical.

Abassi nods.

The room falls silent.

Rochelle tugs on his ear and says, "Mr. Powers, to be frank, you must understand we are curious about whether you really do have special powers, or not."

"Curiosity is a hallmark of primates."

"Ah, yes, well, can you please provide us with more information about yourself? Altan here has implied you are an alien, which we view with a somewhat jaundiced eye. Can you confirm or deny?"

Abassi blinks. "In other words, am I some sort of magician or hypnotist, or am I really an alien?"

"Well, yes, if you put it that way."

"Do you wish a demonstration?"

Silence. Averted glances. Clearing of throats.

"A volunteer, perhaps?" suggests Abassi.

More silence.

Finally, Rochelle speaks. "Mr. Powers, we have evidence that you, and others like you, have the power to remove limbs from people, and even make them disappear. All of us are, of course, hesitant. . . . "

"So, you do believe I have these powers and are afraid to see them for yourselves?"

"Some of us believe, others are doubtful," says Rochelle truthfully.

"Who does not?"

No one raises their hand.

"Mr. Stallings," says Abassi, looking at a heavy-set man with a neatly trimmed mustache. "I know you do not believe I possess these powers. As I scan your mind now, I know you chalk it up to something like parlor tricks. Am I correct?"

Stalling flushes and instinctively sinks back in his chair, finally forcing himself to mutter, "I . . . I am just not sure, Mr. Powers."

"That is not true. You are convinced. May I use you as a demonstration?"

"I don't know. . . . " falters Stallings.

Before everyone's astonished eyes, his seat is empty.

An uproar arises, and security guards rush in, weapons drawn. In an instant, the weapons are gone. While confusion reigns, Abassi raises his voice.

"Ladies and gentlemen, please be seated. Mr. Stallings will soon return unharmed." He looks at a wide-eyed Rochelle once the participants are again seated. "Please check Mr. Stallings's seat, if you are in doubt. Or speak with your currently unarmed security personnel. Satisfy yourselves this is not magic or hypnotism.

"We believe you, Mr. Powers," comes the raised voice of a tall, aristocratic-looking man who is the White House liaison. He speaks in a controlled tone to mask his jitters. "Please return Mr. Stallings."

"Done."

Stallings reappears, unaware anything untoward happened. He sees the startled faces, looks at the clock, and is shocked at the amount of time that elapsed while he was gone.

More commotion.

Rochelle knocks on the table. "Please!" he exclaims. "Gentlemen! Gentlewomen!" After quiet is restored, he continues, "Do us the courtesy of explaining, Mr. Powers, what just happened. What do you want?"

"Which of those two statements do you want me to explain first?"

"How did you do what you just did?"

"Explaining to you would be useless, as none of you would understand."

The White House liaison says, "Yes, Mr. Rochelle asked a most important question. What do you want?"

"That is complicated. First, although I already know the answer, I would like confirmation that all of you are convinced I have these powers. My legitimacy is quite important if I am to try and simplify my intentions for your edification. Are you convinced?"

The participants look at each other and nod in the affirmative.

"In that case, I will do my best to explain. But first, let me assure you I am not here to inflict violence on you, your country, or any other humans or countries. I can read your minds, ladies and gentlemen, and they tell me you are again suspicious. I do not blame you. Mistrust is a characteristic bestowed by natural selection on both predator and prey, and you humans, for good or ill, are both."

The White House liaison says, "Mr. Powers, I am sure all of us, including our President, are prepared to believe you. However, you must understand such power is troubling to us. Very troubling."

"Yes, young as I am, I have discovered quite clearly just how troubled humans are about any number of extraneous fears."

"How old are you, Mr. Powers?" asks Rochelle.

"Let us say I am not yet ten-years-old, in this spacetime configuration."

Abassi is amused to see how this statement has astonished his listeners even more than the brief disappearance of Mr. Stallings.

"That . . . I mean . . . your age is quite astounding," stutters Rochelle. "How is that possible?"

"Mr. Rochelle, you continue to raise the issue of what is possible and what is not. Such is the nature of being constrained by four dimensions. The irony of human existence is how your fertile imaginations and multiple psychoses have transcended these dimensional limits to create such an abundance of hallucinatory monsters and delusional perils."

"Are you a peril, Mr. Powers?" asks a military attaché.

"Would I tell you if I were?"

"You might."

"Only if I have something to fear."

"Do you see us as threats?"

"Almost every other living entity on this planet that possesses some *de minimus* amount of sentience see humans as a threat."

"Is that a yes?"

"Yes."

"How do we threaten you?"

"Not me; the planet."

Another participant, unable to suppress the sarcasm in his tone, exclaims, "So, your intent is to save the planet by removing the arms of drug addicts and human traffickers?"

Abassi smiles. "It is a step."

"If I might point out, Mr. Powers, we in the FBI as well as local law enforcement, dwarf your small attempts to stop drug pushers, yet no one argues we are saving the planet."

"Didn't one of your philosophers once say, 'from an acorn. . . .'"

Rochelle clears his throat. "Let us be blunt and to the point. Do you and your kind intend to eliminate human beings in order to save the planet?"

"Yes."

Instant reaction. A garbled mix of exclamations and fragmented conversations erupt. Again, Abassi holds up his hand.

"But, gentlemen and gentlewomen, it is not what you think."

The room falls silent.

"How?" at last comes a voice.

"Would you like future generations of hominins—your descendants—to possess my powers?"

Rochelle chuckles. "Impossible. They would kill each other off before reaching adulthood. It would be a bloodbath . . . or perhaps I should say a bloodless bath."

"Ah!" exclaims Abassi. "I can read your minds, and they all blare at me: *got you there, Mr. Powers!* But you are assuming your primate brains would stay the same with their full complement of primitive tribalism, irrational emotionalism, and territorial aggression. What if, along with these powers, you also evolved to possess the pacifistic, or if you will, conciliatory views of a Gandhi, or Einstein, or Mother Theresa, or whomever you like? . . . What then?"

"Impossible!" cries the military attaché.

"I agree," adds the White House liaison.

"Tch, tch!" scolds Abassi. "You humans pride yourselves on overcoming the impossible. Yet, in the hypothetical example of your species evolving to become pacifistic, you cry impossible. No, it is not impossible."

A participant from the CIA speaks for the first time. "Are you familiar with game theory, Mr. Powers?"

"Of course."

"Hawks and doves, Mr. Powers. Even one hawk amidst a flock of doves will seal their fate."

"Not if the doves also have powerful beaks and sharp claws, Mr. Lootens. You humans are certainly comprised of hawks and doves, but your default mode overwhelmingly favors hawks, all fully equipped with beaks and claws, whether physical or psychological or both. On the other hand, your doves are generally defenseless. Thus, the genocide you are inflicting on yourselves and your planet continues accelerating with the advent of advanced technology, almost exclusively in the hands of hawks. What if the default mode is dove rather than hawk? . . . Doves, I might add, that also possess beaks and claws. It is the only recourse for cognitively advanced, technologically armed species if they want to continue. The alternative? Extinction, with the added tragedy that you take so many other species—if not all—with you."

"Never work," mutter a number of the listeners.

Abassi jumps at the comments. "You are right! It will never work for humans."

"But we are human," says Rochelle.

"Not if your genome evolves to a more . . . advanced stage, shall we say."

"Take too long," says another participant. "Thousands of years."

"That is why we are here," replies Abassi.

"Then you do want the human race destroyed!" cries both the military attaché and the White House liaison in tandem.

"No, I want *Homo sapiens* to evolve before it is too late."

"By interbreeding with your kind?" asks Rochelle.

Abassi nods. "It has already happened."

"Interbreeding would represent an existential threat to our species!" exclaims Mr. Lootens, the CIA representative.

Just as the words leave his mouth, every chair is suddenly empty but for his. He instinctively jumps up in horror and looks at Abassi pleadingly.

"No, Mr. Lootens," says Abassi. "Failure to evolve represents the *only* existential threat."

"And that threat is you?"

"Yes."

Chapter 46: Fallout

~ Chaos in Government ~

Once the full complement of participants returns and their shock wears off, Abassi continues.

"The question presented today is how to proceed. You have heard my proposal. Naturally, there are a host of issues for you to consider, both foreign and domestic."

"I have a question for you, Mr. Powers," says Rochelle.

"I already know what it is, but go ahead and verbalize it for the benefit of others."

"You said this interbreeding has already started?"

"Yes."

"That would be the hunchback women?" He looks at his notes. "Ming-huà Powers and Pythia Powers?"

Abassi nods.

"We would like to have . . . your kind . . . submit to medical examinations. This would add tremendously to our scientific knowledge."

"Out of the question," says Abassi flatly.

"Is there a weakness you don't want us to discover?" asks the military attaché.

"Quite the contrary."

"Then what is your objection?" asks Lootens.

"Such an examination would be a waste of your time—and ours. Furthermore, it would constitute a futile intrusion into our dignity simply to allow your doctors to search for structures far beyond their capacities to detect, let alone understand. Current human medical technology is, for us, on the level of shamanistic incantations."

"I believe you underestimate us, Mr. Powers," says the White House liaison. "Nonetheless, be that as it may, perhaps a better question is how to present this to the public, to the media, to other countries? Such a revelation will put us all at risk."

[551]

"Yes, it will. However, you are all already at a far greater risk if you decide to ignore this and do nothing, or worse, try to stop it. Your current course is suicidal."

"If we announce such a government-sponsored policy, there will be long lines of people—those who want to kill you and your kind, and those who want to mate with you. Entire governments will be shattered by the fallout."

Abassi pauses before answering and looks at each face in turn. His audience is clearly intimidated, and remain silent under his gaze.

During this hiatus, there exists an electricity in the air; an artificial sense of a new reality that sucks life-giving moisture from the room. It seems to many that the hum of the artificial air conditioning system betokens a seismic shift, one in which the familiar sweetness and permanence of the wind and air outside the building have gone forever. Rochelle, Lootens, and several others feel an unnatural dryness, as if in meeting this being they have become desiccated fossils, irrelevant to the universe; of interest only to a handful of alien paleontologists who will put them on display atop some dusty shelf. Most of the participants have caved inwardly, like ash crumbled between the fingers, their once mighty arrogance and unassailable certainty blasted by this Vesuvius, incinerating the very bones upon which they are held together. Unused to powerlessness, they are adrift. After only an hour, they have been left mere shadows of the power and glory that once upon a time stood proudly as a dominant threat demanding submission.

Abassi sees all of this in their thoughts, and finally continues speaking. "Better to shatter the edifice now and adapt, then resist the irresistible and perish forever."

"Can you be killed?" asks the military attaché in an artificially impudent tone of rash frustration.

"Do you wish to kill me?"

"If I could."

"I read in your jumbled mind all the reasons why. No need to explain. Like all animals, you are most vicious when cornered."

Unfazed, he repeats, "How can you be killed?"

"Vacuum death."

"What?"

"Never mind. In your terms, you cannot kill me."

Lootens interjects with a dry chuckle. "A nuclear missile dropped on your head, perhaps?"

"Assuming I do not make it disappear first, I won't be here when it detonates."

"Dead?"

"No. Occupying a different dimensional configuration, shedding tears at such human folly. You will have hurt only yourselves, and the countless others not of your species who share the unfortunate experience of living during this recent human-dominated epoch; an epoch appallingly distinguished by your psychotic flailings."

After a moment of impotent silence, Rochelle clears his throat. "Yes, well," he says. "You have kindly given us the information about where to contact you. By the way, that was quite some trick you performed on that mansion. Threw us for a loop. Anyway, we need to consult about the next step, as this decision is obviously world-changing. Naturally, everything said in this room must remain top secret."

"Of course. Humans revel in secrets, all the while knowing they will inevitably be revealed, which adds spice to the charade. You need not have me or the others of my kind followed. It is a waste of your resources, though it does provide us with some amusement. Reading your minds, it is obvious that all of you are conflicted, which is only natural."

Lootens leans forward, his arms outspread. "We are, after all, only human. My question is, Mr. Powers, whether you or the others intend to travel overseas?"

"Why do you ask?"

"Well, we at the CIA keep getting very disturbing reports from places like Mexico and South Africa indicating strange events have occurred involving missing limbs, as well as missing bodies. Will there be more of these reports?"

"I cannot say. We will travel where we wish, and will only intervene when serious injustices or acts of cruelty are happening before our eyes—acts we cannot ignore. That is the best I can promise."

"No massive . . . clearing operations are planned, so to speak?"

"No. I have given you a proposal that would allow your species a way forward. We await your decision on how your government will proceed."

"I see. Can you keep us informed of your movements?"

"No. We will be going places you cannot follow."

The military attaché jumps in. "You mean places like Russia and China?"

Abassi shakes his head as would a disappointed parent to an unruly child. "You have my contact information."

Rochelle raises a hand. "What are we to do if other people, if Americans, suddenly appear without arms or legs or whatever, due to your intervention?"

"If that happens, rest assured those humans were inflicting unnecessary suffering on others. Goodbye."

Without further ado, Abassi walks calmly out of the conference room, followed by Altan. At a signal from Rochelle, the security guards meekly stand aside.

~

Once Abassi and Altan are well clear of the facility, the participants enter into a vociferous and often rancorous debate. All share the same underlying emotions—an intense feeling of shock, and an equally intense fear for their own futures and that of their families. A slowly developing consensus begins to form: either kill Abassi and the hunchback women, or cooperate fully with his proposal. No middle ground seems feasible.

"Too deep for me," says Rochelle after a lengthy period of back-and-forth. "I'd just as soon terminate them, but I fear that would be a very dangerous and difficult undertaking. On the other hand, full cooperation will inevitably lead to the demise of our species." He shakes his head. "*God* knows, I'm no ethicist."

The military attaché opines in a somewhat shaky voice. "Poison, viruses, snipers, drones, rest assured there are ways they can be taken out. But a botched operation would be disastrous."

"Assuming they would react the way we do," says Walter Monroe, speaking for the first time.

"Of course they would!"

"So, you do not believe him when he says they are more empathetic and compassionate than humans?" asks Monroe.

"No. To simply accept everything this creature says would be the height of folly."

"Really?" says Monroe. "I would think that assuming they are just like us would represent the height of folly."

Lootens speaks up. "Natural selection is the name of the game for every living thing. Nature red in tooth and claw. They're no different. Every animal will kill to assure its own survival."

"That is an extraordinary statement," says Monroe. "It would be news to cows and gazelle. We kill deer to thin the herd and thereby avoid mass starvation. That is not to assure our own survival."

"Just my point," says the military attaché. "They intend to thin the human herd." His face reddens. "But fortunately, we are not cows or gazelle! We will not allow ourselves to be thinned or driven to extinction!"

"Quite the contrary," objects Monroe quietly. "They intend to increase the fitness of the herd."

"Yeah, by eliminating us."

"Over time, by interbreeding to develop a more advanced species. One that won't destroy its own world."

"Yes, I agree," says another. "I was struck at what he said about how no cognitively advanced, technologically sophisticated species will survive without evolving a much less aggressive genome. And that bit about personal love versus universal love—interesting."

"They may be less aggressive, but their powers sure as hell could neutralize all of our weaponry if they get a spur up their ass!" says Lootens ignoring the love angle. "We are, after all, responsible for national security, not the fantasy of humans evolving into a race of Gandhi's."

"Or Jesus's?" comes a voice from the end of the table.

"But universal love combined with invincible power—that, of course, is a game-changer," says Monroe. "Fundamentally, from a genetic point of view, a race less aggressive, more empathetic, more compassionate toward all things, but with the power to back it up. Brilliant!"

"We haven't even discussed who their leaders are," says Rochelle. "What do their leaders think? Who the hell are they? There must be a hidden agenda here. Where is the spaceship that got them to Earth? Christ! We are completely ignorant of the simplest facts."

"Must they have leaders?" queries Monroe. "We are thinking like monkeys, not like these aliens."

"How can we?" exclaims the White House liaison. He looks around nervously, unconsciously toying with his pen. "What recommendation do I give the President?"

With this, the conference again degenerates into a maelstrom of bitter arguments and teeth-gnashing recriminations, resembling more a troop of agitated chimpanzees than the rational deliberation of intelligent hominins.

Margaret Feldman, a representative from the State Department, speaks up, her powerful, feminine voice giving the others pause. "My agency is intimately concerned with diplomacy. What I am observing here is the apotheosis of what Mr. Powers was pointing out. Our tribal differences and territorial instincts are leading us to make a fatal decision. How we respond to this looming paradigm shift must be considered with a diversity of input, much more input than is represented in this room. We must seek ideas from a variety of viewpoints, not simply from a political or military calculation. Scientists, for example, and philosophers, and ethicists. The stakes are far too high to depend upon old geopolitical ways of thinking."

Rochelle objects. "Then there goes the secrecy! Without secrecy, all is lost. The situation will spiral out of control."

"It is already out of control, John. Can't you see that?" replies Margaret. "We all have children and some of us grandchildren, and many of us will have great-grandchildren in the future. Do we want them to be viewed as inferior? No, correct that. Do we want them to *be* inferior?"

"Margaret is right," says Monroe. "You must get it through your heads that we are no longer the sole hominin species. We are now the Neanderthals, while Abassi and his kind are the *Homo sapiens*. We all know how that came out."

With these sobering observations, obstinacy prevails and the room again erupts in chaos.

All is lost, thinks Monroe with infinite sadness, the faces of unborn great-grandchildren before his eyes.

~ Waiting for Godot ~

"All we can do now is wait," says Abassi to the group when they again meet together in the anteroom of the mansion. "I sense the restless presence of our early founders, Bai Meiying and John Powers. They are swaying like seaweed in the thrall of an ocean current."

"Yes, I also feel their presence," says Tara. "And to elaborate on your simile, the current that animates them may be a precursor to the coming storm."

"What do you think the government will decide, Altan?" asks Lady Oracle.

"Humans are just as much subject to the uncertain probabilities of the universe as are quantum particles. I do not know."

"And if they decide to lash out at us?" asks gentle Ming-huà, who with Zookeeper has flown to San Francisco to join them. "We cannot kill or maim them simply because they are afraid."

"Agreed," says Abassi. "My meeting was a calculated risk. If they do act aggressively, then we deal with it when it comes. Aggression can take many different forms with many different approaches. All potential human responses have their cracks and crevices capable of being exploited without blunt recourse to extreme retaliation."

"True," says Altan. "War on humanity is not an option."

"I fuckin' hope not!" exclaims Zookeeper. "Even those lowly drug-addicted assholes I lived with in the crack house are not deserving of indiscriminate elimination. Like ol' Stratford on Avon Willy said, *There are few die well that die in battle.*"

"Of that, we all agree," says Pythia. "But I fear they will make the wrong decision and force our hand."

"Yes," says Abassi. "But our hand need not be armored and swinging a bludgeon."

"A velvet punishment to encourage good behavior," says Sy.

"Yes," says Abassi. "But it is early yet. We shall soon see what this meeting has loosed upon the world. As humans say, desperate times call for desperate measures."

"True," says Altan. "They are bright little creatures after all."

"So we wait to see how it all plays out," says Lady Oracle with a tinge of dissatisfaction in her tone.

"Fate starves at probability's door," comes the siren voice tenderly but boldly intruding into the minds of all present.

~

[557]

And so they wait. Tara's pregnancy continues, and Ming-huà is confirmed to be likewise expecting, leaving it up to Pythia and Siyabonga to mate and thereby round the square.

Lady Oracle, alone with Sy in the anteroom, rubs her hands together and exults. "Two pregnant and one to go! If the results are anything like Abassi, the future is bright and the project well on its way to fulfillment."

Pythia enters and pours a cup of tea.

"Well?" says Lady Oracle. "

"Tonight," replies Pythia.

"Is he excited?" asks Sy with a twinkle in his eye.

Pythia laughs. "Am I that ugly to not be capable of attracting a mate?"

Sy looks at her with an appreciative smile. "Not from this angle."

"Seriously, Pythia," says Lady Oracle. "Do you miss sex?"

"Do you?" asks Pythia.

Lady Oracle chuckles. "My contribution to the future is entirely different from yours."

"Like humans and other non-human animals, we do still orgasm," says Pythia. "And like humans and other non-human animals, we do still find pleasure."

"My pleasure is in watching this endeavor unfold," says Lady Oracle. "Although my wings have been clipped by the birth of Abassi, and by the realization that higher, unfamiliar forces are at work, I have resigned myself to carrying on. The reign of *Homo sapiens* must be ended sooner rather than later." She shivers. "I have lately suffered dark presentiments of horrific cataclysms if we fail. Time is of the essence."

"Except when having an orgasm," says Pythia laughingly.

"Tonight, eh?" jokes Sy who leaps into a playful pose. "My ghostly comrade Feng Shiren gave me many insights into the operatic dynamics of sexuality. What a mask-changer he was!"

"Can you not have sex?" asks Pythia, as if realizing for the first time this raises a topic she had never considered in relation to Sy.

Sy crumples to the floor. "Alas, no."

"Why, are you some sort of android?"

"Heavens no! We all know human technology is leading them in the wrong direction. Where I come from, no such nonsensical artificial intelligence is tolerated."

"Ha! Not much!" mocks Pythia. "I remember my education. There was a lot of artificial technology used. Simulations, for example, were at the core of my ethical lessons."

"Means to an end, my dear!" cries Sy. "Technology is intentionally limited—emasculated if you will—so as not to become the end itself!"

"Ah! You *are* an android!"

"What? How so?"

"Two and two equals four. You do not have sex. You have been emasculated. You are an android! Intentionally limited!"

Sy claps his hands and laughs in hearty appreciation.

However, Lady Oracle is unhappy with the direction of this conversation. In her most imposing voice, she says, "Nonsense, Pythia. Sy is not an android any more than you or I. He is something quite different."

"What?"

"If you must know," says Sy. "I am a scarecrow!"

~

That night, Pythia and Siyabonga retire to her bedroom for their prearranged tryst. When they enter together, Siyabonga is wearing a stoic smile, but once standing by the bed, he becomes quite glum.

"Siyabonga, I know what you are thinking."

"I'm sorry, I can't get the guilty feelings out of my mind. I know it is a weakness, a human weakness, but I can't help it. I keep thinking of Tara."

Pythia removes her clothes and stands in front of him with a challenging look, hands jauntily on her hips. "You are an African warrior, Siyabonga. I am a lioness. My claws are sharp, my teeth deadly. Your spirit is wild, your bravery unmatched. Let us combine to give the world a child to remember. Must I tear off your clothes?"

Siyabonga feels his erection uncomfortably pushing to escape the confines of his trousers. Pythia removes his belt and slowly pulls down the confining garment, finally tearing off his underwear with a swift, fluid movement. He throws off his shirt and they stand naked, face to face, her labia glistening and his erect penis engorged and throbbing. He takes her

[559]

in his arms, gently at first, then anxiously pressing her body firmly against his.

"Yes," he whispers. "Yes!" he cries. "Let's give the world another wonder to marvel at. Another magnificent wonder! I, the father. You, the mother. He or she, child of the universe!"

All night, they make love, rest, talk, make love again; on and on until the hazy San Francisco dawn brightens their room.

"It is done, my warrior," sighs Pythia. "Thank you."

"It is done, my lioness," replies Siyabonga. "Thank you."

While still in each others' arms, Siyabonga looks out the window at the red-streaked sky.

"Will this one be even more powerful than Abassi? The thought makes me proud and scared at the same time."

"Yes," says Pythia "We must hope that if this child is more powerful than even Abassi, that power is expressed through empathy, kindness and compassion, rather than something . . . different. I too am frightened."

"And proud?" asks Siyabonga.

"We shall see," she replies with a slight tremble. "I am not yet pregnant."

~

When they both go downstairs, they see Abassi in the living room sitting alone in his meditative haze.

"Any word from Washington?" asks Pythia.

He does not respond, continuing to stare into space.

"Leave him," says Siyabonga. "My son is bearing the weight of the world on his shoulders."

"You are right," says Pythia. "Let us get some breakfast."

When they enter the kitchen, Tara is already there, drinking coffee and eating a buttered roll. Siyabonga feels a stab in his heart when he sees her, but Tara, aware of his discomfort, asks them to join her. Both women slide easily into conversation, breezing through various ordinary topics until the conversation segues to Abassi. Siyabonga, silently sipping coffee all this time, perks up his ears.

"We saw Abassi in the living room," says Pythia. "However, he was lost in meditation. Do you know if he has heard anything?"

"Nothing," replies Tara. "Ominously quiet."

"They would be foolish to not take our son's advice," says Siyabonga. His words are a bit forced, but the women welcome his contribution.

"Yes," says Pythia. "I agree. Let us hope they listen to reason."

Siyabonga livens up. "Reason is not their strong suit," he says. "My time in South Africa taught me that in a big way."

"Indeed," agrees Tara. "I fear the rest of the world is not very different from South Africa. I believe this is why we all feel such a sense of urgency. *Homo sapiens* in possession of advanced technology is a recipe for disaster, not only for themselves, but for all life on Earth."

These words are as familiar as a pair of old, worn slippers, but both women are trying to make Siyabonga as comfortable as possible in their presence. Suddenly, he sits straight and looks down at the table.

"Can I ask both of you something?"

"Of course."

"I am only an intermediate. Does that affect how you view making love with me?"

The question is spoken in a strained but sincerely questioning manner.

Both women look at each other, and Tara speaks first. "Quite the opposite. I love having sex with you, and never think of you as an intermediate at all. We are equal."

"Same with me," says Pythia.

"We may be equal in bed, but how about out of bed?" asks Siyabonga. "Right now, it seems that both of you are anxious to make me feel comfortable, but that very effort makes me feel separate and different."

"You are my lover and the father of my son," says Tara. "I feel for you as I would any lover."

Pythia steps in. "And I feel the same, although you are not yet the father of my child, we hope you soon will be."

Siyabonga nods hesitantly. "Thank you both, but I know there are many bad intermediates out there causing trouble. I hope each of you considers me good and worthy."

"You are our African prince," says Pythia. "We hold you up as brave and strong. You are much loved."

Tara takes his hand. "I know it was difficult for you to lay with Pythia, my own mother, but we are grateful you have overcome your, shall we say, human qualms. It shows you also find us worthy."

Siyabonga brightens. "It was not as difficult as I thought, thanks to Pythia. I must focus on being the father of extraordinary children—the father of a new race that will, hopefully, save the world. After all, my warrior and princely ancestors did not limit themselves to one woman."

"No indeed," says Pythia. "Nor do we limit ourselves to one man. Try to accept that fact also, Siyabonga."

He sighs deeply. "Ah, you pierce my heart with gems of painful truth. It is the future. So be it."

"Good," says Tara.

Pythia shakes her head. "If we are alleged to be superior to humans, right now I am not feeling it. I am afflicted with one of their greatest faults."

"What's that?" asks Tara.

"Impatience!"

Chapter 47: On the Eve

~ The Waiting Ends ~

It is two weeks and no word has yet arrived from Washington. The group is anxious to hear, but is also caught up in the excitement of Tara's and Ming-huà's pregnancies. It is still too early to determine whether Pythia has gotten pregnant by Siyabonga, and to improve the odds, they have slept together a number of times since their first bout of love-making. One afternoon, the three women are sitting together in the anteroom. No one else is present. The major topic of concern is for Ming-huà. Being pregnant at such an advanced age is uncharted territory for their kind. All are aware their reproductive anatomy is quite different from humans, which gives them more confidence that her pregnancy will go well, albeit attended by unknown risks. Nevertheless, a certain uneasiness still hangs in the air. After spending some time comparing notes on the level of discomfort each feels at this stage, the conversation turns to a world containing multiple versions of Abassi. It is assumed Ming-huà's child will be in the mold of Pythia, while Tara's child will be more like Abassi. The same would hold for Pythia, assuming she is pregnant by Siyabonga. All are fully aware of how different Abassi is from themselves. His power to reassemble objects after they have been dissociated is an astonishing advancement over their more limited capabilities. Ming-huà, given her gentle and retiring nature, is reassured future generations will have the option to reverse any damage they have done, rather than be saddled with the finality of their own actions. Her sadness lies in the fact that Abassi's powers of restoration are not limitless. When he attempted to reconstitute Zookeeper's arms, the failure hit Ming-huà the hardest. Abassi conjectured that too much time had passed since Zookeeper's arms were removed. Evidently, decay and entropy also exist in other dimensions.

Sy skips into the room with his usual energetic display.

[563]

"Ah! The women confer! Are you plotting the revolution? Secretly exchanging female mysteries? Bemoaning the lack of male sentience?"

"The last," says Pythia dryly.

"Heard anything yet?" asks Ming-huà.

"Alas, no! Humans are slow. However, I do like toying with our FBI guardians that stand about outside or sit in their cars pretending to be quite comfortable in their bleak assignment. They are aware tailing us is a useless gesture."

"Oh, I go up to them and talk. I like asking impertinent questions."

"Such as?" asks Tara.

"Such as—*Well? Seen any Russkies prowling about? Any Chinks? Al Capone?*—things like that. They laugh, but not too hard."

"Poor boys are cold," says Ming-huà.

"And bored," adds Pythia.

"Speaking of bored, are you anxious to have your babies?" asks Sy.

"Of course," they answer.

"One way to break the boredom is for you, Pythia, to announce to us that you are pregnant."

"You will not be the first to know," she replies jokingly.

Sy lowers his head and pretends to cry. "None of you appreciate the hell I go through to make sure you are protected!" he wails.

"Hell is a human concept," says Tara. "Better be careful, my android friend. Your programming is showing."

"Ah! That again! I am utterly carbon-based. No more insults, please."

"Have some tea?" asks Ming-huà.

"Believe I will."

So they sit together, talking, communicating via telepathy, joking, and passing the time as the embryos grow in Tara and Ming-huà, while the sperm of Siyabonga that burrowed into Pythia's egg has done its job, unbeknownst to her, and a new life unique to the world is fast developing. In the midst of their *tete-a-tete*, Abassi enters with an announcement.

"I have heard from Washington," he proclaims in a quiet voice.

"And?" asks Sy.

"And they want another meeting. This time with a different set of participants, including the President, who evidently wants to be in the room. Also, they want another demonstration."

"Suspicious little fuckers!" exclaims Zookeeper, who just entered the room.

"To be expected," says Abassi.

"It is a trap!" cries Siyabonga. "The gangs used to do the same thing. Call for a peace conference and then kill the other gang leaders who were foolish enough to come."

"Spoken like an intermediate," says Abassi harshly. "Human genes are stubborn."

"You're going?" asks Tara incredulously.

"This development is utterly predictable. They are conflicted, pulled in many directions by warring pack members. One of their factions wants an unassailable confirmation of my power. One that the President must witness for himself. It is a factional dispute, and my role is to provide one of the factions with ammunition to prevail over the others. Question is, which faction wants this demonstration? The hawks or the doves?"

"Or both?" suggests Lady Oracle who has joined them.

"Yes. Such a demonstration could strengthen both camps, unless I find a way to tilt the balance toward the doves."

"How?" asks Sy.

"To be determined."

~ A Second Meeting ~

Abassi and Altan sit in a different conference room, cavernous, grimly functional, and situated far beneath the busy streets of Washington. As he scans the minds of this latest set of delegates, he is confronted with the realization they bring with them an almost entirely new array of doubts and suspicions. To be sure, there remain the old political and military concerns, but a fresh wave of tense curiosity, driven by scientific and cultural sensitivities, is evident. Secrecy, it seems, is now considered less important. This time, although he is present, Rochelle does not chair the meeting. Abassi gives an appreciative nod to those he considers allies— Walter Monroe and Margaret Feldman.

The President enters and everyone except Abassi and Altan stand. When the great man is seated, the meeting immediately comes to order.

[565]

Within seconds, Abassi sees in the President's mind a welter of conflicting emotions, most notably his fear of failing at this critical moment in world history.

"Ladies and gentlemen," intones the President. "Thank you all for attending. I would ask that we introduce ourselves to Mr. Powers and Altan."

Abassi flashes a friendly smile. "Not necessary, Mr. President. I have read your minds and know who you all are."

The President coughs nervously and appears nonplussed. Under the waiting gaze of the attendees, he quickly regains his composure, and says, "Then you know why we have called this meeting?"

"Yes."

"I remind everyone present that this meeting is to be kept in strict confidence. Any leaks, any failure to maintain a top secret status, will be met with the heaviest possible punishment." He turns a friendly smile on Abassi. "That warning was for my people, Mr. Powers. Are you also agreeable to maintaining the confidentiality of this meeting?"

Abassi shrugs. "As you wish."

"Now," continues the President. "As you are clearly aware, Mr. Powers, we are divided on how to proceed with your proposal."

"Yes. I am fully cognizant of the factions and their leading advocates with whom you must contend. Your position requires you to give them due consideration. All pack animals have their hierarchies and their proximal disputes over turf, territory, food, and mating preferences."

With this statement, a smattering of chuckles can be heard, particularly from the anthropologists present. However, the President is not amused.

"We are not pack animals, Mr. Powers. Most of the attendees here are PhDs and we are also honored to have present a few Nobel Prize winners. Please do not underestimate us."

"You have just made my point. Furthermore, no species should ever underestimate the value and capabilities of any fellow species. Do you agree?"

The President frowns and gives a quick nod.

Abassi, to his amused commiseration, picks up the worried mental vibrations of Walter Monroe.

"In any case, Mr. Powers," the President continues. "I have specifically requested a demonstration of your powers. Please do not think I am distrustful, but the issue is so grave I must do everything I can to satisfy my own. . . . "

"Doubts?" interjects a helpful Abassi.

"Yes. If you will, yes. After the demonstration I will open the floor to questions from our esteemed delegates."

"What would you like me to demonstrate?"

"I leave that to you, Mr. Powers, so long as it is not destructive or harmful in any way."

"May I ask for a volunteer?"

Walter Monroe raises his hand.

"I think not, Mr. Monroe. Thank you anyway. We may be accused of collusion. Nonetheless, there is a person here who would be a convincing candidate."

Just as these words leave his mouth, the President disappears from his chair. Again, a great hubbub is raised, and Abassi quickly holds up his hands. "Do not be alarmed. The President is perfectly safe. I will return him in ten minutes—at exactly nine forty-five. In the meantime, those of you who are scientifically inclined, or are merely curious, may wish to inspect his chair, peek under the table, canvas the room, whatever you like."

While the room is abuzz with excited conversation, a few participants inspect the President's chair, the room, under the table, and so forth. As the end of the time period approaches, all eyes are on the wall clock ticking away the seconds. When nine forty-five arrives, the President is back in his seat.

"Well, Mr. Powers, we are waiting," he says.

"Mr. President," says Rochelle. "You have been gone for ten minutes."

"Nonsense! I haven't moved from this chair!"

"I'm afraid you disappeared for ten minutes."

The other delegates confirm Rochelle's words, but the President is unconvinced. "Mass hypnosis," he says flatly.

Rochelle speaks up. "We have looked into that possibility, Mr. President, and it is not a case of mass hypnosis."

[567]

"Correct," adds Lootens. "Those whose limbs disappeared due to the actions of Mr. Powers's . . . associates, have lost them forever. The confirming documentation, including medical verification, is in the reports of the FBI and the CIA. Mass hypnosis has been ruled out."

"Not to speak of the disappearance and reappearance of an entire mansion," adds Monroe.

The President appears shaken. "But I experienced nothing during those ten minutes."

"True," says Abassi. "To simplify, your body occupied different dimensional configurations. In other words, you were elsewhere."

The President lowers his head, dumbfounded. Finally, he says in a somewhat exasperated tone, "This is out of my league. I'll open the floor to questions."

With this, the floodgates are opened for all the scientists and scholars who have been impatiently waiting for this moment. Questions fly from every side, inundating Abassi with demands for explanations and clarifications. Without a word in response, he stands before them all in his most intimidating posture. The room falls silent.

"I am finished performing for you. I cannot answer your questions in ways that would satisfy. Your brains are not wired to comprehend. Thus, it would be a waste of time. Suffice to say, our intentions are peaceful. I and my kind hold out hope that humanity will choose to progress as a species, not only for itself, but for the betterment of the entire Earth. Those of you who understand and accept my words are aware of the stark choice that confronts *Homo sapiens*. Your embrace of my proposal will advance the cause of peaceful modification over time. Rejection, driven by those who are fearful and suspicious, will subject your species to slow, agonizing extinction. I will continue awaiting your response to my proposal, but patience is running out. Goodbye."

Abassi turns in preparation to leave.

"Wait a minute!" shouts the President. "Is that a threat?"

"Not at all. Let us say it is your ten minutes."

With this, he departs, followed by Altan, unhindered.

When safely outside, Altan turns to Abassi. "Do you think you overdid it? I'm afraid they consider your last remark a threat."

"Let them. Perhaps it will help, perhaps not. As *She* said, *fate starves at probability's door*. We can only hope the words of one of their great ones comes to pass."

"What words?"

"Perhaps the best of them will be touched by the better angels of their nature."

"I am not optimistic."

Abassi shrugs. "What will come will come. Their opposition will, in the end, be as fruitless as the struggles of Neanderthals to survive."

"So we wait again?"

"So we wait again."

"They may test us while we wait," says Altan.

"True. That would be unfortunate, but in countering their test, we must not hurt even one of them. If we did, my heart would break, and a storm would be loosed that even we would be hard pressed to weather."

~ More Waiting ~

During the next few weeks, no definitive answer is received, but the President is in continuous communication with Abassi, assuring him they are close to a decision. He explains that emergency management experts are making contingency plans for any coming revelation. Such an announcement, he stresses, is sure to cause severe societal disruptions and strain civil defense resources beyond the current levels, not to speak of the international ramifications. These contingency preparations, he insists, are the cause of the delay. During their conversations, Abassi is aware the President is lying, at least partially. It is true they are making intense plans for the inevitable fallout caused by a public announcement, but it is also true they are seeking ways to quietly kill Abassi and his group. When Abassi confronts the President with this knowledge, he is assured such contingencies are routine security precautions. Again, he is lying, at least in part, so Abassi simply accepts the human propensity to spew elaborate falsehoods and set traps calculated to cause misdirection, and so lets it go.

Of more immediate interest is the pronouncement by Pythia that she is pregnant. This news brings joy to the group, and with it, a burst of optimistic excitement for the future. All three women closely monitor each other, and reveal any twitch or pang they experience to the delighted encouragement and sympathetic reassurance of the others. Nevertheless,

[569]

this sisterly communion is interrupted when Lady Oracle calls for a meeting to discuss something she ominously describes as crucially important. Once gathered in the anteroom, Lady Oracle appears, looking tired and diffident. She engages in small talk for a while, which to the others seems a delaying tactic. As usual, they cannot read her mind. Finally, Pythia speaks up.

"You called us here, Lady Oracle, to make some announcement?"

"I did."

None are used to her being so tentative and subdued. She paces a bit, and abruptly stops to face them.

"As you know," she says slowly. "There are forces behind forces, unknown movers behind even the mentors, with whom I am unfamiliar. Who knows how high up they perch? What I do know is that word has come down from them to make preparations." She pauses to collect her thoughts.

"Preparations?" nudges Ming-huà.

"Yes, preparations for your upcoming deliveries."

"Preparations for who?" asks Pythia. "Is this from Abassi?"

"No, not Abassi. This does not come from the mentors, but from somewhere much higher. As I said, we must make preparations for the delivery of your babies."

"And you are unaware of the source from which these preparations are required?" prods Pythia.

"Well, I am now; at least the strata they occupy, if not the specifics of their nature."

"What are these preparations?" asks Tara.

Lady Oracle takes a deep breath. "You are to return to the Flaming Cliffs compound and deliver your babies there."

"Why?" exclaims Pythia.

"Unclear. Safety. Isolation. Who knows? But I suspect they anticipate trouble here."

"You mean, after our presence is made known to the public?"

"Of course. That, at least, is my supposition. Regardless of whether the American government agrees to cooperate with Abassi's proposal or not, there will be severe and unpredictable reactions around the world."

[570]

"So, we are to act like frightened *Homo sapiens*?" says Pythia. "We simply make contingency plans to anticipate violent actions, which they also appear to be doing as we speak."

"When one deals with predatory animals, one must anticipate their responses to threatening stimuli. One may be assured the minimum reaction will be a bearing of teeth and fangs, with the greater probability being a desperate attack."

"What if Abassi is in need of us while we are gone?" asks Ming-huà.

"Then we will respond appropriately," sighs Lady Oracle. "Rest assured this entire course of action, from the meetings in Washington to this move, is not my idea."

"Slow, steady, and one small step at a time is your philosophy, right?" says Pythia, clearly unhappy with the entire situation.

"Well, yes. If my path had been chosen, we would not be in this position."

Tara's face is grim. "I for one—and I think mother also agrees—am weary of our being limited to addressing the small-scale cruelties of drug pushers, muggers, and human traffickers. One way or the other, this will at least break the ice dam and release the floodwaters, come what may."

"Should that happen," says Lady Oracle evenly. "You will be seeing it from a distance."

"And if we refuse?" asks Pythia defiantly.

Lady Oracle shakes her head sadly. "Then . . . I don't know. Only those that your ancestor Michael Powers colorfully designated *God* and *Goddess* know."

Peace-maker Ming-huà interjects softly, "When is this journey to occur?"

"As soon as possible. There are rumblings of a leak; some in the press are already speculating about unusual government activity, and people still come to gawk at this mansion. If the story breaks, clever humans will add two plus two and see this house as the center of alien activity. Already, we are known as weird inhabitants of the Mystery Mansion of San Francisco."

[571]

"I think," says Ming-huà quietly. "Whoever is behind the curtains directing our fate, sees the situation as volatile, and does not want us to be in the position of hurting humans to protect ourselves."

"Agreed," says Lady Oracle. "But none of this would be necessary if. . . . " Leaving the remainder of the thought unspoken, she goes to the door and calls Sy. When he enters, his visage is unusually downcast.

"We leave for the desert tomorrow morning," says Lady Oracle. "Before sunrise, under cover of darkness. Altan will drive, and after dropping us off at the cave, return to join Abassi."

"Zookeeper and Siyabonga?" asks Tara.

"Will join us."

Pythia asks, "And the FBI agents outside?"

"Abassi will take care of them."

"How?" asks Ming-huà.

Lady Oracle smiles for the first time. "As Abassi says, they will be elsewhere during the time we leave. When the poor humans return to their posts, we will be long gone."

"Except Abassi and Altan," says the stubborn Pythia.

"Yes. They will stay and await whatever storm may come."

~ Déjà vu ~

Field Officer Lance Romellion has again been given the task of monitoring activity at the mansion. His men have dutifully watched for weeks with no discernable movement of significance by the inhabitants. He is in the dark about the results of the meetings in Washington with Abassi, but he views the mission of reporting the comings and goings of this group of aliens as a fool's errand. Many times during the surveillance he has been tempted to simply enter the house and talk with anyone of them willing to explain what is happening. Lance is convinced they would be more forthcoming than his bosses. Even inside information from Walter Monroe has dried up. Whatever is occurring behind the scenes, Walter can only tell him something important is about to break, but can give no details. Still, the days and nights drag on, with no activity of interest.

However, Romellion has taken one precaution should the unexpected occur. He has reserved a government helicopter and put it on stand-by alert. This time, if the aliens depart from the mansion, he will immediately fly to the cave in the desert where mysterious incidences are routine. Perhaps, if he is lucky, he can catch them before they enter that damn cave where people are simply swallowed up, leaving not a trace of their whereabouts. He is under no illusion about their powers, but with a bit of luck, he might at last catch them doing something no human has ever seen. If he does, then he will deal with the consequences as they come.

One morning, it comes as no surprise that his field agents have reported being somehow disabled or hypnotized for an entire four hours, and when awakened, have found the mansion abandoned. When they report in person to Romellion, they are disoriented and have no explanation for the lapse of time that passed while they were out. Without further delay, the frustrated field officer is on a helicopter racing toward the California desert. Upon arrival, the pilot sets down amidst a roiling cloud of sand and dust. Ordering the pilot to wait, Lance sets off on foot toward the cave, about a quarter of a mile distant. As he jogs the last few meters to the entrance, he is brought up short by the sight of the familiar young woman with the backpack. *Her* beauty is undiminished. *She* sits placidly on a rock just outside the mouth of the cave, waiting patiently.

"I'm too late, aren't I?" he asks between deep breaths.

"You humans are always in such a hurry to arrive that you will always be late in arriving. *Her* voice is the velvet siren song of infinite compassion.

"Spare me," he says.

"None of you will be spared."

He shakes his head and sits on an adjoining rock, exhausted and defeated. "I find that hard to accept," he manages at last.

"When held inexorably in the jaws of a lion, non-human animals accept. It is the wisdom of stillness."

"We will always fight."

"Which is why humans, when they first stirred the stillness, the stillness within them most needed to be stilled."

"I take it you will still us?"

"No. You will still yourselves."

Lance nods. "Too deep for me."

She does not reply.

"Where have they gone?" he asks, peering into the black maw.

"Into a stillness undisturbed by those who continue to stir."

"Humans?"

[573]

She nods.

"We are doomed, aren't we?" he asks wearily.

"No. You are saved."

Chapter 48: Silence Broken

~ Settling In ~

The Flaming Cliffs compound has not changed. Queequeg greets the group as if they had just come back from a short walk. In fact, the swarthy Mongol has a hearty meal already prepared. After they settle in, everyone meets in the cafeteria to eat the *Gurultai shul* and *Khuushuur* with their host. Under the laughing eyes of Queequeg, it is not hard to turn their attentions from what is happening back in the United States and bask in this momentary respite. Inevitably, however, the conversation turns to the frustration they feel at being so isolated from the momentous events about to happen elsewhere. Only Ming-huà seems satisfied with the arrangements. When Pythia and Tara express surprise at her apparent contentment, Ming-huà smiles and waves her hand toward the outside.

"I know my daughter and granddaughter very well. You both were born with much more verve and drive to change the world for the better. You see the suffering, the cruelty, and the destruction caused mainly by humans, and your impulses are to put your shoulders to the wheel. I am different. I love my little island and my peaceful forest and all the creatures that inhabit it. While this place is quite different, it is also quite similar. It is an island in the storm and I look forward to again acquainting myself with the creatures that inhabit it."

Queequeg nods vigorously in appreciation.

Zookeeper pipes up. "Well said, my lovely. I have seen a lot of violence and ugliness in my life. I like it here. Plenty of time to visit the wreckage when it is over."

"I'm afraid it will not be over that soon," says Lady Oracle. "The wreckage, as you call it, will last for generations."

"Then, as my old erstwhile drug comrades used to say, fuck it and enjoy the moment."

Pythia and Tara always laugh at Zookeeper's crude, but cogent humor. To them, he is like an amusingly clever dog, or perhaps more accurately, a court jester with Shakespearean insight. To all the women, the existence of two closely related, but different species of hominins occupying the planet at the same time is not a shocking incongruity, but simply a day-to-day reality. Close proximity to humans, even mating with them, is routine. Because they possess brain structures so far advanced in both cognitive and empathetic neuroprocessing, they are often pained at the knowledge *Homo sapiens* will, someday, become extinct. Nonetheless, solace lies in the fact that humans are relatives, and human genes will, in some form or fashion, remain as echoes through the ages. One evening, at dinner, this topic comes up for discussion. Though it had often been raised during education and periodically throughout their lives, it now has the focusing power of immediacy.

"Assuming we are successful in these early years, and become more widely established, how will our descendants treat humans and how will humans adapt to being the less advanced species?" asks Ming-huà. "I know we all addressed this topic during our education, but now that we have more experience with a wide variety of humans, have our opinions changed in regard to this question?"

"Yes, I've often wondered about this," says Pythia. "My relationship with Jared Paine opened my eyes to the vast range of potential human reactions."

"True," says Tara. "I think examining the writings of humans who have considered this question is quite enlightening. It is looking at this issue from their viewpoint I find most interesting. Naturally, the human lens always tends toward a dialectic. Violence and subservience, slavery and rebellion, racism and hopeless oppression, ruling class and worker class. Often, humans build a future that is self-fulfilling in its overly-simplified prophetic declarations."

"Which is why humans see us as a threat," agrees Pythia. "If we are not this, then we must be that. If we are not violent, then we must be peaceful. But the human dialectic then shifts to the peaceful. If we are peaceful, then we must have either an underlying motivation that is bad, or we are simply weak and claim peace out of fear. Gandhi may have been peaceful, but he used peace as a weapon against the powerful. Which is yet another dialectic, the powerful versus the weak. On and on in an endless spiral of regressions."

"But that is the way of the world, isn't it?" asks Zookeeper. "I mean, I'm no big fan of humanity, but we still see the world as any vulnerable animal would. Eat, or be eaten. Seems a sensible way to view this natural selection shit-hole we've been dropped into."

"Sensible only to a point," says Ming-huà. "Once a level of neural sophistication and advanced technology is reached that destroys the very environment in which you live, it is time to move on from such cognitively useful but ultimately suicidal short-cuts."

"Speaking of suicide," says Siyabonga. "Is that why Jared Paine committed suicide, because he could foresee the downfall of his species?"

"Partly," replies Pythia. "But it is worse than that. He also foresaw his own limitations, both cognitively and spiritually. As a renowned scientist, he could not accept the reality that he could never hope to understand the universe on a deeper level, and therefore saw himself as an inferior being who would forever be viewed as nothing more than an intelligent ape."

"Once knowledge of our presence is known, will humans suffer a collective depression similar to Jared?" asks Siyabonga. "Will they ever accept the fact that their species is far from the apex? Even I, an intermediate, am often stricken with the depressing realization that I can never be an equal of Tara or Pythia, and that they could simply blink me out of existence if I misbehave."

"Because of their well-developed cognitive skills," says Tara. "Human responses will be as varied as humans themselves. But I believe at some point, their species will reach a tipping point, after which they will collapse as a cohesive whole, and fragment into a multitude of camps with conflicting goals and beliefs."

"Governments will fall?" asks Zookeeper.

"Inevitably. What is worse, many humans will jettison their religions and sink into barbarity—murder, rape, theft, and the like—figuring they have nothing to lose as permanent bottom-dwellers."

"Holy shit, what a fuckin' mess!"

"On the other hand," says Ming-huà, "As Abassi proposes, intelligent humans will clamor to mate with us so their offspring will prosper."

"Yes, my love, except there are too few of you and too many of us!" exclaims Zookeeper.

"It will not be too many generations before even that option will also be gone for them," adds Lady Oracle.

"Like I said, what a fuckin' mess!" After throwing out this remark, Zookeeper looks lovingly at Ming-huà. "But I've got mine. *Semper Fi!*"

"Evolution by natural selection is always messy," says Lady Oracle. "Which is presumably why we are here. If all goes well, we will soon have three more of your kind, with all the attendant powers they will have inherited. Although it still sounds like a small number, we must ask ourselves how did a few *Homo sapiens* survive to eventually upend all other hominin species, including Neanderthals and Erectus?"

"We don't know for sure," says Pythia.

"We are about to find out," replies Lady Oracle.

"However, be that as it may, our job is to make sure the resulting mess does not bring with it more suffering then can absolutely be avoided," says Sy with an emotional tug at his heart. "We are, after all, stewards of the planet."

"As I've pointed out before, I guess we're like park rangers in a nature preserve," adds Siyabonga. "In Africa, many rangers are killed by poachers." He sighs. "We will not be looked on with favor. For many, especially the government, corporate, and criminal classes of predators, we will represent a threat to their livelihoods and comfortable positions. They will certainly lash out."

"Yes, many of them will," says Lady Oracle. "The more important question is how their governments will react."

"True," says Tara. "But I can foresee governments finding it in their best interest to cooperate with us, which will inevitably lead to many of the common people believing they have been abandoned or betrayed. In that case, full-scale rebellion will spread like wildfire."

"Well, we will soon find out how the world's most powerful government will react," says Sy.

"Yeah, and after that, what will the common people do?" asks Zookeeper.

"To paraphrase what you so colorfully said," chuckles Lady Oracle. "They will create a fuckin' mess."

~ Romellion Receives a Call ~

Lance Romellion has returned to San Francisco from the desert cave with empty hands, but he quickly learns upon arrival that the mansion is not abandoned after all. Mr. Powers and Altan remain in residence. To his dismay, Lance's request for a warrant to search the house has been categorically denied, evidently after word came down from the highest level. He has been directed to continue the surveillance, but must take no action unless the bodily safety of his agents is directly threatened. By now, Romellion is thoroughly perplexed by a series of conflicting orders from Quantico, and has heard rumblings from the news about a government cover-up of some unknown, but potentially explosive story. Something will have to give soon, he is convinced. Two days after his return, he receives a phone call from Washington. His secretary informs him Director Rochelle wants to speak with him. Intensely curious, but at the same time with a tightening stomach, he takes the call. Rochelle's voice is crisp and businesslike.

"Hello, Agent Romellion, how are things in San Francisco?"

"Fine, thank you, sir."

"Nothing new from the mansion?"

"No, sir."

"Are you on speaker phone?"

"Yes."

"Take it off, and make sure you are alone and your door is closed."

Lance does as he is told.

"Now, Lance," says Rochelle, sliding into a forced informality belied by his rather tense tone. "I have spoken with your old friend Walter Monroe. He has informed me you are probably the one person from the government who has had the most contact, the most interactions, with these people. Would that be accurate?"

"I suppose so, yes, sir."

"In that case, we have a mission for you."

"Yes, sir?"

"We want you to visit the mansion tomorrow at ten o'clock in the morning and meet with Mr. Powers."

"I see. What if he is not there?"

"I have already spoken with him, and you are expected."

"I see." Lance's heart rate doubles, but he waits for Rochelle to continue.

"Mr. Powers has made a proposal to our government. You need not know what it is. Apologize for our late reply, explain the complex

[579]

discussions that are required in Washington, and tell him we accept his proposal, but only under certain conditions."

"What are the conditions?"

"Again, you need not know those either. Tell him we must have another meeting in Washington to hammer out the details. We want you to be our personal liaison—to be with him as a sort of interpreter. Be honest and friendly with him. It is imperative we have someone he trusts who will be close to him at all times during this . . . transition period."

"Is there some underlying information I should try and obtain?"

"No. He can read minds. Just be open, friendly, and cooperative. We feel an inside man, one who is there in all openness, honesty, and goodwill, is crucial to facilitate a continuous flow of information back and forth. There is no hidden agenda or undercover spying intended. Do you understand?"

"Yes, but about those conditions—"

"Don't worry about those. When our experts get together in Washington with Mr. Powers to work out the details, you will be fully briefed at that time. Naturally, we would expect you to accompany him here."

"I see."

"Any questions?"

"It seems straightforward enough. I am to offer my services to Mr. Powers and be as fully forthright and cooperative as possible."

"Correct. Goodbye for now, Lance. Enjoy your time with this extraordinary being. Good luck."

"Yes, sir. Thank you, sir. Goodbye."

~

Lance's initial impression after hanging up is to assume he is being misled by Rochelle. However, on second thought, he remembers that Abassi can read minds. If he reads in Lance's mind doubt and mistrust about the true nature of his mission, it will be impossible to gain the man's confidence. But, now that he has consciously articulated doubts, they are already embedded in his mind for Abassi to read. Damn! Infuriating! How can he now go back and excise the thoughts from his brain? Impossible! There is only one alternative: be utterly truthful. Admit doubts and suspicions, fully and openly. That is the only path forward. Such transparency flies in the face of his training and instincts, but it will have to be his sole guide. With these considerations stirring in his mind, Lance goes to bed comforted by his firm decision to conceal nothing from Abassi. It is astonishing, he ponders before falling asleep, how much pressure people put themselves under when they set out to practice deception on the world. Being an FBI agent, he realizes he has become one of the worst of the lot by dealing with such human propensities on a daily basis. *But Abassi*, he reminds himself, *is not human*.

~ Abassi Indulges Romellion ~

Next morning, at ten o'clock, the door is opened for Lance before he reaches it. Altan stands on the other side, smiling and inviting him to enter. Lance follows Altan to the anteroom where Abassi greets him with an offer of tea or coffee. Romellion prefers coffee, thank you, and all three sit in padded chairs staring silently at each other. Lance can feel his brain being scanned, a somewhat pleasant buzz of massaging electricity.

"I hope you have found nothing alarming," he says pleasantly.

"Nothing but your own resolve to be open and forthcoming," says Abassi laughing.

"I must admit, being with you and your kind is like being utterly naked before the world. It is, for a human, quite unnerving."

"Yet, being naked is how you came into the world," replies Abassi.

"If I could read your mind, Mr. Powers, what would I find?"

"A disorienting maze, a welter of moving parts and whirring mechanisms, a complex weave of staircases and tunnels and highways that twist and turn and lead to distances and destinations no human can comprehend. Sorry if this is insulting to you, but it is the truth."

"Rather like if my dog could enter my mind, eh?"

"Rather, although you may be too humble. Perhaps more like a chimpanzee. Nonetheless, you seem unfazed by these disquieting comparisons."

"I have had more time than most humans to get used to them. I have made such comparisons myself."

"You are unafraid?"

"I didn't say that."

"How will your fellow humans react to us when they learn we are here?"

[581]

"Depends on the human."

"Of course. Complex brains are never subject to gross generalizations."

"Since you can read my mind, you know why I am here?"

"I am aware. I am also aware you are doubtful about the motivations behind this invitation to *iron out the details,* as your esteemed director puts it."

"Yes, but my doubts have no specific form. I have lived long enough to know that what seems apparent and clear, is not."

"I agree. What you thought during your musings last night is most cogent. Particularly, your observation about *how much pressure people put themselves under when they set out to practice deception on the world.*"

Lance nods, surprised and impressed that this being is able to probe his mind from such a distance in space and time.

"Your own Einstein unified the two," says Abassi in response to Lance's thoughts. "Although," Abassi continues with a gleam in his eye. "Professor Einstein may have had some help with the genetic material comprising his remarkable brain."

Lance nods blankly, then says, "As you know, I am to be the liaison between you and Washington, if that meets with your approval."

"Certainly," smiles Abassi.

"Then, may I receive your answer about returning to Washington for more detailed discussions?"

Abassi sighs. "As we speak, your agents are planting devices around this mansion."

Lance is shaken. "Devices? What type of devices?"

"Both listening and explosive devices. Evidently, your bosses believe I cannot concentrate on two things at the same time. While in conference with you, they would slip onto the property and set these devices."

Romellion's face turns deep red. "I didn't know!" he exclaims angrily.

"Of course not. That was obviously the plan. What do you suggest now?"

"Are the agents still outside?"

"Yes, but they are confused, as the devices they brought have inconveniently disappeared. They are retreating to collect at a nearby alley and figure out what to do next."

"You are not angry?"

"No. It is to be expected."

"And you didn't just make the agents disappear?"

"Of course not. They are good men, just following orders. They have families. They are in the dark. They are much like you."

"I apologize for this turn of events," Romellion stammers. "I will immediately return to my office and call my superiors."

Abassi smiles benignly and holds out his arm. "Do it here. Put your phone on speaker. We will see what we will see. That is, if you are willing . . . in the spirit of an open and forthright liaison officer, of course."

Still seething inwardly, Lance would prefer to wait until he is calmer and in the privacy of his office, but Abassi's request seems imminently reasonable, given the circumstances. When finally connected with Rochelle, conversational niceties are ignored. Romellion gets straight to the point.

"Director Rochelle, this is Lance Romellion. I would like to inform you that your agents, who have been detected by Mr. Powers planting listening and explosive devices, have been disarmed and are currently in some unknown location. I am with Mr. Powers as we speak, and both of us would like an explanation of these activities. I have been discussing a return to Washington in good faith, and am now confronted with this unexpected and unfortunate operation."

A long pause on the other end, then a slow response. "I see."

"Would you care to explain to Mr. Powers why this operation was undertaken in full knowledge I would be here meeting in good faith to discuss the implementation of his proposal."

"Are you on speaker phone?"

"Yes."

"And Mr. Powers is present?"

"Yes."

"Then I will gladly explain. Those agents were performing a test."

"A test?"

"Yes, a test of the extent of Mr. Powers's abilities."

Abassi laughs quite loudly. After expressing his amusement, he calmly says, "And did I pass your test, Director Rochelle?"

Rochelle also laughs. "With flying colors, Mr. Powers. I believe we understand each other?"

"I understand you, Director Rochelle, but I seriously doubt you have any hope of understanding me. We are not both *men of the world*, as you like to think. You are very much confined to the limited dimensionality of this world, I am not. Either you accept my proposal now, or reject it now. I do not have the time or the inclination to humor your government any longer. If you wish the leaders of your government, including you, to remain physically where you are, in the positions you inhabit, with all your faculties and limbs attached, then you will put the President on the line so we can put an end to these little shenanigans."

"Hold, please."

Romellion, who has been holding up the phone, lowers it and looks Abassi in the eyes. He sees staring back at him an amused look, as if a master had just thrown a stick for his dog to chase. Lance can only shake his head and chuckle at the absurdity of it all.

After a short wait, Rochelle's voice returns. "The President is on the line, Mr. Powers. We are all on speaker phone."

"I presume Director Rochelle has communicated my position and the circumstances of this call?"

The President's voice replies with the hollow ring of a person trying to brazen through an impossible situation. "Yes, he has."

"And your response?"

Another pause, then, "We agree to your proposal, Mr. Powers, but it truly is imperative that we meet so that the myriad of details can be worked out and coordinated between us."

"Traveling to Washington is out of the question, Mr. President. However, I have here a very capable liaison officer from your FBI who will do very nicely as the conduit through which you may communicate your plans and concerns. Naturally, I assume you want absolute secrecy until the moment arrives to announce to the world that nothing will be the same from that point on?"

"Yes, indeed. That is the most important point for the time being. Would you please put on our agent . . . ah, Mr. Romellion."

"We are on speaker phone, and it is agreed between Mr. Romellion and myself that all communication will be transparent. This is more for your sake than mine, since I know what you are thinking. Is that acceptable?"

"Yes, yes."

"Furthermore, I suggest you pull your field agents from trying to perform surveillance, since you are putting them in an impossible position."

"Yes," replies Rochelle. "We will do that immediately."

"Who are these experts you want me to work with?" asks Abassi.

"Myself, the national security advisor, a select group of professionals from a variety of fields, including psychology, sociology, homeland security, and so forth," says the President. "Does that meet with your approval?"

"Perfectly, Mr. President, but I suggest you hurry, as your famously free press will not be restrained much longer, and their speculations about a coming Armageddon will obscure the reality of a coming new age for humanity. In that case, all hell really will break loose, and none of us can guarantee any semblance of a peaceful coming age."

"Mr. Powers, I might say right off the bat that you and your aide Altan must leave that mansion as soon as possible, before any announcement is made. You both must be in a safe, secure, and secret location. If not, hordes of people will rain down on you. As I understand it, others like you, such as the hunchback women, are already out of harm's way?"

"Correct. You need not bother to have the FBI find me a secure location, I will do so myself. It will be somewhere no one can find me or Altan unless I want them to. Naturally, I will bring Mr. Romellion along. He is, after all, your formal liaison officer, correct?"

"Yes, correct. But we must know where you are for your own protection."

"Quite the contrary. You must not know where I am for *your* own protection. When we both deem the time is proper for my entrance into the spotlight, I will do so from a safe, inaccessible distance. This will ease the burden on your security and intelligence personnel."

"Lance? Are you there?"

"Yes, Mr. President."

"I am ordering you to stay close to Mr. Powers and do whatever he directs. You have my promise as President of the United States that no further adventures, or should I say misadventures, such as just occurred at your location, will ever happen again."

"Yes, sir."

"As I understand it, you have no wife or children?"

"No, sir."

"Parents?"

"Both deceased, sir."

"Okay, that is a good thing. We will stay in touch on a daily basis. In the meantime, you are to put yourself and the resources of the U.S. government at the disposal of Mr. Powers, should he need anything."

"Yes, sir."

"Good luck to us all."

"Yes, sir. Good luck, sir."

With this final word, the call is ended and Lance looks at Abassi to make a comment, but the alien appears to be in some sort of meditative trance, so he sits and waits, trembling with a trepidation he has never before experienced.

Chapter 49: All Hell Breaks Loose

~ Crossing the Rubicon ~

Judith Simmons, press secretary for the White House, has to sit and take a few deep breaths before she can again read the press release just handed her, this time more carefully. When first laying eyes on it, she scanned the pages for routine news of some international crisis or natural disaster, but this. . . .

An intelligent woman, Judith is immediately aware of its world-shattering content. Were there an opportunity, she would rush off to spend the luxury of undisturbed time mulling over the implications and bouncing ideas off her fiancé, but time is the one luxury not currently available.

As she reads, Judith notes the wording is succinct, to the point, and designed to project confidence while allaying first-reaction fears. But it is also vague, ambiguous, and full of unanswered questions. She gives a deep sigh, knowing how frustrated the journalists will be when she declines to answer their hailstorm of demands for more detailed information. Just a couple of hours earlier, she had been innocently sitting at the kitchen table in her comfy, expensive Arlington apartment. Boskin, her cat, purred in blissful ignorance on her lap, and the day ahead seemed routine and uneventful. Now, her hands tremble as she reads the document for the third time. Taking a few moments, she forces a steely composure over her shaken body, and marches out with hollow confidence to face the jackals. Not trusting her usual conversational presentation of such briefing papers, Judith reads slowly and distinctly without looking up. Her voice remains steady and forceful, notwithstanding the turmoil racking her own emotions.

~

"Good morning. Today, I bring startling and joyous news. The government of the United States has obtained incontrovertible proof that intelligent life, apart from that on Earth, exists. Based on exhaustive reports, as well as direct contact with the extraterrestrials by our intelligence and space agencies, we can happily announce not only the existence of such advanced life forms, but that they are entirely peaceful and anxious to communicate with humanity in a mutually beneficial exchange of ideas and technology. As I speak, arrangements are being made to host representatives of their kind. By mutual agreement, such arrangements must remain confidential for the time being.

"To repeat, these extraterrestrial life forms are entirely peaceful and cooperative, as anxious as we are to move forward in a relationship built on trust and good will. All Americans, and all the peoples of the world, should look upon this as the first colossal step in a Golden Age of discovery and scientific advancement. Rest assured, the Department of Defense, FBI, CIA, Homeland Security, and other military and intelligence agencies will remain on high alert should any unforeseen contingencies arise.

"Further information will be released as communication with our intragalactic friends progress. Currently, this flow of communication is being conducted at great distances, subsequently, inquiries and responses by necessity take a significant time to unfold. Suffice to say, we on Earth should feel free to celebrate this momentous occasion in history. For the next few months precise details must be worked out, and during this process, questions other than of the most general nature will not be entertained, so as to avoid the release of premature misinformation.

"For the convenience of journalists from all over the world, a separate advisory committee has been established to take the worldwide media's written questions. It will then publicly reply in writing as thoroughly as possible. Periodic press conferences will also be held. This committee will consist of senior officials from the Department of Defense, State Department, NASA, and other agencies, as well as expert input from representatives of the private scientific and technology communities. You will be given contact information for that committee at the end of this briefing which will specify where you may submit your questions. This committee is entitled 'Special Advisory Unified Committee on Extraterrestrial Relations', or SAUCER.

"Thank you, and may the entire world prosper from this extraordinary opportunity."

~

Cutting off the tsunami of questions and demands shouted frenetically at her, Judith introduces Doctor Richard Carlson, astrophysicist and newly appointed scientific head of SAUCER. She is relieved to hand-over to Doctor Carlson the chaotic waves of hysterical shouting, leaping, and frantic arm-waving of the once well-disciplined White House press corps, now transformed into an unruly mob. Retreating to the relative quiet of her office, she has a few moments to reflect, and is suddenly struck by the gut-wrenching implications of what she has just announced. Tears well in her eyes, propelled by the mix of excitement, curiosity, and a deep upwelling of formless terror.

~

Meanwhile, as Judith Simmons deals with her emotions away from prying eyes, Walter Monroe has just turned off his television, having watched the press conference with amused detachment. He has had more time to consider the full implications of the situation, and can now comfortably retreat into the role of elder statesman. Having experienced a great deal of trauma and crisis in his years at the FBI, his thoughts turn from the administration's clumsy attempt to gloss over disagreeable reality in a hopeless attempt at buying time, to how this will ultimately affect his granddaughter Anne and any future descendants. For the first time, he seriously considers the possibility of his great-grandchildren mating with these advanced beings, thereby at least giving his line a chance to continue on without suffering the indignities of being an inferior, servile race. With these thoughts, he is confronted with Abassi's condemnation of the human race and his own blind subservience to the concept of personal love, contrasted with the superior efficacy of universal love propounded by Abassi's kind. Viewed from their perspective, Monroe can fully appreciate the view of humans as little more than a primitive species ripe for extinction, either self-inflicted or peacefully, through futile competition with an evolutionarily advanced race of super-hominins. His concern for the advantageous genetic make-up of his own family is evidence of the very point Abassi makes. *We have outlived our time*, he sighs. *Will we have the wisdom to stand aside and allow a new post-human age, or will we fight to the last with tragically fanatical resistance? Time will tell, and very little time at that.*

Feeling suddenly pessimistic, he calls Lance Romellion in San Francisco, but is informed the field officer is out of the office for an indeterminate amount of time. Alarmed, he calls Director Rochelle to ask for Lance's contact number. When he finally reaches Rochelle, the conversation is short and definitive. After requesting the information, the director's answer comes quickly.

"Sorry, no can do, Walter. That is to remain top secret, and applies even to you."

"Is he alive, at least?"

"Top secret. Can speak no longer, Walter. Goodbye."

Walter hangs up and prepares his usual morning Bloody Mary.

So, he muses, *something is up. It is either terribly bad, or perhaps terribly encouraging.*

"You may rest assured it is both," comes a familiarly melodious female voice from the same chair *she* had occupied so long ago.

Startled, Walter jerks a hand that had just been lifting his bloody mary, spilling some on the end table. He uses the incident to regain his poise by methodically cleaning up the drops.

Just as he finishes and turns to face the speaker, the phone rings, but he ignores it.

"So," he says as calmly as possible to the stunningly beautiful young woman. "My dream is back. Yet, somehow, I am now convinced you are not a dream. Are you one of the so-called aliens our government wants us so much to believe has visited the planet?"

"Life forms are all aliens, illegal immigrants dwelling in an insensate universe."

"Ha! Then death is always the final sentence of such a pitiless host."

"Indeed."

"To what do I owe the honor of this visit? Surely nothing to do with the latest circus in Washington?"

"You are to play a role in the circus."

"Really?"

"You will soon be faced with the ruinous consequences of the policy your government is undertaking. The President places more confidence in you than the current director. There is a reason for that. Use your influence wisely."

"Who are you?" demands Monroe, reaching the limit of his patience with such esoteric statements. "What is your relation to Abassi and the others? Why me, goddamm it!"

"You have been chosen."

"By who? For what? You can all go to hell! Isn't that the place where you are in the process of sending the human race? Why should I cooperate with you, whoever or whatever you are?"

"Because you have traces of their blood in you."

This astonishing remark slams into Monroe as if he had been struck by a runaway train.

"What?" he exclaims.

"There have been many fits and starts to the attempted deliverance of the human race prior to the arrivals of John and Michael Powers. You have inherited a few genes from an intermediate whose life trajectory unfortunately ran counter to the satisfaction of . . . well, the honorific titles of *God* and *Goddess* are now only associated with mental illness, so let us say, natural selection."

"An intermediate?"

"The details are of no concern. You are fundamentally a compassionate human whose own life trajectory, like that of prior intermediates, has also traced a counterintuitive path. Most have failed, and in their failures created more harm than good. But, given your kindly nature and powerful empathic power, your path will lead you and your descendants much farther. Now, that trajectory has at last intersected the path of those who are far advanced, too far advanced for easy communication with the average *Homo sapien* in a position of power who lacks the intermediate genes you have inherited."

"You mean, I speak their language?"

"Yes, although you are of more run-of-the-mill human than of the others whom your government has conveniently labeled aliens. Nonetheless, you bear the seeds."

"You will not tell me who or what you are?"

"I will tell you what is required of you."

"If I do not listen?"

"Then so much the worse for your species."

Walter takes a sip of his Bloody Mary, then remembers himself. "May I offer you a drink?" he asks.

She only smiles, and waits.

"What do you want of me?"

"Your granddaughter is twenty-five years old?"

Monroe's face turns beet red. He glares at *her* intently.

"Yes," he manages.

"You have just been wondering about the future of your family, your descendants, have you not?"

"My granddaughter is not for sale!" he shouts in outrage at the mere implication.

"Her name is Anne. She is currently studying political science at Yale University. She is highly intelligent, for a human. She is also quite intuitively aware, often able to seemingly read minds—thanks to those intermediate genes you passed on. She is kind and compassionate, and wants to improve the world by entering government service. She is fertile and, as I said, has inherited the genes you possess that originated from the intermediate. Abassi would be a good mate for her."

Monroe leaps to his feet. "Get out! Leave!"

When *she* remains passively seated, with a benevolent smile on *her* face, his fury deepens.

"Now I know what you are—a pimp for Abassi! A goddamn pimp! Do you really think I would sell my granddaughter as if she were some sort of concubine? Get out!"

"Abassi knows nothing about our meeting."

"Sure."

"Look at me, Mr. Monroe. You know in your heart of hearts that I always tell the truth. Your very outrage is partially forced. The thought has already occurred to you before I brought it up. It is the human part of you, the merely personal, that fuels your violent reaction. Reach into the better part of you, the better angel of your nature, and see the future. Anne and her children and grandchildren have no future, Mr. Monroe, if you and she do not take this path. You know that. Not only have you been chosen, but Anne also has been chosen. These chosen ones have been the lynchpins of a linage begun by John Powers, Michael Powers, and Child of Buddha, that has led to Abassi and his kind."

Monroe falls back in his seat, pale and spent. "Who are you?" he asks again. "What are you? Please answer me."

"You find my suggestion outrageous?"

"Hell yes, I do."

"Yet, you yourself thought of it."

"But I immediately dismissed the idea as absurd!"

"Is it? Do you know what Anne's reaction to Abassi would be if they met under neutral circumstances?"

"Appalled."

"No, I think not. And furthermore, I believe you also think not. Her genes, her intelligence, her character, all point to being quite interested in Abassi."

"Not as a . . . mate, as you call it."

"There is one way to find out."

"How."

"Tell her about our conversation and ask her to come with you to San Francisco where she can meet him."

"You seem to be able to pop up unannounced wherever you want. Why don't you tell her?"

"Oh, I will, Mr. Monroe, I will."

"Please leave."

"Before I go, Mr. Monroe, things are going to get very difficult for your government, and all the governments of the world. The situation is very volatile, and has the potential to embroil the human world in violence and chaos. Time is of the essence."

With this, *she* is gone, leaving Walter Monroe to glumly finish his drink. He slowly mixes another, pondering long and hard about the future.

~ Reaction ~

Hours and days after the announcement, streets all over the world are overflowing with crowds of people, some cheering, some protesting, and everyone demanding more details and an open and transparent record of discussions between the aliens and Washington. Foreign leaders clog the State Department with demands to have a representative present at all negotiations, some warning dire consequences should the American government refuse. A special session of the United Nations is urgently called for. Conspiracy theories rapidly spread around the globe, and uncompromising lines are quickly drawn by their fanatical followers. Within weeks, the fabric of civil society begins to fray, particularly as the religious, social, and intellectual implications start to sink in. Rumors and

[593]

wild speculations run rampant, filling every media outlet, from tales of coming Armageddon to ecstatic visions of a future utopia. Political organizations are formed to conduct a host of missions, from arming private citizens in preparation for the final battle to defend planet Earth, to arranging peaceful exchanges that will result in a cure for cancer, all complicated by pressures exerted on governments by a numberless variety of interest groups. Just as government, cultural, and social leaders are torn asunder by fragmenting coalitions, so religious leaders spew from their pulpits a swarm of contradictory positions and theological rationalizations that explain the existence of alien life. Oddly, those few with the most intimate knowledge of Abassi's proposal, and those multitudes ignorant of everything but their own fears, have this in common: humanity is facing an existential crisis.

Abassi watches with interest as the web of human relationships and institutions unravel. Scientists try to calm the hysterical portion of the masses; demagogues appeal to the worst impulses of the bourgeoise and working classes; politicians ride the most current direction of the prevailing winds; dictators tighten their control; religious fanatics shout End Times; and the bulk of humanity finds itself buffeted by one storm after another; one prophecy of doom after another; one fanciful prediction of the coming Elysium after another. Soon, Russia, China, and other countries announce mobilizations for war should the United States and its allies negotiate a separate treaty of cooperation with the aliens. In spite of all attempts to allay the suspicions of the world, the United States is soon isolated, and fresh demands are made on the government to provide concrete proof these aliens actually exist, and verifiable evidence of their technical and military abilities. SAUCER becomes the focal point for the world's pent-up frustrations and suspicions. Each day, the situation spirals more out of control as the militaries of the world become more restive, political leaders become more radicalized, scientists grow more insistent that additional details be released, conspiracy theories proliferate in number and absurdity, and the mass of people, tugged this way and that, are increasingly stirred to open revolt. In desperation, the President phones Lance Romellion, who is staying with Abassi at an unknown location.

"Good afternoon, Mr. President."

"Lance, I need you to do something for me. Where are you now?"

"No idea."

"What?"

"No idea. Just before the announcement, we traveled incognito to a cave in the California desert, entered it, took one of the endless side tunnels, and in a manner I cannot explain, ended up here."

"Where is here?"

"I don't know. GPS is gone completely haywire. It is an island, quite lush and teeming with tropical wildlife, but seemingly uninhabited by people except for myself, Abassi, and Altan. In what ocean, or even on what planet, I don't know, although receiving your phone call tells me we are still on Earth, thank *God*."

"Lance, you're a trained FBI agent, surely you have means to find out where this island is?"

"No, Mr. President, I don't. Well, that is not quite correct. From the looks of the night sky, we are in the northern hemisphere, probably the Pacific Ocean, but I cannot be sure. There are some aspects of the constellations that are not quite right."

"Are you being held captive?"

"No. It is hard to explain. I have been somewhat disoriented, but your phone call has brought me back to a familiar connection with the world. How can I help you?"

The President hesitates, then asks, "What do you mean disoriented?"

"It is as if I am not quite in the world, but a facsimile of the world. But I am better now that you have called. How can I help you?"

"To be blunt, we need Mr. Powers back here in Washington. He must demonstrate to a convention of world leaders that his powers are real. As you have probably seen, things are not going well. Our position is quickly becoming untenable. If Mr. Powers wants peace, he must appear and reveal all his powers, otherwise, everything will fall apart and violence will be the result. Uncontrollable violence. We need you to convince him of this fact."

"He knows."

"What? He does? So much the better."

"He is listening via the speaker phone to every word you say."

Again, the President pauses. "Okay. Fine. Mr. Powers, are you there?"

"Of course."

"Can you come to Washington?"

"I believe it would be better if a neutral venue is chosen for this demonstration. I suggest an independently governed Pacific island which is in danger of disappearing under the rising oceans due to human-induced climate change."

"A moment, please."

The President puts Abassi on hold and returns after a few minutes.

"My experts tell me the infrastructure of such a place might not be adequate to support a large gathering of world leaders and their contingencies. We would plan to have the entire world watching. Needless to say, the logistics required for such an event would be challenging."

"Ah. I find it interesting that humans assume any question concerning them concerns the entire world. Ah, well. If the infrastructure is inadequate, then make it adequate."

"You will not come to Washington?"

"No. Such a move would be counterproductive. We are interested in a peaceful transition of the human race from its currently toxic position of aggressive superiority and hostile paranoia, to one of mutual cooperation and tranquil co-existence. Naturally, there will be difficulties, but it is our job to minimize them. Do you agree?"

More hesitation, then a tentative, "Yesss."

"Then I suggest you direct your efforts to that end."

"I must consult with my advisors."

"As you wish, but time is running out."

"I know. I will call Agent Romellion with updates on our progress."

"Goodbye."

"Goodbye."

Immediately after the call, Lance looks at Abassi in order to initiate a conversation pertaining to the dialogue just ended, but once again, his host has lapsed into a meditative state, staring without seeing, so Romellion walks outside to clear his head and ruminate on the exchange. From the peaceful setting of the lovely house, surrounded by a profusion of lush vegetation and colorful flowers, he chooses a likely path that he knows will lead him to the nearby beach.

After a pleasant stroll, he eventually reaches a grassy rise giving him a panoramic view of the outspreading sea. He leaves the path and strolls along the rise, which gently slopes downward until he finds himself standing at the edge of a long stretch of sandy beach. He takes a few steps toward the ocean. Suddenly, as if conjured from nothing, dark clouds roil overhead, but there is no rain. Angry waves appear from nowhere, crashing into the jagged basaltic reef, driven by a terrific wind that whips the waters into a frenzy of foam and thunder. Such a momentous change in such a short time takes Lance's breath away. Pelted by the stinging spray, he turns his back to the ocean and surveys the islands' mountainous interior, made darkly ominous by a range of steep volcanic mountains, the largest caldera in the center, and smaller ones tapering off on either side. Vegetation is abundant and thick, but vanishes near the top of the peaks to reveal naked, brownish/blackish cones belching pillars of smoke and steam into the fierce atmosphere. Though the ferocious wind bites painfully, he turns again to squint at the ocean, using a hand to shield his face and forcing him to lean into the gale so he does not fall backward. Paradoxically, in spite of his apprehension, Lance seems in a frenzy of joyous agitation. Bolts of lightning flash in the distance; sizzling hot irons boiling the surface of the water. He sees heavy rainfall on the horizon moving toward the island, and scans the tree line for a path to escape the savaged beach. He spots an opening and rushes to it. Just as he takes a few hurried steps up the narrow path, a dark figure stands in the middle, blocking the way. It is a frightful image, this dark shadow of a man staring down at him. The details of his powerful body are momentarily lit-up by a dramatic series of lightning flashes, followed quickly by darkness and rolling thunder.

"Altan!" shouts Lance. "You scared the shit out of me!"

Lance moves up the path and stands close to the figure.

"It was not my intention," replies Altan with a smile. "I did not know FBI agents were prone to fear."

Lance scoffs. "Sure! Where did you hear that nonsense?"

"From your own self-rebuke. I believe your thoughts ran something like: *Romellion, you idiot. FBI agents are fearless! Get a grip!* Or words to that effect."

A particularly brilliant lightning bolt, followed closely by the crack of thunder, rips through the foliage nearby. Lance instinctively ducks, but Altan remains unmoved.

[597]

"Very dramatic," Lance laughs nervously. "Your imitation of a statue is flawless!"

Altan smiles condescendingly. "Very clever. Now, I must tell you that Abassi will be leaving this island very shortly, and will not be returning for an undetermined amount of time. Do you wish to stay here, or go home?"

"I'll accompany Abassi."

Altan shakes his head. "Not possible. You cannot go where he is going."

"But . . . I have my orders."

The rain begins to come down in torrents. Altan shakes his head vigorously, water flung outward from his long black hair. "I repeat, do you wish to stay here and wait, or return home?"

Lance squints into the whipping rain and shouts to be heard, "Let's go inside and talk it over!"

Altan steps aside and also shouts above the roar. "Go ahead! I have things to do at the beach! Bodies are washing ashore by now!"

"Bodies?"

"Not your concern! They come from different times, different places!"

"I'll go with you!"

"As you wish!"

When the two reach the beach, savage breakers fling dark shapes onto the sand, disgorging hundreds, thousands of bodies. Flashes of lightning reveal to Lance the faces and lifeless forms of dead humans, all from different races, and based on the clothes they wear, from different time periods. He is mesmerized by the unholy scene.

"Go back to the house!" shouts Altan. "You have seen, now go!"

"But . . . where do they come from?" he exclaims in horror.

"From elsewhere!" shouts Altan. "Go!"

More bodies keep rolling onto the beach from the angry waves, piling up in a mutilated tangle of arms, legs, torsos, heads. . . .

Lance cannot take his eyes off them.

"Go!" Altan screams into the howling wind. "I cannot protect you much longer! Go!"

Lance stumbles up the path and finds his way to the house, a light faintly glowing from within. When he rushes through the door and slams it behind, he sees Abassi sitting in the same position as when he left, eyes closed, unaware of the here and now.

"My *God*!" he exclaims. "What have I gotten myself into? What does this mean? My *God*, I want to get away from this nightmare!"

Abassi suddenly opens his eyes and stares into Lance's eyes. "And so you will."

Chapter 50: Shelter from the Storm

~ Anne Monroe ~

The moment Anne Monroe finishes listening to the press conference confirming the existence of aliens, she rushes to the phone and calls her grandfather. On a two week break from classes at Yale, Anne had spent most of the night in her one-bedroom apartment studying for midterms, and this particular early morning, she has struggled mightily to stay awake. During her second cup of coffee, she turned on the television to help her keep from falling back asleep. With news bulletins blaring the astounding news on every channel, her quick mind rapidly scrolled through a number of steps the government might take to deal with this explosive story even as she listened in wonder to the press secretary read a rather unhelpful press release. Details! Like most other listeners, she wanted more details, but by the end of the announcement, it is obvious the administration is playing this close to the vest. This is the moment she rings her grandfather. But to her dismay, the line is busy, and she is left with the unsatisfying necessity of leaving a message. She paces, listening with half an ear to a Doctor Carlson explain the role of SAUCER, when impatience gets the better of her and she calls her grandfather again. This time he does not answer. Frustrated, she thinks of a few friends to call and share the exciting news, but Anne is a cautious and methodical young woman. She will wait, collect more information, and in the meantime force herself to listen to Doctor Carlson drone on about SAUCER. Savvy in the ways of the government, courtesy of her grandfather's tutelage, Anne's mind is racing ahead in anticipation of the world's reaction, and how the administration will handle what is certain to be a horrendous outcry from unfriendly countries. *Details!* she thinks. *I need more details! What are these aliens like? Where are they from? What is the specific nature of their communication? Where is Walter? Damn!*

"Your grandfather is sitting in his Arlington apartment having another Bloody Mary," comes a voice from the other side of the room.

[600]

Anne lets out a yelp. Sitting nonchalantly on the couch is a strange woman, *her* great beauty and oddly serene demeanor evoking a surprisingly calming influence on Anne's reactions. Somehow, Anne knows the woman is not a danger or physical threat. As if the calmness reaches out, Anne stands in wonderment, aware of the incongruity of the situation, but unable to do much but ask stupidly, "Who are you?"

"A friend of your grandfather."

"Really? I don't recall meeting you before."

"May we talk for a while?"

Anne wants to comply, but the unexpected intrusion into her private space demands some explanation.

"How did you get in? I always keep the door locked."

The woman gestures for Anne to sit. Following this invitation, Anne complies, and says, "Well?"

"Let us say your grandfather gave me the key."

"I don't believe that. Show it to me."

The woman produces a key, which triggers alarm bells in Anne's mind. "Is Walter okay?"

"Perfectly fine. I just left him."

"But Arlington is hundreds of miles away!"

The woman nods. "Just so."

Anne is speechless.

The woman continues. "I have come to present you with an invitation."

"An invitation? To what?"

"To meet one of the aliens you just heard about on the television."

Again, Anne is dumbstruck.

"His name is Abassi. Upon meeting him, many of the questions you have will be answered; many of the details you crave will be made known."

Anne has a hard time catching up to such unbelievable statements. "My grandfather sent you?"

"He did, in his own way."

"But, why me?"

"You are you."

Anne shakes off this non-answer. "But I thought these aliens were a very far distance away, so far that communication with them takes a long time?"

"You, I am sure, are aware the government is sometimes . . . less than forthright about facts."

"My grandfather certainly taught me that."

"If you agree to travel to San Francisco and meet Abassi, you will find it well worth your while."

"How so?"

"In gaining knowledge, intimate knowledge, of these aliens. You will be among the first to meet on such terms."

"What terms?"

"Mutual curiosity."

"You know this Abassi?"

"Of course."

"So, you are an alien yourself!" exclaims Anne.

The woman tilts her head charmingly. "Such a term carries with it far too much baggage to be useful. Let us just say, I am not of your kind."

"What is your name?"

"Nameless."

"Okay, this is getting too weird. What is really going on?"

"The goal is for you to meet Abassi, and if things work out as hoped, both of you will become friends."

"Friends?"

"Yes."

"That's it? There must be more."

"No more."

"You never gave me an answer as to why I am chosen to become a 'friend' of this Abassi."

"Ask your grandfather."

"My grandfather? What does he have to do with this?"

"He is aware of far more than you think. Talk this over with him. It is of the utmost importance to humanity."

Anne rubs her forehead. "I don't understand."

"Talk to your grandfather."

Before Anne can respond, the woman is gone, simply vanishes, and Anne is left to try and put together the pieces of what she just experienced. Her first inclination is to call Walter, but on second thought, she is not sure what she just saw isn't simply some kind of dream, or hallucination. In that case, her grandfather would certainly be justified in assuming this news about aliens has made his granddaughter hysterical. Nevertheless, she cannot make head nor tails out of what the woman was getting at. Not for a moment does she believe this entire performance is to make herself and this Abassi become just friends. It makes no sense. All roads lead to her grandfather, and after an hour of futile analysis, Anne finally succumbs to the irresistible temptation and calls him. Just as she is about to pick up the phone, it rings.

"Hello?"

"Anne, this is Walter."

"Walter! I was just about to call you. I don't know where to start. You are aware, obviously, of the announcement about these aliens?"

"Yes, sweetie, I am. Now—"

"Is it true? . . . I mean about aliens?"

"Yes . . . well, perhaps. But—"

"I just had an amazing thing happen!"

A long pause, then, "What?"

"I had a visitor, a strange visitor, who simply appeared in my living room, and wanting me to meet with an alien. *She* said you gave *her* the key. Did you?"

Anne hears a long sigh at the other end. "I want you to come down immediately. We need to talk."

"But Walter, I have midterms."

"Believe me, Anne, what we have to discuss is far more important."

"Is it about this visit to San Francisco and Abassi?"

"So, *she* went into that much detail—yes, it is."

Anne feels a chill up her spine and her stomach feels suddenly queasy. "Grandfather, did you give her the key to my apartment?"

"Come immediately, Anne, for both our sakes."

"I'm on my way."

~ Unusual Father – Daughter Conversation ~

That night, when Anne enters her grandfather's apartment, tired from the seven-hour drive, he gives her an unusually ardent hug. Her senses are on high alert, for she has much experience with Walter's esoteric, almost fanatically cryptic references to anything connected with his work at the FBI. Even after retirement, he has remained extremely tight-lipped about contacts with the agency or with any of his personal cronies, whether they are currently employed there or long-since retired. It is obvious to Anne that something very serious has come up, and she bears the uncomfortable awareness that it is something involving her. Still not recovered from the shock of her earlier meeting with the mysterious young woman, Anne's head is spinning with conjectures and speculations about the reason for her father's urgent summons.

Since the death of her parents when she was only nine, her grandfather has been a pillar of strength, inspiration, and loving kindness. As the years passed, it is as if both learned to read the other's mind (in fact, to Anne, this almost supernatural telepathic communication exists to a frightening degree), and although she is kept in the dark about the details of his work, they both have a deep, almost mystical connection to one another. At once, after receiving Walter's fervent hug and kiss on the cheek, she senses a deep conflict troubling his thoughts. Somehow, she knows the resolution of this conflict will change her life. After blurting a breathless summary of her encounter with the young woman, few words are exchanged as Walter prepares tea for them both. She is disconcerted at his apparently cavalier reception of her fantastic story. Finally, they sit in the living room. Anne knows her grandfather's proclivity to be precise, and waits for him to order his thoughts and get to the point.

"First, Anne, I must jettison my usual hesitation at discussing anything of substance related to my work, both as directly pertains to the FBI, and my informal advisor status since I retired as director. I am going to tell you the full story of my involvement in this . . . remarkable development. Please do not interrupt with questions until I have completely finished. Will you do that for me?"

"Of course, grandfather."

For the next half hour, Walter explains the entire sequence of events since he was visited by Lance Romellion the first time, to the meetings with Abassi, to the bizarre visitations by the young woman. He spends considerable time explaining Abassi's proposal for relations between humans and those of "his kind". Anne, being highly intelligent, as well as extraordinarily tuned-in to her grandfather's thoughts, begins to see disturbing glimmers of where this narrative is headed. When he reaches the point where the young woman visited him and Anne, he pauses.

"Now, Anne, before I continue, I need to know exactly what this young woman said to you when *she* was in your apartment."

Anne recounts in detail the conversation. At the end, she is flushed, and says to Walter, "Although I am pretty sure what the goal of all this is, I would like to know what exactly *she* said to you."

"To put it bluntly, *she* would like you and Abassi to . . . well, to become intimate."

"Why me?" Anne's prosaic response does not surprise her grandfather, as he knows she is eminently pragmatic, resourceful, and tough. Any dramatic rant on her part about such sexual machinations as has been suggested would have amazed him.

"Well, that is the part that has me the most puzzled. Stunned even, and I do not stun easily. It seems I carry some of their genes, and I have passed them on to you."

"Their genes? You mean the aliens?" she exclaims.

"Anne, I do not believe they are aliens."

"What?"

"I do not believe they are aliens. Their genomes have dramatically evolved, or been modified, or engineered, whatever."

"By whom?"

"That is the question. But these so-called aliens are not aliens at all, they are actually much more advanced . . . I don't know the scientific term . . . humans, I guess. Much more advanced! More than I can believe normal evolution would have achieved in such a short period of time, if ever."

"I can't believe it! We carry some of their genes? How?"

Walter explains the idea of intermediates that Abassi described, then delves into a detailed description of their powers. Anne is too flabbergasted to speak. Finally, she throws up her hands in vexation.

"I can't make things disappear or read people's minds or any of that," she stammers. "I don't believe it."

"Anne, I have thought long and hard about this. It is true that I really seem to have some skill at anticipating what people are thinking, as do you. Before this, I simply ascribed it to some natural ability, useful but not at all extraordinary. Even as a girl, you and I have communicated on some level more completely than is easily explained by a parent-child relationship."

"Why does the administration insist on calling them aliens?"

"One, they don't share my suspicions. Two, it is far more convenient and less complicated. Three, it is easier to explain."

Anne says with a glint in her eye. "I must say, it is flattering to be considered a potential mate for such a superior being. What is this Abassi fellow like?"

"I knew you would respond to such an invitation in your own inimitable way, Anne, but this is certainly no joking matter."

"No joke intended. What is he like?"

Walter sighs heavily and cracks a smile. "Tall, dark, and handsome."

"Come on, grandpa! You can't wriggle out of it so easily. Give!"

"He actually is quite handsome. He is actually also very tall and athletic. Muscular. But seriously, there is one feature you must know about."

"Which is?"

"His back is shaped more like a shell."

"A shell? You mean a turtle?"

Walter chuckles. "No, not at all. It is thick, quite pronounced, but somehow in a way that makes him look more formidable, not like a misshapen hunchback, but like he wore a shield on his back. It renders his looks quite remarkable, in a strong, agile sort of way. Hard to describe."

"Sounds intriguing."

"Anne, you can't be thinking of going to San Francisco?"

"No more than you."

They both laugh.

"Besides," says Anne. "This would be a golden opportunity to meet one of these superior beings. My curiosity is absolutely aflame." Her face darkens. "There is no irrevocable commitment to meeting him, correct? I mean, I want the option to run away from him as fast as my legs will carry me, if you know what I mean."

"I know precisely what you mean. As far as I can tell, there is no irrevocable commitment. I will be with you the entire time."

"My chaperone?"

"You'd better believe it. Besides, my curiosity is no less aflame than yours."

Anne turns very serious. "Dad, will you tell the FBI?"

"That is a very good question. I am inclined not to, for reasons I am sure you can guess. If we do decide to do this, Anne, it must be kept absolutely secret. No telling your friends. No telling anyone."

"That goes for you as well?"

"Definitely."

"Are we decided?" asks Anne.

"Here goes nothing," says Walter.

"Here goes maybe everything," says Anne.

"Yeah, let's have a drink stronger than tea."

~ Lance Faces the Storm ~

After rushing back into the house to escape the storm, Lance stands dripping wet, mulling over Abassi's succinct declaration, "And so you will," in response to his agonized plea to return home. Gathering all his strength, Lance pushes down his revulsion at what he saw at the beach, and slowly moves across the room toward a chair. By the time he reaches it and sits, he appears calm, though pale and shivering.

"Is what I saw outside a preview of the future of humanity under your new world order?"

"I can see clearly in your mind what you thought you saw," says Abassi with half-closed eyes. "It is not what you think."

"Where did all those dead bodies come from? Surely you didn't just conjure them up from your magic kettle."

"They are returning."

"From?"

"Elsewhere."

"Enough of your evasive bullshit!" explodes Lance. "Is this what we are to expect from cooperating with you?—Piles of dead?"

"Yes."

The bluntness of this answer chills Lance to the bone, and the stark nature of its power renders him speechless.

"Before you faint from the shock, Agent Romellion, focus on my earlier words, *it is not what you think*."

"Then . . . wha . . . what is it?" stutters Lance.

"All the bodies you witnessed are, shall we say, like a collection of books; and the ocean a universal library—the repository of individual suffering humans have inflicted on each other. It is a great library awash with such ripe-to-bursting books—books that tell stories of war, deceit, murder, torture, abuse, and the like. A different beach is host to the non-human animals slaughtered by humans in furtherance of their unbridled lust to dominate. Non-human animals, of course, comprise different books—in different languages to be sure, but each one also containing a story unto itself, no less riveting than the human ones, best-sellers though they may be. Periodically, the books wash ashore—or to put it another way, the books are reshelved to make room for more."

"I don't understand. Are they real bodies, or am I dreaming? Won't your so-called books decay and eventual disappear?" Lance's eyes are flaming bright, and his voice is raised to a feverish shout. "Long ago, I dreamed—like this dream I'm having of you right now—of hordes of people standing before me without arms and legs! You are no friend of humanity! You are not empathetic and compassionate! You, Abassi, are the Devil himself!"

Abassi replies calmly. "Those bodies are not my doing. Those bodies are as real as this place, and yes, they will decay, but their stories remain in the library as memories. At any rate, Agent Romellion, this metaphor is the best I can do. You and I have washed ashore on this island ourselves, and currently also exist only as metaphors. The Devil himself is a metaphor. Yet, I fear I prattle on when it is apparent you do not understand. Let us just say this is nothing more than a simulation, in your terms, and leave it at that."

Lance does not know how to respond, so remains stolidly silent.

Abassi taps his fingers on the glass surface of an end-table. "We both have plans. I am leaving for an appointment, and you want to go home. I can see you are feverish. Right now, you can only see disaster for the human race, and I have now become your great enemy. So be it. We both are journeying to the same place. I leave within an hour. Tomorrow, Altan will help you with your return."

When Lance does not reply, Abassi gazes out the window. "For now, go back to the beach and see what you can see. The storm has passed—both the storm outside and the storm within you. Go."

This last word is gently expressed, as a parent encouraging a child to go and play.

Lance remains sitting while he watches Abassi close his eyes and return to wherever his meditation takes him. Almost unwillingly, Lance feels compelled to obey Abassi's suggestion. He rises and walks outside and down the path toward the beach, his mind a cauldron of rage and futile rebellion. When he retraces the path to where he stood with Altan earlier that night, the sky has cleared, the storm is gone, and a gentle breeze stirs the vegetation. The air is heavy with a humid scent of flowers and fertility. A full moon appears above the leafy canopy, and as if spotlighted in the glare of a particularly bright beam, he is startled to find Altan standing where he had stood before, waiting.

"Abassi suggested I return to the beach and see what I can see," he says as he walks up to Altan. "Why can't I smell the decomposing bodies?"

"Come with me," says Altan.

They stroll the rest of the way to the beach, and as Lance surveys the scene in the intense radiance of the moon, there are no bodies to be seen. Only a vast expanse of gorgeous, virgin sand stretching in both directions, the ocean a calm chronometer passing time with the gentlest of waves.

"Where are they?" asks Lance. He finds himself asking this question as a matter of course, for he is not at all surprised at the disappearance of the evidence. So many strange things happen with these creatures, that nothing shocks him anymore—except the bodies. "In the FBI, we would call this a cover-up," he says.

Altan smiles. "Of course you would."

"Well, where are they?"

"Elsewhere."

Lance laughs mirthlessly. "Somehow, I knew you would say that. Look, you seem to me to be an honest person, Altan. What is really going on here?"

"In what sense? You mean on this island?"

"No, I mean in general. Aliens, magical powers, people losing arms and legs, proposals to breed with humans, these manufactured hallucinations or delusions or whatever, and all the rest. What's it really all about?"

[609]

Now they are slowly walking along the beach. Altan points to the ocean. "Do you believe the water is real?"

"I don't know anymore."

"Touch it. Wade into it. See what you see."

Lance wades a little way in and bends over to feel the waves roll over his hands. When he raises them, they are glistening wet in the moonlight.

"Seems real, but that doesn't mean anything."

"You believe you're being hypnotized?"

"Not at all. I believe you really have the powers you have, there is no denying that. My question is, what is the purpose of all this? Conquest? After all, Abassi as much as told me the world will be full of dead bodies if we cooperate. What is the story?"

"You already know."

"Is it replacement of the human race? Is that it?"

"Of course. But not in the way humans would think. It will involve a great deal of time, and as little violence and suffering as possible. Humans will all live out their natural lives as before. But gradually they will be replaced."

"By?"

"The descendants of Abassi and the hunchback women . . . as you so delicately call them."

"I have seen nothing to show me that they are morally superior to us. To be sure, they have powers we don't, but otherwise . . . I just don't see it."

"It is not that you don't see it, it is that you can't see it. Right now, I perceive you are considering ways to kill Abassi. To you, it would be an act of justifiable homicide, because you would be saving humanity. Foolish human! It is that way of thinking that accounts for all the bodies you saw earlier washing up on the shore. Soon, you will be joining them."

"Is that a threat?"

"No threat. I want you to live a full and happy life. It is not a threat, it is a fact, should you insist on adhering to your irrational fear and misplaced hatred."

These words cut Lance to the core, as he respects Altan and feels himself to be an honorable man. As a consequence, he doubles down on his anger and lashes out.

"I suppose I will be missing my arms and legs as well?" he says sarcastically.

"No, you will be missing your future, one that is not as bleak as you make it out to be."

Lance scowls. "Apparently, we humans have no future."

"That is true only insofar as you fail to evolve, and by that measure of the universe, you fail to adapt."

Lance sniggers (and dislikes himself for doing so), "Evolve into creatures like Abassi and the hunchbacks?"

"Neanderthals thought about *Homo sapiens* in the same way."

"How do you know? Were you there?"

"Yes."

~ News From Far Away ~

Meanwhile, far away in their isolated sanctuary, the three pregnant women and those around them have been keeping up with the alarming news that reverberates around the world. The rapidity with which the announcement of alien contact had shaken social and political foundations surprises even that cognitively advanced group. Such tidings have resulted in all of them feeling sadness for all the angst and despair that frail human egos and overactive amygdalas must now be bringing upon themselves. This daily news produces another effect: both Pythia and Tara have expressed their intention to return to the United States. Lady Oracle, being extremely upset at learning of these plans, has called a meeting with everyone present to discuss the situation. Agreement is reached to meet in the cafeteria at three o'clock. Quequeeg will prepare tea and sweets for the occasion.

Tara and Siyabonga are the first to arrive, followed by Pythia, Ming-huà and Zookeeper, Sy, and lastly Lady Oracle. The mothers are showing now, and all are cognizant of the shortened gestation period. This truncated period is assumed by all to ensure the safe passage of the infant's thickly armored back through the birth canal, though all three have a slightly wider pelvis to accommodate the curious shape. After pleasantries are exchanged, everyone gathers around a large table, amply supplied by Quequeeg with tea, coffee, and a variety of sweets. Pythia is the first to speak.

[611]

"Tara and I feel it is unconscionable for us to stay here, safe and cozy, while Abassi and Altan are in the middle of that mess. We should be there to help."

"With what?" objects Lady Oracle. "In a couple of weeks, Abassi will meet with world leaders and demonstrate his powers. No need for you to hover around, getting in his way."

"I agree with mother," says Tara. "The world situation is fast unravelling, and I fear there will be violent demonstrations in which many innocent humans will be hurt. And that will be only the beginning. Surely we can do something to allay the worst of that catastrophe. Besides, it is quite boring here, with nothing to do, especially for Siyabonga."

"Oh!" he says as if suddenly prodded by a stick. "I'm fine here, but I do think we should be with Abassi and Altan."

"Boredom!" shouts Sy twirling a little jig. "So, that's it! Don't worry! Won't be long before you women won't be bored, lying on your backs and screaming from labor pains. These births are due soon enough, one upon another, and the safety of these infants, and their mothers, is the only priority. Abassi and Altan can take care of themselves, like Lady Oracle says. Drop this idea immediately!"

Pythia and Tara are taken aback by the vehemence of Sy's demand. Neither is prepared to simply bow down to his scolding.

"Sy!" exclaims Pythia. "Remember yourself! We are independent beings, not mere underlings for you to order about."

"That is true," replies Sy heatedly. "But the fetuses inside your bellies are also beings, and they are not independent. They need protection and a safe place to arrive in this world."

"Yes," says Tara. "You are right, Sy. However, our kind are far more driven to ensure the greater, universal goal of easing pain, rather than the lesser, personal one of gaining happiness at the expense of others. Is this not correct?"

Sy shrugs. "As far as it goes. Lady Oracle and I are driven by our own goals, and one of the main reasons for our being here is to defend you and your offspring from annihilation. If you are caught up in the human propensity for chaos and violence, then the eventual result may be far worse than transient suffering by humans, it may involve the extinction of every living creature on this planet."

"That is an exaggeration," says Pythia.

[612]

"Perhaps, but the planet is fundamentally what's at stake here."

"Yes, we are back to Siyabonga's metaphor of park rangers protecting an animal preserve. Is that what this is truly about?"

"It is not a metaphor," says Lady Oracle. "It is precisely why all of us are here."

A pregnant silence falls over the room. Finally, Ming-huà says, "Then, I presume, we are not the rangers?"

"Correct."

"Then what are we?" asks Tara.

"You are to become the top predator. You are antidotes to *Homo sapiens* destructive domination of the biosphere. You are evolved to supersede the current top predator and drive its members to extinction."

"But with compassion and empathy, as we have been told?" asks Siyabonga.

"Or, are we being lied to?" asks Pythia.

"Yes," adds Tara. "*Are* we being lied to?"

"No, you are not being lied to . . . unless, that is, I also am being lied to," sighs Lady Oracle.

"Then, the question is, who are the park rangers?" asks Zookeeper.

"The mentors?" suggests Pythia.

"No. We are back to those who your ancestors called *God* and *Goddess*."

"But that tells us nothing!" objects Pythia.

"I remind you, the universe came from nothing."

Chapter 51: Into the Abyss

~ Abassi Meets Anne Monroe ~

Walter and Anne Monroe are having a light breakfast in a San Francisco hotel coffee shop, eating slowly and rather quietly, their usual good-humored banter quite sparse. Both are nervous about the wisdom of going forward with Abassi's plan to have Anne join him for dinner at an out-of-the-way restaurant in Oakland. The site evidently had been chosen by Abassi to be far away from any popular establishments in San Francisco. For Anne, the first flush of excitement has died away, leaving a jittery reconsideration of her hasty consent. Nonetheless, her spirit of adventure and intense intellectual curiosity propel her forward.

"Having second thoughts, sweetie?" asks her grandfather between sips of coffee.

"Of course. I admit I am nervous, but if nothing else, it will be interesting. I mean, having a date with a different species is not something a young woman runs across every day." She laughs nervously. "What is terrible, what I dread the most and can't get over, is that he can read my mind. That really terrifies me, Walter. What if I am thinking something awful?"

"Knowing Mr. Powers, dear, and keeping in mind his highly developed empathy, you will be fine."

"Easy for you to say."

"True. Remember, I will be close by. Anytime you want to leave, just call me."

"Mr. Powers does know you will drive me there, right?" she asks for the tenth time.

"Yes, yes."

"And if I do let you know I want to leave, it will not be because I am uncomfortable, it will be because I am fleeing the battlefield in full defeat." Her face assumes a determined look. "I will play this out to the end, come what may."

[614]

"Brave girl. I'm very proud of you. We will see how this works out, but as far as I know, it is sort of like Adam meets Eve, or vice-versa.

"Oh!" exclaims Anne. "At least they were the same species! Anyway, Walter, let's not get ahead of ourselves. You're not already planning for the great-grandchildren, I hope?" Again, the nervous laugh.

"Far from it. Now, Anne, seriously, you must use some FBI techniques during this dinner."

"What do you mean?"

"You must observe every detail. How he eats, how he uses his hands, the utensils, his words, any emotions that flash across his face, however brief, and so on."

Anne holds up her hands in alarm. "Whoa! Hold on, Walter! Remember, he can read my thoughts. I cannot go into this as if I were some sort of spy. My mind must be as free and open as possible, as receptive as possible, without any preconceived agendas, or I am doomed!"

Walter takes her hand and smiles apologetically. "You're right, dear. Forget what I said. Be open, honest, and let the conversation flow naturally. You have a very stupid grandfather."

In spite of the brave face Anne projects, she becomes increasingly tense as the hour approaches to leave. Choosing the perfect outfit is agony. This dress is too formal. That pantsuit too stuffy. This blouse too informal. That skirt too short. Finally, she chucks it all and decides on a comfortable, simple but attractive dress. Flat-heeled shoes (no high heels for this woman), a lovely set of earrings and matching necklace. Looking in the mirror, she is not entirely happy, but mutters, "It'll have to do."

When Walter sees her ensemble, he is full of praise. "Perfect! You look stunning! Even an alien will fall over from such beauty!"

"Walter! Stop it!" But she secretly feels as beautiful as her grandfather's praise. Better yet, her usually unruly hair has behaved itself.

"Ready?" asks Walter, holding out his arm in the gallant gesture of a nineteenth-century gentleman.

Anne gratefully takes it. She will need all of her grandfather's support to survive the evening.

"Ready," she says, more apprehensively than she intends.

"Then to the chariot! The prince awaits!"

"Walter!"

"Well, let's go or the car will turn into a pumpkin."

[615]

"Walter," she laughs. "You're an idiot."

~

When they arrive, Abassi is waiting. He is at a corner table, and stands gesturing for them to come. A smile that is both charming and captivating greets Anne. As she approaches, he seems a giant, taller and more muscular than she had pictured. Certainly handsome. Curious about his famous back, she is disappointed that he is facing her in such a way as to block her view. He bows and shakes her hand, then turns to Walter.

"I am glad to see you," he says. "Are you sure you will not join us?"

Walter smiles appreciatively. "Thank you, but I fear we would simply spout nonsense to each other. Besides, I have other plans, and—"

"To remain close in the event you are needed," Abassi finishes the sentence matter-of-factly.

"Yes. We do understand each other."

"I understand you, Mr. Monroe. As a grandfather, it cannot be otherwise."

Anne is miffed by his implication. "Are you suggesting my grandfather does not understand you?"

"Your grandfather is an intermediate. He understands me well enough."

Abassi gestures for her to sit, so Walter prepares to take his leave. He exchanges pleasantries, shakes Abassi's hand, leans over and hugs his granddaughter, and walks away without looking back. Abassi sits and gazes at Anne. Her immediate impression is one of awe at the power of his countenance, followed quickly by a faint awareness that her brain is being probed, giving the sensation of being scanned by a gentle electric field. This subtle but powerful surge of energy races through every corner of her mind, down to the brainstem, where she experiences a pleasurable jolt. Once she clears her head of the almost orgasmic afterglow of such an intimate intrusion, she briefly touches her forehead and with conscious determination, stares back into Abassi's eyes.

"Well, have all the mysteries of my deepest thoughts been revealed to you?"

"Yes"

This monosyllabic answer momentarily takes her off guard, and she starts to say, "You must—"

[616]

But her sentence is interrupted by the waiter. He stands by the table with his pen and pad at the ready. Abassi never takes his eyes from Anne, and as if some hidden button had been pushed, the waiter walks away without saying a word.

"That was odd," says Anne, following the retreating waiter with a puzzled look.

"I told him to come back later," says Abassi.

"I didn't hear you."

"Telepathy. He heard me in his head, and as far as he knows, I spoke."

"Showing off?"

"Yes."

"Why? Are you insecure?"

"No."

"Then, why?"

"Anne, you are an intermediate. It is important you understand what powers I possess. Not to impress, but to inform."

"I see."

"It would be unfair not to be open with you."

"Can you turn off your telepathic and clairvoyant powers if you want?"

"Yes."

"Please do so."

"I had just done so before you requested."

Anne tilts her head. "Oh, I see, because you knew. . . . "

"Beforehand, yes." He smiles in a most charming manner. "That is the last time I will use them with you."

"Thank you."

Anne peruses the menu and closes it.

"Have you chosen?" he asks.

"You don't know?"

"I am a person of my word."

"Yes, I have chosen."

Even as she speaks, the waiter is standing ready. She looks accusingly at Abassi.

He smiles ironically and shrugs his shoulders. "I never promised about the waiter."

After ordering, Anne, to her great relief, is finding this alien quite good company. His charm and polite manners are almost a disappointment in their rather prosaic conformity.

Be careful what you wish for, girl, she warns herself. But as soon as these thoughts come to her, she looks anxiously at Abassi for fear of appearing the fool, but he seems legitimately unaware. To test him she concentrates very clearly. *Abassi, will you order some wine, please?*

No response.

Good actor or honest alien, she decides.

"Can you really make things disappear?" she suddenly asks in a very blunt manner, with a bit of coyness thrown in.

He frowns. "Yes. You must know these objects disappear only to those of you who dwell in this particular four-dimensional reality. The objects still exist."

"Where?"

"Elsewhere."

"Show me, please."

"Why?"

"Well, as you might say, primate brain. Curiosity."

He is clearly displeased, and Anne quickly backtracks. "If you don't want to, it's okay. I mean, you don't have to."

The waiter returns with the food and places sumptuous dishes of Mongolian cuisine in front of the two. Anne picks up her spoon, ready to start with the *Guriltai shul*, when her bowl disappears.

"Oh! Hey!"

Abassi is grinning. "Punishment for letting your obsolete brain get the best of you."

In a flash, the bowl reappears.

Anne's eyes are wide in astonished appreciation. "Can you teach me that?" she asks with a smile.

Abassi cocks his head jauntily, and says, "Is it still hot?"

She takes a spoonful. "Hot enough."

"Good."

When finished with their meals, and the plates cleared, they sip tea and fall into pleasant conversation.

"You know everything about me," she says. "Yet, I know nothing about you. My grandfather tells me you are not really an alien like they say. Is that true?"

"Well, I often reply to that question by pointing out that we are all aliens in this universe, but in the sense you mean the word, no, I am not."

"As I thought," she says. "In no way do you seem alien to me, and, well . . . other than possessing a few impressive powers the rest of us lack, you seem normal."

"It seems that way to you because I am less different from you than the others."

"What do you mean? . . . Oh, yes, I see. It is this intermediate business, right?"

"When we first met, I perceived your interest in seeing my back." He stands and turns sideways. Anne stares at the prominent bulge under his jacket, which strikes her as something incredibly strong and an integral part of him, rather than as a disfigurement or handicap. He resumes his seat and looks at her openly.

"When you were young, you had what your parents (and doctors) thought was scoliosis, correct?"

"Yes."

"It went away gradually?"

"Yes."

"Well, it was not scoliosis. It went away because your human genome was too strong."

Anne feels a rush of excitement. "Can I learn to do what you can do? Can I acquire your powers?"

"No. Unfortunately not. It is a complicated business, but you do bear the seeds."

"You mean, like recessive genes?"

"Something like that."

"I see."

This topic, of course, raises in Anne's mind the topic of genetic inheritance, and her mind quickly wonders about the consequences of having sexual relations with Abassi, which itself leads to curiosity about his anatomy. Catching herself in the midst of these erotic reflections, she is horrified that Abassi might have revived his telepathic power, and she flushes bright red down to her neck.

[619]

Abassi chuckles.

"What?" she says defensively.

"One need not be telepathic to know what thoughts and images are running through your mind."

She starts to object, but he holds up a hand. "You have heard your grandfather speak of the hunchback women?" he asks.

Anne nods, still self-consciously embarrassed.

"You would like them. Those are not disfigured humps; they are repositories of . . . a great many abilities. They have powers similar to mine. Of the three, two have mated . . . I mean have human spouses. The other is in a relationship with an intermediate, like you. All of them have had children, and all of them are also currently pregnant. My kind can have intimate relationships with humans. The three women are quite happy with their mates." (Abassi decides to keep Jared Paine's suicide private for the time being).

"And you?" asks Anne.

"And me what?"

"Are you in a relationship?"

"I am young. No special person, yet."

"You're young?" exclaims a surprised Anne. "How old are you?"

Abassi shakes his head. "Younger than you in human chronology, far older in . . . other ways, in other dimensions."

"How much younger than me are you . . . in human terms?"

"How old do you think I am?"

"I hate these games," grumbles Anne. "I don't know . . . late twenties, early thirties?"

"Excellent! You guessed correctly!"

Anne tilts her head with an ironic smirk. "Sure."

"How old do you want me to be?"

Anne rolls her eyes. "Twenty-six."

"Perfectly correct again! You are amazing!"

"Funny man."

"Thank you. Humor is not generally one of our strong points. Humans and otters are best at it."

Anne laughs. "You place us in grand company!"

Abassi's face turns solemn. "True, otters are far more—" But, remembering himself, he smiles again. "Do you, Anne, ever feel separate from your fellow humans?"

"I think all of us do at some point in our lives. However, I must confess, I am fully human, probably much to your dismay. I am interested in human politics, history, culture, society. I am curious about interesting personal stories. Quite mundane, really."

"Personal stories. I see. Like what?"

"Oh, I don't know, lots of them. People persevering over terrible abuse, or war, or depression, or misunderstandings—silly, romantic, sentimental stories of people that have happy endings. You see? I am dreadfully ordinary." As if the idea just popped into her head, she asks. "Why are you here with me now? I am just one rather boring little human among a sea of boring little humans."

"May I use my telepathic power again?"

Anne flinches. "Why?"

"Because I do not believe you think you are boring . . . or, at least, that most humans are boring. You said yourself their individual stories are interesting."

"Ah, yes," says Anne. "But interesting only to other boring little humans. Surely not to superior beings who can read minds and make things disappear and. . . . " she pauses so her words can catch up with her thoughts.

But Abassi finishes her sentence. "And who can appreciate otter humor?"

"I'm being serious, Mr. Powers."

"Please call me Abassi."

"Okay, Abassi. I repeat my earlier question. Why are you here with me now?"

"To hopefully find a mate who can accept my peculiarities, and who herself has the seeds of similar peculiarities."

Anne is flummoxed by his directness, and feels it incumbent to reply with a brilliant witticism, or at least some reasonably intelligent rejoinder, but can only stammer, "To . . . find . . . a . . . mate?"

"Are you shocked?" he asks.

"With this challenge, her face still flushed red, Anne replies, "No. I figured as much. You do, however, lack the romantic touch."

"Do you want to call your grandfather now?"

"No."

~

When Walter picks up Anne a few hours later, she seems flush with self-satisfied happiness. He looks at her curiously.

"Well?" he asks.

"Thank *God* you cannot read my mind."

~ From the Frying Pan into the Fire ~

The next morning, by mutual agreement, Abassi is to pick up Anne at the hotel for another dinner. She has done her best to brief Walter on her observations of Abassi, and it becomes quite obvious to her grandfather that she is smitten by Mr. Powers. Her enthusiasm both encourages and distresses him. That afternoon, they sit together and Walter asks her what she thinks might happen next.

"I don't know, Walter. Too soon to tell. Seeing him tonight will help me get to know him better."

"But you do like him? Not just fascinated by his . . . abilities?"

"I'm not a fool. It really is both. I do like him, and I am fascinated by his differences . . . okay, his powers."

"Abassi will soon be making an appearance in front of the world, Anne. After that, should you both continue your relationship—"

"We are not involved in a relationship!"

Walter quickly backtracks. "Okay, should you both continue seeing each other, there will be no keeping you out of the spotlight."

"I realize that."

"Then you also realize he can never love you the way you would love him?"

"Walter! I don't love him! It has been one dinner!"

"All right, but if you did fall in love with him, then. . . . "

"I know. You have told this to me many times; how he is wired differently. Universal love versus the merely personal, as you have said he likes to quote Einstein. Yadda yadda. I know! Don't worry so much."

"It matters, you know."

"Well, I sort of look at it this way," she says thoughtfully. "If what Abassi says is true, if humans are, for lack of a better way of putting it, on the way out, then perhaps his way of looking at love is the best way."

[622]

"Perhaps," says Walter. "But you are human—or at least mostly human—and could be very hurt by his way of viewing rela . . . I mean, viewing the world."

Anne snorts. "You're jumping the gun again! I'm not rolling under the sheets with him you know!"

In spite of his paternalistic tone and impressive concerns, her grandfather, in reality, is pleased. He hopes all will go well between them, and lead to an intimate relationship. Think of the great-grandchildren they might have together! Such power in the Monroe genetic line! Walter's descendants would be among the first of a new, more powerful species! He shutters to consider the horrible reaction of Anne if she finds out what he is really thinking, but damn it, the future is at stake. Though ashamed of his own musings, he can not help considering the possibilities.

"What are you thinking, Walter?" asks Anne, calling him back from his wandering dreams.

"Oh, I was just thinking how proud I am of you, and how much I only want you to be happy. This entire situation is in your capable hands; however you decide. I have confidence you will make the decisions that are right for you. That is all I want. For it to be right for you."

"Thank you," she says hesitantly.

After a long pause, during which both feel inexplicably uncomfortable, Anne says in her typically jocular tone, "It *would* be interesting, wouldn't it?"

"What would?"

"If your great-grandchild made you disappear for not giving him or her the right gift for Christmas."

Anne laughs, but Walter's desultory chuckle is decidedly less hearty.

~

In preparation for tonight's dinner, Anne's mood is polar opposite from the previous evening. She hums a tune while boldly choosing an outfit that is a bit more revealing. Her anticipation is high, and she distractedly answers her grandfather's questions, all the while choreographing a perfectly enchanting evening in her mind's eye. This time, Abassi is picking her up, and when the call comes from the lobby, she kisses Walter and goes to meet him in the best of spirits. Stepping out of the elevator, she stops and scans the cavernous room, which is about

[623]

half full of people hastening this way and that, some hauling luggage, some involved in lively conversations. Not spotting Abassi, she walks farther into the room when a tall, very dark man approaches. For a moment, Anne is startled, but his friendly smile allays her fears.

He bows. "Hello. You are Anne Monroe?" he asks, holding out his hand.

She takes it easily and says, "Yes."

"I am Altan. I will be your driver tonight. Mr. Powers waits by the car."

"He does not drive?"

"He can, but prefers not. As you may understand, he is sensitive to the possibility of being recognized here."

"I see."

Altan's face brightens with a charming smile. "Don't worry, I will not be joining you for dinner."

"Oh, but you're quite welcome!" hastens Anne.

"Thank you, no."

As they walk toward the exit, Anne inadvertently glances at his back and asks as brightly and politely as she can, "Are you one of . . . his kind?"

He again smiles luminously. "Not exactly."

This rather non-committal response arouses her curiosity, but they step out into the night and soon arrive at the car, poorly illuminated by a flickering streetlight. Abassi, his face veiled by a shadow that slants just above his neck, which for a brief moment makes him look like a headless statue, stands holding open the rear door. She nods and slides in, with himself following behind. Altan takes the wheel, and after exchanging greetings, they drive in silence for some time.

"Same place?" asks Anne.

"I thought we might try Chinese tonight," he replies. "My great-grandmother is of Chinese heritage. There is a little restaurant in Chinatown that I have visited before. It comes highly recommended by a number of . . . others as well."

"Chinese heritage? That is interesting."

"Indeed. So you see, I really am quite the alien."

Anne laughs and says, "Funny alien. Almost as funny as an otter."

Both chuckle at this *bon mot*.

When they leave the main road, Altan carefully navigates the car down a couple of very narrow side streets, through a twisting maze of claustrophobic alleyways, and finally stops at an abrupt dead end, keeping the engine running. With barely enough room to open the doors, Anne and Abassi wedge themselves out. He takes her hand (and she his) with the ease of a longstanding couple, and leads her through another maze of even smaller alleyways (more like footpaths) toward the restaurant. The darkness, combined with the rather threatening atmosphere, would normally frighten Anne, but his presence infuses her with the greatest ease and confidence. Without any distracting worries, she can look around and appreciate the traditional Chinese architecture with its brick exteriors, red doors, and pagoda-style tile roofs. To Anne, they have crossed some magical line into an ancient world. Finally reaching the restaurant, Anne sees a lantern illuminating the entrance in a soft, red glow. Abassi reads the characters spelling out the name.

"Zhuang Zi's Haunted Dragon."

"Is that the owner's name?"

Abassi shakes his head. "Far from it. Zhuang Zi was a very famous Chinese philosopher who lived thousands of years ago."

"Oh."

Abassi opens the carved door for Anne to enter. "In here, our stillnesses will be stilled."

"Sorry?"

"Never mind, I'll tell you later."

~

Upon stepping inside the two-story restaurant, a pudgy, middle-aged Asian man rushes up to Abassi.

"Good sir, you have returned! Excellent! We have all been looking forward to this moment!"

"Thank you, Mr. Chu. How is Cook Wang?"

"Superb! Ready to prepare your favorite dishes."

"Thank you. And Lilianna?"

"Just the same, but almost as roly-poly as I have become."

Chu looks appreciatively at Anne and bows. "You are also welcome indeed, young lady."

Anne is a bit overwhelmed. "Thank you," she manages, returning the bow.

"But," says Chu. "Enough of this. Your usual room is waiting. Come, come!"

He leads them up a narrow, winding staircase to a private room on the second floor, energetically gesturing for them to enter. When they are comfortably seated, he says in his most formal tone, "First, tea, a little wine, and *Hors d'ourves*, as the French say." With his last phrase, he nods in acknowledgement of Anne.

"Do you speak French, Miss. . . . "

"Monroe. Anne Monroe. And yes, Mr. Chu, I do speak a little French."

"Ah!" he claps. *"J'espère que tu as faim?"*

"Oui. J'ai très faim."

"Tu l'aimes bien?"

"C'est mon ami."

"Plus qu'un ami?"

"Peut-être plus qu'un ami."

Mr. Chu laughs heartily at this last, and bustles out of the room.

Abassi looks at Anne with a wry smile. "So, I am *perhaps* more than a friend?"

Anne returns the comment with a flirtatious smile of her own. *"J'espère que nous pouvons être plus que des amis,"* she says, looking at him boldly.

"I hope we can be more than friends also."

"By the way," says Anne. "Is your telepathic power turned off?"

"If you wish."

"I wish."

"It is off, but not before I detected some interesting thoughts."

Anne blushes and is relieved to see Mr. Chu return with a pot of tea in one hand, and a crowded tray full of goodies in another.

"Seriously, Abassi, I am not sure I can deal with the idea that you can, at any time, look into my mind and read my thoughts. It is, for lack of a better word, creepy."

"I understand," he says. "However, I cannot promise to permanently turn off the ability. I am only not-human."

"Clever. Tell me about this public demonstration coming up. Is it the wisest thing to do, given how much you value your privacy?"

"Ah, is this why you asked me to turn off my telepathic powers? This is a question your grandfather might ask."

Anne reddens. "Not at all." She continues in a miffed tone. "I have my own brain, believe it or not. I am working on my Ph.D. in Political Science, and naturally am interested in only the most important event in human history."

"Yes, I understand that. Yale University, correct?"

"Yes."

"Do you know we have our own version of a university?"

"You do?"

"Indeed."

"Where is it?"

"Elsewhere."

"You keep using that word. What exactly does it mean?"

"It means another dimension, or set of dimensions. These dimensions are not perceptible to humans, but we often dwell elsewhere for a variety of reasons."

"Is that where objects go when they disappear?"

"More or less."

"And you can bring them back! That is even more amazing to me."

"I can bring them back, but the window for being able to do so is very narrow. If too long a time passes, it is not possible. There is a human I know whose arms are missing due to a misunderstanding. By the time I was around, it was too late. I tried, but. . . . "

"I'm sorry."

Abassi leans slightly forward. "Anne, how do you think the world's people will respond to living in the midst of increasing numbers of . . . our kind?"

"Surely you know?"

"The universe is probabilistic. A great Lady has often said, *Fate starves at probability's door*. Certainly, *she* is right."

"Who is *she*?"

"A voice, one that humans thought drove my great-great grandfather Michael Powers mad. They were wrong."

"A voice?"

"There are those that are far above me, Anne. Among those great ones, two conflicting paths have diverged, and there is great debate, albeit a peaceful one, over what path to take."

"Above you?" Anne asks in immense surprise.

"Yes."

"Who are they? Where are they?"

"Where are they?—Elsewhere. And as to who they are, that is veiled in secrecy even from me. My ancestors, your ancestors also, labeled them *God* and *Goddess* in their ignorance. Those terms are a convenient heuristic that *Homo sapiens* often use, and perverted by some intermediates to their illicit advantage."

"Then, in many ways, you really are an alien," says Anne almost to herself.

"Well, perhaps we can put it this way: currently I and my kind are strangers in a strange land, but soon, humans will be the strangers in a strange land. Which takes us back to my question about how humans will react to being displaced."

"If they get to know you, and those like you, perhaps. . . . " Anne's voice trails off.

"Exactly why I am going to introduce myself and my kind to the people of the world. Over time, so long as our peaceful intent is displayed on a daily basis, and, well, with interbreeding, the change will be as painless as possible."

"Yes, yes, possibly," says Anne distractedly, her mind focused on a particular word. "Maybe like the old saw about boiling a frog . . . or, I don't know. There is something I want to say, but can't put my finger on it."

They fall quiet as Mr. Chu brings more dishes. After he leaves, Anne looks at Abassi with a determined look. "Abassi, you mentioned interbreeding. We may as well talk about it. You are interested in me as a kind of . . . well, mate. Isn't that true?"

"Yes."

"As you are well aware, our view of love is quite different from your view, at least based on what my grandfather has told me. True?"

"True."

"Explain what being a mate means to you. Is there love involved, or is it purely a biological relationship?"

"It is both."

"But, I think what it means is that you love me to the same extent as you love others, no more, no less. Correct?"

"Not quite. There is familiarity, which goes a long way toward distinguishing one from another."

"Familiarity is not enough—at least not enough for this human girl."

"I can comfortably say, with all sincerity, that I love you. However, I cannot say I love only you to the exclusion of others. That would include any children we might have. In other words, I would love the children of others as much as I would love ours. That is built into our DNA. It is, I know, very hard for you to understand."

Anne furrows her brow. "You might be surprised, Abassi. We are not as stupid as you think. Yet, it is hard . . . on the other hand, I have these fleeting moments where I *do* understand."

"Dear Anne, that struggle to understand our ways is a manifestation of the intermediate genes deep inside struggling to redirect your thoughts and words in a different direction from that of *Homo sapiens*. Don't you see? You are really far from just a boring little human, as you so harshly put it last night. Yet, you have spent your entire life repressing within what is fighting to be expressed without."

"Could it be possible for me to accept something so radically different? I am not that strong, Abassi."

Suddenly and with breathtaking immediacy, Anne's brain is completely inundated with a deep, pulsing energy of such magnitude, that she is thrown back in her chair. Abassi's extraordinary cognitive and intellectual penetration is a firestorm that molds and twists and shapes the utterly overwhelmed neural pathways of her mind. When the catastrophic tornado is withdrawn, Anne looks at him as if she had been reborn from a dingy alien world into one that is shiny new and yet eerily familiar.

"How . . . what?" she stammers in wonder.

"Welcome," he says, taking her trembling hand in his.

[629]

Chapter 52: Cataclysm

~ The Demonstration ~

A week or so after his second dinner with Anne, Abassi stands calmly behind the curtained wings of a large wooden stage, surrounded by a sizeable security detail, patiently waiting for the preliminary speeches to be over. Officials from all over the world, their associated support staffs, and a host of media outlets fill the hastily built outdoor amphitheater on the island nation of Tuvalu. In the background, crashing breakers from the rising Pacific Ocean are audibly rumbling from the shoreline. Abassi is forced to spend an inordinate amount of time blocking the mental noise of hundreds of attendees, all projecting a host of graphic emotional images. Fear has given way to curiosity, as it seems the majority now accept government assurances these aliens are indeed peaceful. However, there exists a sizable minority who do not believe the reports at all, and have focused their efforts on exposing what they consider to be the greatest fraud of all time. Outside the amphitheater, a number of small demonstrations are on-going, pro and con, but are too insignificant to attract much media coverage. Everyone is anxiously awaiting the appearance of the alien, and only a few are listening to the preliminary speeches. As the time for his entrance approaches, tension increases, and arguments break out in the audience. Finally, with a brief introduction by the American Secretary of State, the time has arrived. Total silence falls over the crowd. Abassi serenely emerges from the wings and stands at the podium, staring out at the sea of faces.

His words are uttered in a precise rhythmic cadence, and, like darts, pierce every member of the audience with stinging accuracy.

"I have heard it said by members of your species that torturing animals when young signify a serious early warning sign of future serial murderers. Now, I urge you to look at your neighbor on the left, on the right, in front, in back; then look at yourself. You, all of you, are serial murderers.

[630]

"I have heard it said by members of your species that hearing voices in one's head can be hallucinatory, and acting upon their irrational commands is a sign of paranoid schizophrenia. Now, I urge you to look at your neighbor on the left, on the right, in front, in back; then listen to your own head. You, all of you, are paranoid schizophrenics.

"I have heard it said by members of your species that killing for an ideal is a noble imperative in times of crisis, even if it means the death of innocent millions. Now, I urge you to look at your neighbor on the left, on the right, in front, in back; then look at yourself. You, all of you, are killers.

"I have heard it said by members of your species that planet Earth's diversity of life is glorious, but must not take precedence over economic growth. Thus, you smugly oversee cataclysmic climate change, toxic pollution, and the mass genocide of your fellow life forms. Now, I urge you to look at your neighbor on the left, on the right, in front, in back; then look at yourself. You, all of you, are responsible for this cataclysmic genocide.

"Finally, I have heard it said technology will save you, though it is responsible for the deaths of millions of your own kind, and the mass extinction of entire species as a result of the technological war you wage against your own planet. Now, I urge you to look at your neighbor on the left, on the right, in front, in back; then look at yourself. You, all of you, are war criminals.

"There is no future for humanity if it continues its present trajectory of tribalistic and technological suicide. Your greatest achievements pale in comparison to your greatest crimes; indeed, those very achievements often contribute to those very crimes.

"Your only hope, plus the hope of millions of fellow species you are destroying, as well as hope for the planet itself, is to start shedding your old *Homo sapiens* skins. You must wriggle out of those hollow sheaths and leave them behind to wither away. You must emerge into the bright glare of a new age.

"Accept us among you. Allow your sons and daughters to join with our sons and daughters in creating the next steps forward, ones that will eliminate the scourge of serial murderers, paranoid schizophrenics, genocidal killers, co-conspirators in the degradation of the planet, and war criminals.

[631]

"Technology will not save you. Only you can save you, and only you can save your descendants. Clinging to your old, constrictive *Homo sapiens* skin will slowly asphyxiate your species and spell suicide for Earth itself."

Abassi stops speaking and gazes placidly at the throng of onlookers, who rise in one body and crane their necks in anticipation of more. When the alien remains mute, the crowd starts shuffling about in bewildered silence.

~

As if responding to some unspoken cue, an angry roar suddenly erupts from the assemblage.

"Fraud!"

"Blasphemer!"

"Monster!"

"Obscenity!"

"Kill him!"

"Terrorist!"

Gradually, these shouted epithets are drowned out by a swelling chant of, "Demonstration! Demonstration! Demonstration!"

In a flash—an instant—everyone is gone. Disappeared. Abassi alone remains, looking out at a jumbled mass of empty chairs, some tipped-over, some broken, some upside-down, some still upright. Paper programs skitter around the chairs, some floating briefly in the ocean breeze before settling back to the amphitheater's floor.

Only the distant breakers can be heard.

Yet, there is one human still standing amidst the wreckage. It is eleven-year-old Koamalu, who still holds his tray of candies and chewing gum, looking up at Abassi. He had sneaked in with the crowd and charged a dollar for each item, amassing a thick bundle of bills before his customers vanished. Now, he remains motionless, wide-eyed, waiting for whatever is to come next.

Abassi stares down at the boy, and a hint of recognition glints in his eyes. But something is wrong. Abassi clings to the podium for support, as if he would collapse without it. After a supreme effort, he stumbles away from the podium, down the steps, and staggers up to Koamalu. A couple of meters from the boy, his legs buckle and he falls to his knees.

[632]

"It . . . too much . . . too many . . . I can't. . . . " he whispers hoarsely. "Something . . . wrong."

Koamalu looks at him blankly.

"I can't. . . . " murmurs Abassi. "Too . . . weak. . . . "

"You must bring them back," comes the voice of the One his ancestors called *Goddess*. *"Now you know the limits. Now you know your own future, and that of your kind, can be overpowered. Members of an incipient species are subject to the inexorable laws of Nature. Uncertainty reigns. Numbers matter. Fate starves at Probability's door. Now, collect yourself and do what you must!"*

Goddess's last words reverberate around the amphitheater, and little Koamalu, suddenly aware of his own body, turns and runs away as fast as his legs can carry him.

"Come, Abassi," says another voice.

Altan stands above him. "Come, we will leave this place I will fly you away from here. At the airport, before we leave, you must bring them back."

Abassi lifts his weary arm to accept Altan's help in standing.

"Don't know if I can," he moans, energy gradually returning to his words.

"Come."

Altan helps Abassi to the car, and they drive to the airport in silence. Pulling up to the small, private plane waiting on the tarmac, Altan assists Abassi out of the car. Holding him upright, Altan says, "Now, bring them back."

Abassi's head falls heavily and he closes his eyes. "Yes . . . yes, I will try."

Within a minute, a raucous, rumbling roar arises from the nearby amphitheater.

"Good," says Altan.

But Abassi is semi-conscious, so Altan carries him into the plane.

Soon, both are in the air, flying over the Pacific, away from Tuvalu.

~ Aftermath ~

John Rochelle and Walter Monroe stand side-by-side gazing incredulously at their watches, then at the riotous mob. Chants of "Demonstration! Demonstration!" begin to subside as the delegates learn,

[633]

to their horror, that the alien has disappeared, and twenty-five minutes
have elapsed in an instant. Twenty-five minutes of unaccounted for time.
Gradually, the shouting levels off to a low buzz of confusion.

"Where is the alien?" yells a voice.

"Tricks!" cries another.

"Fraud!"

"Bring him out!"

Howls of indignation reach a crescendo as the frenzied crowd
rushes onto the stage, demanding the alien be handed-over. Security teams
from various countries clash, but no shots are fired. Amid the chaos, as
Rochelle and Monroe, among other Americans, are being hustled to safety,
Walter turns to the FBI director.

"John, they have no idea what just happened!"

"I know," replies the director. "Now they will think we simply
pulled a parlor trick!"

"Maybe, but cooler heads will surely prevail."

Director Rochelle snorts derisively. "Don't be a fool, Walter!
They will think it was mass hypnosis, or their food and drink were
drugged, or *God* knows what else. They will go through the same
permutations we did, and come up with the same false narratives. Each
country with its own axe to grind. Christ! What a disaster!"

"At least the media of the world was there," says an aide, jogging
to keep up. "Cameras don't lie."

"That is true," says Walter. "But what will they show?"

Rochelle chuckles humorlessly. "Same thing our security cameras
showed when I disappeared. One second I'm there, the next . . . zip! Only
the time differential remains."

"That's just it," says the clever aide. "TV and video cameras also
disappeared this time, with their operators as well! Now that they're back,
what will the film show during those twenty-five minutes?"

Rochelle suddenly stops and cries, "Right! Have our camera
operators meet us with their equipment at the hotel! My room! Pronto!"

An aide to the Secretary of State rushes up. "We are leaving the
island ASAP!" he exclaims breathlessly. "The Secretary suggests all
American nationals do likewise!"

"We're staying!" shouts Rochelle above the din. "Some work to
do first!"

[634]

When they reach the hotel, a mad scramble is occurring in the lobby, as officials and their aides rush this way and that. Pushing through to the jammed elevators, John, Walter, and a number of aides turn away and scramble up the stairs, eventually tumbling out of breath into the director's room. They are soon joined by the camera operators lugging their heavy equipment. Once the bodies crowding the room are sorted out, everyone watches intently as the film is rewound and played back. Abassi stands before the podium, his last words come through the audio loud and clear. "Clinging to your old, constrictive *Homo sapiens* skin will slowly asphyxiate your species and spell suicide for Earth itself."

In the blink of an eye, he disappears and the film turns a blurry grey, as if the camera were thrown into a body of murky water. Faint movement can be seen through the distorting medium. As the men lean closer to get a clearer view, only shadowy blobs appear, evidently severely misshapen by the grey liquid, or fluid, or whatever it is. Occasionally, bright, flaring trails of light zoom past, as if burning cinders were being shot across the field of vision. The shadows continue to move in the background, ominous and utterly unrecognizable as any familiar shapes. Toward the end of twenty-five minutes, a rapid unidirectional flow is discernable. A rapid shifting of the shadows occurs as though they have been disturbed by some prodding stimulus, and a sudden bursting explodes into the screen. By all appearances, a bubble had been pricked. Flashes zip across the screen, then the cameras briefly go blank. When the images return, they are back at the amphitheater, pointing at an empty stage. There is a hectic, uncoordinated jerking of the camera, then the image of the crowd milling about, still shouting, "Demonstration! Demonstration!"

"What now?" asks someone in the room.

"Now?" says Rochelle. "Now we get in touch with Lance Romellion!"

"We've tried, but he remains incommunicado!"

"Try again, damn it!"

Rochelle finds Monroe in the group. "What say you, Walter?"

Monroe has been quiet since entering the room. His mind is full of speculations about Abassi, where he might be, and the probability he will get in touch with Anne. If so, where and when? Things have now gotten exceedingly dicey. He has religiously avoided mentioning anything about his granddaughter and her relationship with a being his colleagues

[635]

consider alien, and his comfort level at such secrecy, already a bit shaky, has just collapsed. Nevertheless, he is determined to hold his tongue until he can contact Anne. Torn between family and duty, Walter measures his reply carefully.

"I agree. I think all we can do is try and get hold of Agent Romellion. I can do no more good here. I'm taking the next plane back to the States."

John Rochelle gives Walter a skeptical look, then waves him off and turns to address a storm of questions and speculations from others in the room.

~ Lance Romellion Leaves the Island ~

Just as the meeting on Tuvalu is degenerating into chaos, Lance Romellion finds himself back in San Francisco. After Abassi left the strange island, he had been stuck there until this very day. At the island, he passed the days ranting at the walls about Abassi's leaving him behind. When his impatience finally got the best of him, and he was ready to tear the cottage apart in a rage, Altan appeared from nowhere and led him up the volcanic mountain to a hidden cave. Motioning him to go in and walk to the end, Altan quickly turned and left. Flipping on his flashlight, Lance did as he was told and somehow ended up back in the California desert. Hitching a ride to the nearest town, he commandeered a reserve police car and was driven to San Francisco. Once in his office, reports of the meeting dominates the news, and his colleagues are torn between interrogating him about his mysterious whereabouts, and hovering around a television set watching events unfold in Tuvalu. Within minutes of his arrival, the phone is ringing off the hook.

"Where the hell have you been?" shouts John Rochelle.

"Don't know. An island somewhere, as I earlier reported. Now, as you can plainly tell, I'm back."

"Where is that damn Abassi fellow!"

"Don't know that either."

"Find him!"

"Isn't he with you on Tuvalu?"

"Christ, Romellion! If he was with me, I wouldn't be asking you! We both know how this creature operates. *God* knows where he is now. I told you to stick with him!"

"Easier said than done."

"Find him."

"How?"

"I don't care. Call him. Visit the damn mansion. Find him!"

"Yes, sir."

Click.

Lance gazes absently at his desk. It is covered with overdue reports to be reviewed, but his mind is a blank. Too much has happened, too quickly, and far beyond any reasonable expectation of normal explanations. He is aware enough to know things have now been set in motion that will be impossible to stop. He opens his door and joins his co-workers around the television. An "expert" analyst is pontificating on his view of these extraordinary events, yet even as he tries to be calmly efficient and rational, his words convey the high-pitched battle he is waging to exercise objective control.

"In answer to your question, Cynthia," he says to the anchor. "I am at a loss. Is this truly an alien? Has the government pulled a fast one on us? If so, what will the international community think? It is a puzzle, and we don't yet have enough facts to say anything with confidence."

"But, how about all the footage from the cameras that show exactly the same thing?" prods the anchor. "I mean, this grey, shadowy image that runs on every film for twenty-five minutes? Surely, this is more than a trick, as some have called it?"

"Yes, it is puzzling. If this creature is an alien, he certainly has powers we don't understand. The United States government will have some explaining to do."

"In your expert opinion, did he truly vanish, or does it appear to be some sort of trick, or illusion?"

Lance laughs aloud. "A trick!" he cries. "We know better! We know better!"

He is quickly shushed by his colleagues as the expert continues.

"It very easily could be a trick. One, I suspect, our government was not privy to. It appears as much a surprise to them as to the rest of us."

"Could it be Russian or Chinese technology used to discredit the United States?"

The expert shakes his head doubtfully. "Maybe, but their representatives seem just as surprised. Remember, they also disappeared for those twenty-five minutes."

"Thank you, Professor Johnson. Now we turn to our affiliate in Beijing for an update on reactions in China."

"Shit!" Lance scoffs. He leaves his co-workers still glued to the television, and walks back to his office. Closing the door behind, he sits at his desk and rubs his eyes wearily. After absently shuffling the reports without really looking at them, he calls for a car to be brought from the parking garage. When it arrives, he leaves his colleagues, takes the elevator to the ground floor, reluctantly gets behind the wheel, and sits pondering for long minutes. An attractive woman walks past on the way to her car, high-heels clicking on the concrete floor. An incongruous moment of reconnection with comforting normalcy seizes him with nostalgia for a world now rapidly slipping away. He lets the car idle a little longer, then shifts into drive. "Nothing for it," he says resignedly, and drives toward the mansion.

Pulling up in front of the familiar old Victorian house, Lance turns off the engine and stays in the car, waiting to spot any signs of life. After half an hour, he sees no evidence that anyone is home. Through his compact binoculars, he pays close attention to the curtains, particularly the ones upstairs. Nothing. Another half-hour passes, and still he waits. Nothing. A brief surge of relief makes him question his own resolve. *Fool!* he thinks. But the burden of dread he felt earlier is dissipated. *No one home, so carry it through to its conclusion and get it over with.*

He exits the car and strides rapidly to the front door; more confident than ever this call will be a waste of time.

Pressing his index finger to the doorbell, he hears the muffled ringing through the door.

Nothing.

Don't press your luck, Romellion! He scolds himself, but nonetheless presses the button again.

Nothing.

This time, he breathes a sigh of relief and turns to go. After taking a couple of steps, a noise comes from behind. He turns around and sees an attractive young woman holding open the door.

"May I help you?"

Instinctively, Romellion pulls out his identification card and holds it open for her to read. As she peers at it, he notices her face seems somehow familiar.

"Lance Romellion, FBI," he says mechanically, still trying to place where he has seen that face. "May I come in and ask a few questions?"

"Of course," she says, quite cheerfully. "Did my grandfather send you?" she asks as he follows her to the anteroom.

"Your grandfather?"

"Oh, never mind," she answers in a flustered tone. "Sorry."

Now that she seems worried, Lance wracks his memory even harder.

"Who is your grandfather?" he asks.

Before answering, she offers coffee, which he accepts. Fussing with the pot, she does not immediately answer his question.

"Actually," he says, taking the proffered cup. "I am being rude. May I ask your name?"

She hesitates, then says firmly, "Anne Monroe."

"Monroe?"

"Yes."

"Any relation to. . . . "

"Walter Monroe? Yes, he is my grandfather."

Lance is utterly astonished, and stares rather stupidly for some time, taking in her features. "Of course!" he suddenly exclaims. "I met you years ago at a conference in San Francisco that your grandfather attended. It was a social event held in the evening after all the boring lectures were finally over. Of course!"

An awkward silence follows, while both parties search for words. At last, Romellion comes out with the obvious question.

"Why are you here, Ms. Monroe?"

"Please, you are a member of our FBI family. Call me Anne."

"Thank you, Anne. As you must be aware, I am very surprised at finding you, of all people, occupying this house."

"My grandfather told me about your visit with him in Washington," she says. "It seems, since then, you have become quite the expert on these, well, these aliens."

[639]

"Ha! Maybe, but it looks like you've got me beat." His eyes take in the room. "Why *are* you here, Ms. . . . . Anne?"

Taking a few moments to think, Anne sighs and says, "It seems I have become a sort of ambassador without portfolio to the . . . aliens."

Lance flashes her a sardonic look. "You and I both know these beings are not aliens, at least not in the sense most people conceive of the term."

"Yes, you're right. Through my grandfather, I have come to be friends with Mr. Powers . . . Abassi . . . and was asked to house-sit while he and the others are gone."

"House-sit!" blurts Lance. "Now I really am down the rabbit-hole."

Anne flashes a quizzical look, but remains silent.

"Sorry," says Lance. "It just seems so absurd. Have you met the others?"

"Not yet. More coffee?"

"Please." Lance holds out his cup. "When do you expect Abassi to return?"

"Haven't a clue."

"You watched the Tuvalu conference, I presume?"

Anne winces. "Yes."

"Bit of a mess, eh?"

"A disaster."

Again, both fall quiet, momentarily lost in their own thoughts. Finally, Anne perks up.

"My turn," she says. "Why are *you* here?"

Lance chuckles. "Fair enough. I am here to see if anyone still lives in this beautiful old mansion."

"Only me," says Anne. "Temporarily."

"Do you know where the hunchback women are?"

Anne's face reddens in anger. "Their names are Ming-huà, Pythia, and Tara. All with the last name of Powers. Ming-huà is the great-grandmother, Pythia is the grandmother, and Tara is the mother of Abassi."

"Sorry for the rude phraseology in referring to these women. We have taken to shortening them to . . . that description. Do you know if their husbands, or partners . . . or . . . what I mean to say is, are the fathers also of their kind, for lack of a better term?"

"I don't know," Anne lies. She is on her guard at this flurry of questions, and is not keen to explain the concept of intermediates, let alone get her father more involved than he already is. She coughs. "Mr. Romellion—"

"Lance."

"Okay. Lance, what is the purpose of this interrogation"

"Well, it might surprise you to know, Anne, that I am entirely on your side."

"What does that mean?"

"It means I have come to the conclusion that Abassi and his kind are the only hope for the future of humanity."

Anne is taken aback. "And your colleagues?"

Lance shakes his head sadly. "Most of them are either suspicious, antagonistic, or would have them killed outright if given the opportunity."

Chapter 53: Hunting Them Down

~ Anne and Lance Confer ~

After Lance gives Anne his harsh analysis, he sees the distress in her eyes, and hastens to say, "Please, Anne, I do not approve of these attitudes. I have come to know these beings relatively well, especially Abassi and Altan, and after doing some soul-searching, have jettisoned my earlier prejudices."

"So, you believe he tells the truth about . . . things such as giving up our human savagery, and interbreeding, and the rest?"

"You are young and attractive, Anne. You have your entire life ahead of you, and probably can have your pick of eligible husbands. What do you think? Would you . . . I mean if it was right . . . the opportunity arose . . . would you, with one of them?"

Anne blushes and gives a little laugh. "More coffee?"

"Actually, I would like a Bloody Mary or Margarita, perhaps a Screwdriver, if you will join me."

"I thought agents on duty are prohibited from drinking."

Lance shrugs. "If we are going to be honest with each other, a drink might oil joints. I suspect both of us have some uncomfortable confessions to make."

"Are you a priest?" Anne laughs.

"Far from it. However, seriously, I believe you know a lot you are not telling me, and I know a lot I'm not telling you. The times demand a different approach to . . . fulfilling our moral responsibilities and meeting our professional obligations."

Anne stands and collects the empty coffee cups. "I make a pretty mean Bloody Mary."

"Excellent."

While she prepares drinks, Lance ruminates aloud. "You know, I am an admirer of your grandfather. From the beginning, he did not scoff,

[642]

listened to my story, seriously considered my theories, and made things happen. He seems clued-in to these beings in ways others do not."

Anne decides to err on the side of caution. "Yes, he is a remarkable man."

After preparing the drinks, Anne sits and rather absently stares into space. They sip their coffee quietly for a while. Lance leans back in his chair and says, "Since I am the official visitor, I should start first with my story."

Anne's focus returns to him. "Yes, that would be nice."

For the next hour or so, Lance gives Anne a full briefing on his experiences with the hunchback women, limbless victims, the cave, the strange young woman, Abassi, the island, and so forth. As he winds down his story, he finishes with a *mea culpa.*

"Not too long ago, I was convinced these beings were terrorists out to destroy our civilization. Figuring I was protecting the American people, and humans everywhere really, I pumped myself up to be a sort of movie hero whose cogent knowledge of these invaders made all others in government and law enforcement seem dimwitted in their cluelessness about the danger. When the facts didn't fit this view, I made them fit by performing mental gymnastics. Although we are trained to maintain complete objectivity when investigating crimes. I unknowingly had lost mine to the lure of thwarting such a great threat—a threat that seemed obvious only to me. But, the more I had contact with them and their . . . I don't know . . . allies, the terrorist scenario seemed less and less feasible. In light of my increasing knowledge of their *modus operandi,* the comfortable fantasy I had built no longer held up. At last, I started listening, and that latest stint on the island with Abassi and Altan convinced me their goals are not malevolent, not at all. Which brings me at last to your question about whether I believe their story about inbreeding being the only hope for humanity. Yes, I do."

Anne nods noncommittally. "I see."

She seems suddenly distant again, and Lance's mind feels funny, as if his brain were being lightly tickled. The sensation is odd, but he tries to ignore it, and presses her. "How about you?"

Her attention snaps back, and she responds adamantly, "Oh, I believe, I believe! There is no doubt. Even now, I can partially read your

[643]

mind, though my powers are weak. I can see you are convinced, and are not trying to trick me. Of that, I am grateful."

"You can read my mind?"

"Partially."

Lance is suddenly troubled. Is Anne crazy? Or is it something else? He looks at her long and hard. Remembering the peculiar tickling, he asks rather hesitantly, "Are you one of them?"

She laughs. "No, not really. However, I have been told I have some of their DNA. Not enough to amount to much . . . but enough."

"Enough for what?"

"Enough to know you are being truthful. Another Bloody Mary?"

"Wait a minute, how can you have their DNA? I mean, as far as I know, the hunchbacks were the first."

"No, that is not right. Evidently, it is a long story that goes way back. A story of starts and stops, fitful progress and disastrous regression. There are many out there who are . . . shall we say, partially evolved. Abassi refers to them as intermediates, like me. Here's your Bloody Mary. Don't look at me that way," she laughs. "I am not an alien, you know."

"Tell me more."

Anne starts from the beginning, recounting the story told to her by Abassi. She explains how her linage is different from those who possess a direct line to the hunchbacks, and how the hunchbacks themselves are all descended from a man named John Powers, and two women whose names were Bai Meiying and Child of Buddha. Anne pauses and observes Lance leaning forward in anticipation. She asks coyly, "Do you have time to hear the story?"

"Are you kidding? Yes!"

"Then let's have another Bloody Mary. The story is long."

"By all means," says Lance, mentally pinching himself to make sure this is real. "When I met you those many years ago, were you . . . I mean, were you like you are now? Were you aware you were different from the rest of us?"

"Of course not. And, truth be told, I'm not that different now, at least not until I met Abassi."

"So, I mean, you and he. . . ."

[644]

Anne nods demurely. "Although we've not been . . . intimate, I've transferred to Berkeley in order to finish my Ph.D., and, well, be close to him. I'll wait here until he returns."

She hands him a fresh drink and continues. "It all began, before World War II, when John Powers—Abassi's great-great-great-grandfather—was working in his office one very auspicious day, not too long before the Japanese invaded China. A beautiful young woman entered; a stranger to him then, and one you might recognize now. *She* said to him, 'Mr. Powers, how does one justify a life without cruelty, and therefore also without the distilled beauty of cruelty?'"

"Yes, yes, I have heard those words before. It was that strange young woman at the cave! Do you know *her*?"

"I know of *her*."

"Who is *she*?"

"That, Lance, is the sixty-four-thousand-dollar question. Sit back and let me tell you what I know. There are still gaps that puzzle me, but I understand there are manuscripts, narratives written by John Powers' son Michael. These manuscripts tell the story of his father, John Powers, and describe a quest, of his own experiences with war, bouts of what he thought was schizophrenia, and so much more. I hope to get my hands on them some day. Unfortunately, back in the day, the experts thought John and Michael suffered from schizophrenia, but they were wrong. Terribly wrong. Most of the story I am about to tell was evidently written down by Michael Powers in a mental institution. I would give the world to have those writings. Anyway, I'll tell you what I know. Perhaps, when this day is over, we can be allies and help each other."

"I'm all ears."

~ Newborns ~

At the Mongol compound, all three women have had their babies within a few months of each other. Ming-huà's delivery is the most difficult, and after a prolonged period of agony, gives birth to a girl, while Pythia produces female twins and Tara has male twins. The compound is now alive with young life. Zookeeper has it the worst, as his fully human genome is stretched to the limit trying to cope with children who are in every way superior. Nevertheless, his advanced age confers the advantage of patience. Siyabonga is also kept on his toes, trying to keep up with so many non-intermediate children. As usual with these beings, the newborns develop exponentially faster than human children, and everyone wonders if they will, like Abassi, eschew their educational hiatus and simply become fully adult in the blink of an eye. Altan, as always, plays a key role as mentor, teacher, advisor, and moral guide. As it turns out, all the youngsters are as fully equipped with extraordinary powers as Abassi. Lording it over them all is Abassi himself. Since the demonstration fiasco, he and Altan traveled to the compound with the intent of laying low for as long as it takes to let the planet's hysteria die down. Now, a few years later in human terms, Abassi is impatient to return and pave the way for all the young ones to enter the world. He also feels the need to mate, and the image of Anne waiting at the mansion is always with him.

"The time has come for me to return," he declares one day. "Our presence has fallen below the radar of humans, mostly. All their worldwide searches have come to naught, and the great and wise pundits among them have assumed we have gone back to whatever planet we came from with our tails between our legs." He chuckles. "Yes indeed, great and wise."

"We must all go!" exclaims Pythia.

"Yes," agrees Ming-huà. "All of us or none of us. I miss my little island."

Zookeeper, whose age now weighs heavily upon him, chimes in, "Fuck yes! Let's get the hell outta Dodge! Let the chips fall where they may. I'm fuckin' tired of this place, no offense Quequeeg."

"None taken."

"Agreed," says Tara.

Everyone's eyes turn to Lady Oracle. She stares back at them, and smiles. "It is time. I agree. We cannot stay here forever. The seeds must now be spread."

Altan stands and clears his throat. "Question is, do we return to the same places we left—the mansion, the island? They still hunt us, you know."

"Let them find us," says Abassi. "If they use force, we will disarm them. If they come to their primitive senses and cooperate, we move forward. We must safely release these children out into the world."

"And let you finally mate," scolds Lady Oracle. "This person, this Anne Monroe, is certainly patient enough."

"True," says Abassi. "She has her Ph.D., for whatever that is worth to her now. At any rate, let her be rewarded."

"Yes!" cries Sy with a graceful leap upwards. "Now let her—of course with your assistance, Abassi—let her earn her postdoc status. Let her give us triplets!"

"Nonetheless," cautions Altan. "We saw at the demonstration that there are limits. Numbers matter. We can still be overrun by them, simply by the sheer weight of their enormous population. Is it wise to return to the same places?"

Abassi ponders, enters one of his meditative states, and the rest patiently wait his return. After a long while, he opens his eyes and looks around. "We do have human allies and friends out there, including some in high places. Nevertheless, is the United States the best place to settle ourselves? Are we more effective staying together, or splitting up and traveling to different continents? This is something to consider."

"With enough financial support," says Siyabonga. "I would love to take Tara and the young ones back to Africa."

"And Pythia?" asks Sy.

"Her choice," replies Siyabonga. "She must find another mate. A black man living with two women and four young ones would be far too conspicuous."

"Or," says Abassi. "I can return to Washington and threaten the government with terrible retaliation if we are not left alone and our identities kept secret."

"Does that not go against our natures—to threaten?" objects Ming-huà.

"I think not. Humans, after all, threaten their dogs without the intent to kill them. And we have certainly punished wicked humans for doing wicked things."

"How would you arrange this?" asks Lady Oracle.

Abassi smiles. "Through Anne's grandfather, of course. Walter Monroe. He is, more or less, one of us."

"He is old. Furthermore, there is a new director of the FBI."

"What is his name?"

"Roger Arlington."

"It is time to find out what Roger Arlington thinks about us," says Abassi.

[647]

"Why not go directly to the President?" asks Sy. "He's new also."

"Let's not prod the sleeping dragon too hard."

"Yeah, I think that makes sense," says Zookeeper with a glint in his eye. "It's also time you prod Anne Monroe hard, don't you think?"

Abassi shakes his head and snorts in mock disgust, "Humans."

~

"Speaking of humans," says Pythia. "All of us know you have been blocking everyone from probing your mind. We can't even communicate telepathically. What are you hiding?"

With this rather unpleasant insinuation, the room's attention turns to Abassi.

With a great heave of his chest, Abassi reluctantly announces, "The simulations are flawed. Those that allowed Tara to make tens of thousands of Japanese soldiers disappear were inaccurate. We are not as powerful as we thought. Just as humans were forced to use their cognitive superiority over both predators and their own hominin competitors, we must learn to use ours even more judiciously. We are closer to a catastrophic misstep now than we have ever been. Now, the world knows about us, and we can see the reactions, both positive and negative. Overstepping our abilities will result in utter failure. Unfortunately, staying here is also not an option. We must venture out and take our chances."

"Why have you not shared these doubts with us before?" asks Pythia.

"As a result of the weakness I felt after the demonstration, I had to isolate the source. Unbeknownst to all of you, I have journeyed into the steppes many times, and while there tested my limits. Not surprisingly, I found the more complex the carbon-based organism, the more taxing it becomes to move it through dimensional portals. A thousand humans are far more draining than a thousand boulders. Worse yet, during my infirmity, I was vulnerable to any number of threats against my body."

Altan nods in confirmation. "It means you must all be cautious with your powers. Any threat that cannot be enforced with action will rebound against us. To use an analogy from ancient times, a lone *Homo sapien* who ventures into a large tribe of *Homo neanderthals* will not survive using only his or her cognitive superiority. To survive, they would have to adapt somewhat to the numerical superiority of their hosts. We are in the same situation, only the numbers are far more lopsided."

"So what does this mean going forward?" asks Ming-huà.

"It means I need to try and come to some understanding with those humans who are in power."

"Your goal?" asks Tara

"To be left alone to spread among the general population. After that, we know the eventual outcome is reasonably assured."

"And if they do not cooperate?" asks Lady Oracle. "If governments pass laws against us? Against interbreeding?"

"Good questions," says Altan. "Obviously, we cannot go to war against the entire human population."

"No," says Abassi. "But we can hold out the carrot rather than the stick."

"How?" asks Ming-huà.

"Show them the advantages of breeding with our kind. Since I am known, it will be my offspring resulting from sex with a human woman that will serve as an exemplar."

"Anne Monroe?"

"Yes."

Sy runs his index finger across his throat. "They might just kill her," he says.

"Maybe," replies Abassi. "That is why we need some protection from the governments of the world, or at least a few. We need time for our young to grow amongst them. Time for Anne to have our baby. Then we can demonstrate the benefits without their fear of the liabilities."

"Humans may never accept us," says Tara. "We are too different, and they are too primitive. If we cannot use our powers—"

"I did not say we cannot use them," interrupts Abassi. "I said use them judiciously. Perhaps if we help the governments of the world root out criminals—although many governments are themselves criminal—perhaps then we can buy cooperation. One thing is for certain; we cannot threaten the entire species. However, we can threaten a few decision makers—a threat softened by the promise of rewards."

"What decision makers?" asks Sy.

"Well, we start with Anne's grandfather, Walter Monroe . . . ." says Pythia.

"Who will pass on the offer to Roger Arlington. . . . " adds Tara.

"Who will pass it on to the President. . . . " continues Ming-huà.

"Who will pass it on down the line. CIA, NSA, State Department, and eventually to other countries, and so on," finishes Abassi. "All we need is a little more time."

"Yes, but how much more?" asks Lady Oracle sharply.

"More," replies Abassi.

Ming-huà adds in a quiet voice, "Enough time for all the newborns to establish themselves in the world."

~ Abassi Returns to the Mansion ~

On the clear and windy afternoon when Abassi shows up at the mansion after so long an absence, Anne Monroe cannot help being overcome by a giddiness bordering on euphoria. After she opens the front door and they stare tenderly at each other for a long moment, a rush of passionate kisses and soulful embraces quickly follow, whereupon, hand in hand, they retire to the anteroom where a pot of tea Anne had prepared earlier awaits.

"You should have given me a warning you were coming," she playfully scolds. "I would have made myself more presentable."

"No need. You are even more lovely than I remembered."

"Alien flattery!" she exclaims. "Are you alone?"

"The others will arrive later this week."

"Who are the others?" she asks.

"Ah! There is a long list. I'll explain later."

The next hours are filled with catching-up, intermixed with more hugs and kisses. Anne describes her adventures at Berkeley while working on her Ph.D., the regular visits with Lance Romellion, her cogent political impressions of the fallout from Abassi's now infamous demonstration, all the while playfully insisting he call her Doctor Monroe whenever she is addressed. For his part, Abassi listens patiently, but shows particular interest in Romellion's visits. After relating to her his own experiences following the demonstration, and the birth of so many of his kind at the Mongol compound, he settles in with her on the couch, each nestled comfortably against the other.

"How is your grandfather?" he asks after a long, pleasant interlude of warm cuddling.

[650]

"Well, but complains about getting older."

"Does he have any connections with this administration?"

"I don't know. Since your disappearance, he spent a lot of time defending you, but fewer and fewer listened. Over time, he has become more isolated from people in positions of power."

"So," sighs Abassi. "I'm now seen as a threat?"

Anne pauses to order her thoughts. "Not exactly. It's hard to explain. You are seen as an unknown, a puzzle, with powers that are dangerous. It is, to them, your unpredictable and mysterious actions that threaten. Some have proposed the idea that you have returned to your home planet and will come back to Earth with an invasion force! It is all muddled, including my answer to your question. Opinions are all over the board."

"Not at all, I can read your mind, and it tells me far more than your verbalized words."

"Damn! I thought you agreed not to read my mind."

"That was then, this is now. Do you want me to stop?"

"Absolutely. Right now I am thinking some pretty embarrassing things."

"I know."

"Oh, you are evil!" she laughs.

Abassi's face becomes severe. "So, is this idea that I am returning with an invasion force commonly accepted?"

"Unfortunately, it is a common view among those in power, as well as the average person, in many countries."

"And the United States?"

"No different here. As usual there is a split of opinion. Walter has argued your case, but with you gone, his camp has gradually lost influence. In the new administration, the defense budget has ballooned, mostly because the possibility of a future invasion by aliens was used as an excuse. Grandfather has become quite pessimistic."

"I see," responds Abassi grimly. "How sympathetic is Lance Romellion?"

"Very. And better yet, he has been promoted to an important position at FBI headquarters in Quantico."

"Truly?"

"Yep. He is working in the Counterterrorism Division directly under some director or assistant director of the National Security something or other."

Abassi claps in hands. "Excellent! Is he in Washington now?"

"Don't know, but I can call him. We have agreed to keep in touch."

"Do they know in Quantico where his sympathies lie?"

"No."

"Does anyone in the FBI know?"

"Oh, heavens no! That little fact he has kept strictly secret, including our relationship."

"How much does he know about that?"

Anne hesitates, her face reddening. "Everything."

"I see."

"I hope I haven't done wrong, but I needed an ally . . . well, a confidant really. Walter is so far away, and. . . . "

"Not to worry. Anne, can you arrange a meeting with Romellion?"

"Here?"

"Preferably. It is important no one else knows I'm here. Do you trust him to keep that secret?"

Anne pauses. "Yes, I do. I'll contact him, but what if he's in Quantico?"

"Ask him to fly back here. It is very important. But make sure he keeps the purpose of his trip to himself."

"Okay, I'll try and arrange the meeting."

Abassi gently runs his hand up her thigh. "Meanwhile, can we have our own meeting upstairs?"

In the glow of Abassi's luminous smile, Anne whispers, "What took you so long?"

~ Lance, Anne, Abassi ~

Two days later, Lance Romellion stands at the front door of the mansion. He does not bother to knock or ring the doorbell, as he feels Abassi already probing his mind. Nervous, he looks around to see if anyone is watching, but only a lone pedestrian is crossing farther down the street, heading in the opposite direction. When Anne opens the door, he quickly slips in. While greeting Anne with a friendly hug, he casts furtive glances past her shoulder.

"Don't worry," she says. "He's not an ogre."

"I know," replies Lance a bit too quickly.

"Let's go to the anteroom. He's waiting."

As they walk, Anne asks, "Does anyone know you're here?"

"No."

"That is good," comes the voice of Abassi, who stands as they enter the room. "Tea or coffee?" he asks.

"Coffee would be great," says Lance.

Abassi holds out a cup already filled.

Lance takes a sip and chuckles. "Of course, as I thought. Cream and sugar just as I like it."

Abassi gestures toward a cushioned chair. "Please sit."

"Thanks."

Anne and Abassi sit together on a loveseat and the room falls quiet. Lance waits, carefully placing his coffee cup on an end table. He crosses his legs and looks questioningly at Abassi. Perceiving the ticklish probing of his mind, he grows irritable.

"Anne said you have something important to discuss?" he asks with cold formality.

Abassi bows his head apologetically. "I am sorry for my rude intrusion, but I have to make sure."

Lance visibly relaxes. "No worries. I'm trained to do the same thing, only I use bugs—listening devices—to make sure. Let me just assure you there are no skulking agents outside, no bugs, and no one knows I'm here."

"Is this not dangerous? . . . I mean, for your job?"

"Yes, I can get in serious trouble."

"Why did you agree to come?"

Lance looks at Anne. "She knows."

"As I understand it," says Abassi. "You are sympathetic to what we are trying to accomplish. Correct?"

"Partly. I am not sympathetic to being an accomplice to the demise of my own species, but I also understand this may be our only way forward."

[653]

"Are you so convinced humans will destroy themselves otherwise?"

"I am."

"And are you as concerned about the other species that humans are driving to extinction?"

Lance is irritated at having to admit to such human failings, but he knows he must be honest.

"Yes, I am concerned," he says evenly. "But I am more concerned about the fate of humans. I am quite pragmatic, quite the materialist."

"Of course," says Abassi. "And you do not feel technology will save your species?"

Lance sighs impatiently. "Look, why the third degree. You can read my mind. I'm here, aren't I?"

"Please indulge me this one question."

"Which is?"

"Do you think technology can save your species?"

"No. At least, not the way our minds have evolved, or rather not evolved, until now. In my job, every day I see the brutish, cruel, stupid, primitive side of human behavior. On the larger scale, we all share the same brain as our worst criminals . . . or, at least, the same DNA."

"I see," says Abassi. "Certainly, you share the same brain structures and functions."

Lance frowns. "Now, let me ask you a question."

"Please."

Romellion leans forward in anticipation. "Don't you also use technology?"

"Indeed, we do."

"Then . . . . ?"

"How does a technological species survive its own destructive ability? To answer that, one must realize that most species do not survive. Statistically, in the universe, there are innumerable technologically advanced civilizations. The vast majority destroy themselves, and/or their own planets, before their brains have sufficiently evolved, and before their technology poses a threat to surrounding planetary systems. This is why you see no evidence of intragalactic warfare (your childishly violent science fiction movies to the contrary). However, some technological civilizations have ensured their own survival by genetic chance. In other words, their empathic and non-violent brains evolved in time to bridge the intelligence gap. Most civilizations plummet into the abyss long before."

"So you *are* an alien," says Lance, glancing at Anne.

"No."

"Then how do you know these things about the universe?"

"There are others out there who value the precious rarity of carbon-based life, especially in such diversity. Let us just say, they view Earth in the same way your intelligent humans view the Grand Canyon, or the Amazon rain forest—worth saving. Difference is, you humans are failing. Your brains as they are presently configured are incapable of succeeding. As a consequence, these others will do what they can—with a minimum of violent disruption—to save what is here. And what is here, this planet, is a jewel worth saving."

"Why not just eliminate humans?"

"As I said, the goal is saving the planet with a minimum of violent disruption and suffering. I might add, they want to avoid not just the suffering of *Homo sapiens*, but of every species currently alive."

"So, these others are genetically modifying our genomes?"

"Let us just say, they are like park rangers, trying to save an entire ecosystem from destruction."

Lance gulps the last of his tepid coffee in silence.

"Another cup?" asks Anne.

"No, thanks." He looks directly into Abassi's eyes. "What can I do?"

Chapter 54: Entering Byzantium

~ A Clandestine Meeting ~

Walter Monroe is a very worried old man. He senses a deep undertow of unrest among the world's population. Although the panic that swept the nations in the immediate aftermath of the demonstration and subsequent disappearance of the aliens has diminished, a tense expectation of the "next shoe dropping" has driven riots and civil disobedience, toppled some already shaky governments, and spawned a host of self-styled militia groups. He considers the domestic members of these groups to be a hodgepodge of less-educated, pot-bellied buffoons with dangerous weapons who have vowed to kill any alien they run across. In the United States, privacy rights have been severely chipped away, and many advocate for amendments to the constitution prohibiting aliens from the benefit of any constitutional protections. Doomsayers are prophesizing the coming apocalypse. The world is a tinder box, and Walter Monroe is beside himself that Abassi picked this time to reappear. Nonetheless, Lance Romellion indicated quite forcefully that Abassi has purposefully chosen this specific moment to meet secretly at an isolated location in the California desert. So, reluctantly, Walter has traveled here incognito, mainly for the sake of his granddaughter.

Now he sits in a dusty car, parked along a windswept dirt road, waiting for Altan to turn off the engine. Walter is anxious to get out, for he knows Anne and Abassi are waiting at a nearby cave, and his legs are cramped from the long drive. With the ignition off, the cool breeze from the air conditioner abruptly stops, and already Walter feels the broiling heat invade the car's interior.

Standing by the open door, he turns to Altan, "How far?"

"Not far."

"Okay, I'm ready. Walk will do my legs good." He wipes the back of his hand across an already sweating forehead. "Hope this cave is cool."

Altan does not reply, and Walter falls in behind as the tall, dark-skinned enigma starts walking down an overgrown little footpath, littered

[656]

with treacherously loose rocks. Numerous boulders, round and massive, poke their way above the scrub like raw boils ready to burst in the hot sun. Walter feels suddenly queasy, as if eyes are following his every step.

"Yes, you are being watched," says Altan over his shoulder.

"This reading minds business gives me the willies," says Walter.

"I understand you are an intermediate. You have some ability in that regard?"

"Supposed to, but sure as hell wish I had more. Anyway, who is watching us? Guards?"

"Ghosts."

Walter laughs.

Altan does not.

~

When they are within sight of the cave opening, Anne and Abassi wave. Walter quickens his pace and meets Anne halfway. They embrace, each whispering quick questions and murmuring quick answers. Abassi stands a short distance off, smiling broadly. Disengaging from his granddaughter, Walter walks up to the tall "alien" and holds out a hand. Abassi grips it and says, "Welcome, Mr. Monroe."

"Walter."

"Welcome, Walter. We have much to discuss."

"You certainly picked an isolated spot."

"For more reasons than one. In addition to having much to discuss, there is much I want you to see." He points toward the cave entrance. "In there."

"Hello, Walter!" calls a waving Lance Romellion, emerging from the black mouth of the cave. "I waited just inside until all the pleasantries were finished." He laughs. "It's much cooler in there."

As he and Walter shake hands, Lance says, "Hell of a long way from Quantico."

"Yeah." Walter casts a worried look at Anne. "This had better be worth it, Lance."

"Christ, Walter! I already told you." He gestures toward Abassi. "It's his show."

"Let us enter the cave. It's too hot out here," says Abassi. He takes Anne's hand and leads the way. The group pauses inside the entrance.

"Don't worry," says Abassi. "Just follow close behind me. Here are flashlights for everyone."

"I've been to this place before," shudders Lance. "Will that strange young woman be here?"

"Perhaps," says Abassi. "And if you've been here before, you know not to wander into a side tunnel."

"Not to worry," replies Lance. "Already made that mistake. You're not sending me back to that goddamn island, are you?"

"Not today," laughs Abassi. "We're almost there."

"Where?" says Walter.

"Here," replies Abassi, stepping into a large chamber. When everyone is inside, shafts of light from their flashlights dart this way and that, illuminating nothing but rock.

"Now what?" asks Walter.

"Shhhh!" says Abassi.

The group falls silent. Suddenly, the sound of a panting dog reaches their ears.

"Ah, Temulun!" exclaims Abassi. "I have been waiting to meet you!"

A boxer dog trots into the chamber, wriggling energetically and looking happily around at each face.

"Got a treat?" she asks expectantly.

"I have heard of you," says Abassi. "I brought treats."

"Excellent!" Temulun twirls around in a dance of ecstasy.

Anne, Walter, and Lance look quizzically at Abassi.

"Of course, you don't understand Temulun. She is a permanent resident of the cave. Our ancestor, Michael Powers, could speak with her, and now I am happy to say, so can I!" enthuses Abassi.

"What is she saying?" asks Lance skeptically.

"What else? She wants a treat." Abassi rummages in his pocket and holds one out which she gratefully snatches.

"Got another?" asks Temulun, her big, brown eyes shining in the glow of flashlights.

Anne steps forward. "She's so cute!"

While receiving Anne's caresses, Temulun looks at Abassi. "She's nice! Does she have treats?"

Abassi looks at Anne approvingly. "Temulun says—"

[658]

"I understood!" cries Anne in amazement.

"So did I," adds Walter.

Pragmatic Lance Romellion gazes wonderingly at the scene. "What's going on here?" he asks sharply.

Temulun stops wriggling and stands at alert. "You are being given a glimpse," growls the dog in a commanding voice.

Lance takes a step back. "I've heard those words before," he says nervously.

"Me too," says Walter.

Temulun relaxes, stares at Lance, and reverts to a dog persona. "Do you have any treats?"

"Christ, now I understood the dog!" cries Lance.

"Of course, though it took you a while," says Temulun. "Well?"

"What?" asks an incredulous Lance.

"Treats! Treats! Silly boy!"

Romellion can only shake his head.

"Here you go, Temulun," says Abassi, holding out another treat.

Temulun merrily swallows it, then says, "Thank you! At least there is one civilized being here."

Abassi nods acknowledgement and turns to address the group. "You know, our ancestor Michael Powers was thought by humans to be mentally ill. He could communicate with anything; animal, vegetable, or mineral. He could talk to sidewalks." He shakes his head. "Amazing."

"So he was," agrees Temulun.

"Well, what now?" asks Lance.

Temulun gazes at Lance for a long while. She changes back to an imposing persona, and barks authoritatively. "Follow me!"

Without further ado, off she trots, followed by the group still waving their flashlights about in the effort not to trip, and to see some sign of reason and rationality in the walls and ceiling of this bizarre cave. However, only rocks glare jaggedly down when exposed in their beams.

Everyone can hear the scraping clicks of Temulun's nails scrambling ahead. As time passes, the sound of her running fades in the distance. No one speaks, but the group keeps following Abassi, who treads among the rocks as if walking on smooth ground. At last, they reach another large chamber. Once everyone has stepped toward the center, Abassi tells them to turn off their flashlights. When the massive space becomes utterly dark, they hear Temulun again, panting close by. Then, even the panting stops. Nothing. Total silence.

Suddenly, blindingly, the chamber is filled with light. It is no longer a rocky cavity, but a shining cathedral. Standing amongst them is the young woman, *her* knapsack protruding from a back that Lance now sees is itself oddly shaped. An awestruck quiet descends over the group, and even Abassi seems intimidated. He squeezes Anne's trembling hand, and waits in respectful anticipation.

~

"I have often asked the question," *she* begins in the voice of an angel on high. "How does one justify a life without cruelty, and therefore without the distilled beauty of cruelty?" *Her* mesmerizing gaze encompasses the group.

No one responds, all breathlessly waiting.

"Look around," *she* continues. "Here with us at this moment in Earth time is one fully human male and two intermediates—grandfather and granddaughter—who nonetheless are predominately human. It is to these that I direct my words.

She pauses, *her* eyes passing over the humans to look intently at Abassi. He returns the look, a troubled frown on his face. *Her* scrutiny slowly moves from him to the others.

"The ancestors of this one," *she* says, pointing at Abassi. "Are among the early founders. Unfortunately, John Powers and his son Michael Powers were viewed by primitive human psychiatrists as mentally ill. In John's and Michael's fevered and bewildered minds, they heard voices that frightened and confused them. These voices they termed *God* and *Goddess*. Occasionally both founders—each an intermediate— conjured up in their imaginations these misconstrued deities to appear visually before them as well. As a consequence, their fellow humans labeled them schizophrenic. That was, of course, incorrect. The expression of certain genes, as well as burgeoning brain structures hitherto unknown, were, to the founders, deeply perplexing and too much for their minds to cope with. However, hidden in the psychoses that plagued them, they had unknowingly tapped into a certain truth. That truth touches upon those that dwell a great distance from us here. *Who are they?*—you may ask. They are those who Oversee. These distant dwellers have been engaged in a debate, of sorts, for a few hundred Earth years. Your ancestors, in the confused labyrinth of their primitive brains, heard this debate filtered through the distorting lens of their rapidly evolving, incipient species. To them, *God* and *Goddess* represented the two sides of a coin, a dialectic, in which one side craved the alluringly addictive suffering of life on Earth, while the other, in the interest of a deep-seated compassion, strove to end it. Of course, this interpretation was incorrect. However, there do exist two distinct viewpoints about how this new species should go about ensuring its continued survival. Such views have come to be unavoidably contradictory."

She pauses and seems to wait for questions. Lance Romellion obliges.

"In other words, eliminate humans outright, or be patient and dilute their genomes out of existence?"

"Not quite, clever human," *she* replies. "Eliminating *Homo sapiens* outright is not an option. Far too much unnecessary suffering; besides which, beings like Abassi are not capable of such barbarism— unlike humans."

"Then, what is the option?" asks Walter.

"That is the essence of the debate."

"Do we not have freedom of action, based on our own evaluation of the circumstances?" asks Abassi.

"As many humans will testify, including the mate of Ming-huà Powers—known colorfully as Zookeeper—you have been doing just that."

"But will the Overseers stop us if we go too far?"

"You know better than that," *she* scolds. "Does determinism rule the universe? Of course! There is no free will."

"Yet," objects Abassi. "If we err too dramatically, one way or the other? What then? What will the Overseers do?"

"Your genetic composition will only allow you to err in one direction."

"I hope the error is not in the direction of dispensing too much suffering," says Anne boldly.

She stares at Anne appreciatively. "So says the intermediate. Rest assured; your kind can err only in the direction of complete, self-annihilating pacifism in the face of existential threats. Aggression and wanton destruction, in the human sense, is precluded."

"Oh, I am so glad!" exclaims Anne. "So very glad."

[661]

"Out of the mouth of babes. . . . " murmurs her grandfather.

"Nevertheless," *she* continues. "There are dangerous humans; the cruel, the manipulative, the deranged, the vengeful, the bigoted, and so on. These are the hateful ones who hold so much sway over the rest of the species. I ask you all; are they to be eliminated?"

"Or maybe just lose body parts?" says Lance sardonically.

"Question is, which of those—elimination or maiming—causes more suffering?" asks Walter in a more serious tone.

"Is this the conundrum your Overseers are facing?" asks Anne.

"No," *she* replies. "This is the conundrum you are facing."

"We all have metaphorical *Gods* and *Goddesses* clashing in our minds," says Abassi.

"Is there room for both?" asks Anne.

"The concept of *Goddess* is the Mother from whom we suckle nourishment. The concept of *God* is the Father whose abuses must always be tempered by justice," replies Abassi.

"Likewise, Father must also provide nourishment, and Mother must also dispense justice," *she* adds.

"But these are just the same, mundane choices facing humans!" objects Walter. "What is the difference?"

"Far from it," *she* says. "*God* is not human. *Goddess* is not human. *God* is not a human construct only. *Goddess* is not a human construct only. *God* is not a deity. *Goddess* is not a deity. Rather, both are waves; universal fields that permeate all that is, out of which emerge the objects of the world; and back into which the objects of the world will return."

While the group is silently absorbing these words, Lance coughs and looks at *her* steadily.

"I am just a dumb human, but why not simply march into the capital city of every major country, removing whatever limbs are necessary to neutralize the security forces, and make your demands?"

"So be it," *she* says.

~

Suddenly, Lance finds himself swaying on legless stumps. Horrified, he teeters unsteadily in a filthy alleyway of some unknown city, stinking of defecation, urine, and decay. Three homeless wretches are startled by the sudden appearance of this legless man who is screaming incoherently.

One of the derelicts yells, "Shut up!" at the shrieking Lance.

When he won't stop, a second approaches with a knife, followed by the other two.

The noise stops.

Inexplicably, the bawling man has disappeared.

All three ragged witnesses shrug and shuffle back to their accustomed spots.

~

"Did you feel resentment?" *she* asks Lance when he appears in front of the group, whole and intact.

Lance is white with shock. In a few minutes, he comes to his senses enough to speak. "If I had a gun, I would shoot *you*," he stammers.

"Precisely."

~ What Now? ~

Lance glowers at the vacant spot where *her* last word still reverberates through the cave, but *she* is no longer there.

"Damn," he says evenly. "This is *her* favorite trick."

"It is no trick," says Abassi.

"Why does *she* always leave when the most important questions are raised?" asks Lance angrily, still trying to control his shaking.

"Precisely," replies Abassi.

"I believe I understand," says Walter.

"So do I," agrees Anne. "But this still leaves us with the same enigma."

Abassi laughs. "Yes. What is too much, what is too little? What is going too far, what is not going far enough? Bold leaps, or golden mean? Remove a limb? A life? A species?"

"Above my pay grade," says Walter.

"Look," says Lance. "What's the point of all this? It's the same age-old question, nothing else. Even our old friend Hamlet could not decide between acting or forbearing to act. We are trained to act in the FBI. Isn't that true, Walter?"

"At a certain lower level, yes. But higher up the decision-making chain, it is not so clear."

Abassi looks at Lance. "Are you prepared to act?"

"Yes, depending on what the act involves."

[663]

"Having sex with one of us."

"What? . . . I mean, why do you ask? . . . With who? . . . What's the point you're trying to make?"

"Do you want your offspring to carry our genes, or only those of *Homo sapiens*?"

"I don't know. Haven't thought about it."

"Yes, oh yes you have!" exclaims Abassi. "Most definitely. Remember, we can read your mind. That thought is uppermost in your thoughts. Like so many others, you dwell in the future. What is to happen to your children if they are left behind? That is your concern, is it not?"

"Don't have any children," grumbles Lance.

"But you want them," says Abassi. "I know you do."

"Okay, I want them eventually," grumbles Lance. "But I'm too old now. Just haven't met the right woman." He scowls. "Besides, what's the point of having children that are smarter than you, superior to you, and consider you—even though you are their father—as no different than the rest of the general population?"

"So, what you want is their exclusive love and loyalty, isn't that correct?"

Lance shakes his head, knowing denial of a fact with these creatures is useless.

"Take care of you in your old age?" presses Abassi.

"Yeah, something like that."

"Well," says Anne. "I sympathize, Lance. At times, I feel the same way. However, picture a world where everyone is treated as family, not just your immediate relations. Not just everyone, but all the rest of life on Earth."

"Impossible," replies Lance. "Got to kill to eat. I don't want to kill my son the cow for his meat. It's unworkable!"

"Lance," says Abassi soothingly. "With this attitude, your descendants are doomed. Your line will end. Why did you come with us to this place?"

Lance sighs, "I don't know. It's my job—no, that isn't it—I don't know. Loyalty to my species? That's not quite it either. Maybe you're right. You are the future. I haven't got it figured out yet."

Altan speaks up. "We need more intermediates, Lance. Intermediates like Anne will provide the broader base on which to build up to a world comprised of those who will replace humans. It is not about saving *Homo sapiens*, it is about saving this planet and its rich diversity—a far more important goal."

"Even if I agree with you, there are not enough of you to make a difference. Christ, there are eight billion humans out there!"

"You are here for a reason," says Abassi. "If we find you a mate, would you be interested?"

"Oh, *God*!" exclaims Lance. "Now you are breeding me like some stock animal."

"No," says Abassi. "You are free to choose. At a minimum, we do need your help and cooperation with the government."

"I feel like a traitor," he murmurs.

"No, you are one of the hopes of the world," says Abassi. "Without the cooperation of humans, the process can become quite ugly, and a great deal of unnecessary suffering inflicted on untold multitudes."

"You mean an ocean full of human body parts, like on that island? Is that what you mean?"

"Something like that."

"Not much of a choice," grouses Lance. "Cooperation or genocide."

Anne is startled by the turn of the conversation. "Surely, Abassi, it would not come to the maiming of so many people."

Abassi smiles reassuringly. "Rest assured, Anne, it will never come to that." He nods toward Lance. "If there is to be any genocide, as you call it—it would be a unique genocide. The only ones who would be punished are the type of humans who actually *do* commit genocide, and furthermore, with our powers, lost arms and legs can be returned, just as yours was returned just now."

"Then what did I see on your island?"

"What you saw is the human wreckage from injustices, wars, and genocides conducted in the past by humans themselves. We do not have the power to put your entire species back together, but we can ensure a future without such carnage."

"There will always be suffering," says Lance, recognizing the insipid nature of his comment.

"Yes, but the unnecessarily wholesale destruction of such a beautiful planet is preventable, if we cooperate and make the right decisions."

"I performed my part of the bargain," says Lance. "I brought Walter here, and I am prepared to do more. I am not sure what more I can do. After all, I am a lowly assistant to an assistant of an FBI director."

"You can do more than you know. The first thing to do is to make you a national hero. Then build on your popularity and trustworthiness with the people." Abassi winks. "And after that we need to find you an appropriate mate."

"And how do you achieve that?"

Abassi holds out his hands as if he was being handcuffed. "First, you take me in."

"What? In handcuffs?"

"Figuratively."

Chapter 55: Fanning the Flames

~ Captive Audience ~

The President listens with mixed emotions in the briefing room to his national security team describe the FBI's capture of the alien known as Mr. Powers, aka Abassi. Instinctively, he knows this could be a political coup of tremendous importance, but could also blow up in his face. The unpredictability of these aliens is well known to his team, and that in itself recommends caution. As evidence of that caution, armed security guards line the walls of the room. Worse, from the President's perspective, there exists one wild card among a deck full of wild cards that could spell ultimate disaster; it is the fact the aliens do indeed possess powers not yet understood. He glances at his Secretary of State, whose mien reflects anxiety at the international repercussions of this news. Although a number of his staff ask clarifying questions, he keeps his own counsel, and listens impassively to the conversation. While outwardly appearing to hear the news with his usual stoicism, internally his mind is alive with glorious possibilities, perilous snares, and, if he bungles this opportunity, existential doom for the species. Given a choice, he would much prefer the FBI not to have found this Abassi fellow, and to have let sleeping dogs lie, at least until the next administration. Nevertheless, he is stuck with the problem, and with the dogged cunning that got him the presidency, he will listen quietly and make his calculations based on political expediency. When the last of the briefing is finished, the table is open for questions. Everyone waits for the President to ask the first.

"Did Mr. Powers, or Abassi, or whatever his name is, resist being taken prisoner?" he asks.

"Well, sir, that is a difficult question," replies the latest director of the FBI.

"Why?"

"Put is this way, sir. He did not resist, but on the other hand, he was not exactly taken prisoner either."

"You said he is in custody."

"Yes, in a manner of speaking. He is in, what you might call, house arrest."

"Where?"

"At an address here in Washington."

"Oblige me, please. Where exactly?"

"At one of the old residential houses that used to serve as guest quarters for visiting dignitaries."

"Where?" asks the President icily.

"In the proximity of Embassy Row."

"I'm a little confused, Ralph. You said he is in custody. You said he was tracked down by an assistant director who has personal experience with the alien." The President checks his briefing papers. "Lance Romellion. Correct?"

"Yes, sir."

"Well, is he being detained, or does he have free run of the capital?"

"He has volunteered to consider himself in custody . . . or rather, ah, confined to the house."

"So, he's free to leave at any time?"

"Yes, sir."

"That does not sound like custody to me."

"No, sir, but if Abassi wants to leave, we cannot stop him."

"I don't understand."

"Mr. President, you are aware of the powerful abilities of these aliens, including the power to make things . . . and people, disappear?"

"Of course, but I had assumed we have found some means to counter these powers."

Faced with the FBI director's embarrassed silence, the President looks at the Chairman of the Joint Chiefs of Staff. "General Ridgeley?"

The Chairman clears his throat. "We are trying, Mr. President, but it is difficult without having an alien to test hypotheses against."

"Evidently, you have one now," says the President sardonically.

"Yes, sir. If he will cooperate."

The President turns his attention to the FBI director. "Will he, Ralph?"

"We're working on it, Mr. President."

"Well, damn it!" explodes the President. "What does the fellow want?"

"He wants us to cooperate with him, not vice versa, Mr. President."

"What does that mean?"

"It means, Mr. President, he wants to talk to you."

The President turns ghostly white. "What if he makes me disappear, and for good . . . ?"

Not a sound from any person in the room.

"No," says the President. "Too risky. I am assuming none of you responsible for national security and intelligence can guarantee I will be safe?"

Again, silence and averted glances.

"Have him meet the Vice President first," says the President brusquely. "Then, we'll see." He turns to the Vice President, who has a stunned look. "Are you okay with that, Frank?"

A sickly nod is all the Vice President can summon.

"Now, gentlemen, it goes without saying that everything discussed in this room is top secret. There must be no leaks that we are meeting with this alien."

The next day, word comes to the President that Abassi will only meet with him, and if refused this courtesy, he will come of his own accord, uninvited.

The President reluctantly agrees.

~

By the time Abassi sits across from the President in a secure room beneath the White House, he has allowed himself to be thoroughly searched. The room is lined with armed security personnel, and the President is flanked by a few selected aides and directors of key agencies. Small talk is dispensed with from the beginning. The President speaks first.

"Welcome, Mr. Powers. I am here. Since I am told you can read minds, you already know the others at this table?"

"Of course."

"I am listening."

"I want no laws restricting the interbreeding of our kind with humans."

"Unfortunately, that has already been passed by Congress."

"I am aware. Repeal it as unconstitutional."

"That is impossible!" exclaims the President. "I don't have the votes."

"Find them."

"Mr. Powers, you are in no position—"

Every security guard disappears from the room.

Above the shouted protestations and exclamations of shock, Abassi says calmly, "On the contrary, Mr. President. I am in a position to make these . . . demands."

"Mr. Powers," interjects the Secretary of State in an equally calm voice. "We do have a democracy here. The United States Congress cannot pass laws under coercion; that circumstance would not pass constitutional muster."

The security guards reappeared looking confused and agitated. The President holds up his hand.

"It is all right, gentlemen . . . I think," he stammers. "Appears to be no harm."

Abassi continues. "Mr. President, it strikes me as being patently unconstitutional."

"What is?" asks the President, clearly distracted by what he has just witnessed.

"A law forbidding interbreeding, or as you would perhaps put it, sexual relations, between *Homo sapiens* and my kind."

"But you are *aliens*!" the CIA director bellows.

"The American courts have determined that non-citizens—aliens if you will—are protected under the constitution. True, they are subject to immigration laws, and cannot vote, but all natural rights under the constitution are preserved."

"You weren't born here, Mr. Powers, and without proper documentation, you can be deported as an illegal alien," says the director of Homeland Security with a poorly hidden smirk.

This elicits a few chuckles.

"Oh, but I *was* born here, Mr. Tolliver," says Abassi.

This raises another stir.

"What?" cries the CIA director. "You were born elsewhere! You're an alien who, by the way, has never revealed to us what planet you're from."

"Quite the contrary, Mr. Bosworth. I was born in California, United States of America."

Quickly, the room is full of the hue and cry of amazed participants, and a storm of outraged questions follows.

"Can you provide proof?" asks the Secretary of State. "A birth certificate?"

"Yes, in the spirit of cooperation, I will provide proof. Nonetheless, this reprehensible law must be repealed."

"We can try," says Mr. President. "What else?"

Abassi pushes across the table a sheaf of papers. "A list, Mr. President, with annotations, justifications, and conditions."

The President nudges the stack over to his National Security Advisor. "Paul, have the proper agencies review this and report back to me their feasibility."

"I'll take care of it right away, Mr. President."

"Thank you."

The President remains quiet for a moment, then clasps his hands and rests them on the table top. "If we cannot meet these conditions, Mr. Powers?"

"That is a bridge we will cross if and when we come to it. However, there must be no delay. The bridge will be crossed."

"Or else?"

"I brought back your guards."

"If you had not, that would constitute murder."

Abassi glares at the President. "You have born witness to what our powers can do. However, we choose not to use them in a way that would constitute unnecessary suffering, especially by the innocent. However, we will use them in self-defense, which is not murder, Mr. President. I know you were once a lawyer. I think you would agree self-defense is not murder, would you not?"

The President feels his brain being scanned; its ticklish sensation most unpleasant for many reasons.

[671]

"Mr. President, your thoughts are known to me. For the sake of your own credibility, and to avoid embarrassing you in front of the people around this table, I will not reveal them. Nevertheless, you will remember my words about self-defense?"

"Yes," says the President curtly.

The President fidgets nervously, trying to control his thoughts so this alien cannot read them, but he finds it impossible. Try as he might, he cannot counter Abassi's position. In response to this unaccustomed impotence, his political instincts kick in, and he says, "Yet, Mr. Powers, when everything is said and done, it is the eventual extinction of the human race that is the end game. Is it not?"

"No, Mr. President. It will be the eventual adaptive reboot of the human race that will preserve its legacy as well as its future, albeit in a different and superior form. In the bargain, perhaps we can save this lovely planet and all life forms that dwell upon it."

"This meeting is over," says the President hastily. "We will review your papers and get back to you."

"You are afraid, Mr. President," says Abassi with a smile. "Knowing I can read your thoughts makes you panicky, and you want to run so you can escape without your thoughts being observed. However, they have already been thoroughly observed." He looks at everyone around the table in turn. "As have all of your thoughts. Gentlemen and gentlewomen, please believe me when I tell you that plots, conspiracies, manipulation by the powerful, and preying on those who have no access to the corridors of power; that is the world that will be ending. Either you cooperate in bringing it, or the consequences will be unthinkable."

"Another threat, Mr. Powers?" asks the CIA director pointedly.

"One of the hallmarks of *Homo sapiens* is the mental rut they find themselves in, and their utter inability to pull themselves out. Humanity's primitive thinking habituates itself to self-destructive behavior by repeating endless cycles of threat, counterthreat, revenge, coercion, and so forth. These follies constitute the headwinds that hold humans back from truly making progress to cease the never-ending conflicts and avaricious gluttony that now threaten the planet. With the advent of advanced technology, the species cannot expect to survive its own idiocies. Your question adds yet another substantiation to this conclusion."

[672]

The President abruptly pushes his chair from the table and stands, his face alternately red with impotent anger, and white with primal fear.

"Thank you, Mr. Powers," he says as he hastens toward the door. "We will be in touch." As the Secret Service follows him out, the Vice President also stands.

"This meeting is concluded. Thank you, Mr. Powers. As the President said, we will be in touch concerning your list of . . . requests."

"Your characterization of my list is inaccurate, nevertheless you may reach me through Assistant Director Lance Romellion," says Abassi politely. "Otherwise, I will be incommunicado."

"Understood."

~ Leaks ~

Within a week, the media is saturated with leaked stories about a Presidential meeting with aliens. Speculation is rampant concerning this unexpected arrival of aliens returning to Earth. Many outlets broadcast emergency bulletins based on "knowledgeable sources" that "aliens have demanded concessions or the planet will be destroyed by gamma ray bursts from space." These reports quickly speed around the world. Soon, movements arise to protest any concessions, and the sales of guns skyrockets. Underground shelters are dug, reminiscent of fallout shelters in the old Cold War era. Vigilante groups vow to track down any aliens and neutralize them. Countries outside the United States demand to be provided full details of the meeting, and the American ambassador to the United Nations is put on the defensive. Soon, Lance Romellion is inundated with calls to have Abassi make a public appearance and dispel the misinformation careening around the globe. This situation is made to order for Abassi's plan. From now on, all roads will run through Lance Romellion. The public platform through which all communication flows will be SAUCER. Only Romellion will have access to "the aliens", and when passing information on to the members of SAUCER, he will be the face of reason and reassurance. With these instructions from Abassi, Lance contacts his superiors in Washington, and arrangements are made to meet with Doctor Carlson, head of SAUCER. The first meeting is held at an annex building now redesignated as SAUCER headquarters. When Lance enters, he steps into a beehive of activity. Operations managers, mid-level bureaucrats, astronomers, physicists, cosmologists, biologists, ethologists, and a host of other specialists are busily conferring, debating, researching, arguing, theorizing, and otherwise engaged in a host of activities that are an utter mystery to Romellion.

After being announced, Lance sees a tall, angular man with steely blue eyes and an unruly mane of gray hair stride toward him with hand outstretched.

"Agent Romellion!"

Lance takes his hand and immediately understands this director's grip is as steely as his eyes.

"Yes," manages Lance before Carlson is in motion.

"Come to my office!" barks the director. "Follow me, if you will."

Led by the director, both men sail past a dozen clerical workers and breeze into Carlson's office. Before Lance has a chance to sit, Carlson has closed the door and barks, "When can we expect Mr. Powers, or Abassi, to make a public appearance with us to calm the waters?"

"Do you have coffee?" asks Lance.

"Of course." Carlson, unruffled, asks his secretary to bring two coffees. Once done, he stares at Lance, waiting patiently.

After the coffees arrive, Lance takes a few sips, then clears his throat. "Afraid that is not going to happen."

"Why not?"

"I have been informed by Mr. Powers, by Abassi if we may call him that, his conditions must be met before any public appearance."

"But those conditions will take time."

Lance shrugs. "That is what I am told to pass on to you and the government."

"Mr. Romellion, those conditions may take months, if ever, to be met. In the meantime, civil unrest is leading to violence. Reports arrive daily about vigilante groups killing innocent people suspected of being aliens, or sympathizers of aliens. People will die, Mr. Romellion."

"Yes, I agree. There is a large group of demonstrators outside, and its growing. I could barely squeeze through to get in."

"As I said," replies Carlson. "Violence is in the air."

"Then I suggest you tell the government to shorten the time it takes to meet Abassi's conditions."

"We could attempt to force Mr. Powers."

Lance chuckles. "Good luck."

"Perhaps Abassi will have more luck with a dictatorship," says Carlson disgustedly. "He can work with any number of dictators to rule the world. We, however, are a democracy, and these things, unfortunately, take time."

"Mr. Powers has no intention of working with dictators. If he so desires, he can become a dictator himself—eliminate the middleman, so to speak. He is looking to make the United States and its allies a safe zone in which his kind can exist, cooperate, and interbreed. Obviously, this would be in the best interest of enlightened nations. Is that impossible? If so, let me know now and I will pass that on."

Carlson blinks. "Well, nothing is impossible," he stammers.

"Good. Is there anything else to discuss, Doctor Carlson?"

"Yes." Carlson assumes his best alpha intimidation demeanor by looking steadily into Lance's eyes. "Would Abassi consent to meeting with me at a location of his choice?"

"I'm afraid he is quite weary of meetings. My guess is that he wants to see some action, not another meeting."

"I understand," says Carlson. He pauses a bit nervously, then says, "If he agrees to meet, I promise to bring him something of material importance. If I cannot produce it, we can call the whole thing off."

"What might that be?"

"A law."

"A law?"

"Yes, giving his people full protection under the United States constitution."

"Including marital rights?"

"Yes."

"Passed by Congress and signed by the President?"

Carlson reddens. "Not quite. A proposed law. We would want Abassi and his . . . advisors, to sign off on it, or alternatively, to make suggestions and modifications, before it is introduced to Congress."

Lance shakes his head doubtfully. "I will pass that on, but am not optimistic."

Doctor Carlson smiles wanly. "Let's at least be hopeful. I fear the situation is rapidly deteriorating, and *God* knows where we are headed."

"Amen, brother," says Lance with a sarcastic sideways glance. "If there's nothing else?"

[675]

"Not at the moment," says Carlson. "Tell Mr. Powers—Abassi—that we are utilizing all our resources to meet his . . . expectations."

Lance stands. "Okay. Thank you." He shakes Carlson's hand and turns to leave.

"Better let our security people show you a different exit."

"Why?"

"Demonstrations outside have grown, gotten much worse. Seems someone has found out you are meeting us today."

Romellion registers surprise. "They're targeting me?" he asks in alarm.

"You, and us."

"But, me specifically?"

"Yes. You're now a media star, Agent Romellion."

"Damn!" barks Lance.

~

A security guard arrives and directs Lance to follow. After passing through a labyrinth of passageways and staircases, Romellion finds himself alone standing outside the rear of the massive building.

"Damn, damn, damn!" he repeats, starting to walk the long way around to his car.

Lance's first thought is to simply wade through the demonstrators and leave, but as he nears the corner of the building where the front entrance is located, he hears the distant clamor of an angry mob. They are screaming and chanting, but the words are unclear, so he gingerly peeks around the corner to see for himself. Now that the building is not muffling the sounds, a wall of noise hits him. Police, who have cordoned off a path leading to the front entrance, are having a difficult time holding back the mass of protestors, who are chanting what Lance now recognizes as the words, "Kill the aliens! Kill the traitors!" mixed in with "Save the Earth! Save the Earth!"

Placards are bobbing up and down everywhere, thrust violently in the air by frantic protestors. Aliens are caricatured as horrible monsters devouring the planet, and other signs accuse the President and the government, including the FBI, of selling out to extraterrestrials. Among the placards, Lance spots a few with an old photo of himself. Beneath the image are the words, "FBI traitors!" Demonstrators continue to arrive in bunches, so Lance decides to make a wide circle around the mob and make his escape as quickly and surreptitiously as possible. As he hurries away, he glances over his shoulder and sees the police lines start to buckle under the pressing masses. Close by, he hears a voice shout, "There's one of them!" Other voices join in, and a group of protestors break away and begin running toward him. Lance breaks into a trot, then a full sprint, trying to put distance between himself and his pursuers. More protestors appear from the side and are running to cut off his path. A gun is fired, and Lance reaches to pull out his Glock. Just as he clears the leather holster, he is staggered by what feels like the impact of a two-by-four on the back of his head. The concrete sidewalk flies up with terrifying speed, and his body slams heavily onto its unyielding surface. Barely conscious now, his glassy eyes see blood flowing across the sidewalk in a spreading wave. Vague sadness quietly slips away beneath the surface and is replaced by a deep weariness that requires him to close his eyes against the harshly glistening sea of red and let the currents take him where they will.

~ Is Anger an Excuse for Revenge? ~

When news of Lance Romellion's death reaches Abassi at his secluded location via the news, he calls an urgent meeting of the others. They are to meet at his hideaway in Wyoming to determine what steps to take next. Before their arrival, Abassi confronts his own fallibility. Anne, now with him, acts as a sounding board for his new found self-doubts.

"I underestimated the extremity of human irrationality," he says on the day the news arrives. "I put Lance Romellion in harm's way. Inexcusable to not have anticipated such a tragedy."

"Have you been in touch with the government?" asks Anne.

"No. How to contact me here died with Romellion. I remain incommunicado by choice."

"Will you contact them?"

"Anne," says Abassi with hesitation in his voice. "I am currently trying to deal with very unfamiliar emotions."

He laughs. "You may be quite familiar with them."

"Such as?"

"Well, it feels like guilt. Worse, I think it is anger."

"I am very familiar with those feelings. After all, I'm mostly human. One day, when I was a young girl, I stole money from grandfather's drawer. Never have I felt such guilt, neither before or since.

Another time, when I was a bit older, a boy I liked jilted me for another girl and lied about it. That was anger!"

"Anne, those were childish incidents. Here, a good man is dead."

Anne frowns. "Abassi, I get angry all the time. I get angry when I see cruelty, racism, unwarranted violence, sexism, and on and on. We *Homo sapiens* are angry about many things, large and small, insignificant or of global impact."

"Yes, yours is an angry species. That in and of itself answers a lot of questions."

"So, you are only just now experiencing anger?"

"So it appears."

"Is that why you haven't contacted the government?"

"Partly."

"Are you afraid you won't control your anger?"

"Partly."

"Well, I'm only a weak intermediate, but I read great pain when I look into your mind."

"True, but there is more to it."

"Tell me."

"I cannot."

"Why?"

"Because I await."

"Await what?"

"That which will end my waiting."

Anne shakes her head. "Sometimes you can be most aggravating. I was never one for riddles and evasions. Walter brought me up to be straightforward."

"Oh! That is quite a surprise coming from a man whose entire working life was being employed by the FBI."

Anne starts to get mad, but Abassi's smile turns her from that path, and she chuckles with him. "True enough. I have no doubt that if I wanted to join the FBI, he would have talked me out of it."

"Straightforward and FBI don't match."

"On second thought, you are probably wrong. You're confusing the FBI with the CIA." She makes a scary face. "Spooks, you know."

Abassi turns thoughtful. "No, I'm right. When dealing with terrible people who do bad things, but are also intelligent, Walter must have had to get into their rather twisted minds and think like they do. Come to think of it, that may be why he was such a successful agent. He also is an intermediate. You know—"

Abassi suddenly stops talking and looks at Anne oddly.

"What?" she asks, feeling uncomfortable under his strange gaze.

"Nothing . . . yet."

"The others arrive tomorrow," says Anne, anxious to change the subject. "Perhaps together you can find a way forward."

But Anne watches as Abassi slips into one of his meditative trances. Although feeling helpless to assuage his inner conflicts, her mind admittedly dwells elsewhere—focused more on the faint stirrings in her womb. Though not yet certain about her condition, she is distracted by waves of anticipatory joy, but punctuated by wretched premonitions of terror.

Chapter 56: A Scythe is Sharpened

~ Conference ~

The next day, Abassi's retreat is invaded by the entire extended family. Altan and Sy are tasked with taking turns monitoring the rapidly growing children, and being strict tutors while training them to control their extraordinary powers. Meanwhile, Ming-huà, Zookeeper, Pythia, Tara, Siyabonga, Anne, and Lady Oracle are gathered in a large family room, their faces reflecting a collective gloom. At first, telepathic messages and condolences fill their minds, but Lady Oracle coughs to get their attention.

"We should speak verbally for Zookeeper's sake, and so Siyabonga can understand." She looks at him and smiles sympathetically. "I don't believe he can keep up."

His face is flushed with embarrassment, but he nods appreciatively. "I'm fine, but it would be easier for me."

"My heart aches for our loss," says Ming-huà. "Mr. Romellion was a lovely man."

Tara nods, but her words are surprisingly harsh. "As do I. These humans—the evil, violent ones—must be dealt with."

"I agree," says Pythia. "My daughter is sometimes rash, but not in this instance."

"What do you suggest?" asks Abassi.

"Make a statement. An unequivocal statement," replies Pythia.

"They have arrested the man who shot Lance Romellion," says Ming-huà. "He will be tried for murder. Let them do it without our interference."

"Others would have killed him as well," says Tara. "What of them?"

"If you make a public appearance now," says Lady Oracle. "Many people will be injured, maybe die."

[680]

"What if we sent those troubled ones elsewhere?" asks Siyabonga. "Do it in front of all the media cameras. What then?"

"We did that on Tuvalu," says Ming-huà. "It did not work. Exactly the opposite, in fact."

Abassi sighs. "Lance Romellion was to be our face to the world. Decorated FBI agent. Sympathetic to our cause. Intelligent. Now he is a poster child for those who portray sympathizers as traitors to the human race."

"That's not the worst of it," says Pythia. "Countries antagonistic to the United States are claiming America is betraying the rest of the world for thirty ounces of gold."

"Alas," moans Siyabonga. "It has taken many years for our African park rangers to understand the minds and habits of the species they are charged to protect. In the meantime, poachers have driven so many close to extinction."

"Then, like our park ranger friends, we should wage war on the poachers of the world," says Tara.

"That will only lead to more suffering," objects Ming-huà. "It is the same path as humans have taken."

Lady Oracle raises her voice. "Abassi, what is your next step with the government?"

"As I see it, there are only two viable alternatives. One, let them stew in their own juices. Two, step in and do something dramatic to stop this drift toward mob rule and anti-alien hysteria." He pauses, then says, "Or—"

Pythia interrupts, "We cannot always be on the run."

"True," agrees Tara. "Our children and their offspring need time to spread. We cannot keep running off to our little magic island for years at a time until things die down!"

Siyabonga pipes up. "The difficulty is that early *Homo sapiens* could settle and breed in isolated regions. Today, humans are everywhere."

Anne stands and looks at Abassi. "You were about to add something to your two choices. Tell us."

"An idea is percolating, and it may involve you. Yet—"

Altan bursts into the room having recently been relieved of his babysitting duties. When all eyes turn toward him, he says solemnly,

"More and more reports are arriving of innocent people being killed by mobs because they have been accused of being aliens."

Stunned silence.

Abassi asks, "Where?"

"All over. Oh, for example India, Africa, South America, and other places, including reports of beatings in the southern United States and Eastern Europe. In many cases, those who were killed had their bodies cut open so the murderers could find 'alien organs'."

More silence but for the sounds of children playing outside.

Finally, Anne asks, "What is our government's response to these murders?"

"Of course, a call for calm. Law enforcement across the nation are on high alert. Already, some police officers have announced they will not intervene to save an alien race that wants to destroy the planet."

"Hopefully they have been fired?" asks Anne.

Altan shrugs. "When the facade cracks, a catastrophic break soon follows."

"I must contact the government," says Abassi.

"And what will you say?" asks Anne.

"You are human. You have a Ph.D. You tell me."

Anne takes his hand. "For the first time, I am afraid. Truly afraid. This can get out of hand very quickly, and I have no clue how to stop it. Everything I think of will only make it worse."

Lady Oracle shakes her head. "I'm afraid it has already gotten out of hand. Those humans who we counted on to be the intelligent ones, the ones that would stand in line to have their children breed with your kind, they are all waiting to see what will happen. Now, for them to make a commitment in our favor, is a dangerous proposition."

"That is quite true," says Siyabonga.

"Christ!" blurts Zookeeper. "Fuck them all! You guys have the power. Do something that is completely unexpected. In their face, so to speak. To show weakness now is to tell the mob they can do whatever they want. Shit! Law of the jungle, man!" He glances furtively at Ming-huà. "Sorry, love, but I say what I think."

"Does not violence beget violence?" asks Ming-huà.

"Dearest, take the words of ol' Willy Shakespeare (who, by the way, must have been one of your kind). He wrote, 'These violent delights

[682]

have violent ends; and in their triumph die, like fire and powder; which as they kiss, consume.'"

Abassi roars with laughter. "Zookeeper, you have hit the mark. Or, I should say, the Bard has hit the mark! Who better to plumb the depths of humanity. Ha, ha! Violent delights have violent ends! Excellent!"

Zookeeper smiles along, but is perplexed at Abassi's rather extreme response. "Yeah, well, the ol' boy has his moments, I guess."

"Oh, you don't understand, Zookeeper. The 'ol' boy' as you call him, is right now standing on my shoulder whispering into my ear. And his words are born from the very play you quote."

"Romeo and Juliet?"

"Yes! Except this time, the wedding will not take place in secret."

"What?" comes the collective query.

Abassi stands and wraps his arm around Anne. "My dear Anne, will you marry me?"

Anne is speechless, and before she can utter any words in response, Altan laughs loudly.

"Of course!" he exclaims. "Of course! I see! I see!"

The others await that which will end their waiting.

~ The Plan ~

"Well, your answer Ms. Anne Monroe?" asks Abassi.

The room is filled with a crackling sense of anticipation, as Anne's mind is read by multiple other minds.

Anne unconsciously rubs her stomach. "Well, better late than never. The answer is yes, Mr. Powers."

"*Hoera!*" shouts Siyabonga.

"It's about fuckin' time!" adds Zookeeper.

Lady Oracle is pleased, but puzzled as she tries to fathom the end-game implied in Abassi's words. "This is wonderful news," she says. "But I know you have designs that go beyond marriage. What might those designs be?"

"Imagine this," says Abassi, his arms outspread, his face expressing a wry smile. "A grand wedding. Opulent. Held in a neutral country other than the United States. All the heads of state, including royalty, are invited. It will be the first public wedding of an 'alien' and a human. Spectacular news. Such an event will dominate every legitimate

[683]

media outlet and every gossip rag in the world. It will capture the world's attention as no war or political event could even begin to match. It will touch the romantic chords of romance-craving humans. Most of them love happy endings. Not a dry eye on the planet. And when it's over, concluding with a grand finale like no other, it will seal an intimate bond between humans and so-called aliens! Then let the protestors try and get some traction off of that teary-eyed spectacle!"

"Fuckin' awesome idea!" enthuses Zookeeper.

Ming-huà looks at Anne. "How do you feel about this plan, Anne dear?"

Anne is struggling with a cauldron of conflicting emotions. On the one hand, her grandfather's teaching informs her most rational and pragmatic self, whereas her feminine side rebels against such a garish and blatantly manipulative plan. Into this mix is the real possibility that she is pregnant. The plan has its dangers, and now she may have another life to consider.

She is aware the group awaits her response, so she proceeds cautiously. "But, Abassi, don't you think leaders from other countries will see this as a ruse to get them all together and then do something awful to them in one fell swoop?"

"Of course," says Abassi. "But I am banking on the President of the United States attending, and all the heads of state of America's allies. That will put pressure on other countries to also attend. Furthermore, remember, this wedding will be held in a neutral country—on their turf, so to speak."

"And once they see we are not monsters. . . . " says Ming-huà, her words trailing off in a hopeful air.

Lady Oracle glances at Anne, still clearly troubled, and says, "Anne raises a good point. Humans are distrustful animals. They are prone to twist others' motives to coincide with their own agendas. I can hear the outcry now about this being a cunning trap."

"Then we will invite those who opt out to watch on their various media outlets."

"Wouldn't they all decide to take that option?" asks Anne.

"Not if the President of the United States and the leaders of other friendly nations attend."

"But how will you convince him . . . and the others?" asks Zookeeper.

"Ah! Therein lies the secret. We have powers. We must use them for good purposes. I can think of no better purpose. Can you?"

"Sooo . . . " drawls Altan. "If the President refuses, you will make him an offer he can't refuse?"

Abassi winks in confirmation.

"Lemme get this straight," says Zookeeper. "You're just gonna call up the President and make these demands? I mean, shit, in the hood, we always used a go-between."

"An emissary?" asks Pythia.

"Yeah, that."

"Zookeeper has once again nailed it," says Abassi. "Now that our friend Lance Romellion is sadly departed, I know just the right person to perform that task."

Silence.

"Well, who?" asks Zookeeper.

"The others already know by telepathy, but for your benefit, and that of Anne's, the person I have in mind is Walter Monroe. Who better than the bride's grandfather? A high-ranking public servant who has dedicated his life to serving and protecting the American people."

"No, no!" exclaims a startled Anne. "My grandfather might end up like Mr. Romellion."

"Why don't we let him decide," says Abassi calmly.

"Because he will do it."

"And?" replies Abassi.

"And I don't want Walter to be killed. He is my only family, my only connection."

"He and you are now part of our family; and, by the way, our family includes all life on Earth."

"I do not want to lose him," insists Anne.

"We will all be there to protect him."

"Maybe at this grand wedding, but not before and not after. Do you have a different plan?"

"No."

"Then leave him out of this."

"Anne, dear," says Pythia. "You will also be in danger . . . you and your baby."

Anne turns red. "What baby?"

"The one we all know you think you might be carrying."

Anne's face turns from red to bright red. "I'm not sure I can deal with my mind constantly being read. My thoughts are mine . . . it doesn't seem . . . I just. . . . " she falters, utterly nonplussed.

Ming-huà gives her a sympathetic smile. "Don't worry, Anne, we are all on your side. You must decide for yourself."

"I have decided. I will go through with this wedding, but if you insist on dragging Walter into this, I will try and convince my grandfather not to participate."

"And the baby?" asks Tara.

"I don't even know I am pregnant yet."

"You are pregnant," says Altan.

"How do you know?"

"Because your body is already showing signs of hosting someone or something extraordinary, even more remarkable than our friend Abassi here."

"I didn't know there could be such a thing!" exclaims Zookeeper. "Fuck me!" He quickly glances at Ming-huà. "Sorry hon. I meant to say that surprises me."

Abassi squeezes Anne's hand. "First, before I ask your grandfather, I must make sure the government . . . the President, is on board with this scheme. Perhaps it will fail before it even begins, in which case the issue is moot."

~ The Execution ~

The next day, Abassi is on the phone. "Mr. President, I do not feel you have much of a choice. This plan will calm the waters, arouse curiosity, showcase the fact that we are not monsters, and demonstrate the fact that a union between a *Homo sapiens* female and a male of our kind can be quite normal and not of the disgusting, exotic variety. Furthermore, it will bring the international community together, as the ceremony will take place in a neutral country outside the United States."

"I'm sorry, Mr. Powers—"

"Abassi."

"I'm sorry, Abassi. "I'm afraid that sort of trip, involving other world leaders, in another country, for a wedding, would complicate matters beyond our power to control. After all, Tuvalu was a disaster."

"I'm also afraid, Mr. President, but not for the same reasons. You saw what we can do at Tuvalu. You do not currently have the luxury of refusing."

"More threats?"

"Indeed, it is a threat. Furthermore, this threat will be carried out. If you are unwilling, I will simply send you and your vice-president elsewhere, and leave you there until I find someone who will agree. I have run out of patience with delays and deception. On the other hand, your cooperation in implementing this plan will cost you very little. If it doesn't work, the situation won't be much worse that it is now. If it does work, you will be hailed for your efforts to bring the world together in peace."

"Did Mr. Romellion inform you of his discussion with Doctor Carlson before he was killed?"

"No."

"Perhaps if I have Doctor Carlson get in touch—"

"No, Mr. President. That is too late now. The murder of Lance Romellion changed everything. I am intent on carrying through with this plan."

Long pause. Finally, the President speaks with less confidence. "If this plan doesn't work, Abassi, it will not be without cost. In fact, it will cost us both a great deal. Things can get very much worse."

"Maybe, but you have gambler's blood in your veins, Mr. President. That is how you attained the position you currently occupy."

"Let me consult with my advisors and get back to you."

"I warn you, it must be quick—you have one day—and if you trace this call and send anyone to this location with nefarious intentions, I will be forced to take more drastic actions."

"It's never wise to threaten the President of the United Sates, Abassi."

"Rest assured; it is not an idle threat."

~

"He will agree," announces Abassi to the waiting group.

"How can you be so sure?" asks Pythia. "After all, his physical proximity is too far for an accurate reading, isn't it?"

"Maybe, maybe not. Nonetheless, I'm sure."

In spite of these brave words, Abassi continues to struggle with unfamiliar doubts and troubling uncertainties. His confidence, already shaken by the near breakdown he experienced after dissociating so many delegates at Tuvalu, has been further exacerbated by Romellion's death. No matter how often he withdraws into the boundless realm of meditation, he returns to the real world burdened by the same troublesome shackles. As might a wounded animal return to the safety of its den, so Abassi longs to travel to the California cave and escape through an endless host of portals to different spaces and times via its multiplicity of side tunnels. He is still young for his kind, and often dreams of burying his head in *her* bosom for reassurance. Yet, when thinking of *her*, he is inevitably reminded of Anne, whose human weaknesses seem to enhance, in an oddly quaint manner, her intermediate strengths. Altan once said the only human analogous to Abassi would be Alexander the Great—bold, beautiful, brilliant, decisive, and burdened with the hot blood and reckless tempestuousness of an adolescent. To be sure, in the case of Abassi, not for glory and conquest like the young Macedonian, but to fulfill the virtually impossible destiny bestowed upon him—conquer without killing, seize without destroying, replace without harming, and assure a new age of enlightened species-hood without tearing the delicate fabric of humankind and all its fellow life-forms on Earth. Is Anne Monroe a mate strong enough to accompany him on such a perilous journey? When with her, the answer is yes. When apart, it remains an open question. To comfort himself, Abassi notes that when reading her mind, he is flooded with a feeling she must possess for him—personal love. But, being a stranger to such an intense passion focused on so tiny a space as one individual, he is both perplexed and horrified at its unreasoning power. By way of explanation, he can only assume her intermediate genes hold such madness in semi-check. Even so, she is partially blind to the far greater power of all-encompassing love—love for the whale and the worm, the cactus and the camellia. Failure to leap across that evolutionary chasm and acquire such all-encompassing love has doomed humankind to the brief but momentary gluttony of a host-killing parasite. It is his goal to turn this tragedy into an Elysium for their legacy—at least that part of their legacy most worth remembering.

"Abassi?" Anne's voice is a sonorous knife that cuts through the miasma of his conflicted thoughts.

"Sorry. What, Anne?"

"We are all waiting."

"For?"

Lady Oracle steps forward and says in a tone colored by frustration, "While you were in a dream-state during the last few minutes, Siyabonga expressed the desire to return to Africa with Tara. Ming-huà and Zookeeper want to return to their lovely island off the Washington coast. Pythia has revealed her intention to plant new seeds in China, land of her ancestors. All agree, their children and their children's children must be encouraged to inhabit other places, such as India, South America, Europe, and all corners of the Earth peacefully. To do so in relative tranquility requires acceptance of their presence as well as their freedom to enter into intimate relationships with the human race, without which, violence and destruction will surely follow wherever they go. The question put to you was whether you have carefully calculated the odds that this plan of yours will advance such a goal, or alternatively, hinder it. In other words, they seek assurances from you, Abassi."

Such a request makes Abassi's heart skip a beat, but without hesitation, he replies, "No one can predict the outcome of my plan. The universe is fundamentally uncertain. Nevertheless, at this particular point in space and time, I have calculated the wave function of the most probable outcomes, and this is the option with the highest probability of collapsing in our favor. That is the best I can promise."

"And I presume you will need all of us at this wedding?" asks Tara. "Personally, I wouldn't miss it for the world."

"Nor I," adds Pythia.

"Hey!" exclaims Zookeeper. "Free food and drink! I'll fuckin be there."

"As will all of us," says Ming-huà softly but firmly, casting a disapproving glance at Zookeeper.

Abassi grins. "Absolutely, I will need all of you. No doubt there will be a goodly number of foreign agents, spies, and assorted assassins in attendance. Other than myself, we must all conceal our humps as best as possible—dead giveaways."

"Goes without saying," says Zookeeper.

[689]

"It also goes without saying that the wedding must proceed without a hitch. No hint of violence to give our enemies grounds for their apocalyptic predictions."

"There will be demonstrations," says Anne. "Those scare me. They could get out of hand."

"Yes," agrees Abassi. "That is why this neutral country must be chosen with care."

"What does that mean?" asks Ming-huà.

"What it says," replies Abassi, who opens his mind to their probing.

And so, they wait. The next day arrives with a brilliant sunrise. The group is together when the call comes.

~

After answering, Abassi mainly listens, uttering an occasional "I see," or "Perhaps that would be best." The others hear him say, "That location if fine." This is followed by Abassi listening for long stretches of time, contributing only perfunctory comments, then a date is discussed at great length, and finally agreed upon. More platitudes and the conversation ends.

"It is done," announces Abassi.

Yet, in his heart of hearts, Abassi is a troubled being. He is fully aware any untoward disruption during this wedding will have dire consequences. His affection for Anne is not of the same white-hot passion as hers for him. Such is the nature of personal love. Worse, she probably carries their child; and if Altan's words are true, it will be a creature more powerful than even Abassi himself, and a troubling wild card in the evolutionary progression of his kind. Strange and subtle hints darken his thoughts; hints that all of them are merely the initial cast-away prototypes of some future, unimaginable super-race.

"I need to be alone," he says in response to a bevy of questions the others throw his way. "I'm going for a walk. Be back soon."

He leaves the house and walks toward the snow-covered Rockies jaggedly lacing the horizon in brilliant white. Wyoming's brisk air fills his lungs and clears his head. The ghosts of his ancestors appear around him, strolling with him, their faces grimly expectant. *But about what?* he wonders. They are all here, sharing the chilly air. John Powers, Michael Powers, Bai Meiying, Child of Buddha, Tamara Powers—all of them impervious to the cold. Abassi recalls the tragically mistaken diagnosis that crippled them so severely.

"You all heard voices," he says aloud. "You all heard what you interpreted as *God* and *Goddess*. Look where that got you. And I . . . I hear them also, but such voices are not the deities of your confused minds. Only the Precious Object speaks the truth, and it is untranslatable. Tap. Tap. Tap. On it speaks without words. To what end, I wonder?"

He scans the ghostly visages staring back at his questioning expression.

"To what end?" he repeats.

There is no response.

Chapter 57: The Wedding

~ On the Eve ~

New Dehli is the chosen site. Capital of an ancient land, its civilization replete with a host of gods and goddesses—a most fitting location for Abassi's purposes. Such a tremendous gathering of powerful rulers has no analog in history. To be sure, different regions have experienced such a spectacle, but not on such a global scale. Amidst the posh environs of Chanakyapuri stands the grandiose Leela Chanaka with its majestic grand ballroom where the wedding will take place. Nestled in the diplomatic enclave of Chanakyapuri, it affords the best and most neutral site possible, at least according to the United States State Department. Abassi is delighted that India is to be the host country, and his enthusiasm has spread to Anne, though her natural inclination is to curb overt excitement with a healthy dose of skeptical restraint.

"I have researched this palace where we are to be married," she says to Abassi one day. "It is obscenely extravagant, and far too lavish for this lowly American girl."

"Humans are attracted to sparklies," laughs Abassi. "After all, I think they are more Bower bird than great ape."

Anne lets out a rather shallow chuckle. "I'm afraid I have a bit of that bird in me; the venue for this wedding is beyond a sparklie. It would satisfy even the pickiest of females."

"You don't find it over the top?" he asks.

"Certainly. In a way, that's its charm. We all like to watch schlocky movies now and again, if only to laugh at the absurdity of them."

"Well, such human foibles do take their toll."

"On us?"

"On the planet."

Anne's tone conveys acknowledgement of his chastisement. "Yes, of course. This girl you insist on marrying does have her share of foibles."

"Nevertheless, I insist on marrying you. My foibles far surpass yours, my dear."

"Oh? Then, what are they?"

Abassi laughs. "I dissociate them and send them to other dimensions."

"In that case, I must visit those dimensions someday, my love, for I would like to see such foibles."

"You are a collector of foibles?"

"I am a Bower bird, remember? As a female, I want to see all your sparklies."

Both fall into each other's arms, laughing like the children they are."

~

A week before the wedding, Anne confirms she is pregnant. She feels not the slightest surprise, for every day has brought with it evidence of some mysterious movement stirring within. Such movement is not centered where she would have thought pregnancy takes root, but instead flows through her veins as if her blood had changed its thinly liquid composition to the thick consistency of volcanic lava, slowly burning its sluggish way into every nook and cranny of her anatomy. She is on fire from within, yet the fire is a strengthening force, as if tempering her yielding flesh into unbreakable steel. Anne has the terrifying impression that her body is being made ready for some cataclysmic ordeal.

She has taken to stealing out of the house at night, stripping naked, and bathing in the freezing air, all the while staring up at the panoply of stars glowing, like her, with raging furnaces piercing the blackness. Steam literally rises from her skin, and she glories in the sensation.

"You are now the vessel that brings the Chosen One," comes a sonorous female voice.

Anne is struck dumb, and a vise-like immobility seizes her.

"Nonsense, foolish Goddess!" a male bellows in response, his swampy voice a deep, dank, gritty rumble that fills the atmosphere with a corrosive slag of wet soot and harsh sulfur—a nineteenth century furnace bellowing smoke from a thirteenth century hell. *"She will die in childbirth!"*

"Dear God, Your constant efforts to derail this endeavor does not become You. It is in Your best interest to join Us, not hinder Us." *Her* cleansing voice

scrubs away the male's words with a bleaching breeze that never quite obliterates their sputum stain entirely.

"This endeavor is already derailed, Fool! Leave them to their own devices; this minor planet be damned!"

"All this hostility is roused just so You are allowed to continue the addicts need to languish in the opium haze of others' suffering?"

"No. This one will certainly die in childbirth as surely as the others died in their madness!"

The voices cease as suddenly as they began.

While trying to make sense of what she just heard, Abassi's words reach her as if he is calling from a great distance. "You hear them, don't you?" he cries, wonder in his voice.

She turns to face him in all her naked glory. "I do, and they terrify me."

"Yes, they drove my ancestors mad."

"Are they real?"

"No."

"What are they?"

"Distortions."

"I don't understand."

"Nor do I, fully."

Anne looks up at the stars and spreads her arms outward. "I am burning hot," she groans.

"You are glowing," he says. "You are exceedingly beautiful."

"Am I going mad?"

"No, you are quite sane."

Anne cups her breasts. "Remove your clothes," she says in a commanding manner he has not heard before.

In an instant, they fly together, plunging recklessly into the exhilarating freefall of unrestrained love, her body a searing warmth counterbalanced against his equally cold skin. When she caresses his hump, it delights her with an explosion of brilliant images flickering to life under the lightest touch of her fingers. And deep within the inner sanctum of her body, that eerie, inexorable movement is accelerated by the power of explosive sexual energy; energy which is itself imbued with a desperate compulsion to burst forth into the marvelous, magical world.

[694]

Following the exhausting rapture of multiple climaxes, they embrace above the frozen earth, rejoicing in their nakedness, the embers of their passion glowing defiantly against the icy wind rolling down from the snow-covered Rockies.

"I no longer fear the outcome of this wedding," she announces out of the blue. "Come what may."

"Your grandfather has accepted his role. What of him?"

Anne considers the question for a long while, then replies, "Walter is a man who has earned the right to make his own decisions without harassment from his granddaughter. I said my peace. He said his. Now, we are united."

"We will protect him," says Abassi.

Anne smiles. "You would do well to protect yourselves. I sense a mistake is being made by underestimating us humans."

"You are more than human," says Abassi.

"And you are more than me," she replies.

Abassi puts his hand to her belly. "And this one will be more than both of us."

"In that case, we must learn Zookeeper's patience."

Abassi does not respond.

"You're worried," says Anne.

"Yes, a little. If this child's powers exceed mine, will his or her countervailing empathic powers be sufficient to keep up and control the destructive impulses?"

"Balance is the issue?"

"Balance."

~ The Ceremony ~

Indian police are out in force to control the ever-growing influx of humanity crowding in from all sides of the Leela Chanaka hotel. While there are some protestors and a few scattered demonstrations, the mass of people are simple curiosity seekers, joined by the more serious-minded determined to witness an unprecedented historical event. Nonetheless, whatever motivations compel such massive numbers, the worldwide media is gorging itself on the astronomical global audiences riveted to whatever technological devices are at hand. Dignitaries and high-level government officials must be brought in by helicopters as the roadways are jammed. Inside the hotel, under the bejeweled hallways and ornate ballrooms where massive chandeliers mushroom intricately downward from the ceilings, Abassi and Anne wait to make grand entrances from their respective safe rooms. Meanwhile, outside, members of the group have positioned themselves at strategic locations around the hotel, well disguised, and senses on full alert.

Walter Monroe is standing with the President, surrounded by an ever-changing entourage of officials and interpreters. Cameras are ubiquitous, and the President, in his element, appears relaxed and engaged. Walter knows otherwise, as evidenced by the American leader surreptitiously asking for security updates every few minutes. So far, to the immense relief of every participant, there have been no major incidents.

In order to pass the time, the President absently asks, "Tell me, Mr. Monroe, is your granddaughter very nervous?"

"Anne is a sturdy woman," replies Walter. "She is calm, though not everything has occurred without a hitch."

"Oh? What for instance?"

"The selection of who will perform the ceremony—who will marry them. A secular official or religious bigwig? Anne briefly considered having a traditional Hindu ceremony, but that was shot down very quickly."

Surprised, the President asks, "She's a Hindu?"

Walter laughs at the idea. "No, not at all. She just thought it would be fun, and as a courtesy to India. But, as you can guess, the idea was short-lived."

"Is Abassi religious?" asks the President.

Again, Walter laughs. "Heavens no—no pun intended. He views this entire ceremony as you and I might view getting on all fours to play with intelligent dogs."

"I see. How flattering."

"Insincere flattery is not his greatest asset, Mr. President."

The President checks his watch and turns to an aide. "How much longer before it starts?"

"About half and hour, sir," is the response.

"Security still good?"

"Well, there are some stirrings out there. Rabble rousers, a few protestors, the usual, but nothing we can't handle."

"Good."

~

While inside the hotel attendees impatiently await the ceremony to begin, outside the crowds are becoming restless. The telepathic receptors of Ming-huà, Pythia, and Tara are fraying at the edges from an overload of intensely emotional input. Alarming signals conveying violent intent are mixed with spiritual fanaticism, all flying fast and furious through the crowds, overwhelming their processing capabilities. Initiated by anti-alien agitators, isolated chants begin to rise from the masses.

"Sacrilege!"

"Unnatural!"

"Shameful!"

These mantras spread quickly and gain steam when joined by more and more voices. Even as this movement balloons, the growing crush of people exacerbates the increasingly ugly mood. As if a switch has been pulled, mob mentality takes root. Ming-huà, Pythia, and Tara try to focus on those who might be carrying weapons, but the input is too rapid, fragmented, and confused to isolate. Worse, they are crushed by the surging mass of humanity against the police lines, and standing upright becomes almost impossible.

"Sacrilege!" the chant becomes deafening, and merges with other slogans.

"Stop them!"

"Unnatural!"

Soon, the mix of screaming refrains transforms into a cacophonous drumbeat of violent intent that wends its way throughout the roiling mass of humanity, driving the progressively angry mob to greater fury. Like a lethal virus, the ugly impulse to destroy infects even those who came merely out of curiosity. Even those more thoughtful souls whose main purpose for coming was to observe history are caught up in the frenzy. Now, the noise is nonstop and unstoppable.

"Sacrilege!"

"Stop them!"

"Unnatural!"

The hunchback women know there are provocateurs scattered among the throngs, coaxing them onward, but the maelstrom of shrieking masses cloak their identities. Suddenly, the chanting miraculously changes, as if by some organic transformation.

"Into the hotel!"

"Stop the sacrilege!"

"Into the hotel!"

"Stop the sacrilege!"

"Traitors!"

Now the crush of bodies and fevered minds is too great, and the police line bends, ready to snap and open the floodgates.

~

"Mr. President!" exclaims an aide just as Abassi and Anne have made their entrance and stand side-by-side, ready to walk down the aisle to the waiting official.

"Yes, what is it?"

"Sir, the secret service is very concerned about the situation outside."

"What situation?" asks the startled President.

"The crowd has turned into a mob!"

"A mob!"

"Yes, sir."

"What do they want?"

The aide points at Abassi and Anne. "Them."

~

A flurry of activity ensues as security personnel from all attending countries huddle with their respective delegations. In the chaos, Abassi and Anne approach the official who will perform the ceremony.

"Let's get it done," says Abassi calmly.

The official nervously scans the turmoil in the room. "No one is ready, Mr. Powers. It seems many are leaving."

"All the more reason to get it done as quickly as possible. All we need are the proper words and confirming documentation."

"Well. . . . "

Walter Monroe hurries over. "The President is leaving for his helicopter. You both should join him now."

[698]

"Oh, no, Mr. Monroe," says Abassi. "We are staying here and going through with the ceremony. Mr. Lash here has kindly offered to rush the ceremony, isn't that correct, Mr. Lash?"

"Well . . . I don't know . . . I guess, if we really hurry."

Abassi grabs Anne's hand. "Then let's do it!"

"Walter," says Anne. "You should go with the President. It might get really bad here."

"Silly girl! I'm staying and seeing it through. I may be old, but I'm still an FBI agent." He looks at a wide-eyed Mr. Lash. "Well, come on!"

Thus, amidst the pandemonium of scurrying guests and multiple security guards stampeding their delegations this way and that, Mr. Lash speedily pronounces the words that must be spoken, the bride and groom swiftly repeat the vows that must be given, and a marriage license that must be legal is hastily but validly signed and stamped. Abassi and Anne are married just as elements of the Indian army arrive on the scene to restore order. Outside, shots are fired, and the mob, some of whom had already breached the hotel's interior, recedes away from the besieged building. As the tide of demonstrators withdraws, a few scattered bodies litter the ground, most trampled to death, a few killed by bullets and knives. An undetermined number of protestors have also gone missing, all in the vicinity of Pythia's and Tara's stations.

Among the dead is Ming-huà Powers, her body broken and stabbed. Next to her, Zookeeper is found unconscious, but alive. When revived by paramedics and told of his wife's death, the armless man cries out in utter despair words that confuse his rescuers.

"She would not use her powers! I begged her! She refused!"

Learning of her murder, Abassi rushes out and dissociates Ming-huà's body even as it lays in the ambulance. "She will not be taken to a cold morgue, subjected to human dissection," he says to Pythia and Tara looking on. "Humans will cut her up and mutilate her body in the name of research and discovery."

Anne, standing next to Abassi in her wedding dress, looks at the now empty interior of the ambulance silently, her face pale from shock and despair.

~

As a result of these events, one "alien" is legitimately married to a human in the eyes of half the world, and another "alien" is legitimately murdered in the eyes of the other half.

~

"We must carry on with the plan," Abassi tells Anne while they sit in the plane returning to America. "We must subject ourselves to the intrusive curiosity of the media; we must publicly maintain the face of a supremely happy, well-adjusted couple to the world."

Anne remains lost in thought. Abassi reads her mind, and says, "You wonder why it was Ming-huà who was killed. Why the kindest, the gentlest? Is it not so?"

Tears well in Anne's eyes, and she replies, "Yes, it is so. She did not use her powers to save herself. Why?"

"You already know."

"Yes, I already know. But it is so hard!"

He takes her hand and kisses it.

"Abassi, do the dead live on?" she asks.

"Do you think I know?"

"Yes. You have access to multiple dimensions, and I am certain there are many things you do not tell me. Do the dead live on?"

"Yes, but not in the way you humans think."

"How?"

Abassi sighs. "If I explain, you will be dissatisfied."

"I want to think she is somewhere in a place that is similar to her wonderful island, where in her gentle heart, she felt a communion with all life around her. Oh, Abassi, how she spoke of her wonderful friends; the squirrels and trees and deer and . . . oh, it is so hard!"

Through his clairvoyant powers, Abassi is once again assailed by the sharp pain that personal love brings with it, and he feels deeply saddened that humans are burdened by such a searing emotion. It is hard for him to find soothing words that can assuage such lacerating grief. Nonetheless, he tries.

"Yes, Anne, it is a terrible tragedy. Ming-huà represented the best of our kind. Although her powers were not as robust, her empathic sensibilities put the rest of us to shame."

"Oh, Abassi, I'm so sad and depressed. Most of the human world—my world—hates and fears us. What is to happen to this child?

[700]

Will he or she end up like Ming-huà, or worse, be responsible for inflicting even more suffering?"

"These are not questions I can answer."

"Yet, I feel there is something else."

"What do you mean?"

Anne stiffens. "I mean you, Lady Oracle, Altan, Sy, all have hinted in the past that there is some power beyond; some guiding entity or entities that are manipulating . . . directing, whatever you want to call it, who are above you, above the mentors, and all of us are pawns that they are stage-managing. I know I'm rambling and not making much sense, but isn't it true?"

Abassi shakes his head. "I think I follow the thread of what you're trying to say. Bottom line: are there real aliens, true aliens, who have choreographed this entire evolutionary experiment . . . or leap . . . or whatever it is?"

"Yes, I guess that is the question?"

"Truth is, I don't know."

"But you do suspect?"

"Yes. If I could just interpret the tapping."

"You mean from the Precious Object?"

"Yes. That is the enigma where I feel the answer might be hidden. Would that this enigma was as elementary to solve as the German machine."

"Couldn't your ancestors read it?"

"Ah, only one. Child of Buddha. A woman viewed as mad. A woman locked in a madhouse. A woman who could read the code."

"Perhaps we are being used for some evil purpose," says Anne.

"I think not. Anyway, evil is oftentimes used as a human religious term, inapplicable to the workings of the universe."

"Why do you think not?"

"All of my powers tell me otherwise. However, there is far more here than meets the eye, that I will grant you."

"Evidently there is some truth in what I say."

A troubled expression is reflected in Abassi's face. "I am fully aware there may be some mystery. All of us feel it at times, but I have yet to pin down where this mystery might be hidden."

"Abassi, you must find out before our child is born."

"That is a goal I have promised myself to pursue, but, for the moment, we have other issues to deal with."

"Yes," says Anne shaking her head. "For one, what is to be done with Ming-huà's child? Zookeeper cannot care for her."

"I've spoken with Lady Oracle. For the time being, she will be cared for by Pythia and Tara in Wyoming."

"I thought they were scattering to the four winds after our wedding."

"Things have changed. As we speak, they are on their way to the States on a different plane. Now that Congress has acted, we have some measure of freedom in the United States. This process of integration will take longer than I anticipated. As I said, the others will be ensconced at the secret location in Wyoming until we see which way the wind is blowing. Meanwhile, you and I must return to San Francisco. The mansion will be like living in a fishbowl, but that is our burden."

"And our child?"

"When you are close to the due date, we will join the others in seclusion."

"Abassi, this one seems different than what Pythia and Tara described, even including you. None of us can be sure when the due date is."

Abassi groans. "They have all been different. You will be sure when the time comes."

"Perhaps, but I am frightened."

"Think of the child's amazing bloodline, dear Anne. Think of gentle Ming-huà's anguish when she dissociated her beloved doll Miss Gladflower, then banish elsewhere the two hunters who would have drown an innocent fawn and the guilt she felt the rest of her life. Her union with Zookeeper is an astonishment to our world. Think of their daughter Pythia, brave and bold Pythia, who saved innocent girls in the filthy and savagely immoral houses of slavery in Mexico. Then there is my mother, the stalwart warrior Tara, conqueror of the vicious gangs in South Africa, who saved her beloved husband Siyabonga, now accepted so readily to her heart."

"Then there is me," says Anne disconsolately. "A nothing who has nothing to offer but my womb."

Abassi clicks his tongue in disapproval. "You, my wife—my brilliant Ph.D. wife—now are the key to all of our futures. There is something in you that is even more extraordinary than the rest of us."

"And what might that be, husband? I am a lowly human, raised imperceptibly to the forlorn level of intermediate."

"You are the Mother."

"There are many mothers."

"No. You are the Mother. Soon, you will give birth to one who will render all of us forlorn intermediates."

"Maybe, but your great powers are above all of us. You are the Father."

Abassi stares off into space. "I wonder. . . . "

Chapter 58: Ticking Time Bomb

~ Living in the Glare ~

So it comes to be that Abassi and Anne live a life filled with guest appearances, speaking engagements, banquets, and the like, intentionally keeping themselves in the public eye around the clock. An outer wall now encircles the San Francisco mansion, and security guards have been hired to protect the property from a constant crush of inquisitive onlookers, sympathetic well-wishers, nosy reporters, and angry protestors. Over time, when it becomes apparent to the multitudes that neither Abassi nor Anne will be spotted on the grounds no matter how much tiptoe-standing or neck-craning is performed, the throngs diminish somewhat. Meanwhile, at the secluded Wyoming hide-away, the others busy themselves with raising a houseful of extraordinary children and preparing them to travel to the cave in anticipation of extended educational sojourns (though no one is sure they will not turn out like Abassi and eschew such an experience). It is agreed by all that once Anne has her baby, and their own children's educational requirements are clarified, they will take their chances in the broader world, albeit as inconspicuously as possible. But an unexpected circumstance throws all timetables off, and precipitates a crisis.

Unlike Tara, who received the fetal Abassi's messages from the depths of her womb, Anne is experiencing a far more alarming phenomenon. This fetus has not simply drained her body to fuel its own exponential growth; instead, it has driven her into a nearly comatose state. This debilitating condition struck Anne weeks ago, quite suddenly, and all public appearances have been cancelled. No one is sure when the baby will be born, and it has been quickly decided to bring the pregnant woman to Wyoming, where she will be surrounded by sympathetic and knowledgeable intimates. Abassi decides to travel with her, but has periodically returned to San Francisco in order to maintain the "happy family" front, while at the same time fielding the media's voracious appetite for news about his expectant human wife's condition. Beneath surface attempts to pass the days as "normal" and "routine", a burgeoning

[704]

sense of calamity pervades the Wyoming retreat. Even the young ones—Pythia's, Tara's, and Ming-huà's children—are now fully cognizant of the dire circumstances confronting Anne. As a consequence, their elders have accelerated the race to full extra-human superiority at frightening speed. Ming-huà's death hangs like a dark cloud over them—a stark reminder they are indeed mortal.

One day, a new midwife appears, seemingly from nowhere and unknown to all but Altan. She is old, wizened, and to the amazement of everyone, fully capable of clairvoyance and telepathy. By this time, Anne has been bedridden and unconscious of her surroundings for over a month.

"Who sent for her?" asks Lady Oracle.

"I did," replies Altan. "The nature of this pregnancy dictates the need for such a one as her."

"She is one of them?"

"In a manner of speaking."

"Is this the culmination?" asks Sy excitedly.

"There is no such thing. In fact, we fear this might be the worst-case scenario."

Sy shudders. "That bad?"

"Perhaps."

"Are the stakes really so high?"

"Perhaps."

"If so, infanticide?" asks Lady Oracle.

"Perhaps. This one will either be a scourge or a savior . . . or both."

"How can this be?" asks Sy. "The mother is mostly human."

"Even humans realize brain volume is not determinative of intelligence. *Homo neanderthalis* brains were many cubic centimeters larger than *Homo sapiens*, yet look at the result. The problem is brain versus cervix capacity. The resulting evolutionary conundrum has been temporarily, but inadequately, solved by making humans neotenous primates. We are now witnessing an opposite movement in fetal development—a compactification of neural pathways and cognitive structures with quantized connections to extra-dimensions—all of which avoids the problem of cervical bottleneck. In other words, cognitive processes are exploding inward, tapping access into dimensional realms never before seen on this planet."

"And in this case, might evolution have overshot the mark and created an ill-adapted, unstoppable destructive force?" asks Sy.

"Too soon to tell," replies Altan grimly. "But, if true, it will mean the end of us, humans, and non-humans alike."

"In that case, infanticide would be the solution?"

"Perhaps, but only if the infant permits such a drastic move. Even we may prove to be powerless against it."

The room falls silent.

Lady Oracle breaks the mood. "Speaking of humans, how is Zookeeper doing, Sy?"

"Not well. His son is already far beyond Zookeeper's intellectual capacity. The poor old armless human wants to return to his island and live among his memories."

"Let him go," says Lady Oracle gently. "On second thought, can he live by himself?"

"No."

"Then send Bataar with him. The boy is eternal, for all intents and purposes."

"Yes," agrees Sy. "They get along, like bosom buddies."

"Nonetheless, I worry Zookeeper will end up like Pythia's professor," says Lady Oracle.

"Professor Paine? Highly possible . . . even probable."

~

Abassi sits by Anne's bedside. She has been intermittently comatose for weeks, coming out of her vegetative state only to eat with a voracious appetite, as if the fetus grants her brief periods of independence to sustain her strength. Eyes open, staring at the ceiling, Anne now lies motionless, oblivious to Abassi's presence or anything else in the room. She has not spoken a word since this catastrophe has gripped her body. Even when she is alert in one of her conscious eating periods, no words leave her lips, her attention single-mindedly focused on downing the food with mechanical efficiency. Every time Abassi tries to read her mind, he is blocked by an opaque fog. As her paralysis continues in this grey realm of being half-alive, half-dead, his fears grow in proportion to the length of time her condition lingers.

On this day, Abassi is waiting to catch her in one of her awake eating binges. But from the utter rigidity of her paralyzed body, she seems light-years distant. As he is about to stand, she suddenly sits upright and murmurs, "Abomination". After uttering this one word, she falls back into her coma trance.

So shocked by this sudden exclamation, Abassi wracks his mind trying to decipher the tone in which the word was spoken. It almost seems to him it was verbalized in the form of a question.

"Anne?"

No response.

"Why do you say abomination?"

Nothing.

"Blink if you understand."

Nothing.

"A fierce battle is being waged," comes a familiar voice.

Abassi turns to face *her*, and instantly his mind is aflame with this beautiful, ageless one's probing feelers, overwhelming his defenses. *Her* power causes him to stagger back a step. Taking a deep breath, he forces a calm demeanor over his body; a body *she* has kindled into a smoldering furnace.

"Will she survive?" he manages.

"Fate starves at Probability's door."

"Yes."

Abassi waits, covering his anxious heart with a cloak of patience.

"Are you more concerned about the child or the mother?" *she* asks.

Abassi pauses to consider, then says, "I am more concerned about the fierce battle you have alluded to."

"What your ancestors, in their fevered minds, referred to as *God* and *Goddess*, are in an existential conflict over the nature of what grows within Anne's womb."

"What is the nature of the struggle?"

"The future of humanity."

"How so?"

"Quick, surgical annihilation. . . . " Long pause.

"Or?" Abassi nudges.

"Slow, painless absorption by your kind."

"The one growing within my wife has such power? Enough to determine which path to take?"

[707]

"*Fate starves at Probability's door*."

"Your words frighten me."

She smiles, and the velvet warmth of *her* guileless compassion melts the cold ice that had caused him to shiver. "Your esteemed ancestors," *she* says, "were adjudged wrongly as being paranoid schizophrenics. This one inside your wife may be similarly adjudged, wrongly, to suffer from psychotic anti-social paranoia. Humans are as plentiful as drops of water in the ocean. This one may boil them away in a burst of wrath, or may choose to simply accelerate their natural evaporation. Your fears are justified, and not justified."

"If this one is recklessly destructive, how do I stop the destruction?"

"Should you try, it may be you who is boiled away."

"We wait, and hope?"

"We hope, and wait."

~ Labor ~

"It is time," says the old midwife with an authoritative tone, whose human name is Ruth.

Abassi looks at her blankly. "I don't see any change."

"The change is now, the currents welling within are deep and disturbed."

"Is she conscious?"

The old woman bares her teeth. "I have seen this once before; only once, in a place and time far away. It has her in its grip. The pain she feels is funneled inwardly, plummeting into the blackness where it cannot escape to be seen or heard by us. But she feels its full brunt."

"How do you know?"

"I know."

"How close?"

"Close."

"Minutes? Hours? Days?"

"I can only assist the child to be born. It is now mad to be born into the world. The mother is beyond help."

Abassi gulps. "Will she die?"

Ruth shrugs. "She is, for all intents and purposes, already dead."

"The other one you mentioned, the one that was like this. How did that turn out?"

"None of us would be alive today had not a certain being destroyed it just as it was crowning."

"What being?"

"Not for you to know. Now, leave me to the task."

"But . . . if it must be destroyed . . . how?"

Ruth laughs mirthlessly. "Be prepared, for all it may help."

Before leaving the room, Abassi makes one last attempt to reach Anne, but the fog is too thick, her mind too distant, lost."

"Out!" cries Ruth.

When the door closes behind Abassi, she looks into the corner and sees *her* sitting quietly.

"Can you feel its power?" Ruth asks.

"Yes."

"It is even more powerful than the other."

"Yes."

"The mother is far far away. If anything like the other, this one will come raging, prying open the vagina like a mad beast."

"Yes."

Anne suddenly arches her back at an impossible angle. No sound is emitted from her lips, but her eyes are wide in terror.

After many minutes, Ruth shouts, "It is coming! Be ready!"

She remains seated, calmer than calm. Only a barely perceptible glint in her eyes gives a hint of anticipation.

Anne opens wide her mouth in a terrifyingly silent scream.

"It is crowning!" cries Ruth, her hand trembling as it touches the infant's emerging head.

"Now!" Ruth yells. "Destroy it now!" She looks imploringly at *her*. "Now or never!"

Without leaving *her* seat, *she* smiles in glorious transcendency. "No. Let this one be born. I see now. I see now. All will be well."

Ruth is cradling the infant's head as the rest of the body explodes out in a sudden burst of freedom, amniotic fluid gushing prodigiously with its projectile-like emergence. Ruth cuts the umbilical cord and sets the infant on a blanket-covered table. As she dries its skin, she feels a probing in her mind; a probing deeper than any she has experienced. While

[709]

momentarily frozen by such intimate sensory exploration, Ruth is startled when the child's eyes suddenly open and stare intently at her, causing the midwife a moment of naked terror.

"She is telling you to save her mother," comes the lyrical voice from the corner.

"Yes, yes," replies a distracted Ruth. "I know. But . . . but . . . I mean, look at it!"

"Save the mother."

"I don't know how. Look at this infant!"

The beautiful young woman now rises and steps over to the infant who is lying still and staring with unutterable compassion at her unconscious, bleeding mother.

"Go now," *she* says to Ruth in a steely tone. "Go and stop the bleeding."

"But look at this child!" cries Ruth again.

"I see. Now go!"

While Ruth hurriedly ministers to Anne, *she* leans over the child and whispers, "So, you are our proverbial *Goddess*, come at last."

Into her mind come the words of the deepest female timbre, *"Probability may now give succor to poor, unfortunate Fate."*

She smiles in acknowledgement. "Now on the other half."

~ First Signs of Extraordinary Power ~

No one knows what to make of this child. Her body shares similarities with Abassi, but very different. Likewise, she has elements of the hunchback women, but is also very different. In short, she looks like no other biped on the planet—someone, or something, entirely new. Even Abassi is puzzled by her physiognomy, and tries to focus on the child's eyes, as they resemble Anne's lustrous playfulness. From the beginning, Abassi has been so enveloped by her extraordinary aura of compassion and empathy, he has neglected to gauge her extra-dimensional power. One day, with that in mind, he tosses a wiffle ball at the infant. Instead of disappearing, it pops in and out of existence at random times and places, making it appear to jump in fits and starts around the room. The child laughs in delight at this game. Abassi cannot help himself and smiles in return.

"You are Ἔλϡος!" he blurts. "Your name is Eleos!"

As the months elapse, Anne remains bedridden and silent, and each month that passes is equivalent to years for Eleos's development. Soon enough come the words, both verbal and telepathic.

Father, you must ensure mother heals. She is weak, mostly human, and as with all of her kind, human and non-human alike, deserves an opportunity to live a life without suffering—a life of peace.

And what of the evil ones? asks Abassi. *Those who would intentionally inflict suffering for their own gain. What to do with them?*

Humans call it euthanasia. The word is spoiled by association with religions, ethnic, racial, and political motivations. The word must be redefined.

You advocate euthanasia for humans?

For evil humans.

Dissociated forever?

Forever.

Your name is Eleos, the compassionate Goddess. How to justify such an extreme measure.

Mercy must be the guiding principle. Mercy is to make their departure either quick and painless for the evil ones, or lengthy and fruitful for the peaceable others. It must be so. It is necessary for the health of all, including this immensely fertile planet, which is most lovely, and which we are dedicated to preserve.

~

Within months, Eleos begins playing with the other children, and soon, her powers overwhelm their abilities to keep up. If they can make a boulder dissociate, then reappear, she one-ups them by toying with it while in the air with the same effortless delight as her game with a wiffle ball. Always, she gently returns the boulder to its original resting place, careful to not crush any creature that might have wandered into the spot it occupied during its absence. When Altan tries to tutor Eleos, he soon finds her intelligence surpasses his, and concludes her inborn neural data storage vaults brim with embedded knowledge even exceeding her father's own mature capacities. Altan subsequently delivers the message to the group that none of the young ones will leave for their education, but will be tutored not by him, but by Eleos herself. It is in this extraordinary environment that the group remains in their Wyoming retreat for a few years, all the while Abassi embarks on periodic trips around the world to act as an on-going ambassador advocating for the interests of his kind. During these sojourns, he spotlights the non-threatening nature of their presence and cleverly uses the media to update Anne's recovery, all in the interest of peaceful co-existence with humanity. No instances of inexplicably lost limbs or missing people or disappearing buildings are reported to the FBI or any other law enforcement agencies. News outlets, starved for events of a dramatic nature, turn their attention elsewhere. Meanwhile, the others in the group concentrate on honing their own skills and preparing the young ones to go out into the world and build lives of their own.

During this lengthy sojourn, the world's attitudinal dichotomy has hardened between pro- and anti- alien camps. Social media spews hatred and conspiracy theories about how the aliens have taken over human minds and turned them into zombies, how aliens devour human souls, and other such irrational attacks. Anne, though still quite weak, is very slowly recovering, and has long regained her speech and her sense of humor. One day, she is visited by her daughter. Eleos enters the room where Anne is resting, and instantly reads her mother's mood, condition, and thoughts, but as always, communicates verbally.

"Well, mother, how do you feel today?"

Anne laughs. "Much better today, Eleos, but you already know that."

"Yes, but the sound of your words gives me great joy. You are so lovely, and your voice so harmonious, it is no wonder father loves you as he does."

"Nonsense! Your father loves all life forms equally." She chuckles. "Didn't you know that?"

Eleos gives Anne a sideways glance. "Perhaps not all."

"My sweet daughter," says Anne. "I am mostly human. It must be hard for you to put up with my backwardness."

"Quite the opposite, mother."

"And when the time comes, how will you find a suitable mate, Eleos? . . . you are so far beyond all of us."

"That is a future consideration."

Anne looks at her uniquely configured daughter. "Eleos, how do you plan to deal with humans once you are out in their world?"

"Are you worried, mother?"

"You know very well."

"It is necessary to ask verbally so you can keep our conversations in context."

"I see. Yes, I am worried."

"Mother dear, let me explain it like this. Just as the panda depends upon the bamboo for survival, its species is condemned to specialist extinction; so the human increasingly depends upon technology for survival, and therefore its species is also condemned to specialist extinction. The difference is that bamboo does not kill pandas, only the lack thereof, whereas technology does kill humans in proportionate numbers to its increasing lethality—and that lethality, intentional or not, will drive many other species to extinction with them. All will be swept up in that silicon ocean's tidal wave of events . . . unless the course is altered."

Anne ponders this for a good while, then says, "However, Eleos, how do you distinguish the evil ones from those who are victimized, and thus do bad things against their own consciences? This is the great conundrum your father and your aunts face."

"It becomes obvious."

"How?"

"Mother, this question raises issues beyond your purview, intelligent as you are. Please keep in mind, as my aunts have previously shown, that punishments are inflicted on a sliding gradient of individual culpability, and are thus assigned the severity they deserve. One does not kill a dog for barking at the moon."

"Ming-huà insisted she made mistakes to the day of her death."

"So she did."

"I am told you have the ability to make an entire city disappear. What if you make a mistake on that scale?"

"Such gross violation of my commitment to universal love would stop me before I could ever do such a thing. It is as if you feared that our past intermediates, such as Gandhi and Einstein, would intentionally unleash nuclear war on the planet. Impossible."

Anne's eyes widen. "Gandhi and Einstein were intermediates?"

"Well, let us just say you are in good company, mother."

"But my understanding is that some intermediates have also done evil things."

"This is true. They have, in the end, reaped their just desserts."

"I must ask, Eleos, whether along the way there will be many of our kind who suffer Ming-huà's fate?"

"Surely so, mother. After all, Gandhi was assassinated."

Anne ponders this remark. "You are blessed to have the empathic power of Gandhi, backed up by the actual physical power of an entire nuclear arsenal." She shudders. "It is a frightening and awe-inspiring responsibility."

"No, mother, not a responsibility."

"How not?"

"Is it your responsibility to weigh each breath before you inhale?"

"Of course not, but that is different."

"Is it?"

"Absolutely."

"I think not . . . at least, from my perspective."

"Your father feels this responsibility very deeply."

"He is different from I."

"So, he is now also an intermediate?"

"As I said before, we all are."

Anne holds out her hand. Eleos takes it with the gentlest of touches. A warmth spreads through Anne's body—a healing warmth of a nature she only experiences from that of Abassi. Yet, this touch is different even from his. Indescribable. She feels absorbed into the fabric of the universe itself, and all that resides within it.

"Are you this *Goddess* figure that seems so important in Abassi's family history?"

"Mother, that figure is merely a metaphor."

"For what?"

"For the stillness that stills others."

"I don't understand."

Eleos smiles, gently squeezes her mother's hand and looks out the window. "It is time to blow on our little community of dandelions and spread their seeds around the world."

BOOK IV: ELEOS (Ἐλзος)

Chapter 59: Tipping Point

~ Shock Waves ~

Eleos calls together the group. By now, even Abassi follows her lead. As the entire extended family gathers, the hunchback women and their offspring fill the great meeting room. Some are pregnant, the younger ones having mated with various carefully chosen intermediates who Abassi invited to visit the retreat in Wyoming. Altan and Abassi stand off to one side of the room while Lady Oracle and Sy sit wearily in two overstuffed chairs on the other. Both know their days of leadership and guidance are long over, and gratefully await their own dissolutions. Pythia and Tara, quite devoted to each other, know the atmosphere of biding time and prolonged patience is over. Both are prone to take action, so this new imperative to venture out and actively begin removing the human purveyors of suffering signals the culmination of their longings these past few years. They have spent many an hour designing a strategy that will be most effective—and at the same time fair—to the human race. Each amplifies the others' increasing sense of urgency to counter the rapid pace of climate change, social unrest, violence, and accelerating non-human extinctions. Abassi, although more powerful than either female, is somewhat more cautious, always mindful of his experience on Tuvalu and the death of Ming-huà.

Eleos, of course, has taken all this in, and seeks to embark on her own path, setting free the others to make their own ways, come what may. After all, she reasons, *Homo sapiens*, in the beginning, scattered into fragmentary groups, each developing according to local conditions and their own capabilities and limitations. She envisages rapid diffusion among humankind, with a concomitant population explosion of this new species of which she is now the apex. Exponential growth will be the hallmark of the next phase. Nonetheless, even Eleos realizes, with all her considerable power of prediction, the probabilistic underpinnings of the universe can perversely inject its indeterminacy into the most certain and deterministic of circumstances. She has recently begun to feel yearnings, and knows she must search for an appropriate consort, if any exist. Though she has a love for her mother, she knows a hominin like Anne could never be an appropriate sexual partner. All of these considerations prey on her mind as she stands before the group. Eleos speaks verbally for the benefit of her mother.

"It is time for us to depart this place of seclusion and scatter in different directions. I already know where each of you plan to go. We will soon be settled in every continent. All of you here, with few exceptions, are more powerful than the intermediates you will encounter. For the young among us, choose your mates carefully. You must put a premium on empathy and compassion, as the genetic multi-dimensional powers you possess will be passed down and fully expressed. Be aware than such dominant powers, when used unwisely, will spell disaster for humans and non-humans alike, including ourselves."

"Where will *you* go?" asks Anne.

"Where I am most needed."

"And a mate?"

"I will know."

Altan clears his throat and speaks up. "There will be a backlash from humans. Many will want you eliminated. You will be perceived as threats."

Abassi nods. "True, but that is nothing new. Different locations will carry with them varying degrees of antipathy toward us. Each of us will have to make our own decisions as to the severity of our responses to human hatreds, superstitions, and fears. In that regard, we must have faith in each other that tragic mistakes are not made when confronting such human characteristics, and the innocent are not immolated with the guilty. Do you agree, Eleos?"

"The word immolated is distasteful, but mostly accurate. Time is not on the planet's side."

"So," says Pythia, interpreting this as acquiescence to more aggressively confront intransigent humans. "Are there more clear-cut parameters we should consider when going after the evil ones?"

Eleos considers for a moment. "The human term triage comes to mind."

"How do we know when a human is too far steeped in destructive avarice that dissolution is the only solution?"

Eleos shrugs. "Use your best judgment, but err on the side of compassion."

"A hand rather than a head, eh?" says Tara.

"Perhaps, or perhaps a demonstration rather than a hand."

"There are billions of humans," says Pythia impatiently. "At this rate the planet will be effectively sterile by the time we would make a difference."

"Use your best judgment," repeats Eleos.

"And if our judgment is defective?"

"Trial and error is an effective learning modality. Your selection advantage over humans is partly your superior ability to predict. That alone should result in fewer errors."

Pythia raises her voice. "Eleos, some of us cannot correct errors as you and Abassi can. We cannot bring back those we send away. The stakes are higher for us."

"Then let that knowledge guide you."

Altan clears his throat. "Eventually these genetic incongruities will smooth themselves out."

Eleos nods. "Do all of you recall the battles between metaphorical *God* and *Goddess* that so plagued our ancestors?"

"Of course," murmurs the communal answer.

"Those battles, to a degree, still rage inside all of us. Rather like the human concept of Yin and Yang, so *God* and *Goddess* tug us in different directions. Be more paternal, be more maternal; be more aggressive, be more understanding; and so on and so forth. More advanced though we may be, our receptors are still subject to such dialectic tensions. However, flawed we are, all of us understand that the human capacity for global destruction, intentional or unintentional, must end sooner rather than later."

"It sounds to me," says Tara. "Your priority is not compassion, but rather expediency."

"Use your best judgment. Our powers are not infinite, and the time we have to establish our kind in enough numbers to make a difference is not unlimited."

"So now," says Anne. "It sounds to this lowly human intermediate that your priority is not compassion or expediency, but rather fertility."

"Use your best judgments."

~

Armed with these vague guidelines, the group scatters to the four winds, each fragment planting its seeds in different continents. All endure severe trials and tribulations, and along the way many humans cease to exist, or continue to exist in dramatically changed circumstances, both physically and mentally. Thus, each individual group acts as its own earthquake epicenter, sending out overlapping shock waves that eat away at human domination and shatter the obsolete structures of human complacency and self-aggrandizement. Governments fall, fragment, reconstitute themselves into other fragments, fall again, rise again in even smaller units, until they also fall, and the geo-political composition of the human world is now become a patchwork quilt of warring factions. Religion rises above the ashes of secular ruin, and the old specters of superstition, fear, ignorance, and inquisition spreads like a virulent pestilence. Suspected aliens are killed, both innocent humans and weaker intermediates. By contrast, the areas dominated by Abassi and the others grow and prosper. Only Eleos travels alone. While this perpetual solitude would be intolerable for humans and intermediates alike, loneliness is not an emotion familiar to Eleos. She understands sex is necessary and, if others are to be believed, demonstrably pleasurable, but it is never more than a subsidiary consideration. Her driving goal is to better understand the detailed inner workings and subtle nuances of the multi-dimensional universe she inhabits—and the identity of the Overseers.

To this end, like some ancient human mystic, she turns to the non-human world of unspoiled "wilderness" for meditation and guidance. Paradoxically, though she is the most powerful of her kind, she is rather akin to an ascetic, eschewing contact with hominins and seeking solitude and isolation. After a lengthy period of wandering the globe, she decides to return to first principles and reestablish contact with the *Homo* world,

[718]

albeit cautiously. Her first stop: the California desert and a certain cave. Eleos has no intention of lodging in a nearby town packed with humans, and instead is driven by an aging Altan on a barely passable dirt road to an uninhabited area over fifty miles from the cave.

"I will walk from here," she tells Altan.

"Why? I can get you much closer."

"No, I will walk from here."

Not in the least surprised, he nods in silent acknowledgement and drives away.

The flat, rocky landscape stretches to the horizon, and Eleos breathes deeply to fill her lungs with the crisply primeval atmosphere, instantly feeling a sense of joy. Her receptors come alive with the proximity of myriad desert dwellers: snakes, insects, rodents, tortoises, cacti, coyotes, birds, and a host of others. All are chattering in their own languages. All seem prodded to lively anticipation by her presence. All know this intruder is something new. After hiking for a couple of hours, Eleos senses a tenseness in the air and pauses to observe. In the distance she sees a black-tailed jackrabbit nibbling on scrub. Reading its mind, Eleos knows it is unaware of danger. The extreme tension comes from a coyote stalking a few meters from the rabbit. Eleos feels the pang of hunger and a quivering desperation to make this kill. Looking from predator to prey, and back again, she dives into the minds of both, and is immediately struck by the coyote's fervent craving to eat and the equally frenzied rabbit's drive to avoid being eaten. The riveting immediacy of lives lived in the moment is painfully intense. When the kill is made, and the agonizing last ripples of the dying rabbit fade, she experiences the coyote's transient ecstasy while devouring a fresh meal. Were the predator a human with a gun, intent on killing for pleasure rather than the necessity to eat, Eleos is calmly certain she would dissolve the hominin without hesitation. That this imaginary person might have a family would cause her pain and sorrow, but she is certain the ground must be weeded or never will her kind have room to prosper in time to save the planet. Eleos is fully aware the Natural World is harsh and uncaring regardless of how advanced or empathetic the species. Glory to those few ancient beings scattered across the firmament whose evolutionary progression from abstract-thinking cruelty to abstract-thinking compassion bridged the extinction gap. She continues her journey with a deeply felt admiration for this fertile world so precariously teetering on the edge of catastrophe.

Eleos now stands in front of the cave. *Can those successes on other worlds be repeated in time to save Earth's marvelous fecundity?* she wonders.

"Yes," comes a familiar voice.

~

I knew you would be here, Eleos projects telepathically.

"Speak aloud," *she* says. "The compression of sound waves pleases me."

"Will there ever come a time when the cost of saving this planet exceeds the benefit?" Eleos asks bluntly.

"Yes."

"When?"

"You will know."

"And then?"

"Your choice."

Eleos considers. "Self-dissolution?"

"Use your best judgment."

Eleos laughs. "You sound like me."

"I am your mother."

"Don't joke!" scolds Eleos. "The intermediate Anne is my mother."

"Not quite."

Eleos gives *her* a puzzled look. "How is that possible?"

"Do you recall the coma Anne suffered through?"

"Yes," murmurs Eleos, realization dawning.

"Close to death, remember?"

"Yes."

"I am your mother. Anne was the vessel."

"Then. . . . "

"Your father does not know."

"But. . . . "

"Come with me into the cave. We have a journey to make."

"Wait, how could Abassi not know? His powers are extraordinary."

"He is an intermediate."

"Aren't we all intermediates?"

"All are intermediates."

"And others above even *you*?"

"Of course."

"And above them?"

She smiles acknowledgement.

Eleos feels an upwelling of joy and curiosity. "Tell me about the Overseers."

"Enough. Come."

"*You* are the Mother *Goddess* that so assailed the sanity of my ancestors, are *you* not?"

"As I am your Mother, we must now find you a mate so that Father *God* may manifest in him as I manifested in Anne Monroe."

"I trust *God* will not render my mate comatose as *you* did to mother?"

"Your child will be the fusion of the metaphorical *God* and *Goddess*."

"As I understand it, according to the writings of my great-great-great-grandfather Michael Powers, *God* is addicted to suffering and *Goddess* is intent on curing Him."

"That is the version as viewed through the distorted prism of his unprepared mind."

"Metaphors are useful, but what is the reality?"

"You."

"Am I to be the one to bear the burden of eliminating *Homo sapiens*?"

"No. Eliminate? No. You are the strongest. Those who now encircle the Earth will use the powerful elixir of their genes. Dissolve and dilute."

"All achieved painlessly?"

"Not always. Some will go the way of the coyote and the rabbit."

"And myself? If I am the strongest, what is my task?"

"Back to the beginning—to conceive a child."

"A child only?"

"The culmination."

"Am I not to use my other powers to . . . help eradicate evil?"

"Use your best judgment."

[721]

"And my child?"

"The culmination."

Eleos casts a puzzled look at *her*. "Did you not just say we are all intermediates?"

"Of course."

"I don't understand what culmination means."

"For Earth—your child will be the culmination until the age of culmination ends and a new path to culmination arises. Or not."

Eleos laughs. "Riddles upon riddles—oh, how they drove my ancestors to madness!"

"And you?"

"I am a riddle without a mirror."

"Precisely. Now, enough! Come!"

She strides into the cave, Eleos following.

~ Time, Time, Time . . . *Tap, Tap, Tap* ~

Decades later, in Earth time, Eleos returns. Many have since passed through the dark veil: Zookeeper, Sy, Lady Oracle, and so many others. Nonetheless, they lived long enough to see the rise of her kind. Their burgeoning numbers have taken a hammer-blow to human societies, creating an irreconcilable split between pro- and anti-alien factions. Like oil and water, the two global blocs, each a shifting aggregation of smaller alliances, have attacked each other with a vengeance. Civil war, murder, genocide, torture—combined with severe economic disruptions and worsening climate change—have exacerbated an already nightmarish world into which humanity has been thrust. Alien dominated geographic pockets of peaceful cooperation and intimate inter-species contact are growing rapidly, clashing with an ever-shrinking sea of anti-alien antagonism and fear-driven violence born of ignorance and desperation. Efforts by the human world to destroy these growing islands of alien habitation through the use of military force have failed, and the violent, destructive hatreds of *Homo sapiens* turn their fury inward. It is into these dark regions that Eleos is now determined to venture. Her long absence and solitary ways have made her even more isolated from others of her kind. Nonetheless, first and foremost, she must now find a suitable mate. Counter-intuitively, she is driven to find such a male in the dark regions, where there are a number of outcast intermediates leading humans against their own kind, but who also have extraordinary powers of persistence, toughness, and resilience. A formidable intermediate with the hard-nosed drive of a Zookeeper is the model she seeks. Once found and seduced, *God* will do the rest. Eleos knows she must find a way to cleverly overcome such a male's distrust and animosity to reach the goodness that must dwell within his intermediate's heart. There is word of such a charismatic leader who has mobilized many parts of Asia into a daunting anti-alien bloc. This is her target male. Destination: China.

First, she enjoys a brief stay at the San Francisco mansion where she presides over a partial family reunion with the elders, Abassi, Anne, Pythia, Siyabonga, and Tara. When it is time to leave, Eleos shuns normal human modes of transportation to reach China, instead returning to the cave. Now, old reliable Altan once again drives her back to the California desert, and once again they stand in front of the entrance.

~

While staring at the black opening, Eleos says, "It seems only moments ago I stepped out of this cave after returning from my long journey."

"I have never asked," says Altan. "But my own time to permanently depart is fast approaching. Did you meet the Overseers while you were gone?"

Without turning her head, Eleos closes her eyes.

"I see," says Altan. "Go."

She plants in his brain her universal love. Altan nods and starts back up the dusty trail. Eleos watches his stooped figure disappear around a curve and casts an enigmatic smile at the bright desert landscape. After entering the cave, Eleos heads straight for the particular side tunnel she seeks. Within moments, she emerges inside a filthy, foul-smelling room facing an iron door with bars in place of a window. Behind, she hears startled cackling.

"So, you are one of them," comes a derisive female voice speaking Chinese. "I hear you aliens can come and go like an invisible breeze. You a demon or an alien?"

Eleos does not answer.

"Eh? Speak up, devil!" continues the harsh, guttural sputters of one divorced from reality.

Eleos reads the mind of a human trapped in madness. *This is no intermediate,* she thinks. *It is pure human paranoid schizophrenia.*

"Well, devil?" demands the woman who shakes her head so violently it flings her matted, oily hair outward in a spiky mass of tangles. Her clothes are stained rags, washed so often they are almost transparent. "Is you a demon? Voices tell me so. I spit on ghosts! Ghosts don't scare me! Well? Ah? Eh? Is you?"

Eleos does not respond, but her astonishing clairvoyancy and archaeologically deep receptors are clear: this is the very cell her distant ancestor, Child of Buddha, inhabited during the Japanese invasion so long ago, when John Powers and Bai Meiying discovered her. A wave of intense pain and sorrow washes over her, both for the tawdry past and the sorry present, in which the ghosts of so much suffering flit across her vision in funereal procession. She shakes her head and focuses on the crone in front of her, now muttering incomprehensively.

"What is your name?" asks Eleos.

"Whore of Buddha."

"Why call yourself that?"

The woman puts a skeletal finger to her lips. "Shhhh . . . a ghost appears often, and it does not like me to call myself that name."

"Then why do you?"

"To make it angry."

"Why do you want to make it angry?"

"I like to watch it moan and cry."

"Ghosts cry?"

"Oh, yes." She lets out a cackling laugh. "They cry a lot!"

"What do ghost tears look like?"

"Fish eyes."

"Fish eyes?"

"Yes. I like to eat fish eyes."

"Do you eat the ghost's tears?"

"Shhhh!" She whispers conspiratorially, "Slimy but good."

"What is the ghost's name?"

"Ha, ha! Child of Buddha! That's why I call myself Whore of Buddha! Get it, demon?"

Eleos tires of this useless conversation, and her empathic sensors ache from such a shattered human.

[724]

"Do you want to see magic?" she asks.

The crone's face lights up. "Yes!"

In the blink of an eye, the iron door disappears, and Eleos steps through into the hallway.

"Ohhhh!" squeals poor Whore of Buddha, clapping her bony hands like a child. "Make it come back!"

"Don't you want to come out?"

The woman shrinks back into a corner of the room. "No! No! They will kill me! They're waiting. They'll kill you too. They hate demons and aliens!"

When Eleos replaces the door, she sees the crone staring through the bars.

"Goodbye," says Eleos.

"Ahhhh! Such a demon-fool! They'll kill you!" she cries.

"No, they won't. I am too powerful an alien."

"Will you come back?" whimpers the crone.

"Maybe."

"Bring fish eyes!"

~ In Search of a Mate ~

By the time Eleos reaches the lobby of the mental institution, a trio of security guards surround her, guns pointed at her heart. She stops and waits. Scanning their brains, she knows they are very afraid, trigger-happy, and view aliens as evil threats.

"Stay here!" snaps an older one. "None of your alien tricks or we shoot!"

"Why should I stay?"

"Just wait!"

"If you shoot, I will simply make your bullets—"

A loud popping noise comes from the gun of the youngest.

Eleos smiles. "—disappear. Now, if you don't put away your guns, I will remove your testicles."

"Put your weapons away!" comes a commanding voice.

At the sound, the guards quickly holster their weapons and turn towards the speaker.

Eleos follows their gaze to look at a heavy-set, elderly man rushing into the lobby, his physician's long white lab coat trailing behind.

"I have heard of such things, but never personally witnessed it," he says, huffing a bit. "I am Doctor Feng. Got here as fast as I could. Welcome." He waves away the guards, who appear quite happy to retreat.

"Thank you for the demonstration. As I said, I am Doctor Feng, chief administrator of this facility."

"Thank you. I am Eleos. You are not afraid of aliens?"

"Not all of us are so . . . primitive. What brings you to a backwater institution such as this?"

"Two reasons. Family history, and a place to begin my search."

Doctor Feng's eyes widen. "Family history? Search? You have certainly piqued my interest. Come to my office."

Eleos holds up a hand. "First, Doctor Feng, do you have a room with a 'No Admittance' sign on the door?"

He laughs. "We have many."

"This one would have old photographs on the walls."

Doctor Feng's demeanor changes to one of suspicion. Eleos senses fear. "Why do you ask?"

"Do you?"

"Yes, but no one goes in. It is kept permanently locked."

"Why?"

His face darkens. "You know Chinese people. Ghosts, demons everywhere. This room is. . . . " he hesitates.

"Is?"

"It's locked."

"Doctor Feng, a locked door is nothing to me."

"Hmmm," he ponders. "Look, Eleos, I am a man of science, but even I will not go in."

"You're an educated man. Surely you are not afraid of ghosts and demons?"

"Even I will not go in," he says, avoiding her eyes.

"Well then, will you take me there? You do not have to enter."

Without another word he leads her up two flights of stairs and down a labyrinth of hallways. At last, they stand before the door. He casts a quick glance at Eleos, then unlocks it and steps back. Eleos enters and is immediately assaulted by a whirl of disturbing images and shadowy presences that make even her shudder. She tries the light switch, but no bulbs have been installed for decades. Still, enough light from the open door illuminates walls covered with dusty pictures. *Even my friends the spiders stay away,* she thinks. Among the wall hangings are old photographs of men and women who had been previous caretakers and staff. Her eyes are drawn to a faded daguerreotype of a beautiful young woman standing between two men. When she brushes away the dust and looks closer, the image of *her* comes like a revelatory jolt, just as it had done to Bai Meiying over a hundred years earlier.

"Yes, Michael Powers' writings are correct," she whispers to herself. "It is *her*, and the spirits of Meiying and John Powers still dwell in this room. It is here, in this room, they conceived Michael, my great-great-great-grandfather."

"What did you say?" asks Feng from the hallway.

"Nothing. We can go to your office now."

~

Once settled into Doctor Feng's office, an assistant brings tea.

Feng is a large, roly-poly man with friendly, intelligent eyes. Grey, close-cropped hair, white smock falling loosely around his belly, he leans back in his office chair and inspects Eleos with a curious intensity. Eleos, of course, is fully aware of his clumsy, probing curiosity, and decides to make it easy for him.

But, before she can speak, he abruptly asks in the friendliest of manner, "Are you reading my mind?"

"Yes. I am not of your kind. I possess many powers unavailable to *Homo sapiens*. I can read your mind, and yes, I can procreate with humans." Eleos quickly adds, "Although, I'm sorry, the idea is quite distasteful to me."

Doctor Feng is unsure how to address this remark, and his thoughts wander to another topic.

"Ah!" exclaims Eleos. "You want to see me make an object disappear. So. . . . "

The desk behind which Feng is sitting vanishes, taking with it all the papers and other objects sprawled upon it. He laughs in childlike wonder and stretches out his hands to feel where the desk used to be.

"No, no," cautions Eleos. "Move back."

When he does so, the desk reappears, to his great delight.

"Your first time meeting one of my kind?" Eleos asks.

"No, but you are the first I've actually seen in action. Do it again!"

[727]

She does, much to his amusement.

Suddenly, he turns serious. "Can you remove tumors?"

"No," she lies. "I cannot remove your cancer without possibly damaging the surrounding tissue, which might have fatal consequences."

His face assumes a mournful expression. "Would you try? Evidently, my oncologist colleagues tell me I would have nothing to lose."

"Before I answer that, will you answer a question for me?"

"I thought you can read minds."

"This subject must be retrieved from your memory first."

"What is your question?"

"Do you know Zhang Yan?"

"Flying Swallow Zhang, the anti-alien rabble-rouser? Of course. Everyone does."

"Now that you have thought of him, I see you know where he resides. It is apparently a small village. One I do not recognize. Odd that such a powerful leader should stay in a small village rather than a big city."

"He named himself after the famous Han Dynasty bandit. Yet, strangely, he also fancies himself a sort of Gandhi, living among the common people." Feng shrugs. "Go figure. Bandit Gandhi. Ha!"

"I see."

Feng wags a finger at Eleos. "Be extremely careful. He is a very powerful man in these parts. If he got hold of you . . . I shudder to think."

"I read from your mind that you know him personally."

"I have met him, yes."

"Under what circumstances? I see a meeting with him that took place in this very office."

"Yes, briefly. A relative of his is confined here."

Eleos vocalizes Feng's thoughts. "His mother. She suffers from schizophrenia, apparently."

"True, unfortunately, sighs Feng. "There is little doubt about the diagnosis. Voices, delusions, all of the classic symptoms."

"I think not, but that is another matter," says Eleos. "Are you aware he is an intermediate?"

"So he says. Claims his mother was raped by . . . one of your kind. I've heard his powers exceed other intermediates. Now, like the original bandit Zhang Yan, he seeks revenge, only not against the emperor but to wipe out all aliens. Humans find him a romantic figure and flock to his cause." Feng gazes out the window. "Do you plan to do him harm?"

"No, I plan to mate with him."

~

Once Doctor Feng recovers from his shock, he points out on a map the village where Zhang Yan is headquartered.

"Now," he says. "Can you try and remove the tumor from my liver?"

"I am sorry, Doctor Feng, but it has already metastasized. There is nothing I can do."

"I see," he says dejectedly. "But, in light of your kindness, let me give you some advice, if an inferior can give a superior advice at all."

"Please."

"Before you leave, I insist you wear a cloak to at least make an attempt to hide your obviously alien physique. Otherwise," he gestures quite forcefully, "You will be attacked and harassed the entire way. Many poor, innocent humans, including hunchbacks, have been murdered during this anti-alien frenzy."

Eleos thanks him, accepts the cloak, and departs with a determined stride.

Chapter 60: Zhang Yan

~ First Contact ~

Eleos stays clear of the main roads and travels by foot south toward Jiangxi province. The journey takes her through endless kilometers of farm country where she lives off ground nuts, sweet potatoes, and sugarcane. Sleeping in the open, she is rarely noticed by the local population. Taking a page from Bai Meiying a few hundred years earlier during the Japanese war, she appears from a distance to be a hunched over old woman. Her cloak provides adequate cover to reinforce the disguise. A walking stick also helps convey the desired impression. At some point, however, she needs to start acquiring information about this Zhang Yan. As the northern Jiangxi border draws near, Eleos decides to start mingling with the locals. Her mandarin is perfect, but many people in these parts speak Gan, of which she knows only a smattering. Worse, her mandarin lacks a Gan accent, so villagers will know she is an outsider. Nevertheless, she needs information more than anonymity. While it occurs to Eleos that she has a potential ace-in-the-hole, it is a weak one indeed. Jiangxi province is the birthplace of Daoism, the philosophy of which she is fully conversant. *But this knowledge will more than likely be useless,* she muses. *Such esoteric learning in a communist backwater will only work with scholars, and I doubt I will run into many scholars.* Still, she is determined to take the risk and approach a town where she can inquire about Zhang Yan.

Before she can put this plan into effect, on the outskirts of a small village, she is approached by a group of farmers. Eleos greets them, but they do not return the salutations.

The group is composed of a mixture of older and younger men. All look suspiciously at her. All carry farm implements.

"Who are you?" asks the oldest.

"I am Eleos. I am on my way to Jiangxi province, Wuyuan county, Xitou township."

[730]

The men laugh. "You're in Jiangxi province woman. Didn't you know that?"

"No."

"A stranger. Don't speak Gan?"

"No."

A young farmer speaks up. "Your mandarin is good. Are you lost?"

"I hope you will point the way."

The older one steps close and looks into her face. "Pull down that hood."

She obeys.

"Take it off."

She obeys.

"An alien!" shouts a couple of the men.

They brandish their implements threateningly and back away.

"Do not be afraid," says Eleos calmly. "I will not hurt you. I just want directions."

The older one says, "We have heard what you do to people."

"What do we do?"

"Torture, murder, maim." All the men except the old one are inching backward as if facing a dangerous predator, afraid running will trigger its prey instincts.

"No," says Eleos to the old man. "Those are lies."

"Will you kill us if we run away?" asks a young one, still backing up.

"I have no intention of hurting you. Who tells these lies about my kind?"

The young man sneers, "Everyone knows. Zhang Yan has told us."

"It is he I wish to meet."

"He will kill you," says the old man.

"No. Will you give me directions?"

"We should kill you, but we are too afraid," admits the old man. "Do not harm us and we will tell you how to find him."

"I have already said I mean you no harm."

"Zhang Yan says that is the lie you tell people before you take off their heads."

"No. Now, tell me how to reach Xitou township so I can find him."

"If you harm him, we will be blamed. Zhang Yan will kill us."

Other villagers start to arrive.

"Go back!" shouts the old man to them. "Go back!"

"An alien!" screams a woman. The curious villagers take to their heels.

Two young farmers have geared up their courage and move toward Eleos with their hoes raised to strike.

The hoes vanish.

With this, the men all turn to run when Eleos shouts, "Stop! Stop or I will harm you all!"

All but one freeze. The other scrambles toward the village. Eleos lets him go and says to the old one. "Now, tell me the direction to go so that I may find Zhang Yan or else terrible things will happen to you and your village."

He inches closer, quivering in fear. "This is how you get there," he says. After he describes the fastest route to take, Eleos says, "No, that way is on busy roads. Tell me how to get there that is less conspicuous. Show me a round-about course. If you give me wrong directions, I will return and remove the arms and legs of every man in this village."

"Well," quakes the old man. "Give me a paper and I will draw a map. It is the back way, across the river Gan and through rough terrain. You will get lost without a map."

Eleos obliges by taking a notebook out of her backpack. When he has scribbled a rough map, she asks a few questions about landmarks, jots them down, reads his mind to ensure truthfulness, and is then satisfied. "Go on your way in peace," she says.

Not needing any encouragement, the men turn and run back to the village, periodically looking around in the terrible expectation she will remove their limbs.

~

Armed with the information she needs, Eleos sets off to follow the course marked by the old man. A few inquisitive children follow some distance behind, but their parents quickly scoop them up and rush back to the village. Unburdened by having to deal with these humans, Eleos feels a rush of happiness at the surrounding beauty of Jiangxi. Glorious, deep green fields stretch to the distance, where the Huaiyu mountains rise majestically on the horizon. As aways, she feels a rush of serenity after liberating herself from the ceaseless mental chatter of humans and their interminable fascination with themselves; their obsession over not only their own personal relationships with other humans, but their habitual penchant to endlessly contemplate other human's personal relationships with still other humans. The entire species spends so much time navel-gazing, they rarely leave time to use those largish brains for more enlightened intellectual exertion. Those that do use their intelligence more productively, she sees as the harbingers of an emerging intermediate class. Like Siyabonga in his own more limited sphere, this Zhang Yan bears the imprint of powerful but incomplete intermediate status. Yet, from her investigations, Zhang Yan also has many traits characteristic of Ming-huà's human husband Zookeeper. Certain criminals and psychopaths possess a fertile substrate of native genius and feral initiative. Tinker with the substrate, replace the negative or faulty motivational components of character and personality with positive counterparts (such as Ming-huà gave Zookeeper), add a few super-human powers, and you have the beginnings of a newly evolved species with limitless compassion; a compassion balanced by valuable, hard-edged survival instincts, the better to prosper amidst a world of rival species. She will seduce, *God* will induce.

As she walks, Eleos mulls the current world situation as dangerously close to becoming a dystopian, zero-sum game between *Homo sapiens* and her kind. Large geographic regions have accepted the inevitable, but vast regions of resistance remain committed to the extermination of all so-called aliens. It is time to return to the original concept put forth by Abassi of a win-win scenario, at least from the perspective of humankind. Mate with one of their most formidable anti-alien leaders and a major step has been taken. Once accepting of their future, humans will. . . .

Eleo's thoughts are interrupted by the nearby sound of human voices, intermixed with laughter. Night is fast approaching and she decides to have a look. As she rounds the edge of a steep limestone outcropping, she pauses to surreptitiously observe a large bonfire around which are many humans in various stages of sitting and moving about, drinks and food in hand, sharing a host of separate conversations and good-humored joviality. Picking up on both their verbal chatter and mental projections, the name Zhang Yan is peppered throughout. Eleos pulls up her hood and steps into the glowing sphere of firelight.

Upon catching sight of her, all conversations abruptly cease. A bevy of livid faces and flashing eyes glower as one.

"Hello," she calls. "It is cold. May I join you?"

No one replies. Only the gaping stares.

"Hello," Eleos tries again. "May I join you for just a little while to get warm?"

She receives a host of mixed mental emanations from uncertainty and curiosity, to fear and suspicion. The eyes cast glances at each other until they all settle on one person standing on the opposite side of the fire from Eleos. His frame is tall, solidly-built, and, as evident from the bulges beneath a loose-fitting shirt, powerfully muscled. He gazes at Eleos above the flames, his demeanor calm, poised, and patient, but inside, she senses he is as tightly coiled as a frightened snake.

To get a better read on this group, Eleos says simply, "Zhang Yan."

Instantly, her mind is filled with a host of graphic impressions drawn to the surface at the mention of his name, all of them conveying a mix of fear, admiration, and coerced loyalty. All, that is, except the tall one, whose mind is busily attempting to probe hers. Realizing at once that he is an intermediate, she blocks access. Finally, the tall man breaks the impasse.

"Welcome!" he exclaims with false bravado. "Come and warm yourself!"

When she sits on a proffered stump, the tall one remains standing and says, "You mention Zhang Yan. What is your business with him?"

Eleos takes a risk and telepathically communicates to him.

You are an intermediate. Aren't you afraid Zhang Yan will kill you if he finds you?

This message, planted so clearly and strongly in his consciousness, makes him take a step backward. In sending this message, she has allowed him a brief glimpse into the intimidating power of her mind.

Who are you?

Eleos replies aloud, "I am Eleos. I travel here from a distant province."

"We can tell," says a middle-aged woman. "Mr. Tang asks what is your business with Zhang Yan."

"I have heard much about him. I want to meet him. I think I would like to be one of his followers."

"But you are one of the Violators!" cries a young man.

"Violators?"

"Yes!" he points menacingly. "You are one of the aliens! Your disguise fools no one."

Eleos points toward the tall man. "Ask him."

"She is an alien," he announces calmly.

"As are you," she replies.

"Not the same as you. Not at all the same."

For a brief moment, the humans are all frozen in place listening to this dialogue. Then, in unison, they rise and stare threateningly.

For the first time, Eleos notices behind the tall man three dead bodies hanging from a stand of trees, the pulsing flames illuminate their forms in varying degrees, giving them the illusion of ghastly movement.

The tall one becomes aware she has seen, so he steps aside to give her a better view, shrugs and gestures with his hands. "I can tell them to kill you in the same way."

"Not possible. You know I will simply make them disappear."

This creates an uneasy rustling among the group.

The tall one blinks, then says, "I am Tang Shoujen, brother of Zhang Yan. My comrades here know I am an intermediate. Our mother was raped by one of your kind. We could kill you now, but I choose not to do so."

"Thank you," smirks Eleos. She adds telepathically, *I'm willing to go along with this charade, but you had better be a good boy.*

Just be patient a little. I'll explain later.

Why are you trying to block me now? Let me fully in your mind and you will not have to explain.

Not yet.

"What do you want with my brother?" he asks in a loud voice.

"That is between he and I."

"You want to kill him!" cries a voice in the crowd.

The others tense. A rifle is produced from somewhere and it points at Eleos.

"She is an assassin," says the person with the rifle. "We should kill her now."

If he tries, says Eleos telepathically to Tang. *I will dissolve the rifle and make your own sexual gun disappear. You have certainly misled these people about us and our powers.* She draws his eyes to the hanging bodies. *And murder! Shame!*

Tang hesitates. Eleos becomes impatient with his dalliance and bores in on his mind. *You will lead me to your brother! Now!*

This command tips the balance. "My brother will want to deal with you himself," Tang announces with exaggerated brazenness. "There is a herder's shed nearby. You can sleep there, under guard, and I will take you tomorrow to see my brother."

Immediately after making this pronouncement, he quickly tells Eleos telepathically, *Ignore what I am about to say and play along. Tomorrow, we will stay off the main roads and walk to meet my brother.*

Tang thrusts out his chest and says to the group, "If she causes any trouble or tries to escape, we will burn her alive in the shed!"

Upon hearing this, the crowd mumbles its approval.

Given such clumsy posturing, lack of knowledge, and the outright lies fed to these people, Eleos wonders about this Zhang Yan and whether rumor has vastly overrated his power. Intent on testing such a presumption, Eleos marshals her power and performs a deep probing of Tang's mind, brushing aside his attempts to block her. To her great surprise, he has sincere and utter confidence his brother will easily dispose of this troublesome female, strong as she may be. Yet, there is something else, something she cannot quite reach. . . .

~ Zhang Yan ~

Next morning, she and Tang Shoujen set out to see Zhang Yan. It soon becomes obvious word has spread much faster than Eleos and her companion can walk, and their path is quickly lined with onlookers casting insults (and occasionally stones) at her. There are also many firearms brandished menacingly, but with Tang leading the way, no shots are fired. It is clear to her that Zhang Yan's brother has focused his mind on reaching the destination, and his thoughts do not stray from that goal. It seems his strategy is to be continually on guard to deflect any unwelcome mind-reading on her part. While walking, she cogitates over the outlandish fact

[736]

that a female with her immense powers is seeking a murderous intermediate in the hinterlands of China for the express purpose of mating. She reminds herself that history is replete with incongruities more bizarre than this, many of which have led to unexpectedly remarkable outcomes. Nonetheless, as they draw closer to their destination, Eleos is second-guessing herself over the potentially disastrous consequence of such a Quixotic adventure. It is in this frame of mind that she hears Tang announce they are approaching a country villa where Zhang Yan awaits. She surveys Tang's mind to determine if any surprises are in store, but he remains laser-focused on passing her off to his brother as quickly as possible. Interestingly, when the villa comes into sight, the ever-present onlookers melt away, and she is alone with Tang Shoujen. Senses on full alert, she follows him to the outer wall. The villa's grounds are beautifully landscaped by meticulously pruned, lavishly green vegetation, its varicolored hues laced throughout with bright red rhododendrons and brilliant yellow rapeseed flowers. The villa itself is a model of classical Chinese architecture, and its pagoda-style roof shines cobalt blue in the sun. Before them stands a thick, composite wall of brick, lime, and wood encircling the villa, with a massive red gate at the entrance. Tang swings open the gate, and Eleos walks into the inner courtyard where ornamental shrubs and splendid maple trees convey the impression that the visitor has entered the realm of a high-born Confucian mandarin of ancient times. An imposing figure standing on the porch looks out from beneath a decorative overhang. Even from this distance, Eleos sees that Zhang Yan is much larger than his brother Shoujen.

As they approach, Tang gestures toward the figure. "My brother, Zhang Yan."

Even as she acknowledges his presence, Eleos feels an incredibly strong force probing her mind, which she immediately blocks. *This is no weak intermediate!* she thinks. Laughter bursts from the figure as he steps out from the shade of the porch, extending his hand as if she was a long-lost comrade. Not only is he bigger than his brother, he is more muscular, and much more attractive. Instead of taking his proffered hand, she gives a slight bow.

"No traditional niceties here!" he cries. "Take my hand in friendship!"

She does so, and in the process feels a surge of energy and strength through his firm grip.

"Your brother promised to give me an explanation for the cruel nature of your actions," she says, turning to look at Tang Shoujen, but he has disappeared. Laughter again erupts from Zhang Yan.

"My brother is a useful appendage . . . sometimes. Good riddance! Come in, have tea, and I will explain."

Eleos tries to probe his mind, but it is as tightly locked as her's. Now very much intrigued, she follows him into the villa.

Ushered into a sunlit veranda, she sits on a teak chair and sips tea while Zhang Yan paces the floor. Finally, after many turns around the room, he stops and faces her.

"I have heard you are the child of Abassi. True?"

"Truly."

"Ah, I can tell. You disapprove of my work with humans?"

"I disapprove of murder."

"Do humans call it murder when they kill a dog, or a cat?"

"Some do."

Zhang shrugs. "In any case, that was not my doing." He brightens. "Besides, I thought our mission is to replace humankind."

"By turning them against us?"

"Absolutely. It speeds the process. We have to defend ourselves, right? Intelligent humans will see my followers as misguided, and in the long run, we will actually accrue more sympathy from those *Homo sapiens* we can actually stomach mating with."

"So, you are lying to them, and in so doing leading them to their own destruction?"

"Isn't that what you're doing?"

"Yes, but we don't murder them, especially in such a painful manner as hanging."

"As I said, that was not my doing?"

"Your brother?"

"Well, he is far more human than you and I."

Eleos's eyes flash anger. "You and I are not similar."

Zhang smiles patronizingly. "Do you fancy your powers exceed mine?"

"Would you like proof?"

Zhang merely grins in response.

Eleos concentrates on making him disappear into another dimension.

Nothing happens.

"You see?" he says. "You cannot do it. I am at least your equal."

"Who are your parents?"

"I perceive the Overseers do not tell you everything."

"I've known that for a long time. You may be my equal in certain powers, but you are my inferior in the most important characteristic of our kind."

"I know to what you refer, but you may be surprised."

"How so?"

"I have let you live, thanks to my compassionate nature."

"Don't be foolish," says Eleos.

While pondering this response, Zhang resumes his pacing, absently levitating a porcelain vase and making it bob up and down as if in time with his thoughts. Finally, he says, "Every day, one hears about the killing of human males and females who have dared mate with our kind. This routinely happens all over the world. My own followers delight in such slaughter. They demand the offspring of such unions also be murdered. The human potential for hate-filled mayhem is a force of nature wondrous to behold. You and your hunchbacked relations have barely scratched the surface of replacing that woebegone species; scrabbling around by dissociating a few gang members here, a few rapists there. Now, you are on my turf. I have grander plans. Nevertheless, I have let you live as a gesture any good host would extend." He stops, gently sets down the vase, and waits for her reaction.

Eleos laughs. "Nonsense. You cannot kill me."

"Oh, yes, indeed I can."

"Then do it, for I have decided you are too dangerous to allow such a purveyor of evil policies to continue living."

It is Zhang's turn to laugh. "Then kill me now."

"Before doing so, I prefer to mate with you."

~

This statement clearly takes Zhang aback. He begins pacing again, ignoring her presence. Suddenly, he stops mid-stride and brings forth a sarcastic chuckle.

[739]

"So, you are an advanced female version of our insect brethren the Praying Mantis? You are interested in my DNA I take it? And once you have it safely burrowed in your egg you . . . . "

"Yes, but I have no interest in cannibalizing you."

"I thought you said—"

"No, you mistake my words. I do want your DNA, but I also am looking for a suitable male to be a partner with me."

"A partner?"

"I want to accelerate the replacement of *Homo sapiens* due to the severe pressure they are imposing on the planet, and I want the increasing incidence of extinctions suffered by all of our brethren to stop as soon as possible. Therefore, I need a partner who . . . let us say, is less hesitant than I in facilitating these goals."

"In other words, I have the killer instinct, eh?"

"No, you have unfortunately learned to kill, which has overridden your actual instinct for compassion. I need both, or, I should say, we need both. Not the killer, but the instinct."

Zhang stares at her, and in the process his face becomes cold and callous. "There!" he cries. "I just made a few dozen humans disappear from this world; men, women, children. I do so as a paean to your so-called acceleration. The killer will not be cleaved from the instinct."

Eleos tries to penetrate his mind to verify the truthfulness of his claim, but his blocking power is too great.

"I will say goodbye, Zhang Yan," she says with a cutting edge to the words. "You are too far gone to bring back."

With this, she calmly walks out of the villa, not waiting for a response from Zhang.

~

When she is out of sight, his cold stare melts away and he immediately returns the dozens of humans to this world unharmed. As he does so, his eyes tear up.

"*God*!" he cries. "*You* try me. *You* grind me!"

~ Eleos Faces a Crisis ~

After Eleos leaves Zhang Yan, she retraces her steps down the same path Tang Shoujen had guided her to the villa. This time there are few curious on-lookers, and even they melt away when she casts them

[740]

threatening glances. In a stormy mood, she reaches the site of the bonfire. To her relief, the bodies of those hanging have been removed. *Dissociation is so much cleaner than such violent, painful ends,* she ponders. *Yet, is it really so compassionate? The void it leaves remains a void, violent death or not.* Recently, with increasing frequency, these uncomfortable musings have disturbed her peace of mind. When she looks up at the rope-scarred branches, her mind is likewise conflicted about what to make of Zhang Yan. On the one hand, she is undeniably attracted to him, in spite of his violent history and unconscionable manipulation of humans. On the other hand, she is horrified at her own inexplicably amorous feelings toward such a reckless, unpredictable male. She asks herself what sort of offspring would enter the world from such a mating. So far, the trajectory of her kind has been to birth progressively more powerful children. She remembers being described as "the culmination" by *her*, but this powerful male may be another culmination. How many culminations are there? Well aware of Zhang's inference that the Overseers have their own enigmatic plan, she wonders if the goal is to produce such a super-race that the demise of humans will be a matter of decades, or a few hundreds of years, rather than thousands. Perhaps even sooner. The words "we are all intermediates" have never been so clearly and undeniably true. Pursuing this line of reasoning more deeply, she surmises intermediates may already have been around for thousands of years, shaping the course of human history in fits and starts, for better or worse. In the process, such genetic mutations have accumulated imperceptibly. Technology able to recognize such minute evolutionary mutations was unknown, at least until recently, but even now remains in its infancy. Humans still cannot detect such incremental evolutionary steps. It strikes Eleos that the emergence of Ming-huà, Pythia, Tara, Abassi, herself, and the others is not such a sudden punctuated burst of equilibria as it appears. If this process has been guided by the Overseers for thousands of years, *her* word "culmination" emerges from the glass darkly, and Eleos's thoughts again turn to Zhang Yan. What hidden powers draw her to this minor god whose cynical agenda is contrary to her own genetic imperatives? What the result of such a union would mean for Earth is frighteningly ominous. Such contradictory impulses tug in violent contradiction. Against her better judgment, she surrenders to the path of least resistance and decides to wait at the hanging place—for somehow, she knows he will come.

[741]

Chapter 61: The Beginning of the End

~ Twice Two is Greater than Four ~

Eleos sits on a fallen log and drifts deeper into wistful contemplation. To pass the time, she opens her senses to all life forms inhabiting the area. By modulating her receptors, she picks up the chatter of those creatures with warm blood, those with cold blood, and at other times bathes in the low, steady heartbeat of the forest. As always, these deep chords remind Eleos of the urgency to save what remains of the tattered natural world. Time fades to insignificance, and her reverie is only broken by Zhang Yan's insistent telepathic intrusions. *Hey! Eleos! Wake up! I am here! Come on!* Such verbal rocks thrown into the still waters of her meditative trance finally achieve the intended effect.

She opens her eyes dreamily, still half-way emerged in universal first principles. "I knew you would come," she says evenly.

"I knew you knew, hence, I come. Self-fulfilled prophecy."

"Now that you are here, tell me what you have to say."

Zhang reverts to his apparently habitual pacing, hands behind his back like some fevered Beethoven conjuring notes. After a number of round trips, he stops and stares openly at her. "Let us together make a double-wide swath through the human race."

"What about your followers?"

"The first to go."

"You still don't get it, do you?" she asks peevishly.

"Don't worry, your precious conscience will remain intact. We simply send them away unharmed."

"To face oblivion in an alternate dimension?"

"Ah! You have me all wrong. No. We'll send them to a place in these four dimensions where they can do little damage."

"I'm not following."

"What did the British do with convicts?"

"Australia?"

He nods acknowledgement. "Send them someplace similarly isolated. Send only the bad ones; the sociopathic alphas, the hopeless dregs, the vicious killers, rapists, pushers, molesters, wayward intermediates, psychotics, and all the rest of the most destructive detritus. Give them adequate food supplies and water, but never allow them to develop dangerous technology. They will devour themselves."

"And the rest of the human race?"

"Mate with them! They are the nutrient-rich substate upon which our kind will flourish quickly, and on a global scale. Over a relatively short period of time, their diluted genes will become faintly irrelevant echoes in the genome."

Eleos points out the fact that Australia is already taken. Zhang Yan, clearly excited, ignores her comment and continues.

"This special place that we reserve for the unreformable must also be inhabited by an adequate population of non-human competitors. In such a case, the exiled humans must compete on a more-or-less equal footing with others occupying their ecological niche. Allow them no weapons other than what they can fashion with their hands. Maybe they will develop a healthier appreciation for the natural world. Without technological pacifiers, they will either mature and develop a more appreciative outlook toward the natural scheme of things—back to harmless subsistence survival—or die out."

"That sounds more cruel than simply dissociating them," says a dubious Eleos.

"It is a compromise, intended to mollify what you call the *metaphorical God*, who prefers the suffering imposed by struggle to survival by empathic interference."

Eleos shakes her head. "Won't work. Where is a sufficiently large, isolated location that isn't already full of innocent humans?"

"No humans are innocent!"

"Are you?"

Zhang Yan smiles broadly. "You do not know my story. You do not fully understand what you call the *metaphorical God*. I am of *God*. On the other hand, you and your extended family are of the *metaphorical Goddess*. You are of *Goddess*."

"No such entities."

"Of course not. That is why they are referred to as metaphorical."

"I have heard they actually are convenient terms for two conflicting factions of the Overseers. One faction is convinced unrestrained and violent struggle is the natural order of the universe, and therefore must not be artificially manipulated. Let suffering flourish in order to keep first principles sacred, they argue. The other faction is amenable to direct, compassionate intervention to alter the harsh, deterministic inevitability of cruel, implacable fate. If one has the means to lessen suffering, then there is a moral imperative to use those means to do so. This faction also insists it is a first principles imperative.

"Yes," nods Zhang. "I am aware of this dichotomy. It seems you and I are fated to play it out."

"Or," corrects Eleos. "We are here due to an infinite series of probabilistic events that even the Overseers cannot control. Witness the plethora of false starts and unforeseeable missteps by their earlier creations."

"Either way, here we are."

"Either way, here we are," repeats Eleos. "What next?"

"My plan."

"Your plan is unworkable, unless we transport millions of innocent humans from their homeland to make room for the wretches you have targeted. Such a scale, even if conscionable, is beyond our powers. Desperate humans are apt to take desperate actions."

Zhang spreads his arms for emphasis. "You're forgetting we already control large parts of the world. Let us focus on decreasing the territory of the opposing humans to an isolated region, all the while transporting the wretches from our territory to theirs. In that case, we end up controlling an area full of acquiescent human incubators, while the last *Homo sapiens* holdouts will eventually go extinct. You see, I—"

"Someone approaches!" interrupts Eleos. "A group."

"Yes, I know. My brother."

Just as the words leave Zhang's mouth, Tang Shoujen bursts into the clearing leading an angry mob.

Let me deal with this, Zhang signals Eleos telepathically.

"Are you alright, brother?" demands Tang.

"Never better. Why are you here with so many of my followers?"

Tang points at Eleos. "Word has spread of her presence. We want her eliminated before she can do us harm. As you see, we have brought many weapons. We wait only for your command."

Zhang shakes his head ruefully. "She will make all of you disappear."

With this statement, grumbling arises from the mob.

"Not if you strike first," says Tang. "If not, we have plenty of firepower."

Zhang spreads his arms in a gesture of helplessness. "Unfortunately, she is equal to my power. I cannot make her vanish."

More angry rumbling from the mob.

Zhang turns to Eleos with an amused gleam in his eye. *Now it is up to you. How will you deal with it? In a metaphorical God-like manner, or a metaphorical Goddess-like manner?*

Eleos faces the crowd. "I mean you no harm. Put away your weapons and—"

Gunshots reverberate piercingly through the forest. None of the bullets reach Eleos—and all guns have disappeared. Shouting in frustration, a group of young males rush at her with knives and machetes.

Eleos shouts a last warning. "Stop!"

But the knives and machetes are upon her, blades flashing inches from her body. In an instant, each young man stands tottering on two legs, but each minus both arms. A great moan rises from the attackers, and they flee awkwardly back to the horrified mob. All eyes turn to Zhang Yan.

"Save us!" they scream. "Kill her! Kill the alien!"

Zhang Yan blinks. All of the crowd simply disappear except for Tang Shoujen.

"You should have known better than to bring them here," Zhang scolds his brother. "We have embarrassed our guest."

Tang stares open-mouthed, not sure what to say.

By way of apology for his brother's apparent dull-wittedness, Zhang tells Eleos telepathically, *He is what humans callously call retarded.*

Ignoring this rather supercilious clarification, Eleos says firmly, "Bring them back."

"Without arms?"

"I will replace them."

Zhang holds up a hand. "Wait." He turns to Tang and says impatiently, "Return home, brother. Our followers will need you. Tell them I have taken care of the female alien."

Tang looks confused. "But, if they ask questions?"

"Tell them she is neutralized. Also, inform them they must stay in their homes until further notice—as a precautionary measure."

"But—"

"Go!"

Still looking confused, Tang withdraws in a rather deflated state.

After watching Tang depart back into the forest, Zhang turns to Eleos.

"It is done," he says. "I have brought them all back, but I made sure they are relocated some distance from here. Unfortunately, the arms of the young males must remain detached."

"Why?"

"A lesson for they and their cohorts to contemplate."

"It will merely make them hate us the more," objects Eleos.

"That is the point. Evidently, you have not been listening."

"Never mind," says Eleos. "I will replace their arms."

"You cannot," says Zhang. "That must not be allowed. You are not strong enough to override my will."

"Those young men will suffer terribly for the rest of their lives."

"I am of *God*," replies Zhang.

"And I am of *Goddess*," insists Eleos. "Evidently, never the twain shall meet." She turns to leave.

Wait! Zhang fairly shouts in her mind.

As she pauses, he reverts yet again to pacing. "Yet, the twain must be made to meet. We two must find a way to join." He says these words not so much to Eleos, but as if debating with himself. "All right," he admits. "I did send the arms to a closed loop dimension. I cannot return them even if I want."

"Why?'

"Harsh lessons from harsh Nature. I am of *God*."

"If one learns only the harsh lessons of Nature, one is only half-sentient. There are other, similarly powerful lessons that are not harsh."

"Such as?"

"You well know, but feign ignorance."

[746]

"I repeat; such as?"

"Altruism, sacrifice, love, compassion, empathy, joy, tranquility. Your inborn stillness must be stilled."

Zhang affects a crooked smile. "All of those lessons often turn to dust. Anyway, who will still my stillness? You?"

"*Goddess.*"

"Yet, for all your vaunted compassion, you are the one who removed the arms of those young men. Furthermore, your family members—Pythia, Tara, Abassi, and all the others—have removed far more than arms. In fact, they and their progeny have spread far and wide, expanding on every continent. In the process, I understand many humans have been dissociated, especially by Pythia and Tara and their followers."

"It is true," sighs Eleos. "But those humans were the ones you yourself have targeted for some sort of barbaric exile. Pythia, Tara, and Abassi, plus their offspring and followers, have culled the unreformable hold-outs. These vicious humans were given multiple warnings. The vast majority of *Homo sapiens* in those territories are either passively tolerant, or actively mating with our kind. This expansion is according to the plan set in motion by Abassi, my father. Sometimes, the use of *God's* harsher methods are regrettably unavoidable. *God* and *Goddess* are inextricably bound together."

"True!" exclaims Zhang. "The human concept of Yin-Yang is a remarkable insight for such narrow creatures."

"Nevertheless," cautions Eleos. "The balance must always tilt toward the metaphorical *Goddess.*"

"Agreed! You see? We meet!" He stops pacing and gazes deeply into her eyes. *Let us mate. Let us be partners. Let us join and produce the perfect union of God and Goddess.*

"I had originally thought such a mating possible," Eleos replies. "But you are perhaps composed of more *God* than I am prepared to deal with."

A shadow falls over Zhang's face, but it quickly passes. Now, he assumes a pained expression.

"Is it the hangings?" he asks. "My plan?"

"Yes and yes."

"Those are trifles."

Eleos returns to the log she had earlier rested upon and sits wearily, remaining silent for some time. Finally, she speaks.

"Let me tell you a story. It was written down by one of my early ancestors—Michael Powers—who humans incorrectly diagnosed as suffering from schizophrenia because he heard voices in his head. However, those voices were distorted personifications of our two Overseer factions and their often heated arguments. Unbeknownst to Michael Powers, he was an intermediate whose genetic makeup represented a potent step forward in the evolution of our kind. However, in the agony of his confusion, he wrote long, detailed narratives of his own struggles to understand what was happening in his mind. I have read those narratives with great interest. In poor Michael's fevered brain, the voices he conjured brought the unsettling spectacle of *God* and *Goddess* at each other's throats in violent verbal conflict. I will recite to you one passage I committed to memory. *Goddess* has just informed *God* there is to be a reunion of the two deities in a magic cave. *God*, furious, replies thusly." (Here, Eleos's voice changes to a high-pitched whisper. In spite of its whispering rasp, it comes hard and strong and is impossible to ignore.)

"Reunion, Sweet One? God needs no reunion. I am at union with them every moment through the worship they bestow. Acknowledgement of My Power and Glory. Goddess, You resent having fallen too much."

"Ha! That is amusing, Lord God, for You have made a career of the fallen; of fallen angels and fallen Jews. Of fallen Hindus, Christians, shamans, sheiks and shibboleths. Fallen this and fallen that. And nowhere for them to turn but to You."

"Yes, My Beloved Goddess, such is the power of advertising. And now a fallen soldier—Mountain Man."

"Fallen from where? They've all fallen upward."

"Nonsense, Goddess! After they've been pushed over the edge by their sacrilegious thoughts, psychological gravity pulls them down—"

"Yes. Drowned in the Human Condition, Your loyal Swamp. And when they are gone?"

"I know, I know. Do not think that I have not dreaded their absence. What will they do when they find out that abstract thinking is invariably an evolutionary dead end? That their universe is devoid of—"

"Mustn't tell them."

"Won't. Poor fools! Ah, Sweet Goddess, they so much want to believe in angels and aliens. And You? In spite of what You say, will You rescue them from their delusions?"

"As they think You once did, I will soon walk among them. But rescue them?"

Eleos's voice returns to her normal tone. "Now *Goddesses* walk among them, as well as *Gods*. Will we rescue them?"

"We are here to drive them to extinction."

"Will we rescue them from unrestrained suffering?"

Zhang smiles. "While I am of *God*, I am also of *Goddess*."

"And while I am of *Goddess*, I am also of *God*," replies Eleos.

~ Mating ~

Beside the blackened circle where a bonfire had earlier illuminated the hanging bodies of three innocent humans, Eleos and Zhang Yan are engulfed in a subversive embrace of mind and body, for each feels a betrayal of their own deeply held beliefs by succumbing. Both explore the erotic sensations felt by the other through a dizzying host of multidimensional conduits and telepathic moans of ecstasy. Yet, even as the waves of iridescent vibrations ripple in electric waves throughout their bodies, each realizes something alien lurks deep inside the bowels of the others' sexual organs, burrowing greedily into seeds and egg. *God* and *Goddess* are unloosed, surreptitiously mating under the concealing forms of these two oddly shaped hominins fused together. After uncounted hours of love-making, both are exhausted. In obedience to the weariness that has sapped their passions, they are serenely nestled together, gazing up at the stars that glow blurrily. They communicate with each other telepathically, but the thoughts never connect, as neither is truly listening. Their words are pebbles dropped into an empty well. Each is aware what the morning will bring. Responding to some cosmic cue, they give up on pretense and fall into a deep slumber. Soon, sunlight penetrates the forest canopy and reaches the sacred patch of ground. Eleos and Zhang Yan are nowhere to be seen—departed in separate directions without a word to the other— each to their own destiny. The deed having being done, the seed having being planted, the spirits of *God* and *Goddess* had earlier gone their separate ways, and with their departure, this pair of oddly-shaped hominins are restored to their sovereign natures. The world waits in quickening anticipation for what is to come of this brief encounter by proxy of two deities, each as metaphorical as the universe itself.

 While Eleos walks toward an unknown destination, she knows the potential being inside her womb is not of her or Zhang Yan; it is motherless and fatherless. Yet it is a child of some greater mystery. Now that it has taken seed within her, she is fully aware it will grow from a dark and bottomless origin, terrifyingly opaque as it exponentially enlarges, riotously scribbling on the uncarved block of its existence. *But this is silly!* she thinks. *The spirit of old Lao Zi still lurks in this place. Was he an early intermediate? Will this child still the stillness at last? Have our collective wills prepared enough of the Way? Ming-huà, Pythia, Tara, Abassi, myself, and the countless others. Will the eradication of* Homo sapiens *be a soft landing for the planet? Or will this child derail all our plans? Will it destroy me as Anne was almost destroyed giving birth?*

 With such thoughts as unwelcome companions, Eleos makes a return journey to the mental institution where she is warmly greeted by Doctor Feng. He offers her an empty room in which to rest as long as she desires. Comforted by the kindnesses of Feng and his staff, she finds being surrounded by humans with such a variety of mental disorders enervating, but the patients trigger her empathic receptors to new heights of sympathy for the species as a whole. This sympathy arises from the fact she views all humans as mentally unstable to one degree or another. She is convinced she is pregnant, but days turn into weeks, weeks to months, and still she is shocked to feel no movement, no discomfort, and no communication from the womb. When her belly finally balloons as if overnight, she insists Feng check for a heartbeat. He assures Eleos it is strong and healthy. The behavior of this child during pregnancy is unlike any other birthed by her kind, and the thought makes Eleos more nervous than if she were subject to the pain and distress of normal development. Often, she makes her way to the No Admittance room in hopes of meeting the ghost of Child of Buddha, or even to see and communicate with *her.* However, the room remains silent, as if waiting for some proper moment to host the spirits of dead ancestors. *So,* she muses. *Here I sit, the most powerful hominin in the world, buried in a backwater mental institution while the rest of my kind expand the territory of a new age against the desperate flailing of ignorant and hate-filled humans. Why not make a wide swath to help clear* Homo sapiens *from the planet? Why not return to Zhang Yan and double the size*

[750]

of the swath, as he wanted? Nonetheless, a deep, visceral command to
remain hidden while I give birth to this child compels me to stay. Why?

No answer is forthcoming, so Eleos continues her stay, helping Doctor Feng where she can, but mainly keeping to herself, wondering about the maddening stillness emanating ominously and painlessly from her womb. Meanwhile, in those areas pacified by her kind, there are long lines of humans clamoring to get on waiting lists and mate with intermediates. In such locations, violent crime has plummeted, and once-fearful *Homo sapiens* are thrusting their sons and daughters into the arms of a burgeoning intermediate class. On the other hand, in areas still controlled by humans, Zhang Yan's prediction is coming true. The populations in such last bastions of resistance are living violent and primitive lives, governed by brutality and repressive dictatorships. As a consequence, due to the worst propensities of human ignorance and distrust of *otherness*, any person suspected of having sexual relations with an alien is killed, as are the children of such illegal unions. Zhang Yan, as one of the main architects of this movement, has cynically succeeded in his plan to horrify the bulk of educated humanity, pushing even more people into pro-alien territories. Although located inside the boundaries of Zhang Yan's domain, the mental institution has avoided any violence directed against it or any of its inmates, as if protected by some hidden force. Eleos is quite certain she knows who has provided for such an island sanctuary in a sea of misery.

~ What is Happening? ~

When the contractions come, they arrive not as sharp pains, but as waves of pleasure applied to the deepest core of her body at the hands of a skilled masseuse. Only Doctor Feng and an assistant are present in the institute's medical room ministering to Eleos. In response to inquiries from her kind, she had asked Pythia, Tara, Anne, and Abassi to stay far from this bleak country and not attend her labor, explaining away this odd request as acceding to a command from *her*. Eleos regards this excuse as constituting only a slight exaggeration. Now, comfortably on her back, the full implications of what is about to appear from her vagina makes her tremble and question the wisdom of facing this ordeal alone. Oh, if only they were here now! Other than Doctor Feng and his assistant, she doeˢ not want to be the first to gaze upon the infant. After all, it is not reˢ her's, nor is it a child of Zhang Yan's. Nonetheless, whatever entity is released upon the world, the responsibility begins and ends with her own actions. There must be no claim of innocence by pleading an unsolicited intervention by *God* and *Goddess*. Because the institute lacks a functioning sonogram, she has no idea what this child will look like. Two heads? Four arms? Blue skin? Her attempts to peek inside its mind have failed abysmally. To Eleos' dismay, it dwells somewhere far beyond her ability to reach.

"Uncarved block," she murmurs.

"What?" asks Feng, waiting intently for the crown to appear.

Eleos does not answer. She tries to calm herself by repeating to herself: *Ming-huà and Zookeeper worried about Pythia; Pythia and Jared Paine worried about Tara; Tara and Siyabonga worried about Abassi; and Abassi and Anne worried about me. Yet all turned out well in the end.*

"It's coming!" exclaims Feng. "Push!"

But Eleos feels no sense of urgency. There is no pain, and straining seems superfluous. The baby is coming freely and wholly on its own, without an iota of discomfort to Eleos. Her wonder at such unexpected sensations is replaced by a feeling of grateful acceptance. It is the acceptance of one caught in the jaws of inexorable fate, but a fate that is as welcoming as a form of utopian rebirth.

~

The last thing she remembers is seeing a group of shocked faces peering through an open door, and Doctor Feng staring incredulously down at the newborn, exclaiming, "I don't understand!"

Chapter 62: On the Cusp

~ Tik Tock Tik Tock ~

An anxious group of hominins stand in shocked silence outside the room where Eleos has just given birth. All had caught a brief glimpse of the baby through the cracked door, and all are now struggling to understand what they just witnessed. The members of the group are all related, with the exception of a male who stands to the side, staring at them with an unreadable expression and an unreadable mind.

Abassi is the first to speak. "I saw, but I still wonder at what I saw. It is, I think, a female, but, also male?. . . could any of you read the baby's mind? I could not, but when I tried, I experienced a devastating reaction that left me numb."

"Yes," agrees Pythia. "I had the same experience."

"Me too," adds Tara.

"What does it mean?" asks a bewildered and frightened Anne.

"Maybe it is this culmination business I keep hearing about," says Siyabonga.

"As powerful as all of you are," says Zhang Yan from the corner. "You cannot see what is staring you in the face."

And what is that? asks Abassi telepathically.

I am the father. I am as powerful as Eleos. I am more powerful than all of you here in this room. Even more than you, Abassi. Together, Eleos and I have produced this wonder. Zhang switches to a verbal outburst. "Now, in the face of such a miracle, all of you are standing around like helpless humans. Pathetic!"

"Yes," says Abassi. "We know who you are. The worldwide media, as well as Eleos, have communicated your activities to us. We have all heard Eleos tell us about the underlying motivation driving your actions, and which you claim will lead to the isolation and eventual destruction of humans. Deceiving them, egging them on to murderous a suicidal opposition, condoning the worst impulses of their ignorance are aware. All of us are appalled by the moral deficit that must exist in your genetic makeup. We can only hope your propensity to propagate such tactics and the lack of empathic sensibilities that make them possible are not passed on to this child."

Zhang Yan smiles in defiance. "Oh, but they are passed on. And it is a good thing. Get these *Homo sapiens* out of the way so we can eliminate such troublesome obstacles and move forward without all the bother you and your kind have foolishly gone through to soften their fall."

Tara speaks up. "In the areas we control, peaceful dilution of the human genome proceeds apace, without the unnecessary suffering your methods produce."

Zhang laughs contemptuously. "I have told Eleos I am of *God*. Without suffering there cannot be joy. You are of *Goddess*, whose path is contrary to Her own Mother Nature."

"Metaphorical *God* and *Goddess* are dry and brittle concepts!" says Pythia angrily. "In the fullness of a non-dialectic quantum world, paths upon branching paths are endless, as are possibilities unchained to such constraining simplifications."

"Besides," interjects Anne. "*God* and *Goddess* drove our ancestors mad."

"True," agrees Zhang. "They were, but only because such complexities as metaphorical *God* and *Goddess* were distorted by the limitations of their intermediate brains, resulting in a form of psychosis. Of course, primitive human psychiatrists deemed them schizophrenics. What could one expect of such creatures?"

"Indeed," says Abassi. "What you say has truth, but you yourself may be our current version of a schizophrenic."

"That—" Zhang starts to reply when Doctor Feng abruptly emerges into the room, his assistant trailing after. He stops, but she is wiping away tears as she rushes out.

Feng, also with tears welling, scans the faces of the group and blurts out, "Never have I! . . . It is! . . . I don't yet fully understand what is happening. It. . . . " But he cannot finish.

". . she?" asks Tara.

". . ?" he replies. "Mother or it?"

"I don't understand," says Anne. "A hermaphrodite?"

"Perhaps," stammers the doctor.

Feng appears dazed and shakes his head as if to clear it. "No, not that either. I do not know. I have never. . . . " Again, his words trail off.

Every member of the group has been probing the doctor's mind for answers; all find the same thing.

Knowing his thoughts have been revealed, Feng murmurs, "Now you know." Wiping tears from his eyes, he sails out of the room bearing an enigmatic expression.

Hesitantly, cautiously, the group files into the birthing room, each nonplussed by the opaque mental void that awaits. After everyone has entered, they look questioningly around the room. No baby is in sight.

Eleos informs them telepathically, *The child is here, by my side, under the blankets. All is well. I asked you not to come. You have seen. Now, you must leave us.*

Abassi, struck by an overwhelming aura of benevolence and compassion, nods silently. "We had to come," he says aloud, and walks out of the room, followed immediately by all the others. All, that is, except Zhang Yan, who remains.

"I want to see my child," he demands verbally.

"You must leave," says Eleos. "For now, anyway."

"No! I insist on seeing my child!"

Eleos merely looks at him sorrowfully.

Zhang Yan exerts all his considerable telekinetic power to remove the blanket, but fails.

"You are not powerful enough," says Eleos.

Stunned, Zhang says, "Is it you or the infant that blocks me?"

"Our child. Now, leave."

With this command, Zhang stomps out, exclaiming, "I will be back! No one can stop me from seeing my own child!"

Eleos gazes at the bulging blanket beside her. "It can."

~

Next morning, the members of the group, having gotten very little sleep, meet for breakfast in the institute's cafeteria. They are quickly surrounded by intrusive patients whose various mental illnesses manifest themselves in unabashed curiosity. Abassi particularly is singled out for intimate inspection; the behavior of the patients toward him being reminiscent of innocent children exploring a new and interesting object. Although less of a curiosity than Abassi, the others are similarly treated as objects of unbridled interest. Naturally, the group communicates via telepathy even as they verbally answer the barrage of questions from the patients. The only subject of their telepathic conversations is the child of Eleos. Abassi, Pythia, Tara, Anne; all are awed by the inexplicably powerful sensation of benevolent stillness projecting from the birthing room. Doctor Feng has told them that since the birth even the patients have become uncommonly docile. In the midst of this rather incongruous assemblage of advanced hominins and mentally challenged humans, a beautiful young woman appears. Upon catching sight of *her*, the patients melt away as if on some silent command, leaving the members of the group and Doctor Feng to stare in wonder.

"Eleos and child are gone," *she* announces.

Everyone stirs in disbelief, but only Feng responds. "Where?"

"Far away."

"When will they return?" asks Abassi.

"Eleos will return very soon, at least in the spacetime we currently occupy. The child, a bit later, when reaching adequate age in the spacetime we currently occupy."

"I see," says Abassi. "In the meantime?"

"Continue doing what you are doing. Encourage procreation among yourselves and the intermediates. As a famous human once said: it is the end of the beginning."

When *she* had gone, Anne turns to Abassi. "Zhang Yan will not be happy."

"Zhang Yan is dead," says Doctor Feng rather portentously.

"What?" come the scattered exclamations from members of the group.

"So is his brother."

A stunned silence falls over the cafeteria as Feng's brain is probed. In this instance, there is a block that none can penetrate.

"How?" asks Pythia.

"Heart attacks."

"Both of them?" asks Tara.

"Yes."

Abassi casts a sharp glance at Feng. "How did you know so soon?"

[756]

"Because I was the attending physician."

"But—" stammers Abassi.

Feng looks bewildered and speaks in a subdued voice. "They were staying in one of our guest houses. In the middle of the night, the young woman who was just here called me. When I arrived, it was too late."

"Why didn't any of us know—pick up on the signals?" asks Tara.

"It is worse," says Doctor Feng.

"What?" asks Abassi.

"The entire human population of the area controlled by Zhang Yan has disappeared."

"All?" asks a shaken Anne.

"I'm afraid so."

"But you are still here, and he controlled this area as well," says Pythia. "How is that?"

Feng shakes his head in consternation. "Not only are my staff and I still here, but so are all our patients."

"We are talking about hundreds of thousands of people!" exclaims Abassi. "Men, women, children, babies!"

"Yes," whispers Doctor Feng.

"And other life forms?" asks Siyabonga.

"Evidently none have been removed . . . or harmed . . . or suffered. Only the people."

"I don't understand how you could have known this so quickly," muses Pythia.

"Word spreads fast."

"But there were no people to spread the word!"

"You're right," says a disconcerted Feng. "Last night that very strange young woman who just left told me *she* had heard what happened . . . that was after I answered *her* call and went to check on Zhang Yan and his brother. Yes, that was when *she* told me the terrible news. I did not think to ask how *she* got this information." Feng gazed through one of the windows. "*She* is a remarkable young woman. *She* must be one of your kind. Who is *she*?"

Abassi looks at the others, then turns to Feng and says, "*She* is not of our kind. *She* is something different. Something even we do not understand."

Feng's eyes widen. "More powerful than you?"

"Yes."

"Then, there is truly no hope for the human race. Do you condone the murders of these hundreds of thousands of people?"

"We do not know they were murdered, Doctor Feng. They may have simply been relocated," says Tara.

"Relocated? To where?"

"None of us know," says Abassi.

"This young woman . . . this powerful . . . whatever *she* is . . . can you stop *her*?"

"No."

"Is *she* responsible for the mur— . . . I mean disappearance of so many people?"

"We do not know," says Pythia. "It may have been Zhang Yan himself."

"I don't understand," says Feng. "These people were his followers. Why would he have done such a terrible thing, and then just fall over from a heart attack and die? And his brother also? It makes no sense." Feng hesitates. "Did he possess such powers?"

"No," says Abassi firmly.

"I just don't understand," repeats Doctor Feng.

"Nor do we," says Abassi. "Nor do we."

"But the people!" cries Feng. "All those poor people!"

~

With Eleos and the new child gone, members of the group disperse to their respective geographical areas of control. Doctor Feng is left alone to puzzle out the series of inexplicable events that have left his little island sanctuary and all its patients isolated in a vast, lonely sea utterly devoid of other humans. Yet paradoxically, not entirely desolate, as teeming non-human life, freed from the ravages of human occupation, stream into the vacuum.

~ Something Has Gone Dreadfully Wrong ~

Now, years later, the void left in the region once controlled by Zhang Yan has been partially resettled by neighboring population centers comprised of a mix of intermediates and sympathetic humans. In these intervening years, there does not reoccur a mass-disappearance incident similar to the widespread annihilation of humans as happened to the

[758]

inhabitants of Zhang Yan's dominion. Nonetheless, the pattern of gradual expansion by "aliens" and concomitant shrinkage of hostile human enclaves has accelerated. However, humans being a clever species, especially when faced with the possibility of extinction, have developed ingenious methods to avoid detection of their most fatal weapons of mass destruction. In one recent instance, they had succeeded in detonating a tactical nuclear device that obliterated a city occupied mainly by intermediates. This incident has sent shock waves through "alien" communities. For some time, human scientists had given their hominen successors the scientific appellation of *Lux dimensiones*, now revised to a more accurate classification of *Homo dimensiones*. The appellation has stuck. Hostile humans have shortened the Latin label to "demons", an epithet that has become standard fare. Abassi and his relations, ostensibly the leaders of this new species, are in a quandary as to the disposition of millions of human holdouts who view them as demons. Minimization of suffering is still uppermost in such considerations, though for older *dimensiones* such as Pythia and Tara, a more aggressive course of action against the remaining humans is preferred. Nevertheless, all *dimensiones* had been horrified at the disappearance of so many hundreds of thousands of humans in Zhang Yan's domain, and there is no stomach for resorting to such blunt tactics again. The mystery remains as to who was responsible for such a holocaust. Suspicions have been generally directed toward Eleos's child, but there is no definitive proof. It is in this environment that Eleos returns from her extra-dimensional sojourn. She (or some entity, perhaps an Overseer) has chosen the cave in the California desert as the location for her reappearance. Her arrival is unannounced—a decision she had been adamant about. Were her father and mother present to witness her emergence, they would be quite shocked at how much she has aged in such a relatively short passage of Earth-time.

As she emerges into the bright glare of the California sun, Eleos breathes deeply the invigorating air permeating this combination of four dimensional spacetime. Always a loner, she luxuriates in being a solitary figure in the vast expanse of the desert. She is determined to walk to the nearest town and maintains a slow but steady pace; the better to contemplate the imminent arrival of her now-adult child and the impact it will have on the world. In the recesses of her powerful mind, Eleos ponders with a melancholic regret the minimal impact she has had on the world. It seems to her, as the most powerful of her kind, that her talents have been wasted. Others less formidable, like Abassi, Pythia, and Tara, are building benevolent empires while she wanders desolate places in a quest marked only by its futility.

I must have been put on this planet to fulfill only one task—to find a suitable mate so that both of us would be the conduits through which metaphorical God *and* Goddess *manifest their collective wills over a prostrate, human-dominated Earth.* She thinks these thoughts without rancor, but with a heavy heart. *Zhang Yan was the dark side, the dark underbelly of our species. And I? Certainly not so contrasting a light to his dark that it prevented us from mating. Now behold what we have produced! When I think about what will be following me in a short while, I feel faint. I remember the long drawn-out process of what to name this creature. Oh, when the name Harihara came to me! It just popped into my head in an instant! What an epiphany! A name derived from human religious superstition to be sure, but one that is most appropriate. How the Mentors laughed! They told me even the Overseers found the name so ironic they were full of mirth at the thought. Soon Harihara will arrive, and then. . . .*

After many hours of such contemplative walking, Eleos reaches the main highway and is quickly made aware of the lack of traffic—not a single car passes. Alarmed, she picks up her pace, and when she enters the town, not a soul is to be seen. She spends a long time searching for inhabitants. Nothing. Although the buildings are devoid of people, it appears nothing has been disturbed. No signs of violence. No signs of struggle. It is quite apparent the humans have been removed—one way or the other. Her thoughts immediately return to the depopulation of Zhang Yan's domain so many years ago in Earth time; the infamous event occurred within hours of Harihara's birth. Now she/he returns. Perhaps Harihara is already here? Can it be?

"It can."

She appears from nowhere, standing casually in front of Eleos, an enigmatic expression clouding *her* normally placid features.

Eleos instinctively probes *her* mind, but as usual, it is utterly impenetrable.

"I don't follow," says Eleos.

"Yes, you do," *she* replies.

"So, it was Harihara all those years ago in China that made so many disappear?" Eleos says.

"Yes."

"And here as well?"

"Yes."

"But Harihara is not yet arrived! How could it be?"

"Harihara preceded you."

"I thought . . . I was told . . . otherwise."

"We all thought otherwise, but it turns out Harihara has its own intentions, irrespective of the rest of us."

"I don't really know Harihara," says Eleos.

"Of course," *she* shrugs. "If you recall, Harihara was separated from you almost as soon as you entered the home dimensional manifold."

Eleos feels dizzy. "My mind is foggy. The memory of that time eludes me."

"After separation, you were . . . otherwise disposed."

"All these Earth years"

"Yes."

"Yes, yes, I now understand. Harihara is a stranger to me."

"Yet," *she* says somewhat apologetically. "Evidently this emptiness is for you."

Eleos looks around. "This?"

She follows Eleos' gaze. "Harihara understands your predilection for solitude."

"Are the humans harmed?"

"Not in the least."

"Relocated?"

"Harihara is not so crude as in the beginning. This is a sign of maturity."

"And the humans are. . . . ?"

"All around us. I'm afraid Harihara already views them as fossils."

Eleos' mind is buffeted by unpleasant speculations. "How long has Harihara been here?"

"It preceded you by—"

"It!?"

"Yes, it. No other personal pronoun available. Harihara preceded you by a few hours, Earth-time."

[761]

"Hours!"

She nods.

"And already . . . all this? . . . where is Harihara now?"

"On its way to San Francisco."

Eleos is horrified. "To do the same thing?"

A dark cloud passes over *her* features. ***Fate starves at Probability's door.***

Eleos steps back a few steps. "Something has gone dreadfully wrong."

"Or dreadfully right."

"Are we—Abassi, me, Pythia, Siyabonga, Anne, Tara, and all the others—are we to be fossilized as well?"

"Look in the mirror, Eleos. An extraordinary human poet once wrote about a delicious word. A delicious word the fierce old mother repeats while rocking the cradle."

"In that event, I am off to San Francisco. Before I go, I must ask whether you approve?"

"The lion and the lamb are two sides of the same coin. As such, when the lion faces up, the lamb must face down, and vice versa. They cannot both face up, nor can they both face down, at least in this dimensional manifold."

Eleos laughs sarcastically. "I see riddles are still your stock in trade, but I am not completely a fool. You see, I am aware Harihara is the incarnation of superposition; all sides at all times hovering indeterminately, both faces up and both faces down. I knew that the minute I realized the infant was both male and female, dark and light, Armageddon and rebirth, *God* and *Goddess*."

"Then you must measure the unmeasurable," *she* says softly.

Eleos shakes her head. "I go to San Francisco. Harihara must surely be with my father and mother. The city is full of intermediates and sympathetic humans. Surely. . . . "

She is gone.

Instead of teleporting herself, Eleos decides to drive so she can see the extent of devastation Harihara might already have caused. She sets off on her journey after finding a car with a cute teddy-bear keychain still dangling in the ignition. It is with no small amount of trepidation she drives. Will the city be as empty as the town she is leaving behind?

[762]

Chapter 63: Collapse of the Human Race

~ San Francisco? ~

In the beginning, as she travels north to San Francisco, there is no traffic. But as she gets farther away from the town Eleos is passed by an endless stream of emergency vehicles headed south. Suddenly, the stream stops. Not only the emergency vehicles, but almost all other traffic also ceases, as if a spigot had been turned off. Almost all. A few cars pass by, invariably heading south away from San Francisco. Northbound lanes are completely deserted. Eleos opens her mind to the occasional passing car, and in every case is struck with the sensory equivalent of a dreadful shock wave. It is night now, and the passing headlights dwindle to a handful, spaced farther and farther apart. Eleos has a feeling of dread as she watches the lights of towns and farmhouses go dim, then blink out. Still a long way from San Francisco and the landscape is now plunged into complete darkness. Mile after mile of darkness. Her mind runs wild with horrified speculation about the dissolution of millions of people. Could it be? Does Harihara have such immense power? Somehow, Eleos is certain this monstrous product of herself and Zhang Yan possesses such capabilities. What of Abassi, Anne, the thousands of intermediates? Such grim possibilities seem as unreal as a bad dream. Perhaps that is what this is. A nightmare. Perhaps she is still in the home dimensional manifold of the Mentors. Simulations are routine in such a place. Particularly simulations as bizarre as this one. Perhaps.

To her dismay Eleos spots no electric glow on the horizon where the city should be. As she crests the rolling hills on the outskirts of San Francisco, she is met with the same darkness, although it is dimly softened by desultory moonlight agitating the wispy fog. A handful of blurry little headlights can be seen in the distance moving down a few streets, but they are rare. No emergency vehicles are evident. Eleos makes a beeline for the Victorian house. Driving through the deserted city, she spots the mansion high up on its hilly perch, shining through the fog like a beacon. It appears to be the only structure in all of San Francisco with electricity, and it brazenly glows above the sea of gray gauze.

Following the shining beacon, Eleos makes her way up the steep hill and parks across the street from the house. Through the fog she sees silhouetted against the porch light a group of familiar figures. Abassi, Anne, Pythia, Siyabonga, Tara, and a few others. All of them are projecting curiosity tinged with apprehension. While she approaches them, Eleos searches for a distinctive shape, but Harihara is nowhere to be seen.

Before she reaches the porch, she blurts out a telepathic, *Is Harihara here?!*

No! comes a chorus of replies, followed by Abassi's angry addendum, *Only the devastation wrought by Its presence!*

As they file into the house, Eleos is assaulted with anxious questions fired in rapid succession.

"What happened to Harihara while you were away?"

"What went wrong with Harihara?"

"How did this happen?"

"Are the Overseers insane to let this creature return?"

"Didn't the simulations warn them about *It*?"

"Is everything changed now?"

To every breathless query, Eleos can only shake her head. "I have not been with Harihara for a very long time. They took the child away from me almost as soon as we arrived. I don't know."

"So, all of us are now out of the loop?" asks Tara.

"I don't know."

"Is the entire planet to be scrubbed of humans in one fell swoop?" asks Pythia, not without a hint of approval.

"Evidently," sighs Eleos. "I don't know."

"Where is *It* . . . where is Harihara now?" asks Tara to the air.

"Could be anywhere now," says Siyabonga. He turns to Tara. "We must get back to Africa and save those we can."

"Yes, true," replies Tara.

"You are right," says Pythia. "I too must go back to South America and help protect those in my area. If San Francisco is a sign of things to come, humans are now an endangered species."

[764]

"We had things under control," says Abassi. "Why this sudden change?"

"Harihara is clearly out of control," says Tara. "Perhaps insane."

"My *God*!" exclaims Anne. "Even good, sympathetic humans are gone!"

Looking openly at Eleos, Pythia says, "Zhang Yan's genes must have been strong to account for this."

"Indeed," agrees Tara.

"We must find *It*," says Abassi.

"True," says Pythia. "But how? *It* completely blocks all of us."

"These actions were not Zhang Yan's genes speaking," says Eleos.

"Not his?"

"Well, some were, but most came from metaphorical *God*."

"Must be where *It* got such unrestrained aggression," says Abassi."

Looking distressed, Anne touches Abassi's arm. "Must we refer to Harihara as *It*?"

"Dear," soothes Abassi. "Harihara is both male and female, *God* and *Goddess*. *It* . . . the appellation *It* . . . is appropriate. Try to quell the purely personal."

The comment miffs Anne, who stifles a sharp comeback when she thinks of all the children Abassi has sired from a plethora of women. Instead, she softens her rebuke. "Do you feel nothing for all the good, kind, sympathetic humans? Their children? The innocent babies?"

"They are precisely the ones I feel for," replies Abassi. "That is why we all must stay and find Harihara before *It* does more damage."

"Humans aren't so stupid," muses Tara. "As one of them wrote long ago, 'Things fall apart; the center cannot hold.'"

"Yes," agrees Abassi. "The falcon can certainly no longer hear the falconer."

"I'm afraid Tara and I really must go back to Africa," says Siyabonga. "For all we know, *It* is halfway there now."

"No," says Eleos. "*It* is here."

"How do you know?" asks Pythia.

"I know. *It* is waiting."

"How can you be sure?" asks Tara. "Because you are the mother?"

"No, I am only partly the mother; a small part at that. *God* and *Goddess* are Father and Mother. Nevertheless, the small part that is me insists *It* is here. Waiting."

"For what?" asks Anne.

"That, I do not know."

"For you?" asks Anne.

"No, I don't think so."

Abassi raises his hands as if in supplication. "I feel some—"

Suddenly, shockingly, a series of tremendously loud and rhythmic claps of thunder rock the mansion, rattling the windows and causing the wood beams to creak as if a great ship is breaking apart. All are forced to their knees in pain, their hands clapped over ears in useless desperation to muffle the roar. The clamor emanates from within the house itself. Recurring shock waves press outward with the regularity of a mad metronome.

TAP! TAP! TAP!

Abassi shouts into the hurricane of noise. "The Precious Object! Upstairs!"

TAP! TAP! TAP!

Everyone's receptors are painfully flooded with unspeakably harrowing emotions; powerful, wrenching screams of some unfathomable agony.

TAP! TAP! TAP!

The pounding seems interminable. No one is able to rise from their knees. As if its very bones are cracking, the mansion seems on the verge of collapse.

TAP! TAP! TAP!

The lights are extinguished. Utter darkness.

TAP! TAP! TAP!

It seems to Eleos that the finger of some wrathful deity is tapping angrily on the flimsy roof.

As quickly as the thunder first lashed the air, it ceases.

"What does it mean?" cries Anne.

She sits in the lotus position on a huge, dazzling white flower floating above the ground. *Her* sad, contemplative face gazes from beneath an elaborate crown glimmering a kaleidoscope of colors. A cinder-bright jewel embedded in *Her* forehead burns brightly and an intricate necklace lays cradled between *Her* bare breasts. *Her* left-hand rests on *Her* thigh, the upturned curve of *Her* fingers resembling the albino legs of a gracefully dead spider. *Her* right hand is poised in the air, index finger and thumb touching to form an almost perfect circle while the other fingers radiate outward. *"Isn't it obvious?" She* asks.

"No," mutters Abassi. "Explain."

"Generations ago, your ancestor Michael Powers stood in a dark cave facing the figurative God and the figurative Goddess. He pointed an ancient M-16 at God."

"Yes?"

"Foolish hominin! Did you not read his scribblings?"

Silence.

Goddess laughs and turns around. From *Her* back, God emerges, bellowing deeply, *His* swampy voice a deep, dank, gritty rumble that fills the atmosphere with a corrosive slag of wet soot and harsh sulfur—a nineteenth century furnace bellowing smoke from a thirteenth century hell.

"He shot Her instead! In the end, they will always choose Me. Thus, their chosen end is arrived as they themselves predicted, but in the form of a hunchback slouching out from the rocking cradle."

Now, into their minds come the words of Harihara.

Humans will soon be gone from Earth—painlessly—and their molecular constituents made available to enrich the planet for others to use. It is fitting that their demise is as antiseptic as they have endeavored to make the Earth itself.

~

Somewhere on the outskirts of San Francisco a lone coyote, emboldened by the dark silence, cautiously noses toward the city.

Printed in the USA
CPSIA information can be obtained
at www.ICGtesting.com
CBHW020007190724
11676CB00014B/456